Born in the Bahamas but raised in four of the five New York boroughs, excluding the Bronx, from age seven onwards, Neil J. Smith was the fifth child of ten children. He says "I was ill-educated in as many schools" and did not receive an education until he discovered the library system. He started boxing at the age of 12 and went on to win various amateur awards for the next 12 years, including the All Army Champion. He organized for various civil rights groups, the 5th Avenue Peace Parade Committee, and finally The Black Panther Party. After that sojourn, Neil studied creative writing, literature, and poetry at NYU with William Packard, author, editor, professor, and founder of the prestigious New York Quarterly, where Neil was vice president for 15 years. He now lives upstate with his wife where he continues to write.

Neil J. Smith

ON THE ROPES

A TALE OF THE '60S

AUSTIN MACAULEY PUBLISHERS™

LONDON • CAMBRIDGE • NEW YORK • SHARJAH

Ordering Information
Quantity sales: Special discounts are available on quantity purchases by corporations, associations, and others. For details, contact the publisher at the address below.

Publisher's Cataloging-in-Publication data
Smith, Neil J.
On the Ropes

ISBN 9781645369431 (Paperback)
ISBN 9781645369448 (Hardback)
ISBN 9781645369462 (ePub e-book)

Library of Congress Control Number: 2020912481

www.austinmacauley.com/us

First Published (2020)
Austin Macauley Publishers LLC
40 Wall Street, 28th Floor
New York, NY 10005
USA

mail-usa@austinmacauley.com
+1 (646) 5125767

I would first of all like to acknowledge the late professor, editor, poet, and playwright, William Packard, for the years of friendship and mentorship in which he encouraged me. I am also beholding to Barbara Iuviene for her friendship and editorial work on my behalf.

The ring hovered in a flood of lights at center stadium swathed in rend bands of smoke from the cigars of fat cats, big time spenders and high rollers with their fur draped, powder puff, kewpie-doll-face molls, seated up front at ringside. Two bloodied, sweat-sopped combatants climbed out of the ring: one was downcast, defeated, whereas the other, the victor, was exultant. The roar of the crowd dwindled to a murmur as two other fighters made their way ring ward from the locker rooms below. The ravenous, beer guzzling fans drew back, eyeing each fighter cagily, trying to gauge their mettle by the cut of their jib. They resumed their seats as the fighters climbed into the ring and threw off their robes revealing sculpted, gladiatorial physiques.

The ring bell tolled: "Ladies 'n gentlemen," the official barked into the microphone, "our next semifinalist in the hundred-n-sixty-pound division of these 1968 Olympic trials – on my right, in the blue corner, weighing in at a hundred 'n sixty pounds 'n a half, from Chicago, Illinois, Josh Slade!"

Slade whirled out of his corner, hard and black like anthracite coal, throwing a whirlwind of punches to the air, muscles gleaming under the hot lights of the ring. "Slade," echoed the ring official. The fighter wheeled round and tossed up his hands, bouncing on the balls of his toes, flashing a glance at his opponent. He then back peddled to his corner, as the fans whistled and hollered.

"In the red corner, from Brooklyn, New York, weighing in at one hundred and sixty pounds, Percival Jones!"

Tall, taut, sinewy and brown, Percival stepped forward and raised a lone gloved fist. He fixed his gaze on the apron of the ring and the blank, hovering faces at ringside. "Jones!" stated the official once more, as a rousing applause rose from the crowd. Percival was the hometown favorite. He pivoted, lowered his fist and returned to his corner.

The referee beckoned the two fighters to join him at center ring. "I want a clean fight," he began, placing a hand on each fighter's back. Percival's eyes fell over Slade's broad shoulders, pectorals and corrugated stomach, as Sled's eyes fell over him. "I want you to break when I say break," the referee continued. The two fighters then locked eyes. Percival was half a head taller. "If there's a knockdown, I want the standing fighter to go to a neutral corner.

Shake hands 'n at the bell come out fighting." The contestants slapped gloves and returned to their respective corners.

"OK, we know this guy's a brawler," Percival's trainer, Punchy, said in the final seconds before the bell. "Box this guy. Work off your jab, in out, move, move, move." Percival nodded, half listening.

The opening bell rang! "Box-box-box!" Punchy shouted.

Slade sprang from out his corner with all the ferocity of an enraged bull, looking to rend and lay Percival cold on the canvas, in his corner, with a single blow. He had devised this method of attack to surprise and overwhelm his opponents at the outset of a fight: a tactic that had helped catapult him to the semifinals of the '68 Olympic trials. Percival, however, deftly slipped away, and though thrown off balance, stumbled beyond range of a follow-up, slashing left hook. With an eye to a quick kill, Slade threw blow after blow, looping them up from the canvas as Percival, unable to catch his footing, toppled backwards, trying to stay out of range and off the ropes. His heart was caught in the well of his throat when self-preservation, 'fight or flight,' seized hold of him. Though under attack he knew, in the words of Joe Louis, "You can run but you can't hide." Besides these were the Olympic Trials and 'flight' was not an option.

The fans were screaming as Slade, snorting with every blow, pressed him.

Watchfully the referee stood aside. Punchy had stiffened halfway to his stool. Slade's opening attack was surprising in immediacy and ferocity. He was a bruiser who enjoyed trampling his opponents from the start. His every blow was packed with fury. It was not meant for Percival to last beyond the first minute. And surely, reeling as he was, like an off-balanced top, he would have to fall. For the first time in his seven years of boxing and with 97 wins in 102 starts—he had been All Army Champion for two years, Inter-Service Champion one year, and was currently the New York Golden Gloves Champion— Percival knew, as did the howling fans, that he was in danger of being knocked out.

This was Percival's dilemma, bicycling backwards under Slade's assault, trying to find ground on which to build a defense. Then, to his relief, his shoes gripped the canvas under foot and he lashed out with three spitfire jabs, rallying back, catching Slade flush in the face. He paused and shook his head like a wet, dumbfounded dog. Percival made him pay for his befuddlement with another whiplashing jab. The blow only served to annoy. Again Slade came at Percival like a runaway truck in a bad dream. But he was only able to land glancing blows, while Percival struck him over and over with cobra like accuracy.

Slade's cornermen looked on dumbfounded. After such an overwhelming and surprising attack, the fight should have been over. Instead they looked on in awe. Percival was giving Slade a boxing lesson.

Punchy plopped onto his stool. This was the Percival he knew! The spectators, on the other hand, could not quite grasp the situation, as Percival had so nimbly taken command. Though he'd lost the moment, Slade was savage in his fury and not to be dismissed, but as the fans continued to watch, they found themselves looking at the best boxer of the trials, Percival Jones!

The referee began to circle the combatants. Slade had trouble pinpointing his target. He could not figure why he had not nailed Percival in the opening seconds after the bell and drop him like a ten pin. Slade was unable to find his man with a single blow. For every blow he missed Percival countered with two or three of his own. Slade grew anxious, reaching for the one punch that would lay his opponent cold.

Percival could smell Slade, feel and taste his body heat in the rancid spray of salty sweat. He sensed Slade's every move before he made it, as if dancing a hot tango. Slade followed Percival's lead to the best of his ability, throwing blow upon blow. Then of a sudden, Percival sidestepped, leaving him to hurtle forward, pummeling the air. He waited for Slade to swing round. Full of wrath, Slade swung round but, as he did three more crackling jabs ricocheted off his nose, eyes and mouth. Blood trickled cross his lips from his nostrils, and, as he prepared to fling himself at Percival, the bell rang. Angry and dumbfounded, Slade wandered back to his corner. Percival fell onto his corner stool, breathing soundly. Punchy entered the ring and removed Percival's mouthpiece, saying, "You're doing fine. jus' fine." He squeezed a sponge full of water over Percival's face. "Keep boxin' 'im."

Percival could not rightly hear Punchy, his only thought was, *This guy's fucking trying to kill me.*

Slade sat at the edge of his stool, anxious for the start of the second round. The ten-second whistle blew. Punchy left the ring. Percival looked at Slade, steeling himself for the fray. Slade returned that look with a scowl, and began to stand. The bell for the second round sounded.

Disdainful of his opponent's finely honed skills, Slade fell upon Percival at center ring, even before the bell's echo had faded and the roar of the fans took its place. Slade raised welts on Percival's shoulders and arms with walloping blows, but Percival weathered the attack, throwing lancing jabs again and again; moving, using the ring, avoiding the ropes where Slade wished to pin him. Slade set him up for his right, but Percival slipped away.

The fast pace of the bout kept the referee panting.

Slade was relentless, a pitbull, dogging Percival's every step. He was unlike any fighter Percival had ever fought before. Percival slipped in and out, as skillfully as a sneak thief, catching Slade with blow after blow, staving him off. But Slade was unstoppable and kept coming and coming with a taste for blood. Percival was on the defense, but ably kept Slade on the receiving end of his fist. Again, he caught Slade with a right to the gut, and followed up with a hook to the head. He dodged Slade's counter and drew his head up with a crisp upper cut, then sidestepped and leaned in with a sizzling right cross, rocking Slade on his heels. He had engaged Slade in a matador's waltz that kept the fans screaming, jumping, and applauding wildly.

The bell rang for the close of round two.

The crowd remained standing, screaming for more. This was a classic boxer versus puncher, the matador and the bull.

The instant Percival collapsed on to his stool, Punchy jumped through the ropes, removed his mouthpiece, splashed his face with water, and broke a cap of smelling salts under his nose. Percival shook the fog in his head and blinked against the sharp ring lights. Surges of adrenalin pumped through his body in larger doses than usual. He breathed mightily, genuinely aglow with anticipation and exhilaration.

"If you don't catch 'n knock this guy out, you're gonna lose," Slade's corner informed him.

"I'm a get him! I'll get the son of a bitch, you'll see," Slade swore, spitting into a water bucket, eyes aflame.

The bell for the final round tolled. The fight commenced without letup. Slade was enraged, ready to throw his life away on crushing the life out of his opponent. Percival continued to ward Slade off with timely side-to-side maneuvers and sizzling left jabs. Nevertheless, Slade was determined to upend him. He was fierce. Any other fighter would have been picked up in a heap in the first round. But as Slade was discovering, Percival was a technician. And as Slade furiously pressed on, he used that skill to control him.

Percival seemed to be everywhere at once, though Slade labored mightily to cut him off. Unable to catch his opponent in any one spot, Slade grew reckless. Percival wanted to laugh, but Slade was no one to be laughed at. In the next instant, Slade was back on the attack, fist pumping. Percival smothered the blows as best he could on battered shoulders, elbows and arms, rolling with each blow. Still he kept Slade on the receiving end of his jabs.

The fans were jubilant. Suddenly, Slade struck Percival a blow that opened his eyes in dumb surprise. His knees caved. Slade caught him again; and Percival staggered, one foot over the other, dropping his guard.

Punchy's heart leapt, and his eyes searched for the clock: forty-one seconds to go. Time enough for Slade to win by a knockout. Punchy hoped Slade had not realized his advantage.

The crowd fell silent. Leary of Percival's many tricks, Slade hung back. His corner shouted him on, "Take him! You've got him. He's yours."

Percival was in a fog and his fist hung low. With seconds to go in the fight, Slade reached for the punch that would up end Percival and win him the bout, but he was only able to muster enough strength for a blow that caromed off Percival's forehead. Before he could take a second swing, Percival seized him, tying him up. Slade thrashed wildly, trying to break loose, and for the first time that fight, the referee had to separate them. They swayed from exhaustion as the final bell tolled.

The crowd broke out in an exultant roar. Punchy scrambled up the steps and climbed into the ring. Percival was mostly surprised that the fight was over. Punchy threw a robe over his shoulders and guided him back to the corner. Percival eyed Punchy's smiling face through bleary vision. He tried to smile in return. Punchy massaged his shoulders as they awaited the decision. The waiting seemed endless, and Percival longed to be off his feet.

"The winner," the ring official proclaimed, "from Brooklyn, New York, Percival Jones!"

The fans went wild. Percival could barely lift a victorious hand; the fight had drained him utterly. He lowered his hand and started for Slade's corner to say, "good fight," but Slade had fled the ring. Swaying, Percival turned for his corner. Punchy spread the ring ropes for his departure. He climbed out of the ring and down the steps to the hoopla. He was a hero. And as he made his way to the locker room, the following bout on the card was being announced.

"You're the best! You're the best!" The fans assured him, shaking him by the hand as he passed. Then one after the other they took their seats and gazed at the ring. On entering the downstairs locker room, which he shared with three other fighters who were preparing for their upcoming bouts, he could still hear a faint roar of the crowd from the arena above. Without a word Percival collapsed onto his cot and pulled his legs up after him like dead things. As he stretched out, it felt as if a weight were on his chest, and each new breath came with a struggle. His arms dangled over the sides, touching the floor, and his mouth hung loose.

Punchy stood aside, leaning against a locker, and looked proudly at his fighter. That was how he thought of Percival, *my fighter*. Percival was one in ten thousand – no, one in a million. They were on the way, and nothing foreseeable could trip them up. The Olympics was theirs for the picking. Then following that who knew? Who knows, Punchy wasn't speculating that far ahead. The thrill of the moment was enough for the moment. Other trainers eyed him with envy as they looked in to congratulate him, "Nice win," they said.

Punchy smiled, saying, "Thanks."

One looked at Percival and said, "It's in the bag!" Percival simply waved.

A trainer looked up at Punchy from bandaging his fighter's hands: "You must 'a wooed 'em out there."

"I'd be lying if I said we didn't."

"Ummmmmmmmmm," murmured Percival.

"Don't lay there too long," Punchy advised. "You don't want your sweat to dry on you."

"I'll only be a minute."

"Jus' a minute."

Percival groaned and lowered his legs over the side of the cot as he sat up, knowing that the time would spend him more than rest him. As he leaned over to unlace his shoes a shadow fell between him and the overhead light, causing him to look up into the troubled face of his younger brother, Sam.

"What's with you man, I won?"

"I know. I saw. You were great, the best. That's not it. it's…" his voice faltered and, leaning forwards, he withdrew a hand from his pocket, upturned, beseeching. "It's…"

"It's what," Percival pressed.

"This is the wrong time," Sam uttered.

"Wrong time? Wrong time for what?"

Sam hesitated, then said, "telling you Martin Luther King's been shot n killed!" Sam blurted for all to hear.

Punchy started forward but stopped to see who had overheard, and noticing everyone had, he lowered a tremulous hand on Percival's shoulder and looked at Sam aghast. The news had passed like a shockwave among the occupants of the locker room. Percival stiffened, clinging to his shoelace, blinking back tears in stark disbelief. A fighter stalking up and down came to a halt as the other fighters and their trainers, turned their heads, gazing up at Sam in alarm. In that moment all motion ceased, as if time had circled in on itself. And only the insect like hum of the fluorescent lights could be heard. Observing the query in their eyes, Sam felt compelled to go on. "I jus' caught it on the radio at the food stand myself. At first I couldn't believe it, – people saying 'What? Who?' Others asking, 'King's dead?' Still I didn't know what the fuss was 'n try to ask, 'King? King who?' Like it could be the King'a England? But someone say 'shrrr.' N everybody fell silent 'n the newscaster say, 'Dr. Martin Luther King Jr. has been killed.' That's when I come," said Sam, resignedly.

"You were right the first time," said Punchy, irritably. "This was not the time –"

"I tried saying so."

"Is there such a thing as the right time?" asked Percival, lowering his head into the palms of his hands.

"What's done's done," sighed Punchy.

Percival slumped backwards on the cot, moaning as though he'd been struck with a vicious body blow.

A man poked his face into the locker room. "Chauncy Wells," he called, startling all but Percival who lay on his back in a state of gloom. "You're up in two," called the man.

Punchy, as well as the others, felt intruded upon in a moment of trial, more so since the man was white.

"Coming," Chauncy's trainer finally responded, and the man departed before Chauncy could gain his feet. "You best whip this white boy good t'night," said Chauncy's trainer, as they headed for the door.

"You know that boy ain't white," Chauncy replied.

"Never you mind, you jus' make believe he is," his trainer responded.

"Good luck," called Punchy as they went through the door.

"Yeah! Good luck," the other trainer added. Then, cocking his head sideways, he said to no one in particular, "it'll burn hot as Hades in Harlem t'night."

"If it ain't waxing hot already," Punchy added.

"If that ain't the truth," said the other.

Percival could barely breathe. He felt a vague coldness creeping over him. "Oh god," he broke out in a piteous cry, "not now!"

Punchy watched helplessly, weighing his own shock. But he knew, as had Sam, how fond Percival was of Dr. King, having met him in the past. He had first encountered Dr. King on the march from Selma to Montgomery and again on the long march following the assassination attempt on the life of James Meredith. He had worked in the South with the Student Nonviolent Coordinating Committee and had been much affected by King, despite SNCC's Chairman, Stokely Carmichael's call for Black Power, which, of itself, was a compelling thought but left one hanging. It was a phrase in dire need of an explanation. They were both fearless, no doubt, but Dr. King had been anointed by fate for this task. It called for a Moses not a Messiah, a descendent of slaves raised high by divine appointment.

Percival slowly swung a dangling leg as if to a funeral dirge. He listened to a muffled drum roll that turned out to be the distant roar of the fight crowd. *I lost,* he thought, sitting up as if waking from a dream. "I've been knocked out 'n I'm jus' coming to." He blinked and looked round in near panic, as if coming to. But on sighting Punchy and Sam, he recalled, "no," he had not lost. Worst still, Dr. King was dead and he had won.

"I'm sorry to be the one to say," said Sam, looking at his griefstricken brother.

Looping an arm round Sam's shoulder, Punchy started him for the door. "You've caused enough mischief for one night!"

"If you want me to go I'll go."

"Go," Punchy whispered into Sam's ear as he ushered him through the door.

Sam broke away. "I didn't kill nobody!" he spat, then said over his shoulder, "Catch you after t'morrow's win bro or is it Champ?" And with a slight laugh, he was gone.

Punchy viewed Sam's departure with mild disdain. "You best hit the showers," he told Percival.

Percival made his way to the showers feeling more in a state of suspension than exultation, or even remotely himself. He felt drained, detached, in a kind of limbo; grief stricken. He looked up and was somewhat startled at finding Slade showering off. Slade caught Percival's eye, scowled, and turned into the blast of water from the spout. Percival stared at Slade's black back, buttocks and legs glistening under rivulets of water cascading over him, and almost felt ashamed for having won out over such a fine specimen. Suddenly he felt Slade's disappointment as keenly as if it were his own; he knew how hard Slade had worked and knew that Slade had never imagined losing – No more than he had!

But Percival also knew himself to be the stuff of which champions are made and he had no reason to feel abashed and would not have were it not for the ghastly feeling welling up in him since being informed of Dr. King's death. He had recoiled from believing but the effort was as daunting as was the reality from which he would escape. Moreover, the real question was, "What in hell was his brother thinking?" Sure Sam had his problems, but Punchy was right, "this was the wrong time." There must have been a better way, if not time – there must have been. Then came another question, "Would it be appropriate to tell Slade?" Percival shook his head at the absurdity and stepped into the shower stall, turning his face into the pulsating water. He sighed deeply and turned his back on the current. He dropped his head and looked between his feet where water ran and felt a portion of his soul swirled down the drain, as had Martin's life swirl down the great American toilet.

Slade stepped out of the shower and without toweling off, threw his robe over his shoulders and left. Percival felt as if something more should have

16

passed between them. He soaped down and washed off vigorously. Before he left the shower, he turned off the hot water and turned up the cold. He danced a jig under the icy burst and chattered, "brrr!" He then snapped off the faucet, grabbed his towel, and drying himself quickly, threw on his robe, and, feeling more himself, started down the corridor.

The word of King's assassination was out. And while it did not seem to affect the mood of most fighters, the black fighters fighting white fighters felt themselves to have a strong moral edge over their white opponents. One more reason for their winning. Percival saw one black fighter preparing for his bout with a white fighter, pounding his gloved fists together in front of his opponent and pacing back and forth like a cat taunting a mouse. How strongly his opponent felt this—and felt it he must have— is not easy to say since all black fighters fighting white fighters felt as though they had a score to settle. No white fighter worth his salt could doubt that.

"Looks like the word's out," Punchy noted, as Percival entered the room going to his locker.

"It's 'n ill wind –" lamented the other trainer, smearing Vaseline on his fighter's face, chest and arms.

"Yes 'n ill wind," Percival agreed, pulling on his shirt.

Punchy strolled over in his leisurely fashion and sat beside Percival, dressed and tying his shoelaces. Punchy watched, hands clasped and thrust between his thighs. He then said, "I'm sorry. It's no damn good. It's wrong. All wrong. Been wrong all my life. Go home 'n get some rest. You can use it. Take 'n ole soldiers advise. Let's get these trials behind us. Let's do what we do best," Punchy implored. "Now get outa here. Go home 'n get some sleep. You'll need it come tomorrow."

"Where's there to go but home?" said Percival closing the locker door with a soft "bang" that went through him like a wisp. *It must'a happened that quick,* he thought with a start. A cold chill took hold of him, as if death had paused in passing. He blinked and looked at a stoical fighter, robed and ready to be gloved up.

"Good luck," said Percival, starting out.

"Thanks," said the fighter dourly.

Punchy got up slowly. "I'll walk you out," he said and, laying a hand on Percival's back, they left the locker room. The fighters in the corridor were warming up, shadow boxing to the tune of their trainers bellicose, "Punch! Stick! Move! Punch!"

"Sam's timing is the worst," said Punchy. "He should'a damn well known better."

"He didn't do anything," Percival responded, eyes downcast.

"He only tried doing what Slade couldn't do – take the starch out'a you."

"It's not his fault."

"Let me fill you in on something: news is not only who, what, where 'n when, but who you hear it from 'n why. It's no good to make excuses for him."

"He's young, a kid, 'n got no father."

"Unless I miss my guess, you've got no father either."

Percival looked at the older man with a wink and a smile. "That may be, but I've got you."

Punchy could not have been more pleased; the feeling was mutual. He squeezed Percival's shoulder warmly. "Go home 'n get some sleep." As they reached the exit, the rumble of New York's subway system below brought the ground to life under their feet. "I'll see you here tomorrow. Try not to let this get to you. It's been a long haul, 'n we're finally on the upper rung."

Looking solemnly over his shoulder at Punchy, Percival opened the door, the night lit city and 34th. St. to his side. He said, somewhat estranged, "I'll hang in there for all my ass is worth."

"You're prime beef. You're jus' about the finest honed fighter in the world, 'n soon enough everyone else'll know it too."

"I'm glad you're so damn confident."

"I've every reason to be."

"I'll see you here tomorrow then," Percival said, stepping out.

Turning away, Punchy concurred, "Tomorrow it is."

As the door shut at his back, left on the sidewalk to his own devices, Percival looked up at the tall city, adrift and without a life line back, assailed by Martin's untimely death. He felt his negritude press in on him, dark as pitch, grim as death. Yes, dark as Martin's passing – black as sin: A void into which the collective Negro psyche, his psyche, would be flung. The subterranean depths of the American negro despair. A sulphuric hell hole out of which escape was dim. It all came back to him, as he leaned against the building: it was his night to shine, and hell itself could not take it from him. "It's my night," he spat, looking beyond the street lights, but New York was too noisy and the night lights too bright to be affected.

A couple strolling past caught sight of the black man in the shadows. The man paused. "Are you okay fella," he asked. Before Percival could reply, the woman tugged at the man's arm, "let's go. He's probably a junkie!"

Percival shook his head and laughed angrily loud at their departing backs. The couple picked up speed, propelled on by his pernicious laughter. "Fucking pathetic," he uttered under breath, stepping from out of the shadows into a flood of street lights, looking skyward with sinking heart. The sounds of passing traffic whizzing by and the glare of street lights gave him a dizzy, uneasy sense of being.

"Why, when on the verge of seizing the greatest prize in all amateur sports, the Olympic Gold which I've struggled long 'n hard to capture, this happens? Killing it; killing it in me; in my soul; increasing my cup of sorrow by half! How? Why? for what? Haven't I paid the piper the price of a dance 'n more?" He gnashed his teeth, galled by it all. "Hell, they'll 'ave me pay 'n pay again," he lamented. In that instant the skyscrapers around him seemed to twirl before his eyes and begin to tail spin in on him. "Damn it! There's something god-awful in a situation where you must first fight off a hell of another's design before you're free to break out on your own." He lowered his head, searching about, trying to gain his bearings, and restless in his skin, started for 8th. Ave. His steps betrayed his uncertainty. After such a telling win, his strut was usually exuberant, cocky, and self-sure. That evening it was anything but.

A second equally troubling thought, *Bestir thyself for action on the field of Sacred duty,* a quote from the "Gita," one of India's more sacred text, which he was introduced to at a "Sit In" in the deep South, intimated, as had Ghandi and Dr. King, that nonviolent passive resistance is, by far, the better way. A fellow Activist had read it aloud to remind other fellow Activist, facing a rout by the police, to hold firm to their convictions in the face of bodily harm. He wondered at himself, "What's it to me now? It was a long time ago." It was three years ago to be exact! The incident had proven him unsuitable to be a pacifist. However, he could at least say he'd tried. "What of it?" he mumbled irritably, forging on.

He was to catch the "A" train into Brooklyn, change for the Lexington Ave. line at Hoyt & Schermerhorn, ride on into Crown Heights, walk the last three blocks home and topple into bed exhausted or, at least, that was the plan.

Meanwhile, the muffled roar of the fight crowd still rang in his ears. Every muscle of his body still strained under the fray; he still felt himself reeling about in a macabre dance of life and death; slipping and countering, escaping the broad swing of the reaper's scythe. Although the exhilaration of the fight was short lived, it would return after the lassitude had left his mind and body. But for now, the sting of Dr. King's death kept him off balance, squeezing all else out of him, and working its tortuous roots into his soul.

A blare of horns shook him out his reverie. Cars were grid locked at the cross section under a traffic light. A taxi driver stuck his head out his window, shouting, "Move it!" Then leaned on his horn. Still more shouts, more car horns, finally the grid lock broke and the traffic rolled on. Strange, as full of vehicles as the street was, the sidewalk was deserted. There was no pedestrian traffic in sight.

19

As Percival approached the 8th. Ave. subway entrance, his pace slowed, reluctant to descend. He peered down the gloomily lit stairwell and drew back, looking for an easy escape. The roar of the fight crowd was behind him and the long train ride home lay ahead with only the agony of Dr. King's death to dwell on. With welcome relief he sighted a neon sign "Shamr ck" over a barroom door. He decided to enter and have himself a beer. Besides, his throat was so dry he could barely spit.

The tavern door creaked open under his hand like an infant crying, but none of the patrons watching baseball on T.V. turned from the game, though the bartender faced his way. The room was not much brighter nor more comforting than was the street. The few customers not watching the game sat apart in the shadows at separate tables; night people, colorless and gray; they looked like leftovers from a distant New Year's Eve party, grown estranged from one another over the years. They sat quietly as they downed their drinks or stared forlornly off into space.

It was very much like a death watch or sitting shivah. The fetid air smelled of age, beer and loneliness. Worst of all there was not a black face, or a woman, in the joint.

As Percival observed these lost and lonely men, he came to realize that his longing to be with people stemmed from a desire to be among black people. At that moment white people could only play on his nerves. Still, he had no wish to face the long subway ride home. And so he swallowed a bit of bile and trudged up to the bar, taking a stool at the far end.

The men at the bar sat watching the game on T.V. in conspiratorial silence, listening as the commentator drone on. The bartender watched from his side of the bar, then came to life as Percival sat and the bartender started toward him. "One more," a customer called as he passed. The bartender responded, "be right with you," then came to a halt before Percival.

"What'll it be," he asked, wiping the bar with a damp cloth.

"I'll ave a beer."

"A beer it is."

"Make it a mug, will you?"

"Indeed, laddy."

Percival winced at the word 'laddy' and flashed the bartender a quick, furtive glance, but he had turned away. He seethed below the surface: He had grown accustom to the abusive misuse of the word 'boy' in the mouth of racist white America by which to denigrate black men, whereas the lyricism of the word 'laddy' was, however, not so offensive as it was sentimental. It evoked an all at once disarming and bittersweet refrain of lost innocence for which, in his fragile state, he was ill prepared.

Percival sighed, trying to rest his guard, but was much too keyed up to let go.

The bartender plopped the beer in front of him.

"Fifty cents."

Percival lay the coins in the bartender's palm with the care of one paying the 'Ferryman,' Charon, passage across the River Styx, down to the House of Shades. The atmosphere palled on his spirit so. Indeed, he felt the inescapable coldness of death encased in his bowels tightening its grip.

Regardless, the bartender collected the coins (as does the 'Ferryman'), then passed on to the next customer and then the next, before returning to his spot in front of the T.V. screen.

Sighing softly Percival recast his gaze on the silent, blotchy faced men reflected in the mirror behind the bar through a veil of cigarette smoke, watching T.V. as they downed their drinks between balls and strikes. The silence went unbroken except for a fan balking at a bad call or two.

Percival was uneasy, watching T.V. between sips of beer. It was not the game nor the T.V., but the company into which he had strayed. These were an impotent and bloodless breed of men. And here they gathered to forget. He tried to shuck the desolation, taking a long swig of beer to wash it down. Yet, after he had smacked his lips and run the back of his hand across his mouth and put the mug down, his gaze followed the course of least resistance to the screen of the T.V.

The door opened with a plaintive cry, drawing his interest. He rolled his eyes from the T.V. to the panoramic bar room mirror and saw beyond his dusky reflection, a florid-faced, burly man, clinging to the open door, cigarette in hand, smoke rising, masking his face. The door creaked to a close behind him as he brushed in. He looked about with the familiarity of a regular, recognizing everyone without noticing anyone, and brought his gaze to rest on Percival's unfamiliar presence. He was struck by the fierce gleam in the fighter's eyes as Percival stared back through the smoky interior of the mirror.

The man paused, sucking on a cigarette, considering Percival's reflection, eyeing his shoulders and back in vague recognition, trying to jolt his recollection.

The bartender turned his head toward the sound of the closing door, and smiled on recognizing the new arrival. He glanced back at the T.V. to catch the tail end of the last play. He then called, "Hey, Mike, how was the fights? How was our lads."

"The fights," the man began, starting forwards, "there was this lad, Jones –" He paused mid stride, snapped his fingers, and turned towards Percival with a look recognition stealing over his face. "Of course," he exclaimed, "you're

Percival Jones! Harry! Come here a minute," he summoned the bartender. "I want you to meet Percival Jones, the best fighter of the trials! Fellas," he grandly announced, "This is the next captain of our Olympic boxing squad." He approached Percival with hands outstretched.

Percival chortled, facing the stranger. All the eyes of the barroom crowd focused in on him.

The burly man took Percival's hand, shaking it vigorously. Percival smiled, the exultation of the fight passing over him once again like a sweet dream.

"I'd like you to meet some pals," said the man of those leering at him. "If you don't mind, okay?"

"Not at all."

The man called the bartender again. "Harry, here's the finest boxer pound for pound since the Sugar man quit the ring. As they used to say, the Sugar man could give you diabetes. Well, I'll tell you, Harry, the lad's fight was a treat fer me ole sweet tooth."

Percival accepted the bartender's hand, smitten by the flattery.

"Glad to make your acquaintance," said the bartender. "If Mike says ya a good a fighter since Robinson, lad, take it as a complement. Mike here knows fighters better than most. It's good to meet a lad representing the American side of things at the games. It's an honor. Really an honor," repeated the bartender, as their hands parted.

"Give the lad another beer, Harry," said Mike. "And I'll 'ave me usual scotch n soda."

"Coming right up."

"I'll thank you kindly too."

"No! No more for me," insisted Percival. "I gota keep ta my weight."

"Right you r, lad. Harry! We'll pass on the beer," Mike shouted.

"Okay."

"Come here Pat Mahoney, you son of an Irish Mick n meet Percival Jones," said Mike as his eyes fell on a mottled face imp of a man, whose eyes sparkled lustrously from drink. He climbed off his stool and started over, paunch preceding. "Use to do some pugging in his day, before your time. No more than a fly weight. He's little more than an overstuffed fly weight now. He was called Irish Pat, 'cause he always wore green trunks with a shamrock embroidered on it."

Somewhat amused, Percival smiled as the fly weight advanced on spindly legs and feet no bigger than those of a child. He wore the sad expression of a pug who'd heard one bell too many.

"A Ray Robinson r you?" said Irish Pat tauntingly, holding back, looking Percival over, arms akimbo. "Maybe you 'r 'n just maybe you isn't. Ya got his shoulders sure enough. Ya tall n lean 'n you got the look of a wolf but 'r you mean? Do you 'ave the killer instinct? Let me feel you're grip," said Pat, seizing Percival's hand. Percival bore down mercilessly on the smaller man's hand, looking him keenly in the face. "Ay," Pat yielded, "you got a right strong hand."

"Ya ought to see the lad fight," interjected Mike.

"I'll see him tomorrow in the finals."

"You'll not regret it either."

Among the growing knot of drinkers was a late arrival, a man with bifocals who, on adjusting his glasses, sidled up to Mike and, leaning into his ear, asked, with a strong Irish brogue, "Who's the spade?"

"Nobody I'd wish to 'ave hear me call him that," said Mike, having recognized the newcomer from his reflection in the bar room mirror. "But if you must know, O'Shay, the lad's bound to be captain of our Olympic–" but as Mike started to explain, he was suddenly interrupted by the staccato like urgency of a teletype machine resounding throughout the room from the T.V., tick-a-tick-a-tick, with the words News Bulletin emblazoned thereon, followed by the voice of the program announcer, "We interrupt this program to bring you a special news update."

Then there appeared the familiar face of a popular newscaster: "Good evening ladies and gentlemen, currently in the wake of Dr. Martin Luther King Jr's assassination, there have been widespread outbreaks of violence in the Negro communities across the land –"

"What's that," cried Percival, staring up at the T.V. as if into diminishing space.

"'bout time King 'coon' got his!" O'Shay spouted for all the bar to hear.

Percival shut his eyes at the blasphemy, forcing back hot, angry tears. He knew the barb was meant specifically for his ears. And it came like a knife thrust, a cruel, ill-fated blow. He gasped with despair, as a blinding surge of blood rose to his head. Once more he bore witness to Martin's passing as played out like an endless loop in a "film nouveau," tightening his temples in a vise like grip. Suddenly, unable to bear it anymore, he stiffened, glowering at the scarlet faced stranger. A lightening flash of contempt crossed his face, enraging him.

The bar was uneasily still and all eyes curiously set on Percival and O'Shay, while the news broadcast throughout the room: "In New York, Harlem and Bedford Stuyvesant riots have broken out –"

23

Mike stepped aside, leaving O'Shay exposed. The other onlookers dropped back as well.

Seething with anger Percival stared at the ashen faced stranger as if he would throttle him, recounting, as he did, the many scars from racial slurs, insults, and wrongs accrued over the course of his young life, and there were enough to break a heart, wound the spirit, and stunt or belittle a lesser person. Nevertheless, he felt empty and used up, sapped by the monstrous stupidity of it all.

Whereas O'Shay saw Percival's feline strength; the fierce intensity and glint of rage in his somber eyes. He felt naked, vulnerable and afraid. In a word, alone. He began to sweat. Strangely enough he was embarrassed, caught in a trap of his own design. Therefore he became contrite, ashamed of himself for losing face in the eyes of his drinking buddies.

Percival turned away, and, trying to keep the tremolo out of his voice, said to Mike, "It's nice to have met you."

"The pleasure's mine, lad," exclaimed the burly man, looking to break the tension filled air.

"But on that crass note," Percival declared, looking wildly at O'Shay, standing dead still, "I better git going."

"Pay O'Shay no mind."

"No, I won't do that. I made the mistake of walking in here. I should'a known better. T'night of all nights. I think it's best I be going," said Percival, slipping off his stool. He eyed O'Shay in a fury and pushed past him, heading for the door.

"What did I say? Did I say King Coon instead of Dr. King Coon?" said O'Shay in false humor.

"Listen to yourself, man."

"I thought the fool nigger was gonna jump me!"

"Thank your lucky stars he didn't."

"Why? Who the hell is he anyhow?" O'Shay demanded.

"Only the best up 'n coming fighter on the scene t'day; 'n sure to be captain of our Olympic boxing squad."

"Ya don't say?"

"I do say!"

"I'll be damned!" O'Shay swore, sweating anew.

"The F.B.I. have been called in to conduct the investigation into the slaying of the Civil Rights leader and Nobel Peace Prize laureate," the newscast continued to blare out in the otherwise quieted room. Percival grappled with the door handle and drew it toward him, feeling the numerous eyes at his back. He looked out on the noisy street, and overheard the broadcaster say:

24

"We go to a tape of Senator Robert Kennedy, taken earlier today at a campaign stop after receiving word of the assassination."

"For those of you who are black and are tempted to be filled with hatred and distrust at such an act, against all white people, I can only say that I feel in my own heart the same kind of feeling " came the voice of the self-assured Bostonian Senator from New York, as he addressed a black crowd. "I had a member of my family killed, and he was killed by a white man…

"My favorite poet was Aeschylus. And he once wrote, 'In our sleep, pain which cannot forget falls drop by drop upon the heart until, in our own despair, against our will, comes wisdom through the awful grace of God.'"

"That was the Senator from New York. Robert Kennedy. Brother to the late President – John Kennedy. We now return you to your local broadcast."

An instant later the drone of the baseball commentators voice filled the bar room like nothing of consequence had occurred outside a foul ball, strike or run batted in.

As he fought to suppress the welling anger in his throat, street and car lights seemed to meld in a dazzling confusion before his eyes, and car horns blared relentlessly. The noise came at him like a jungle cry. He then leapt from the barroom doorway and dashed for the corner subway like a thief in flight. He hastened down the steps two and three at a time, borne on by a subterranean stream of air. When he reached the turnstile, he turned back to see the face of the man in the token booth. And when he was sure that he had caught his eye, he leapt over the turnstile, and was somewhat disappointed that the man had not shouted out after him. He laughed out loud at himself; and his laughter rang throughout the chamber with a resounding echo that came back on itself before fading down the long corridor of tracks over which a rattling train was quickly approaching.

He flew down the last flight of stairs, wild-eyed, looking to see if the train was his. It was the 8th. Ave. A, going into Brooklyn. The train rolled into the station, coming to a stop. Its doors opened with a hiss. He stepped in. The subway car was empty. The train doors closed at his back, and it pulled out with a tug from which his body swayed. He grabbed hold of an overhead strap. The lights in the car dimmed as the train rolled into the tunnel.

He plopped on to the nearest seat, clenching and unclenching his fist. His thoughts lurched along with the clattering train wheels, "'bout time King coon got his. 'bout time King coon. 'bout time'," resounded in his head, setting him on edge. He was angry with himself for not having struck O'Shay. *I should ave,* he thought. *I should've.* He balled a hand into a fist and struck his open other palm, wishing the more that it had been O'Shay's face! "Son of a –" As these thoughts crowded his mind, he became more and more angry with himself for not having responded out of his initial rage, but to have up and fled. He sighed, rolling and unrolling his fist.

The rotating wheels of the car against the tracks kept repeating in his head as the train hurtled through the tunnel, screeching to a halt at each station that other passengers might embark or disembark, then pulling out once more with a strenuous tug, lights dimming, rattling on into the darkened cavity ahead. He propped his elbows upon his thighs and lowered his chin into a palm, rocking with the train, trying to console himself. The comforting words of Martin's "I Have A Dream" speech spread through the pain filled caverns of his mind like an unguent, keeping cadence with the clattering train wheels: "I have a dream that one day," th-thump, "little black boys n little black girls," clatter, "will one day sit down at the table of brotherhood," clatter clatter, "with little white boys and little white girls," clatter clatter, "that one day my children will be judged by the content of their character 'n not the color of their skin," clatter clatter,

"I have a dream today —"

Clatter clatter.

When Percival first got on the train, he had every intention of going straight home. He was to have changed trains at Hoyt & Schermerhorn but his thoughts had run astray and he had missed his stop. When he realized it, it was too late; hence, with an indifference that befitted his mood, he rode the "A" on into Bedford Stuyvesant, and as he stepped out onto the empty subway platform at Kingston & Throop, an unexpected gust of smoke, wafting by, filled his nostrils. He coughed and choked and frantically tried to regain entrance to the safety of the departing train but, too late, the train had closed its doors and was well on its way out of the station.

Subsequently he found himself stranded and confused, amidst ribbons of smoke, in the gloomily illumined bowels of the Brooklyn subway system.

As the train faded rapidly down the corridor of tracks at his back, an eerie, muffled noise reached his ears which he could not place, any more than he could the smoke that trickled past in tatters. And as the smoke billowed and rolled towards him, his apprehension grew. He broke out in fitful sweats, sensing danger. The tumult from above at that hour on a workday was disorienting and as foreign as the patches of smoke wafting throughout the station. He realized he could not just stand there. He would have to move. Get out! He covered his nose and mouth in the crook of his left arm and inched his way toward the exit with the outstretched fingers of his right hand pressed against the subway wall through which he could sense the vibrations of the overhead commotion. It convulsed in him, shaking him in all his parts. Smoke seared his eyes and clawed at his throat, forcing him to wretch, to cough, to choke, batting his eyes, fighting back hot, scalding tears. He could barely see.

He stumbled along careful of his every step, afraid of what he would encounter when he hit the streets. The uproar from above grew. Shriek followed shriek, resounding off the station walls along with the tramping of feet, causing the hairs to bristle at the nape of his neck. The clamor was such it rattled the skeletons in the family closet. All the many years of repressed rage contained in the American negro psyche had been unleashed tenfold. That, or it was the fracas of thrill seekers at an amusement park raising hell. But this was not the noise of an amusement park. It was too sour and full of bile. This was Bedford Stuyvesant, not Coney Island.

"The inner cities of black America are in turmoil following the assassination of Dr. King. In New York, Harlem and Bedford Stuyvesant are in flames –" The news update came back to him fully blown. Black America was in crisis, licking its wounds while counting its mounting losses.

Martin Luther King Jr. would not go to the grave alone.

Police sirens and fire bells added another discordant note to the hullabaloo, causing Percival to slacken his pace. He exited through a turnstile and headed up the stairs to the street. A garbage can came toppling down the steps, rattling, spilling its contents as it flew past spattering his shoes and cuffs as he pressed himself against the stair wall to avoid being struck. "What the—," he spat, watching as the garbage can bounded down the steps beyond him and rolled to a crashing halt beside the vacant token booth.

"Anybody down there?" shouted a boy at the top of the stairs at street level, peering down.

Percival looked up through a haze of smoke, the sky over the youth's head was a ruby glow.

"Ain't nobody down there, lil' brother, but chickens," clucked an unseen voice.

The youth sniggered, starting off.

He emerged from the subway as if in response to the crackling flames, caught up in a dreadful nightmare from which there could be no easy escape; drawn on as if by a chorus of lost souls. The sky was alight with flames and acrid with smoke. A wild writhing cluster of angry rioters could be seen shaking fists and shouting obscenities, tossing rocks and bottles. Police cars and fire trucks interlocked at the intersection to offer cover for firefighters and policemen who hung over the hoods of their squad cars or stood in defensive posture behind them. Many a windshield had been shattered and the flashing lights atop squad cars were less than glaring in the rosy flames.

After regaining his breath, along with his vision, Percival stood on the sidewalk in mute disbelief, panting, and shielding his eyes with the back of a hand against the incandescent hallucination pouring in on him from the surrounding blaze. He swooned. There was a fire behind him on Kingston and another further down on Fulton, but the fire closest to him was on the corner of Throop, catty-corner to the subway from which he'd emerged.

The rioters, pressing in on the police blockade, were straggled out across the street. One caught sight of Percival stumbling over a "Do Not Enter" sign hung on a chain across the subway entrance. "We giving whitey hell soul brother," the rioter chortled. "Here, ave a brick on me."

Percival accepted the brick with reluctance.

The bar on the corner had been closed down with a steel curtain covering both windows and doors. A florescent sign was painted on the steel: "Black owned," saving it from the wrath of the rioters. But the unfortunate white owned stores on Fulton & Throop were ablaze. Long tongues of flame licking out from stores on both sides of the road created an intense updraft that brought the overlapping flames together into a column of black smoke. These were buildings the rioters were trying to stop the firemen from saving.

"This fucking place is like the bloody Congo," one cop complained to another, leaning on the hood of a car, shotgun at the ready.

"I just got home from Nam 'n it feels like I'm damn well back –"

"It's guerilla warfare all right."

"What pisses me off is the goddamn spooks got the bleeding-heart liberal politicians tying 'r hands."

"That's how it is," lamented the other.

More, perhaps, like Mardi gras in hell there existed an element of madcap revelry. The flames danced, sizzled and spat like a pit full of venomous snakes under the watery assault from fire hoses. But the fire raged on out of control, making everything shimmer in its leaping light, giving an appearance of instability to all it cast its eerie glow upon. The rioters were so grotesquely distorted by the coloration of crackling flames that they looked like members of a cast in the rousing finale of a burlesque show, as they jumped and spun about like whirling dervishes, whooping gleefully, "Burn, baby, burn!" And the flames soared higher and higher into the night sky. The roof of one of the buildings was heard to crash in on itself, sending sparks and flaming debris shooting off in all directions.

The firefighters were having a devil of a time fighting the stubborn blaze.

"Let's get a move on. Let's get more hoses on those fucking flames," shouted the fire Captain to his beleaguered men, trying to avoid being struck by missiles coming in from rioters.

Percival half expected to turn about and see Lucifer himself orchestrating the debacle.

Stones flew over vehicles, but most fell short of their mark or struck fire trucks and police cars. Under orders by the Mayor's Office to demonstrate restraint, the police were in a tizzy trying to hold rioters at bay, as weary firemen pointed hoses on roaring flames. Striving to keep within bounds of the Mayor's guidelines, the police were having a difficult time of it with projectiles constantly falling in on them. The rioters seemed hell bent on taunting them to recklessness.

A police officer shouted at rioters through a bull horn, "Okay, the excitement's all over and you can clear the streets and go home."

"We is home, mother-jumper, you're the ones who need go home," cried a woman shrilly.

The rioters laughed hilariously, and a hail of stones followed.

"Take that you white sons-a-bitches," screamed someone, flinging a Molotov cocktail that broke into flames at the blockade.

A deep sense of dismay clouded Percival's mood. He had longed to be among his own people. He had wanted to commiserate, to comfort and be comforted; in 'this' their hour of mutual grief; to reflect on Martin, the man, the dreamer and his dream. Yet the only solace available was of flames soaring skyward, and rioters dashing aimlessly about, and the ear-splitting wail of sirens. Hence, he said, as would a carnival barker under his breath, "Welcome to the fantastical, topsy turvy world of Alice –!" The thought was absurd, and he laughed, finding it reassuring. His next thought was, in the disturbing words of Malcolm X, *Here's King having dreams while the rest of us Negroes are having nightmares.* And this, inarguably, was the unfolding of a nightmare.

A police officer asked the fire Captain to have a hose raised over the rioter's heads. The fire Captain, more than glad to comply, instructed two of his crew to point a hose on the rioters. This they did with gusto. As the water cascaded downwards on the rioters, dampening their ardor, a volley of bullets was fired into the smoke-filled air.

Cursing, wet, and half scared rioters broke ranks and ran, some descended the subway steps. Dropping his brick, Percival was swept along in the mad scramble down Fulton St. A youth fell as he fled and was badly trampled; his back broken in the stampede. His mournful cry for "HELP" went unheeded until the fire hose had been redirected on the fire and police came and dragged him away.

Percival finally managed to disentangle himself from the fleeing band of rioters and, as they slowed down and came to a halt, he was able to slip off. The rioters began to regroup, collecting their courage. A few of them pulled whisky bottles from shirts and hip pockets and, taking long slugs, passed the bottles around. When the last drop of alcohol had been shaken from the bottles, they were flung at police on the blockade.

Stealing off, Percival slipped into the shadows. The smoke was cloying. It was hot. The fires raging. He was sweating profusely, and felt his safety threatened by the ongoing pandemonium. He hastened along fearful lest 'the devils of his lesser nature' escape their bands and bid him join the horde of howling rioters, looters and arsonists, expressing their grief, misery, and frustration with this nation, the country of their birth. Despite it all, they retained a remote, deep down, gut bucket sense in that they were the lost descendants of the African Sun god Ra, of pharaohs and kings, rulers of ancient empires of which the United States is but a pale shadow that had ruinously managed to subjugate them, reduce them in stature, turn their skin color into a curse against them, and, far worse, vilify them, as a people, before the altar of Heaven. As such, a just but long-awaited retribution, of which Dr. King's assassination was the spark, broke into flames. And the outcry, "Burn, baby, burn," was heard loud 'n clear across the land! Percival felt as if his fuse had been lit and he too was about to ignite. He picked up his pace, trying to distance himself from the clamorous mob.

Everywhere he looked stores had been gutted and glass strewn up and down the street. Cars were lying on their sides, their wheels gone, and anything else of worth gone with them. Then the cars were set ablaze. As he made his way uneasily along, feeling like a voyeur, Percival was more than shocked at how much of a battle zone Fulton St. had come to resemble in a few short hours. Stores had been sacked, gutted and left smoldering. Steel grates had been ripped from casements and dashed to the pavement under glass they previously protected.

The ominous wail of sirens was unceasing and inescapably nerve wracking, keeping Percival on his toes, alert and in the shadows, his mind and heart racing at full gallop.

It was growing late and the violence had barely subsided. Some rioters had sated themselves and taken their loot and gone home. Still a hardcore majority remained on the streets to give "the man" a respectful hard time of it. Looters were climbing in and out of ransacked stores like pack rats with stolen goods.

Cast adrift amidst a sea of flames, crossing the river Styx, facing, as he was, the fangs of Cerberus, the three headed dog guarding the gates of Hades, Percival realized, on reflection, that he had not paid the Ferryman, Charon, back in the bar, for a tour of Hell for naught. Indeed, he'd found himself trapped in the outermost nether regions of Hades—the ninth circle of Hell!

Every step he took thereafter filled him with trepidation. His heart throbbed so heavily in his ears he could barely hear the crunch of broken glass under foot. His eyes flared hot from dripping sweat he could not brush away fast enough. He felt down in his soul like a man about to be lynched, avoiding lighted areas like the plague, and watching looters from shadows as they fled sacked stores with all kinds of foodstuff and appliances. One such man left a furniture store with a lounge chair turned upside down atop his head and disappeared down an alley way, chuckling to himself, self-satisfied, "He-he-he-he-he-he-he-he."

Percival observed a teenager from close up as the kid crawled from a gutted store and was seized by a cop in front of a well-lighted storefront church. It was one of the only storefronts left in Bedford Stuyvesant with plate glass window intact. And from the ring of voices emanating from within, it was apparent that Church was in session. The minister's voice, reaching the ears of passersby on the street, rolled like thunder,

"'N though my brothers falter 'n fall 'n the fires a hell rage round, still I'll be found in the House a God praising the Lord –"

"Praise the Lord," came the consensus from the Amen corner.

"Hallelujah," replied the congregation.

A golden curtain draped the storefront window and gave a semblance of privacy to the faithful. A cross was inscribed on the window with the words "Sanctified Church of God in Christ."

It was the sudden appearance of a solitary cop from out of nowhere that caught Percival off guard and brought him to a halt more than was the wild, sickly look of panic in the abducted boy's face, though the boy's panic was far from lost on him. Percival looked around for where the cop had sprung from and where other cops might be.

An empty squad car with flashing lights, driver's side door thrown wide, and police radio crackling statically, was left standing in the street, front tires abutting the curb and motor running. The cop was solo, rogue, on his own.

"I know time's 'r hard and I know hell fire's all too near b't the nearer hell fire n damnation come the closer heaven's gate is for us who's made 'r souls ready for God's coming –"

"Let me go! I ain't done nothing nobody else ain't doing," cried the boy, dropping a radio and toaster to the ground where they smashed at his feet. "Let me go. let me go."

"I'm gonna put your face through that fucking church window, boy! N if you live you'll be so damn ugly no Jamima's gonna want'a make any little tar babies for you."

31

"No, man! What you want'a hurt me for," protested the youth, struggling against the cop's grip. "No, man, don't hurt me. What I ever do you, huh?"

The cop's back was to Percival, but he could see the distress in the boy's face and felt his grief as sharply as if it were his own. The cop's words came as a vexation, filling him with anxiety and rage.

"Oh, man, please don't," begged the youth.

"Shut your face you fucking punk," shouted the cop, drawing the boy back, flexing to fling him through the Church window. "Are those folks ever gonna be surprised when you come flying through that plate glass at em face first," the cop laughed.

The boy shut his eyes against the eventuality, drawing his arms protectively against his face to shield himself from the impact of his skull against the plate glass. He visibly quivered, aware for the first time of the sermon issuing from the Church, "Yeah though we walk through the valley are the shadows at disfateful time we'll not fear evil, 'cause like Daniel in the lion's den the Lord's angels r with us."

"Praise the Lord –"

As the cop began to swing the boy through the plate glass window Percival moved, acting spontaneously to the crisis, and before the cop could toss the boy Percival seized him by the shoulder and wrenched him violently round, fist raised for the knockout blow.

But the punch never fell.

Taken aback, Percival blinked in recognition, "My god, no! Not y-you," he blurted. "It can't be."

"Seems it is," uttered the equally startled cop.

The boy dashed off, not looking back.

There in the glow of street fires and light from the storefront church (most streetlamps had been smashed), Percival stared with dismay into the florid, shame-faced gaze of an old army buddy; a former comrade in the Paratroopers. They had undergone Airborne training together and were assigned to the same unit in Europe. Though not of Percival's caliber, he'd shared a second spot on the Division's boxing squad. They had bridged the color barrier and had downed many a beer, laughed, whored, and talked man-to-man of their future aspirations, private doubts and youthful regrets. Brothers in Arms, they had been friends.

In that instant of uncertainty Percival relaxed his guard, losing his edge, fist shaking, trembling indecisively, and without a moment's delay the cop drew his pistol, shoving it deep into his gut. Percival's eyes fell on the .38 chafing his navel, little able to believe the absurdity of the situation into which he'd stumbled. He grimaced, shook his head in disbelief and took an agonized

32

look into the cop's grim but troubled face. His old Army pal had obviously been shaken up as well.

Percival saw his former white friend's face contorted with frenzy, fear and rage in the lurid luminosity from nearby flames. No doubt, if he were shot and killed under these conditions there would be no one to fault but himself; and, all at once, he was horribly afraid, embarrassed and ashamed for the both of them.

"Steady Jones," cautioned the cop. "Just lower that fist and fucking back off e-a-s-y."

His fist menacingly aloft, Percival did not immediately respond. It was as though, looking through the cop, he had not heard him.

"God damn you, Jones, do as I say. I don't want to spill your fucking guts here on the streets in the middle of a damn riot but I'll blow your black ass to kingdom come if you don't drop that fist now," the cop spouted, cocking back the hammer of his service revolver.

Percival heard the menacing click, but as if from far off.

The cop nudged the gun barrel further into his gut. "Drop it now!"

Percival lowered his eyes dazedly and looked at the weapon, as from dream filled sleep. His lips tingled, turning numb. And a queasy feeling spread throughout his gut, as if his stomach would lurch.

"For ole time sake I'm holding back, but I wouldn't count on ole times too much, if I was you – not to say you're not my boy," the cop sniggered, derisively.

Percival blinked nervously and shook his head, feeling wave upon wave of emotion spiraling outwards from his center in concentric circles, verging on nausea.

"You don't much like that, huh? You'll like it or like hot lead more."

Sickened at heart, Percival's legs faltered under him and with a short gasp his balled fist loosened and fell limply to his side.

"That's better. I wouldn't want to kill you. You know that. I'm fucking fond of you, man. I've been boasting about you, telling the guys down at the precinct that you're gonna take these Olympics big 'n then go on to become middleweight champion of the world. 'n you know, Percival, I don't want'a kill off my prediction. It just wouldn't be right, would it? No, man, it wouldn't. I suggest you just back off 'n get the fuck out'a my face before I forget myself 'n waste your god damn nigger ass any fucking way," the cop concluded, shoving Percival back with the barrel of his gun. "Take to your heels. I want'a see you run Jones – Run!" "let's not forget to pray for those children on the street t'night raisin hell n carrying on causing pain and untold grief not cause they mean spirited, spiteful and bad like some wants us ta believe but cause they in the pit of desolation and jus' can't see to find their way –"

"Damn it," the cop swore as he, retreated to the safety of his squad car, gun raised on an advancing mob of rioters. "Get back," he yelled in to the fray, waving his pistol recklessly. "Get back or I'll shoot!"

It was not the gun that made Percival reel, but the face of an old friend behind the weapon, cast in a lurid ring of flames, with a menacing gleam in his eyes. He trembled with fear at the sight of the Devil in the guise of his old Army pal. The threat was all too real to go ignored. Of all people, a former Army pal whom, on another occasion, he would have entrusted his life to and vice versa! Yet, caught on opposing, contradictory sides of a race riot tearing at the nation's fabric, old ties come undone and friendships break apart. Moreover, deep racial wounds resurface. Suddenly more afraid than ever before, he found himself sinking under a tidal wave of doubt. He was less than nobody under the circumstances and could easily be killed on these parlous streets, in these deeply troubled times. Without raising a stir. His story would be dismissed as bittersweet. A man who'd lost the chance of realizing the highly desired and globally envied American dream. Thus shaken, he turned and ran, though not from the gun!

Sirens blared; fires raged; the madness was wild, unrelenting and all around. He had no sooner turned the corner onto Nostrand Ave., when more shots rang out: Bang! Bang! Bang! He stiffened, wavering in his tracks. There followed the ominous crash of glass and weird shrieks. He did not turn back but walked faster, sweating all the more, out of breath. Rioters rushed frantically about, this way 'n that, in a mad dash scramble to avoid the next round of gun fire, which followed soon after: Bang! Bang! Someone slammed into him without apology, twirling Percival about. Half dazed he continued on his way, thinking to himself, "This is fucking war. But if war where is the enemy? And where the allies?" Then, before him, as if in reply to his query, a sign "Black Panther Party For Self Defense," appeared on a storefront window riddled with bullet holes, many having passed through a poster of The Minister Of Defense, Huey P. Newton, regally ensconced in a high back wicker chair with spears in one hand and a rifle in the other. Percival almost laughed, but opened the door instead. A bell over the doorway rang, announcing his entrance.

A fearless looking young man, a boy actually, in a black leather jacket and beret looked up from a front desk on which a nameplate, Duty Officer, stood in front of a typewriter. "Power to the people," chanted the youth, as he came from behind the desk and met Percival under the glare of a bare light bulb that hung from the ceiling by a frayed cord.

"I'll have to frisk you, bro."

"You'll what?"

"He'll have to frisk you," said a woman brassily, standing in the doorway to the back quarters. "We got'a maintain a tight security. N besides, not all pigs come to a barbecue all dressed up for the roast."

A peel of laughter erupted from the room at her back.

She too smiled, seemingly amused.

Rattled as he was from the aftershock of the near fatal run-in with his former Army-pal-turned-cop, Percival was not amused. He rolled his eyes and gritted his teeth. He steeled himself and glanced sidelong at the woman posed in an inner doorway wearing a black beret with a Free Huey button, an unbuttoned leather jacket over a powder blue turtleneck sweater and black slacks. He was generally not partial to women in uniform, and the Panther costume gave her more the appearance of a biker's moll than a freedom-fighter. But, as far as he could see, that was her only blemish and did little to detract from her allure. In fact, he was pleasantly surprised. She cut an exceptionally fine figure, shapely, tall, buxom and pretty. She gazed at him with penetrating eyes, eyes that gleamed in her honey-colored face. Her lips were sensuous and full.

He had been fully prepared to be angry but his eyes widened as he stared over his shoulder and, smitten by her, found himself flustered instead. She was a troublesome presence given the circumstance and, with the thrill of his earlier ring triumph having all but vanished, he felt vulnerable.

She leaned her shoulder against the doorjamb, revealing the butt end of a holstered .45 below her jacket, and eyed him as the Duty Officer frisked him. Somewhat startled by the gun Percival raised his eyes to hers in faint surprise, like a lover who's recently come to learn of his sweetheart's infidelity. She returned his gaze without apology, seeming to know what he was thinking. As the hands touching him passed up his thighs, reaching for his crotch, he suddenly became acutely aware of them and would have drawn back but, not wishing for her to see him flinch, remained stoically still, despite feeling violated. More so since she stood sentinel over this vaguely rude and obscene procedure.

"He's clean, Captain," pronounced the Duty Officer, rising from his haunches.

"Captain?"

"I'm the Defense Captain, yes. Have you any objections?"

"No, only I'd think you'd be more interested in what's going on out there on the streets, than frisking unarmed people," said Percival indignantly.

"N if we were less concerned with what's going down in here we'd sure as hell be remiss wouldn't we?"

"They're not jus' drunk punks out there, you know, but kids."

"Who else you expect to be out there? Some Uncle Tom handkerchief head, doorag wearing Nigger?" She scoffed.

No, jus' some Panthers ta defend 'em."

"You think we're do nothing revolutionaries, ay? That this is a' kind a' blind? Meet some kids who've come in off the streets to escape the pigs."

She stepped aside allowing Percival to approach. There were a group of kids, street urchins, mingling with a small number of the Panther membership, all armed and similarly attired in berets and leather jackets. One zealous member read quotations of Chairman Mao to the kids from his "Little Red Book."

"Power flows from the barrel of a gun –"

Percival smiled lopsidedly and thought, *Why not quote Al Capone, 'A gun and a kind word will get you far.'*

A boy seated apart raised his head from out of the sports page of the Daily News and stared with a glimmer of recognition at Percival, then lowering his eyes back on the sports page he sought his likeness among the photos. He grinned, gleeful to see that they were one and the same. He flashed Percival a smile of recognition.

"Did you win?"

Percival gave him the "OK" sign.

"All right!"

The Defense Captain eyed the boy, then Percival. "As a rule, we don't pack but t'night the pig might try vamping on us 'n, like the boy scouts, being prepared is half 'a what's meant by being a Panther. If we got'a go down, some pigs 'r gonna fry."

"Right on, sister," chanted the cadre.

"You don't look much like a rioter to me," she said, speculatively, studying him, his body language. "So if you ain't no undercover cop, what might a strapping young man like yourself want with us if not hook up?"

"Obviously nothing," said Percival, turning to go. The tumult on the streets was, however, more harrowing for being inside where, through the plate glass window, despite the fires raging out of control on the avenue, one could more readily see in than see out. "I was jus' stepping out'a line of fire." He felt stuck, reluctant to leave, to go back on the streets swarming with rioters and cops, was, in his estimation, insane; though, too, this store front, which these Panthers would presume to defend, was no more defensible than a matchbox in a firestorm.

"Wait, brother man! Wait!"

Doubtful, he hesitated.

"Everybody's edgy," she went on, "the cops have been vamping on us all evening, trying to find any excuse to bust in, 'n keeping em at bay ain't been easy. They want us to lose control so in the heat of the fray they can waste us. A score a' them bullet holes in that window we got from pigs driving by trying to incite us. So yeah, we're jumpy, dig? But we ain't closing 'r door, we gonna stay open through this wild west show – gun fight or no!"

"A symbolic gesture, ay?"

"This is a riot, brother, not a revolution. You think this shit's in somebody's best interest? Well it's most certainly not in 'r's."

"It's probably in no one's best interest but that's not the point. To do nothing – I mean, to simply keep watch –" Percival stammered, befuddled.

"Bear witness while keeping the pigs at bay, "she interjected, "ain't exactly nothing, brother. 'He too serves who waits.'"

"What that mean? They're 'r our people – struggling for their liberty no matter how badly expressed."

"No-, no, – no," she corrected, "they're expressing they frustrations; they grief; they pains; they're not rebelling, they expressing something more surface. Yeah, a surface reality, man!"

"Come again? A surface what?"

"I mean 'r grief's as deep as a pit'a fire; dark as a crypt. Ancient as d' River Styx; 'n as painful to cross as the rivers of hell. That's so but come t'morrow they'll be shucking, laughing 'n jiving 'bout the loot they got; frustrations spent, Martin 'n the ground, 'n memory lost. But those who 'r sincere will realize how superficial this shit is 'n will come round to joining us, a really advanced revolutionary group."

"Right on, sister! Right on," sang fellow members in attendance.

"In the meantime, you sit it out? What a surface excuse. What about those getting their heads cracked, being hosed down the streets—you telling me they don't count? They got'a wait? I've jus' been hosed down! I'd climbed out'a the subway 'n, before I knew it, I was being bowled down the fucking gutter by water cannons! That's why I'm out'a sorts 'n pissed off by your lame dialectics!" He was still off balance from the encounter with the cop, an incident he wished to forget and was loath to mention. Their friendship was a thing of the past, and that night saw to its unmasking. "No, I'm not rioting, but given the color of the skin I'm in I, too, stand in the dock accused!"

"You stand in the dock accused, do you?" said the lovely defense captain curtly. "Well unlike you the rest'a us stand on the gallows condemned!" He blushed. "No!" She shook her head apologetically. "Wait, brother! I feel your

37

pain. I see your out'a joint. So 'r we all out'a joint. We're sweating in here, man, not jus' killing time. We're on the street. This is the street if you can dig it –know? We're no safer for being in here than out there. In fact, we might be in even greater danger. In here we're corralled. This is no safe house. The only reason the pigs haven't moved on us is they know we'll shoot back 'n shoot back we have 'n will continue to do so in self-defense. That's why we got gun men posted on roof tops above 'n across the street. No, we do jus' as well to wait for the pigs to come to us; that way we can pin 'em down in a crossfire! That, in fact, is 'r only safeguard.

"If you ran in here for cover, you took a wrong turn. I don't mean to belittle your concerns, brother-man. But don't trivialize 'r's either," she said, disconcerted. "What we're talking here is strategy. What you're talking is subjectivism. 'N when it comes to that what can I say? T'morrow is the only hope we ever had on this continent, in this country – this god forsaken western world in which we've been held captive since day one. If our hope rest in t'morrow it's 'cause we, as a people, 'r not yet prepared for revolution. T'day we're only prepared to riot. There's jus' nothing else for a vanguard party to rightly do. Let's face it, soul brother, all us lost Dr. King t'night – all! White folks as much as black folks. We know for a long while he was the spearhead of all 'r yearning's to be free – 'n right or wrong, the people gonna grieve in they fashion. Besides, they're thousands out on those streets. Thousands a' angry black folks 'n all the Uncle Tom politicians, Democrats 'n Republicans, begging em to go home; respect King's memory 'n denounce this display'a violence. But they there. They know all government handouts been given, taken, 'n 'spent, 'n they ain't seen a penny'a it; but these do-rag wearin', Uncle Tom, ass kissin' preachers 'n politicians 'ave!" She scoffed. "'N if we're gonna advance a step further it's 'cause we're gonna put 'r lives on the line differently. Nonviolence, pacifist action, died with Dr. King t'night! As a revolutionary, we don't approve of rioting. As for ourselves, we ain't gonna riot, we ain't gonna grieve, we gonna sharpen 'r knives, strap on 'r bandoliers 'n wait till t'morrow when we can pluck the fruit a this riot, marshal 'r forces 'n carry 'r banner forward. Ain't no sense doing this thing prematurely."

"The fist of my hands 'r the only dialectics that concern me," Percival snarled, shaking his fists furiously, but dropped them just as abruptly as he'd raised them, embarrassed at his bravur. He felt that he'd been seen through— revealed. That is, he had not knocked the cop out on the streets, nor the Irish Mick, back in the bar who'd insulted him by insulting Dr. King's sainted memory. He curled his restless hands at his side into fists once again, attempting to drive the nails into the flesh of his palms. He knew his argument was faulty: "More emotional than rational," as she had said. However, he was much too conflicted in himself to recognize the contradictions. "'N the best you have to offer is hope for a day's reprieve? This, you say, is the strategy of a vanguard party? O' Lord, deliver me," he exclaimed, inching towards the door. The night was not turning out as he'd thought.

"Yeah, come t'morrow we'll roast some pig," voiced a fellow Panther.

"You're too anxious, brother. When I say tomorrow, I mean it figuratively. Since day one, this nation's had us bound in a socio/political trick bag we Panthers 'r determined to free ourselves of, dig? We say, 'Whatever the Man's for we're against, 'n whatever he's against we're for.' Therefore, we got'a first reeducate 'r people to the need for armed socialist rebellion. As Che says, 'The only difference between a bandit 'n a revolutionary is that the revolutionary educates.' No, come tomorrow, we'll bury 'r dead."

"In that case you offer no more hope than brief mention in the obituary column," Percival grumbled, bracing himself for the streets.

"One moment," called the defense captain. "We're out there but we're in here, too. T'morrow revolutionaries 'r on those streets too! 'N while we're not rioting a good number of 'r cadre 'r out there, putting they lives at risk, trying to get these damn fools safely off the streets, 'n see they heads don't get cracked cause come tomorrow we're gonna need whole heads 'n not cracked skulls to pull this revolution off."

Percival cast one last flirtatious glance her way and said, "Anything's possible come tomorrow, pipe dreams 'n all!" He then turned out onto the riot torn streets and was hastily swallowed up by rioters and looters wreaking havoc as they went.

On passing the lighted office, a number of rioters saluted the Panthers inside with raised fist and chanted, "Seize the time!" While the majority sang, "Burn baby burn!"

The urchin with a copy of the Daily News approached the defense captain. "Look," he said, showing her Percival's photo in the paper. "He jus' won 'n fights in the finals t'morrow."

She took the paper from the boy and stared at the photo in disbelief, but when the boy had said, "t'morrow," she laughed hilariously, while others clamored round. "So that was Percival Jones." She shook her head, laughing the more. "I wonder how the hell he found himself in the middle of this shit?"

"I suspect, he must'a fallen down the bunny hole," someone said from the ranks.

"Wrong end," uttered the defense captain.

Said another, "I wonder how he's gonna find his way out?"

"God spare him," she said.

"For t'morrow?" asked the other.

39

"Percival Jones? Of course. He won? Good. I knew I knew him the instant he raised his fists," the duty officer remarked. "I've seen him work out at St. John's gym on various occasion. They say he's the best fighter to have ever come out of Brooklyn. And Brooklyn's had its fair share of fighters."

"I thought you had perfect recall," said the Defense Captain? "You might 'ave said something earlier, little brother."

"My mind was elsewhere," said the duty officer. "Such as on the immediate situation in which we find ourselves trapped, caught in the middle of a fire storm, with no means of escape save fight, kill or die," he replied, as a new burst of gunfire rang out close by. "We'll not walk away from this unscathed."

"These are hard choices, lil brother. This is 'r hour of truth!"

"And it might just prove our undoing, too. A fateful first, if not last, stand."

"It's the risk we run."

"I know," he said, then quoted Che, "'death is a concept a thousand times more real, a victory, a myth that only a revolutionary can dream of.' And so we dream," he exhaled.

"That 'bout sums it up, lil brother," she said ruefully.

"I'm not your little brother," the other fervently objected.

"Sorry Jamal, no offense intended."

Much to Jamal's regret she had roused his ire, challenged his masculinity, causing him to flush with emotion – rankling him. He had had no wish to be seen, as she had so vexingly put it, as "her," or anybody else's, "lil brother," particularly hers. He was seventeen and about to graduate Brooklyn college, far ahead of his years, at the top of his class, "summa cum laude," with a fellowship to MIT in his hip pocket. And he was already a lieutenant in the people's revolutionary army, The Black Panther Party. He was a scholar par excellence, worthy of her attentions. He had wanted to be looked up to. Moreover, he had wanted to be her one and only. In a word, her "guy." However she only saw him as a precocious, callow youth with his first beard not fully in, and, unlike Percival Jones, far too wet behind the ears. Though she did not say nor indicate it, she felt almost certain Percival would return.

Grateful for his safety, Percival found his way out of Bed-Stuy and the ongoing riot. By the time he reached Eastern Parkway, which bordered Bed-Stuy and Crown Heights, he was emotionally and physically spent. He had taken a roundabout route out of the ghetto, trying to avoid roving bands of rioters and further skirmishes with police.

He then crossed the majestic Parkway, paying small heed to the rush of oncoming traffic. At least one car swerved and honked, catching a glimpse of him in flight in its headlamps. A crowd of people were clustered in a knot on the far side of the parkway, pointing at the roseate sky and wreath of smoke overhanging the ghetto, much like the belching forth of the crematoria at Austchwitz, Belson, Ducheau, et al. It was an ironic twist of fate that had not escaped Percival's notice, that most of the onlookers were Hassidic Jews witnessing, in the flames over hanging Bedford Stuyvesant, their own more recent catastrophic past. It was, ironically enough, their neighborhood, Crown Heights, into which he had escaped. Indeed, a neighborhood into which the occupants of Bed-Stuy were fleeing with ever increasing frequency creating, in its wake, an underlying tension between Blacks and Jews. Percival took a backward glance at the plume of smoke rising over the ghetto. Much to his relief, the ominous wail of sirens and chilling cry of the distressed were at his back in the distance.

He slowly trudged the last blocks home on weary legs. He entered his apartment house and dragged himself upstairs. He entered the darkened flat and switched on the hall light revealing a narrow corridor off which a closet like kitchen stood. Then, without delay, he strode into the living room, throwing on that light, too. He continued down the corridor past the toilet and on to the bedroom. He flipped on the switch, as he stepped into the room. The conflicting sounds of radio and T.V. poured in through the air shaft. Underneath the howl of Eric Burdon's "a' house in New Orleans they call the rising sun," the latest newscast with the day's body count in Vietnam was heard along with an update on the assassination of Dr. King. But the garbled voice of Burdon would drown out the news, "it's been the ruin a many poor boy and god I know I'm one."

"Mothers, tell your children n't ta do what I ave done."

Percival stood still listening intently while looking about. The bed was empty. The sheets rumpled and in disarray. The faded smell of Joleen's perfume was stale on the air, like a wilted sprig of flowers, or the scent of baby powder. His eyes came to rest on an empty crib in the corner gathering dust, and his heart sunk in his chest. Small wonder he had had no wish to rush home. He flushed with the realization that in truth it had not been so much that he had wanted to be in the streets, but that he had, in fact, wanted to avoid coming home to an empty, loveless apartment and again being accosted by the pity of it all.

She was gone! The sweetheart and love of his life, Joleen, was gone. She had taken their son, Malek, and gone these past weeks to her mother's. And not a day went by that he did not hurt or try to make contact with her. For some unknown reason she would not talk to him or allow him to see his son. Or so her mother gladly informed him whenever he called. It seemed hopeless their ever patching it up, though he didn't know just why. One day they loved, another day they had a child, then came estrangement followed by abandonment. She had up and taken their son, the pride of his life, and left without a word. And that was all there was to it. No, there was also Joleen's mother, the family matriarch. "That black hearted witch," as he was wont to call her. She had been a constant source of conflict from the start, and had manipulated her daughters as ruthlessly as a Svengali.

Joleen had been her mother's plaything and took her mother's every word for gospel and had broken her commandments but once to his knowledge. That was when they had first set up house against her mother's wishes – not that her mother would have approved any more had they married. Indeed, she would have approved far less. But Joleen had repented her sin and returned home to her mother's house with their child in arms.

He wagged his head wearily. Despite it all, he could not understand other than to think that they had been too young. Still, other young couples made it; fought through it, and made it without their parent's blessings. So why not them? He could not rightly say. No! No! For as much as he would want to dismiss it, there was the ugliness of it, the brutality of it, the anguish. There was little or no compatibility between them. He had to admit that now. Nonetheless, they had had a child and *"that,"* to his thinking, *"must account for something."* They had had a son. His son. And his grief was all-consuming.

He fell across the bed face down before his mind began to reel. He buried his head in the pillow. A tear rolled out of the corner of his eye onto the back of the hand on which he'd cushioned a cheek. He tried not to think, to fall asleep. Gradually he fell into an uneasy, fretful slumber, filled with dark and brooding symbolism.

***

Bring – ri-n-g – i-n-g. Percival stirred, laden down with sleep, the phone insisting, i-n-g. "Uh," he uttered, fighting back like a fish thrashing on the line, being drawn up through murky layers of consciousness, breaking the surface of thought – gasping. The ringing was without cease. Ri-n-g – i-n-g. His eyelids rolled back, as he groped for the phone on the table by the bed, "ello," he sputtered, his sleep-filled eyes ached in their sockets.

The response was short, "Percival, that you?"

"Was las I checked," he yawned into the mouthpiece, feeling sore from the bout the night before and at the thought of having to repeat the effort again that night making him groan, "ugh," wanting to roll over, pull the covers over his head and go back to sleep.

"Who's this?" he asked instead.

"It's me, Morty, caught you at a bad time, huh?"

"Ya woke me."

"Couldn't be helped. I don't have much time. Got a bunch of calls to make. The Peace Parade Committee, War Resisters League and Veterans Against the War, will be sponsoring a Memorial Service later this morning in Sheep Meadow, Central Park, for Dr. King. Know the place?"

"I know it."

"Never know what you Brooklyn cats know."

"I know; we don't get out'a the sticks much. I'm sure that's funny but you'll pardon me if I don't laugh," Percival yawned again.

"Humor aside. Should we look to see you?"

"I'll try, sure. What time is it anyway?"

"Oh, yeah, it's to start at eleven-thirty."

"What time is it now?"

"Round eight-thirty."

Percival sighed heavily. "I'll catch ya later."

"By the way, congratulations."

"Yup," Percival emitted, ready to hang up and fall back asleep.

"Excuse me. Hold on. Someone wants to say 'hello.'"

"Sure thing," said Percival, clinging to the phone while Morty transferred the call; a fuzzy, electromagnetic tickle in his ear. He rubbed his moist, sleep filled eyes with the back of a hand and drawing his knees up formed a tent of the rumpled sheets. He closed his weary eyes and waited restlessly on the line.

"Hull'o," came a fluty voice, coursing gently through him like a sweet thrill, somewhat allaying the anxiety to which he had been rudely wakened. He opened his eyes wistfully, smiling. It was Racine, the thought of her face illuminated the gloom of the darkened room. He would recognize that trill-like gush of her voice anywhere. He wished just then that she were near that he might roll on top of her.

"Racine," he said groggily. "Hey, girl, how you be?"

"As well as any of us, I guess."

"Yeah," he said, fraily.

"Congratulations! Your win last night was the second most important feature in the news after the riots and Dr. King's death – for me, anyway."

"Thanks but given the order of events it doesn't seem like anything ta be congratulated on."

"It's more than most of us have."

"I wouldn't know," he said, gazing off into the sable dark. From the turbulent store of images cast in his mind's eye from the night before, coupled with the assassination of Dr. King, came a desire to escape it all; be done with

43

it all. Yet here he was, on the phone, having been awakened in response to it – corralled by it!

"The thing is I got'a fight again t'night, n I don't know I'm up ta it in the face of all that's going on."

"The timing must be awful for you."

"It couldn't be much worse. I don't want this thing screwing up my game but I don't see how it can't. I mean, t'night's all too soon."

"Maybe you should stay home and get it together and forget the Memorial Service, you know?'

"I can't see sitting here all day sulking either."

"In that case, care to meet and we can go together?"

"Sounds good. Where 'n when?"

"Say 59th. Street and Columbus Circle at eleven-fifteen?"

"I'll be there."

"It'll be good to see you. I only wish circumstances were different. I've got to get back to work. Care to have me put Morty back on for you?"

"No, I'll catch him there."

"And I'll see you at eleven fifteen."

"Count on it."

"By for now," she chimed and hung up.

Percival lingered on the line in melancholy reflection, and as he lowered the receiver, he thought it good to be seeing Racine. She would be someone with whom he could share his grief; someone who cared for him, loved him even, although he could not reciprocate. He was black. She was white. He was a fighter. And she a flower child who had rejected the promises of the American dream as a decadent, bourgeoisie fallacy which she knew something about. Conversely, he had been trying to gain a toehold in the very society from which she had fled. Except the closer he came to attaining it, the more mirage like it appeared on the horizon; to wit, the carrot before the mule. He shook his head, trying to rid his brain of the cobwebs. But once more, he was given over to a whirlwind of doubts, finding it all too easy to lie in bed in the dark cloaked in anger and brood. The words of the evangelist, "death where is thy sting," sprang to mind, hence the reply: "Today 'death's sting' is lodged in my heart along with the bullet that killed Dr. King and lay waste the hopes and dreams of countless black Americans, long yearning to be free."

Tossing the covers aside, naked but for a pair of briefs, he swung his bare feet to the floor. He snapped on the bedside lamp, casting a jaundice, fan like glow about, exposing the drab, sparsely furnished room in dire need of a coat of paint. Roaches scurried into hiding, but the more brazen crawled on as before.

It wasn't just King's death that haunted him so, but the long train of associations it engendered, longer than the castoff chains of bondage, longer than recorded history, than time itself. This dreadful uncompromising thing called death, the frigid big "D" left him cold and isolated; crawled up his spine and fixed itself at the base of his brain like a nagging afterthought, and left him wondering how many blacks had been killed the night before on the riot torn streets of America. Luckily, he himself had escaped unharmed and had not been wasted on the streets of Bed-Stuy. He could still see the flames reflected in the eyes of the flustered cop's face. And felt the horrible sensation of the open end of the gun barrel pressed against his navel. The mean-spirited dig, "I'll blow your black ass to kingdom come!" sprang to mind.

"Son of a—" he growled and swung his cloudy gaze from the empty crib to the vanity against the wall at the foot of the bed with a partially open draw from which a lone stocking hung to the standup closet beside the door and finally on the narrow air shaft window which allowed a modicum of light through the tightly drawn blinds. A conflicting trumpet of noise from morning television and radio crisscrossed one another in the air shaft, warring for space. The sounds came together through his bedroom window in a cacophony, as if a brawl were brewing outside his window.

The poverty of the room had come to shame him. When he first took the apartment for himself, two and a half years back, he was grateful for it. It was a pad – his pad – a place to hang his hat, call his own, lock the door and shut out the world. He would fall on the couch and look up at the ceiling and feel as free as a bird under a vast sky for it was his place, and no one could deny him access. That was until Joleen moved in with him six months later. Then the poverty of the place became apparent with each new stick of furniture she brought. He grew to despise it and would no longer have come home but for her. Though he too began to feel somewhat lessened in her presence, as though the poverty of the place was his mirror image. He was made to feel this even more acutely when Joleen became pregnant and gave up her job, staying home and watching soaps half the day, internalizing these serials and translating them into real life situations. She began to look and react toward him as if the grit of poverty were on his hands and would rub off onto her with his touch. And she carped at him more and more for it.

"I don't know why I ever moved into this dump with you in the first place," she brayed at him. "How are we to raise a child in this place?"

"What 'r you talking 'bout? We was raised in no better."

"Not my child. I want more for my child."

"Our child."

"Not while it's in my belly," she flung at him.

"What do you want from me?" he hopelessly asked.

"From you?" she sneered, laughingly. "I don't even know I want you."

He walked to the living room window in confusion and peered out on the darkened quadrangle below with an empty feeling in his gut, wondering what his life was coming to?

Joleen was so taken in by appearances that substance eluded her completely, and he felt certain that it was more the appearance of poverty than it's reality that had compelled her to finally take flight.

Joleen's reaction to what could only amount to a temporary setback baffled him. After all, he was employed, in night school and the best boxing prospect to come along since Sugar Ray Robinson. Their fortune was well in the making and sure to be had with a little patience. After all, they were young and full of possibility and had not yet plumbed the depth of their resources. Therefore it was difficult for him to understand, especially since she too had been raised in Bedford Stuyvesant and came from a lower middle-class family. Though with pretenses to the contrary. Her mother saw them, 'as millionaires temporarily embarrassed.' But no matter how hard her mother tried to conceal, the surrounding reality of Bed-Stuy, from her daughters the eventual outcome was a foregone conclusion.

Her father was a peach-brown Georgian; a retired civil servant; a tragic non-entity his wife treated dismissively, his youngest daughter, contemptuously and she, Joleen, ambivalently. At one time he had been dashingly handsome but was now emasculated in his own home and spent his declining years perpetually drunk and snoozing in front of the living room T.V. with his pants open and penis protruding snail-like out his jockey shorts. His wife and daughters came to view this pathetic soul with vast indifference. "Don't mind him," they'd say dismissively.

His wife, Mrs. Reel, on the contrary, labored ceaselessly at keeping up appearances. Mr. Reel was the one drawback in this charade. But she, Mrs. Reel, excused him, saying, "he pays his freight." Besides, as stupefied as he was, he was out of her hair and she was left to run the show, which was all to her liking. She thought herself a bourbon, high born, in other words too good to be a Negro. In fact, she was as much Indian and white as she was colored. Otherwise known as high yellow. She could have squeaked past, but confident of her superiority, she didn't try.

Slender, tall and elegant, Mrs. Reel's hair cascaded in silky black and gray waves about her shoulders. Her voice was sultry, redolent of Virginia honeysuckle. She worked in a fashionable upscale mid-Manhattan boutique dressing mannequins. And she dressed with such fine taste herself that it was not quite beyond the realm of possibility to see her at work in the boutique window and mistake her for one of the mannequins.

She had once told Percival, in all sincerity, pointing from the terrace of their new Ebbets Field apartments (to which they'd moved to escape Bed-Stuy and its predominantly black population), at a group of young blacks lazing in the courtyard below: "They ought'a take coloreds like them, line em up n gun em down." She was angered that she had moved to no avail; she had hoped instead to have been able to look from her balcony and see white people gamboling merrily over the diamond that had once been Ebbets Field, former home to the Brooklyn Dodgers, Holy Ground.

Horribly surprised, Percival responded, "they'll kill us all."

"Oh no," she reassured him, "the better of us will be spared."

"Who'd decide?" he asked, glancing at Mr. Reel drunk as usual in his lounge chair.

Moreover, Percival believed that had he the money, nothing including mother love, could have taken Joleen from him. But, had he the money, obviously Mrs. Reel would not have objected half so strongly. Which was too bad because one day, he vowed, he would have the money and plenty of it too!

He gazed at the vanity beyond the darkened room which was reflected in the lamp light as it glowed on the mirror's surface. It conjured up numerous intoxicating illusions and unquieted thoughts and feelings. The mirror beckoned to him like the come-hither hand of a gypsy fortune teller, and his reflected image stared back at him. The more his weary eyes tricked him, the more his attention was drawn to the glow of light, and he was swept away by dark suggestions drawn from the wellspring of his subconscious.

He dreamily observed Joleen as she brushed and combed her raven black hair a thousand strokes each before bed, often using the ritual to avoid sex and, if he were still awake after she was done, she would then mask her face with cold cream as a further deterrent. In the morning she would wipe off the faded cold cream in front of the vanity and apply make up to her lovely face, with a careful an artist's eye. The end result was always spectacular. Already lovely, her beauty now shone forth as if from the cover of a fashion magazine. This transformation never ceased to amaze; for as pretty as she was, as fair of skin, she became even more so. She was like Moby Dick, whiter than white, Snow White with ruby lips, rose petal cheeks, and raven black hair. All she lacked, as far as he could tell, was a glass coffin in which to be lain.

She smiled at him from the mirror in a wicked cock teasing way. It was a smile that held out every promise but was quick to renege on delivery. She then laughed at him toyingly like a capricious child – it was the very laugh with which she mocked her father. He blinked and shook his head as peals of

47

laughter issued through the air shaft from a morning talk show and, shifting his sleepy focus, he was startled to discover that Joleen was not there and that he had fallen asleep.

He reached behind him, seized a pillow and flung it at the vanity. "Bitch!" he swore, as the pillow struck the mirror and fell harmlessly to the floor. He was taken aback at the unusual display of temper and thrust his hand dejectedly between his thighs, wondering how it was possible to be denied that to which one is born. Although he had come to realize, intellectually anyway, that it had all too tragically become the plight of black Americans. *So much so it's taken in from infancy with our mother's milk,* he thought. *Just as now Joleen feeds it into our son's gut, blood n brain; pours it in through his mouth from those succulent, warm, Nubian breasts of hers.* He felt a pang of envy, for he too longed to drink from those magnificent orbs. He caught himself and laughed with hilarity for being jealous of his own son when, in fact, he no longer knew whether he loved or hated Joleen. All he knew for sure was that she was a recurring source of conflict in his life. Wagging his head, looking dishearteningly about the drab, cheerless room, it's walls closing in on him, he leapt to his feet, anxious and somewhat claustrophobic, but no matter which way he turned no immediate avenue of escape presented itself. He felt trapped. And the longer he stood the more he came to doubt his senses and felt that his legs would drop out from under him. As such, he sat back on the bed, his body sagging forward.

He caught sight of the phone on the bedside table and eyed it as if it were a life line. He reached desperately for it and dialed the first number that entered his head and held on with baited breath as the phone rang on the far end.

It rang repeatedly.

"Come on," he implored, face contorted. Then came a click on the distant line, followed by a florid, "Hello?"

"Lily," said Percival, thankful for a friendly voice on the other end.

"Percival," she responded, buoyantly, "I'm glad you called."

"I'm glad you're glad."

"Tell me – how 'r you?"

"I'm only half sure myself."

"That's better than most, honey. Cause, honey, the papers say you last night's big win," she chortled.

"What the papers don't know ta say is I might well ave been last night's biggest loser."

"T'day's not much for congratulations is it?"

"N't when everybody else is waking up more like it's the morning after a horrible night before – no, I'd say not."

"My way of being lighthearted."

"That's why I love you so. You have a feeling for things."

"'N one is when to get off the phone," she said, teasingly. "You gonna talk to Rufus, aren't you?"

"If I ave ta."

"Ya ave ta."

"If you say so."

"But I do."

"How's he doing?"

"Much like the rest of us, though he won't admit it. You know that man'a mine almost as well as me," she sighed. "Jus' can't get him to do right; stop getting high so much n going to work steady, n well, you know, you the one got him this las job."

"Can't fault him for not going to work t'day."

"Not today but yesterday n the day before?"

"Mmm," Percival murmured.

"Lord knows what, but he's got something," she laughed, "that man'a mine."

"Yeah, he's got you. Let me tell you, I wish I had a sister like you ta not give up on me."

"I could love you for that, Percival," she blurted.

"If only," he mused.

"Let's not," said Lily, as if she had already dismissed it. "T'day's dim enough without piling up 'If onlys."

"You're right – you're always so right."

"Quit that," she scolded.

He blushed.

"Before I call Rufus, ave you been able to see your son?"

"No," he replied dryly.

"What sort'a woman is she?"

Percival's face warmed with blood and, blinking back tears of anguish, he was even more reluctant to speak to Rufus. He asked, "' n how's your pregnancy coming?"

She sucked in deeply, galvanizing herself.

He felt he'd struck a tender nerve.

She slowly replied, "I honestly can't say. I'm under too much stress. I'm always edgy. I want this baby. I want it for Rufus. I want it for the both of us. But I'm torn. It's been nearly five months n it's not progressing as it should. I'm afraid. I mean, really afraid. I feel much sicker than I ought, n sometimes it feels more like a tumor developing than a fetus."

49

"Have you seen a doctor?"

"Who can afford a doctor?"

"I got some spare cash."

"Thanks, but I can't allow it."

"Why not, I'm like family ain't I?"

"You know the song, 'Mama may have n papa may have/ but God bless the child that's got his own."

"On that note, I'll talk to Rufus," said Percival feeling, overly exposed.

"Rufus, telephone," Lily called out fetchingly.

"I ain't in no mood to talk to no fucking body," Percival overheard Rufus shout in response to Lily's summons.

"It's Percival," she shouted back.

There followed a short thoughtful silence, then Rufus gruffly conceded, "Okay, okay, I'm coming. Got'a git my pants up, damn it!"

Percival smiled to himself, "same ole Rufus."

"Percival," said Rufus curtly, having taken the phone from Lily. "What gives?"

"You know, man," said Percival thinly, well accustomed to Rufus' curtness. "I know I need not say."

"Say what the talking drums saying all night long? Shit's brewing 'n the natives 'r restless in they skin, man. So yeah, I know what's jumping off!"

"Small surprise there," Percival agreed. "No, man, what I want'a say is there's gon'a be a Memorial in Central Park –"

"That too the drums playing."

"Ya making it?"

"What for? Malcolm's the cat I dug, dig? I mean, man, I hardly dug King when he was alive preaching his pacifist shit, 'n I ain't gonna mourn or bury him now he's dead – But, if you like, I'll lend you a shovel." He laughed, nervously.

Percival listened gravely.

Rufus could be rash, thoughtless, insensitive and cruel believing that that was how a man was supposed to act. Moreover, he was tough, querulous, vulnerable and moody with a tendency towards truculence not wishing to appear soft, racing, as he was, headlong, to an early grave – as was the inclination of every other young black man running, trying to outstrip the demons of the nation's past, the hounds of hell that bedeviled them like the mythical Furies of Greek folk lore, pursuing their ill-fated victims to their inevitable doom. What terrible crime had they committed to deserve such a fate? They were born in America, the wrong country, the wrong color. And so they ran, ran in a blind, ran into objects that would spin them about. They ran

50

without cease and would not stop until overtaken by the pernicious forces that characteristically lurk in the darkened corners of the status quo. They ran for a freedom that was not to be had. Hence, they ran directionless and scared. "Nowhere to run. Nowhere to hide," as the song goes.

"There's no such thing as an old black man," Rufus railed, "except them uncle Tom so called negroes; n you can't rightly call them men! They've betrayed they rights to be called men," he claimed. Frayed at the edges, Rufus' strings were more tightly wound than most. It was not at all surprising that he had been dismissed from the military on a Section Eight following an extended stay in a military mental facility after a breakdown on the battlefield which resulted in the assault on his squad leader while under hostile fire:

The incident occurred on a routine recon operation in the Macon delta, the jungles of Vietnam, on one of many such missions for Rufus. Suddenly his squad came under enemy fire. Scrambling frantically for cover as did the others, Rufus tripped and fell, his rifle getting away from him in the underbrush. He groped about on hands and knees, panic stricken, sweat cascading down his grim face. He had not looked long when he found himself at the feet of a young VC, a boy, certainly no older than he, staring down on him through his rifle sights. Rufus stiffened, looking back at the VC for what felt like an eternity – a span of time in which his life twirled hallucinogenicaly before his mind's eye. He was in such panic that he had lost awareness of all else taking place around him, his heart pounding explosively in his chest. Sweat bejeweled his frightened black face under his steel helmet.

"Oh g'd not now," Rufus pleaded, trying to shield his face with his hands, tears leaking down his coffee colored face shining wetly in the Asian sun. "Not like this," he implored.

The heat from the overhead jungle sun was so intense that the air shimmered vaporously as if the jungle itself was about to ignite.

"Why you here black man. not enemy. go home. go. go." the VC shooed him away. "Go," he snarled in broken English above the confusion of the fray to Rufus' befuddlement and terror that had held him fast. And for the first time in his life his color had not automatically sentenced him, been an object of derision, hostility, a misery for which he felt obliged to apologize, a Cosmic joke, but, of all things, a lifesaving asset. It was more than he could bare, more than enough to shatter his psyche and shame him for having been thus spared. For how was he to now look his white comrades in the face and try to be just another one of the fellows – though that pretense had long since failed Or, for that matter, face his black brothers in arms. After all, they too were killing Vietnamese. But, far worse, how was he to fire another shot at any one of these people, America's enemy. Gooks? He was at his wits end, giddily wafted away on the sultry jungle air.

Strangely surprised at still being alive, Rufus removed his hands from his face, his heart having sunk out of him and cautiously watched when, as the young VC turned away, a solitary shot rang out above the others, reverberating through him like a thunderclap. "Ugh," he gasped, and almost felt the plash of blood as the bullet ripped into the guerrilla, tearing flesh and smashing bone, ripping a substantial hole through his torso and pitching him face forward to the jungle floor.

Rufus' squad leader, having noticed his predicament, killed the Cong.

Rufus was stunned out of his wits, as if twice over a witness to his own death. He then scrambled over to where the body lie and, tears in his eyes, turned the fresh corpse face up. As he gazed into the dead youth's sightless eyes, he wondered, how many of these people had he killed? How many graves had he helped fill with their broken limbs? Strangers! And now all those strangers stared back at him in the lifeless gaze of this one broken boy. There too, he saw his own cruel fate reflected and he wanted to scream and scream and not stop screaming.

"Saved you worthless ass, didn't I?" his squad leader said, coming up on Rufus from behind, and slapping him soundly on the back.

Then Rufus screamed, "Ayyyyyyyyyyyyyyyyyy," leaping to his feet, seizing his squad leader by the throat, and together they toppled backwards to the ground. Rufus' fingers were like a steel trap on his throat, thumbs pressing into his wind pipe, trying to crush it to jelly. It took half the squad to pull him off, hold him down and tie him up. And while he screamed, wept and intermittently laughed, they pulled back to safety amidst the rattle of gun fire, and radioed in for a Medevac. On its arrival, Rufus was strapped into a straightjacket and, like so much freight, packaged aboard the chopper and evacuated from the area.

"Save the bastard's worthless ass," choked the shaken squad leader as he watched the helicopter lift off, "'n the fuck tries to strangle me. If that don't beat all," he swore, still feeling Rufus' claw-like grip on his throat.

The other squad members looked on dumbly, uneasy, not talking, disquieted at having witnessed yet another aspect of war aside from loss of life or limb, but one of mind; and, moreover, the spectacle was chilling.

At first Rufus was flown to a field hospital, then transported to Saigon and finally airlifted back home to the States where there were proper facilities for such problems. He had drawn into himself and had become unreachable, "catatonic," believing himself dead and finally rid of the white devils who could no longer do with him as they would. For no matter how deeply they

52

probed with their icy instruments to retrieve him, he was far beyond them and their sterile analysis. And for the next year, Rufus remained in the mental ward of an Army hospital. An obsessive paranoid with definite schizophrenic tendencies, he was put on medication and released on outpatient care and discharged from the Army with a disability, granting him a small pension.

Rufus' military sojourn had taken him through slaughter, landed him in an Army mental hospital and, finally, on separation from the Service, led him to join the clamorous ranks of dissenters on the streets of America in protest of the Vietnam war. He had joined a Vietnam Veterans Organization against the war, and like so many Vietnam veterans who opposed the war, Rufus felt uncomfortable with the Movements anthem, "Hell no, we won't go," as did other Vietnam Vets. But with time, its sting became less venomous and more a reminder of why he now stood in opposition to the war. Indeed, it was primarily because he had served there.

Percival first met Rufus at a meeting of dissimilar Peace groups, in lower Manhattan. It included the Vietnam Veterans Against the War; The 5th. Avenue Peace Parade Committee; The War Resisters League; The Dubois Club; Youth Against War and Fascism; and the notorious Students For a Democratic Society. It was somewhat ironic how few blacks were in attendance, considering the topic under discussion was Mobilization of The Black Communities. It was even more amusing since the proposal on the table, one of countless others, called for simultaneous rallies to be held in Harlem and Bedford Stuyvesant in support of Muhammad Ali, the deposed heavyweight Champion, stripped of his crown by a white American Boxing Commission as a direct consequence of his refusal to be inducted into the armed forces, stating, "Ain't no Vietcong ever call'd me nigger!"

A suggestion was made that it might be prudent to call off the rallies at that time. Since it was doubtful that the police would issue parade permits, and that the possibility of arrest was almost a certainty under the circumstance, dealing with the police in the ghetto was a risky business at best, and, for whites thought of as outside agitators, it could go badly.

"Let's go to jail! It's moral cowardice to do less," Rufus said sharply, standing abruptly, scrutinizing the crowd closely in his cross-eyed gaze. A breathless, numbing silence followed. No less bemused than intrigued, Percival raised his eyes, anxious to hear what else Rufus would say. He did not have long to wait. "'N there's not much hope'a 'r getting more blacks downtown either," Rufus continued. "We's here or don't you see us? We is who you got 'n you who we got! Let's not bicker," he said. "Who's surprised more blacks ain't here – downtown? Who? I don't see any'a y'all running uptown to no meeting," he said rudely. "Downtown's white man's land. We isolated 'n cut off. Besides, we all too damn busy being conscripted 'n getting 'r asses blown off in Vietnam, the war we here to stop, 'n there jus' ain't gonna be no easy way'a doin' it, dig?

"Fact is it's more necessary these rallies go on now than ever. Too many blacks die every day in Nam ill informed. It was so in my case. I live in a ghetto. Raised in a ghetto 'n poorly educated or, that is, educated to the man's purpose. The white man's, that is!" Again he paused, his eyes roving the room, trying to gauge whether his words were taking effect, sinking in. He weighed his audience as they measured him. He was of an unknown quantity, virtually unreadable. If, however, looks were any indication, his sensuous, wine red mouth gave him an air of wanton sexuality. And his cross-eyed stare was that of a predator capable of inciting lust in women's breasts and fear in men's hearts – particularly those afraid for their women's sake. He was the personification of the stereotypical "bad nigger"— cunning, angry, crude and menacing. A trickster, Stagger Lee—the Afro/American folklore equal of the Greek, mythic hero Odysseus— who'd incurred the wrath of many. As such, he was feared. Appearances to the contrary, Rufus was well read, an autodidact, and working, in fits 'n starts, towards a bachelor's degree. It could be said that he was a closet intellectual, an anti-intellectual intellectual, disdainful of academia and academics. He was especially indifferent to white people. He felt he could not trust them; therefore, he had no reason to like them.

He was furious at the god-awful world into which he was born and the misuses to which it had put him!

Save for the dead in Vietnam, he saw danger all around. He sucked his burgundy lips between his teeth, then went on to say, "I could hardly read. Still hardly read." He had no qualms fabricating in order to gain a point. "What I know comes from experience, 'n experience tells me more 'n more blacks will die in 'Nam 'cause they can't get a college deferment. 'Cause they poorly educated, ill informed 'n hungry. 'N one gets three square meals a day in the military 'cause a' Army runs on its guts 'n must be well fueled in order to fight.

"If I fought, 'n fought I did, it was for three square meals a day. If I killed it was to keep my belly full. When you grow up hungry you develop no more ethics than it takes to fill your plate; no more ethics than a rat scrounging round your baby sister's crib for a morsel'a food, even if that morsel turns out to be your baby sister! Sadly, that selfsame lil sister became severely brain damaged from eating flakes of lead paint off the apartment 'n hall walls of 'r tenement to stay the hunger pangs of growing up poor in the city slums. What saved me was I was quick with my hands, fast on my feet, 'n could sneak in 'n out those small Mom & Pop grocery stores like an Apache. But, yeah, as soon as I could

54

I ran off to join the Army— who wouldn't? Only, as I came to learn, a decision such as going into the Army should be made on a full stomach not an empty one— as was mine when I join'd! After high school, rather than face the man, I took to the streets as had many of my friends but saw, early on, some of 'em crack, land in jail, or end up dead from an overdose in some back alley with a spike in their arms. Worse yet, others married, entering into lifelong relationships that would sink them as surely as they had 'r parents. Friends I loved like family gone to seed shortly after stepping out of high school. I had no wish to share in their fate. So it struck me as if the Army was a safer bet. Little did I know the depth of the circle of the pit into which I would descend was far more horrible than any Dante, in his wildest dreams, could possibly imagine awaited me."

The Vietnam Veterans in attendance against the war eyed each other darkly, and nodded knowingly, in concert with Rufus' last words.

Percival recognized that the hunger of which Rufus spoke was similar to the hunger that fired his ambitions as a fighter.

"Am I on drugs?" Rufus asked, "Yeah, I'm on drugs, prescription drugs mostly. I need 'em to cope with what I did 'n saw in Vietnam. 'N sometimes it's not enough. I don't eat half so much anymore either since developing a bad stomach, 'n bad conscience to go with it. I'll bet none of you ever had to make a decision based on having missed a meal," he said, with impudence, rolling his eyes slyly. "I missed scores 'n scores of meals as a kid growing up in the ghetto! Scores! Some people see me 'n confuse me with being slim. Hell, I'm not slim I'm malnourished is what I fuckin' am!" he growled. "It limits your scope, that's for sure. Back'd against the wall in the 'hood, hungry all the time as I was, I'd'a kill'd God himself for a crust of bread. No, in fact, I did kill him! Kill'd him in Vietnam along with my soul! But I've since come to learn that if you're well-off, well educated, 'n well fed you'll kill him for far less," he said knowing full well his remarks would upset both atheist and agnostics alike, all of whom were well off, educated, and possessed student deferments. As Rufus saw them, they were middle class, white, college age kids out slumming. Therefore, he felt justified in dismissing them out of hand. His anger was such, however, that he had unintentionally disparaged veterans from the international peace organization, "Global Peace Project," there in support of the American peace initiative. If it were his intention to grab their interest, he'd certainly done that. They were riveted, all eyes were unswervingly focused on him.

"Anyway," said Rufus, "my belief in God was kill'd in 'Nam along with my belief in my soul; even belief in myself. All of which I'm trying to recover. I mean, trying to believe in God again; trying to believe in my soul again;

55

trying to believe in myself again; trying to retrieve my life, my self-worth, my sanity, from out'a that which has since become the American void." Rufus paused as outside street noises entered the room through an open window fronting 9th. St. & 7th. Ave. South, looking out over Sheridan Square. Someone got up and lowered the window, muffling the street noise. Rufus smiled wanly, appreciative. "If through 'r efforts we spare the life of one Vietnamese person, I will be relieved for much'a the ugliness that haunts me because a' the crimes I committed in the name of 'r country against those ancient people. I suffer. All us Vets suffer 'causea the hand we played in Vietnam," he said, stirring the communal pot of emotions. "So let me say, while we talk, they die; while we debate, they perish; while we speak, bombs 'r exploding all over Vietnam; while we go 'bout 'r daily rounds, the Vietnamese people 'r catching hell. A hell of r nation's making. A hell we're suppose to be committed to stopping.

"So how do we wait? Seated on 'r hands with 'r conscience in check? There must be more to a peace movement than that. We're damn well obligated to seeing this war to an end. It's gone on far too long already. Jail? What day in America's not a sentence for blacks? Jail for us in America's an everyday affair. I guess when you shout, "Hell no, we won't go!" ya not only mean you won't go to Nam but you won't go to jail either. I was in Nam, like the rest'a the vets here against the war. It was not out'a conviction that I went. But I tell you, if I can go 'n kill out'a lack of conviction, I can readily go to jail out'a conviction. The hell with jail. For us it's only a few hours out'a 'r day, for them being conscripted, being sworn in, being shipped out, them on the battlefield, 'n for the Vietnamese people it's not prison, but death! A death of 'r nations making! We can't delay 'n call ourselves a peace group, a' antiwar movement – not in good conscience anyway.

"The hell with it, let's go to jail 'n be done with it!"

Rufus' comments were met with overwhelming approval and resounding applause, broaching no opposition.

Percival, like everyone else, had been favorably impressed. But in the weeks and months to come, aside from the periodic flights of prophetic inspiration of which Rufus was capable, Percival came to know his other side, the deeply disturbed, paranoiac, Jekyll n Hyde-like personality disorder; the sump into which his soul would descend, a depthless chaos which the glassy surface of his cross-eyed stare gave only the vaguest hint. The side to him that had yet to leave Vietnam.

It occurred to Percival as they spoke that dark day, that Rufus was in a mood swing and, perhaps, stoned – his words were smoky if not gruff or,

56

maybe, like himself, he had not as yet shaken the comatose, drug-like effect of sleep, and, less than entirely himself, garbled his speech.

"This shit's like dragging a dead horse after beating it to death," Rufus grumbled with regard to King and the Memorial to be held in Central Park later that morning.

"Perhaps," said Percival, irritably.

"What y'll ever loving pacifists gonna do in Central Park – hold hands 'n sing?"

"I've no claims to bein' a pacifist."

"Ya jus' flirting with em like intellectuals used to flirt with Communist, ay?"

"I seem to recall you holding hands with those pacifists yourself."

"No shit, man, that was a phase."

"A phase?"

"Yeah, you remember those rallies we put together fer the Ali defense fund?"

"Sure. We worked on that together."

"But do you know what happened ta the money?"

"It went for the Ali defense."

"That's your story. Now let me hip you— 'r white radical friends used that money we raised for Dr. Spock n Rev. Coffin's defense instead!"

"Where'd you get that from?"

"Ask Morty next time you see him. 'ave your white friend tell you 'bout how he betrayed his black friend, 'n now they want'a sing with you at King's Memorial."

Percival winced. "I'll do that."

"You do jus' that."

"You don't mind if, in the meantime, I act sensible?"

"If waiting, watching, n singing is sensible, then niggers 'r the most sensible people on the face a' God's green earth."

"If you don't bear witness t'day, how 'r you gonna give testimony tomorrow?"

"Testimony? The only testimony I 'ave to give is with a Molotov cocktail."

Percival chortled. "The Panthers said 'this is a riot not a revolution' last night when I briefly ended up with em in their headquarters in Bed-Stuy. N, if you recall, Malcolm was calling for a revolution, not just another riot."

"You? How's that?"

"I got lost in the fracas."

"Caught in the riot?"

"Yes, on my way back home. I missed my stop 'n stepped into the middle of the riot."

"Had yourself a night of it, ay Golden Boy?"

"Could'a gotten killed," Percival said, vividly recalling the previous night's adventure.

'The Black Panthers, ay!" Rufus said, excited. "Now I can get into them. They something else."

"I suppose."

"We can use em here on the island, man, especially New Brighton – niggers here in need of'a wakeup call. Somebody set off a pack of firecrackers las night. The dumb mother fucker mistook it for the 4th. 'a July! 'n that's 'bout their notion of a riot, man. I fucking miss Brooklyn baby. Miss Brownsville. My ole stomping grounds, know? the ole neighborhood. The bunch I use to hang with fucking dead, in jail, or Nam. The situation here is worse than Bed-Stuy n Harlem for years of neglect, n these fool niggers shuffling to a Jim Crow tune. They think that nickel ferry ride's a visa to Oz, or some shit, you know?"

"Yes, we talked 'bout that at length if you recall," Percival said. He had come to know Staten Island somewhat, New Brighton more especially since his mother had moved there from Brooklyn to within walking distance of Rufus. When he had asked, "Why?" she had fretfully replied, "Bed-Stuy's no place to grow ole by yourself." Thus she moved into a low-income project fronting the river, off Richmond Terrace, along with his younger brother, Sam, and their sister, Lois who was engaged and trying to save money to start out on as well as working her way through college.

Racine also lived in another depressed area on the island, Stapleton, at the bottom of Canal St., across from the only pier still active there. From the windows of her cold-water flat, the Verizzano bridge was visible, casting it's shadow across the joining tides of the estuary. Rufus' observations, from Percival's experiences, were not far off. Staten Island was, at first blush, like a lazy, once pretty backwater with all the unseemly elements of its racial discontents festering below the surface, yet markedly apparent in the faces of its stifled black population.

"This fucking place is locked in a' kinda time warp, n I'm going out'a my ever-loving mind which, I'm told, I'm already outta," Rufus cackled uneasily. "I fucking miss my ole pals, especially on days like t'day," he said, dolefully. "Oh man, everything's become a haunt. At times I jus' want'a give up, throw up my hands, you know? 'N other times I want'a hang tough once again with 'the Bloods,' as we use to call ourselves. They was some down brothers, you know?"

"I hear you, man. Ya can always come back."

"Ta what, worn out welcomes? How's that song go?' Those wedding bells 'r breaking up that ole gang'a mine?' In my case, the story is the street life's broken up that ole playpen a' mine, dig?"

"In spades. You're thinking you might wanta tough it out with the Panthers?"

"It's better than singing."

"It's your play, baby."

"I'm simply looking to go out with'a bang," said Rufus melodramatically.

"I'm sure the cops won't mind setting that up," Percival added.

"Tell me, man, where they located anyway?"

"My recollection's hazy but I think it's somewhere between Fulton n Eastern Parkway."

"That covers some ground."

"It was confusing."

"I'll find it."

"Easier than finding your way back to work," Percival taunted.

"I'm a pressure cooker 'bout to erupt 'n you talking 'bout work. You, you on your way to the Olympics, what I got, a two bit job as a guard at the Museum of Modern Art on your say? Well screw you too. Who you think you 'r, my ole lady?"

"Hardly but it don't mean I'm not thinking of your ole lady 'n expectant child."

"Don't talk to me 'bout my ole lady like it's something I don't know. N what business is it of yours anyway?"

"It's not."

"Jus' keep it that way."

"It's your thing."

"Hey, man, you called me, I didn't call you!"

"Yeah, I know."

"Good luck t'night, man," Rufus blurted, suddenly apologetic. "I'm glad somebody I know's on the way up 'n not all us faltering, dig? Stumbling 'r way sidewise to the grave."

Percival was unsure as to how he should take Rufus' remark, but he thanked him nonetheless. "Look," he said, "before the games start, want'a let's hook up?"

"Lily'll like that."

"I'll call."

"Do 'n don't forget to keep your fist high."

59

"Shall do," Percival sighed, placing the phone on the hook with relief. Talking to Rufus was always an ordeal, he thought, eyeing the phone on which his hand rest. He wondered to himself, *Do I dare? dare I do? Why not? She the one took our child and went away, wasn't she?* Thus he dialed a local number, but lost heart and dashed the receiver back on its hook, thinking, "it's too early." He shook his head, "No, it's too late!" And urgently dialed the number again.

It did not ring very long. "Hello," said Mrs. Reel on the start of the third ring. He was unprepared to respond. "Is anybody there," she demanded in a honeysuckle twang. His first impulse was to hang up, but he caught himself replying.

"Ay, yes, Mrs. Reel, it's me, Percival –"

"I could 'ave guessed," said the peeved voice on the other end.

"Can I talk to Joleen."

"My daughter don't wanta talk to you."

"Is there a reason?"

"Ya jus' don't know do you?"

"I can't say I do."

"You're a lot bigger fool than I took you for," she chimed, and before he could respond she hung up, the line going dead in his ear.

He clung angrily to the deadline, listening blankly. She had treated him as if he had been a nuisance caller and not like he and her daughter had had a child between them with a lot to work out. It was to have been expected, he supposed, but it stung just the same and, blinking back tears, he slammed the phone back in its cradle with a bang, rattling the table lamp. He got off the bed and started out of the room and down the hall to the front room. It could not properly be called a living room; it was much too small and sparse for that. It was more like a Monk's cell, but less neat since Joleen had left. He turned up the volume on the radio, trying to blot out the processes of his thoughts with an overkill of news.

He also wanted the rooms to resound with noise, as much as he wanted to be versed on every grim detail of the previous night. He retraced his steps down the hall and turned into the toilet. The difference of being out of the bedroom and in another part of the apartment was telling, and as much a mental relief as was emptying his bowls and bladder a physical one.

He stared into the mirror as he washed his hands. The mirror surprised him and, as always, his reflection was baffling, somewhat like hearing one's recorded voice for the first time. Likewise, neither did his image ring true. Mistrusting mirrors, his scrutiny took on a comic vulnerability. He was boyishly handsome with a devil-may-care look about the eyes, and a certain cunning in his smile – though of late, out of sorts with himself, he was also at odds with his reflection. He tried to shrug it off but he knew what it was. It was her. It was him. It was the child they had between them. It was the death of Dr. King. It was the finals of the Olympic trials. It was everything. It was nothing.

As he left the toilet, the empty songs playing on the radio and the vapid chatter from a neighbor's T.V. combined to confound him. He couldn't make heads or tails of it. He hastily decided to change and get the hell out'a there, before losing his sanity along with Rufus.

***

When Percival emerged from his apartment house, Carroll Street, the side street on which he lived, was empty and the mid-morning sun had yet to surmount the tenement rooftops, thus the street was cast in shadow and well reflected his somber mood. The leaf bare trees along the block thrust their budding branches skyward like so many yearning dark skeletons, and the ripe, fecund smell of uncollected garbage wafted on the early spring air.

He descended the stoop somewhat haunted by his previous night's adventures. He strode to Kingston Avenue like a somnambulist. As he approached the intersection of Kingston and Carroll, he was jostled out of himself by the rumble of heavy traffic along the busy road and blinding sun coming up the center of the avenue, rising like a dazzling affirmation, it's rays resplendent on his face.

Kingston Avenue was busy as usual and seemed to be preparing for a parade. It was a national election year and every candidate smiled photogenically from red, white and blue bordered posters of themselves, plastered on the graffiti-scrawled building walls and the forest of telephone poles that stretched to the horizon. James Farmer, the former national director of C.O.R. E. was running for congress on the Republican ticket against local Democrat Shirley Chisholm, and he had opened a campaign office on the corner of Kingston and Carroll where Percival was stuck waiting for the traffic light to change.

Impatient with the traffic light and ceaseless flow of buses, trucks and cars, he darted into the street, weaving in and out of the two-way flow of traffic, inciting an angry blare of horns. "Ya fucking asshole," an enraged trucker swore, hitting his brakes, bringing the traffic behind him to a screeching halt. Percival glared round at the driver and flipped him off, then continued on without breaking stride.

He quickly reached Eastern Parkway. Eastern Parkway had an old-world appeal and could easily have been a major thoroughfare in any modern

61

European City. The majestic promenade was lined on either side by stately trees and turn of the century brownstones that jutted out of the concrete like reflecting palisades. The busy, heavily trafficked parkway was divided by a landscaped median, displaying a colorful array of tulips amidst various deciduous shrubs and evergreens. The south side of the parkway was the northern face of Bedford-Stuyvesant.

Kingston Avenue, as it narrowed in the distance on the Bed-Stuy side of the parkway, was deserted. A police cordon closed off the street and rerouted all traffic. The street was littered and nowhere was there a garbage can left standing. The sunlight gleamed off myriad shards of broken glass strewed up and down the empty street. A broken liquor store sign hung by a hinge like a hand attached to a limp wrist. The fire escapes on the old tenement fronts looked like excessive, top-heavy scaffolding. A lone newspaper page, tossed by the wind, hovered kite like over the rubble sprawled street.

Percival was disturbed by the disparity he saw between the two sides of the street, in a way he previously had not. Disenchanted with Bed-Stuy, the place he most thought of as home, he turned on his heels and descended the subway stairs.

Racine waited patiently on the southeast corner of Central Park West, her back to the park's many budding, though leafless, trees. She cradled her love child in her arms or, that is, her child out of wedlock, her bastard, made more poignant for its being black, her sky-blue eyes on the watch for Percival.

"Where is he?" she wondered aloud, looking on the infant in her arms. But the child was busy sucking it's thumb, too self-absorbed to care.

The streets crisscrossed one another at Columbus Circle from half a dozen directions. The flow of traffic around the circle was too dizzying to watch. There was also a half dozen subway entrances and exits, including one in the central circle itself on which the Gallery of Contemporary Art stood at sharp angle to the coliseum. The world renowned Essex House was to her left and overlooked the park, as did other fine Central Park addresses.

Racine watched the comings and goings of the beautiful people in and around the circle, thus the words of a Beatles song, "You keep all your money in a big brown bag inside a zoo/ nothing to do," sprang to mind. She herself was poorly attired and though she felt out of place, more especially as wealthy, well dressed women eyed her critically in passing, she nevertheless embraced her poverty, and despised those women no less than they despised her. She held the child protectively to her bosom against their cold glances.

Percival arrived soon after and sighted Racine instantly. She stood alone, rocking her child gently, and looking anxiously about, a slight breeze tugging playfully at her skirt. He couldn't help but notice that not all the passersby viewed the contrast between mother and child entirely indifferently, taking more than a casual second look: Whereas Racine had a petal soft, peaches and cream glow, flaxen blond hair and lucent blue eyes, the infant had a chocolate brown complexion, hair black and fine as silk, with midnight blue eyes. But the child's nose, unlike her mother's Nordic one, was Negroid. Apart from that, the child was the image of her mother in black skin.

He had also observed on more occasions than one that black women with white babies were not so scrutinized as was Racine with her black child. Of course, the black women were assumed to be maids whereas the other conjured up images of miscegenation much too taboo for words. But more surprisingly than not, the looks came from blacks as well as whites, and their expressions were usually more hostile than kind.

Racine waved frantically on sighting him.

He started across the street from the central circle but the snarled, bumper to bumper traffic coming from every direction frustrated his aims.

He gestured with upraised hands, in comic defeat.

She laughed with gaiety at his antics, her round, voluptuous shoulders shaking with hilarity under her tawdry thrift shop bought blouse – a style much in vogue among flower children and hippies alike, and was as much attributable to the then emerging counterculture as was it a rebuke of middle America's value system and the war in Vietnam.

Moreover, Racine dressed, as did all the Flower Children, like one of a growing sect of mendicants foreign to American soil. She had gone through the cloth bins of various thrift shops with as much care as would a woman of refined taste, but no resources, so she looked stylishly ill-kempt, as did all the flower children. Or, as Leonard Cohn, a voice of that culture, sang, "She is wearing rags and feathers from Salvation Army counters." Contrarily, the poverty of Racine's dress did little to disguise a heady sexuality that lurked beneath her tawdry garb, a sexuality she wore forthrightly, without affectation, raw, like a princess wears a diadem for the world to see. She was substantial; she had flesh on her bones and, like a milk maid, all in the right places. She was, in a word, as Fielding might say, "a lusty wench." And few men, without exception, ever encountered her without taking notice, drawing in the heady draft of her sexuality, which she exuded in abundance.

Indeed, where high fashion would have concealed, poverty revealed. Joleen, on the other hand, was beautiful in that fashionable sort of way, but Racine exuded a passion on which high fashion would have gone to waste. So unlike Joleen, Racine wore her sexuality without check. A facet of her character Percival most enjoyed.

An artist friend had once said of her, most prophetically, "She's beautiful in an odd sort of way – but beautiful! She's a model artists look for and fall in love with after it's too late. She's as much wreathed in mystery as in tragedy."

Percival finally managed to join her on the park side of the busy intersection. "It's good to see you," she said, as he stepped onto the sidewalk.

"It's good to see you, too," he acknowledged, kissing her bright mouth, her eyelashes catching the sun.

"It's good to see Percival, isn't it, Dakota." Racine bent her face in the direction of the infant who, recognizing his voice, looked round. As he came into view, she smiled, stretching out her dumpling brown arms for him.

"Sometimes I think she likes you more than me."

Percival suspected Racine might be right. Whenever he was near, the child's eyes would widen and follow him like a sunflower follows the sun. Racine laughed, passing him the child.

He accepted the infant gladly from her mother. She lay her head contentedly against his shoulder. Racine laced an arm through his, and they turned into the park, joining a trickle of mourners on the way to the Memorial Service. They bypassed the bird sanctuary, alive with the springtime songs of birds, and the sun dappled trail on which they tread wended its way through a grove behind the zoo. Dakota perked up at the strains of the organ music floating on the air from the carousel, but the jungle-like cries from the zoo— the trumpeting of elephants and roar of a lion— made her pout as if to cry.

Percival smiled at her and softly said, "it's okay, don't you fret – they can't hurt you they're toothless."

Comforted by his reassuring tone, Dakota became less tense.

"It's not my place to ask, I know, but have you been able to see your son? "Racine asked, as they came in sight of a massive crowd beginning to gather round the open amphitheater fronting Sheep Meadow, bedazzled with sunlight.

"No," he said, as much surprised by the flood of mourners converging on the amphitheater, as to Racine's query. "No," he repeated, scanning the interracial composition of the crowd. "I've not seen him."

She sighed, drawing closer.

They came slowly from all directions of the park, wearing their grief like a shroud. Starting with J.F.K., they were becoming accustomed to mourning their fallen leaders. They came in clusters; they came in couples; they came one at a time; they came silently in long trains; they came across the meadow in droves. Their greetings as they met were one and the same, soundless and empty. Their burden was heavy and they had no words to express their loss, only a grief to be borne. Percival took Racine's hand, and they joined a slow train of people linking up like Pullman cars heading for a central rail yard.

As the crowd advanced on the amphitheater, they were greeted by flower children passing out sunflowers and proclaiming, "Peace!" A girl with an oval face, almost beatific smile, garland of sunflowers strung through her hair, and love beads dangling at her throat, offered Percival a flower from a profuse bouquet in her arms, which he silently accepted. He then tucked the flower beneath Dakota's ear. It cast a yellow glow on her creamy brown cheek. Other flower children were busy tossing petals into the air which they rained down on the train of mourners again like spattered paint on an artist palette.

It was good to be there. It was so unlike the agony on the streets of Bed-Stuy the night before.

All the seats around the amphitheater had been taken and the vast crowd sprawled out, spilling onto the meadow where they squatted on their haunches or sat crossed leg in the lotus position.

Stage technicians were adjusting the sound system and setting up microphones. A loud electrical screech rang out across the meadow from a speaker like the cry of a prehistoric bird. Dakota screwed up her face and began to cry.

Racine and Percival tittered.

An elderly white-haired woman with a crown of braids atop her head and a wry, care-worn smile said to Percival, as he quieted the whining infant. "Your baby is lovely."

Percival eyed the woman measuredly, then looking at Dakota he said: "She is isn't she?" He accepted the complement, not for himself, but for the child and it's mother.

"She's my child not his," Racine indelicately interjected, taking Dakota from Percival, piqued that the woman had only seen the obvious and jealous that the woman had missed all resemblance to herself in the infant.

Percival readily handed the child to her, sympathetic to Racine's point of view.

"Oh, ah," the poor woman stammered in surprise, looking keenly between mother and child for a knit of identity, before becoming lost in the faceless sea of people pressing in from all sides.

"I feel such a rush of envy when people do that, mistake Dakota for your child and not mine. It makes me feel insignificant in her life when I'm the one who brought her into this world against the objections of practically everyone. She's mine," she said sharply, gazing possessively on the infant smiling cherubically up at her.

Percival did not reply straight off but took his time. "I hate to say we know why that is but we do," he said softly. "We live among the blind. What else can I say? 'N yes, I find it objectionable, but for other reasons."

65

"Other than you love Dakota more than you do me?"

"That's not fair 'n you know it," he objected. "Far from it. Besides, I thought we'd settled that? Anyway, it's different, if not altogether untrue."

"That's hopeful," she said frailly, avoiding his eyes. She had made the mistake of falling in love with him despite his warning her not to. "Should I look to see you after your fight tonight?"

"I'd like that, yes." He smiled, wanly, then said, "Look, Racine, I think I'm coming down with pre-fight jitters n I'm in need of sleep, so I can't say how long I'm gonna stick."

"I can't stay but so long either," Racine admitted. "I have a two o'clock appointment with my analyst."

"Oh," he said archly, lifting his eyes. "How's that going?"

"It's more or less like I've told you in the past. I suppose it'll work out in the long run. I hope so for Dakota's sake, as much as my own,' she said, resignedly.

"Yes! Yes!" he recalled. She had told him. How could he forget? It was one of those things that had struck a sympathetic chord in him beyond the yearning she had stoked in his loins. She had been a new face around the offices occupied by various peace groups located in lower Manhattan. She had been employed as a secretary to the organizations that shared the same floor. In his hasty comings and goings they had bumped into one another but had not had the chance to strike up an acquaintance. It was at a party thrown by Morty for friends from the Peace Coalition that she had finally accosted him,

"I could like you, Percival Jones," she had said." I might even be able to love you. God knows, I could certainly fuck you," she gushed, reddening from the throat up, her lucent blue eyes engaging his.

Percival blanched, staggering back, not unpleasantly surprised. He had almost laughed. No woman had ever propositioned him quite so brazenly before. She then pressed a hand to his groin, holding his eyes, all along. She was tall and ungainly, ripening beautifully, Nineteen. And yet there was a surprising younger girl's vulnerability about her.

Her forthright manner, though startling at first blush, was not simply surface bravado. Moreover, below this overt display of raw sexuality lurked a gaping black hole into which constellations might be lost. Thus, like a stray star, he would wander further into her sphere of influence than he would rightly have liked. But, alas, she was the most sexually alluring woman he'd ever encountered. Suffice it to say, the die was cast.

"I'm afraid I'm involved," he felt compelled to say.

"Oh?"

"Yes, her name's Joleen."

66

"And I'm three months pregnant and unmarried – what of it?" she charged, matter of factly,

"Oh?" he said, flabbergasted? "I have a child too, a son."

"Are you two married?"

"No."

"Are you in love?"

"It's more like I'm in difficulty than love."

"How old is your son?"

"He's going on seven months."

"And does he have a name?"

"It's Malek."

"African, is it? My child's father is also African – someone I'd met in college, an ambassador's son from Nigeria."

"So your child will be black."

"In as much as its father is African, only. But in as much as I'm white, German, no. After all, I'm it's mother," she said, poignantly.

Percival chortled.

"By the way, is your difficulty—Joleen you say her name is—with you tonight?"

"No, we've been on n off much of late n presently it's been off."

"Then no one can fault us for dancing real slow," she suggested, swaying languorously to the music, tempting him on.

It was a temptation he could little resist.

From then on Racine became impossible to avoid. In any event, he had had no wish to avoid her. In fact, he liked her, although her directness could be a nuisance at times, especially since he could bandy the truth with the best of them to suit the occasion. Apart from a nuisance, he also found that her honesty did not necessarily make her a better person. It simply made her a more vulnerable one. Then again, that's what she had wanted from him, an ear, a champion, "a Parzival," as she was to inform him on a later occasion.

"Do you know the story of Parzival?"

"Who?"

"Parzival, your namesake, from the Grail Mysteries?"

"Go on."

"It's from the Arthurian legend, Camelot. Of all the knights to go off in search of the Grail, some going mad, others dying on the quest, the only one found morally equipped to recover the Grail was Parzival. He was a strong, splendid fellow, a guardian of the defenseless, and arch champion of women's honor. That's who you are to me— a knight in shining armor. My Percival."

"Well," he teased, "I've been called black as night before so, maybe."

"You're joking and I'm being serious."

It wasn't long after he'd won her trust that she felt compelled to bare her soul and reveal to him her darkest secret. It wasn't so much that he had not wanted to hear it, but he feared he run the risk of becoming too emotionally entangled when, in fact, he had only wanted an occasional bed partner. He had had no wish to be burdened down with any additional emotional complications or be introduced to the family skeletons. Hence, when she raised the subject, he had said, off key, "I don't mind an occasional sin of omission. In fact, I hear it's good fer the soul."

She wouldn't hear of it. "I've not spoken of this to a soul other than my analyst."

"So why tell me?"

"I told my analyst I was going to tell you. He thought it would do more harm than good, especially because, as he put it, 'you're already involved and have a child to complicate our involvement.' He thought that since our relationship is so tenuous it might not withstand the strain. And he wondered whether or not this was my way of driving you away. I thought about it and told him it doesn't change the truth, and you have every right to know."

"So you're gonna tell me," Percival sighed like a deflating balloon.

"Yes, I have to risk it. Besides, I think I know you better than that and I'm vain enough to want you to want me, despite myself," she coaxed. "Besides, one woman too many has lied enough to you as is."

"What 'r you talkin' 'bout?" he snapped.

"Joleen."

"You have no right!"

"I only refer to what you yourself have said."

"I said too much. I didn't mean to flare up at you. Please, continue."

"You sure?"

"If it's important."

"It's important." She paused her eyes fixed solemnly. "The best way to start is to tell the most difficult part first." She began with a shyness and sadness in her tone. "When I turned thirteen my father seduced me. I don't mean to say he raped me or anything of the kind," she insisted softly. There was no pain or tremolo detectable in her voice. "It was a methodical seduction, almost natural. It started innocently enough," she said.

It had started back from before she could recount, she told him. They had always taken baths together, she and her parents. It was a marvelous venture, splashing about in the tub, learning how different boys were from girls, the secrets of their nature. They would lie in bed together, the three of them, and sometimes her parents would make love as she watched. Afterwards, she would clap her little hands and they would scoop her up between them and hug her up.

Percival gazed at her in mind-numbing disbelief.

She spoke with lowered head and averted eyes, her flaxen hair hung in disarray about her face, and her voice was low, like that of a troubled child's. They were German. Her father was a second generation American but quite the elitist, and though he hadn't cared much for Hitler, he strongly believed in maintaining the purity of the Aryan stock. He thought the only way left to retaining racial purity, under the circumstance, was incest. He had said often enough, 'Incest is both biblical and mythological, and the most natural thing known to man.' He also claimed, 'It sustained European aristocracy for over a thousand years.' Her mother had been born in Germany and had immigrated to America after the war. She had briefly served as a member in the Hitler Youth Movement and was much in accord with her husband's views on racial purity.

"My mother had very much been a part of this ritual until the other children came along," she said, dryly. First came Thomas, her brother – that was when she was already five. Then came her two other sisters, Karen and Shelby. At the time her mother became wrapped up in the younger children and she was left to her father's lecherous designs. "I think my mother came to see her error and did not wish to repeat it with the other girls."

She paused, considering how to proceed. "As I began to develop, I began to feel self-conscious that I still bathed with my father while none of my girlfriend's father's ever bathed with them. Then again, it also bolstered my image of myself as a woman, and it made me feel even more special. The secrecy of it helped flame the passion of it. At the same time my father's touches became more probing, and no longer simply made me titter and blush, but stirred me deep down with unknown urges, urges of which I was at first tremulously shy. Yet my body, despite itself, began to respond to his caresses in ways that I couldn't fathom, and I would find myself swooning. On one occasion, I blacked out. Daddy would say what a beautiful woman I was becoming. I was paradoxically proud that my father enjoyed looking at me. Watching me unfold, he called it and spoke of the delights which awaited us when I came of age."

Still her mother said nothing. "I suspect that I was the sacrificial goat, and so long as daddy's attentions were on me, she could protect the younger ones. Or so she thought.

"My father you must understand is well thought of in his profession and in our small cloistered midwestern college community. He is someone of prominence; the head of the college English department. Our house was constantly full of his colleagues and admiring students. My mother was considered the perfect academician's wife, as well as a gracious hostess. As you can imagine, ours was a perfectly lovely family. And daddy was above suspicion.

"In fact, I was so taken with our wholesome family image that if I were somebody else, I'd have envied us." She shook her blond locks ruefully. "If only I were somebody else," she sighed, her voice issuing up through congested tears in her throat and out between quivering lips.

"The day finally came when my body, ripe with desire, responded favorably to daddy's every caress. *'Like a finely tuned instrument,'* he had said, then promised: *'My little girl is to become a woman today.'* I was all of thirteen. He swept me up in his arms and carried me off to his bedroom like a child bride. I lost my virginity that day in my mother's bed, beneath my father's writhing corpulence." She blushed, turning crimson to the roots of her scalp.

"It wasn't at all as horrible, as people like to paint, and that's what, on reflection, makes it so difficult. It couldn't have gone better, I'd responded as would a girl in love, with mixed frantic-emotions, passionate, adoring. If incest is horrible, it's horrible for different reasons.

"Afterwards, I felt as if I'd been given the keys to a city, a kingdom. I was shamelessly in love with my mother's husband – my father! I was so filled with his love at the time it's a wonder I didn't burst from the joy of it or, for that matter, spill it to the world I was so beside myself. Other than my father insisting on it remaining our secret, I must have known something was terribly amiss to have kept it locked away, as I have all these years. Yes, I guess I knew.

"I've as much as confessed I was infatuated with my father as any young coed could be with the star player of the high school varsity football squad. And I was indifferent to the advances of the pimply faced pubescent boys who'd wanted to date me, and I got a reputation for being stuck up. Had they only known I was getting it at home from my father. But good," she added sarcastically. "For two years I was the most deliriously happy girl on campus. Then darkness entered my life and I was plunged into the pits of despair. A despair out of which I am still finding my way.

"I had come home from school earlier than usual one day when my mother was away, and entered what I'd supposed was an empty house, but on hearing my father's voice from his study, I thought to tip toe in and surprise him. His study door was a jar, and, to my own surprise, I found him coddling my butt-ass-naked, eight-year-old sister, Shelby, who was fondling him, as he coaxed her along. My heart stopped, stuck in my throat. When it began to beat again the blood surged explosively to my brain.

"I-I was stunned. I couldn't believe it. It was cinematically, surreal, base and ugly – me, my father, our family," she moaned. "I couldn't bear to look, the sight of them. I covered my face and turned away, crying into my hands. It had all come crashing in on me like a flimsy house of cards and I had no one to complain to. I certainly couldn't complain to my mother. I grew bitter and resentful for his betraying me, betraying our love."

"I stole back outside unheard, and I sat on the garden swing, crying myself sick.

"It was then that I first glimpsed my mother's dilemma. And became ashamed, and my eyes began to avert hers, much as in the same way hers had averted mine. Suddenly I began to feel put upon, abused, as if something of value were being denied me, something within that had perhaps once been my soul," the words seemed to come from the darkest reaches of her heart. "On the surface I looked no different, but on the inside, my identity had begun to teeter. And that remains the scariest part of my ordeal today, not knowing who I was or if I was or even if I am. In fact," she inclined her head, "at one time I was daddy's little girl, but now I'd become his little whore; his mistress; his concubine and my own mother's competitor for her perverted husband's wayward affections. I'd even thought I'd somehow become my own mother, and, in some distorted way, given birth to myself. As well, my mirror image became unbearable to me."

Percival sank forward with a groan. His strong hands hung limply between his sprawled thighs, and he stared vacantly at the floor between his feet. It was like listening to a cry for help.

"By the time I turned sixteen he told me that when I married my first child should be his and would be our secret. No one outside ourselves need know. The thought of it was repugnant to me; there was to be no escaping him, not even in wedlock! I'd become trapped in a nightmare. Oh don't think I didn't think of suicide. I thought of it all right, thought of it a lot." She looked up, her lips trembling, and her eyes red with tears.

Percival felt empty, his breast barren. Horrified by Racine's account, he wore a startled, hang-jaw expression. He tried to find comforting, reassuring things to say, but words failed him, and he could only gesture helplessly, pitiably.

She continued in a barely audible voice, "By then I thought that I had grieved my mother more than enough for one lifetime, and I was also growing fearful that my mind was coming apart, and there was absolutely nobody I could talk to without ruining my whole family.

"With every passing year I could see how much my relationship with my father had deteriorated us as a family. And though mama still said nothing – I

71

knew. Consequently, I grew closer to her, emotionally and felt our relationship shift, as if I had become the mother and she the child, and I was the only one able to act.

"I often think that suicide was not my response because I was afraid that the reasons would come out. After all, one commits suicide so that the worms might get out, but I had had no wish to scandalize my parents and destroy everyone's illusions of what a wonderful family ours was. In many ways that was all they had. I think, deep down, despite it all, I too so wanted to believe it myself. Isn't that a lark?" She laughed, through sobs.

When it was finally time for her to go to college, her response was to accept the first offer and flee as far from home, and her farther, as possible. And that's what she did, though she continued to love him. "I suspect I shall always love him, if for no other reason than he is my father, but I can't forgive him or myself for having injured my mother so," she sulked.

She had left home gladly and ran as quickly, and blindly, into the arms of Tabiso, the African who was to father her child. "His blackness was my deliverance, and in his arms I felt freer than I had in years. 'Tabiso,' so my analyst says, 'is the personification of my shameful black secret.'" She shrugged, indifferently. "Maybe there's some truth to that I don't know, I can't say. I never thought of it; but in the context of American life I can see his point. More importantly to me, it allowed my mother to know that I had no further designs on her husband."

Percival fixed her in his gaze, as if to ask, "N what does ya analyst say 'bout me?"

"Anyway, Tabiso and I were busy fucking our brains out and did not come to our senses until I discovered that I was pregnant, though somewhere in me I knew that I'd have his black baby to spite my father's face and for this I'm somewhat ashamed, but not overly. I shall be a good mother and hope that 'the end justifies the means.'" She smiled faintly.

When she informed Tabiso that he was to be a father he told her, "That can't be!"

"But it can and is," she responded. "And I have every intention of keeping it."

"You can't," he balked. "My father would disown me," he argued. "My people would cast me out."

"Spoken like a true white man." She laughed that their roles had reversed. Aryan as she was, her father a professor, a man of learning and stature, and still she wasn't good enough for his aristocratic, African ancestry. In truth, Tabiso had not seen her as white in the same way black Americans see whites— that is, *as the other* – but saw her as exotic, scarce, a rarity as she similarly, but naively, saw him. She was an innocent. In any event, he distanced himself from her, and once more they became total strangers. They'd simply ceased to exist for one another. That was fine with her. She had accomplished her purpose, and for the first time in her life she had successfully managed to thwart her father's will. It was a sacrifice, even a selfish one, but she knew of no other way of proving to her mother that she loved her. Yet in so doing, she lost her entire family. They could not forgive her having a black bastard.

"It's ironic that how I feel like I've wronged my mother so, and I continue to feel that, despite my analyst telling me otherwise. He says it was her duty to safeguard me, and she failed in fulfilling both her legal and moral obligations to me. Well n good," her voice grew strident, then broke into sobs, "but how in hell is that supposed to make me feel any better?" She lowered her chin to her bosom and made a faint effort to smile.

"Percival, I loved my father like I've loved no other man. I guess I tell you this because I was finally able to run from him, but I'm not able to run from you. If anyone must go, it'll have to be you. I need you and I'm going to cling to you for dear life if you don't," she said tearfully, facing him eagerly, waiting anxiously for his reply.

He was speechless. He did not know what to say. They stared at each other in an awful pause. There was an abysmal silence at the bottom of his mind, a dreadful weight that lay there like a coiled, venomous snake. Born and raised in Bed-Stuy, a black ghetto, an outpost from civilization, he had assumed that he had witnessed every depravity known to man or beast. He couldn't have imagined that the hallowed halls of the academia would, unwittingly or otherwise, harbor one who had added a twist or two of his own to the screw. His heart broke for her, went out to her. He reached for her and pressed her blond head to his breast, but his overriding concern was for the unborn half-black infant that she would hazard to bring into this world, alone.

"One more thing," she sniffled, as he ran a hand through her hair. "I want you to name my baby for me," she said, looking up at him, pleadingly. More than her words it was the expression of anguish on her face that made him stiffen.

"Me?" he wondered. "Why me? I'm not the baby's father," he protested, abashed.

"I so wish you were."

"But I'm not," he said, stiffly. "Besides, I'm trying to work out some related difficulties of my own."

Choosing not to hear him, she persisted, "Will you?"

"I'll be straight with you, I can't say how long I'll be round cause with Joleen n me it's like 'Porgy N Bess,' when she touches me things stir in me for which I can't account n I must have her – body n soul."

"Maybe she'll fade out of your system like my father's fading out of mine," she said, hopefully.

"Maybe," he said, doubtfully.

However, he and Joleen were still estranged at the time of the baby's arrival.

All the nurses on the ward took him for the infant's father, and, having fallen in love with the child at first sight he was loathe to dissuade them of the notion. Hence, he consented to naming the baby, as asked, and chose to call her "Dakota," after his favorite female jazz vocalist.

"I like it," Racine smiled wanly from her maternity bed, petered after the strenuous delivery. "I like it a lot." And looking on the wizened faced infant nursing at her breast, she tenderly cooed, "That's you, little one, Dakota."

***

As late arrivals settled in among the host of mourners spread fanwise from out the shadow of the amphitheater to sunny Sheep Meadow, a voice rang out over the microphone, "Hello!" A stately, full figured black woman in a wide brim sunbonnet clasped the mike and looked out over the multitude. "Friends, we meet again on another dark day, as if these days are not dark enough; but there are elements in our society that would conspire to steal the light out of the day and the sight out of our eyes," she said, with burning sadness that passed like a sharp pang among the body of mourners. "This is what I'm feeling today, this is how it feels today as though I can't see the sunshine, and sunshine a' plenty is falling.

"And I don't know when sight shall be restored me my eyes have seen enough misery for one lifetime. I know that in the heart of the most venial today there stirs a sense of loss," she said gravely, in helpless fury. "You can bet there's no rejoicing in good ole Dixie today, for yesterday Dixie plucked it's eyes right out it's senseless head."

She spoke awhile longer, briefly recounting the history of the struggle. She recalled others who had fallen in the cause and warned, "Others are bound to follow. Christianity and non-violence have ceased to be bargaining chips, as the wanton slaying of Dr. King attests. This nation is all too tragically suckled from crib to grave on violence. And as last night's riots confirm, our black youth are growing impatient."

She then said in teary-eyed conclusion, "I thank you all for being here today. Last night was the longest and loneliest of my life, and I deeply appreciate your presence because it makes this dark day more bearable."

A smattering of applause arose from out of the ranks of the otherwise awkwardly silent assembly, but quickly died out. Everyone, without exception, identified with the speaker's distress, and felt, for the most part, that applause could not possibly reflect the depth of their sorrow and was suspended as though it were an intrusion on their mutual grief.

Morty Levinsky, from the Peace Parade Committee, took the mike as the distraught speaker departed. He thrust a hand into a pocket of his blue jeans, and nervously brushed his straggly, shoulder length hair from his downcast, mournful face. It had been a long night, and his eyes were red from fatigue and tears.

"Hi, I'm Morty Levinsky," he said, in a wary, raspy tone of voice. "I'm with The Peace Parade Committee. Our first speaker was Julia Banks from The Harlem Youth Project. Before we continue, I'd like to say, there's no need to applaud, we understand, we're in this nightmare together," he said solemnly, confirming the overall sentiments of the gathering. "And, as Julia stated, there's no rejoicing today, not in Dixie, not for any of us."

After Morty's brief remarks, he was followed on stage by an array of speakers, starting with a city official who apologized for the Mayor's absence. He explained, "The Mayor felt compelled to tour the scene of last night's riots in hopes of allaying any further outbreaks of violence."

Then a woman who was the Secretary of The Peace Parade Committee, took center stage, but could not find words in which to frame her grief and so she publicly wept – and much of the gathering was moved to weep with her.

Then Borough President, Percy Sutton, appeared and said a few words, "Martin would have us reject last night's display of violence, no matter the provocation. Panic is no solution and violence small consolation for such monumental a loss."

Congresswoman, Bella Abzug, garbed in mourning, as if for the interment of a dignitary, followed the Borough President to the mike. She was as eloquent and graphic as were the many glamorous hats for which she was known. "Dr. King's work will not be undone. There is much to be accomplished, and much we need do." She spoke of the upcoming Poor People's Campaign, inaugurated by Dr. King. She begged all present to participate. She thanked the crowd, then departed.

A young Blackman from the newly formed Peace and Freedom Party, sporting a burgeoning Afro, wraparound dark glasses and wearing a dashiki, strode boldly up to the mike, much like a young Jason, righteously indignant, coming to claim his patrimony, his murdered father's stolen crown. He seized the mike by its stem and – the lions of rage having all been unleashed – bellowed explosively,

"If you're not tired a' swallowing the appeasers swill, then I'm tired for you. T'day I don't address myself to 'r friends but to 'r enemies," his voice, cavernous as a crypt, rose from out of the groundswell of his sorrow. "I'm angry beyond belief! I'm sick 'n angry as a body can be 'n not be hospitalized. My mind is hell bent on vengeance. My hands long to drip with the blood of vengeance. Now we've all heard the self-righteous ministers 'n self-serving politicians say 'Martin wouldn't want it that way." A rage washed over him, and he said in a voice thick with fury, "I say, Martin's not with us to want it any other way!" He then railed against the powers that be, against the bitter cup that had long been his people's; the long, bloody years of darkness through which they had groped, the groaning under the interminable yoke, the awful travail through which they had passed and were yet to pass. The disgrace that was this nation's. He expressed Percival's misgivings almost to a fault, which worked like salt on a raw wound. "This savagery. This butchery. What else can I say? This accursed deviltry! I swear I have a dark mind to poison the reservoir. I mean drop a ton or two of L.S.D. into the fucking reservoir, n give New York a' taste of my despair!"

These remarks traveled like electricity from person to person, causing a small stir, as the speaker abruptly abandoned the stage.

Then as the stagehands readjusted the mikes for him, folk singer, Richie Havens, guitar in hand, mounted a stool at center stage and, without any introductory remarks, fitfully strummed his guitar and opened his mouth in a ghostly song,

"The countryside was cold n still, there were three crosses on the hill/ Each one wore a burning hood to hide it's rotten core of the wood/ n I cried father, I hear n iron sound, hoof beats on the frozen ground/ Downhill the riders came, Lord it was a crying shame to see th blood upon their whips ta hear th snarlin from their lips/ n I cried mother, I feel a stabbin pain, blood flows down like summer rain, summer rain/ Each one wore a mask of white ta hide his cruel face from sight/ Each one sucked th hungry breath from th empty lungs of death/ n I cried sister, raise my bloody head, it's so lonesome ta be dead Ummmmmmmm ta be dead/ He who rides with th Klan is a devil n not a man, fer underneath his white disguise I've looked inta his eyes/ n I cried brother, stand by me, he-y it's not so easy ta be free/ Brother, sister, he-y mother, he-y father, stand by me/ it's not so easy ta be free ta be fre-e-eee."

The song went through the hushed crowd like the winged Angel of Death, and the stark imagery of its haunting lyrics ("Father, I hear n iron sound./

Mother, I feel a stabbin pain./ Sister, hold my bloody head./ Brother, stand by me, it's not so easy ta be free.") set the assassination before their collective mind's eye like nothing else could, and left them just husks of themselves. Many wept unabashedly.

Percival couldn't take it and said, matter-of-factly, to a teary-eyed Racine, "I got'a go," kissing her and Dakota lightly in parting. He had the night ahead of him to consider, the Olympic Trials to win, and he could little afford to be emotionally spent on entering the ring later that evening.

"I'll look to see you later on," Racine said, choking back tears. "Good luck."

"T'night," he assured her, then turned and waded into the sea of mourners, and, having to excuse himself every step of the way, he cautiously advanced with careful an eye for every foot fall. Richie Havens was well into his final song when Percival finally broke free of the assembly, and started back across the park for Columbus Circle, no less troubled than before.

All the reassurances that Dr. King's work would carry on, despite the assassins' bullets, had a hollow ring and echoed deafly on his ears. Sadly enough, Percival felt as though an assassin's bullet had ended Martin's work in him. Certainly he could not feel as if nonviolence were an acceptable option for Blacks to accept in their quest for full citizenship. No, he had only been reassured that Malcolm was more right than wrong when he had said, "Let your blood flow in the streets!"

The memorial service had proven anything but consoling, and his soul cried out for solace.

He caught the subway back into Brooklyn, growing increasingly weary from stop to stop. His soul was agitated, deeply disturbed and of a dual nature. Belonging neither to hell nor heaven, vacillating between two worlds, between going home and catching up on some well needed rest or trying to see his son, Malek, for whom his soul pined. The more he brooded over it, the more he realized that his small apartment was much too claustrophobic to contain the contents of his grievous heart.

The train lurched into the Franklin Avenue. station, Joleen's stop. He leapt to his feet, about to exit but caught himself, drawn back as if by an invisible hand. "What am I thinkin," he asked? Still he yearned to get off, to follow his aching heart, walk the distance to the Ebetts Field apartments and, if only, gaze up at Joleen's window in hopes of her sighting him on the sidewalk below, taking pity on him and bring down their son, Malek, for him to see. As much as he loved Dakota – and loved her he did –, she couldn't replace Malek, his son, his lifeline, his link to immortality, in his heart. But he realized that the best he could hope from Joleen, under the circumstance, was an eruption, an outbreak of temper, a heated exchange of words with nothing to show for it.

He waited for the train to pull out, he wondered, muttering under breath, "how'd we ever get so close we could fly so far apart, of a sudden, like that? Light years away? N the child of r union, r bond of love, become a grudge match between us – how? How?'

He threw himself back on the car seat with grave reluctance and, looking about the sparsely populated car at the drab, vacant faces, he sighed bitterly, resignedly as the train pulled out.

He arrived home and paid no attention to the lightless rooms through which he passed on his way to the bedroom. He kicked off his shoes and other than that he didn't bother to change, but collapsed face down across the bed, fully clothed, and instantly fell asleep.

He slept the sleep of the dead or, more aptly. "the just." He wakened, in a fright, his body thrumming. He was disoriented, in a mindless fog, fearful of having overslept and missing his fight; his chance at the Olympics for which he had long striven. He reached for the bedside clock and cursed himself for not having set the alarm. Much to his relief he still had time. He scampered to his feet to dress but found, except for his shoes, that he was fully clothed. He slipped on his shoes, then hastily left the building. He just had time for a meal before having to meet up with Punchy outside Madison Square Garden. He found a small roadside cafe, on his way to the subway, where he took a light meal, then hastened to the city.

Punchy waited mid-way upstairs to Madison Square Garden and watched the pedestrian traffic below out of which Percival emerged. As he mounted the steps the sun slipped beyond the Jersey skyline plunging the city into nocturnal gloom. Then, just as suddenly, and as if by magic, the city lights went on from block to block and building to building, once again setting the city ablaze like the candles on an octogenarian's birthday cake.

"How r you?" asked Punchy, restrainedly.

"Okay, considering," said Percival, evasively, having detected a note of tension in the older man's tone.

"Considering? Considering what?" asked Punchy, irritably. "Ya left here las night the top Olympic prospect 'n you show up t'night looking like something the cat drag'd in."

"I know I must look a' fright, but I'll pull it off."

"I told you last night to go home 'n get some rest. I call'd on several occasions las night 'n t'day 'n you wasn't in. So where was you?"

"Ya don't want'a ask."

Punchy eyed him crossly, silently. "I jus' hope you ain't blown you chances."

"Have I failed you yet?"

"You can be sure King's death won't frazzle Juarez any," said Punchy, without equivocation. "I'm sorry, it had to be said. The stakes r too high."

"Juarez?"

"Ya opponent, Chico Juarez, the Latino kid from California, the one they call the razor. Las night he sliced his opponent up like a ripe tomato."

"Well I'm no tomato."

"This is a fight. This isn't something owed you, to which you're entitled. This is 'May the best man win'; n, no matter, the best man doesn't always win."

"I can handle it."

"You know the score as well as anyone."

"I like to think so."

They each lay a fraternal arm on the others shoulder – they were in it together, no matter— and climbed the remaining steps to the sports arena like father and son. They entered the lobby and, as always, a sense of awe, evocative of the wonder one feels on entering a cathedral, came over Percival, filling him with an impending sense of the spectacular.

They were ushered along by a guard to the locker rooms beneath the arena. The locker rooms were similar to desolate train depots or starkly lighted holding cells, where fighters awaited their uncertain fate in nerve wracking introspection till the first bell of their bouts rang. Meanwhile, they roamed the rooms listlessly, tentatively, seminude and bare ass, like astronauts in depthless space or, as it were, in a dream like sequence.

Only one of the other four fighters who had shared the locker room with Percival, Chauncy Wells, had survived the previous night's cuts.

"Hey, man, it'll be a gas being on the Olympic squad with you," Chauncy said, offering Percival his hand.

"Likewise," said Percival, drowsily, taking Chauncy's hand.

The finalists eventually began jockeying for position online outside the official A.A.U. weigh-in room, wearing but a towel to hide their shame. Each fighter was into himself, and the line inched along slowly, with little or no conversation to speak of. Percival followed a flyweight onto the scale. An official adjusted the balances. "One fifty-eight pounds," he called, as another jotted it down.

Percival proceeded to step off the scale and found himself, as he turned, face to face with Chico Juarez. He was struck by his honey, golden brown complexion, a gift of the Californian sun, no doubt. They glowered at each other, eye to eye, like circling dogs. Juarez threw back his curly black head of hair, stifling a laugh. He had the surly, insolent good looks of bandito, a curly haired Aztec Adonis. He was a pretty boy who had learned to protect his looks on the gang infested streets of the southeast Los Angeles Barrio. He stuck out his chest, drawing breath. He was manly, fiercely proud, contentious, and piqued that Percival had been favored over him to win the trials. Hence, it was his intention to prove his detractors wrong.

"They say you the best," he rashly accused, his upper lip curled impudently. "I show you. I show them all. You're nothing. Nobody. I kill you." Juarez knew that he would have to rattle Percival, if he were to stand a real chance of beating him. Startled, the other fighters and officials looked on curiously, silently, expectantly.

The pulse in Percival's throat quickened. He gazed unflinchingly in Juarez's pitted, black eyes. Punchy draped his robe over Percival's shoulders, and there rest his hands. "Kill me, you say," said Percival, deadly calm, overcome all of a sudden by a sense of lethargy. "I won't kill you, boy, I'm jus' gonna whip you till you call me daddy. If you don't mind, son?" He brusquely pushed Juarez aside, and drew his robe tightly about him with a strangle hold on the sash.

Incensed, Juarez made to lunge for him, but his trainer constrained him. "The fight'll be soon enough."

Chico growled, "I'll cut him to ribbons!" Then climbed onto the scale.

"Don't let it get to you," Punchy advised, on the way to the locker room. "It's water off a' duck's ass."

"Don't discount him either."

After Percival had slipped on his trunks, he took a seat on a bench against a side wall and extended a hand over the back of a chair on which Punchy sat facing him, about to wrap his hands.

"Ya hands 'r unusually cold," Punchy noted, as he grasped the hand to be bind it.

More than cold, Percival's fingers were bloodless, like those of a corpse. He grumbled noncommittally, with sweat flowing liberally down his flanks, unable to dismiss Chico's wild boast, "I kill you!"

Punchy wrapped Percival's hands with alacrity, folding strips of equal length back and forth over his knuckles, then he drew the gauze lengthwise between the separate fingers of his hands and secured the wrap with tape, making a staff of forearm and fist.

A man stuck his head in the room, holding out a fresh pair of gloves. "Jones," he hollered, "Ya up in four!"

Punchy accepted the gloves, then had Percival shove his taped hands deep into the mitts, working his fingers, clawing for the win, feeling for the K.O. contained therein. Punchy tied the strings about the gloves at the wrist, tied the laces and secured the tie with tape.

After Punchy was done, Percival stood up, shucked his robe, and, having cast off Juarez's threat as no more than an idle boast, he started to warm up, moving slowly at first, like a kitten at play, pawing the air. Sweat began to trickle down his taut brown face; his vision had turned inwards, and his movements were like a ritual dance, everything about him had suddenly become electric.

Punchy observed Percival with a discerning eye, Percival's muscles rippling under a sheen of sweat. He moved with the stealth of a big cat. He was a splendid fighter, a fascinating fighter, developing from fight to fight, and growing from strength to strength as he progressed. And though Punchy felt certain that Percival was the best fighter to come along since Ray Robinson, Chico's threat, "I kill you," had an equally disquieting effect because, as he knew, Robinson too had lost a few, as had Percival. And now, offset by the death of Dr. King and whirlwind sequence of events sweeping the socio-political landscape affecting every black person in America to their soul and, all too tragically for Percival, Juarez was not black, but Latino, and unless he was more sensitive than they had had a right to expect, Martin's death could, under the circumstance, prove to his advantage.

Punchy passed a hand over his timeworn brow, his watchful eyes never forsaking Percival. It had been a long, wearisome day, following a short, restless night. He had stayed home all that day glued to the T.V. screen, watching the news unfold in an agony of spirit, the crisis through which the nation was passing, his people were passing. Had he been a young man he too would, no doubt, have been out on the streets venting his spleen despite his having been a second world war hero – or more possibly because he had been – distinguishing himself in combat, in the European Theater, in service to his country – a country that had denied him and his ilk more times than had Peter denied his Christ.

Indeed, he was no less justifiably outraged than were those youths firebombing the inner cities of America, the ghettos in which their countrymen had hoped to abandon and forget them. The burden of being black in America produced, in its people, an intolerable bitterness of spirit; one which age did not lessen in the least. In fact, it only further served to deepen the cup of sorrow. He too was no less troubled over the death of Martin than was Percival; but he did not have the added dilemma of having to climb into the ring that night.

Percival continued to shadow box until his muscles were sleek and warm with sweat and his breathing came soundly, like that of a runner's after a good dash. Punchy wiped him down, helped him into his robe, wrapped a towel about his neck scarf like and tucked it beneath the neckline of his robe.

Punchy threw a towel over his own shoulder next, stuck a couple of cue tips behind his ear, and checked the contents of his medical pouch. Then it was fight time, time to head upstairs.

"Good luck," called Chauncy.

"If luck's what I need," said Percival, tersely, turning out of the door with Punchy and an A.A.U. second at his back and on either side of him. The roar of the fight crowd above increased in volume as they ascended the stairs. The arena was no less packed than it was the night before. The preceding bout was over and the contestants had left the ring. Percival passed the beaten fighter in the aisle on his way ring-ward. There was a considerable stir among the fans as Percival climbed through the ropes and stood in the flood of lights which encircled the ring in a theatrical glow.

The crowd grew impatient waiting for Juarez to show. Chico shortly entered the ring. The fans settled down. Juarez pranced about the ring as if he owned it. Percival strolled to a neutral corner and grounded the soles of his shoes in rosin dust.

The bell tolled; the mike was lowered. "Ladies n gentlemen," an official hawked like a carnival barker, "the next contestants in these '68 Olympic trials: On my right, in the blue corner, weighing in at 158 pounds, from Brooklyn, New York, Percival Jones!"

The crowd cheered lustily.

And without leaving his corner or exerting any unnecessary effort, Percival raised a sole gloved fist in acknowledgement of the fans. They cheered the louder. He had become the crowd favorite. But, on the other hand, when the official announced, "Chico, the razor, Juarez." Chico bounded out of his corner and threw up his hands, slashed the air viciously with his fist, then back peddled to his corner and tossed off his robe contemptuous of the "boos." His muscular, sun baked body gleamed lustrously under the hot, ring lights.

There were as many wolf whistles and cat calls as there was applause for this Adonis, this curly haired competitor from the West Coast up against the hometown favorite – Percival Jones proving himself to be the best fighter of the trials.

The combatants were summoned to center ring for the referee's instructions. "I want a clean fight," he stressed, laying a hand on each fighter's back. "When I say break." Chico tried to engage Percival's eyes, but Percival chose to gaze at the canvas between Chico's feet and forego the staring contest. "Shake hands now and at the bell come out fighting," the referee concluded.

Percival stuck out a gloved hand. Chico waved him off. "I'm'a kick you ass not shake you hand," said Chico roughly, his mouthpiece causing him to slur his words.

Percival shook his head. "Okay," he said, and returned to his corner, anxious for the first bell, having developed a healthy dislike for Juarez.

"Put a' hurting on the pretty boy," a fan shouted from ringside, which caused considerable laughter among fans in surrounding seats.

Then a momentary lull fell over the crowd as the first bell rang, sparking the action.

Percival spun from out of his corner like a dancing top and met Juarez at center ring, circling. He instantly fired off an upturned jab, bypassing Juarez's guard, determined to punish Chico for his insolence, and struck him flush in the face. Chico countered with a jab, which Percival picked off. Chico followed with a looping right cross. Percival slipped the blow and dug in a right uppercut to Chico's gut and followed through with a slashing left hook which threw Chico off balance.

Percival pressed Chico hard. Chico swung a blow desperately, wide of its mark. Percival drove a right into his gut. "Ugh," he grunted, flailing back. Percival broke through a volley of Chico's blows with a right cross, catching him on the chin. Chico stumbled, upended, and landed on his butt, looking up at Percival from the canvas with chagrin.

The crowd rose to its feet in a roar.

The referee picked up the count over the felled fighter, ".3.4.5."

Chico shook his head as if he'd stubbed his toe and struggled to rise. The referee wiped his gloves and signaled the fight on.

Percival bolted from the neutral corner and resumed his attack. He was unrelenting, allowing Chico no quarters in which to escape. Chico fought back, both fists flying, trying desperately to beat Percival off, but Percival was unstoppable as he out maneuvered, out boxed and out fought him; beating Chico to the punch at every hazard. Percival feigned Chico out of position, then caught him with a vicious hook to the heart and crossed over with a right that took Chico's legs, and left him on the canvas in a daze.

Percival pranced to a neutral corner as the referee took up the count. ".3.4.5."

The crowd was going wild, whistling, cat calling and screaming, "Kill d' bum!"

Chico regained his feet, but the bell rang as Percival began to pursue him.

Percival fell on his corner stool. Punchy removed his mouthpiece. "This guy's a piece a' cake," Percival claimed, breathlessly. "I'll waltz him around n take him out in the third."

"Don't play with him. you got him," Punchy countered. "He's more dangerous now than ever. Take him out n let's go home," he advised, but Percival was too busy gloating to listen.

Chico's trainer broke a capsule of smelling salts under Chico's nostrils, sprinkled water on his bruised face, then toweled the blood from his mouth and nose. He solemnly said, "he thinks he's got you beat. He thinks he'll beat you easy. He thinks you got no balls. He thinks you'r a pussy. He thinks you've got no fight, no heart. Go at him hard, go at him like a bull. Gore him. Cut out his heart 'n spit it back in his face. You promised to kill him. Do it!"

"Si, I do," Chico responded, more determined than ever. "I kill him." He spat a gob of blood into the water bucket beside his stool. "I do it." He swore, with spit 'n fire in his voice, "I kill him!"

The bell for the opening of round two rang.

Chico broke from his stool like a cyclone, raining blow after blow on Percival, who was unprepared for such an assault following the drubbing he'd given Chico the previous round. He had smugly assumed that Chico should have known that he had been "whupped', mastered, and would, as a matter of course, go on the defense Hence, he could, as he had told Punchy, "waltz him." But, to the contrary, Chico had gone on the attack and so, to Percival's dismay, he was forced to give ground. Juarez was, in turn, giving him the beating of his life.

Taken off guard, Percival was having a devil of a time responding. His fists would not do as bidden. And as more and more punches rained in on him, the more frustrated he grew. And as the peppery blows ate at his resolve, he became increasingly discouraged, disheartened even. He was receiving such a pummeling he felt as if he'd been swept up by the blades of a windmill in a high gale. He felt his resolve slipping as an easy win eluded his grasp.

The crowd was stunned, groaning with every blow. Chico's corner was thrilled. Punchy sat breathlessly on the edge of his stool.

Percival was suffocating under the assault, unable to draw breath, fearful lest he not escape. His face was contorted in bewilderment. He was easily exhausted but held his frustrations in check. He fought back the urge to chuck it, throw up his hands and quit. Then, as he groped for air, Chico struck him with a right cross that exploded in his head like a thunderclap threatening to split him along the hemispheres of his brain, down his spine to his coccyx's. He squeezed his eyes shut against the flash of pain and rolled with the blow. He fell from the ball off of his right back foot onto its heel, off of which he

84

then recoiled with a murderous right cross that caught Chico coming in fully in the face, eyes, nose and mouth, and fell him in his tracks, spouting blood as if from a severed artery.

As Chico hit the canvas, Percival thought to himself, *Get the fuck off'a me!*

The crowd rose to its feet as a body. "Hurrah!" Percival was back in the game. Punchy leapt from his stool to the apron of the ring with a gasp of relief. Chico's trainer fell back on their stool in silence, aghast. The fact that Percival withstood the impact of Chico's last blow and came back, on the instant, and dropped Chico in place was attributable to the untold tale of the tape, the unaccountable regions of the human heart encased in mortal coil. With that explosive punch, Percival had all but ended the fight.

He hovered over Chico, his anger welling like a riptide. The referee waved him to a neutral corner before picking up the count. ".3.4.5."

Percival followed the count closely, ".4.5.6.," every nerve ending in his body scintillating with rage and, eyeing Chico maliciously, he felt a bitter resurgence of the day's agony along with a throbbing in his jaw. Far beyond the pain, all he saw was rage. A rage that had been building since his first hearing of the death of Dr. King.

Somehow, to everyone's surprise, Chico managed to regain his feet. No sooner had the referee signaled the fighters on, than Percival took pursuit, moving with the efficiency of a big cat on the attack, his fists working like pistons, taking Chico to task. Although hurt, Chico was no less game and fought back recklessly if not valiantly, much like a wounded stag, as much out of blind animal instinct as mortal pride, no less determined to fulfill his promise and "kill" Percival still.

Punchy looked on raptly as Percival went to work on Chico, starting to pick him apart like a locksmith picking a lock. Percival had found his stride.

He snapped Chico's head back with a spit fire jab. Chico responded with a flailing right; Percival side stepped and countered with a hook that positioned Chico's jaw in range of his right, and he followed up with a crippling right cross. Chico felt something snap, his cerebral lights flickered, and his legs went out from under him as he crumbled to his knees. A blood curdling howl rent the air, looking to the kill the crowd was in a frenzy.

Chico slumped forward to his outstretched gloved fist, feeling nauseous, his head lowered like a whipped dog's, his face bruised and body sore in every joint. His breath came in short, painful gulps, and his mouth was full of the taste of his own blood. He could little hear the referee counting over him, ".5.6.7."

Chico wagged his head. He knew it was over but his game heart would not give out. Thus, lacking all hope, he rose gamely to his feet.

85

"You okay?" the referee asked, gazing into his bloodshot eyes.

Chico nodded, senselessly.

"Want to go on?"

"Si," he insisted, wagging his curly, sweat laden locks.

The referee gave the combatants the go ahead. Without hesitation, engaging Chico's eyes, Percival went at him. He threw a feint, Chico raised his guard, and Percival fell below his upraised arms with a vicious blow to his rib cage. Chico groaned and started to fold, but Percival straightened him up with a left uppercut and came across with a decisive right that drove Chico against the ropes. Then Percival caught him with a body blow that doubled him over; and, with a swift right cross, he drove Chico spread eagle through the middle strands of the ropes to which, semi-conscious and trapped, he clung. Before Percival could get off another blow, the referee threw himself between the fighters, waving the fight to a close, and embraced Chico, standing him aright.

The fans were in an uproar, whistling, hollering and applauding heartily.

The day having finally caught up to him, Percival's body surged like an overheated engine.

Chico's trainer hopped into the ring to help the referee carry his semiconscious fighter back to his corner stool. The ring physician entered the ring to examine the badly battered fighter.

"We did it," Punchy exclaimed. "You did it!"

"We did," Percival breathed strenuously, as he slipped on his robe.

Meanwhile the announcer barked, "Winner by knock out, in two minutes n thirty-seven seconds of the second round, Percival Jones!"

Stomping their feet in unison, the fans shouted, "Jones! Jones! Jones."

Percival acknowledged the acclaim with upraised fist, then crossed the ring to see about Chico, but the doctor and his trainer were administering to him. Thus, feeling superfluous, he turned away exhausted, spent like a thin dime, unsure of himself, of his ability to navigate back to his corner. And when he finally left the ring, his jaw was pulsating with such fury that he thought his head would split. All the fans were on their feet, shouting at the top of their voices, "On to the Gold!" They were jubilant, celebratory. Percival had lived up to all their expectations.

"On to the Gold," kept ringing in his ears even as he paced up and down the locker room, having not yet sat, though his legs were wobbly.

Chauncy Wells had been scheduled for the seventh bout of the evening and was already at ringside, and so the locker room was empty but for Percival and Punchy.

Unable to place his distress, Punchy observed Percival with concern.

Suddenly Percival ceased his frantic pacing and swung round with a guttural outcry and struck the nearest wall locker full force with bare fist, rattling it. "Damn!" he swore, striking it again. "Damn!"

"What gives?" asked Punchy, with alarm.

"It's my jaw," Percival moaned, facing him. "It's fucking killing me." He grimaced, caressing his injured face.

"Your jaw?" Punchy observed him closely.

"It could be a tooth."

I best get the doctor," said Punchy, hastening out the door.

Percival was slumped in a chair when Punchy returned with the doctor.

"What seems to be the problem," the doctor asked. "I'm told it's your jaw?"

Percival nodded, looking up at the doctor with dolorous eyes.

"Let me see," said the disheveled, silver haired physician, as he sank to his haunches and placed his soft, odorless white hands to Percival's face, working his fingers. "Does that hurt? At one point, Percival drew back with a whimper.

"Try shifting your lower jaw from side to side."

Percival was unable to comply.

"Draw your lips over your teeth and clamp down," the doctor instructed.

The doctor sucked inward, frowning. "It doesn't look good. I won't know for sure till your jaw's been X-rayed, but it's my guess your jaw's been fractured."

Percival was stunned and in too much pain to show any emotion.

"You sure?" Punchy asked, dispiritedly.

"We'll need X-rays, but I'm fairly certain," the doctor responded, standing.

Sick at heart, Punchy collapsed in a nearby seat and lowered his face, blinking, trying desperately to swallow this new disappointment.

"It's over," Percival groaned, too exhausted to cry. He slumped in his chair, his jaw causing him considerable pain, more so, as he strove to drive away the bitter thoughts of a pyrrhic victory. He had won to no avail, and Martin was no less dead, despite it. The dream, his dream, King's dream, the sweet dream, was dead!

***

The X-rays confirmed the doctor's suspicions. Percival's jaw had been fractured and would require wiring. He was admitted to the hospital and arrangements were made for a plastic surgeon to perform the procedure the following morning.

In the meantime, he was escorted by an orderly to a men's floor and assigned a bed in a ward of sixteen. It was late and all lights were out but for a corridor night light by which he observed, as he gazed from his bedside into the gloom, forms resting corpse-like. He was suddenly filled with dread that he had inadvertently stumbled into a mortuary, but the intermittent rattle of snoring soon dispelled his morbid fears.

He breathed easier and changed from his street clothes into a hospital gown, then climbed into bed. The night nurse arrived and gave him a sleeping injection from which he sank away, as deathlike in sleep as the others.

No sooner had he yawned upon waking the next day, when he received another injection, a local anesthetic, was hoisted aboard a gurney and taxied through the corridors to an operating theater and deposited onto a surgical table where, for the first time, the surgeon stared at him beneath his mask, under an overhead circle of lights.

The surgeon inquired as to his morning so far, while an assistant covered him with a sheet up to his neck.

The local had produced an insensate effect on him, and he lay helplessly on the table, incapable of a response, and though his thoughts and feelings were anesthetized, his eyes roamed limply, lacking curiosity. If he had foggily imagined that he would have been etherized, then he had been sadly mistaken and was to remain conscious throughout the procedure. Although there was some pain, he was vastly indifferent to it as if it were someone else's.

"Forceps," the surgeon requested above him, threading wire between Percival's upper front teeth and drawing it through with a firm tug. "He's got good teeth to work with," he heard the surgeon say, as he ran more wire between his lower teeth. "His jaw should knit just fine."

Percival sensed more than felt the wire cutting into his gums, bleeding them, and he recognized an inordinate strain at the root of his teeth as the doctor deftly secured a bind, wiring his mouth shut. He closed his eyes before he was drawn into the glow of overhead lights like a dizzily circling moth, trying to distance himself, taking comfort in the fact that the surgeon liked his teeth. The procedure was not long, and shortly afterwards he was back in his ward bed fast asleep.

Percival would awaken on scenting the perfumed presence of someone standing impatiently beside his bed. He was still groggy from the anesthetic and numb throughout his body. His face felt like a pin cushion and his tongue a wad of cotton in his parched and wired mouth. He rose to his elbows, vaguely recalling where he was and how he came to be there, and found, to his chagrin, Alfonse McGraw, "Al" for short, a fight manager and promoter who had a string of fighters – some more than mere journeymen, too – wavering hazily before his cloudy gaze like an unclean spirit. Percival had no more cared for Al than had Punchy. In fact, he had inherited his dislike of Al from Punchy who had often warned, "be sure to count you fingers after shaking his hand."

Al was a middle aged, Irish Italian – "the worst kind'a mix," Punchy had uncharitably claimed. He wore a pin stripe, tailor made suit, silk tie, and patent leather shoes in which he could see his pampered, well fed face clearly enough to shave, if he so liked. His stubby, manicured hands were adorned with finger rings which served as brass knuckles. He was not a man to be trifled with. He had the overall appearance of a successful shyster. His hair was pomaded, slicked back and parted on the side, and his facial features cleanly shaven. All of a piece, he looked and smelled like a man freshly out of a barber's chair.

"How r things," he casually asked, as Percival labored to sit up. "You was las night's big win again. too bad lady luck threw you a curve, though you batted it out'a the park," Al blathered, tossing a copy of the Daily News on his lap, sports page up.

The headlines ran: "P. Jones, breaks jaw in spectacular win!"

Percival tried to read the headline through a fog, unable to make sense of it. He looked up slowly from the page, his expression frozen, unaltered, wondering what this shady fight promoter, reputedly connected, married as he was to a Bronx Don's daughter, might want with him this time of day; all too early for a visit? It could not be said that they were friends, far from it, they were hardly on speaking terms. Although, it was known that, Al would frequent the gyms and fights scouting out new talent for his stable. Always self-serving, he was brief with those who could not benefit him and fawned over those who could. And occasionally, when Punchy's back was turned, he would approach Percival: "Whenever you're ready ta go pro, kid, give me a call," he'd say, slipping him his card.

Percival would seldom respond, but when on occasion he had, he'd say, "Talk ta Punchy, not me!" Then ditch the card at his earliest convenience.

"What's the verdict, how's your jaw?" Al asked.

"It's broken," Percival swallowed, garbling his words, he could barely get them out and gazed at Al in perplexity.

"Some fluke breaking your jaw like that, but taking Juarez apart says it all. I've never seen a fighter come back from a broken jaw – never! N the way you did it, so methodical, every instinct razor sharp," he said, with gusto. "It was something to watch."

Percival gave Al a dazed, lost look directly in the face.

"Which brings me to my visit," Al went on, looking down on Percival, his face hanging on the brink. "I wouldn't want you to think I'm trying to take unfair advantage of a man on his back, but it's only good business to run ahead of the pack and stake you claim—something someone of your caliber can appreciate. I've had an eye on you for some time now. You have real potential and r bound to be the crown jewel in anybody's stable. Well I want it to be mine, and I'm willing to pay. I'm talking a quarter mil to start," Al proposed with a saccharin smile. "I know we'll make a bundle together – I'll make you rich."

"Ave you talked to Punchy 'bout this," Percival asked, eyeing Al seriously for a moment.

Al guffawed, then leaned closer and said more intimately, "I've got trainers of my own. It's not Punchy I want, it's you. I've got the pull. The connections. I can make you a champion."

"No dice. We're a team, Punchy n me. We got history," Percival said, trying to get the words out from behind a mouthful of wire. "I go where Punchy goes, that's the way it is." He longed to roll over, close his eyes and go back to sleep. He struggled to yawn with his jaw and mouth locked in place.

"You're telling me you need a babysitter? I'll be damned, I'd think you'd be wantin ta talk to an accountant," Al said, waving a hand in exasperation.

"Punchy ought'a be here," Percival groggily insisted, in a distant voice, lowering lazy eyes.

"I guess I figured you wrong. I thought you were your own man."

"I'd be yours if I sign any papers, now wouldn't I?"

"No, you'd be on your way to being a rich man and a world champion."

"Go away, Al. I'm in no shape to read anything let alone sign it."

"Look, Punchy's amateur. Your amateur days r over as of las night. I'm pro. I can see you to the top and make you rich in the bargain – that quarter mil is just for starters," said Al, producing a contract for Percival's signature, to prove his sincerity. "It's all made out, all you've got'a do is sign."

Distraught, Percival snickered, the sound emanating from behind his wired teeth. His jaw started to ache. "If that ain't a bitch. You don't hear," he chided, placing a hand to his jaw, wishing Al would stop tempting him, leave him alone so that he might drift off. "Money's a partial solution I confess, but…" he said it, as an afterthought, thinking how he could entice Joleen, if he so cared, with such lucrative a contract offer. But it wasn't worth the thought. He felt dead, empty, unable to concern himself. He just wanted to be left alone to sleep and to forget.

"What r the words to that pop tune? 'If money can't buy it, then it's not worth having?' You're talking crazy or you're delirious from whatever they've been giving you. Or worse," Al scoffed, an idea dawning on him. "There's a skirt, isn't there? A sucker for the broads, r you? Well? And what do dames like more than money? Money makes problems go away faster than anything else." Al winked knowingly. "N there'll be plenty a' that. Hell, you can have all the broads you want." Al smiled, toothily, as eloquently as would a shark.

Groggy, Percival had wished to object but it was lost on him and passed like a vapor before his mind's eye.

Presently, the head nurse peered in and surveyed the scene from the doorway. She stormily entered, and clearing her throat peremptorily, "harrumph!" She firmly asked Al to leave.

"I'm only trying to make your patient here a rich man," Al explained, a tight smile playing on his lips as he folded the contract and discretely put it back in his inner jacket pocket.

"A fortune he might enjoy as soon as he's conscious enough to do so, I'm sure," said the nurse in reproof, looking at Percival, his eyes wilting. "If you would be so kind." She gestured to the doorway with an outstretched hand.

Al cast a critical glance around the drab ward, as he turned to go. "You shouldn't be in a ward full of sick people, who knows what you might catch," he said in distaste. "You should be in a private room by yourself. If you want, I can see to it for you."

"I won't be here that long," Percival declined.

"Please," the nurse begged, "there are others to consider. You may return at regular visiting hours."

"Think it over, sport, see if you don't come round n see it my way. No one's gonna make you a better offer, you can be sure of that. If you're holding out for a better deal, you'll only be wasting your time," Al said, as the nurse ushered him out.

"I'll remember that," said Percival to Al's departing back. Then unable to close his eyes and drift back to sleep as he would have liked, he instead considered the congested, eerily still ward and its occupants. It was a discomforting scene; so many men on their backs, sick, aged and isolated from the world; estranged from family, friends, and each other, absorbed, as they were, in a hell of their own. Out of a youthful, morbid repulsion of anything sick or weak, he could little find it in himself to empathize with these old, decrepit specimens of humanity, broken on the wheel of life, belonging more to the other world than this one. Some were installed in oxygen tents, others attached to i.v. hook-ups through which, drop-by-drop, life giving sustenance was provided. A few others had tubes up their nostrils. But the most disquieting was the skeletal old man in the bed across from him breathing his last, his breath coming angrily and in short, rattling gasps from his scrawny throat. He was having a wretchedly difficult time of it dying. And overcome by a winnowing, heartfelt sense of remorse, Percival found himself horribly fascinated.

Eventually, he lowered his eyes on the newspaper Al had left behind, turning to the front page. The King assassination was still cover story. The F.B.I. was closing in fast. Percival's eyes drifted sleepily from the page, the paper slipped his grasp and his eyes closed. He would drift in and out of sleep for the rest of the morning till visiting hours later that day when friends and family began to arrive bringing a buoyancy with them that was otherwise lacking. Some brought flowers and candy; some tears and laughter; and one came to hold the hand of a dear one who could not consciously respond.

Punchy arrived amidst a crosscurrent of cautionary chatter. "How r we?" he asked, drawing up a chair.

At a loss for words, Percival grimaced, eyeing his trainer with the beseeching eyes of a sick child.

Punchy's eyes met his, his expression mixed, elusive. It was difficult to fix Punchy by his looks; his cool poker face, mirthless smile, turbid, deep-set eyes, his broken nose flattened across his face and balding pate or, for that matter, the blue collar worker garb he habitually wore when, wholly, he was not a laborer but, in fact, a landlord, though it could be said in his defense that he did most of his own janitorial work, if only to keep himself occupied.

He was single, a lifelong bachelor, dedicated to sports, boxing most particularly where, in his prime, he had vied for the lightweight championship twice, but had failed to capture. He had invested his winnings in apartment buildings, some of which he owned outright and a few of the more fashionable he owned jointly with an old Army buddy, an international gambler and boxing aficionado, Derrick Rafkin.

Punchy was a sportsman, light on his feet, good with his hands, and someone to be reckoned with despite his fifty odd years. He was not a learned man by any means but he had a vast store of experiences on which to draw. He was a straight shooter, believed in fair play and would not cheat another out of his due. He was a gifted trainer, known in boxing circles as an oddball, a man who would not pimp his fighters. In fact, his nickname had been ascribed him by a boxing underworld that was highly suspicious of anyone who failed to misuse a fighter for profit. Hence, they concluded that he must be "Punch drunk." Ergo, the nickname, "Punchy," which he was anything but.

"How you feel?" Punchy asked.

"Like I blew it," Percival rejoined, blinking. "If only I'd listened."

Punchy winced. "It wouldn't have mattered. Juarez was virtually unstoppable, n not ta be denied his pound of flesh. Ya got'a give the devil his due. The truly amazing thing is you got it together enough to come back as you did. That said, I saw your doctor on his way in. He says your jaw'll knit jus' fine. Concentrate on getting better n get that fool notion out'a your head. You did yourself proud las night, no mistaken it. If you've any doubts, here." Punchy started to hand him a copy of the Daily News when he noticed an edition on the bed stand. "Ya got a copy, I see."

"Al McGraw left it," Percival drawled.

"Al McGraw?"

"The same."

"What that thief want? Or was he here to check yo pulse?"

"Ta offer me a deal."

"What he offer?"

"A quarter mil to start."

Punchy whistled. "That can buy a lot of groceries."

"N every mouthful tasteless," Percival mumbled, unable to project his voice fully.

"Al's no fool, it'll keep other bidders away once word's out. Ummmm," Punchy mused, scratching his grisly chin. "Al's bad enough news but his silent partners r far worse, they bury their mistakes."

"He wants me to ditch you in the bargain."

"That son of a bitch," Punchy spat. "But that's ta be expected – it's par fer the course."

"I won't deal with the likes of Al."

"In this game it's not so easy. People like Al don't crawl back under their rock cause ya disapprove of him."

"I told him, I go nowhere without you."

"What he say to that?" Punchy asked, pleased.

"The head nurse came 'n drove him out for sneaking in before visiting hours."

"Good for her," Punchy approved.

Racine swept into the ward sylph like, casting a benedictional glance this way and that, looking to locate Percival. She spotted him seated up in bed engaged in a conversation with a diminutive, balding, brown skinned man whose back was to her. She strolled over in her pert, unassuming fashion, catching the eyes of all she passed, even the elderly man on his death bed, gasping for air, stole a peek. She perfumed the air with sexuality; the spark of life. "'ello," she said in a sultrily voice, leaning forward and kissing Percival familiarly.

"What you doing here," he asked, gazing up at her, embarrassed by a consuming passion that entered his face and eyes, raising his blood. He flushed all the more, suspecting Punchy's inquisitive gaze.

"When you didn't come last night, I got worried and read in the morning paper that you had broken your jaw. I called around and found out what hospital you were in, and here I am and there you are."

"You've not met my trainer, Punchy," Percival said hurriedly between clamped teeth. "Punchy, this is Racine. A friend, sort'a."

"Hello," Punchy smiled, indulgently, admiring the tall, voluptuous, rosy cheeked blond with eyes only for Percival.

"'ello," she gushed, flashing a sensual smile by him.

"Look, let me leave you youngsters to yourselves. Two's company, they say. I'll be back tomorrow 'n we can finish 'r talk then," Punchy said, swayed by the suggestive play between the two, in which he felt out of place.

Racine blushed, not objecting, averting her eyes. Percival hoisted his gaze, extended his nostrils and smiled mutely.

"Don't worry," Punchy said, rising, unable to take his eyes off Racine. "Tomorrow'll be soon enough."

"Thanks for coming," Percival uttered.

"Sure thing," Punchy said, eyeing Racine for a final time. "It was nice ta make ya acquaintance."

"Likewise," she chirruped, fixing him in her blue eyes. "Too-da-loo." She wriggled the fingers of a hand in farewell.

"Tomorrow then," said Punchy, taking his leave.

Once Punchy had gone, Percival rebuked her: "Ya shouldn't'a come without my calling."

"Why not?"

"For one thing, Punchy 'n I had stuff to talk about."

"Do I embarrass you?" she asked, candidly, lips quivering.

"Can't you see, you're white n I'm black?"

"You keep saying that like it's supposed to mean something."

"You don't get it, do you? Punchy knows me, knows Joleen. Knows her family, for that matter. So yeah, it increases the possibility for conflict."

"I'm sorry, I wasn't aware of your feelings," she said in a bruised voice, heart near breaking.

"God, Racine, suppose Joleen shows up, what then? I swear, I wish it wasn't so," he said contritely.

"How is it that woman's so under your skin?"

"It's not what you think."

"Oh?"

"She has my son. Malek is the bargaining chip."

"If only I can believe that."

"It's true."

94

"That woman sticks in my craw."

"She shouldn't."

"But she does."

He smiled wanly, defeatedly. "I'm terribly sorry."

"You needn't be."

"I feel my life's become an apology overnight," he wailed.

"But you've nothing for which to apologize," she said, soothingly, taking his limp hand in her own.

"Oh Racine," he uttered drearily, "if only things had worked out."

She cradled his wooly head to her sumptuous breast. "Shhh," she calmed him. "It'll work out, you'll see, I promise. I'm with you. For you. Whatever it takes. Now just hush!" He succumbed to her charms, knowing it for false hope, but what else did he have left?

Brows stormily banked above his eyes, Punchy returned the next day as promised. If, since his visit of the day before, he'd clung to any illusions they were all dispelled. There were none now left on which to base any hopes or dreams. Moreover, his fighter, Percival, was in a hospital bed, sedated and with a broken jaw, all too tragically the winner! It had been a long grueling haul, ten years in the making. And no church bells announce the death of a dream so loudly as do their sustained silence.

Punchy was dispirited. So much so, in fact, that desiring numbness he had had, what for him, was an unusual number of drinks before coming.

"Hello," said Punchy in a cracked tone of voice.

Percival smiled feebly from his bed; his face having become visibly lopsided in the last twenty-four hours.

Before launching into the unfinished discussion of the previous day, Punchy drew up a seat, scratched his bald pate, and eyed Percival, alarmed at how corpselike he appeared against the fluffy, white pillow beneath his head.

"You okay?" Percival mumbled sluggishly, as with a mouth full of marbles.

"Yeah, sure, why not? You the one on your back, ain't ya?" said Punchy. "N I'm on my feet. We-l-l, barely." Their dream derailed, it was time to own up. They had clearly arrived at a difficult pass, and what they now had to decide could alter the course of their relationship. He was more aware than Percival of the degree to which his career had slipped as a consequence of his having broken his jaw, casting a shadow over what had otherwise promised to be a splendid future; Punchy's foremost concern was that Percival not enter a tail spin out of which he could not pull himself, as was common with fighters on suffering such a reversal of fortune.

Champions were a breed apart, no doubt. Then again, how many had he seen over the years broken, become stumble bums? shoeshine boys, derelicts, alcoholics or border line psychotics? Then there were those who became Kings, ambassadors of the sport, the sweet science – men of the world. Much a source of Punchy's pride, Percival was undoubtedly championship material. He had it all. He was easily the best fighter he'd ever handled in his thirty odd years and the best fighter he'd seen since Robinson. It wasn't so much that their hopes had been dashed but that their dream been derailed! Under such conditions, who could think of going on? Who cares what bleeds out of a man shipwrecked and with a drowned dream to bury?

Sick at heart, Punchy felt like crawling into bed beside Percival, but gamely said, "Slade 'n Juaraez 'r going to Mexico. They're gonna decide who'll compete in the games between them in ya place." No sooner had Punchy spoken than he felt like someone who'd shot a favorite horse on breaking it's leg winning the Derby.

It took a while for Punchy's remarks to sink below the surface of Percival's codeine addled brain. Rising on his elbows like a fighter trying to beat the count, he blurted, "huh?" reeling from the memory of the blow that had hospitalized him and Juarez's taunting remark, "I kill you. I kill you." ringing in his ears.

"Juarez won after all?" Feeling as if his life had become one long dizzy spell, Percival's head sank back on a long, outpouring sigh, echoing his dying neighbor's fading breath.

"No, you won alright."

"What's it matter if someone else collects the prize?"

"If that was all. Al's gone 'n leak'd his offer to the press. It's in t'day's paper," Punchy said, setting the paper on the bedside stand. "Read it for yourself when you get a chance. It's meant to pressure you into accepting, as well as warning others off. In fact, it goes so far as to suggest you've already signed,"

"Sh-e-et!" Percival sneered.

"It was bound to happen, there 'r big bucks involved. Till now you've been busy following the Olympic trail 'n sacrificing to do so but the rides come to a bad end. I know how much you sacrificed 'n for it to ave tanked like this – I know it stinks! 'N Al's banking on your accepting his offer as a consolation prize. I know you got some problems that if you had some money to throw at things'll go easier. I know the prospects of continuing poverty is not pleasant. I know. But money in boxing's a reward, not an inducement; being champion, winning' the championship, that's the inducement. Money too quick, too soon, can spoil you; dull your edge; cut your hunger. Make you too soft to soon," said Punchy frankly. "I wouldn't want'a talk you out'a going pro but there 'r lots a' easier ways of making a buck than taking it on the chin. Hell, you can surprise your mother, for that matter, 'n go finish school.

"This might not be the best time for us to talk, but it's on my mind," said Punchy, voicing his concern. "We been together ten years 'n during that time I don't think I ever steered you wrong. Over time I've come to regard you as a son," he said, with a surge of pride. "Remember, this is boxing we're talking, 'n it's too easy to leave this sport damaged. I've seen too many good fighters left penniless, brain-dead 'n in some godforsaken back alley with only a bottle of cheap booze for company, forgotten by fans, managers 'n promoters they made rich. I know it's a' hell of an offer to turn down. But it's the sharks like Al with their twenty-five-dollar cigars, dressed like Hollywood pimps 'n gangsters who end up in the mansions 'n the fighters forgotten in some back alley sick 'n broke. Boxing's a profession where it's all too easy to come apart like a jigsaw puzzle that don't quite fit together so good an more. I don't know why I love this sport," Punchy admitted. "Maybe it's cause I like my violence confined to a squared off area 'n less random like in society.

"I've said what I wanted, more or less. You decide what you're gonna do. take your time, get focused, let your jaw mend, don't rush. The sharks that infest these waters will still be there after you've made up your mind.

"But if you should want'a turn pro, I'm with you, but no Al – he's in I'm out! Now I can get you fixed up with good management. Derrick Rafkin, my business partner would be glad to manage you, but no inducements, no quarter mil. We stick together, you got'a fight your way back', y'all ave to keep a sharp edge on your killer instinct.

"Ya got'a rely on the carnivore, 'n the instant that beast ceases to be hungry, ceases to run ahead of the pack, ceases to seek a championship or hold on to it for its own sake, you get out, call it quits while your brain's still intact 'n before your body's been reduced to one big ache, as it must feel right about now."

Percival's eyes roamed limply over Punchy's unshaven leathery face. "I guess I understand," he said, swallowing dryly, wishing he could turn back the clock. "For now I'm'a try forget, sleep 'n not dream. As for the rest, so long as we're in it together, I don't care."

Punchy slapped Percival soundly on the shoulder. "Count me in—I'm with you— 'All the way'—as you told me the paratroopers say."

"All the way!" Percival echoed, flat on his back from a hospital bed.

***

Percival was released from the hospital Monday morning. The same morning the old man in the bed across from him breathed his last, the day before Dr. King's funeral. The overcast city, on smog alert, and, as best he could tell, it's usual frantic self. Due to the effect of the medication he was on, and less the disposition of his afflicted soul, it felt like a recurring dream from which he could little rouse himself. A lingering doubt, a sense of oppression, which he could not shake, haunted him on the subway ride into Brooklyn. Overall he felt as if the fates had conspired against him, to cheat him out of that which was rightly his. "The best man doesn't always win," he recalled Punchy saying. Yet he was no doubt, the better fighter, if not the better man and, to his regret, he'd won! "If that ain't a bitch," he muttered unguardedly.

He gained his feet with difficulty as the train swayed into his stop, his face wilting from the drugs he was on, the pain killers, which left him dopey, and slow witted.

He disembarked, exited the subway and headed home.

He arrived at his apartment and clumsily managed to unlock the door. He then entered the darkened passageway which opened on both the closet size kitchen and front room. He could not recall having left any lights on and so he was surprised to discover the front room lights ablaze down the hall, but he was even more surprised, nay, aghast, shocked out of his torpor, to find Joleen ensconced on the couch, cigarette in hand and smoke spiraling from her mouth.

"Hello stranger," she sang, exhaling, breaking the emotionally charged silence that crackled electrically between them.

"J-Jo –" he stammered, trying to keep his composure.

"Surprised?"

"Not happily."

She crossed her legs, rustling her floral print dress as she did, striking a peevish pose. A faint scent of perfume reached him across the room. "Don't be that way." She pouted.

"How'd you expect me to be?"

"Glad to see me."

"Sh-e-et," he snarled.

"Is that any way to greet someone whose been waiting for you since Saturday?"

"You've been here that long? Why? What'a you want?"

"To see you."

"Don't," he challenged her assertion as a fabrication.

"I guess I have no right to think you'd believe me."

He breathed in sharply, his breath cutting into his lungs with fiery intensity. He eyed her darkly, searching to find fault, fix blame for so much that had gone wrong in his life of late, starting with her. It further rankled him that though he knew better than to trust her, he had never desired her more. Besides, he knew she wanted something and so she must be there to seduce him, there could be no other explanation. He could see it in her face, beyond the veil of smoke. It shone in the reflected light of her eyes, eyes he knew and that knew him.

Deriving satisfaction from his surprise, Joleen watched him coyly, his eyes resting on her, fixed on her. She was unprepared for the hostility of his gaze, and gasped. She knew how swiftly he could overpower her; rip off her clothes and do with her as he would. Although she was as childishly intrigued with sex as afraid of it, she was not unaware of the passion she aroused in him, nor was she above using her adolescent female wiles to beguile him. She continued to smoke, engaging his softening, bewildered eyes, her saucy lips pouted into a wistful smile.

"Say something, won't you," she peeped, laying her cigarette aside. "You are glad to see me, aren't you?"

"Why should I be," he asked, his voice quavering.

"Don't be that way," she urged. "It's so. Oh, you know ungallant." She uncrossed her legs, rose from the couch to her stocking feet and approached him. She embraced him as if for a dance, her face tipped up below his. "Baby, believe me, it's not been any easier for me," she said, with a nasal twang, feeling him out. "I didn't want to hurt you, but I thought I was in your way. I've grown. I know better now. But at the time I thought I was an encumbrance." He so wanted to swallow her story, believe her lie. She gazed into his remote eyes, raising a hand to his jaw. "Does that hurt?"

"No more than losing my shot at the Olympics."

"I'm sorry about that."

"I jus' bet you r."

"You're so cruel," she accused, averting her eyes. "Why can't you love me. You did once, remember? Don't be so heartless, you still can. if only you would. You still do, I know you do, just like I do. So why can't you say it? I want to hear it from your lips, your own sweet mouth. Oh, say it for me," she implored, holding him tightly against her.

Percival's eyes strained in their sockets with disbelief. Yes, he had considered this encounter on numerous occasions in the past, but he had never resolved it satisfactorily and it appeared he would fair no better now. She was beside him, palpable, real, a flame in his veins. Moreover, her perfume, much like her pliant body pressing irresistibly against him, overpowered his senses, and was as good an intoxicating counter argument to any he might propose. However, before he could respond, she pressed a silencing finger to his lips. "No, don't," she said. "Just kiss me." Succumbing to her wishes, he thought

99

What the hell. She tilted his chin as she raised herself on tip toes, and the instant their lips locked all else was forgotten. He could curse the wiring behind which his tongue ineffectually lay, but still their mouths raised ample sparks enough; and together they toppled onto the couch. She strung one leg over its back and the other she bent up from the floor, thus he collapsed between her thighs and folds of her up-raised skirt. But with so little space in which to maneuver, they shortly adjourned to the back bedroom, groping, as they did, to free one another of their clothes.

It was over no sooner than it had begun. And with a groan of dissatisfaction, Percival rolled off Joleen and onto his back like a beached whale, thinking of Racine and hoping Joleen would get up, collect her clothes and go. For being so alluring, Joleen was certainly a disappointment in bed. He found it odd, to say the least, that she was as good a dancer as he knew. She could really cut a rug, shake up a dance floor. Yet, in the bedroom, she was inapt, a wallflower, frigid and unyielding. In a word, frustrating.

Sex for Joleen was a dilemma froth with social consequences, biblical injunctions and racial taboos, which were of little consequence to Racine. Whereas dance, in as much as Joleen had taken it from early childhood on – both ballet and modern – was a cultural expression worthy of social recognition. But sex, to her mind, was a function lowlife Negroes participated in all too often, scandalizing the race. Guided by her mother's archaic lights, she had been given to believe that sex was something to be frowned on. And besides, to enjoy it overly was to succumb to the dark forces of blind necessity. Again, the lesson had been reinforced, in church, from the pulpit, by the pastor who had informed his flock, "it's a curse, a sin second only ta the eating of the forbidden fruit, which brought death to a fallen humanity. Beware the snare of Satan, my children, set for the everlasting run'a many; the devil's own tainted daughter, the Whore of the World!" To which the congregation had replied, "Amen!"

Joleen felt certain that the virtuous, stern faced women in the amen corner, "the community of Saints," as they were referred to, had never succumbed to such temptations. They always looked, from week to week, as spotlessly virtuous as the starched white dresses they habitually wore, symbolizing the whiteness of their pristine souls despite the blackness of their skins. That is the curse of Ham, which had befallen his offspring and had been inscribed on their countenance like a Scarlet Letter.

Consequently, Joleen had been made afraid that if she enjoyed sex overly, that she would become lost to the seductive sway of the jungle that beat like the savage rhythms of Africa which coursed through her blood and was to be denied, at all cost, on threat of eternal damnation. Thus she was forced to deny all racial memory of that primal spark from which creation sprang. It was one thing to dance like a jungle bunny, but quite another to fuck like one.

"You can't expect too much from men. They're all alike – like your no-good father," so Mrs. Reel had informed her since early childhood on. "Jus' look at him, the sot." And what Mrs. Reel had not taught Joleen about men, her father's spineless example had. Subsequently, she thought it prudent to see that Percival not stay poor long, for both their moral and spiritual welfare.

Joleen laced an arm over Percival's sloping shoulder and curled up spoon like against the contour of his broad back, inciting aversion in him. She sighed languidly, "You're delicious, Mr. Jones."

"Why didn't you come see me in the hospital?" he asked.

"I would have, but I doubted it was the right place," she said coyly. "Besides, I thought this would please you more." She tittered, nipping him playfully on the nape of his neck.

"Don't," he carped. "Anyway it's jus' as well," he added, recalling Racine's visit.

"Percival," she cooed next to his ear, snuggling cozily against him, listening to his breathing, "can we talk? I'd like to come back, try again. I've missed you something awful these weeks. I'd like so much if we can give it another go. Malek needs a father and I need you. I really do. We can be a family. Won't you say yes?"

"Don't ask me that," he said, irritably, pressing the side of his swollen face into the pillow. "I can't consider a thing like that jus' now. I'm not feeling well. I'm in considerable pain. My jaw's busted 'n my dream's lost," he said, in remorse.

"I'm sorry for your loss, truly I am, but you made love nonetheless."

"Is that what it was? Well I didn't realize it was gonna cost me anything."

"We have a son and that cost!"

"Had you only considered that before you walked out."

"Let's not argue. Can't you see I'm trying to make amends?"

"You left with 'r son without a word 'n wouldn't take my calls."

"On the surface I know it looks bad, but you don't know the whole of it, how I was here alone by myself all day every day, going crazy with a crying baby on my hands and suffocating in this wretched place. I couldn't bear it. I was so miserable, so lonely, and every time Malek cried I'd cry too. I felt so low, so downcast, my school days gone all so suddenly, so painfully, and the responsibility of motherhood thrust upon me and the promises of yesterday behind me at the ripe old age of twenty. So yes, I panicked and ran back to my mother's."

"Only two years ago you came running here seeking shelter cause'a what you said were irreconcilable differences between you two."

"Where else was I to go? You were my fiancé. Was I to turn somewhere else?" She charged him with lovelessness. "If you loved me, you'd not question me. It's so awful."

"Oh, I see, my loving you justifies your sticking it to me, ay?"

"You can be so hardhearted."

"We could ave married had it not been for that mother of yours."

"It worked out for the better, we didn't have the money then."

"It spared us the cost of a divorce, that's for sure."

"Since we're on the subject, why didn't you send any child support? It takes money to raise a child you know?"

"I told you I wouldn't support anything under your mother's roof, n I meant it."

"Malek's still your responsibility, no matter the roof under which he sleeps."

"If you'd wanted me to support him, then why'd you haul him off to your mother's putting us in this spot? 'N not returning my calls either?"

She said, evasively, petulantly, "I was afraid we were going to end up like all the other people in this neighborhood leading penniless, empty lives; lives devoid of hope. I was afraid that that was all there was in store for us, but now I see we have a chance – a real chance for a better life."

"What 'r you getting at?"

"You know what I'm getting at, that quarter million dollar contract offer," she said giddily, squeezing him tightly, unable to contain her excitement further. "I can see it now, can't you? We can get out of this dump, finally. Move to St. Albans among a better class of Negroes." Curious, he listened anxiously. If he had not been alert before, he was certainly all ears now. "We can have a yard in which I can grow flowers and Malek can play with his little friends," she prattled on like a self-indulgent child ticking off it's Christmas wish list. "It'll be so cute. I can see it now. It'll be wonderful. We can get married. Mama couldn't object. And who'd care if she did anyway," she tittered. "I'll be good to you, the way you like – wasn't I good to you just now? Oh Percival," she implored, "can't we?"

"Jesus Christ, you obligate a man before naming your price," he snorted, casting off her arm and throwing his legs over the side of the bed, and sitting up with a hand to his throbbing jaw. "Nothing's ever straightforward with you." The prospect of spending a life of bourgeoisie respectability in the suburbs with Joleen horrified him, inflaming the intensity of the ache in his face. "If that's what this is about you could'a saved yourself the bother cause I can't take that deal."

"What do you mean you can't take that deal," she yelped, sitting up abruptly, panting, her breast heaving. "Are you just going to throw our future away?"

"R future? What future is that?"

"The one you're evidently so willing to throw away."

"All you care for is the money."

"Shouldn't I? Since I'm the one who ends up living through you, rich or poor. Pardon me if I'd prefer we do it richer than poorer, okay? If I must live through you, be known through you. I mean, ever since we began dating back in high school people always identified me with you and they'd inevitably ask, first off, how's Percival? When is his next fight? And then only incidentally, how I was, as if I were an appendage and didn't have a life apart from yours. How do you think that makes me feel? My life's become an afterthought, insignificant beside yours. I've little else to look forward to these days but your coming home nights, so why shouldn't I be able to do it comfortably? With respectability?"

"You'd sell your soul 'n sell mine along with it."

"What's soul to do with it," she said scornfully. "And since when did you find religion?"

"Religion has nothing to do with it," he parried, eyeing her in the bureau mirror, her breast quivering. He focused his gaze. They had known one another since childhood, dated in his last year of high school, exchanged letters during his stint in the Army, and now after two trying years of having lived together and having had a child, they could hardly speak to one another without producing sparks, inciting loathing. "Soul has to do with keeping faith with those who've kept faith with you. You ave not, where Punchy has, 'n that deal does not include him," he said, caressing his jaw.

"What's Punchy to do with it?"

"Everything, he's my trainer."

"S-so?"

"If he ain't in I ain't either."

"That's all right for you to say, but Punchy's not putting any money in your pocket, is he? No food on your plate, or paying your bills," she voiced. "Hell, why should he care? He's got his, but what of us? Of you? You're supposed to take care of us. And we can make it now. All you got to do is sign that contract!"

"N become beholding to the mob? No thank you! As for us, you took care of that when you walked out the last time without a word, avoiding my calls – now you show up like a bad penny cause you smell money."

"Yes," she confessed brazenly, "because there's finally money. What else have you to offer? Love? What's that got us but a child we can't afford. Seems to me love is a counterfeit, no more than an excuse to produce unwanted babies without much else to show for it," she said hysterically. "It's all around us, strung out from block to block in this slum you're content to call home for some god unknown reason. Is this what you want for our son? For Malek? Or have you forgotten him, too? See it from my angle, I'm the one who must make a home for us, for our son. A woman in a man's world must fight with what she's got to make a place for herself and family. So why should we spend the rest of our lives pinching pennies, especially now we don't have to?" Joleen said soberly? "You can't fault me for wanting more for us, for our son."

"No, Joleen, I don't fault you," Percival conceded, "but I don't love you anymore for it either. I owe everything to Punchy. If there's a golden egg, he's the one laid it."

"The goose that lays the golden egg is not the one to profit from it," Joleen argued. "Somebody else does. So why not us?" she urged. "My father's known Punchy going back a way now and Punchy's not hurting, but we are."

"Yeah but what the hell does your father know 'bout fighting," Percival rejoined?

"Cause that's what this is about, not money."

"No! No, it's everything about money; it's about the little we don't have," she contested. "What we don' and what we can have if you weren't so mule headed!" She drew her knees up under her chin and clasped her arms about her legs, sulking. They had not bothered to switch on the bedside light, thus the room was cast in shadow but for a lattice of light that filtered through the slats of the blind over the air shaft window. Percival sighed, slumping forward like a crumpled paper bag. His back to her, Joleen crouched at the top of the bed in the room's obscurity and stared vacantly, unable to fathom the disquiet of her wretched heart.

"Won't you at least consider what I've said," she beseeched him, fighting back tears, unable to understand why she couldn't control him the way her mother controlled her father. "Is what I ask so wrong? Is that old man more important to you than your own son – your precious Malek, the one who stole your heart from me?"

Percival was taken up short, surprised to find that Joleen knew something about him after all, though he dismissed her comment saying, "you're doing the talking."

"No one throws that kind of money away," she said, angrily, in stark disbelief. "You got a better deal going or something?"

"Don't be tiring," he drawled.

"I don't get it. I just really don't," she admitted, seething, fastening her gaze on his back in the spectral gloom. "You're supposed to love me, help me raise our son, Malek. You don't have a contract with Punchy, have you?"

"The contract I ave with Punchy is inscribed here," he said, tapping his chest over his heart. "The contract's right here! As for a better deal, I wish to god there was one," he said dryly. "If you think the only trouble between us is money, then you're sadly mistaken. Sure it's money, but it's everything else too. It's lack of understanding, mostly. You don't think of the sacrifice, the dedication it takes to box; the grueling day to day, sweat popping task of it, not jus' for me but for Punchy too. Boxing's not a hustle, you know? The bond struck between a fighter 'n his trainer is one forged in the crucible of the ring, 'n more binding than that of blood! A fighter must put himself in the hands of his trainer without reservation. He must have the utmost confidence in him. He must place himself entirely in his trainer's hands. Utterly! The nature of the game makes it so. One being this broken jaw which, had I followed Punchy's instructions, would not 'ave occurred."

"He says otherwise, trying to console me, but I know different. I was sure I could do it my way, 'n here's the result," Percival said, self-effacingly, wrenchingly. He could have wept and would have wept had Joleen not been there, but he had no wish to appear weak before her, or leave himself vulnerable, open to attack.

"If I'm a good fighter it's all because Punchy's a great trainer," he said. "I'm no more than he is. No more than he's made me. In this game he knows me better than I know myself. It's a relationship born of trust. I owe Punchy more than I can repay. But who the hell thinks of a fighter's feelings?"

She eyed him hatefully, wanting to laugh but, to her credit, she restrained herself.

"N despite it all," he resumed, "I can't say I don't love you!" Despite it all he still desired her, yearned to fulfill his hungriness on her, awakening her to her full potential like Prince Charming rousing Sleeping Beauty.

"Oh Percival," she sang, soaring.

"Wait! Wait," he said, staving her off, in a more sorrowful than angry tone. "You don't know how I wish I could give into you, believe your fantasy – but it's not my dream. It never was. 'n what about what I owe Punchy?"

"Maybe you can –" she started to say.

"Gal, won't you let me finish!" he demanded!

Startled into silence, her face was strained.

"Punchy's been there for me forever. from the very beginning, from the time I lost my father, n that's about as far back as I can clearly recall," he said, searching his memory, trying to find reason beyond his broken jaw by which to explain himself. "Punchy's been there with me every inch of the way, every step of the road. But you you've left me hanging on more than one occasion, left me in situations I can't rightly excuse. Punchy's been straight with me, like a father to me, he's never let me down. You on the other hand," he stopped, deciding to drop it. Why *bother*. "Yes, from the very start there was that ole man, as you so indelicately put it," he said.

"I didn't mean anything by it," she interrupted.

"Girl, I've seen a thing or two, enough to know things ain't what they ought'a be with us for us to base a future on." He sat restively on the edge of the bed with a dismal glow in his eyes, and then faced her, his eyes drawn to her exquisite breasts, luminous in the lattice of light that filtered into the darkened room through the blinds that covered the air shaft window, stealing his breath away. He was ready to fall down and worship at them they were so lovely to behold. She was undoubtedly beautiful, and he so wished that he could buy into her siren song.

She blushed self-consciously, and, reaching for the bed sheet, covered herself.

"Ya know where I've been these days?" he asked, casting his eyes downward, breathing heavily in spite of himself. "Know what I'm going through."

"I can well guess. It's no secret you've broken your jaw, you've lost your chance at the Olympics, you've been hospitalized, and yes, you've decided to throw a quarter million dollars away. Does that cover it or did I leave something out?" She said this sourly, clutching the bed sheet to her bosom in taut, defiant fingers.

"Yeah 'n you weren't there. Neither at the fights or come to see me at the hospital. Instead you hatch this little scheme hoping to seduce me. But when I really needed you, I was left to pull it together on my own."

She swung her eyes—Eurasian eyes, cruel eyes— scornfully on him, feeling cast down and cheapened by the shameful aspect of poverty from which he refused to rescue her.

"So it wasn't a bed of roses for you," she cuttingly remarked.

"Jus' like you to miss the fucking point," Percival said, his jaw throbbing. "I was trying to say something 'bout loyalty, 'bout paying dues."

Joleen riffled her scheming brain for an apt reply. "What about our son? What about Malek?"

Don't hold 'r son up for ransom like that. If I give into you – crumble 'n give into you – what kind'a man would that make me?" he demanded, eyeing her over his shoulder. "What kind'a father could I hope to be? The kind'a father your's is?"

"At least he pays his freight."

"He pays his freight out'a his hide, out'a his flesh 'n blood, out'a whatever's left of his ever-loving manhood, which is not much," Percival rejoined, rising to his feet. "I'm jus' now home out'a the hospital, jaw broken, hurting like sin, hoping to collect myself, 'n here you show up like a haunt 'n in less than 'n hour I'm in a scrape with you. If that don't beat it all. How in hell you suppose that's possible," he asked, pulling on his trousers. "You're fucking tiring, you know that?"

"Tiring," she emitted with hostility. "You say that now that you've gotten what you wanted from me! After you've done the foul deed. Stuck that thing of yours in me, and this is the thanks I get."

"What I wanted," he guffawed, "Don't flatter yourself. I got what it pleased you to give. What I wanted was to see my son, Malek."

"When was the last time you contributed to his welfare?" she quipped, irked at having been seen through.

"Ta live under your mother's roof n in her care? Never!"

"I'll have you know the day I left here – left you, this house, these rooms, this miserable existence," she said scornful, furious. "I found a roach crawling on Malek's sleeping face; crawling on my baby's face. My mother tried to tell me that it would always be this way with you," she said, attempting to cut him where it hurts. "You ought to be thankful my mother took us in. I mean, from the looks of things you've still not made your fortune or am I deceived? This place is the same roach infested dump I ran off and left," she said spitefully, flicking a cockroach off the bedside table to the floor, where it writhed on its back, legs flailing, trying to right itself. "You want to kill it or should I?"

Clasping his head in the outspread fingers of his hands, Percival staggered from the sting of the barb, his eyes on the roach which had righted itself, taking flight. He wagged his head somberly, reminded of how cruel she could be.

"Just like a nigger to bring a child into the world and not give a damn once it's here to care for. You call that loyalty? But me having to go downtown to the welfare department to beg assistance for your son, isn't loyalty?"

"Don't lay that at my door. You the one who left. I ain't forgotten nothing 'n don't think I have cause I ain't. I remember coming in from the gym the night before you split, Hi-Fi playing songs we used to dance to back in high school, n you sulking 'n nursing a pint of scotch 'n Malek crying his head off.

107

Sparks flew that night too. N that was the night before you cut last time, so don't try snowing me."

"That's your story but it doesn't make mine any less true," she said, as tears welled in her eyes. "As for your being snowed, I feel I'm the one being left out in the cold, taken advantage of. You make me ashamed of having been born colored. Colored men treat colored girls like crap," she flared. "You wouldn't treat a white woman like that, now would you?"

"What the hell you talking 'bout?"

"You think I don't know don't you? I know. I was there. I saw her, that white Hippie bitch! What's her name? I remember now, Racine. Would you treat her like that? You black son of a bitch," she spewed, watching him with bitter eyes. "You think I don't know what this is about? You think I'm not good enough for you – that it? You think I didn't get to the hospital but I did. I came. In case you're interested, I just missed Punchy as I stepped off the elevator going up and he stepped on the one going down. Then I saw you with her; that white Hippie looking bitch crawling all over you like a slut."

"She wasn't crawling over anybody," he said, anger filling his throat. "You lied 'bout not coming, did you?"

"What was I to do, make a spectacle of myself? Humiliate myself more? I couldn't even go back to my mother's, how could I tell her about your white whore? That's why I came here. I had the keys so I let myself in thinking I'd confront you, seduce you. I'll bring you round to your senses. I'll make you mine again. Once here I plotted my revenge while I waited. I turned the place upside down for evidence of her. I eventually found something better, your little black telephone book," she said tauntingly, viciously, her voice hoarse.

"What the fuck 'r you saying," he ejaculated, eyeing her steadfastly. "I don't believe you."

She reached for the lamp stand draw beside the bed in careless haste and the bed spread, formerly covering her, slipped her grasp, stripping her of all pretense to modesty. She took only casual notice of her nakedness, as she retrieved his little black book from the draw. "Don't believe me anymore?" she asked, pale with anger, and holding up the book to him like a red flag. "I called her too. Hell, I called every woman's name in it I didn't know. But Racine, her ears caught fire. I saw to that," she said mockingly, brutally. "It was her reserve that gave her away; she's the one who didn't hang up, the one who wanted to know more. Well I gave her an ear full you can be sure of that!"

Percival was so taken aback that had his mouth not been wired shut, his chin would have hit his chest in gaping disbelief. "You had no right – no fucking right at all," he said, nostrils flaring, burning.

"I had every right," she retorted, her face discolored with rage. "I've your son. I've Malek to protect, to look after, and I'm not going to let another woman have what's rightly mine."

"You'll not hang a millstone round my neck, bitch!"

"Bitch, now is it?"

"That's the last straw," Percival growled, glaring. "I want you dressed 'n out'a here before I forget myself," he declared, snatching his black book from her.

Crying softly, Joleen lowered wet eyes and gazed indolently on her plump breast, and the apex of her sexuality, the mons Venus, the root source of so much shame in her. And so, like Eve on awakening to her difference, she turned raspberry red, furious for having been born a woman; inferior, inadequate, "a nigger," passed over for a far less attractive white woman.

"You used me, fucked me, had your way with me and now you want to toss me out for your white whore," she cried, in hate and desperation, her face purpled with rage. "This is what I get. You're thinking of marrying that bitch, aren't you? That's it, isn't it? You're going to throw all that money away on that slut and leave Malek and me on our own. You don't love us. You don't love your son. throwing our lives away like that? Well I won't let you do it, you hear? If you can't do right by us, I'll see what a lawyer has to say about that. I'll sue your black ass. I'll drag you from court to court to court till you do right. Don't think I won't you stinking bastard you, I should have known my mother was right about you all along. She's always right! You're just another worthless nigger like the rest of them," she flung the word at him, crying inconsolably.

"One way or another I'll see you don't get away with it. If you think you're going to, you got another think coming. I'll plunge a knife into your black heart first. I swear to God I'll kill you. You know I will. Don't think I won't cause I will. No woman's gonna take you from me no woman, you hear? I'll see you dead, you son of a bitch!"

"You best take control of yourself. You're talking crazy 'n you don't want me any more pissed than I already am, you hear me, girl? Don't make me think about killing, don't do it," he said, raising a warning finger to her.

She observed the outstretched finger of his hand as if it were something vile, like Medusa's head, or a snake about to strike. Brushing hot, angry tears aside, she laughed maniacally, causing him some doubt. Then, without warning, she sprang from the bed for him, wild-eyed and snarling. She raised her fingernails, sharp as thorns, and raked his chest with them, peeling his skin like ripe fruit, drawing blood. He staggered, wavering dumbly, horrified. "Wh-what the fuc –" he gasped, watching the rich, red blood rise to the surface of

109

his chest like fizz. Before he could think, his open hand shot up and came down flat across her laughing mouth, knocking her off her feet. She felt herself in free fall, then struck the ground, senseless as to her whereabouts. She looked ashen, drawn and spiritless. Slowly her focus cleared, and she recognized the awful truth of her position. She wept the more, hand pressed to her smarting cheek.

His rage was unabating. He drew back his foot to kick her teeth in but caught himself, recalling that she was the mother of his son, sparing her. This was a parting of the ways for him. He had never struck a woman before, and he felt a light go out in him as a consequence.

"Get up! Give me my keys! Get your clothes on 'n get out'a here or you'll be the one to die here t'day!"

Joleen remained crumpled where she fell, crying more out of self-pity than pain. She beat the floor in front of her with balled fist, sobbing convulsively. She was supposed to have handled it differently, thereby handling him. She had calculated badly, and, as a result, felt doubly wounded.

"Get your fucking things 'n get outa my sight!" he ordered.

She collected her clothes and, standing on shaky legs ran into the bathroom off of the corridor and locked herself in. He trailed after her, trying the door.

"I want you out'a here," he barked. "I want you dressed 'n gone, hear me?"

She sobbed behind the locked door, leaning her weight against it. "You'll never see Malek again," she cried, in a voice shaking with malice. "Never! I swear it!"

Percival started back for the bedroom, droplets of blood seeping down his chest from the wounds inflicted on him by Joleen's fingernails. He then proceeded to collapse on the bed with a heartrending sigh, and raised an unsteady hand to his pulsating head, listening impatiently, waiting for Joleen to get dressed, get out of the bathroom, out of the apartment and out of his slowly crumbling life.

***

Gathered round the living room T.V. in the small project apartment Percival's mother, Hattie Jones, shared with his younger sister, Lois, and brother, Sam on Staten Island, in New Brighton, the most depressed and densely populated area in the borough—they focused on the televised proceedings of Dr. Martin Luther King Jr's funeral.

Typical of so many Negro homes then, a picture of a white Jesus occupied a place of prominence on the living room wall above the T.V. console with a photo of Jesus' modern-day disciples, John F. Kennedy to his right, and Martin

110

Luther King Jr. to his left, and a photograph of the late Mr. Jones sat atop the console. "Cleanliness is next to Godliness" was Mrs. Jones' motto, thus her apartment was spotless and not an article of furniture out of place or a cup improperly hung; though a faint odor of fried foods issued from the kitchenette and clung innocuously on the air. Aside from this short coming, Mrs. Jones' home was as immaculate as a house of worship.

Presently, the diva, Marion Anderson, sang, "The Battle Hymn Of The Republic" over the casket of the slain Civil Rights leader; and, as the mezzo-soprano's angelic voice soared, filling the church from vestry to eaves, the T.V. camera scanned the deeply affected faces of mourners and dignitaries in the front pews. Everyone's heart in the small room leapt as the camera focused in on the irregular, boyishly good looks of Presidential hopeful Robert F. Kennedy in an otherwise sea of black faces. There were many other white mourners in attendance of course, all the other Presidential hopefuls, as well as world leaders, but, after Martin, Robert embodied the hopes of black Americans more than anyone else. As the diva's voice spilled "Mine eyes have seen the glory of the coming of the Lord –" over the air waves, it was especially warming to see Bobby counted among those in attendance.

As they watched the T.V. screen, their thoughts were cast back on a similar scene five years earlier following the assassination of then President John F. Kennedy; nor had his words been lost on them that, "The torch has been passed to a new generation." As such, like most blacks, they too had come to rest their hopes for redress on the late President's stalwart younger brother's shoulders.

"Glory glory Hallelujah –"

Mrs. Jones hugged herself and rocked back and forth like a mother cradling a still born child. "Lawd – Lawd," she said tearily, as the T.V. cameras passed from Bobby's soulful face. "Thy Kingdom's yet to come."

Then came the recorded voice of the martyr as the pallbearers carried his remains from the Church, "I just want to leave a committed life behind. Then my living will not have been in vain."

Coretta Scott King, garbed in spectral black, a picture of mourning, was nobility itself. And nobility had seldom been carried with more dignity. Her children beside her, they followed the coffin of her heroic husband from the church to a waiting mule cart outside on which his remains were to be borne. Slowly, slowly, with a train of weeping mourners following, the mule cart pulled out with a strenuous tug.

Mrs. Jones rose from her armchair as if the weight of the world were hers to bear. "Oh Lawd," she groaned, standing erect under the burden, clicking off the T.V. She sucked her teeth in arrant disgust, staring absently at the blank screen and then fell back in her chair, her hands to her face.

111

Percival sat motionless, morbidly preoccupied, as were they all. Sam rashly said, breaking the silence, fighting back tears, "He was only jus' a man, jus' a man."

"After all," Percival conceded. "Still, like Malcolm, dead though they may be, I envy them."

"It's sad when we're left to envy the fallen," said Lois, horrified.

"It's an ugly fact of American life," Percival proclaimed.

"Amen to that," Sam agreed.

"I suppose it's so," Lois conceded.

"Ya do so put me in mind'a your father," said Mrs. Jones softly, casting a reflective gaze on Percival – there was infinite sadness in her cloudy gaze.

"H – How's that?" Percival wondered aloud, unaccustomed to his mother speaking of their father. She had buried him deep, once and finally, and seldom made mention of him. Indeed, a conspiracy of silence seemed to have grown up around his memory, so much so that they, the children, knew little of him. Little more, that is, than a sad black face in a discolored photograph atop the living room T.V. set, a missing heartbeat amongst them. And for fear of opening Pandora's box, they dared not question her too closely. Instead they tacitly agreed to close ranks against any intrusive memory of him. Ironically enough, Percival had, long ago, given thanks that he had not turned out like his father. Hence, his mother's remark struck a raw nerve.

She considered him. "I know, child, you think you father's Booker Jones. He's your younger brother n sister's father all right but you're his adopted son but Booker wasn't your father, your biological father." She paused wearily, settling back in her chair, clasping her hands.

Lois, Percival and Sam looked at one another in stupefaction, then redirected their inquisitorial gaze back on to their mother's solemn face.

"It's nothing I intended to keep from you, but I didn't know how to tell you neither.

It's no easy story to tell, but after King's death, after his lynching las week – I mean, what else can you call it— it all come back to haunt me like a bad dream from which I can't waken. As if, after all these miles, all this time, I'm still running. N it come back so clear to me, the time after the Army, you went south to work with that Civil Rights group, what's they call now?"

"SNCC," Percival reminded her.

"That them students for non-violence—they ain't so much up for non-violence no more is they? It scared me night 'n day you down there. I was senseless with grief at not seeing you alive again 'n my hair jus' 'bout turn white from fright. N now this – this, O God it terrifies me so, pouring in on me like yesterday's rain, making me relive those times all over again, reminding me why I'd never go south again." She tearfully turned her face away, wringing her hands. "They made it so I wouldn't go home again even after my father got sick 'n died, though your grandma begged me to come. I wouldn't go. It wasn't I didn't want'a, but them crackers so stinking evil! For a time Martin made me hopeful 'bout going back home to see my people after all this while – But no, the truth is— the truth always as I've known it— n the terrible truth 'bout your father, Percival, n how they lynch him. Lord! Lord!" She covered a gasp with her hand, her startled eyes set as if on something unspeakably foul.

In her forties, Mrs. Jones had been quite lovely, but worn out by work she had tired, let herself go, grown overly plump and had aged perceptibly. She was still however quite dignified. Capable of love, she lavished it freely on her children, hoping to keep her small family intact.

"It tormented you younger children's daddy so it kill him too," she uttered in dismay, taking her hand from her lips. "Memory can be a curse, n memory stretch it's long hand from Alabama to kill poor Booker in Brooklyn!

"Sure y'all think Booker got himself killed stepping in front a truck but that jus' a postdate to the actual event." She fretfully paused, sucking air, girding herself. Then, "Since nobody dies all at once any more than they born all at once, it really happened more like this: I shouldn't'a loved your pa, Percival. But I couldn't help myself. He was lovable 'n jus' 'bout everybody did. He was mischievous 'n they love him all the more; he become devilish, 'n they wish they had the nerve. But when he became a bad nigger, they fled his company. I did too, I suppose." She sniffed, brushing aside a solitary tear. "It was said all his life, 'That boy gonna end up bad.' They say when they bury him, 'the undertaker took his measurements early on.' Ya pa, Percival, Lucius Sims, was the middle chile a seven; four girls 'n three boys. N he was the middle boy. A ole crone live down street a piece use to say, 'the boy born with the sign.' She never say what sign, though. Anyhow, he was the son'a 'r local Baptist Minister 'n his aloof, Caribbean born 'n Boston bred wife who was 'r schoolteacher. N Lucius was much his parents favorite – I think his father love him so for religious exercise, 'n I know it took religion to forgive him cause I ain't rightly forgive him yet.

"His mother was a free spirit 'n all the shackles a' the south couldn't constrain her high mindedness, her lofty spirit. She was held in esteem wherever she went, even white folks address her with respect. Them crackers, those envious so-called Belles, call her 'The nigger minister's fancy, high toned, Yankee wife.' The Cracker men though always tip they hats in passing – they so hypocritical. She was above it all. It's said she was from that school of New England transcendentalist founded by Mr. Emerson 'n Mr. Thoreau. She was a bigger influence on Lucius than his father, Pastor Simms, ever was.

Like I say, Lucius was smart, dangerously so, a blossoming intellectual I guess you'd say. Anyway he was too smart for the south – that is, for his own good.

"Lucius was easy ta love, too easy! N he could also be a good-for-nothing rake! A gambler; foot loose n fancy. A rollin stone n smart a student who ever opened a book. A good looking, sharp dresser, he could sweet talk a girl's bloomers off. We girls use to call him luscious. It suited him better. Anyway, we girls thought so." She blushed, surprised at herself. "But he was baptized with the name Lucius. It means, bearing light. Anyway, he was at the top a his class at school, a good athlete, 'n popular as sin, 'specially among us girls. But he was reckless, a driven soul, all too willing to risk it all on a trifle.

"'If only I could be myself; equal myself in this climate'a hate 'n fear, then I'd be content,' he would say to Booker 'n me. We didn't know what he meant exactly. We took him to mean he wanted to be like white folks. It took us awhile to figure out that's not what he meant at all, that he jus' meant what he say. The problem is, he was himself!" She sighed. "He jus' didn't know it yet, 'n the south wasn't gonna give him time to realize it neither!"

Percival listened attentively, clasping and unclasping the fingers of his hands, weighing his mother's every word. Lois and Sam meanwhile, were much distressed. They felt a sense of loss, ambivalence, and betrayal to learn that Percival was their brother by half and that his bloodline, other than their own, branched off radically, like a bolt of lightning, in an entirely different direction.

"Lucius the only colored boy I ever see fight white boys. Most of em jus' cut 'n run. Uh-uh, not Lucius, not your father, he wouldn't let white folks push him but so far. He paid people no never mind when they say, 'boy, keep that up, see if you don't end up dead.' I used to hate hearing it, it scare me so. But Lucius, if he scared, he sure didn't run. Hell, that boy so obstinate he wouldn't get off the sidewalk downtown to let white folks pass or say 'Yes sum' n 'No sum' like crackers like they colored folks to say. They say it cause his mother fill his head with her fanciful northern notions. Maybe, I don't know. I know they certainly had a time keeping her from following his coffin into the ground the day they bury him.

"Cause Pastor Sims well thought of, even white folks, some'a the leading citizens come warn him, 'That boy'a yours is too uppity for his own good, 'n if he don't learn his place 'n fast folks talking 'bout taking action.' The Chief'a Police was the main spokesman. That's why they come, to wipe they hands'a it. The reverend thanked the hypocrites 'n promised to act decisively. But Lucius had his poor father, Reverend Sims, wrap round his pinky fingers 'n the Reverend know it. He thought it best to get Lucius out'a Laurel n send him up north to college. Like I say, Lucius was bright, some folks say brilliant. He was too smart for his own good, that for sure.

"It was already the summer'a the year Lucius graduation roll round 'n he found he was accepted to a prestigious college up north for which his folks was grateful. The summer I found myself carrying his chile, Lucius' chile, my first born. You, Percival. I was too scared to tell him, after all I wasn't his only girl – though I was his steady girl. The one he always come back to. I held out hope, but I wouldn't hog tie him, I couldn't.

"It was that summer, too, Lucius 'n his father, Rev. Simms, got into difference of opinion 'bout religion. He tell his father, the Rev., 'I won't believe in a God who won't believe in me; who'd allow ignorant crackers dominion over me 'cause I'm color'd 'n they white. I won't 'ave such a' God as my God.'

"His father, Rev. Simms, was livid:

"He say, 'Son you ain't so ole I can't lay a strap to you yet!'

"'You do,' Lucius say, ''n I won't step foot in this house again!'

"Reverend Simms know that boy ain't lying either. He know Lucius good enough. He jus' say, 'Son, I hope you know what you 'bout cause I sure don't. You're more your mother's chile than any other of my children. Maybe it's best you go to school up north. It's best you get out'a the south. You got too much'a your mother's temperament for a colored boy down here. Lucius don't say nothing. But the summer had yet to tell it's story.

"Lucius become more reckless than ever that summer, knowing he was leaving, taking to drinking 'n carrying a pistol in his belt under his loose shirt tails. They would'a sent him to his mother's folks up north but he wouldn't hear it. Another thing, the crackers would go out what they call themselves "coon hunting." That is, they'd scare up some poor colored boy for sport 'n, as they'd say, 'beat the tar out'a the Sambo!' Trying they best to cripple him. "N often they did too. Well Lucius wasn't gonna stand 'n let that happen to him. Hell no, you could be sure'a that. 'If them white boys come mess with me, I'll deal with them in a way they sure to understand,' he'd say, brandishing his pistol. The way he carry on at times could scare the beejezus out'a you.

"Then there was this pretty little white girl Candy who took a shine to Lucius. They call her Candy cause she the color'a pink cotton candy 'n the boys say she look good enough to eat.' Maybe, but for a colored boy, she was a rope 'n a grave," she said, sadly, visibly pained. "She was like forbidden fruit in the garden'a Eden. Ya can look but not touch, 'n barely look at that. But that only made her more desirable. Try say something to Lucius 'bout it n he jus' laugh it off like it wasn't nothing. If she'd been a colored girl, pretty as she was, I'd'a jus' been jealous; but she was white, so I wasn't jealous, I was jus' plum scared.

"All the boys wanted to sample her fruit, her honey pot, colored 'n white alike. They didn't ave to say it, you knew it. The way the colored boys, for fear'a being caught looking her straight on, lowered they heads 'n strain they eyes to see her as she pass. Them white boys use to laugh, splitting they guts cause they know them colored boys aching for her the same way, jus' like them. Lucius though, he look her every which way he please, the way he look at any pretty girl, making em blush, feeling delicious, like a ripen Georgia peach. N it no doubt, excite her.

"'What y'all looking at boy,' a peckerwood say to him one time. Lucius snap back fast, 'not you cracker, that for sure.' That boy's face drop as Lucius turn 'n go, sauntering, head cocked.

Candy fancy that, she knew Lucius wasn't afraid 'n it tempted her. She would lay in wait for him at times in some out'a the way place to flirt 'n tease him. But it was more than jus' teasing. She wanted him, but southern customs such it wouldn't allow it. So she had to try tempt him to rape her. That way, if discovered, she could save her respectability 'n say, 'He rape me!' But it wasn't Lucius' way to steal what he could get free elsewhere. It cause her a dilemma a sorts however.

"There was this one-horse cart bridge across a canal that separated the white part of Laurel from the colored section, 'n trees grew along either side it's sandy ledge. White folks generally didn't cross that rickety old bridge cause they didn't have no big reason to visit 'r shanty side'a town, but us coloreds used it often enough.

"Candy sometimes come over to the colored side 'n wait for Lucius in the bush or under the bridge, if she thought he had reason to pass that way. That was one place they could safely meet 'n sit 'n talk under the bridge in the shade near its murky waters.

"Lucius 'n me was crossing that ole bridge one day that summer when I hear a hiss underneath it's planks. Till then I'd only heard rumors 'bout their goings-on. But sure enough, Candy step out from under the bridge, looking sassy 'n every bit annoyed at me.

"'Is that your lil pickaninny,' she asked testily?

"'I ain't got time for your foolishness t'day,' Lucius say.

"'Well jus' send'a along then.'

"'Lucius wave her off n we kept walking.

"'You best get back here quick, Lucius Sims, for I scream,' she say fuming.

"'Scream,' he say, 'see if I care.' Of course we wasn't in ear shot'a nobody, but in the south a white woman's yell carries. Lucius took my hand so tight in his it hurt. I was so proud I lost all sensea the potential danger with my hand wrapped in his. But it was then I knew Lucius didn't love me, couldn't love me, not the way I needed a man to love me if we to raise a family. He was too wild to love anything much else than danger. I should'a known it, but wouldn't admit it, no more than I could admit to Lucius that I was carrying his baby." A tired sadness crept into Mrs. Jones' misty eyes, a sadness which echoed in her plaintive drawl. "Lucius knew his women well. Candy stood on that bridge, arms akimbo, boiling mad, but she didn't scream.

"It was Thursday'a the followin' week toward evenin' on a lazy day in mid-July that Lucius, Booker n me was out walkin' the rural, sun bake back roads lookin' at sharecroppers workin' the fields on into dusk. Lucius was drinking a little, I suppose, n wishing he'd listened ta his folks n gone north for the summer. Thursday, the slowest day'a the week downtown, was colored night at the movies, so Booker suggest, to distract Lucius from his gloom, we go downtown n take in a picture show. 'See how much better white folks act on the silver screen,' Booker had us laugh. 'Laurel,'" she repeated, reflectively, "that was r town; the town I grew up, a backwater sump. But that's what comea the south following the Civil War.

"Like so many a' other hick towns, Laurel was jus' another whistle stop down the line. They had 'lectricity downtown, so it was sort'a fun to see Main Street aglow against the descending night sky; n enjoy the movie stills under the marquee while waiting for the next show. The followin' day, Friday, pay day, was the big night downtown n the white folks want'd downtown to themselves weekends. N with as few whites as come to the movies colored night, we still had to sit upstairs in the balcony t not offend the sensibilities a white folks who wasn't even there," she said, snidely.

"Slowly people began to cumulate n form a line. White folks up front n colored folks to the back. A southern rule'a thumb," she said idly. "But wouldn't you jus' know, as the ticket taker was setting up, Candy show up with some white boy on her arm n, without a by-your-leave, cut in front'a us. Candy laughed, shaking out her hair – hair a little colored boy or girl dream'a caressin' in a darken movie house. His vanity injured; Lucius was mad. Candy had taken no notice a him.

"'Cause you white ain't no excuse for being crude,' he scolded, attracting Candy's n her dates startled gaze.

"'Pay him no mind,' she say trying to brush it off.

"'Do what? No, this nigger's got'a pay,' that boy flared. 'He been getting away with this crap too long for it to go on anymore.' Then he snarled at Lucius, 'Who the hell y'all talking to, boy?'

"'Since I don't know y'all, y'all can suppose I'm talking to Candy,' Lucius snapped back. 'But if yaw want'a be included, feel free.'

"'I know y'll, that's what counts; y'll that smart mouth Sims boy, jus' a hair's breath short of 'a lynch rope!'

"When that cracker say 'lynch rope' every colored person heart on line failed n r skins crawled with fear'a certain Klan reprisal," she relayed gravely. "Scared we took cover away from the telltale street lights, not wanting to be identified. Never more in my life I wish'd to escape the circumstance'a my race; the burden a what I knew in my heart was sure to follow –

"True to form, Lucius flung the fatal insult, 'Y'all not the one to put it round my neck, peckerwood!'

"Well that boy must'a thought Lucius crazy cause he give Candy such a robbed look but, unsympathetic, she just shrug. He look to the few other white folks there for support, but they looking at him – n that boy, scared as can be, was pale as chalk. But when he see the eyes'a all us colored folks milling round in the dark, he knew he couldn't back out or he'd be accused'a singlehandedly losing the cause a the Confederacy; a cause so long lost already," she intoned dryly.

"Hell bent Lucius was possessed! No doubt it, n when he got like that he was like somebody having a fit, 'n there was little to do but wait for him to come out'a it himself.

"Jus' as the ticket taker raise his head, that white boy took a round house swing at Lucius, but Lucius fast, too fast for that boy, 'n wham he laid into him quick, fist flying, giving us something to consider. No one dare really believe they eyes. Lucius was bloodying that boy good!

"Candy stood aside lookin' on in glee while, in a state of shock, I clung to my belly n the new life formin' in me, Lucius chile, my lover's chile stirring in me. Can't y'all see?" she implored, hands outstretched, casting a teary-eyed glance at each of her three children.

"The ticket taker shouted, startlin' everyone, 'nigger y'all drunk? I'll fix you, you dirty black bastard!' Was Lucius drunk? Not as you could say, but he'd been carrying a bottle in his back pocket from which he'd been sipping from time to time. I think it created a false image. Well Lucius caught that cracker with a whoppin' blow, spillin' that boy on his ass. N them white folks stood huddle, lookin' on Lucius like they worst fears come round, then lookin' nervous at us other coloreds backing off slow. All us scared, looking over r shoulders for those hooded demons to show up outa the ground, knowing there was gonna be a killing that night, wonderin' if we should fight or run?

"As might well be expected, self-preservation won out! The ticket taker dash'd outa his booth bearing a cudgel, going to bash Lucius' brains in n we

118

jus' kept backin' away, too stricken with fear to utter a cry. But when Candy see Lucius in danger, she scream, 'Lucius, behind you!' Then clasped her hands ta her mouth too late, eyes wide 'n darting, hoping no one else had overheard her.

"Lucius heard her sure, like everyone else, n swung round, the club coming down on his shoulder, missing his head. He stumbled to a knee but quickly regained his feet, pullin' his pistol from his belt under his shirt' n jammin' it in that ticket taker's puce face, a known Klansman too. That man drew to n abrupt stop, eyes bulging on the bore a Lucius' gun. Had Booker not caught me in his arms, I would'a fainted dead away. But Booker had hold'a me, drawing me back silently as possible, trying to figure the fastest way out'a town.

"'Swing now you fucking fat ofay – SWING!' Lucius urged the ticket taker. 'Try me, see if I don't squeeze the trigger!'

"How my heart sank when he cock'd the hammer a that gun!

"Some frantic white woman passing stumbled on the ruckus n run helter skelter down Main Street yelling 'n screaming, 'Help! Help! The niggers' gone crazy – the niggers' gone crazy; they gonna kill us all in r sleep!'

"That's when I scream'd too, Booker tried to shush me; 'Run, Lucius, run; we're gonna have a baby – r baby, Lucius! R baby, can't you hear me? Dear God, Lucius, run. I'm pregnant with your child,' I wept, collapsing in Booker's arms. If Lucius didn't hear me, Booker sure did n caught firm hold'a me, draggin' me off to Lucius' parents' house. Others were there before us n had told the Reverend. But they say Reverend Sims look'd like he already knew what they'd come to say 'n poor Lucius mama cryin' hard as me. The Reverend wanted to fetch help but they say, 'Where's help to be had? We do best to lock 'r doors cause once that Klan got they hoods on you doing business with the Devil, 'n Reverend, you' a all people know 'bout dealing with the Devil!'

"'Absalom! Absalom! My son, my son, would God I had died for thee,' Reverend Sims groan'd before gathering his family into church 'n locking them 'n us in behind closed doors – praying n waiting, as we all abandoned Lucius to his fate," she confessed, staring out with a black female grievance, still resentful after all these years that the colored men of Laurel stood impotently by as Lucius, the father of her unborn child, was being lynched!

"Lucius never got home that night, as well you can imagine. Next day, they found his naked body face down in the canal not too far from the bridge. The story go he pistol whip'd that ticket taker unconscious 'n left that other white boy cowering, 'n back off pointing his pistol.

"'Come on, Lucius,' Candy cry, stepping over the ticket taker, 'let's run! N they fled, never to be seen alive again. That is, Lucius was lynched n Candy

119

disappeared. They say when the Klan caught Lucius no trace'a Candy was found. They accused Lucius a having raped, kill'd n disposed a' her body. They dragged n dragged that Canal, though nothing'a her ever showed. Still they say he raped n kill her.

"Dissatisfied with their grim night's work, the Klan come looking for Booker cause they know Booker Lucius friend. But Booker had gone into hidin', so they shoot up the place n torch Bookers folks place for good measure before they finally leave. They would'a torched Rev. Sims place too, but his was a house a worship n they love they darkies on they kneesa praying. 'N though I go to church Sundays, I never insist on y'all comin' with me 'cause'a that. One ought'a go to church from a feelin' born a' the heart 'n not the strap.

"After Lucius' burial Booker come to me n tell me he always loved me. 'Who better,' he say 'to raise Lucius' child than his best friend? Ya don't want the chile to be born no bastard, Hattie. Y'll don't want that for Lucius' chile, do you,' he implored? 'Come north with me, we'll marry. Y'll don't wanta stay here with no illegitimate baby, not now!' Booker was persuasive n to the point, 'n I had no argument against what he say. So yes, I ran north with Booker cause he wanted me, not cause I was in love with him, I wasn't, but he taught me something 'bout love over the years. N I come to love him for his many kindnesses. He loved Lucius 'n wanted his chile to ave a name. He didn't want Lucius' chile to be no nameless bastard. N he love me enough to want'a marry me n bring me north with him so no one could call me a tramp, out'a my name.

"A little more than a year later, shortly after you was born," she continued sadly, looking directly in Percival's eyes, "I got'a letter from my ma saying Reverend Sims become a broken man n his fragile wife, Lucius mama, had gone out'a her head with grief, insisting to all that Lucius couldn't rape or kill nobody. Things got so with her they finally lock'd her in a mental hospital.

"No sooner we got north, Booker took up drinkin' – not all at once but slowly. He was no alcoholic but come to find comfort in it at times. It was easier to find drinking companions than friends, Booker discovered. It was no wonder, hell, too many'a us were fleeing a similar past! Small comfort for'a nagging sore. We tried not to talk 'bout it but it was obvious that that night had sealed r fate along with Lucius'. Everybody back home in Laurel thought Lucius kill'd Candy. Booker too, though I had my doubts. The truth is, what I remember a that night n what Booker couldn't forget made strangers of us in the long run.

"Don't get me wrong, Booker wasn't a bad man. In fact, he was as good'a colored man I know. I mean, he did the kind'a do right things a woman wants a man to do. He was sincerely Lucius' best friend n a faithful husband. He paid the bills n kept us all in shoes. He never threw stuff up in my face. He was kind like that.

"But twelve years later, as misfortune would have it, Booker was working in mid-Manhattan round Forty second street n Eight Avenue, sweeping streets, when he saw Candy on the arm of 'a colored pimp. She look at him like she knew him too, but couldn't fix where from – But Booker, he knew. He come home that day pretty much upset 'n babbling. At first I thought he'd lost his job. N so I ask'd him what's wrong? He wouldn't say nothing right off but got a bottle from the cabinet n pour himself a glass full n swallow it in a gulp, tremblin' as it went down. Then he say pourin' a second glass, 'I-I s-seen er – S-she s-she's alive!"

"'Who that?' I ask'd mystified.

"'Candy, w-who else woman? S-she's selling herself on the street.'

"'How's that?'

"'S-She's alive, woman! C-Candy's alive!'

"'That can't be!' I insisted.

"'W-Why not? You always say Lucius never kill'd her; so why not?'

"'Yes, b-but,' I stammered, doubting myself. 'If she's not dead –'

"'Then Lucius couldn't'a kill her,' he finished the thought for me. 'I been wrong 'bout Lucius all these years,' he mournd, pourin' another drink. 'How it break my heart.'

"'Ya believed no more than anybody else, Booker, what more could you do?'

"'He was my best friend,' he wailed. Booker finished that bottle, shaking every drop loose. Then he went out n didn't come home for the next few days n when he return he was sopping drunk. 'Ya got'a get yourself together,' I scolded him.

"'Woman leave me alone,' he brushed me off. Booker went to work the next morning but they sent him home 'n told him if he should ever show up for work like that again they'd fire him!

"'Hell,' he complained, 'Mr. Charlie's got ya coming 'n going.' That's the last I saw Booker alive. He left the house n never come back. I went n identified him after that truck run him down later that week, n buried him. The only other man I ever love beside Lucius, put in the ground early by the same woman. Uh-uh," she shook her head, ruefully. "I had to know," she said. "So I went to try 'n find her. It took me a few days, but I found her, jus' where Booker say he saw her. She was a prostitute alright, a little too old for her age but, nevertheless, ripe for picking as always. A little too ripe maybe," she added scornfully.

"Dizzy n half trippin' over myself, I hesitantly approached her. "'Candy?' I stammered? She lookd at me long n hard.

"'Do I know y'll?' she finally asked.

"'Laurel!'

"'That's a long time ago,' she sneered, indifferently, paling. 'I don't remember y'll.'

"'Lucius,' I replied, catching her attention.

"'Who y'll?' she suspiciously intoned. 'Oh yeah, the pregnant girl back on the bridge.'

"'Ya knew?'

"'Was there something not to know? All you had to do was look,' she drawled. 'I saw it in the possessive way y'll took Lucius' hand n look'd so reassuringly over y'll shoulder at me when y'll walked off. Lucius hurt me so that day! I'd never wanted anyone more. Now, what can I do for y'll?' she asked curtly. 'As y'll can see, I'm'a working girl.' She gestured broadly, indicating to the mill a men on the sidewalk 'n lurking in doorways a peep shows 'n dirty book stores.

"'They say Lucius kill'd you.'

"'Who the hell say that?' she demanded.

"'The paper's. everybody!'

"'Y'll mean they say what the Klan want em all to say, don't you?' She scowled. 'Yeah, they would'a said that – the bloody bastards,' she swore.

"'Since y'll not dead like they say, tell me, what happened?'

"'They caught me with Lucius, that's what happened. N after they half way kill him, beat him so his coffee skin run red with blood, they cut off his cock 'n told me I can have it now. I couldn't hold my stomach for years to come, still can't. But was Lucius scared? Not as you could tell. He fought back like the horse on which the devil rides. They had they hands full, I can tell you. N he laughed demonically as they did they worst before they kill him. But I-I wanted to live. In that miserable stifling dark all I wanted to do was live on for one more second, I told myself, n tell myself. But it's been twelve years breathing on n on ain't it? Strange, I feel I've become so grotesquely unrecognizable that it almost pleases me y'll can still see me some place in here from such'a long way away. Let me get back to my story, that's what y'll here for now, ain't it? Y'll can't imagine the terror I was facing.' I reassured her I could. 'The horror those ugly people. I knew I'd died n gone to hell! Then one'a them took his hood off n looked at me in the headlights a surrounding cars 'n trucks—'n I became more frantic than ever when I realized it was my daddy staring at me like some hideous monster! I screamed n screamed, trying to waken, trembling in my bare feet. I was never more horrified in all my born days, n full'a self-loathing. After all, these were my people, my neighbors n kinfolk. They kill'd everything decent in me that night, making me so dirty I could never wash clean again. They told me I should disappear n never be heard from again. N let me tell y'll, I was glad for the reprieve, so when they drop'd me off beyond the county line I kept going. So here I am in this meat market, a bit more dead than alive, selling my overused but much desired ass,' she said, as a man came along and picked her up. 'So much for ole times, sister,' she teased, turning away. Then I ran for the subway n came back home, as out'a my head as Booker had been, trembling in all my limbs, shaking with grief – Oh, God, how cold, alone n terrified I felt. But I've come through till now, 'A breath at a time,' like Candy say, n that's as much as there is to tell!"

***

Lois rose from out her chair clinging to the armrest, her eyes swimming with tears. She observed her mother as if for the first time, the sickle moons under her eyes; her hair streaked with gray, and work worn hands folded in her lap. Seeing her with a past, a history, a life separate from theirs and no less similarly desperate.

"Anyone for tea," Lois asked, turning from her mother, unable to bear the pathos in her haunted face down which a solitary tear rolled.

"It'll 'ave more than tea, sis," Sam scoffed. "How 'bout'a scotch?"

"Hush boy," Hattie admonished, raising moist eyes. "Thank you, Lois. If it ain't too much bother."

"Shoo," Sam grumbled. "I ain't said nothing out'a place."

"Care for tea, Percival?" Lois asked, haltingly.

He brushed her query aside with a wave of his hand, staring blankly, self-absorbed, altered in himself, afraid for the first time— afraid for himself, of the stranger within him and with whom he must now become acquainted.

Lois started for the kitchenette but turned back and threw herself face down in her mother's lap, sobbing. "I didn't know. I didn't know."

"Ya wasn't expected to, chile." Hattie comforted her as best she knew, looking across at Percival with deepening concern.

Chin at rest in his open palm, and jaw throbbing mightily, Percival felt a dark confusion blanket his soul. Ever since learning of the death of Dr. King he had found himself on an emotional roller coaster down which he had precipitously plummeted into the unfathomable depth of a torn heart. And with his mother's equally disquieting revelation, there appeared before him no foreseeable end in sight. Nor could he digest this new store of information any more than he could unlock the mysteries of the Seventh Seal. At best, it was a wild card tossed into an already high stakes game of chance. And at worst, it was more undesirable baggage for which he could little account. Either way, it didn't much matter.

"N that's why you left the south," he asked, in an accusatory tone.

Before responding, Hattie took Lois' face between her hands and planted a kiss on her brow. "Care to fix tea now?" she uttered. Lois regained her feet, and, wiping away hot tears, entered the kitchenette to prepare water.

"Yes, yes, that's why," Hattie rejoined, looking guiltily past Percival.

"So Booker wasn't my father?"

"Not as you can say."

"N my real father was lynched, that it?"

"That's right," said Hattie, pained.

"Why didn't you tell me before?"

"How you tell'a chile'a thing like that?"

A strained silence followed in which Percival grew increasingly restless, wanting to get up and go but he didn't know how to do so gracefully, and so he sank further in his seat with a long-winded sigh.

Sam got up with a yawn and went to the toilet.

"I'm thinking of working for the Kennedy campaign on campus. 'Students for Bobby,'" Lois said from the kitchen area. "There's a lot to be done."

"It cain't hurt," Hattie remarked, glad for the distraction.

"I like Bobby," Sam chanted, returning from the bathroom from which the sound of a toilet gurgled. "I like his style. How 'bout you, bro? What you say?"

"Say?" Percival frowned, uninterested. "'bout what?"

"'bout Bobby, bro –, 'bout Bobby."

Percival shrugged as a matter of indifference.

"I thought you liked him?" Lois spoke out, pouring Hattie and herself a cup of tea.

"I got other things pressing on me," Percival stormily said, rubbing his chest through his shirt with a feverish look of anguish on his face.

"What's bothering you, son?" Hattie asked.

"It's nothing. A token, a memento from Joleen," he said, with a bitter, ironic laugh.

"It's something to complement my broken jaw."

"You saw Joleen, then? How's my grandson?"

"She didn't bring him, only her siren song."

"What she want?"

"Something I don't ave to give."

"Money?"

"What else."

"That chile's so predictable."

"She's a witch," Lois supplied. "What can you expect?"

"She ain't got no shame," Sam stated. "Them pretty ones seldom do."

"I got'a go," Percival said, rising, in a fluster. "I got some cats I got'a see."

"I was hopin' you'd stay 'n eat," Hattie proposed.

"How can I," Percival emitted, curling back his lips, exposing the wire framework which bound his mouth shut.

"What am I thinking," said Hattie, ruefully, and setting her cup of tea aside, she scrambled to her feet to see him to the door.

"I'll walk you out," Sam offered, starting for the elevator.

"Okay."

"You're not leaving already?" Lois sounded genuinely alarmed."

"Gott'a sis, gott'a," he said, despairingly.

"Oh Percival, you know I love you," Lois wailed, embracing him before he fled.

"Well, son," Hattie intruded, as he wormed his way out of Lois' embrace before the opened door, "I'm sorry 'bout the Olympics. I know how hard you tried." She clucked, sadly. "I would' a come see you in the hospital, but my feet been ailing me 'n I jus' couldn't do all that walkin', standing 'n waitin' round."

"I didn't expect you too, maw," he assured her, pecking her lightly on the cheek, trying to escape.

"I wouldn't wanta let you down."

"Don't worry 'bout it, you didn't. I did that on my own," he lamented. What you gonna do now? Go back to school—I hope?"

"Someday, maybe, who knows."

"Ya'd rather get you brains scrambled, that it? Look at you with'a broken jaw. What next?"

"I said nothing 'bout what I was gonna do."

"Ya don't ave to, I know you."

"Mama, please!"

"Education's a good thing to ave, you know that."

"No I don't 'n neither does anybody else. Sure it's worth something but it's no cure-all. I mean, if everybody in this country, no, this world, woke up tomorrow with a PhD., 'n if all the other social ills ain't been cured we'll still be in the same fix we're in right now. Only we'll all be scholars in the mix," said Percival in a tone of arrant disgust, looking anxiously down the hall to where Sam waited for the elevator. "The prisons would be jus' as full; the ghettos jus' as overpopulated; the rich as rich 'n the poor no less so, 'n the police will still be cracking heads –"

"That's ruinous thinkin'. Keep that kinda talk outa my house."

"Mama, it's education, not religion."

"Humph," Hattie snorted. "Tell that to the Jews."

"'N they haven't solved their problems, either."

"Maybe not, but they're prosperous."

"If being consumed in the flames of a Nazi war machine is prosperous, they can keep it."

"Boy y're irreverent."

"With no intention of being so."

Sam beckoned to him. "Come on, man, let's do it, the elevator's here."

"Love you, ma," Percival said, escaping out the door.

"You too, son."

Percival raced for the elevator and, as its doors closed, he breathed a sigh of relief. He wiped his brow. He had begun to sweat. The pain in his jaw was irrepressible. He was finally forced to pop a pain killer, which he jostled, with a forefinger, to the back of his mouth to the well of his throat, between the inside of his right cheek and molars, then he swallowed it. Sam pressed the button for the lobby. The elevator, which reeked of urine, rattled in its grudgingly slow descent. "Ya lucky you out, man," Sam said, querulously. "I get that stuff all the fucking time. Always telling me who I is or ain't. Maybe not so dramatic as with you jus' then but it's sure a nuisance. I must say that was one hell of a story 'bout you pa though, wasn't it?"

"Some hell of a story," Percival agreed, not wishing to pursue it.

"We don't ave to talk 'bout it if you don't want know?"

"Let's not."

"Mind if I light up?"

"I can't stop you."

"Well you know me big brother, I respect my elders," said Sam, sucking on the joint, and shaking out the match. "Want some?"

"It won't do on top of my medication."

"Ya loss, baby."

"So how's school?"

"The only thing good 'bout it," Sam said, exhaling the pungent smoke, "is next month the shit's over."

"I thought you was enjoying it?"

"I say that crap for mama's sake."

"I see."

"So dig, you 'n Joleen ain't gonna make it, huh?"

Percival didn't respond.

126

"Ya looking for a roomy, man? Cause I ain't at home here on Staten Island, you know? N it's time I get out from under mama's wing, dig?"

"N move in with me under mine? My place wasn't big enough for Joleen 'n me 'n we shared the same bed. What makes you think you 'n me can share'a place where two who 'r suppose to live as one can't?"

"Maybe that's the difficulty, trying to live as one."

Percival guffawed. "Maybe, lil brother, maybe."

"So y'll think on it?"

"I ain't promising nothing, man," said Percival, elusively.

The elevator opened onto the lobby and they exited the building on to Jersey St., the most infamous 3/4-mile stretch in all the borough. It was an ugly strip with a seedy past and no redeeming features to recommend it. It was pockmarked with bars, and dilapidated tenements fronted the street. Back in it's heyday, it was something of a honky-tonk; a redlight district and, before repeal of prohibition, an outlet for bootleg hooch, as well as a thriving seaport. But when the docks closed down following the Second World War, employment dried up and local businesses died off, a belabored wave of indigent southern blacks poured into the area seeking cheap housing. Thus, Jersey Street and environs quickly became a fetid, crime ridden slum.

"Ya going over to see that freaky white chick, Racine, huh? I love them flower children 'n hippies, man, especially the chicks, they make some freaky love," Sam said, knowingly.

"N how would you know?"

"Shit, man, I can read it in their eyes. N I know they want some black dick, too. N I got some to give em, dig?"

"You're a wonder, man."

"Tell me I'm wrong?"

"You know better than me."

Sam left Percival at the bus stop and turned back for the project playground and a game of hoop. Percival caught the bus and then disembarked, several minutes later, in Stapleton, on the corner of Beach Street, across from Tappin Park. A few doors up was the coffee house, "The Missing Link," with a cutout of an ape's paw holding a broken chain link over the entrance: "Where People Connect," read the logo under its claw. A hotbed of social activism, The Missing Link, was cause for concern among its conservative neighbors. Many wondered why this disparate element of intellectuals, poets, artists, peaceniks, beatniks, radicals, hippies, flower children, students, professors, blacks and would-be revolutionaries of every ilk, would appear, overnight, to settle in the midst of their otherwise tidy American community, where families had sons' in uniform and homes patriotically flew Old Glory.

The spacious interior of the coffee shop was artistically decorated. The fresh brewed flavor of espresso and various other coffees, along with homemade pastries, wafting on the air, was, on entering, welcoming.

There was a goodly crowd. They couldn't have appeared more morose or was it his somber mood? He thought not. The ghost of Dr. King was abroad! Percival spotted Rufus with Felix, a Muslim, and a young man— the duty officer in the Black Panther Party Office from the other night, the night of the riots, if memory served— attired in full Panther regalia and beret with a "Free Huey" button.

Percival also caught sight of a dear friend, Nina Koestler, an angelic, rosy-faced woman, and childhood victim of polio. She was having coffee with a woman seated in profile at a corner table. Nina was a fine artist and editor of a socialist rag, The Responsible Citizen, which harkened back to what remained of the spirit of Walden in the second half of the 20th. century. They had met a few years back in the deep south on a civil rights march. They had liked one another considerably and became fast friends. They had since tramped the pavements together at various anti-war and civil rights marches, where he would invariably hang back with her when she had had difficulty keeping up. He admired her courage and stamina, and how ably she wielded her misshapen legs for miles at a stretch on crutches, no matter the distance, without losing heart. And they would discuss all manner of things from poetry to philosophy, trailing the marches. She was extremely well versed in the humanities—as well as was she herself a humanitarian.

She had two children, a girl and a boy, and harbored a nearly invisible spouse— invisible in that he was seldom seen but haunted the upper rooms of their home and made a nuisance of himself by stamping about overhead, rattling around like a ghost, whenever she had company. He knew both her children well and loved them as would an uncle, and they, in turn, loved him.

Nina waved, beckoning him over. He bypassed a few tables to reach her's. A folk musician strummed her guitar in song, "ain't gonna study war no more," she sang. Nina seized him by the arm with all the strength at her command, which was considerable, and drawing him downward kissed him passionately on the cheek. "My dear, dear friend," she said, folding his hand in her's, and engaging his eyes. She collapsed her lips in sorrow, and her eyes misted over. "I'm oh so sorry for your loss. But I'm even more sorry for our mutual loss. Your loss, as difficult as it must be for you, is only a temporary setback, but the loss of Martin, at this ungodly hour, is irreversible."

"I can't agree with you more," he confessed. "It's a bitter pill to swallow."

"It is," she agreed, caressing the back of his hand. "It is."

"That sums it up," he said, for want of something to say.

"By the way," she said breathlessly, releasing his hand, "I want you to meet Beverly, a friend of mine. Beverly, this is Percival, I must have mentioned him to you."

"No more than a dozen times." Beverly laughed and extended a hand across the table, which Percival readily accepted. "It's good to finally make your acquaintance."

"A pleasure," he returned.

"Beverly writes for the local paper, The Advance, as well as contributes to my small effort, The Responsible Citizen, which you refer to as a rag."

"Not jus' a rag but a socialist rag," he teasingly corrected her.

"But you read it nonetheless."

"I wouldn't miss it," he said, looking Nina fully in the face. "I got'a previous engagement. I'll give you a call."

Casting a glance at the corner back table where the three black men clustered, Nina whispered, "The revolutionary brotherhood is holding a cabal, eh?"

"Can't get much by you," Percival winked, backing off.

"Good to have met you," said Beverly.

"Likewise."

Percival then crossed the coffee shop to the table where he was anxiously being awaited. He drew back an empty chair on which he sat, and acknowledged the others with a sweeping gaze, then his eyes came to rest on the young man across the table from him, sporting his Panther beret at a jaunty angle. He looked like an elite soldier. Indeed, a paratrooper, and for a second Percival was unsure of his footing. He had this uneasy feeling of being drawn into a revolutionary vortex, which the Black Panther Party had come to represent. That is, Black men and women formed into a paramilitary phalanx opposed to the all-pervasive status quo! And as their Minister of Information, Eldridge Clever, had said, to that status quo, "Stick em up motherfucker, you're under arrest!"

"You don't remember me do you," said the youth, sticking out his hand.

Percival regarded him with pursed lips. "Yes," he said, spreading the fingers of his hands. "You were the Duty Officer the night of the riots – for'a second there I thought we were gonna get physical," he said, frankly.

"As hot as things got that night we couldn't slack off," said the youth, coolly. "I didn't recognize you and I've seen you work out a number of times at St. Johns."

"Where I train." Percival clasped the young man's outstretched hand, and as they went through the publicly secret ritual black power handshake, they searched each other's eyes for the required spark, the flash of empathy, on which to found a trust.

"I'm Lieutenant Jamal Ibrahim," the youth introduced himself, as their hands parted. "After talking to Rufus, it's really quite an honor. I'd not realized what a strong activist background you've had in the civil rights movement. Someone of your stature would prove invaluable to the Panthers at this juncture.

"I should also say our defense captain, Lakey Sako, when she heard you would be here wanted to come herself 'n apologize for the rude manner in which you were received at our headquarters the night of the riot but, I assure you, it couldn't be helped," he said off key. "So here I am in her stead." He grimaced. "It would be good for you to meet her. She would like that," he said, with a pang of envy.

"What can I say? I'm flattered," said Percival, flattered, recalling to mind the near faultless beauty of the pretty defense captain. "Till now Rufus only told me he'd wanted to talk but didn't say 'bout what – If you'll pardon me, before we go on," Percival broke off and, shifting to his right, acknowledged Felix. And though they had not been well acquainted, they had known each other peripherally. Percival had always admired how well Felix carried himself, like he was the tallest person in the room. He seemed to stand apart, aloof, and as erect as a cigar store Indian. And there was also a cold, hard, shrewd look in his eyes, and a fixed, menacing scowl on his lips which could be intimidating – as was also true of Rufus.

"A salem alekum," said Percival in greeting.

"Wa alekum salam," Felix returned the welcome. "It's good to see you, my brother."

And without ceremony, they shook hands.

"Rufus baited my invitation by saying you'd be here. I am here." Unlike the others, Felix was conservatively dressed, sported an insignia Black Muslim bow tie, fez, and a ring with a crescent moon and star adorned a finger of the hand on which he also wore his college ring.

He was twenty-seven, had served three years in prison on a five-year sentence for beating a man within an inch of his life – a crime for which he was unrepentant. The fact that it had been a white man, his landlord, rather than a black was, for Felix, a matter of honor. He was currently a sophomore at Wagner College and President of The Black Student Union on campus, and he had established a reputation throughout the black community for being resourceful.

"I'm glad you're here," said Percival, deeply appreciative.

"That's really all according to what the fox has up his sleeve," Felix said, rounding on Rufus.

"Well," said Percival and, facing Rufus, lay his right forearm on the tabletop and dangled his hand over the edge. "What's the urgency?"

"Let's first get some coffee before we start," Rufus suggested, his cross-eyes on the doorway, as if expecting someone. "I wanted this meeting as far from my place as possible cause for as long as I can I want'a keep the cops at bay – especially since Lily ain't been fairing so well of late." He broke off, calling, "Waitress!"

A fleshy young coed, a hippie type, rapidly responded. "May I help you?"

"See what they're having," Rufus said, casting a handful of bills on the table. "On me, fellas," he offered, receiving no objections.

"Tea for me," said Felix, frostily, his eyes cast upwards at an acute angle, looking at her askance, his face tense with suspicion, causing her to pull back.

"Espresso for me, Cindy," said Percival, smiling vaguely, wondering what was eating at Felix?

"I'll have the same," Jamal intoned.

"Freshen up my cup while you at it," Rufus said, handing her his empty cup, a sly, twinkle in his eyes. They talked idly between themselves until she returned with a tray of tea and coffee. Then, as she departed, Rufus began, "Like Mailer says, 'a shit storm's brewing,'" Felix winced at the crude, but apt, description of the social milieu. "N we're in the middle of it, 'n if we're gonna deal with it or, as the Panther's say, 'Seize the time,' then we're gonna ave to ave 'r shit together."

"Excuse me," Felix interrupted, "but I'm ill at ease talking so openly as we 'r in a white enclave, such as this."

"That's the beauty of it," said Rufus, with mirth, his eyes rolling towards the center of his nose. "Most important right now is how out in the open we appear to be, see? N here, in this nest'a would-be intellectuals 'n white radicals, we've a cover. The best under the circumstance – white folks! It's almost like hiding out in the middle of a Ku Klux Klan meeting," he laughed. "This place was made for a black cover up."

"I'm at a loss."

"Since King's assassination," Rufus resumed, "I've been in constant touch with Defense Captain Lakey Sako, the sister in charge'a the Bed-Stuy branch of the Panther Party, as well as with Chairman Jacob Bishop, the brother in command'a the northeast; 'n we're agreed that an office would be beneficial here on Staten Island, on Jersey Street"

"But to what end?" Felix challenged, playing devil's advocate.

"Well first off, with a view to putting these honkeys on notice," Rufus said, "'n shaking these so-called Negroes outa their somnolence into the militancy a' the 60's, for a start."

"Well 'n good," Felix annoyingly persisted, "but what does it mean?"

"It means," Jamal plunged in, "that we must develop a strategy for revolutionary action. We must engage the people in social debate. We must create a forum for discussion in which the masses become involved, then take our story to the people; black voters especially, and enfranchise as many a black, lumpen proletariat as possible."

"A southern style voter registration drive, that it? N with what alternative to these white devils seeking political office?" Felix scoffed. "You must be joking, little brother!"

"Not at all," Jamal said, disregarding Felix's reference to his youth. "We'll simply add Rufus to the ballot on The Peace and Freedom ticket. It'll give em Eldridge Cleaver for President and Rufus for Congress. At the same time, we'll have laid a foundation on which to base a radical program of social reform. We're struggling to transform our communities into vibrant cultural, intellectual, economic, political, educational and social oases in which our people might thrive."

"No revolution has yet to produce the idolized state it's imagined," Felix said, bluntly.

"Neither has any religion brought the Kingdom of Heaven to earth. Still we fight and pray in the hope that someday one of the two will work," said Jamal in harsh rebuke. "On the other hand, social reform is within reach."

"We've not brought heaven to earth but we've managed to bring our Gods to task," Percival lamented. "We've weighed them in the balance and found them wanting," he said pensively, his thoughts elsewhere. "No Gods! No heaven! How tragically sad."

"There's no Santa Clause either," Rufus chimed in. "Where's the sadness in that?"

"Once you've cut off the source of life, then what?" said Percival, sibilantly.

"We won't 'ave the man on 'r fucking backs – that's what," Rufus said.

All, with the exception of Felix, laughed. Instead he considered them dubiously, but more disturbed by the scamp than not, he pressed his advantage, "'N what program might that be, or should I ask?" he persisted.

"No, not at all, glad you did. It's figured Staten Island's a microcosm of the nation and all its social ills. It's estimated that fewer blacks here than any other borough in the city will graduate high school or attend college because the district has created a tracking system that gears blacks into general education and vocational training requiring less academic skills, and, as a result, are forced into menial job related situations such as hospital orderlies, garbage collectors and all around social failures," said Jamal with rancor. "Hopefully, to answer you, what we're doing is seeking a strategy for redress."

"With due respect, lil brother, ours is a crisis of inner moral decay," said Felix provocatively. "A hatred of self-festering in 'r souls since slavery, which stole 'r manhood 'n cannot long go unattended."

"That's a crock, if ever I heard it," Rufus spat.

"Yes 'n no," Percival interposed, stirred from a brooding silence. "In the northern cities, yes, but in the south, as the civil rights movement proved – not so much. Blacks in northern cities, 'The Cities of destruction,' as E. Franklin Frazier put it— 'r, for the most part, in transition, locked in mortal combat with a racist, amoral society. It's more the racial struggle shifting north from south that's created this illusory climate. To be sure, the civil rights movement brought out as many moral people there 'r in this nation. But, at the end of the day, we've simply decided that there wasn't enough among em, black or white, to constitute a majority."

Percival held back as the others laughed. He then added, "the awful thing about black and white Americans is—joined to the hips like Siamese twins as we 'r— in 'r hatred of each other we end up by paying the price of hating ourselves for it."

"What a chilling thought," Felix snickered.

And as the laughter subsided, Jamal said, at last, "We, the Panthers, feel there's a benefit to opening a branch in every borough, to encourage freedom fighters wherever they are. We want to reach a broad range of black Americans wherever they may be! We'll be here to provide guidance when needed. After all, we're a vanguard party. This conversation, by the way, isn't taking place in absentia but is occurring in every ghetto, on every street corner, and every hamlet across the country in one guise or another. And following the slaying of Dr. King, the people are beginning to realize that they are corralled, hemmed in, or, as our Minister Of Defense, Huey P. Newton, puts it, 'Occupied by an outside brute police force.' The people are coming to see that, and are beginning to recognize a need for constructive, revolutionary action.

"About finances, you'll have to work that out yourselves. We all must, realizing, of course, that we're guerrilla fighters obligated, as Chairman Mao says, 'to not steal a needle or piece of thread from the people.' By the same token, we say, 'whatever the man is for, we're against, and whatever he's against, we're for.'"

"If that ain't pure unadulterated sophistry," Felix uttered in disgust, shifting his gaze from Jamal to Rufus.

"It's a call to action," Rufus stated bluntly.

"How convenient," Felix replied, with a look of disdain.

"No less so than five hundred years in irons," Rufus retorted.

"That statement, lil brother, is no vague hint at resorting to illegal methods," said Felix, openly critical, if not hostile. "What you're proposing is a recipe for disaster. Why not do something like opening small businesses in 'r communities 'n create job opportunities for 'r people, as we Muslims do?"

Jamal considered Felix along the rim of his raised demitasse cup. Felix's insistence on calling him 'lil brother' began to grate on him. It was one thing for his defense captain, Lakey Sako, with whom he was infatuated, to refer to him as 'lil brother' but quite another for someone he was only recently acquainte to address him so familiarly. "You put me in mind of my father," he said, lowering his cup to its saucer. "He too is a Muslim. A member of the F.O.I., in fact."

"Now you shining me on, lil brother."

"No, not at all. I respect my father deeply."

"Only you don't mean it as a complement."

Jamal had recognized in Felix, as in his father, a similar moralistic, holier-than-thou conservative, bible-thumping tone of righteous indignation, no less exasperating for its black nationalist bent than any zealous religionist spouting salvation on a street corner. He himself had been raised a Muslim and had only broken ranks on recognizing the legitimacy of Malcolm X. "That apostate," as his father had branded him, which subsequently alienated him from his father who he truly loved and respected, as a person and, especially as a black man.

"My father," Jamal went on to say, "took the black identity as far as his lights allowed, but it's my duty to outstrip my father's grasp, is it not?

"We're revolutionaries, not capitalists," Jamal said, riled at himself of late when thinking of his father, whose face was his own and mocked him in the mirror. "And I don't think you believe any more than my father does, that selling Shabazz bean pies qualifies as a job opportunity, as if our grievance stops there."

"Until now we've not had much else," Felix countered acidly.

"That's not my argument! It's our intention— the Panther's that is— believing 'The spirit of the people to be greater than the man's technology,' to restore the means of production into the rightful hands of the people! How, you ask? As Malcolm said, 'by any means necessary!'"

Disliking this scamp, Jamal, more and more, Felix bull doggedly persisted, "as yet, I don't see how I fit into your little scheme."

"Very simply," Rufus responded, facing Felix. "We basically want'a be able to work round you 'n with you in areas of mutual concern without conflict."

"I see," said Felix, lolling back in his chair. "Ya want me to remain neutral where the Panthers are concerned, that it?"

"More or less," Rufus agreed.

"I appreciate the gesture but I'm not sure I'm deserving of it." Felix arched his brows. "You all seem so self-sure. So why do you need me?"

Percival stirred his coffee listlessly, his head cocked in an attitude of listening.

"I know you, Felix, you can be an asset if you choose. I want you for an ally, recognizing 'r differences up front." Rufus reached for a packet of cigarettes on the table. He shook one out between his teeth, then fired it up, inhaling. "Ya position at Wagner College gives us n "in" with the black students on campus, if you'd allow, 'n I suspect some will want'a extend a' hand in the community, as you yourself often do. N I also suspect, such 'n alliance would bolster your popularity among the students on campus considerably."

"Clearly not with the administration."

"No risk exists only for those who won't dare," Rufus retorted, smoke trickling from his fat pink lips. "N that's not you. I mean, man, it's obviously apparent, you, of all people, a fervent cultural nationalist, reaching across the divide, out'a brotherly affection, to us misguided, godless, amoral materialistic brothers' who've gone woefully astray."

Felix smiled, cynically, considering the angles, these were troubled times, even for student organizations on campuses.

"You were invited cause you're a shrewd operator," Rufus said, appealing to his vanity, which was considerable.

"Ummmmmmm," Felix murmured, pondering the dilemma. He was not at all sure he liked these Panthers.

"Excuse me," said Percival, insistently, swinging his eyes from left to right. "I don't know if you quite know it, but this is no kid stuff you're talking," he remarked. "Do you know what the Panthers represent? They're at the opposite end of every law enforcement agents' gun in the land. They're brigands, outsiders, threatening to be pushed out of all existence by the powers that be. For starters, the F.B.I. has labelled them the most dangerous threat to the internal security of the United States! It's sheer lunacy to which you've invited us to descend. It's the uttermost echelons of the pit, man. It's the nth degree of insanity," he said, nostrils flared – aching.

Jamal leaned over the table on his arms, and whispered conspiratorially to Rufus, "I thought you said he'd be with us."

"I didn't say he'd be hog tied 'n gagged. We gotta pull his coat, man – school him, dig?" Facing Percival, Rufus then said, "Listen, man, don't talk crap. The guns of the law enforcement agencies have been pointed on us forever, 'n the lynch rope is old hat, nothing new there. We've been dying like flies without putting up much resistance till now. What's new is 'r turning the tables – that's what's new! Where you been, man, while the cops been cracking heads? You been living that Olympian dream so long you've forgotten what hell the rest of us niggers been catching? Climb down from your ivory tower, brother man, 'n see what's going on at your feet below!"

Percival flinched and eyed Rufus morosely – distressed, recalling the episode of the other evening, the night of the riot, with his old Army buddy, the cop, and enmity rose within him like a rip tide but he had no wish to raise the subject, to speak of it – no more than he wished to speak of his mother's nightmarish excursion into the death of his father, Lucius, a father he never knew. The memory of it galled him, inflaming him to anger, his jaw.

"Don't, man! Don't," Percival warned Rufus off with a forestalling hand. "My dreams 'r my dreams, as 'r my nightmares – dig?" He blinked back hot, scalding tears.

"Ya can't deny it, man, if not 'r dreams, given the nature of the culture we reside, we share at least one nightmare in common," Rufus said.

"I won't argue that," said Percival, irritably, looking off.

"Believe me, bro, I feel your pain. I can only guess how hard your fall must feel. Your hope was my hope, too," said Rufus, sotto voce, empathetic. "No matter, you're the best. You're golden, man. They can't rob you a that." He eyed Percival in his unnerving, cross-eyed stare. "My man!"

Jamal interposed, considering Percival anew, "Revolution is a difficult process. If you recall, Rap Brown said, 'with dollars you can buy guns but with pennies you can buy matches.' To better illustrate my point, let me recite from the Declaration Of Independence." Then, "'When in the course of human events, it becomes necessary for one people to dissolve the political bands which have connected them with another, and to assume, among the powers of the earth, the separate and equal station to which the laws of nature and nature's God entitle them, decent respect to the opinions of mankind require that they should declare the cause which impel them to separation."

The others leaned in, trying to catch Jamal's every word. "'We hold these truths to be self-evident," he went on, "that all men are created equal, that they are endowed by their creator with certain unalienable rights, that among these are life, liberty, and the pursuit of happiness. That to secure these rights, governments are instituted among men, deriving their just powers from the consent of the governed; that whenever any form of government becomes destructive of these ends, it is the right of the people to alter or abolish it, and to institute new government, laying its foundation on such principles, and organizing its powers in such form, as to them shall seem most likely to affect their safety and happiness. Prudence, indeed, will dictate that governments long established should not be changed for light and transient causes; and accordingly all experience hath shown that mankind are more disposed to suffer while evils are sufferable, than to right themselves by abolishing the forms to which they are accustomed. But when a long train of abuses and usurpations, pursuing, invariably, the same object, evinces a design to reduce them to absolute despotism, it is their right, it is their duty, to throw off such government, and to provide new guards for their future security.'

"If these words don't apply to the condition of black people in 1968, then these words aren't valid for the existence of the United States. And, to be sure, from the native American perspective this document represents, at best, no more than a used scrap of toilet tissue. In short, there is no moral justification for the existence of the United States!"

"What'a Indians mean to me?" Rufus said.

"I don't think you mean that," Jamal challenged, backing Rufus down. "They ought to mean the world to you, to us all. First off, you're seeking freedom on their land – not the white man's land but their land, dig? The white man has no land outside Europe. Everywhere else he goes he comes like a thief in the night. This here is Indian land, Native American land, and let's not forget it! If not for any other reason you should be respectful for that. We are also asking them to join in on our struggle. It was the failure of the civil rights movement to have not included them in their cause. We are not the only oppressed people to be considered. And we won't allow their plight to go unrecognized. Secondly, when we say 'Power to the people,' we mean you to understand just that! And to not recognize the rights of native peoples everywhere, particularly here in the United States, is to undermine the worth of our own struggle."

Percival nodded in assent, the pain in his jaw resurfacing, causing him to want to scream out loud. He reached for his medication, and downed a pill by dissolving it in his coffee. "For native Americans it was vast extermination proportionately more momentous than was the Jewish holocaust, which lasted less than a decade, but the murderous crimes against native Americans went on for generations, which resulted in the total loss of their homelands and ancestral way of life. If the genocide of the Jewish population had been carried out with equal fervor and over as equally long a period, there would be no

Jewish people left of whom to speak. The pogroms across the centuries were harsh, but sporadic, and there was never a doctrine such as Manifest Destiny put into play until Hitler's manifesto, 'Mien Kampf, came into being.''

"Our story is no less horrific," Felix interjected.

"Yes, true, only different. Slavery was indeed a product of Manifest Destiny – no doubt about it – as was the expropriation of Hawaii and the Philippines a byproduct of that doctrine, too. Unfortunately for us however, we are adopting the white man's ways, taking to ourselves his value system, his false gods, his idols, lucre, of which he himself will eventually fall prey – victim of his own success. And by our efforts we hope to hurry that day. That is why the Black Panthers are needed at this time, to offer our people a way out. His is the error we must strive to avoid."

Felix crossed his arms stolidly, despite their differences in ideology, the scamp knew his catechism and was not to be taken lightly. "You have a facile tongue, lil brother?" he said testily.

Jamel strummed the tabletop with the tips of his fingers, glowering at Felix.

Circulating the room, the waitress, Cindy, approached their table, as the folksinger broke into a new song,

"How many roads must a man walk down before they call you a man –"

"Everything okay?" Cindy asked.

"Jus' fine," they concurred. She began to remove the empty cups.

"How many seas must a white dove sail before she sleeps in the sand –"

"Can I get you anything else?"

"Nothing," Rufus took it on himself to dismiss her.

"Yes, and how many times must the cannonballs fly before they're forever banned –" the song wafted softly through the room, like a gust of wind.

Percival's gaze wandered listlessly over the interior of the coffee shop and, latching onto Nina Koestler, he smiled, reassured by her presence.

"The answer, my friend, is blow-i-ng in the wind. The answer's blowing in the wind."

"Revolutions are not fought with a national war chest but on a shoestring and the will of the people to win," Jamal said, confirming Percival's suspicions. "It was Victor Hugo who said, 'All the armies in the world can't stop an idea whose time has come.' Well I say our time is at hand, so let's seize it!"

"I don't disagree with you entirely, outside the cost in blood, since blood is all we've got to give 'n always what we've given," said Percival disconcertedly. "What the hell can revolution mean to a black minority in a predominantly white nation?"

"Which is why we Muslims disagree with the idea and opt instead to separate," Felix argued, raising an admonitory finger, "'n so spare 'r people the cost in blood."

"This Country's not gonna grant us three states any more than they did forty acres 'n a mule. Or, for that matter, grant Marcus Garvey's organization, The UNIA, to mount a successful exodus to Africa. No God came down with a bible from on high to offer us no land, as he did the Jews. The Honorable Elijah Muhammad is dreaming in technicolor, I'm afraid. No, we got a' better chance a' winning a' revolution," said Rufus, nasally. "Or the fucking lottery, for that matter."

"I'll take whichever comes first," said Percival, the words rolling glibly off his tongue encased, as it was, behind his teeth, in a scaffolding of wire.

"It's a point but it's an insane one," said Felix, irked.

"These are crazy times in which we live and they call for drastic measures," Jamel interjected. As if to echo those sentiments the minstrel in the background broke into a new song, "Come gather 'round people wherever you roam/ and admit that the waters around you have grown –" Rufus eyed Felix angrily, as the lyrics filled the room, "and accept you better start swimming/ for the times they are a changing –".

Rufus went on to say, "Besides, people 'r not so apt to leave a place in which they've put down roots. In that sense they 'r much like plants 'n, whether we like it or not, black Americans' 'r a peculiar hybrid, the Strange Fruit of which Billie Holiday sang. My experience in Nam convinced me'a that," Rufus claimed, frowning. "I'm talking 'bout people in villages caught in the crossfire of three different armies, devastation all around, it would behoove em, so you'd think, to collect the little they got 'n move on, but no, they'd stay, farm, live 'n die amidst a political chaos not'a their choosing. N we blacks 'r no less like those hapless peasants – except we don't ave no water buffalo, no rice paddies, no forty acres 'n a mule. In short, we got nada!"

"What we got is the hard end of the policeman's nightstick," Felix snarled. "I don't deny that."

"Nada, indeed," Jamal agreed, pressing a forefinger to his temple. "And so we, in our ten-point program, ask for a United Nations supervised plebiscite for the purpose of determining the will of black people as to our national destiny." He paused thoughtfully, then said, "In the meantime, we've made overtures to our radical white brothers, trying to press home an agenda to redress our historic grievances."

"N have they offered any more than the usual lip service?" Felix quipped.

Fed up with Felix's polemics – or lack thereof – Jamal said, rashly, "We're not so frightfully paranoid of white people as Muslims seem to be!"

139

Felix scowled at him.

"What presently concerns us, 'n to which we must address ourselves, is the overpowering occupation of 'r communities by a brutal, racist 'n mercenary police force," Rufus broke in, trying to quell the flair of tempers. "N one way to start radicalizing the people is getting "The Panther Speaks," into their hands.

"In this week's edition of the Panther Speaks, our Minister of Defense, Huey P. Newton, wrote on why the gun is a symbol of the Party. I'll read you a few lines," he offered, withdrawing a copy of the paper from a jacket pocket. "'As the aggression of the racist American government escalates in Vietnam, the police agencies of America escalates the repression of black people through the ghettos of America. Vicious police dogs, cattle prods and increase patrols have become familiar in black communities,'" Rufus concluded, passing his copy on to Percival.

"I've breezed through 'The Panther Speaks,' in the past and it reads like a comic book version of a paper," said Percival, irreverently, casting his gaze on the front cover.

"Yes," Jamal chimed in, facing Percival. "Huey's a fine theoretician, and equally true, the paper has its faults, but publishing isn't one of them. Our's is a simple paper; a people's paper that employs the vernacular of the street where the people gather and get their news. We have a larger population of blacks in jail than school who can barely read. We're not publishing for the black bourgeoisie, but for the lumpen proletariat, the field Negroes; and they don't read the New York Times, but the Daily News, the picture newspaper full of comics, sports and photos," he explained, dismissing Percival's objections. "And we tailor our paper to the skills of the overlooked blacks, the ill-educated, illiterate, imprisoned and working class. If we use illustrations and language accessible to their abilities and understanding, I think we're to be forgiven, if not congratulated."

"Tell me," Felix asked, slightly off-key, "how old 'r you, little brother?"

"If it matters, brother man, I'm seventeen."

"N what does that make you, a senior in high school or something?"

"I don't know you," Jamal said with rancor. "So why do you keep baiting me?"

"Jus' testing the waters, lil brother."

"And will you please stop calling me lil brother!"

"As you like."

"No, as a matter of fact, I'm not a senior in high school," Jamal said, his patience exhausted, "I have an above genius I.Q. to start – far above. It's among one of the highest in Mensa, to which I belong. I shan't bother you with the numbers. I'm sure they won't mean anything to you, anyway" He smiled, fleetingly, annoyed. "I graduated Brooklyn Tech three years ago at the top of my class, and I'll graduate Brooklyn College early next month, in May, also at the top of my class, in physics. And I'm scheduled to do my graduate work at MIT, on a fellowship. Had I not been black I would already have had my PhD; but for the longest time my intelligence quotient went unrecognized because I'm black and a product of the inner city school system, which, as you know, is utterly racist and held me back as a matter of course!" He looked at Felix sternly, with utmost sincerity. "I was raised Muslim, so I know where you're coming from," Jamal said, like a gawky, self-conscious kid.

"May as well tell em the rest," Rufus said.

"As for my value to the Panthers, I have perfect recall – nothing written down, all filed safely upstairs," Jamal said, tapping his brow. "My hobby is explosives. There's very little I can't do with them. For instance, I can turn a bar of soap into nitroglycerin, and a book of matches into enough explosive force to rip Wall Street off the international Stock Exchange," he said, impishly, eyes sparkling.

Felix felt uncomfortable, his face crumpling into a grimace. The scamp's veracity was irrefutable. "You think a lot of yourself, don't you?"

"Think a lot of myself? Don't you? You're a Muslim aren't you?"

Shamefaced, Felix threw up his hands, smiling darkly.

"Any more questions?" Jamal asked, resting his elbows on the table and his chin atop clasped hands.

"I guess I understand why Felix was invited to this meeting, but I'm at a loss as to why I was," said Percival. "After all, I live in Brooklyn not Staten Island."

"That's a question for Rufus to field," Jamal replied, deferentially.

"For one thing, you're politically astute 'n you've worked with peace people from the island in the past, 'n so you not unfamiliar with the lay of the land, but most important, you organized in the south 'n escaped with your scalp," Rufus slyly began with a brief summary of his background. "So I thought, since I'm gonna make a bid for congress, 'n you ain't going to the Olympics after all, what better way to distract you from you than ave you run my campaign, dig?"

Percival curled his lips as if to laugh. Instead, he emitted, "you're kidding of course?" He thought he'd never heard anything so foolhardy in all his life.

"Not at all," Rufus retorted, indignantly, "not at all! As you've pointed out, this is no joke. When King was killed, I couldn't respond. I was only able to numb myself. You know the state I was in. You talked to me." Percival nodded. "Only the further I sank into my despair, the louder the cry of the Mau mau's welled up in me, shaking me to my ancestral core. 'Uhuru, uhuru,' repeated itself in my delirium like the pulse of Mother Africa in my veins. I could hear the call, just as I hear that singer in the background now, to paint my face with mud, don a freshly killed leopard's skin, pronounce some voodoo incantation or other, then hunt the hated enemy to extinction, exorcise him from my soul! I've killed on orders from the government for 'r country in Vietnam, 'n now I'm ready to kill again, if necessary, in the name of 'r people, black people, here in this country, dig? There's some bloodletting to be done! No, Percival, this is no joke," Rufus eyes looked off-center with a dementia-like gleam. "I'm committed to the death! Like Eldridge Cleaver said, 'We shall have 'r manhood! We shall have it or the earth will be leveled by 'r attempts to regain it!.' N I intend to follow through. I'm gonna need all the competent help I can get, so I can't afford to let you off the hook. With you I won't 'ave to watch my back. What'a you say? I can use your help?"

"There is some bloodletting to be done, no doubt. But I hope it's not ours." Percival sucked his teeth. "Shit," he spat, "it's not that I oppose the Panthers on principle but they're a paramilitary group 'n frankly, after the Army, I've had it with following orders. Granted, much of what the Panther's stand for is inarguably necessary. But on this point, I'm adamant!"

"Unlike Jamal or Felix, you 'n me were in the military," Rufus argued, "n arguably you're the best fighter in the world, admittedly one with a broken jaw," he teased. "You see my point? Let's face it, had the man called on you to serve in 'nam, as I was, you'd'a gone, no question."

"Meaning?"

"Well your called on to serve again. This time it's in a black revolutionary army—The Black Panthers! You 'n me ave a far greater obligation for having served in the man's Army. Like Malcolm said, 'When the man sends you to fight in Germany, you bleed; when he sends you to fight in Korea, you bleed; when he sends you to fight Hitler 'n Tojo 'n anybody else you don't know, you bleed. But when your children 'r being killed 'n your women brutalized 'n your leaders shot down in broad daylight, you got no blood!' N I, for one, won't ave that said of me."

"Your points well taken, despite my opposition to the contrary." Percival spread the fingers of his outstretched hands fanwise. "It's something I'll reluctantly consider. But I'm not gonna commit myself like that, either. I can't. I'm sorry. It's outrageous."

"Will you at least head up my campaign?"

"In as much as I can spare the time," he said, doubtfully.

"I'll take that as a yes."

"Take it as you like."

"Before I forget, did you ever call Morty on that Ali defense fund thing?"

"Ain't seen him yet."

"Next time you go see that pretty blond thing you got tucked away on Canal street, jus' walk 'n extra flight'a stairs, knock on his door 'n ask. Thought I didn't know 'bout Racine, huh?"

"It wasn't a secret."

"In case you're interested, Joleen called saying shit like you'd abandoned her 'n Malek for some white bitch name'a Racine. Well, Lily took the call, 'n she told her where to go."

"Excuse me, do I hear right?" Felix interjected, eyeing Percival as if observing a lower form of species. "What about that beautiful black sister, Joleen? You left her for the white devil's whore? Is that possible? I must'a heard wrong. Is that so, I heard wrong?"

"You expect me to dignify that?" Percival said, agitatedly.

"What's shaking?" Rufus asked, concerned.

"You should ask," Percival uttered.

"You disappoint me," Felix said, in disgust, gaining his feet, his hands flat on the tabletop. "I came here for you, 'n it turns out you're sleeping with a scarlet woman, the white devil's tainted daughter; fouling 'r sacred black manhood; shirking your responsibility to your race. How do you expect 'r sons to respect 'r women if we pass em over for the white devil's temptress? What do you think it does for the self-worth of 'r women? R mothers who bore us? R sisters? R daughters? You of all people, a fairly well-known athlete, a role model. If you scorn 'r women, so will others. I guess I don't know you. I thought you were a strong, righteous black brother who stuck to his own."

Rufus and Jamal shot a look at Felix in alarm, then swung their startled eyes on Percival.

The musician in the background was strumming her guitar hard and wailing,

"Where have all the young men gone/ gone for soldiers everyone/ when will they ever learn/ when will they ever learn –"

Percival's eyes flared up, and the blood rose in his face and ears as if he'd been slapped. "How dare you," he said, sourly, rallying his internal forces. "R you some kind'a fucking fool? What gives you the right to talk to me like that? Not your crackpot religion, surely. A faith based on the absurd conviction that the white race was conceived by an evil black scientist in a test tube? Which makes the scientist no less evil than his creation, 'n illustrates, more than not, the potential for evil in us all! A ridiculously childish concept of religion for a cat as intelligent as you're suppose to be! Come on, man, we're all college here. The Black Muslims! What kind'a pseudo religion is that? It's certainly not in keeping with the Prophet Muhammad's call for unity of all, a brotherhood of mankind. Besides, brother man, you're not so clean yourself. You may ave cleaned up from heroin, but you've not cleaned up from the American induced stupefaction of racism!

"Don't talk what you don't know man. I refuse to entertain this conversation further," he cautioned, his voice menacing. "As they say, 'A word to the wise should be sufficient.'"

"I have nothing else to say to this brother," Felix announced, a shadow of uncertainty clouding his gaze. "If you should want me, you know where I can be found." Without further ado, he did an about-face and strode briskly from the coffee shop.

"It can be terribly difficult dealing with Black Muslims," Jamal said, thinking of his father.

"Damn, Percival," Rufus said, "you're sure one pissed off motherfucker. I knew inviting Felix would be risky," he claimed.

"The funny thing is I can't fault him. True, I don't much know him; but I like the way he carries himself, so self-certain, as if he's got all the answers in his hands."

"He doesn't! He's jus' a guy having a hard'a time of it as the rest of us. 'N that religious fantasy in which he's cloaked, insecurities 'n all, is the superiority you think you see," Rufus said, with scorn. "He was going for Jamal but struck a brick wall 'n went after you 'cause he smelled blood," he surmised. "He was only looking to find fault."

"Funny, I knew he felt that way, what Black Muslim doesn't? But I don't think any less'a him for it."

"So long as you don't think less of yourself," Jamal said.

"Less of myself? Nothing of the sort," Percival snorted. "It's simply dealing with yet another aspect of a dream deferred or, does it, like Langston Hughes say, 'explode?'"

"Far worse," Rufus stated, "it could implode!"

"I got to go," Jamal declared, rising abruptly. "I got to get back, check in, then go out on police patrol."

"That is?" Percival asked, following Jamal and Rufus out. He searched for Nina's face among the growing crowd. She had apparently left. He waved to the singer as he passed.

She followed him out with her eyes, her voice soaring, "Out under the winter sky – Out under the winter sky/ Stars come trembling on my eye/ Stars to tremble my eyes/ n I feel like something's gonna die/ Hand me wings for to fly –"

"It's more or less routine, seeing the cops follow procedure on making an arrest and not brutalizing the brothers and sisters in the process," Jamal explained, as they paused on the sidewalk outside The Missing Link, the sky purpling overhead. "It makes the pigs wish they'd not obstruct passage of The Police Civilian Review Board."

"Consider my proposal," Rufus said at length. "I mean, man, with you I stand a chance of staying alive, dig?"

"I'll get back to you," Percival promised, shaking hands with Jamal in parting.

"Power to the people," Jamal said in farewell.

"Power to the people," Percival said, echoing him.

"I'm counting on you," Rufus said, slipping in behind the wheel of a beat-up Chevrolet.

"I hope you'll be joining us," said Jamal casually, settling in on the passenger side. Rufus switched on the ignition, set the car in gear and, before Percival could respond, the car eased into the flow of traffic. As the car rounded the corner adjacent to the park, Percival spotted an unmarked car as it pulled out from the curb behind them.

***

In a transport of thought, Percival strolled through the lamp lit park and crossed the street at the intersection of Bay and Canal. He continued along Canal and, on passing under the S.I.R.T. trestle, kept alert for the German shepherd that had taken a dislike to him. The street was dark but for the stark light in front of the pier at the bottom of the street and entrance outside 30 Canal. This secluded end of Canal St., the other side of the tracks, consisted of a row of boarded up warehouses, cold water flats, a vacant lot, and terminated at the waterfront dotted with abandoned, rat infested piers that jutted out into the murky river like skeletal fingers under the encroaching cover of night.

He entered the bleakly lighted hallway of 30 Canal, and climbed the stairs to the 2nd-floor landing over which a window looked out on an unkempt back yard where cats prowled and stray dogs overturned garbage cans in search of food. He entered Racine's flat at the far end of the hall, at the bottom of a flight of stairs leading up to the third floor. He stepped into a cluttered, semi darkened front room with a coat rack felled over a musty Morris chair; a tailor's dummy; sea chest, and various other objects scattered randomly about as if someone had hastily left in the midst of packing. Moreover, the woman from whom Racine was subletting was storing her belongings in the front room while she, with knapsack and blithe spirit, went off to see America up close with no idea if, or when, she would return.

Racine appeared in the inner doorway with Dakota in arms. A light from within silhouetted her voluptuous form through her cotton dress; and though her face was cast in shadow her lustrous blond hair glistened like spun gold from the light at her back. The infant, Dakota, focused her wondrous eyes on him, smiling brightly; delighted at him, her cherubic coco brown face aglow. She gurgled like a brook, stretching forth her arms.

"Percival," Racine uttered gladly, overjoyed. "I so hoped you'd come."

He paused for a moment, looking her in the eyes, startled, as if he'd entered the wrong room; shrunk back, offended by her color, her whiteness, as if Felix had cursed her, cursed him. *So you're the white devil's temptress,* he thought, *suckling your pickaninny love chile to your breast.* He shook his head, trying to dismiss the uninvited sentiments; but, like saccharine, it left a cloying after taste. He could hear Felix laughing, laughing like the Devil! Then, catching himself, he thought, *Oh hell,* and kissed her nonetheless. "Hello," he finally said, stepping into the room past her.

"Koochie, koochie, koo," he cajoled, pinching Dakota's plump cheek.

"How are you? You look a little peaked," Racine said, standing aside that he might enter the drab whitewashed kitchen, bath and dining area.

"My jaw's busted," he sullenly replied.

"How is it?"

"God awful," he wailed, then fell listlessly on one of the four chairs at the dining table, and casting a blind eye over the bleak, ill lighted utility room; bare but for the chairs, table, and tawdry curtains over the high windows. The oven to an antique stove was open and on, providing the flat with its only heat. The toilet was located against a side wall in a space no larger than a broom closet alongside the bath which doubled as a kitchen sink; and, off to the side on his left, were two adjoining bedrooms.

Cast precipitously into poverty, Racine's situation – though she didn't seem to realize it –, was grave and less than certain. She owned no more than the clothes she wore, all else was borrowed, left behind or acquired from the streets. And her job, as a typist for The War Resisters League, paid a minimum wage, thus she qualified for a Welfare Subsistence grant which supplemented her meager income. Despite difficulties she seldom complained, nor cried sour grapes. Perhaps it was because the experience of poverty was so relatively new to her that she could romanticize her plight. Besides, thwarting her father's designs gave her a measure of satisfaction, if not control. She had likewise learned in early childhood to keep the family's dirty secret, hence she was not inclined to rattle on overly of her misfortunes – of which the burden of poverty

146

was now one! She was also absorbed in her child, Dakota, enamored of her antics, and so in love with Percival too much care. Finally, driven from the lap of her nuclei family, abandoned like a waif to her fate, she was, perhaps, emotionally insecure, too afraid to complain, afraid of losing him. After all, Percival and Dakota were her family now – her raison d'etre.

In this she was unlike Joleen, she did not shy from her poverty so much as embrace it.

"Can I get you something," she asked?

"Like what?" he bluntly asked, fully aware that her cupboard was no less bare than was Mother Hubbard's.

"There's not much, but I do have tea."

"I'd rather scotch 'n soda," he said blankly.

"That I don't have. But if you like I can get some?"

"Don't bother," he declined. "I was jus' joking."

"Many a truths are said in jest," she reminded him good naturedly. "I'm sure I can get some from Morty upstairs." She was as solicitous of him as she was in love. "I'll be right back." And with Dakota in arms, she was out the door and up the stairs and back before long with a pint of scotch.

"Morty says he owes you."

He smiled deceptively, accepting the bottle. "He owes me alright, damn him! But," he said, unscrewing the cap, raising the bottle to his lips, "I'll drink now 'n complain later."

"You're cheerless," she said in mild reproach, handing him a glass of ice.

"What's there to be cheerful 'bout?" He sneered, swallowing. "The death of the death of the death?"

"I suppose that says it all," she conceded, recalling Dr. King's funeral earlier on. She breathlessly sighed, as she strapped Dakota into a baby carrier and angled it in a position on the table facing him. She enjoyed the interplay between them, thinking it delightful. She drew up a chair, and, folding her skirt in her lap, sat beside him. She crossed her legs under the seat at the ankles and cupped a cheek in the palm of a hand like a flower.

"Care for some?" he asked, holding the bottle out to her.

"Not while I'm nursing, no!"

He shrugged, pouring a drink over the ice in the glass.

"Did you see the funeral?"

"With my family. N you?"

"I saw it with Linda. I thought Dakota should witness it. At least be present. I think she sensed the urgency, as she did at the memorial service."

"I wouldn't be surprised." He considered the infant with ineffable tenderness.

147

"I felt, I feel, as if God no longer looks favorably on us as a people. We've become undeserving," she said soberly. "It was so oppressively sad to see Dr. King's family mourning his loss; his brave wife, Coretta, so noble. But I think Jackie Kennedy's presence made it even more poignantly sad, don't you?"

"Was she there," he asked, surprised?

"You didn't see her?"

"It was despairing enough without taking a head count," he said, lifting the glass to his full lips and downing its contents in a gulp. "Ahhh," he ejaculated, slamming the glass back down. "N how's my little angle face?" he inquired, changing subjects, tweaking Dakota's toes through her pajama booties.

She gurgled in that playful tongue infants employ to convey their joys: that is, the splendor of their unabashed selfhood. She smiled at him adoringly, as if his face contained within itself all the diffuse rays of the sun. Dakota flailed her arms and wiggled her toes.

Percival laughed, as did Racine.

"I'm somewhat concerned about her, since you ask," said Racine, with a frown.

"She's developed a cough that won't go away. You must have noticed it, didn't you?" He acknowledged that he had, feeling the effects of the alcohol as it spiraled to his head, suffusing his face. "I suppose this flat's much too cold with only that oven giving any heat," she gravely said. "I think I'm going to have to do like the other tenants and get a kerosene stove."

Racine had scarcely concluded, when Dakota began to cough, her frail lungs rattling.

Racine removed the coughing child from the carrier and, strolling back and forth, lay her on her shoulder, rubbing her back. "There, there, mom's here. hush, hush. Shhh," she quieted the infant's cough.

"Those stoves can be wickedly dangerous."

"I know but if I'm to keep Dakota healthy, what else can I do," she said with a look of poverty that was revealing. "I certainly don't have money to move into an apartment house with central heating."

He conceded her point, pouring another drink.

"I'm going to put Dakota in her crib."

She vanished into one of the two side rooms and reappeared shortly after putting Dakota to bed. She paused for a moment by the door, listening to the infant breath beneath the hum of a vaporizer. She was such a perfect child; a quiet, uncomplaining baby; an absolute blessing, and it rend her heart to see her suffer in the least. She turned from the door and came back to the table and stood behind her chair.

148

Percival looked up from his drink at her with a droll, self-effacing grin. "What is it," he asked, recognizing her reticence from the brooding expression on her face.

After a moment, she seated herself and said uneasily, "it's been preying on my mind, and I think you should be aware: Joleen called the other day. It seems she saw us together in the hospital after all."

"Everyone's heard from her so it seems – except my family," he said satirically, rolling his eyes ceiling ward, assailed by the memory of Joleen crumpled on the floor before him and his foot raised to kick her. He shuddered, taking a hasty gulp of scotch to dispel the awful memory.

"She loves you, Percival."

"Loves me?" he spat, eyeing her obliquely. Heart sick, he sighed, overcome by an agony more wrenching than death. "She-e-t, you don't know what you're saying."

"A woman has an intuitive grasp of these things," she said in a melancholy voice, looking round at him slowly. "especially if she has a love interest in the same man."

'Geese g'd," he said in a huff, screwing his face darkly and up ending the glass.

"Seems to me that word gets bandied 'bout a' lots. Love is gonna conquer all, ah? Well you best think again, woman, cause none'a us 'r in the shit we're in cause'a the truth'a that assumption. Didn't you jus' finish saying, 'God ceased to look favorably on us?' Is God not suppose to be love? N if his eyes 'r turned away, isn't it cause that love's been denied us? N love without God is an absurdity! If there is a God, which I doubt. By the same token, I know the Devil exist cause I see the evidence of his handiwork on display everywhere 'n nothing of God's!"

"The possibility of life without God is equally absurd, if not impossible, isn't it? But that's not the point, is it," she said outspokenly, darting a defiant glance his way. "Besides, I meant it metaphorically."

"Well I don't, I mean it factually!"

"I don't know why you allow that woman to torment you so; to harden your heart against the world. The very mention of her name sours your whole mood."

"You may be right," he said with impotent rage, "though I don't believe all within me's yet been calcified. But where in me that is I don't know."

"Those are just words," she said, passionately. "Words! I know you better than that."

"Both you 'n my mother," he said sarcastically. "Well accept it on the strength of what it is you think you know."

"You can be exasperating," she petulantly said. "I guess I need not ask whether you've been able to see Malek or not?"

"Right you 'r," he said bitterly, refilling his empty glass. "But, for what it's worth, I saw Joleen."

"Oh," she blurted in surprise, stiffening. "And how did t-that g-go?"

"It didn't. It was a fiasco."

"I should have thought that she would have brought Malek along," Racine said, unable to suppress her glee. "I would have. At times I'm so afraid you'll go back to her if only for him."

"I'd rather go to jail. No, not again – not ever, uh-uh; the prospects all too fucking scary."

"I thought I'd never hear you say you were afraid of anything."

"Did I say that? Well I only meant it metaphorically," he jocularly amended.

She laughed despite herself. "Have you spoken to a lawyer as yet?"

"I have about as much money for a lawyer as you have for a luxury apartment," he said, and, looking at her with stark eyes, passed a cold hand over his damp brow. "In truth, I feel like a man caught up in a Kafkaesque fable without whatever it takes to get past the outer chambers of justice, n if I get beyond that outer door there'd be another beyond that 'n on 'n on. As if lack of money isn't embarrassing enough; as if coming apart inside oneself isn't; but as if money's the stuff by which we're redeemed. As if, in the meantime, one hasn't given oneself entirely to the devil!" He raised his glass. "Here's to going to hell on a hang glider," he grimly proposed, taking a long swallow, starting to feel somewhat inebriated. He wiped his moist lips with the back of his hand and looked around like a man suddenly bewildered.

"You scare me when you talk like that." Racine trembled. "Shouldn't you slow down drinking? You're on medication too, aren't you?"

"I don't need reminding," he said curtly, downing another swallow. "My jaw's reminder enough."

"I'm very much confused," she said, changing tact. "Morty says you've been offered a considerable amount of money for your contract."

"All of which Joleen's afraid I'm gonna spend on you." He laughed mirthlessly. "Well, Morty's the voice of authority, so I guess he should know? Yeah, I was made an offer; but no, it's not one I can accept. On one hand money solves problems but on the other it worsens 'em. That's not to say I can't be corrupted; g'd only knows if I could accept it I would."

"Then you've not given yourself entirely to the devil?"

"No, but we've got'a discussion going," he said tersely, glowering.

"What are you going to do now that the Olympics have fallen through, and you've refused that lucrative proposal? Will you not box anymore?"

"Not box?" he said with a start. "Not boxing? It's in my blood; it's who I am. I've always boxed. For me to say I'll not box is ridiculous. I spoke to Punchy 'bout it but nothing's been definitely decided. For now, I'm gonna jus' take his advice 'n heal – that's it!

"One thing sure, starting tomorrow I go back to work instead' a going into training for the Olympics. N for another," he added, "I met with Rufus, a Black Muslim 'n a Black Panther earlier on, at The Missing Link, jus' before coming here."

"Knowing Rufus there must have been a dark purpose to that meeting; one most likely not in your interest," she said, anxiously, annoyed. "I don't know how he hold on to a fine a person as Lily."

He fixed her fiercely in his gaze, brows constricted and looks perceptibly hardened. "They're opening a branch a' The Black Panthers here 'n Rufus is gonna run for congress on The Peace and Freedom ticket, 'n he wants me to run his campaign."

"You mean he wants you to fight his fight."

"What's it to you," he reflexively asked, in a stupor? "What's it to anyone?"

"Don't do it! You'll kill somebody or get killed yourself –Please don't do it," she implored. "It's – it's dangerous. those Panthers are scary."

"Don't get so worked up. I didn't say what I was gonna do, did I?"

"You'll do it," she said in a voice hoarse with tears, her facial expression waxen. "I'm sure you'll do it, but not out of black pride or black love or black is beautiful or anything else like that black thing. You'll do it out of that masculine ego of yours; out of going to hell on a hang glider; out of not going to the Olympics," she said in disdain; and, taking up short, he gazed at her with uneasy eyes. "Oh I know you Percival, don't think I don't. All you black radicals, you're all on a suicide mission. None of you will be satisfied until you're rotting in the ground with Malcolm and Martin to either side of you, in your shared manhood, which you all wish to prove so badly. You'll kill me yet. You'll kill my love for you, then you'll kill me!"

Which was just as well with him, sadly enough: if Joleen could not love him, then he would love no one and, in turn, would have no one love him. He said, "everybody knows me, so they say, better than I know myself evidently. Jesus Christ," he involuntarily exploded. "What's with you, woman? Don't try make me feel guilty for something's got nothing to do with me, hear? She-e-t," he swore, angry, swallowing the last of the scotch from out the bottle. "Without god life's not worth living if there's nothing you won't die for."

"You were for non-violence once; you worked in the Civil Rights Movement; you organized for the Peace Parade Committee; you, up till now, have been a strong Kennedy supporter. So how can you possibly think of entertaining joining the Black Panthers? How? It makes no sense to me."

"What you say's true but it doesn't tell the whole story," he said, and felt the blood in his veins mounting to his brain. "Not even half a' it!"

"Okay, tell me, what's the story?"

"I fought as best I knew under the circumstance for Civil Rights. Non-violence was a strategic weapon. A kind'a sword. I jus' didn't know how blunt the blade was. now I do, 'n the tip of the sword's been broken 'n buried in the chest of Dr. King. Besides, I used to think of myself as a citizen of this country 'n those crackers, despicable as they 'r, my countrymen. now I'm not so sure we're even of the same life form," he said with loathing, feeling his skin crawl. "Yes, I like Bobby. He's the only thing standing between me 'n not joining the Panthers t'day! Meanwhile, I'm gonna bide my time."

She reached across the table. "Give me your hands," she urged, to which he reluctantly complied. "Your hands are cold," she observed, squeezing them. She searched his bleary eyes, then bleated, "I know how much your son means to you; and know he would love you if only he had the chance. But," she insinuated, "Dakota knows and loves you and needs you just as badly, can't you see that?"

"But he's blood of my blood!"

"And Dakota's not?"

"I wish she were."

"It's not so simple apparently."

"It's suppose to be!" He withdrew his hands from hers, and, in a stupor, clasped his woozy head as the room began to oscillate before his gaze, and a dreamlike strain of a Siren song beckoned him. "Look, Racine, it's useless, I'm too far gone," he owned, his words slurred and mood somber. He then proceeded to fold his arms atop the table and plop his head on them with a groan. "It implodes," he heard himself say before passing out.

"Percival, Percival," she snuffled, eyeing his slumped, unconscious form balefully. "I need you too!" And gaining her feet, she looped one of his arms about her neck, coaxing him to rise and, tottering under his weight, she dragged him into the bedroom where Dakota had again begun to cough. She stretched his body across the bed and proceeded to undress him. She noticed, with a start, the vertical, jagged, unattended cuts gouged out and crusting over on his chest, which she would see to on undressing him.

***

152

The radio alarm went off with the most popular song of the day: "It was the first of June another sleepy dusky day of the week." Percival rolled over with a groan and found himself bestirred by Racine's morning breath. She murmured, pressing her knee between his thighs, beginning to stir. He had, in the meantime, developed a piss on that wouldn't stop. He started to turn, to swing his legs over the side of the bed, but Racine's raw breath conjured up other urges in him, forestalling him. She parted his thighs with her knee, then took firm but cautionary hold of his cock. Their lips met. She rolled him on his back and mounted him without breaking stride.

"N Billy Jo McAllister jumped off the Talachachie bridge," the song continued.

She gurgled merrily, throatily, laughing triumphantly like a girl riding a rocking horse at breakneck speed. She began to toss her head to and fro, crying as she did, "Oooooooo," her body quivering convulsively, uncontrollably. "Jesus God," she wailed, lurching forward, coming to a shuddering, climactic halt, collapsing atop him as he, in turn, erupted mightily inside her, groaning his all – the rocking horse coming to a standstill. He hastily rolled her off, satisfied in all his parts, but a scalding piss was building and he had to get to the toilet fast. He climbed out of bed and found his way to the toilet in the dark. He breathed a sigh of relief, passing one of the hottest pisses of his life.

When he left the toilet, he found Racine by the kitchen sink, fully naked. She kissed him, fondling his genitals as she did. "You're scrumptious," she cooed, coaxing him back to bed. He would have her again before washing up, dressing, and having to leave for work. He laughed afterwards while washing his armpits and crotch at the sink, recalling the whores he'd known back in the Army and their hasty routine of cleaning up after servicing a John and heading back out for their next trick. He shut the water off, and entered the cramped bedroom, and found his clothes on a chair where Racine had neatly folded and left them.

Racine asked purring from bed, stretching herself, "Can you see the time?"

He yawned and cast a bleary-eyed glance at the radio's luminous clock. "Five thirty," he groggily replied, stepping into his pants.

"This is Ten-Ten WINS New York, your wakeup radio station," the disk jockey informed his listeners. "And we're in for a fine spring day, according to our weather report –"

"I'll walk you out," Racine offered. She rose from bed, slipped on a shift, strapped a pair of sandals on her feet, threw a shawl over her shoulders, and strapped the child, Dakota, in a harness to her back, like a papoose.

"Whenever you're ready."

"I'm all set."

They left the flat. She took hold of his hand as they emerged from the building and stepped out under the pale aureole of the house light. And though the sun had not yet risen, seagulls cawed hungrily in the predawn gloom, wheeling overhead like primal birds of prey. The morning felt like it must have back when the world was in its misty, predawn infancy.

They made their way to the elevated train station, then trudged up the darkened passage of stairs to the platform. And as the last shade of night contended with the first rays of morning, they stared across the tracks beyond the sluggish river at the steady flow of car lights and streetlamps dotting the Parkway on the Brooklyn side of the river.

"Will I see you tonight?"

"I can't say. I don't know what might come up."

"Then I won't hold supper."

"I can get a cup of soup most any place."

"I'll wait up in any case."

"Suit yourself."

"I love you, Percival," she said, addressing his shadowy profile.

He winced, facing her slowly. "You're too kind."

"I don't mean to be kind, I mean for you to love me too."

"I don't wanta deceive you. I don't know if I can love anybody. The best I can hope to do is satisfy you."

"And you do."

"Then we're even," he said, a curious smile on his face.

She started to respond but the rumble of the train careening round the bend, it's blinding lamps lighting the station, drowned her out. She kissed him with urgency and hugged him fiercely. And her arms gave way reluctantly as the train came to a halt. "I'll be seeing you," she said cheerlessly, as he climbed on board.

Percival waved as the train doors closed. Few people were on board that time of morning, and so he had no difficulty finding a seat. The Staten Island Rapid was an old train with reversible wicker seats, and retained a conductor, dressed like a tattered drum major, who collected fares. He approached Percival, collected thirty-five cents and gave him a punched receipt stub in return. The train made one more stop, Tompkinsville, before arriving at the St. George Station. Here everyone disembarked and walked through the indoor terminal which incorporated the Staten Island Ferry. He picked up a copy of the New York Times at a nearby news stand. The next ferry out would arrive in ten minutes, which gave him time to get a cup of coffee and doughnut at the terminal coffee shop. He ordered a doughnut and cup of coffee. "Make it dark, will you?" But the counterman gave him a cup of milk white coffee instead.

Percival returned it saying, "I ask'd for dark coffee." The counterman stared at the contents of the cup. "Isn't that dark enough?" But Percival insisted, "When I say dark, I mean no lighter than me, dig?" The man looked at him, then back at the cup and, without uttering another syllable, he took the cup emptied out half its contents and returned with a considerably darker cup of coffee.

"I knew you'd get it," said Percival and, handing the counterman the exact change, he turned away with coffee and doughnut in hand. A moment later, the bell signaling the ferry's arrival rang. He continued on through the opening doors toward the ferry.

He sat outside on the back facing the Verazanno Bridge under which the sun hung over the river, it's brilliant light glittering jewel like on the foam capped waves. He quickly went through the New York Times, then turned to a book, "Soul on Ice," by, former convict, Eldridge Cleaver, currently Minister of Information for The Panthers and Peace and Freedom candidate for President. It was one of the many books by black authors he'd been reading of late – of whom James Baldwin, his essays more particularly, was his favorite. Seagulls circled restlessly overhead, as the boat cut through the waves churning up fish, which these sharp-eyed birds plucked up in their bills and, perching on the waves, swallowed whole.

The boat first passed the Statue of Liberty and shortly thereafter Governors Island and, within minutes, struck dock and slipped into its pier guided by grease pilings. The ramp was lowered, the gates drawn back, and the early morning commuters disembarked on the Manhattan side of the river. Percival continued on to the subway station located under the terminal, fished a token from his pocket and dropped it in the turnstile, then descended more steps to the 7th. Avenue line.

The hands on the station wall clock stood at 6:45. The station was empty but for another commuter. The train rolled into the station a few minutes later. Percival took a seat and resumed his reading, to which he gave much thought; much as in the same way he gave his full attention to the paintings on the gallery walls of the museum on his rounds at night. He would often throw on every light in the gallery to discover the mysteries behind the symbolism imposed on so many an abstract work of art. He labored, grappled, and often felt on the verge of discovery; but then, he'd grow faint, seized by vertigo, and once more his soul would topple back into chaos, and there he would begin his reflections anew.

Percival raised his eyes from the pages of the book, as the train slowed into Forty Second St. He had one more stop to go. He closed his book, dog earring the corner of the page. And sat until the train pulled into the fiftieth St. station, where he emerged from the subway.

The city around him was cast in the pastel hues of dawn; and the peak of every building glittered in the light of the rising sun. The streets were also beginning to awaken: Vehicles were racing back and forth. Pedestrian traffic was slow that time of morning, 7 O'clock, the polite time of day, when nearly everyone said, "hello." He stopped off at a roadside juice bar for a glass of orange juice, and looked into the confectionery store window at the vast display of candies as he downed his freshly squeezed juice. He then checked his watch and moved on. He enjoyed the charm of the mid-Manhattan neighborhood in which he worked. It was picturesque. He approached Rockefeller Center and turned up 6th. Ave. toward Radio City Music Hall. And though he'd never been inside he felt a thrill of remembrance course through him like it were an old friend; beyond Radio City, across the street, was the Time & Life building. He passed C.B.S. and turned up 53rd. St. at the corner of the New York Hilton and approached the Museum of Modern Art just off 53rd. St. and 5th. Ave., across from the 666 building and Donnelly Library.

Watching out for him with one eye and impatiently observing the clock with the other, the night guard unlocked the door for him on his arrival. "Good morning," he said, stifling a yawn, anxious to go.

"Morning," Percival responded, signing in.

"Take care," said the other, signing out.

"Shall try," Percival returned, as the other left. "See you next week."

Percival found no reason for changing into his uniform so early on in his shift, and since no one was there to question his decision he assumed a position on a stool behind the information desk in the front lobby. It was unusual for the phone to ring so early in the day but, to his annoyance, it rang. "Museum of Modern Art," he said into the mouthpiece, "good morning."

"He-l-l-o," came a panting, sultry reply.

"Hello?"

"I like your morning voice, it's so sexy and virile."

"I've no complaints with yours neither."

"Keep talking, you're making me hot." She breathed warmly.

"Sweet'art, please."

"It's too late sugar I've stuck my hand in my drawers and I'm diddling my clit, OoooOooo a-h-h –"

Click! And suddenly the line went dead.

Somewhat amused Percival recalled how unpredictably wild Racine was earlier on that morning in bed and found it disturbing that, despite her attempt at anonymity or because of it, he had not been any less aroused this time either.

"Fantastic," he uttered to himself off guard, hanging up, "I can see it's gonna be one'a those days."

Again he took up his book and was fully engrossed when the front door bell rang. He looked up. It was Carl, a guard, a soft spoken, elfin German gentleman about to retire. *The antithesis of the blond beast,* thought Percival, as he went over to open the door.

"Goot morgen," Carl said ever so politely, his clear eyes twinkling, as he entered the spacious, well lighted lobby.

"Good morning," said Percival in response, and returned to the information desk and his book, while Carl had disappeared only to reappear fifteen minutes later in uniform.

"What are you reading, may I ask?"

Percival handed Carl the book and studied his wizened expression as he took in the jacket cover and portrait of Eldridge Cleaver posed behind the walls of a high security prison with a gun tower to his back. Carl looked up with a puzzled frown, then turned the book over and read the raves. Next he opened the book to the introduction and followed by examining the table of contents. "This man is a rabble rouser, is he not?"

"Maybe I'll know after I've read the book," Percival declared, smiling ironically.

"Jah, I've heard of him," said Carl disapprovingly and, returning the book, took a seat alongside Percival behind the front desk. Carl habitually brought a shoulder bag with him out of which he retrieved a thermos bottle and bible. He poured himself a cup of dark coffee and asked, "Would you care for some?"

"Why not," said Percival and reflexively held out a paper cup into which Carl spilt coffee. He grimaced as he took a sip. He had never liked Carl's coffee, but, out of regard for the older man, he had routinely accepted it.

Carl sipped his coffee and opened his bible. Percival leaned back and stared contemplatively at him for a moment; observing the manner in which he read: Carl silently pronounced every word with his lips and would often blurt a word out loud. When they had first started working together, Percival had found himself turning suddenly to Carl and asking, 'You say something?' To which Carl would bashfully look up and reply, 'Nine! Nine! I am but reading.'

Stirred from his musings, Percival stood up. "Well," he said, "I best be seeing to my rounds."

"Jah," Carl said without looking up.

Percival wrapped the time clock strap in his fist and started off, swinging the clock at his side, He waved to a maintenance man mopping the first-floor east wing gallery. "Sorry 'bout ya jaw," the man called, as he passed. Percival punched the key in the time clock and pushed on to the next gallery and the next; pausing occasionally to observe some work of art which particularly interested, disturbed or puzzled him, as many of the paintings had. He then descended the basement stairs and passed through its gloomy corridors and storage rooms. He checked the doors to see if they were properly secured, then punched the clock and continued on. After he'd finished, and it usually took him no more than half an hour unless, of course, he got caught up in a painting, then it might take him forty-five minutes or more. Finally, he returned to the front desk.

"Why do you read the bible every day," he asked Carl in earnest?

"Because of all the sins I see in the world."

"Sins?"

"Jah," Carl responded, "even here at the museum."

"Sins here?"

"Those paintings and sculptures."

"I don't see it."

"You are young and your eyes are not yet opened."

"They're not," Percival responded curiously?

"Jah –"

"I don't follow that."

"You are older in many ways – beyond your years even, but in this you are an infant."

"How do you figure?"

"Well this museum is a prestigious place. It has a big name for itself and so that makes it all right. And young people are always discovering new things, and all these paintings seem so – so new. So modern. But that's not so, these paintings were first in Babylon. The bible tells you that "There's nothing new under the sun." And as you know God destroyed Babylon because of its wickedness."

"If that's so, Carl, why do you work here?"

"Because a man must eat, and it was here where I first found work when I came over from Germany after the war, and even then I wasn't such a young man."

"I see."

"You should read the bible more, Percival, and read less of those rebels who get your people in trouble and try to turn the world over to the communist."

Percival suppressed his rage and scornfully asked, "What do you know about my people?"

"That they wear the mark of Ham!"

"Oh g'd," Percival wavered in place.

"So you see, the Negro race was born out of Ham's offense and was eternally cursed."

Percival turned a hostile gaze on Carl, and said on a discordant note, "So we blacks r cursed with the mark of Ham, is that it?"

"Jah, this is true –"

"If the black man was born of the curse of Ham," Percival argued, "then it follows that the Germans' bear the mark of the beast 'n 'r the anti-Christ?"

"I've heard that before, and nine, that is not so. Ve Germans were Gods instruments, always. Only now do people say it was wrong what ve did, nobody say otherwise then. The Jew had been disobedient to God and so he punished them."

"You really think God meant for that to happen?"

"It did happen, didn't it? It could not happen without God permitting it, could it? If it were wrong he would have stopped it, but the Jew had gone their own way and become money lenders and idol worshippers and all God told them not to do. And he used them to tell the world, through Ve Germans, to listen to his word or else," Carl said softly.

"Oh?"

"Vell, you know, Hitler was not so evil as people now like to paint; no more evil than F.D.R. with all his communist programs, like welfare. It makes your people lazy, you know? But look at yourself, you a hardworker; a student; a boxer and you hold down a job."

Percival visibly flinched, casting his reflections on members of the black crew of maintenance workers there at the museum who held down two full time jobs to pay off mortgages, provide for their families, offer their wives a little extra and be able to send their children to college. These men labored daily to exhaustion under Carl's eyes but Carl couldn't or wouldn't see them but saw instead all the surrounding evil and drew justification from the bible for his nations blood lust.

"No," he surmised, "Carl wasn't the blond beast but it didn't much matter that he wasn't."

"It's unpopular to now say so, and that is because the Jew has gained so much influence here, especially in New York City," Carl continued. "But all of Europe at that time had no use for the Jew and the problems he was creating – like communism and such. I know it seems wrong to kill so many people, but they got it because they were disobedient. God told them, through Moses, that if they didn't listen to him that he would scatter them across the world and destroy them. But they laugh at him, and he did what he say he would do."

"I see," said Percival dubiously.

"Don't you see, ve Germans were not all wrong. Though war is a terrible thing, God uses war sometimes to purge the world of its wickedness. So, you see, ve Germans were not all wrong – though ve now take the blame."

"You don't tell this to everyone do you, Carl?"

"Nine, but you a nice boy and I don't want to see you go wrong, so I confide in you – Jah?''

"I dig," Percival gravely exclaimed, wondering what he'd done to deserve such dubious an honor?

Carl opened his bible and resumed his studies, silently forming each word with his lips. Percival continued to observe him; to scrutinize his tranquil expression and serene gaze which, incidentally, made him wonder, especially since he'd never ventured to read but the four gospels himself, what could this otherwise kindly old man find in those pages to justify Hitler's persecution and attempted near genocide of the people for whom the book was written in the first place? The thing which disturbed him most was that the persecution of the Jews was synonymous with the persecution of blacks in the United States and the disease of fratricide globally – the curse of Cain more surely than the curse of Ham was what plagued the world, as far as he could see! No, Percival could not fathom it and so, with a careless shrug, he returned to his own reading.

The morning passed and by ten thirty he had changed into his uniform, and the women who worked the front/ information desk were setting up before the museum opened its doors at eleven O'clock. A half an hour later, he opened the museum doors to the public, and took his place in the lobby as the guest poured in.

Shortly after he was relieved for lunch. He took a stroll. The midday sun was high and bright over the city; and the otherwise hurried city streets had slowed to a civil pace. Women, divested of their winter apparel, bared pale limbs to view, and the raised hem lines of min skirts caught the eye of every passing, would be Casanova. Percival removed his jacket and loosened his tie, craning his chafed neck. The day, as forecast, was glorious.

He sat on the steps of the CBS building and watched, amidst the swirl of passersby, one of the city's most peculiar if not fascinating characters, the blind, eccentric poet/ songwriter, Moon dog, arrayed in the furs and horned helmet of a Viking, as he leaned unwaveringly on a staff as tall as himself in his usual spot on the busy corner of 53rd. St. & 6th. Ave.; poems tucked in a leather pouch at his side. The fine spring day was considerably mild for such apparel; it was, nevertheless, what he wore in all seasons. He looked only somewhat like a beggar with his craggy, wind burnt face obscured by an unkempt, grizzly beard and sightless eyes. His costume was often mistaken for a come on or a beggar's gimmick; but, on the contrary, it was more the garb of a lone poet crying in the wilderness. In as much as New York City could be perceived as a wilderness. True enough, he accepted money for poems when offered, but much of his verse had been turned into hit songs. It was rumored

160

that he was wealthy. In fact, he had made several appearances on "The Tonight Show" with host Johnny Carson. Yet even New Yorkers accustomed to seeing everything did a double take on first encountering Moondog and would exclaim, as often as not, like every other out of Towner, "Now I've seen it all."

Percival eventually rose, brushed off the seat of his pants, checked the time, and headed for the nearest deli wondering what variety of broth to have for lunch. His stomach gurgled in protest; the thought of more broth sloshing around in his gut was indigestible. Yet he could eat nothing with his jaw wired, and so decided, "What the hell," and had a cold beer before returning to his post in the museum's main lobby.

His jaw began to throb spasmodically, and he longed to be off his feet, to remove his shoes and socks and massage the bottom of his sore feet. But it would be indelicate to do so in the heavily trafficked lobby. In exasperation he reached into his pants pocket, withdrew his medication, popped a darvon in the side of his mouth, and clasped his jaw waiting for the pill to take effect. Hence he wondered, "how does Moon dog stand all day on the fucking street corner as old as he must be in all-weather wearing nothing else but sandals on his feet?" He glanced up wearily at the clock over the front/information desk. It was time for him to relieve a guard in the east wing gallery on the second floor.

He bypassed the elevator and took the stairs. Quintos, a short, portly guard, a flame, was waiting when Percival entered the gallery. "There you are, sugar," he lisped as Percival advanced, skirting a cluster of art aficionados. "They tell me you broke your jaw? Boxing, tch-tch, such sexless brutality," he uttered with a wand like wave of the hand. "It's so, so, you know, primal," he drawled. "Don't get me wrong darli-n-g," he coyly advanced, devouring Percival with his eyes, "after all, some pain is desirable, if you follow my drift?" He smiled lasciviously. "Anyway, honey, I'd find other outlets for my aggression if I were you."

"I'll consider it."

"You do that."

Quintos was a child of the South who'd fled North in fear for his life before the Klan discovered his dirty little secret. For, as he'd learned early on, the KKK dealt with "queers" in similar a fashion as they did "niggers," without mercy. Therefore, for safety sake, he dare not take on white lovers. And so, as he'd said, "I had to seek out black boys for my pleasure. The danger being the same for them as it was for me. Only I could trust they would keep our secret." He went on, "When I was a boy the Klan found two white boys, teenagers, having sex. They took those boys and tied them hands and feet and shackled them to a barge in the middle of the Mississippi and set the barge afire. I can

161

still hear them screaming in terror as the whole town watched from the bank of the river, while they, and the sinking barge, whooshed into flames." He tremulously recalled, "You could see them flailing on the burning barge, writhing in agony against their bands—as the flesh fell off their bones like melting wax. You could smell them roasting like pigs on a spit. The sweetness of the odor was cloying. That's how close they were. It was all so surreal. It was like I was standing outside my body observing the scene. I was in a swoon and saw them as vapors in a mist; tormented souls writhing in the flames. The older boys, at the prompting of adults, jeered and threw stones, while the minister preached 'damnation and abomination in the eyes of The Lord.' Then the cries from the barge went eerily silent, and the barge submerged, leaving only an oily, smoldering spot on the surface. I wanted to run but my uncle held me fast. Nobody did anything to save those boys. Not even their parents! No protest in the name of sanity was raised! I was never more terrified in all my life and pissed myself, trembling in my uncles grasp, tears washing my bewildered face. It was horrible! Horrible! I fell sick and was confined to bed for some time after. It gave me to know, in no uncertain terms, that my rude nature would get me killed if I didn't flee. And so I ran from the south as soon and as quickly and as far as my feet would carry me."

As a consequence of his experiences, Quintos's sexual preferences became young black men. "What can I say," he winked. "I've since developed a taste for dark meat."

"Oh well, I'm off to lunch," said Quintos. "Unless, of course, you want I should eat you?"

"Goodbye, Quintos," said Percival flatly.

"Have it your way, sweet cakes," Quintos pouted, slapping Percival's ass as he flounced off.

Percival stiffened, eyeing the queen over his shoulder with concealed amusement. "What'a place," he mused, recalling Carl saying to him, 'this place is a den of inequity.' He could not help but laugh. He turned to his duties and strolled about the galleries observing the people as much as the paintings; the charming girls more than anything else. Whenever he became fed up with working at the museum, he found that he could always be grateful for the hordes of beautiful women who religiously streamed through its revolving doors: Girls from Vasa; Brandies; Wesleyan, etc. Then there were debutantes, socialites, artists, et al.; young women from every imaginable walk of life whose minds were blossoming in direct proportion to the degree to which they were also willing, like calipers, to spread their legs; making MOMA, for the cognoscente, the best spot in New York to pick up women. On numerous occasion Percival had met some rather attractive women in these galleries; and though he had not succeeded in seducing them all, there had always followed a pleasant exchange of ideas. They invariably talked art, and many of his questions on modern art were put to rest, temporarily at any rate. Little by little, he became versed in the language, discovering cultural and historical references in paintings that he could not on his own have guessed. But with his jaw now wired, he had little interest in speaking or overly taxing the muscles of his jaw. He walked his post with silent purpose.

Quintos returned from lunch and Percival quickly departed. Quintos blew him a kiss. "Goodbye, sweet cakes," he called. Percival chuckled and went on to relieve his friend Courtney, a short, dark West Indian, in the south gallery.

"Ay, mahn," Courtney hailed him, "I made it de finals. I saw you, mahn. Ya was spectacular."

"If that were the whole story."

"Fate played you a dirty trick."

"It was fate 'n not Juarez, was it?"

"Ya got reasons to be pissed, mahn."

"I'm trying not to think 'bout it."

"I'd be pissed!"

"What at – fate?"

"Well, mahn, I see I best be going."

"I'll catch you on the rebound."

Percival was there no more than five minutes when Rufus appeared: "So ya made it ta work after all, did you?"

"Yeah, thought I'd scare you up on my break," Rufus looked more suspiciously mischievous than usual.

"Everything's everything, is it?"

"He-he," Rufus tittered, pointing over his shoulder with a backward jerk of a thumb. "Know that painting with the dude stepping bare ass into a bath next wing over?"

"Cézanne's "Bather," you mean?"

"Yeah," Rufus chortled, smacking his lewd lips. "I could'a sworn he turned round 'n gave me a' wink as I was passing."

"You stoned or what, man?"

"That's an idea, I wish I'd thought'a it," Rufus stubbornly said, his cross eyes glazed with a crazy glint in them.

"I should care," Percival cried in disgust, "it's your job not mine!"

"N don't you forget it –"

"It's always like this with you. I'm not disputing it's your job or your life for that matter. I jus' don't like the idea of swinging in the wind on account of you, dig? I mean, las night you're talking Marxist dialectical materialism n t'day your talking outta your head, 'n you expect to put my life on the line for someone as unstable as nitroglycerine?"

"I hear you, bro," said Rufus uneasily, embarrassed. "I hear you."

"Do ya?"

"I said as much, didn't I-I'm jus' playing with you, ay? Ya lose your sense'a humor along with your shot at the Olympics," Rufus taunted? Percival fixed him with an indignant, icy stare. "Okay, okay, I was out'a line. But tell me," Rufus continued, "you really think cats like Picasso ain't stoned on LSD or something else painting stuff like this? Wouldn't you be? I mean, you got'a be tripping outa your fucking skull to come up with shit like this," he snorted, casting an amused glance at the paintings on the gallery walls. "N if you want'a dig where they're coming from, really dig where they're coming from, you gota be stoned as they was when painting em, dig? So yeah, I'm flying." And he clucked and flapped his arms like a rooster. "But make no mistake 'bout las night," he more soberly added. "I meant every word of it; trust me, ya can bet ya life on it."

"That's exactly what I don't wanta do."

"Ya could do worse."

"Not in your wildest dream."

"It don't change shit, being here, looking at this chicken scratch day in n day out is enough to unglue anyone," Rufus said in defense.

"I don't wanna hear it," Percival angrily quipped. "Jus' don't go feeding me your lame fucking excuses."

"Hey, man, ease up."

"You asking me to put out for you 'n you show up actin' like you're outa your fucking skull."

"Okay, man, I catch ya drift."

"I hope so cause I'm the one got you this gig in the first place."

"It didn't take long for you to bring that up."

"Aaah, man, get outa here." Percival waved him off.

"Adios, I'm gone." Rufus backed away with hands upraised, bumped into a visitor, apologized, then offered his back as he tramped off. "Lily's expecting you to call," he shouted before turning in to the north east gallery.

"Sh-e-et!" Percival swore under breath, watching Rufus as he bypassed the viewers in the gallery on his way out. He couldn't figure it: they were always at loggerheads, always at odds, like kids scrapping over marbles. However, they loved each other and would go to the ground in defense of the other against all opposition.

Courtney returned from lunch a few minutes early:

"Not to interfere in your affairs, mahn, but out'a curiosity what you gonna do now," he asked? "Rumor has it you not gonna accept McGraw's offer. Where that leave you, mahn?"

"With not too many options."

"R you gonna go pro?"

"Right now, man, I feel like a cornered rat," Percival said, choking with emotion. "N after the killing of Dr. King 'n with all the other fucking shit going down, like the rest of us, I'm sick 'n fed up with groping in the dark."

"These be trying times."

"Ever so trying."

"Amen to that."

"Last night I was talking to Rufus 'n a couple brothers –"

Courtney broke in sharply, "I know Rufus your mahn but you best tell that cat, mahn, that he best shape up cause he's on they shit list. They jus' waiting for a' chance to fire his ugly ass."

"He's a Vietnam vet, man."

"'N that why he still got a' job."

"I know he's volatile like plastique but, I mean, his wife's pregnant, dig? Besides, man, the guy's been queered over by Army shrinks, you know?"

"Mr. Charlie ain't interested."

Percival lay a hand on Courtney's shoulder, looking him sternly in the eyes. "Well maybe it's time Mr. Charlie becomes interested!"

"What you gonna do, hold a gun to his head?"

"Don't go giving me ideas!" Then, lowering his gaze, Percival dropped his hand from Courtney's shoulder. "Later," he irritably said, turning away.

"Watch your step, mahn," Courtney warned as Percival walked off.

Percival returned to his post in the front lobby for the remainder of his shift; following which he would usually head straight for the gym, and then after a rigorous work out, race off to class. But since his jaw was broken and the Olympics cancelled for him as a result, the gym was out and school, even had it not been shut down by the student strike against the war, would still be a distant few hours off. Therefore, without a direction in mind, he stood outside the museum in a quandary, feeling sorry for himself and wondering what to do? He had no immediate wish to return to his Brooklyn apartment, nor had he a desire to see Racine again so soon. "Though it had its compensation," he thought with a Satyr like leer; but he had no wish to travel all the way to Staten Island again so soon either. He sighed forlornly and began to feel somewhat self-conscious, as though passersby could read his thoughts – he'd obviously been standing undecided for a while. Hence he scurried off and found his way to the nearby subway stop below the mezzanine and sub-basement of the 666 building. He bought a copy of The Journal American and The New York Post at the subway newsstand, then caught the downtown G train. He emerged from the subway at 4th. St. & 6th. Ave. in front of the Village's well used basketball court where a hot game was always under way. He watched awhile from his side of the fence along with other viewers, then turned up 7th. St. and strolled eastward to Washington Square Park and NYU, feeling more and more at a loss.

The park was full of various activities: chief among which was chess; and musicians, gathered round the ornate fountain, sang and played instruments, as couples strolled through the European style park with the Grand Washington Arch (reminiscent of the Arch d'Triumph in Paris) which stood at the terminus of 5th. Ave. In front of the University, across from the park, a straggly band of protestors carried signs declaring war on the institutions of war, while shouting hoarsely, "1-2-3-4 We don't want your bloody war!" And, "Hey, hey, LBJ, how many kids did you kill today?"

Percival ensconced himself on a bench by the fountain for a while listening to the musicians and reading the papers. He discarded the papers after going through them, then ventured across the street and joined the protestors. Soon wearying of this fruitless exercise, he wandered off under cover of dusk and found his way to Figuroas, a cafe on Bleaker St., where he lingered over a cup of coffee. After which he journeyed a few blocks up town to the Strand Bookstore on 12th. St. and roamed among the rows of floor to ceiling bookshelves, as well as browsed through the bins full of used, dusty old books. He finally left empty handed.

By the time he hit the street it was past 9 O'clock and fully dark, and, still avoiding going home, he turned his footfall in the direction of the Village Vanguard, a basement Jazz Club, on 7th. Ave. South. He descended the narrow steps to the basement club and took a seat at a table on the side, catching alto saxophonist Charles McPherson and trio, piano, base and drums, arrayed on the band stand up front. The small atmospheric club was structured somewhat like a railroad car with tightly fitting narrow tables and a bar snugly tucked away in the back. It was a small appreciative mid-week crowd. A waitress approached him. He ordered a scotch and soda, then settled back for the duration.

McPherson's horn soared on the Jazz standard "Cherokee," and his trio entered at a breakneck tempo which retained its coherence throughout as the music skyrocketed on patterns of irregularly resolving chords. If not the technical genius of Parker, McPherson possessed his lyrical grace and while Bird's influence was recognizable there was no attempt at imitation, and therefore his sound, paralleling but not parroting, was fresh; possessing a distinct tone, quality, voice and beauty which, incidentally, was the name of the piece that they had just then broken into, "But Beautiful." And McPherson's rendering of it was, indeed, beautiful.

Percival closed his eyes, gazing speculatively inwards, as the music washed over him, entered the blues of him, and bore him aloft on the lyrical wings of song.

***

The ring lights were stark. He could little see. His unnamed opponent had not yet entered the ring, and yet he was afraid. His defense was low, nonexistent; his hands were bound at his back and the referee paraded him about the ring to the hoopla of the crowd, as one would a slave to be sold at auction. He was alarmed to find that it was a hangman's rope to which he was attached, and the fans a better part of a lynch mob. But he was unable to figure, despite the tightening noose, who was about to be hanged when, out of the corner of an eye, he was distracted by a fleeting young blond flitting imperceptibly by, eluding recognition. Was it Racine? Was it Candy? Candy? He abruptly lost interest as the noose, tightening more firmly, choked him; and, taken up short, he recognized his old Army pal, the cop, tugging at the other end of the rope as he observed, to his dismay, that the faces at ringside were hooded; thus he stared on in sickly fascination as one removed his hood and, to his horror, saw Juarez shouting, "I kill you – I kill you!" He realized that he was caught in the grip of a terrible nightmare from which he then struggled to waken; but in trying to escape, the noose only tightened. As he grappled with the bed sheets, his heart flailing, he heard a sultry voice call from out the substrata of his consciousness, "Lucius!" He woke of a sudden, in a panic, panting, and sat up in a cold shuddering sweat, confused as to his whereabouts. A constellation of sweat beaded his brow and his night shirt clung to his dank, throbbing chest. This same dream had awakened him on several occasions over the past few weeks, distressing him considerably. He was about to switch on the bed side lamp when a hand took hold of his arm, and, pulse quickening, he drew back in a start.

"You okay, love," Racine dreamily asked?

"It was jus' a bad dream," he muttered, his mind wheeling, so he was in Racine's bed?

"Want to tell me about it?"

"There's nothing to tell." He could hear his heartbeat in his chest. He had not as yet told her or anyone else, for that matter, about his father, Lucius, and his tragic end; he had not quite digested the revelation himself, as well as had

167

he not yet found words in which to frame the story: That is, he was his dead father and himself alive, fearful of their mutual impotency.

"Try get some sleep then," Racine suggested, turning on her side.

He lay back down staring off into the dark, too afraid to close his eyes; this had been the first that he had seen Racine since starting back to work the previous week. He had been avoiding her much as in the same way he had been avoiding Rufus. And that evening when he had shown up at her door, she had greeted him coldly, silently.

He smiled shamefacedly. "How r things," he asked, unable to bear the silence in which she looked at him. "ello stranger," she quipped, choking back tears. "Things have been better." There were a thousand things to plague a young mother with a first child and no one to turn to but an indifferent state agency, a cold, indifferent bureaucracy. "I tried calling you, oh how I tried."

"Well I'm here now, ain't I?"

"How you hurt me," she complained.

"Ya know how it is with me."

"As well you know how it is with me," she said, arms crossed under her bosom.

"Should I go," he asked, starting to turn?

"I didn't say that." She stamped her foot imperiously. "I didn't say that at all," she insisted. "Why do you do this to me?" She threw her arms about his neck, stopping him. He scooped her up and carried her into the back bedroom and deposited her on the bed where they talked and made love for the rest of the evening – but mostly they made love.

After wakening from the nightmare, he could not fall back to sleep and, slipping in and out of consciousness, he tossed and turned for the remainder of the night. Then rising the next morning, more tired than rested, he had to get to work. It was Friday, the end of the work week, and, having to be at the museum by 7:30a.m., he had to run, and so left Racine in bed undisturbed and silently stole off.

Rufus accosted him later that day in the second-floor east wing gallery. "You avoiding me, bro?"

"No more than usual," said Percival flippantly.

"You gonna give me 'n answer or what?"

"I've got questions'a my own I need answers to, dig? I got'a be able to see my way clear, you know?"

Rufus stared stonily off, then said of a sudden, "you promised Lily you'd drop by but you haven't so far either."

"I've been inundated with my own shit, man," Percival tried to exculpate himself.

168

"Yeah, I dig!" Rufus continued to stare off. "She lost the baby," he said shortly, piteously. Percival stared at him aghast. "Lily lost 'r baby, man, you know?" he emitted, near tears. "'R baby, man, 'r beautiful black baby –"

"W-What?" Percival dubiously stammered. "No! How? When?" he asked, staring into Rufus' woeful eyes with a pang of regret, his thoughts on Lily. "Poor Lily," he uttered under breath, not quite able to believe it; not wanting to believe it; not wanting to have fallen short in Rufus' eyes nor Lily's estimation and certainly not his own. But fallen short he had, at least in his own eyes.

"I got her outa the hospital Tuesday, so it was las Friday. N that's why I wasn't at work yesterday."

"I hadn't noticed," Percival claimed absently.

"I thought you thought you was my keeper."

"No, man, jus' your brother."

"Well, bro, you fallen down on the job."

Percival shifted uneasily, at odds with himself. "Sheet," he snarled, feeling much like a heel. "Is Lily okay?"

"Okay? How okay can you be if you jus' lost your baby 'n they cut out your womanhood for good measure?" Rufus said, his voice ringing with anger.

"Keep your voice down, will you?"

"I don't give a fuck who hears me – fuck all these white people anyway!"

Heads of gallery visitors turned in their direction.

"Ya talking to me not them, remember?"

"I'm so fucking pissed, man, I can kill!"

"Ya best pull yourself together, man, before you lose it," Percival cautioned. "Besides you've already killed too often – remember Vietnam?"

"Sheet," Rufus exclaimed, lowering his tone. "I'm apt to forget myself." A small growl escaped his lips.

"Ya gonna be okay?"

"'R you?" Rufus strode off for fear he'd break down and cry, leaving Percival in a dither.

"I'll call Lily," Percival called but Rufus was beyond ear shot.

He called Lily on his break: "I'm sorry," he apologized. "Rufus told me. I know I promised I'd visit –"

"It's okay, Percival. I know you got'a load you're carrying yourself – I don't fault you, not at all. But them doctors," she started to cry, "they gut me, Percival. They gut me like a fish, 'n I can't hope to have a baby no more. They only do that cause I'm black, you know? Oh Lord! Oh Lord! Why my color such an affront to them? Why, Percival, why? I want'a know!"

169

He didn't know how to respond, and she couldn't stop from crying. He softly said, "goodbye," and hung up; his anger overwhelming him, deciding him. Before he had thought Rufus running for congress farcical, but now he didn't care. He was ready to give Rufus his reply.

Percival was a consummate newspaper reader: He read both the Times and Post daily. He followed the burning questions of the day and swallowed every morsel of information like food, discovering most of it, in the long run, unpalatable. It was small wonder that he had not developed an ulcer, he was so consumed by it and spoke little else.

By late May the hunt for Dr. King's assassin had become back page copy while the front-page news was that of the upcoming Presidential primaries and Vietnam. A recent Gallup poll revealed that 53% of the American voters wanted to see an end to the war. Richard M. Nixon, the Republican presidential candidate, "On his way to a coronation," as one pundit put it, had said that he had a plan to end the war but could not reveal it because of the delicate nature of the present Administrations peace initiative.

Meanwhile every adult of voting age had turned their eyes on the upcoming Democratic California primaries in early June where, in the straw polls, peace candidates, Eugene McCarthy and Bobby Kennedy were running neck and neck. Hubert H.

Humphrey, the current Vice President, was laying low, hoping to get into office on the coat tails of his boss, L.B.J., who, having failed to win the peace or stop the Vietnam debacle, had stepped aside.

A televised debate between Kennedy and McCarthy was to occur June 2nd., a few days before the California June 5th. vote. The anti-war people in both camps were holding their breath; although it was inconceivable to the Kennedy people that the dull McCarthy could rattle Bobby in a debate. The Kennedy people felt assured of Bobby's debating skills. He was a candidate on top of the issues with as sharp a trenchant Irish wit, as had his elder brother, John, before him.

McCarthy, on the other hand, while holding the right view on the war, was a stuff shirt, a one issue candidate; whereas Kennedy was well rounded for a man of his years, forty-two. He understood his time like few politicians seldom do; he sympathized with the voiceless yet understood the reins of power. He also believed, as had King, that America had fallen short on fulfilling its promises. And to these issues he brought the oratorical skills of a Cicero and concern of a confessor. He was loved in one camp, disdained in another, feared by his enemies and respected by all.

Alex Burton broke in on Percival reading the morning papers behind the front desk: "You better come," he beckoned. "It's your friend Rufus. He got in a scrape with Keough and busted Biglow's lip as he tried to stop it," said Burton, the guard who had taken over Carl's shift on his retirement." It took three of us to drag him off Keough. Carlson had me take Biglow to the infirmary, then told me to get you."

"What Keough do to trigger him," Percival asked in disgust, trailing Burton?

"Got me!"

Percival couldn't work up any sympathy for Keough. He was unlikable and probably got his just desserts. He was universally disliked and avoided all around. Percival had briefly worked the night shift with him and had found him close mouthed and distant with a penchant for looking through keyholes. It was the night crews' constant complaints against him, brought on by his reporting of their dereliction of duties (sleeping on the job and punching in for one another) which landed him on the day shift for which the day crew was no more thankful, including the supervisors for whom he snitched.

Having recently been transferred over to the day shift, Keough could not have known Rufus or vice versa. Similar in character, they were natural enemy types: Deeply suspicious, they were both mistrustful and as wary as a one-eyed alley cat; and from opposite ends of a crowded room they would gravitate toward each other and come to conflict.

"That's it, huh?"

"That's all I know. I jus' came on them as I was finishing my rounds."

"Okay, we'll see."

Burton led the way upstairs where a loud exchange of voices could be heard overhead. And when they reached the second-floor landing, Percival saw two guards restraining Rufus with some difficulty. Rufus bellowed, frothing with rage, "Let me go cock suckers!" He yanked and tugged at the arm locks strenuously applied. "Let me go!" Carlson, the Chief Security Officer, stood in front of him, blocking his view of Keough, who stood next to the open freight elevator, trembling violently, his face as colorless as an albino's, calling to have Rufus arrested:

"Call the cops," he shrieked. "I'll press charges!"

"Let me at him," Rufus implored.

"What gives," Percival asked, stepping up, looking from Rufus to Carlson and back?

Rufus quieted on seeing Percival, but his cross eyes remained intensely fierce.

"Talk some sense into your friend," said Carlson coolly. "I can't."

"Get these jive mothers' to turn me loose," Rufus said evenly.

"If you're not gonna call the cops, let him go. N if your gonna call the cops, you best keep'a tight hold on him. But I suggest letting him go cause I know Keough's not blameless in all this."

The two guards looked at Carlson.

Carlson shook his head. "It's okay"

"First get Keough out'a here," Percival interjected.

"He's the one who should be gotten out of here," Keough railed shakily, on the verge of tears. "He should be arrested. I'll press charges myself if the museum won't."

"Take Keough to the infirmary," Carlson ordered, turning to Alex. "Keough," he added by way of an afterthought, "I'll talk to you later."

"Come on," Alex coaxed Keough, placing a consoling hand on his shoulder, and, escorting him onto the freight elevator, closed the door and they descended.

Rufus was released once Keough was gone, and like a wild beast free of its constraints he looked furiously about wondering who to attack next.

Percival held up a forestalling hand. "Let's try to remember where we 'r, bro, 'n who we 'r, dig? Ya want'a walk from this without getting your ass thrown in jail for assault, man. So let's fucking can it right now! Besides, I'm in no mood to have to explain this crap to Lily, dig? She's been through enough for one month, you know?"

"I should'a killed that red neck neo-Nazi son of a bitch," Rufus lamented, snorting.

"Snap out'a it, man, we got more important fish to fry than that snitch."

"Okay, okay, I'll be all right," Rufus bristled, pacing back and forth. "Son of a bitch!"

"Let's take this down to my office," Carlson suggested, glancing at his watch. "The museum's about to open and we don't want to have a scene." He summoned the passenger elevator, dismissed the two guards as it arrived but asked Percival to remain. They entered the elevator and, on request, the operator dropped them off on the basement level. Carlson led the way down a long passageway past storage rooms; the maintenance office; the mail room; and the packing room to the security office.

"I'll talk Keough and Biglow out of pressing charges. But you'll have to go," Rufus was informed after Carlson had seated himself behind his desk and invited Percival and Rufus to do likewise.

"I was tired'a looking at all that crap they call art any fucking way," Rufus sneered. "Who understands that chicken scratch, anyhow? Do you? I know I don't!"

"We're paid to guard it, not explain it," Carlson reposted.

Touché, Percival thought, surprised by Carlson's acuity.

"Jus' gimme my pay n I'm gone."

"Shouldn't you at least know what happened before you fire him," Percival asked?

"Very well," Carlson conceded. "If you care to tell your side of the story, I'll be all too happy to hear it."

"Yeah, I'll tell you," said Rufus angrily, casting disdain to the world. "I'll tell you all right! That guy, what's his name again?"

"Keough," Carlson informed him.

"Anyway he was operating the freight elevator 'n I was going up on it n I ask him for the time 'n he look round at me like dirt under his fucking nails 'n turn away without'a word back, ignoring me. I say, woe, 'Can't you talk?' N he say, 'I ain't got the time.' N I see his watch on his wrist, you know? N I say, 'You ain't got the time for me or you ain't got the time for'a nigger?' N he say, 'Take your pick.'

"My jaw must'a hung slack, I was so taken aback by the nervea the prick! So I say – 'n I'm fucking pissed now – 'I ought'a kick your ass you scrawny bastard.' N he say, cool as ice, 'I'll have no swearing on my elevator.' His elevator, can you beat that? His elevator! I had to laugh. 'What 'r you Captain Ahab or some fucking shit,' I say? 'I ain't start to swear, you red neck maggot son of'a bitch!' Well that caught him cause he brought the elevator to a halt n flung the doors open n grab me by my lapels to throw me off. I tried shaking loose but he held me tighter, n so I clocked the son of a bitch n he toppled out'a the elevator n tumbled to the ground, my hands on his throat trying to strangle the wretch," Rufus said his voice ugly, full of contempt and rage. "Then Biglow come from outta the gallery n grab me from behind, like he's helping him cause he's white. So I slammed him in the face with my elbow, n he fell back with a loud outcry n that's when all you swarmed from out the woodwork on me n dragged me off that puny white boy's ass," he gruffly said. "N that's 'bout it, I guess.'

Carlson shook his head in dismay. "Even if your story is true, which I have no reason to doubt, it changes nothing. I still have no choice but to let you go."

"What about Keough," Percival argued?

"Keough is Keough, unfortunately. But Rufus, on the other hand, is volatile and blatantly irresponsible."

"Thanks for the vote of confidence."

"Your record speaks for itself, I'm afraid. Whenever I fire a brother, it's done with much trepidation. But I have an obligation to my office, staff and position here at the museum beyond any one person's consideration."

"Spoken like a true white man," said Rufus rashly, to his black supervisor.

"That remark was uncalled for," said Carlson with ire, catching Rufus' eye. "But that's my point exactly: You're volatile and apt to strike out irresponsibly without regard for who gets hurt!"

"Jus' get me my fucking money n, like I say, I'm gone!"

"We'll have to mail it to you, it's a matter of policy."

"You'll have to break it cause I'm not leaving without my money in my hand," Rufus demanded.

"Very well," said Carlson, picking up the inter office phone, "I'll see what can be done." And he looked at Percival as if to ask, "This is your friend?"

Rufus' check was summarily drawn up and he was escorted off the premises with a firm but polite warning to not return.

***

In that Sunday's California primary debate between Robert Kennedy and Eugene McCarthy it was the opinion of the political pundits that Robert Kennedy had won. But it was now up to the electorate (always assumed to be fickled) to officially decide in the upcoming June 5th. vote. That Wednesday, June 5th., Morty had invited a group of people, friends, associates and political activists to watch the returns at his flat on 30 Canal St., a floor above Racine. His flat was better heated, furnished and decorated. It was humble, bohemian and cozy. Then again, Morty was editor of "War Resisters" magazine for which Racine was part time secretary, and his wife, Estelle, was a professor. Estelle was preparing tea and coffee while Morty placed crackers, cookies, carrot sticks and a cheese dip out on the dining room table.

No one would get stoned that night. They all wanted to be clear headed and lucid as the returns came in; so instead of the pungent aroma of marijuana there was the acrid smell of cigarette smoke adrift throughout the room and clinging to the ceiling in a blue haze round the light fixtures.

The room was crackling with the polemics of the day and a-hum with speculation. Racine stood off to the side cradling Dakota and talking to Lily, who, admiring the infant, was grievously jealous; yet no shade of it clouded her countenance nor colored her mood – tall, slender and dusky, she appeared her usual bright eyed, effervescent self. Rufus stood in a semi-circle in front of the T.V., which was on but turned low, talking to students from Richmond College's BSU, SDS, a professor and representative from the Peace and Freedom Party, smoking a pipe. Other guest were seated on chairs, bean cushions or standing about in animated conversation.

"If Bobby wins tonight, the war is all but over," someone announced over Rufus' shoulder. "But if McCarthy wins, the party machinery might well close ranks and deny him the nomination."

"We've fought bitterly hard to bring an end to this awful war," said another. Everyone in the room felt as if they had a personal investment in bringing this war to a close.

"Yes," added still another, "then we can get back to the business of remodeling our society in such a way as to be proud of."

The room was packed with a diverse group of radicals.

There was Dr. Osgood, a pediatrician and Communist who had been burnt out of her home in Louisiana because of her Civil Rights activities, and one of the best strategist the Movement claimed. She was hardly a fan of Robert Kennedy but she was less a fan of the war in Vietnam. Ergo, politics makes for strange bedfellows.

Percival was seated in a sling chair across from Nina Koestler who, her lifeless limbs tucked beneath her on a bean cushion, leaned forward on a crutch and said, "unlike the well-ordered Republican convention will be, the Democratic one is bound to be noisy, disruptive, and take place on the streets of Chicago as much as in convention center."

"Well you know," Percival remarked, "Abbie Hoffman claims 'The streets belong ta the people.'"

"Yes," Nina exclaimed, toying with her crutch, "but I don't think Mayor Daly is of the same opinion. Besides, the issue of law and order is very much on everyone's mind."

"Yes, that silent moral majority wants law 'n order so that they can catch up on their sleep."

Estelle brought Nina a cup of tea. "Here," she said, reaching down so that Nina would not have to reach up.

"Thank you," said Nina, accepting the cup. "How thoughtful."

"Would you mind terribly if I borrowed Percival for a moment," Estelle asked?

"For a mere cup of tea," Nina teased, as Percival slowly gained his feet. "It hardly seems fair."

"I'll only keep him a moment," Estelle promised, leading him away by the arm. "Would you care to work with me for the neighborhood youth corps this summer?" she asked as they paused in front of the kitchen stove beside Morty, pouring himself a cup of coffee.

"The neighborhood youth corps?"

"It's a federally funded anti-poverty program to give ghetto teen summer jobs."

"I'd take you up on it if I didn't have a job already."

"These kids can use you. You're someone they can look up to."

Percival winced.

"Can't you take a leave of absence? It's only for the summer. It'll be worth it. I can have you work in New Brighton on Jersey Street. It'll allow you to put your finger on the pulse of the community, especially as you'll be helping Rufus start a Black Panther Office there."

"It's something to consider."

"I can give you two weeks. We start July 5th., a month from today."

Percival nodded. "I'll get back to you."

"I see you finally got your braces removed," Morty observed, laying a carefree hand on Estelle's round shoulders while sipping his coffee.

Percival stretched his jaw. "Yeah, jus' the other day." He grinned broadly, showing his bare teeth and, starting to go, stumbled into Lily. "Excuse me," he apologized. "I'm sorry."

"There's no excuse for you," Lily parried, smiling up at him.

"I see ya was talkin ta Racine."

"Yes, she's circulating. Dakota is such a lovely baby. But is she well?"

"How do you mean?"

"Oh, I don't know a woman's intuition?'

Percival shrugged it off, thinking it no more than Lily's morbid preoccupation with the recent loss of her own child and having been sterilized in the bargain. "She's had a cold but no more than that."

"Jus' thought I'd mention it."

"Looks like Rufus is holding court."

"Yes, he's in his element," Lily agreed.

"What'a you thinka his running for congress?"

"It's what he wants to do." She shuddered, looking across at Rufus, frightened by it all; as he addressed the black and white students of BSU and SDS, respectively, on the subject of Franz Fanon's "Revolutionary Native," whom the Panthers had adopted as a symbol of defiance and struggle.

The students from the BSU were amply excited by Rufus' run for congress. "This is the way to stir things up," one was saying, "this is how you get whitey to take notice. We can raise money for your campaign through the social commune on campus, as well as have you address the black student body –"

"I think we should have him address the entire student population," the SDS President, Bob Fischer, broke in. "In fact, this is exactly what we've been looking for."

The professor and Peace and Freedom Party representative was a bit more cautious: "True, you'll need student support, as few others will welcome your candidacy, that's certain," he claimed, removing his pipe from out his mouth. "More to the point, the argument must be made and the issues brought to the fore. You'll have to challenge the political machinery; it's well entrenched and will do it's best to silence you. If your campaign can do that, gain a hearing and receive local media coverage, then you'll have done much of what you've set out to do."

"Pardon me," Morty interrupted, sidling between them to turn up the volume on the T.V. Stepping aside, they all turned their faces toward the screen. The commentators were talking back and forth from the candidates' campaign headquarters, analyzing the returns as they came in. That year's democratic primaries had drawn more public interest than any in recent memory, noted a commentator. And there in California, the black and Chicano vote was at an all-time high, accounting for the larger than expected crowds. "Blacks and Mexican grape workers have well-oiled the wheels of the Kennedy band wagon," a commentator observed.

"Looks like it's going to be an early night," Morty interposed.

"I would have thought that McCarthy could have closed the gap," said Bob Fischer.

"The Kennedy appeal is much too strong," Dr. Osgood declared.

"Well that's being borne out here tonight," they all concurred.

As conversation died down and the voices of the commentators carried through the room everyone turned their focus on the T.V. screen. Robert Kennedy had gained a considerable early lead in the precincts polled and appeared to be unstoppable. It was expected that Senator McCarthy would concede the victory to the New York Senator at any moment. That announcement was not long in coming. McCarthy told his workers that "It's evident that the victory belongs to the Senator from New York." And said, "I have just finished speaking to him and congratulating him."

Shortly the T.V. camera switched to the jubilant Kennedy headquarters where the Senator was making his appearance, waving to workers as he approached the rostrum. He graciously thanked them for their support and hard work, brushed a lock of hair from his forehead, raised a hand in a victory sign and said, "Now on to Chicago!"

All the workers threw up their hats, laughing and cheering as Bobby made his way among them for the kitchen exit. Everyone in Morty's flat was equally euphoric, yelling and screaming and kissing each other; leaping off the floor in jubilation. There were tears of release and joy on their shining faces. Someone giddily threw open a window and declared, "The war is over! The war is over!" Such was their jubilation. And they cleaved to each other in their joy, their mutual victory.

Morty then shouted, startling all, "Quiet! everyone, quiet!" The T.V. commentator, his voice strained and low, said: "They've wrestled the assailant to the ground."

And as they regrouped round the T.V., the announcer reported, "Senator Robert Kennedy has just been shot –"

Horror stricken, Nina yelped, "No!" her thoughts racing back to the balcony scene where, six weeks earlier, Dr. King was killed. "Not again!" She raised her hands to her face aghast at the sight of the body of the felled senator from New York on the T.V. screen and, losing the support of her crutches as a result, she began to fold in on herself like a collapsed accordion. Luckily, however, Estelle, who was behind her, caught her in mid fall. She was light as a child. Meantime the professor gasped, "Good God, no!" Scarcely surprised, Dr. Osgood snickered, "So this is what we've become—a nation of assassins!" The camera zoomed in on the felled Senator and, in a gasp, they all reeled from the T.V. screen. Both the BSU and SDS students grasped their heads in bewilderment, reduced to tears over the dark, unforeseen fate of the nation. Rufus painfully laughed. Sickened at heart none dare look the other in the face for, in a sense, they all felt culpable. Percival grunted, "Ugh," like he'd been kicked in the groin. The unsavory words of the sleep walking Lady McBeth, "Out, out, damn spot," was indelibly inscribed on all their hearts. Morty snapped the T.V. off in dismay. Stunned beyond belief and without word of "Farewell," his guest began to stagger lifelessly out of the flat, sickened to the point of nausea.

***

Rufus stopped to talk with Percival, in the hallway, by Racine's door, while she went inside with Dakota, and Lily continued on downstairs, as did the others, to wait outside in the fresh night air. "I'll only be a moment," Rufus called. With a hand on the knob, Percival stood with his back against the door for support, feeling as though he'd aged perceptibly in the last few minutes.

"What about this shit," Rufus asked? "Will it be possible for all the King's horses 'n all the King's men to put this country back together again?"

"'Turning and turning in the widening gyre; the falcon cannot hear the falconer; things fall apart; The center cannot hold; mere anarchy is loosed upon the world…'" Percival quoted from William Butler Yates' poem, "The Second coming," shrugged and fretfully smiled. "This will reverberate for some time to come. It might well reverberate for all time to come."

"And that's the riddle, isn't it?"

"In spades."

"As for the Panthers, they're calling the furies down on 'em."

"You scared or something, man?"

"Scared? What kind'a question's that? They've just killed a white man of prominence, Robert F. Kennedy, a presidential candidate, on primetime T.V. for an international audience. Doesn't that make the hairs stand up on the back of your neck? Mine do. So yeah, I'm scared. Aren't you?"

"Sorta," Rufus said with a shrug of indifference.

Percival eyed Rufus with curious detachment, unable to fathom the murky depths of the man behind his unnerving cross-eyed stare, who he referred to as 'friend.' He pressed, "You know what this means, man, don't you?"

"It means they'll kill you 'n me without question. Hell, man, that don't scare me, they already left the best'a me for dead in the jungles of Vietnam, " said Rufus bitterly, nostrils flared.

"Did they?"

"You know me, my story, I'm jus' tryin' to maintain."

"You know that then? This is the enda the line?"

"Dr. King's dead, ain't he?"

"They're killing us like buffalo alongside railroad tracks."

"The rivers 'r swollen red with the blood'a color'd folks."

"Or it's 'r nation coming to terms with itself. It's ugly, god awful past."

"Where do we go from here?"

Percival threw up his hands. "I don't know. You tell me. Down a blind alley, I suppose?"

"You fill me with confidence."

They were distracted by a slight rustle that caused them to look upwards, in the jaundice luminosity of the hallway light, and saw Dr. Osgood, at the top of the stairs, cast in shadow, about to descend—the last out. Dressed in medical blues, she was on her way to work. In her mid to late forties, she was an attractive, stately woman of Bostonian/brahman stock going back to the Mayflower, but with all the taste and sensibilities of a modern woman. She descended the stairs slowly, gracefully, lost in thought, and shortly alighted on to the 2nd floor. "Oh!" She looked up in surprise and exclaimed, "Rufus! Percival!" She was startled, having come upon them unexpectedly. "Pardon me but I was abstracted," she explained, her eyes shifting between the two. She then grasped Percival by the arm. She was fond of him. "Brace yourselves," she cautioned. "Nixon's bound to become our next president. He's an awful person. I never trusted Bobby but he'd changed since his brother's death. Alas," she windily sighed. "You can be sure, trouble's afoot." She looked them squarely in the face, then excused herself, "sorry, I'm running late." She hastened off along the corridor and down the final flight of stairs to the 1st.

179

floor landing leading from the building onto the sidewalk where Lily wait under a streetlamp.

They could hear the hurried tread of her footfall from the resounding echo of her heels as they rang upwards, 'clack-clack-clack,' between the side walls of the narrow corridor.

"You should get to know Dr. Osgood," Percival said, at last. "She knows stuff I can only guess at. She's the most politically astute person I know. She managed to survive the McCarthy era with her scalp intact. She knows a lot."

"You mean—like how to survive?"

"Yeah, why not?"

Rufus watched her as she descended the stairs, then turned his gaze on the floor between his feet, ruminating. "I'm tired'a surviving, man," he said to the sound of the front door closing below. "I wanta stab at living, dig?"

Percival sighed. "Man, I'm too damn well sick 'n disgusted," he spat. "I'll 'ave to talk to you some other time. Goodnight."

"I best get going myself," Rufus said, at last, releasing Percival. "I shouldn't keep Lily waiting."

"Later!"

Rufus started downstairs and Percival turned inside.

Silently taking Racine by the hand, he led her to the bedroom. As they settled in under the covers for the night, she asked, "What do you suppose is going to happen?"

"Simply the worst! All hope's been screwed. "

Following Percival's terse prognosis, a funereal silence descended over them.

Senator Robert F. Kennedy, Bobby, was more than simply the Senator from New York, he was also the last authority figure that the left had felt that they might trust – though he himself was not of the left – and would, perhaps, have come to terms with; if only for convenience's sake. He was quite genuinely a man of talent who knew the issues and, as such, was a fearless ambassador of social reform. He was a cunning, brave, outspoken captain – his detractors thought him ruthless. And for that – and kismet – he was killed.

Racine fell asleep holding Percival's hand for fear of losing him in the gathering storm. Her breathing grew sonorous, and her hand relaxed and slipped his grasp.

Percival felt alone, desolate, struggling to fall asleep as the picture of Bobby dead on the floor of a California kitchen hotel some 2,913 miles away, stirred his fevered imagination. He was in a state of shock, sicken with grief— as was the world stricken over the televised slaying of presidential hopeful, Robert F. Kennedy. He felt revolution—the *Founding Fathers road*— the only road open. He lay awake in the dark lost in thought, vaguely aware of Racine in bed beside him, and Dakota asleep in her crib oblivious to any external threat. As he grew groggy, tears welled in his eyes. "Mercy, mercy," he moaned into his pillows, "you were 'r very last hope – 'r one last chance for redemption! It's a whole new game 'n a lot more blood's gonna spill on account." He sighed, succumbing to a fitful, nightmarish slumber.

He did not hasten to waken the following day and had as difficult a time motivating himself to get out of bed later on as well. On his separation from the military—which for him was but "a boys' last hurrah"— he shortly found common cause with the peace and civil rights struggle, which, unlike the Army, nourished both his spiritual and intellectual life alike. As such, his heart quickened and every day he awakened to the promise of a dream, but then the movement came under heavy governmental scrutiny and attack, whereupon every night thereafter he went to bed with a dream deferred. Still his spirit soared until on yawning that morning, as he struggled to rise, the "dream" was torn asunder before his feet could touch the floor. He sank back in bed, heavy as a stone, incapable of rising. It was Thursday and luckily enough he did not have to be to work again until 4a.m. When he finally opened his eyes, he felt that he'd made a dreadful mistake and turned his face back into the pillows with a groan to hide from the light squeaking in the room through the partially drawn curtains.

"Are you going to get up some time today," Racine boldly asked?
"What for?"
"It's nine thirty, if you care to know," she said in a tone of indifference.
"Well I don't."
"Besides I've got to practice my cello," she reminded him.
"Have you ave no pity, woman?"
She reconsidered him a moment further before turning out the room and closing the door after her.

By the time he dragged himself from bed, yawned, scratched, dressed, said "good morning," and had himself a cup of coffee it was well past ten O'clock. Racine had been waiting patiently for him to rise that she might practice her cello. He irritably sat at the table with the cup between his hands, warming them, and listening as Racine scratched out a maudlin Mozart sonata. He smiled at Dakota seated in a highchair at the table, but he could little endure her bright, cherubic face.

"Have you seen the papers," he asked?
Racine lifted her eyes off her music sheet. "No," she responded. "I'll see it after you I'm sure. But I didn't go out and get one, if that's what you're

181

asking." She bowed on, her lustrous blonde hair tossed about her face, masking her sorrow.

"I'll go get it," he said, starting for the door, anything to escape the noise of her infernal practicing.

The day was gloriously bright and the sun warm on his face but, despite himself, his pace was unsteady and his heart sunk all the more in his chest, as he recalled that it was only a little over a month ago that Dr. King had been killed and that his killer had yet to be apprehended. He was suddenly seized by terror, chilled to the bones, looking about as if every stranger was a potential assassin.

The papers were almost sold out when he reached the newsstand; people held newspapers to their faces and on every cover appeared a photo of the late Senator from New York. Percival could not tell whether the papers were held so high because they were being avidly read or because the readers were crying behind them, bemoaning the loss of one of two of the nation's favorite sons, Martin and Bobby – within months of each other – at the hand of assassin's; and, as a consequence, themselves, too, on whose shoulders the fate of the nation had unceremoniously come to rest.

The following days found Percival wondering listlessly, disoriented, rootless, having lost his compass, circling on himself and hearing the relentless drone of Racine's bowing on her cello, framing his somber mood. Nothing could hope to make sense anymore. The evidence of which was borne out that Saturday when he arrived at a political education class at the Black Panther Party headquarters in Bed-Stuy, where the discussion soon turned from Franz Fanon's "Wretched of The Earth" to Robert Kennedy's untimely demise, which was met with mixed feelings:

"It's well he's dead," hailed a rabid revolutionist, "he appealed to the reactionary spirit rampant in the black community, 'n with the black savior, King, in the ground, they turn to a white savior out'a desperation. Any fucking savior so they won't ave to rise up 'n take a' revolutionary stance. It's that ole Uncle Tom syndrome at work. But now they'll ave to think twice!"

"Or not," said Percival.

"In any case," voiced another, "a President can't do but so much. I mean, hell, he's only a status quo figurehead. It's not like a benevolent dictator or anything. It's more dancing a jig on a fucking party line while the people 'r kept on hold four years till next election."

"What's scary," interjected Defense Captain, Lakey Sako, "was his sophistication; his cool under fire 'n ability to pull the rug out from under you to vast applause; like a magician waving his cape. He was the most sophisticated of New York's politicians; 'n New York has the most

182

sophisticated politicians in the nation from Javits to Lindsay. And that unbeatable Kennedy charm, combined with his sense of duty, noblesse oblige, ennobled him. Blacks empathized with him because we feel that John, his brother before him, took the bullet as much for us as anyone else 'n so we wish to think Bobby understood as we understand. Yes," she smiled sorrowfully, "along with brass balls 'n brains the man had style!"

"Is that a woman's opinion or a dialectic revolutionary stance," chided the revolutionist?

"I'm not gonna apologize for being a woman," said Lakey with fervor. "If not a revolutionary stance, it was an objective view of how black people see Robert Kennedy. And with the war in Vietnam at an end there would'a been a peace dividend we could'a cashed in on as well."

"In truth, it's more like what Malcolm said when his brother, John, was gunned down 'bout 'chickens coming home to roost.'"

"Somewhat," Lakey granted.

"It's still too bad he's dead," Percival lamented.

"Huh?" uttered the revolutionist, staring Percival down. "You some kind'a closet liberal or something?" he accused.

"What I am 'n what I'm not you don't wanna know," said Percival with raised eyes. "It's simply too bad good men 'r being killed 'cause they're good men! True, he may 'ave made it more difficult to appeal to a revolutionary spirit 'n that's because much'a what we're after might 'ave been accomplished without resortin' so heavily on use'a the gun."

"That's the point," claimed Jamal, "he'll have done the work we're suppose to do for ourselves – We've got to liberate ourselves; no great white father can liberate us. And to think otherwise is to postpone the work for another day. No, we must 'seize the time,' as our Minister of Defense, Huey P. Newton, commend."

"Right on, brother," sang the cadre. "Right on!"

"I don't think," Percival countered, "that he would 'ave liberated us. Only that he would 'ave liberated us from having to rely so much on use of the gun. Cause you're right, no one can liberate another anymore than he can eat for him!"

His comment went unchallenged.

That Monday Percival joined the countless mass of mourners outside St. Patrick's Cathedral hoping to pay their last respects and file past the casket of the slain Senator.

The crowd was so overwhelming, however, that the streets were impassable, and all regular traffic had been rerouted, as the teeming multitude spilled from the doorway of the Cathedral down the steps onto the sidewalk and out into the streets in a sprawl. It was impossible to advance in any direction but in increments.

It was another luminous day and the sun's rays slanted obliquely on the congestion of people moving in a tidal wave towards the Cathedral, but were forced back by mounted police, trying to direct the flow into specific, orderly conduits. And the control they exerted over their steeds in the execution of their office was carried over in the control they exercised over the populace. In any event, Percival was growing apprehensive, trapped, as he was, in the midst of the tight, restive crowd. He had wanted to say 'farewell,' but had slowly come to realize that he and Bobby had gone separate ways; that, in fact, he was going to forgo reform, take up the assassin's gun and travel the blood spattered road to revolution; his crucible; his trial by fire; it was the only thing that would now give meaning to his having lost his chance at the Olympics. Hence, with down cast spirit, he jostled his way back out of the crunch of people and returned home by subway in a feverish state of mind.

He would later learn that day that Dr. King's assassin had been captured in a London airport in flight to South Africa. And that his widow, Coretta, had been informed of the arrest by the Secret Service earlier on at the funeral services of Senator Robert Kennedy, at St. Patrick's Cathedral.

How tactless, thought Percival, as the station resumed its regular broadcast.

Percival was unusually preoccupied, focused, as he was, on everything but his job. In fact, he was trying to figure his way out of it: the constant standing, the debilitating swing shift which enfeebled him week after week and left him exhausted on his days off which he then used to recover for his next week's 'bout with work. The thought of working with Estelle that Summer for the Neighborhood Youth Corps was becoming more and more appealing. It would allow him leisure to conduct Rufus' campaign and organize for the Black Panther Party. What bothered him most, however, "is" what would he do for work after the summer?

These were the questions troubling him when a limousine drew up to the curb in front of the museum. The chauffeur stepped out from behind the steering wheel and held the back door open as an elegant, stylishly clad white woman in her mid-fifties, followed by two less stylishly attired black women in their Sunday go to church best, clutching their handbags to their bosoms in tight fist. The white woman was tall, and carried herself with poise born of assurance, wealth, education and class. Whereas the two black women, obviously hirelings, were ill at ease trying to look grateful.

They entered the museum. The socialite took her scullery maids coats and handbags and left them waiting by the entrance to the galleries while she checked their things in the cloak room. Percival observed the two women as they looked about the lobby in mute fascination. He could see that they were out of their element as they looked at one another every so often, mystified. He also imagined that they had not been to The Modern before and most probably had but the vaguest notion of what modern art was; certainly no more of an idea than had he on his first entering these galleries a few years back. He chuckled, amused, wondering what might have possessed this rich white woman to bring her black servants to The Museum of Modern Art the very day after Robert Kennedy's funeral? A need to explain one-self? What?

The socialite reappeared, flashed her membership card to the guard at the entrance, and escorted her guest into the galleries. As they passed from view, they also passed out of Percival's mind, thus he returned to his gloomy musings. He was then relieved for lunch by Quintos. And after his break, he resumed his post in the front lobby. Shortly thereafter, the three women reemerged from out the galleries. The two black women's expressions were stark, while their white patron's was sober. She left the two women to retrieve their belongings from the cloak room. She was no sooner out of hearing than the two black women gaped at each other in marked stupefaction. Then, matter of factly, one said to the other, "didn't I tell you white people r crazy?"

The other shook her head in ascent. "If that ain't the truth."

Percival walked off, chuckling under breath. "If that ain't the truth," he echoed. The three women passed him on the way out, and he followed them speculatively with his gaze: "I've been here three years racking my brains trying to make heads or tails'a most'a the art work hanging on these famous walls; listened to more hype, swallowed more swill in the name of expressionism, abstractionism, dadaism, modernism, etc., n t'day, right now, two fucking scrub women come in n in less than two n a half hours put their finger on it, supplying me with'a damn well irrefutable answer – 'White people r crazy.'" He could barely contain himself, this was too funny and revelatory. It was a fairly accurate analysis in light of the conditions in which most black people play out their lives. *Son of a bitch,* he thought, taken up short, "We're all fucking crazy! But still, I've been duped; hoodwinked; taken in, hook, line n sinker! In short, I've been had!"

Within the next twenty four hours Percival had decided to quit his job at the museum and work that summer with Estelle for the Neighborhood Youth Corps; hence, that day, during his lunch hour, he went upstairs to the office building next door to talk with his friend, The Personnel Secretary, Yuki Ahoshi, a Japanese-American, who had spent two of her childhood years in an American internment camp during the Second World War with her family. Consequently she was sympathetic with the expression of rage coming out of the black urban centers of America.

Percival began by informing Yuki, "I got'a quit!"

"Is anything the matter?"

"It's me, Yuki."

"Do you want a leave of absence?"

"Yuki, I'm gonna be straight with you."

"Yes?"

"I'm angry –"

Yuki laughed. "I thought that was obvious."

"I'm about ta explode."

"You've had a lot of pressure put on you. What will you do?"

He covered his mouth with a hand and breathed heavily through his nostrils. "I suspect," he said, removing his hand, "I'm going to jail."

Yuki leaned back despairingly her lovely oriental face twisted in confusion. She then raised her hands with a look of sympathy and sighed.

"Yuki," he continued, "you know what's going on, I jus' can't stay tucked away from it anymore. I've no choice. I've got to quit. I'm wasting my time here for a dollar bill, when I'm badly needed elsewhere."

"How can I help you?"

"If you can see your way clear to telling the New York State Unemployment that I was laid off, so I can collect unemployment benefits for the next six months I'll be grateful."

Yuki blanched, astonished, leaned back in her swivel chair and eyed him in mute surprise. Then said, clearing her throat, "You're asking me to break the law. I've never broken the law in my life. Were it anyone else I think I would be insulted and request you leave this office immediately! But I do know how things must stand with you; as they stood with my family when I was a girl and we were placed in internment camps during the Second World War. I'll do it," she decided, leaning forward. "And I'm going to wish you the very best of luck, though I should hope you won't land in jail."

Yuki rose with Percival as he stood and gave him her small hand, which he brought to his lips. "Gracias," he exhaled. Then, reaching over her desk on tip toes, she kissed him fondly on both cheeks in farewell.

He raised his brow slightly, blinked once or twice and backed out of the office, his lips clamped. Next he went downstairs to the Security Office in the basement, gave Carlson a two-week notice (which was accepted with much regret), and then he returned to his post in the front lobby.

On his final day of work he walked out of the museum free—emancipated. It occurred to him on his way through the teeming streets of Manhattan as dusk settled in over the city but was lost again as he entered the subway. It then returned as a glimmer: He could well have been lighting a cigarette for an alluring beauty, observing her face in the glow of flame, and as the match flickered and died out so too had the enchantment. It could have happened in that fashion. But, no, it was in the packed IRT station trying to survive the crush of the rush hour crowd as they pushed to board the train that he felt a light, airy, ebullient sensation of liberty caress him; the impulse for everything else that would occur in his life.

***

Lakey Sako, Defense Captain of the Brooklyn/ Bed-Stuy branch of the Black Panther Party, lived on Herkimer St. on the third floor of a five story walk up, a few blocks from Panther Headquarters. Security around the office was primitive and Lakey thought the office was bugged. She was certain that the phone was tapped. And though the Panther Party was relatively new to New York the police already had a strategy in place to disrupt, cripple and render them ineffective. They arrested members on false charges and jailed them up to forty-eight hours before bringing them before a judge who would then release them. The process would be repeated ad nauseam.

Lakey was playing it safe and had invited Percival to her apartment to discuss Rufus' campaign, as well as leaks in security and his own future in the Party, since he had high visibility and his organizational background could prove useful.

Percival leapt at the chance to be alone with her. He found her fascinating and hoped that she had found him no less so. He was rakishly attired for the occasion. Indeed, he looked like a Black Power ad for radical chic. He wore a planter's hat which shaded his face like a sombrero, a freshly starched safari jacket, a maroon shirt with wide lapels, a violet scarf knotted at the throat, a pair of khaki trousers and sandals. The only thing lacking was a shoulder holster and .45.

He took the stairs to Lakey's apartment with a jaunty swagger but when he reached her floor, his antenna went up. He felt something sourly amiss as he approached her door. The door swung in on his knock. It had been forced, it's bolts and locks snapped. He entered the room with a strong sense of foreboding and looking searchingly about he was struck by an eerie desolation. Nothing was right side up; everything had been tossed. The windows were knocked in and glass scattered about. The furniture was spilt and a gutted mattress lie on the floor. All this Percival observed from the doorway. He knew it was pointless to call out and suspected that it must have been the work of the police. Beads of sweat formed on his brow and upper lip. He slowly backed out into the hall wondering what the hell he was getting himself into. A door creaked.

He turned to face an old wrinkled faced man with a wooly, cotton white top who'd stuck his head out a door. In addition, Percival felt eyes set on him from every doorway peephole on the floor.

"Ya'll one'a them Panthers?" the old man asked.

Percival considered him awhile before responding. "Could be."

"Ya too late then," the old man snapped. "They got her. Dragged her out in cuffs. They come with a SWAT team. Broke in her door n go through her windows. I never seen the like, cept on T.V., uh-uh. They brought out guns n such. Who'd'a thought such a sweet girl like that had enough explosives in there to blow us all to hell 'n back? Tch-tch, I never seen the like." He shook his head, woefully.

Others dared to open their doors and interjected themselves in the conversation: "What y'all Panthers doing giving descent colored folks'a bad name?" A woman carped, "Y'all suppose to uplift the race not drag it down."

"That's right," another scolded. "Y'all outta your minds. Y'all need get some religion rather than going 'bout scaring God fearing people with all your irreligious shenanigans."

Suddenly the hallway was filled with disputant voices. Percival took the opportunity to escape down the stairs, leaving the tenants to argue among themselves. Telling himself not to run, trying not to appear conspicuous, he hurried along the street, his heart in his throat. Shortly, he reached Panther headquarters. Jamal was the duty officer. Percival was about to speak when the phone jangled. Jamal looked up, as he reached for the phone.

"Black Panther Party Office. All power," he stopped short and listened intensely, his brow knitting as a stern expression masked his face. "Shit," he spat, slamming the receiver down. "They took Lakey!"

"That's what I was about to tell you," Percival said. "I was jus' at her apartment, n it was tossed. A neighbor said they took guns, grenades n dynamite from her crib."

"I'm almost sure they did," Jamal said, nostrils flaring.

"The question is, how'd the cops know? They went there with a SWAT team; that means they knew what they were after – they knew she had weapons. How? Someone informed, that's fucking how! You've got yourself an informer in the ranks!"

Jamal looked up from his seat behind the desk, his eyes indicating that he understood perfectly what Percival had said. "Tell me something I don't know," he said with asperity, his face wrinkled in a villainous grin, "like who? The pigs are hitting us where it hurts. We don't have the community behind us yet and, at this pace, we never will. Hell, they hardly know what we're about. They think we're all about guns and killing cops."

"So what's to be done?"

"We're going to have to get our heads together. We'll have to contact Harlem. Though they got their own problems, too. Shit! For now I'm in command and I'm not Lakey. No, we're going to need some serious help to regroup. This is a major bust. That was Lakey just then on the phone. She's going to renounce any Party affiliation to try and draw fire off us. There'll be no bail. Shit man, she'll be incarcerated for the best part of her life for all the military hardware she was stashing!" He bit his lower lip, drawing blood. "Shit! Shit! Shit!"

An assemblage of black faces appeared in an inner doorway, peeping over each other's shoulders.

"Lakey's been busted?" one gasped.

"Yeah, she's been taken," Jamal confirmed, waving them back. "I'll fill you in later." They withdrew, mumbling among themselves.

Unable to speak, Percival stood listlessly in the doorway.

"Consider that you've been sighted, Percival. It's well you go into seclusion, you're too well known. We don't want the pigs picking you up under any circumstance. If you can remain out of circulation, do. I'd suggest staying away from your apartment, too. Go to a girlfriend's or something. Just make yourself scarce for awhile but stay in touch. Call, dig? And, by the way, ditch those threads they'll spot you coming a mile away."

Percival flushed crimson, momentarily embarrassed, thinking of how he was going to impress Lakey. "I'll ave to go home 'n change."

"Make it snappy!"

Starting out the door, Percival paused. "'R we really going to abandon Lakey 'n let her sink?"

"She knew the risks, man. I don't see we have much choice."

"Hell, if we're working so fucking hard to free Huey, why not work a little harder to free Lakey?"

"For one thing Huey's our founder and Minister of Defense."

"Shit," Percival exploded, "The Minister of Defense, why not god? Ain't Lakey 'r Defense Captain?"

"I understand your concern, but sacrifice is the name of the game, dig? Lakey knows the score."

"Yeah, all too sadly I'm sure. But I got'a tell you, there was never a time in SNCC where we'd let one of r numbers go unaccounted for."

"Different situation, brother."

"No, that's what you'd all like to think. But it's the same struggle jus' different emphasis."

"So why you trying to get in so thick then?"

"I'm not trying to get in so thick, as you think. I'm jus' trying to balance accounts, dig?"

"I can accept that," Jamal nodded as Percival left.

Within two and a half hours after changing clothes and leaving Brooklyn, Percival stepped off a bus on Staten Island in front of Stapleton Park at the intersection of Bay & Canal St, hatless and wearing a faded dungaree suit. He proceeded down Canal Street and spotted his old rival, one of Racine's neighbors German shepherd, prowling the otherwise empty Street. The cur would gladly have sunk its fangs into Percival long ago and, sighting him then, drew to a standstill, braced for an attack; tail unflagging, it's lips curled back in a snarl. Percival picked up three heavy stones as he passed under the SIRT trestle, never taking his eyes off the dog. He tossed a rock at a garbage can beside the dog, causing it to flinch and turn in the direction of the clank. He then chucked another stone short of its mark in front of the dog, forcing the animal to give ground. And the third stone he tossed back and forth between his hands like a ball. Suddenly he wound up like a pitcher about to toss a strike, but the dog had instantly slunk off between two buildings. Percival smiled with relief but held onto the stone just in case.

When he entered 30 Canal his ears were assailed by the howling of a young child on the bottom step, hands pressed to her splotched face. Her sobs were racking, and her howling ear splitting. Percival recognized her. It was Nadia. She was usually quite the precocious imp, as coquettish a rascal three years can produce.

"What's wrong, Nadia," he asked consolingly, stooping on his haunches before her. Nadia looked up, startled to find anyone else present. She eyed him coolly, and said through sobs, "G-g-go f-fuck y-yaself!" Percival rose, stunned, wide-eyed and chary, staring fixedly at the imp as if to say, "Well, I never –" But undaunted, Nadia cried louder than before.

A clamorous shout thundered through the hallways from the fourth floor above, causing the brat to flinch and take heed. "Nadia, you stop crying this instant before I come down and drag you upstairs, you hear?"

Percival recognized Nadia's mother's voice. "She don't but I do," he called out.

"Percival, that you?"

"One n the same."

"Hold on! Don't move! Wait right there!" she called back, starting downstairs, heels clacking as she descended the marble stairs. She reached the bottom step, picked Nadia up and straddled her over an out thrust hip. She straightened, her pert breasts straining against her tank top, nipples erect. She eyed him dreamily as if something else were in the back of her mind, which she never got around to revealing. She was no beauty, but she was a temptress.

"What gives?" Percival asked, slyly looking her over.

"Dakota's in the hospital," she said, gravely, eyes glimmering. "She's sick, and Racine's been at the hospital with her all day so far."

"What is it?"

"I'm not certain," she responded. "All I know is she took Dakota unconscious to the hospital this morning; she couldn't get her to wake up." She turned furiously on Nadia, who was still bawling, and shouted, "For Christ sake, girl, shut your fucking mouth!" And facing Percival calmly once again, she said with gravity, "that's all I really know. But you'll find Racine at Staten Island Hospital, I'm sure."

"Thanks, Linda," he sighed.

She turned upstairs, Nadia whimpering on her shoulder, and he hastened out the door, watchful of the German shepherd. He dashed up the street and caught the no # 5 bus and within ten minutes alighted in front of the hospital, which sat back on a hill like an asylum. At the information desk he found where the children's ward was and the room in which Dakota was tenanted. He bypassed the elevators and climbed the stairs, two and three at a time. He raced through the corridors, looking at the room numbers until he sighted Racine in a room standing over a small oxygen tent that looked as much like an infant's casket as not. His heart stopped for a moment, and he entered the room cautiously.

Sensing his presence more than hearing his approach, Racine turned around. Her face was ashen, tear stained, and lower lip turned down in consternation.

"Oh, Percival," she wailed, flying into his arms. "Oh, Percival, they can't save her, Dakota's dying."

"What r ya talkin 'bout," Percival demanded, stupefied.

"Dakota," she sobbed, "she's i-in a c-coma and t-they c-can't save her, it's too l-late."

Percival gently pushed Racine aside, and looked down into the oxygen tent at the gray form with eyes closed and head rolled facing him, as the machinery strained, pumping oxygen into the frail lungs. The infant had lost her honey brown complexion and was as drained of color as a corpse. Her frightfully frail chest would convulsively shudder and collapse. The poor child struggled in every limb, even as death closed in.

"Well w-what – what happened?" he asked, stunned.

"I brought Dakota to the hospital yesterday because she just wasn't holding down her liquids; she was belching everything up. So I brought her here to the emergency room," she wept, "and this arrogant, young, white, male intern looked at me as if I were a slut and my black child an orphan and treated us as such. He gave Dakota a cursory examination and told me everything was all right, and that I could take her home. 'It was nothing to concern myself with,' he told me. So I did. I brought her back home. Then this morning when I got up, Dakota was gasping for air, cold as a fish, and wouldn't open her eyes," she said through hot tears. "I had Morty race us to the hospital a-and a fucking doctor had the gall to now tell me that had I only gotten her here twenty-four hours earlier, they could have saved her," she cried frantically, wiping teary eyes with a palm. "They said she was dehydrated. I-I told them I'd had her here yesterday and I was told I had nothing to worry about. 'Well,' they replied, 'Whoever told you that was mistaken.'

"Oh, Percival, had you only been with me; had you been here they could not have dismissed us so easily. But since I'm a single, white woman with a fatherless black child, they ceased to see my infant as a person. Oh, Percival, had you only been here they wouldn't have dared – they wouldn't have!"

"You say they say she's gon'a die?"

"The oxygen tent is the only thing keeping her alive. She's in a coma, a death sleep –"

Racine hiccoughed between sobs.

"Ya sure?"

"I've been here all day talking to doctors and doctors. They say there's nothing to be done. They asked how I wanted to dispose of the remains. 'The remains! My Dakota a corpse, a remains. That's how they said it. I couldn't believe it. I didn't know how to respond. I don't have money for a coffin or a burial or anything. They said I should sign her remains over for medical research."

"You didn't did you?"

"I did. I did what choice did I have. My baby, my precious Dakota," she wailed, "all but gone from me." She broke down, trembling, and thrust her forehead against his chest.

Percival's eyes were fixed on the frail, withered body of the infant he'd named, wondering how it was possible, Dakota had been such a breath of fresh air; a dazzling ray of life; and he adored her and had often wished that she were his own.

"There's nothing to be done then?"

"Nothing," she moaned, "but for the doctors to turn off the oxygen."

"Well," he said, passing a hand over his woozy head, "it's pointless ta stand n helplessly watch." And so he led her out into the hall.

"What now?" she asked.

"I'll be damned if I know," he responded wearily.

"Percival," she began, looking up at him wistfully, her tear stained face a rosy hue, "w-will – I mean, w-will you marry me?"

"Huh?" he gasped, raising his eyes in astonishment at the question. "Marry you?" he emitted with an ironical leer, glowering at her. "Jesus g'd, I mean," he faltered, looking wildly about, searching for something to say, "w-what reason could I want'a marry you or you me? Cause your child's about to die? Jesus g'd, don't do this to me! I mean, you put me on the spot, telling me shit like Dakota would live had I only been here yesterday to intervene. Hell, the truth more is, she'd live were this country less fucking racist. That not being so, what kind'a chance you think we'd stand? Those forces – those fucking very forces," he blinked, pointing to the room in which Dakota lie comatose, "that'll bury your child 'r already at work to kill out any possibility for us. Let's face it, we're a one-night stand at best, two ships passing in the night," he said dryly. "We've had 'r fun, sure. But marriage? I can't see it! Come on! Besides, what's between us except Dakota that'll make us want ta marry, n even as we speak she's becoming a ghost?"

"Percival! Percival!" she pleaded, "don't!"

"No! No!" he retorted, slowly backing off.

"Percival, Percival, don't go – d-don't leave me by myself."

"Hell, I've got my own son I've not seen since I can't say when n I'm gonna see him t'day if it's the last thing I do!"

Sobbing hysterically, Racine collapsed against a wall, her hair in disarray about her face. She clasped her brow with one hand and stretched forth the other, pleading. "Please, Percival, don't do this," she beseeched him, as he moved hastily for the exit.

Dusk was settling over the suburb as he dashed from the hospital, his soul writhing in agony. He didn't want to think, he only wanted to act, to be out in the open air; and so he directed his steps toward the Staten Island Ferry, a brisk two and a half mile walk at least. He felt an uncontrollable rage brewing in his chest and longed to strike out and kill someone. Tears leaked from his eyes as he hurried down Castelton Ave., shoulders hunched, and head low, mumbling to himself in response to some nagging doubt, not noticing passersby, though they got out of his way as he stormed past.

He reeled through the streets like a drunkard; his mind in turmoil, racing.

He knew that he had been cruel to Racine, though he had not intended to be but her remark that he could have saved Dakota 'had he been there' cut him to the quick and made him indirectly responsible for her death as was the intern directly responsible; and so he struck back at her out of blind rage.

He turned left onto Jersey Street tramping swiftly toward the river and Richmond Terrace, with savage resolution. The streetlights were bright, and Jersey St., was, as usual, raucous: the wail of sirens; fights over drug deals gone sour; crap games in dark alleys; the spate of drunken lovers – all through which Percival heedlessly plunged. He was breathing rapidly and had broken out in sweat. He passed Carlton Street, Brighton Ave., and charged through a group of men milling about outside a bar, The 2nd. Step. "What's with you ya blind fuck," a drunk swore at his receding back to the hilarity of his friends. He passed Carlyle Street a short block on which Rufus rented a cottage at the upper end of the hill. He swiftly approached the New Brighton Projects and, as he passed the lighted playground, his brother, Sam, who was shooting hoop, saw him and hollered, "Percival!" But he either ignored him or didn't hear him, and continued on without facing round. Sam shrugged and went back to his play. Percival turned right on Richmond Terrace along the river which wound its way snake like toward South Ferry. A welcome breeze issued off the water, as night came on.

Percival encountered Morty at the St. George Terminal, and they took the Ferry into Manhattan together:

"You've seen Racine?" Morty asked.

"I just left her."

"And how is Dakota?"

"Dying," Percival said, with a melancholy air.

"What's that suppose to mean?" Morty exclaimed with a searching glance.

"Just that!"

"No! Dying from what? How? Why?"

"From dehydration," Percival answered, seemingly distracted. "Seems some racist intern misdiagnosed her yesterday 'n now it's too late to save her."

"And what about Racine?"

"What about her?"

"What about her?" Morty asked. "You didn't leave her by herself, did you?"

"N if I did, what of it?" Percival muttered irritably, shifting uncomfortably, looking out over the turgid dark river under cover of a starless sky. "I got my own problems."

"That's pretty damn selfish, wouldn't you say?"

"Don't give me that look – I've a kid of my own I've not seen for months." Percival blinked back angry tears. "N I'll be damn'd if I'm gonna go another day without seeing him, dig? Besides you the last person to talk to anybody 'bout selfishness. Hell, you think I don't know 'bout what y'all did with the money we raised for the Ali defense fund?" he said with a rueful look. "Put it

194

in the Sloan/ Spock fund instead!" An expression of sarcasm played about his sullen mouth. "Don't talk to me 'bout selfish, tell me about the politics of racism – that which Dakota's dying from more surely than not!"

Morty lowered his eyes, and sat speechless, breathing noisily. "You're right about the money being transferred," he ventured to say, coloring. "But that's not the whole of it. We tried to give it to the Ali defense fund but they wouldn't accept it. We were told that our money wasn't required. We tried to explain the circumstances under which the money was obtained but they were indifferent. So what could we do? We couldn't give the money back, and since it was raised as anti-war funds, the conclusion seemed obvious."

"The thing was, you didn't mention it to me, 'n I was a major player in raisin that fucking money."

"I guess we didn't consider it necessary."

"That's a bitch now ain't it? Or did you think I'd ave other ideas on that score? Shit, man," he uttered with disdain, "don't jerk my chain, will you?"

Approaching Manhattan, the Ferry rapidly bypassed the Statue of Liberty and skirted Governor's Island on the starboard side. The city lights sparkled in the distance offshore like a King's ransom stacked against the night sky; it's reflection glittering jewel like on the dark surface of the waves as the Ferry positioned itself to enter it's slip.

Percival and Morty parted company at Bowling Green & Broadway in front of the Custom's House across from Battery Park. Morty continued on foot up Broadway to the WRL Office on Park Row and Percival went on into Brooklyn by subway. He called Joleen from a telephone booth across the street from the Ebbets Field Apartment complex.

The phone rang twice before it was picked up. He listened for the voice, "Hello,"

and thanked god it was Joleen.

"Jo, it's me, Percival. I've got'a talk to you."

"We've nothing to say to each other."

"Wait! Don't hang up. I've signed that contract," he fabricated. "I've done as ya want."

There was a brief pause. "You signed the contract?"

"Yeah, I ave."

"I knew you couldn't be such a fool as not to," she said, drawing a welcome breath. "Where are you?"

"I'm downstairs across the street."

"I'll be down in an instant."

"I'll be here," he assured her, then hung up.

195

True to her word, Joleen was downstairs almost immediately. He sighted her through the full plate glass window of the well-lighted lobby as she exited the elevator, cigarette in hand and as well poised as a model coming down a walkway. He crossed the street to greet her as she exited the lobby. She was more lovely than ever.

"You didn't bring Malek?" he asked.

"I was in a hurry and would had to have dress him."

"I was hoping you'd bring him," he said disconcertedly.

"You'll have plenty of time to see your son. You'll have me; I'll have you; we'll have each other. Oh, Percival, I can see it all now, just as I pictured. We'll get married. We'll have a home in St. Albans. It'll be so wonderful," she gushed, taking his arm.

For a moment he felt like a genuine heel; like the "no good bastard" she would soon be accusing him of being. She still retained the capacity to make him feel guilty.

"Where shall we talk?"

"Why not Ebbets Field Bar & Grill?"

"They'll do as well as anywhere, I guess."

Afraid of making small talk they walked in silence to the bar. It was a musty old place with regulars reliving the glory days of Dodger baseball. There were a good many yellowing photographs of old time Brooklyn Dodger players hanging on the walls. The floor was well worn, and the jaundice light cast an enfeebled glow. They drew out two seats at a back table. He went to the bar and ordered two double rum and cokes, then returned to the table with drinks in hand.

"Well," said Joleen, excitedly, as he sat, "do you have a copy of the contract?"

He smiled, indulgently. "It's nothing you carry round in your pocket."

"Well how much of an advance were you allowed?" she hazarded to ask.

"It's all in the works," he said, evasively.

"You didn't get me down here under false pretenses, did you?" she bristled, stirred by familiar misgivings.

"I want'a see my son."

"You're not saying there isn't any deal, any contract, are you?"

"All I'm saying is I want'a see Malek!"

"There is no contract is there? You miserable black bastard, you," she screeched, starting to rise, but falling back abjectly in her seat. "You've shattered my life." Crestfallen, she was on the verge of tears. "No, I won't cry. I won't give you the satisfaction." She picked up her drink and downed it in a swallow.

"So I'm a motherfucking miserable bastard, am I?" he said, leaning back in his chair, away from her.

"You added the motherfucker on your own," she said contemptuously. "You should know who you are better than me, I suppose."

"What I know is you won't let me see my son," he shot back.

"You don't contribute to his upkeep, so why should I?"

"Ya argument lacks merit," he declared. "I can't contribute financially right now, but I can in other ways."

"Other ways don't pay the bills," she snapped.

"Other ways develop character."

"Look who's talking character. You're no sweet deal; you're a fucking dead beat; nothing but a slacker," she charged, darting a bitter look his way. "And you can add liar to that tab too!"

"No matter, I'm his father!"

"Don't make me laugh," she snarled.

"Laugh as much as you like, I'm gonna see Malek t'night."

She laughed mockingly in his face, causing his blood to rise. "Like Hell you are!"

He smirked, nostrils dilated, eyeing her with suppressed rage. "Watch n see."

She pushed her chair back and rose. "Goodbye," Joleen said, tartly and left. She was no sooner out the door than he was beside her.

"Where do you think you're going?"

"I already told you."

"Hymph!" she snorted.

They approached the entranceway to the Ebbets Field complex. She drew out her key, and as she entered, tried to block his passage, but he was too fast and strong and she was easily pushed aside.

"That's as far as you'll get."

"We'll see."

"You think my mother's going to let your sorry black ass through her door?"

"Don't mistake me for your father."

She chose to take the stairway, and he followed closely after. At each landing, she looked back to see if he were there; reassured, she continued on. They turned in from the stairwell exit onto the 5th. floor, and in a few steps stood outside her mother's apartment doorway.

Rather than use her key Joleen rang the bell. A honeysuckle drawl asked from within, "Who is it?"

"It's me, mama," Joleen rejoined. "Percival's behind me."

"What's he want?"

"He says he wants to see Malek."

"Well, that's too bad, isn't it?"

"I told him that but he followed me up anyway."

"Does he think I'm going to let him in?"

"I think he thinks he's going to push his way in."

"Just let him try," said Mrs. Reel, opening the door for Joleen to slip in, but Percival struck the door with his shoulder and Joleen and Mrs. Reel toppled over one another, as he entered the foyer.

"Now that you're here, what the hell are you going to do," Mrs. Reel demanded, positioning herself in front of him, hands akimbo. "Take Malek into the bathroom and lock yourself in and call the police," she instructed. Joleen's sister, Delia, swept Malek up in her arms and raced into the bathroom along with Joleen and Mr. Reel, the more panicked of the three.

Percival brushed past Mrs. Reel, and raced down the hall, but she had slowed him long enough for them to lock themselves in the bathroom with the hall telephone.

Mrs. Reel flew down the hall after him, and inserted herself between him and the bathroom door, her sharp features drawn taut and her lips compressed into a loathsome sneer.

"Will you get out of my home before the police get here?" she requested.

"Not till I see my son!"

"I could hate you for this," she shrieked, raising an open hand above her head with which to slap him. He caught sight of her descending hand, and, before it struck, he caught her with a vicious left hook to the chin, dropping her in a heap at his feet. She never knew what hit her. Taken aback at himself, he considered her inert form on the floor with some anxiety and watched her as she slowly began to stir, to regain consciousness. She did not look up but traced the pattern in the tile with a finger like a child. She then looked up, bewildered by his unexpected presence. She stuck out a hand. "Could you help me up," she asked meekly, confused as to how she got there in the first place. He complied. Once again on her feet, she looked about, slowly regaining her wits.

"Percival," she said now with a honeysuckle sweetness in her tone with which he was unfamiliar, "do you care to have a seat? Let's be calm and talk this out."

He allowed himself to be maneuvered as if he were the one regaining consciousness. She led him into the living room and had him take a seat on the couch beside her, but neither of them knew what to say. In a few minutes the doorbell rang and she scurried to answer it. When she returned there were two policemen with her: one black and the other, at whose sight Percival's heart leapt, his former Army pal, was white.

"There he is," she pointed an accusatory finger at Percival, livid with rage. "Would you remove that worthless piece of trash from my home."

"They won't let me see my son," Percival pleaded in despair, looking from cop to cop. As they positioned themselves on either side of him, he clutched his head tightly in both hands.

"Then you should support him like a real man," Mrs. Reel carped in response.

"You mean like that real man of yours hiding out in the bathroom?" he threw in her face, his savor for the fray abating.

"Get him out of my sight," she shrieked, as if she would be struck blind were they to do any less. "Get him out of here!"

"He's my son," Percival objected.

"That and my daughter's ever-loving mistake," she amended spitefully.

"Do you care to press charges, ma'am?" interjected the black cop.

"I just want him out of here!"

"We understand, ma'am," said the white cop, laying a hand on Percival's shoulder. "Come on, let's go."

Percival rose from the couch like a somnambulist and allowed the police to escort him out. Once they were downstairs in the lobby, the black cop turned to him and asked,

"You're Percival Jones, aren't you? Damn, but I've not seen you since High School – years now." Percival looked at him, drawing a blank. "You don't remember me, do you? We used to go to the same high school. I was a year behind you. I'd go to St. John's gym on occasion to watch you work out. A lot of us guys did. You were one of my idols. My father and Punchy are old friends." Suddenly he asked in a confused change of voice, "what gives with you? Why are you in this predicament?"

"Ya recall Joleen Reel? Well she n I had a child, a son –"

"Yes, I recall hearing something said about that," the cop said. "Bob," he addressed his partner, "this here is Percival Jones."

"We're ole Army buddies aren't we, Jones," the cop said, half mockingly.

"That was a lifetime ago," Percival said, sourly.

"Well what'a you know," exclaimed the black cop. "You're old comrades."

Percival grimaced, embarrassed on his own account; here he was once again at the mercy of the police.

"Let's take him to the precinct," the black cop suggested. "I know his trainer. He'll come pick him up. He's an old family friend."

"Fine with me," said the white cop.

At the precinct they placed Percival in a cell, while the black cop called Punchy. He explained the situation briefly and shook his head. "Fine, fine, he'll be here. If you can have a heart to heart with him, I'm sure it'll come in handy – thanks, see you shortly."

Meanwhile the white cop had approached Percival seated on the cell's solitary cot. "Look, Percival, what went down during those riots was nobody's fault. Let's let bygones be bygones, ok, buddy?" The cop asked, extending a hand through the bars.

The memory of that night had galled on Percival, festered like a sore wound, and left him unreceptive to the offer. Indeed, he could still feel the barrel of the gun pressed against his navel. "Let's say we did but don't," said Percival, acidly, refusing the hand.

"We were friends," the cop stated.

"Friends don't threaten each other's lives," Percival said in hot rebuke.

"I could 'ave killed you," growled the cop.

"But you didn't," uttered Percival, near despair.

"For ole time sake," the cop rudely insinuated, looking Percival over before walking off. "Next time you get in my way you're dead!"

"You're a gambler, as I recall. You won't risk losing a bet," Percival snarled.

"Bet, be damned! I'd rather take revenge than win a lousy buck!"

Percival's stomach lurched. "You're someone I no longer need to know."

Punchy arrived within less than half an hour. The police released Percival to Punchy. "Why not spend the night at my place," Punchy offered, receiving no rebuttal. "We'll talk in the morning; thing's will look less bleak in the light of a new day," he said, characteristically optimistic.

Percival was agreeable.

They took a cab back to Punchy's home. He lived on Hancock Street in an old, turn of the century brownstone, in Bed-Stuy, on a tree lined road of private homes in a well-tended, upper middle-class neighborhood. His apartments were meticulously kept, with Spartan like sensibility. He let the two upper floors to a distant relative and retained the lower half for himself. He led the way into his home through the downstairs hall which had been converted into a showcase for his many trophies, medals and awards. The centerpiece of his collection was The Silver Star awarded him for valor on the field of battle in The Second World War. Percival had visited Punchy's home many times in the past and every time he passed through this gallery he was struck by an overwhelming sense of pride at Punchy's many accomplishments as an athlete, soldier, and man. Punchy showed him to a room on the second floor. "We'll talk in the morning," he said, as he departed. "Good night."

"Good night," said Percival, half-heartedly. He stripped to his briefs and slipped under the bed covers, thoroughly frustrated by his failed attempt to see his son and an overall feeling of ineptitude.

The phone at Percival's apartment on Carroll Street rang incessantly, as he lay sleepless in Punchy's home. Racine was desperately trying to reach him. She rang repeatedly, hanging up only to try again moments later. After trying for over half the night, she determined that he had had no wish to speak to her, and so she gave up trying.

Percival rose early that morning, slipped on his clothes, and left Punchy a brief note: "Sorry, we'll have to have that talk some other time." He signed his name and left.

He hurried through the predawn streets of Bed-Stuy for the subway in distress over Racine. He could not make the transit system move fast enough, though his heart insisted that it should. "Faster, faster," beat his tempestuous heart. "Faster still." And finally, in a tortured state of mind, he reached Canal Street on Staten Island and raced blindly down the block, heedless of the prowling dog, thinking wildly, "Why shouldn't we marry? After all, as James Baldwin wrote, 'If she can't raise me up to her standards, then maybe I can raise her to mine.'" He dashed up the stairs of 30 Canal, and was disturbed on seeing Racine's door ajar. He stepped inside and climbed over the clutter in the front room, his hair bristling at the nape of his neck as he entered the kitchen, bath and living area mindful of Lakey's tossed apartment the day before. He instantly noticed that the side of the tub was incrusted with dark stains as was the floor beside it. His heart pulsated in his chest, but he refused to acknowledge what it was he felt. He glanced at his watch, his temples aching, it was 7:45, Racine would, of course, be in bed. He tip toed into the bedroom but, strangely enough, she was not to be found. In a sweat, he was drawn back to the tub and with tremulous finger scraped the stain. He recoiled, aghast, it was blood! And there must have been plenty of it too. What could it mean? He dare not guess, Morty and Estelle would know! He fled the flat, dashed upstairs and pounded furiously at their door.

"Coming! Coming!" a quaking female voice cried out inside.

Percival scarcely recognized the timbre in Estelle's voice it was so oddly out of pitch.

The door was drawn back, and Estelle stood there in her bathrobe, clasping it tremulously at her throat. "Percival," she gasped, perceptibly shaken. "Come in," she invited him, standing aside.

"You ok?" he asked, entering.

She pawed at his chest with an outstretched hand and moaned, "No, I'm not!"

"What is it?" he asked, looking about.

"Racine's dead," she bleated. "Racine's dead and Dakota's dead. They're both dead. And it's so wrong," she wailed, shaking her fist. "It's so dreadfully wrong! What kind of world do we live in anyway?" she asked, her eyes swimming in tears.

He faltered, stupidly, turning aside to avoid the scrutiny of her stern, but sad eyes.

"Racine killed herself. She slit both her wrist. She got in a hot bath and cut her wrists and bled out her life a floor below us." Her breast heaved in anguish, and she stamped the ground with a foot. "Here," she yelped, "here," taking a note out of her robe pocket and passing it to him.

He accepted it with all the reluctance of someone receiving a court summons. He stood chilled and palsied, as he read the brief note: "Goodbye – Goodbye," it read. "Don't fault me overly; for, no matter, the worms win out." It was simply stated and signed, "R," no date. His eyes had become bleary and stuck on the page, leaking tears. His senses swam and he kept repeating key words as if trying to digest them, the page trembling in his grasp.

Slowly he raised watery eyes and asked, choking, "W-where's Morty – i- is he in?"

"No, he went with the police to fill out a report and notify her family. Morty found her," Estelle sobbed. "He faults you! He feels your leaving her alone at the hospital amounts to criminal negligence! He knows it's irrational, but since he's an atheist and can't fault God, he needs a human agent to take responsibility. And, in this instance, that's you – sad to say."

Percival swooned, tottering in place, starting to feel the room twirl, as the note slipped his grip and sailed to the ground. "N-no," he shook his head in a cold sweat, his legs grown rubbery under him. In despair, he collapsed onto a nearby sling chair, his head thrust dejectedly in his hands, and his body racked with sobs as he bitterly wept for the mean-spirited part he'd come to play in this tragic affair.

***

Taking stock of the cramped quarters with wary eyes, they filed into the room one after the other like suspects in a police lineup. They were Black Panthers though, would-be revolutionaries all.

Rufus asked, "has the room been debugged?"

"I saw to it myself," Jamal responded.

"Then you won't mind if I take a second look?"

"Suit yourself."

Rufus then combed the room for any electronic listening devices, while the others greeted one another solemnly, feeling the burden of the occasion and escalating tension between themselves and the law enforcement agencies. FBI director, J. Edgar Hoover, had come out and called the Black Panthers "The most dangerous threat to the internal security of the United States." As such, they felt the noose tightening. And this high strategy conference was long overdue.

They wore black berets with a button of a springing Panther attached; some wore quarter length leather jackets, powder blue turtlenecks and black slacks. Others, like Rufus, wore jeans. Percival wore a safari jacket and planters' hat which, once seated, he parked under his chair.

There were a few present who would later be arrested in a conspiracy plot and become infamously known as the New York Panthers 21! One of them was Bob Collier, who took a seat on a corner windowsill overlooking the street below, as the Sun began to tilt westward in the afternoon sky. It was Saturday, the day after school had let out for summer and the street below was filled with children; and their whoops sporadically entered the room through open windows. Collier attentively observed the street, the cars, passersby's, idlers, and frequently scanned the rooftops across the way, sighting an armed Panther standing watch from a rooftop, while missing little else of what was occurring in the room.

Others who would be counted among the 21 were Lumumba Shakur, one of the original organizers of the New York Panthers; and Michael 'Cetewayo' Tabor, an urban guerilla theoretician, as well as Sekou Odinga, Defense Captain of the Bronx branch of the Panthers, who would elude pursuit and go into exile. Afeni Shakur, Lumumba's common law wife, also counted among the 21, could little abide "whitey," as she commonly referred to Caucasians and could be quite voluble on the subject, but on this occasion she was meditatively silent: She had recently learned that she was pregnant and was distressed by the thought of bringing a child into this troubled world. She saw life as a war zone—that was her experience of it—and felt herself on a kamikaze mission.

She was also, as were most ghetto blacks, self-conscious of her education or lack thereof. Although she had attended Music and Arts— one of the city's finer and more integrated schools—she found she could not quite 'fit in,' for, as she'd admit, "I was one fucked-up chick." She would briefly attend City College as well. She was also ill at ease expressing herself dialectically. She was no less suspicious of syllogisms; sensing both to be tricks of scholasticism.

As such, she felt both anger and resentment at the inadequate education received in the primary schools she'd attended growing up in ghetto settings— which stifle imagination and centers the 'Will' on resentment, malice and rage, inciting revenge! All her primary grade teachers, with few exceptions, were white, and believed their students incapable of learning, stigmatizing them. Hence, they trained them as opposed to teaching them, with an insistence on conformity. Foremostly knowing their proper place in *polite* society. Moreover, that is, *white* society!

As a result of such fine an education most of these revolutionaries were graduates from some of the more brutal street gangs in the city such as the Bishops, Chaplains, Sinners, Cheyennes, etc. Some had spent years behind bars for gang related activities, including murder. But that which had attracted them to the Party was the undercurrent of social reform sweeping the nation, and could not be divorced from the vast student movement, the free speech movement, which had its roots in the California "Berkley Campus" and had spread like wildfire across the country, hopping from University to University, inflaming the minds and hearts of Black Panther founders Huey P. Newton, Minister Of Defense, and Bobby Seale, Chairman, two college students from the California ghetto of Oakland. Coupled with the Civil Rights Movement and burgeoning Peace Movement, the infection spread into the ghettos and inspired it's youth, as the rebellious students proved to the disenfranchised, "lumpen proletariat" – as the Panthers classified themselves – that they were not at all wrong in their conviction that the prevailing social order had singled them out for persecution and/ or genocide – as evidenced by the devastation the illegal and immoral Vietnam war was having on the black American male population against which Dr. Martin L. King Jr., had lent the moral authority of his voice, and that their initial impulse to rebel was more than justifiable (but sanity itself). Thus liberated, inspired by Malcolm X's heroic example, these otherwise criminal types found a meaningful outlet for their aggression and, through the Black Panther Party, a means of expressing a nobility of spirit hitherto unknown to them. Hence, they could say, in the words of Franz Fanon,

"Toward a new humanism.

Understanding among men.

Our colored brothers.

Mankind, I love you." That despite Nietzsche's denying "Mankind's existence," in the first place. And to this very cause they would give "the last full measure of devotion." They had thought of themselves as outside the Church beyond God's grace and in the devil's clutches. Therefore they chose revolution as an alternate course of redemption. Revolutionaries, yes, criminals no more! It was surprising how learned, politically astute and versed in Marx these jail house scholars were; but Malcolm, of course, had been their inspiration and they saw themselves, not so much through their own eyes but his. That is, through the grave. They thought of themselves as Malcolm's heirs. And in prison they had learned to bend the back of books, as had Malcolm before them; and straighten their own backs in the process. At times their polemics would slip into the garrulous slang of the jail yard and would, no doubt, have caused Marx to blush but, most assuredly, he would have approved of their revolutionary zeal.

The Panthers also counted among its members scholars, PhDs', and professionals from various fields; people such as Joan Bird, an RN who was there at the strategy conference and would be numbered among the 21, as well as Clark Squire, a teacher. Ali Khan, defense captain of the Queens branch of the Panthers, and the largest group in the city. A later addition was Curtis Powell, a physicist. All were attracted to the Panthers for different reasons, but the prevailing motivation was that the Civil Rights Movement was singly a southern strategy and not applicable in a northern setting where blacks were corralled in "colonies," as said Minister Of Defense, Huey P. Newton, "inside the mother country," and dehumanized by the socio/political economic structure of racism enforced by an occupying brutal police force.

There was also, at bottom, a deep-seated conviction that capitalism was the root cause of their subjugation and with its removal all other chains would likewise fall away. However, it was felt that capitalism was so deeply ingrained in the pathology of the nation that, as Ali Khan said, "It's a malignancy that's got'a be surgically rooted out of the people's belief system."

All the New York Defense Captains with their Lieutenants were present along with a few others whose observations, it was thought, might prove useful, such as Percival. They sat on folding chairs in a semi-circle round Jamal and a secretary, Rosemary Bird, Joan Bird's cousin. The atmosphere was bleak, almost funereal, as they waited with pressing urgency for the meeting to commence.

Rufus could find no listening device, and so Jamal called the meeting to order:

"All power to the people," he said, saluting them with raised fist.

"Panther power to the revolution," they chanted in unison, fists high.

"Thank you for coming. It's been harrowing," Jamal resumed, a tremolo in his tone. He appeared far too overwrought for someone of his age, seventeen, trying to balance the pans of revolution on his narrow shoulders. He balled a hand into a fist to stifle a yawn. His bleary eyes roved back and forth over all their faces: all of whom were older than he, though not by much, and any one of them was far better suited to chair *this* emergency, high stakes meeting— as far as he was concerned: that is, all the defense captains and their lieutenants were collected under one roof at the same time and thereby subject to unwanted, premature exposure to the police, which was undesirable while trying to gain a toehold in their respective communities. Therefore, Rufus' caution was not unwarranted. High risk or no, this meeting was a calculated necessity. And since Chairman Bishop had been inconvenienced by the police and was not able to attend, the chair had fallen to Jamal as second in command, after Lakey, of the Brooklyn branch of the Black Panther Party. Though he felt at sea, he could not find a trace of objection on any of their faces to his raw, untested youth. He finally said, wading in somewhat self-consciously, "I know some of you come from upstate and have got to get back as soon as possible. I also know we're all plagued by various difficulties, but it's my hope we might be able to be of use to each other, as we move forward. Let's get to it!

"Since Lakey's bust last week, the pigs have been swarming 'bout like flies on shit; doing all they can to harass, disrupt and intimidate," he said angrily, fearfully, spittle flying, his adolescent voice cracking under the strain. Then, too, everyone else in the room was under similar a strain, intimidated, uncertain of the cruel fate that awaited them: uncertain though that fate maybe they knew, no doubt, it would prove cruel. "We can't move without the pigs sniffing 'r asses." He continued in despair, "they're questioning our neighbors like Gestapo, approaching our landlords; trying to kick us in to the streets – roll us like stumble bums out into the gutter," he said, a snag in his voice. "They've been coming down on us with everything they got; trying to push us out of existence!

"Just the other day, for example, at a hearing for Lakey, in a downtown Brooklyn Court House, after we'd been searched for weapons, and knowing damn well we were unarmed, the pigs jumped us in the corridors and proceeded to club us without mercy, with undue provocation. They clobbered us 'n clobbered us, landing some of us in the hospital. We fought back but suffered head wounds and contusions in the fracas. The pigs fought us with nightsticks, while we only had our fists," he said, angered to tears. "Not just vamping on us, attacking us openly. They've been calling in markers, reminding the reactionary element in the community of the side on which their bread is buttered," he said, his face damp, anxious. "And we're having a hell of a time getting a toehold in the community. Which puts us in kind of a nether land –"

"Excuse me," Percival broke in, and though gaunt, bloodless and sallow from grief, his face was known by all. "That assessment's not altogether accurate; the people 'r more mistrustful of us than not. Why be surprised by that? We're in the process of finding 'r footing even as we speak. Few of us 'r veterans here. We're learning as we go. The only advantage we've got over the community's suspicions of us is that we're something new; something they've not seen before; 'n the base animosity they feel for cops or 'pigs.' But if we allow Lakey to go down, we'll 'ave confirmed their worst suspicions of us," he said, his voice hollow as a crypt.

Since the loss of Racine and Dakota, the two great loves of his life, his soul lay in ashes, and left him in a state of near mental despair; his heart rend with unconscious melancholy. When he and Racine had first met they were both in such deep personal pain that they had missed seeing each other for who the other truly was. Hence they sniffed each other out like dogs in heat and commenced to rut, more fiercely than passionately; despite racial difference or because of it. What did it mean? More's the pity, it didn't much matter anymore anyway. Except, of course, that he was left alone to endure the vacuum of her absence, along with Dakota's, her child; lost to the world and from him forevermore. Consequently he was forced to summon all the forces at his disposal to hold himself intact. But for that which most grounded him in reality, flooded his blood and brains, was rage at the unacceptable barbarity of life; the injustice of it; the brutally idiotic, unsparing and irreducible cruelty of it. In addition, he bore the unresolved burden of his son, Malek, with deep resentment. He was not feeling the least bit religious of late. Indeed, he was at odds with God and all his angles, and he was just as eager to storm the citadels of hell. Ergo, he was in distress; in agony of mind and heart. He wanted to rage but restrained himself with near superhuman effort. He had lost control once too often, particularly his slipping at the Olympic Trials. He recalled Punchy having said, 'You lose control, you lose!' And he had grown unaccustomed to losing and had no wish to lose again:

"There's a woman's issue here we can't escape," said Percival. "As I see it, Lakey's not Huey but she is New York," he said with outstretched hands, recalling to mind, (ashamed of himself for it), how badly he had mistreated Racine when she had loved him beyond all others. "'N I ask, if she were a man would we let her take the fall without raising a hue 'n cry? I mean, we're raising money hand over fist for Huey, 'n rightly so, yet, at the same time, we're losing 'r members here in New York, on the east coast, 'n let me say that it's no incentive for future members to risk their necks for Huey if we're not gonna risk r's for each other," he said, craning his neck, looking at Jamal between the heads and shoulders of two Captains seated ahead of him. "If we can't spring Lakey, we should not allow her to go down without the community knowing we're four square behind her, dig? We must face up to 'r obligations to her, which is 'r revolutionary duty." And, as he concluded, his voice rising, "I mean, how can we call ourselves a vanguard party if, by that, we mean for the men to advance to the front of the bus while 'r women continue to ride in the back?"

"The brother has a point," said Bob Collier from his window perch, where, with a glance, he could see Jamal over the heads of all those in the room. A plume of smoke swirled from a cigarette in his mouth and wreathed his head in a blue haze then wafted out the window in tatters, at his back. He swiveled his head like a bird of prey. One felt that he had spent a lifetime sniffing out cops. He was a scholarly, stern face, clean shaven, cream-colored man of mixed blood and average height; full, not thick lips, and eyes the color of copper pennies. He seldom smiled. At a time when most young black men were sporting Afros,' he wore his hair customarily short. There was an unparalleled strength in the overall contour of his bearing. Although he appeared more the solid citizen than a crazed Bolshevik, he was no one you'd wish to cross. Philosophically he was a nihilist more than a socialist, a conviction he embraced because it gave voice to a revolutionary impulse born of an estrangement suffered at the hands of his countrymen. He plucked the near-finished cigarette from his teeth and flicked the flaming butt out the window to the near empty street below. "When I was in Cuba back in '64," he went on to say with a shrewd, amused, speculation in his eyes, "the women's issue was a burning one 'n everywhere you went women were on equal footing with men." Bob had returned from Cuba singing its praises and extolling its successes. And everyone to whom he spoke was impressed save, of course, the F.B.I. He was arrested and indicted on conspiracy to "blow up The Statue of Liberty, The Liberty Bell, and The Washington Monument.," respectively. The relationship to Cuba was never made. Nevertheless, he was sentenced to ten years in prison, subsequently released after serving two, and became one of the co-founders of the New York Black Panthers.

"It's good to hear some strong brothers voicing such concerns," Joan Bird, petite, tan and with a full-blown Afro, spoke up, smiling secretly. She had never felt so self-assured as in the company of these Panthers; these righteous black brothers. "It's nice to hear brothers refer to sisters with such regard, like we count!" She paused, then resumed, "We black women have been, from day one, at the forefront of our people's struggle for freedom, from Harriet Tubman to Sojourner Truth to Rosa Parks and now sister Lakey Sako." She opened her eyes speculatively wide and, with a wistful smile, draped her arms as would a swan its wings on descent; or, for that matter, when as a girl she'd dreamt of becoming a primer ballerina and performing in Tchaikosky's "Swan Lake," at Lincoln Center. But, as she would come to learn, for ghetto blacks, life seldom delivered on such dreams. Nevertheless, youth is 'the stuff on which dreams are made.' As such, Dr. King shared his dream with the world, and was killed for his trouble. Regardless, it gave heart to both the hopeless and downtrodden. And more than a few were in that room that day—of whom Joan was one. Joan's fingers fluttered birdlike, then came to rest in the folds of her lap as she said in conclusion. "It's also good to remember that in Vietnam the Vietcong women are fighting side by side with their men and have done so traditionally for centuries."

"Don't suggest for a moment I want to see Lakey in jail," Jamal responded over the outside street noise, his swarthy face nervous, a young man roused to passion. "The simple fact is, we don't have a fucking bail fund. Why hell, we barely got enough money to keep our door open. We don't have any means by which to stage a response!"

"That's a problem we're all faced with," Cetewayo interposed, with a scowl of displeasure on his boyishly rude lips. He was a roguishly good-looking youth with flecks of red diffused throughout his otherwise sable complexion; his eyes were those of liquid melanite set within a prominent brow, that betokened an underlying, acute intelligence, made more so for its roots, the Harlem ghetto. He wore a bushy Afro adorned with a barrette to which a "Free Huey" button was attached. He further said, surveying the faces of those around him, "The pigs 'r fully aware of the fact that we've not had time to build a network as yet with the outside radical community 'n that's why they're vamping on us so hard, so fast, dig?" he said coolly, deliberately, jabbing the air with a purposeful forefinger. "They don't want us to get 'r act together for the good reason they've seen what's going on in Oakland 'n they want'a stop us before we can produce a community consciousness that'll develop into a true community liberation."

"Right on, Cetewayo," agreed Zayd Shakur, Lumumba's younger brother, a bantamweight who looked more like an African poet than a revolutionary, with his intelligent bovine eyes, Fu Manchu beard and mustache, and hair braided in corn rows. "They must stop us now or the snowball effect will be much too much for them to deal with down the line."

"Hell, let's face it," said Rufus shrilly, his inflamed ego an eternal source of agony, "right now, as it stands, we've little else to offer 'r people but sacrifice of 'r lives!"

"What an awful waste of life if we can't first teach 'r people how to live," Percival forcibly interjected.

"You hold the key to such knowledge do you?"

"You know damn well what I mean."

"What 'r people need to fucking learn is the power of the gun," Rufus wrathfully exploded.

"No! Rufus, no! We want to transform 'r communities into desirable places in which to live 'n raise 'r children. Oasis' of hope, learning, worship, art, music, thought; hotbeds of culture such as was Ethiopia's, Timbuktu's, Mali's 'n Egypt's. Civilizations in which 'r people flowered 'n passed on the fruits of their labor to a thankless world before they'd passed out of memory, history, 'n existence. A song they gave birth to which, for their descendants lost on these shores, became 'The Blues.' In short, we want communities in which 'r people may live healthy, productive lives. Somewhere we can live in dignity 'n pride of place." He weighed his next words carefully, with a stony face, and said, "If, other than folk lore, 'r stolen past can't be restored us, then the rights 'n privileges of 'r humanity must. For this I'm willing to fight, but to jus' shoot cops? 'Pigs,' as you say. That's meaningless. Uh-uh. If death is the outcome of my decision to fight, then I'll accept it. Otherwise, no! I mean, if I'm gonna do this I have to justify it to myself, 'n killing 'pigs' isn't justification enough," said Percival wryly, his forehead restless. "I'm not interested in adding another body to the death count. We've done much to much dying as is, both sides of the divide."

"Neither is it justification enough for any of us," Joan Bird piped. "And I don't believe, for a moment, Rufus meant it quite that way."

"I'm jus' saying," said Rufus, "we can't escape the gun!"

"That's the dreaded truth of it," said Zayd forthrightly.

"The danger's real enough," Bob Collier said. "The gun is an inescapable fact of American life. It's the cornerstone on which this nation stands; without which there is no country. Violence 'n violence alone gave birth to the United States. As H. Rap Brown reminds us, ''Violence is as American as cherry pie!'"

"And the ongoing threat of violence sustains it. This I know," Percival admitted.

"Impossible!" Rufus threw up his hands. "For a fighter you've one heck of a pacifist streak," he sullenly balked.

"We're struggling against impossible odds, so why not dream it? If we happen to prevail—all the better."

"You're an idealist," said Ali Khan mirthfully.

"Would you be doing this if you weren't?" Percival reposted. "Isn't everyone who's advanced the cause of freedom one iota not an idealist? Including the founding fathers who failed in its execution which brings us to this bitter pass?"

"Touché," sang Ali Khan off key.

"Yes, I want the cops off 'r backs too—primarily, however, I want a life worth living, dig? What I'm hoping for, what we're doing is trying to enrich 'r people's lives, help make their passage from crib to grave more bearable 'n less grievous; so we're not short changed at every turn," Percival reposted, looking at Rufus with furious exasperation. There were times he didn't like Rufus very much, and this was proving to be one of them.

"Boxing's a dangerous game but not half so dangerous as what we're trying to do here; but it'll prove especially more ruinous, for all concerned, if we fail. Then again boxing's not meant, like socialist revolution to produce, along with control of the means of production, a living art form such as only the humanities can 'n revolution must in order to justify itself," he arguably said! "Let me tell you it's never easy entering a ring but, when you do, baby, it's for yourself 'n on mutual terms. On the other hand, when passing through that door it's not for me but for 'r people," he gestured to the doorway on which they all swung expectant eyes. "It's to address 'r concerns, the wrongs done us. The dreams destroyed! The lives crushed under boot 'n heel! We're sacrificing too much to accept anything short of 'r self-worth, dig? If it's to be done by the gun, then let it be the gun. But don't forget the gun no less than the sword, must biblically if not dialectically," he coughed, "Ug-ugh, be beaten into plow sheers, if we 'r to achieve 'r ends.

"We must extract from this pseudo, godawful culture that has stolen 'r birthrights, killing 'r Souls from early on, from crib to grave. Apparently, as if 'r lives aren't worth a damn – sucking from 'r core all the love 'n joy life has to offer. Making 'r lives, as Hobbs put it, 'brutish, cruel and short.' Sad to say, the powers that be 'r content to keep it that way! We must look to ourselves, draw from the reservoir of Self a culture of life! We must look elsewhere. I'd worked at the Museum of Modern Art for a few years," he said, without making mention of Rufus. "And in that period it taught me, culturally speaking that the West is barren; has nothing to offer and I don't just mean artistically either. As Pop savant Andy Warhol puts it, 'Everybody's gonna be famous for fifteen minutes.' And this bourgeois, Micky Mouse culture's run its course!"

They laughed lustily with full throated gusto.

"Or, more precisely, as Poet Laureate Allen Ginsberg asks, 'America, why are your libraries so full of tears?'" He halted, then went on, "It's a people's culture to which we must appeal! We must look beyond the cultural norms; the cultural matrix. And face the fact that this culture is dead to us! A blind alley! A fucking cul-de-sac! We must resort to 'r own devices, 'r inner senses. We must create a new culture. A society in which there is no need for charity, dig! We must strive to create wholesome communities in which to live. Communities which enhance life, foster life, nurture a love for life, a reverence for life, 'n all too clearly, this culture does not. This, all too sadly, is a culture of death which we must struggle against while, at the same time, harbor no wish to emulate," he said, addressing Rufus directly, who rolled and banked his eyes like dice, snake eyes, toward the center of his nose. "Neither should the State be richer than any of its citizens nor any citizen richer than the State! We need something like an egalitarian society where hopefully, the GNP falls nothing short of happiness and, of course, Soul survival since happiness, of itself, is not the fulfillment of life. No doubt, love expresses itself in happiness, joy 'n wellbeing. However, the true spirit of freedom is the liberty of a rational order reflected in the common good. We must, in our efforts, work to establish a community of man right here, right now, on these shores. The only purpose of a State is to ensure the wellbeing of all its citizens without prejudice! That should be the aim of governance, otherwise it's a cold hearted 'n predatory sham. As such, America is a criminal state. Huey didn't overlook this, but anticipated it, where, in the ten-point program he wrote: 'We want land, bread, housing, education, clothing, justice and peace.' The means by which one may obtain, as the Declaration of Independence assures us, 'Life, Liberty and the pursuit of happiness.' N that, in sum, baby, is what this struggle's about for me!"

He was roundly applauded.

"Well said," Clark Squire intoned. "Well said!"

"As it is for us all," Joan Bird chanted, facing Percival; intrigued by his cunning, ruthlessly fierce, animal beauty. She watched, electrified, as a storm subsided in his face. "You've the soul of a true revolutionary; it is the spirit of educating our people, heeding the words of Che, who was a physician. Yes," she raised a hand to her brow, once again facing round, smiling, her earrings catching the light, "I'm a nurse. And it's my business to heal, and so I've had to discard, for the moment, my pills, thermometer, and stethoscope, and take up the gun – as did Che before me – not so much to kill as to cure – that is the foul nature of the diseased society in which we live. As Dr. King often observed the closer he came to death. I, for one, have seen too much in my twenty-one years, to wait and watch anymore. It's easier, in all honesty, to become a full-fledged revolutionary. I no longer wish to endorse the criminality of this country. The wrongs perpetrated against so many people in its name. I don't want it on my conscience!" She said, "I've since come to believe in the need of a communist state; and I don't mean the kind of communism Russia became under Stalin and is today." She sneered, "that is no more than a form of state capitalism!" She nervously laughed. "But I think something more Christian is required," she said, with forced hope. "I mean, the soul of socialism is inarguably Christian. The failure of socialism in Russia and China today is they're no respecters of the intangible in man; much as, in the same way, capitalism deadens the spirit of Christianity with its system of organized greed." She stated, looking steadily at Jamal. Her words were polite, respectful, but their significance was unmistakable. Jamal shifted his gaze uneasily. "If, as Huey says, 'The spirit of the people is greater than the man's technology,' it's because Huey recognizes something of the primacy of spirit over the physical. And that is: materialism is not the primary substance of life but soul force must enter the equation. It would seem," she went on, shifting in her seat to face the others, "Dr. King's recognition of socialism evolved out of his religious perspective, as did that of brother Malcolm's. And it's these intangibles, as expressed through the humanities, as Percival said, which can't go overlooked as we address the social issues which plague our communities on a day-to-day basis."

A silence followed in which the room filled with smoke, and cigarette after cigarette flared up. Percival observed Rufus as he inhaled, filling his lungs tentatively, sucking as if on a stick of marijuana. Rufus felt Percival's eyes on him and so cast a quick, cutting glance his way, then faced away with a look of base envy, smoke curling from his nostrils and lips. There was something brutal in his expression from which Percival shrank, and, looking back, raised his head. He crossed his legs at the ankles, folded his hands in his lap, and watched the smoke spiral ceiling wards in a blue haze. He did not smoke but had grown accustomed to being among smokers in the Army. He observed the haze in melancholic reflection: There was something eerily reminiscent of the Army in all this, something hopeful beyond measure yet, in a word, painfully sad; something which he could not hope to recover; something most certainly lost among his fellows; something he wished he had been able to salvage but, sad to say, was no more than a boyish dream, a vacant longing.

Unlike the Paratroopers where there had been a strong sense of bonhomie, esprit de corps, among the Panthers there were few deep friendships struck. Then again, the military was, at bottom, a boy's last hurrah, whereas with these Panthers, retrieving their manhood from out the desolation of the American void, their lives (to that moment) a crap shoot, could not be otherwise – given the inescapable dilemma facing them; and went a long way in explaining his relationship to Rufus. Wrote Eldridge Cleaver, "I've entered the den and seized my balls from the teeth of a roaring lion." Where, on the contrary, Percival was easily at home with the lion – the lion being his shadow self – hence, to scratch the one was to wrong the other. In short, he felt favored in a way Rufus did not: he felt his manhood, that elusive, indefinable something or other, intact, his balls secure, despite the fact that his life, to that moment, was a shambles that had brought him to this pass, seated him among this band of wooly headed revolutionaries, instead of in Mexico City where Chico Juarez, instead of him, was poised to win the Olympic Gold.

213

No, the question for him was, as it were, one of life, its meaning and value. In other words, the right to move about in society freely, unmolested and without abuse. Inarguably, as he saw it, the first principle of life is, "Nature is economical, abhors a vacuum, and is not wasteful." Therefore, contrary to the base, conventional view that, "Life does not owe you a living," the more persuasive, natural law view, "Life must owe you a living otherwise you could not exist!" And the New Testament substantiates that proposition where, in the words of Jesus, it says, "Behold the fowl of the air: for they sow not, neither do they reap, nor gather into barns; yet your heavenly father feedeth them. Are you not much better than they?

"And why take ye thought for raiment" Consider the lilies of the field, how they grow; they toil not, neither do they spin:

"And yet I say unto you, that even Solomon in all his glory was not arrayed like one of those.

"Wherefore, if God so clothe the grass of the field, which today is, and tomorrow is cast into the oven, shall he not much more clothe you, O ye of little faith?" Hence, lack of sufficiency is artificially produced for the benefit of the few and the regret of the many.

It was solely because of his ability as a fighter that he had become accustomed to being held in high esteem and that he had mistaken, until going south, freedom of movement his due but, in the deep south, he had come to learn otherwise, and it had scarred him like only first-hand experience can and left an indelible mark on his soul, blemishing his notion of citizenship: He had left the Army, the paratroopers, and gone south with the best and brightest of his generation and courage and convictions of their youth and the promise of democracy that had gathered on the eve of social reform, the likes of which the nation had not seen since the close of the Civil War. Yes, the children of his generation, inspired by the King, Kennedy and Johnson years, had gone south to liberate, once and for all, the down trodden, long suffering, disenfranchised blacks, laboring under the yoke of racial oppression; their feet held to the flames by their brutish redneck neighbors who gave them no quarters and were as wont to snuff out their lives as that of a candle. And when they left the south, more tattered and torn than crowned in glory, disillusioned, the inner cities of the north had burst aflame and the nightmare of racism in America had come full circle. In addition, the war in Vietnam had spiraled out of control and the citizenry split over the issue; and he, along with others who had gone south to work for social reform, picked sides. Needless to say they chose to join ranks with the then fledgling Peace Movement. Hence a moral dilemma engulfed the land.

"…the main cause'a 'r people's suffering," Lumumba was saying, drawing Percival, lost in thought, back to the present, "is as racial as it is economical." He righted himself noisily in his seat, his tone one of urgency, "We're low man on the totem. 'N as the saying goes, 'las hired/ first fired.' Hell, if we'd been granted the forty acres 'n a mule after the Civil War, as rightly we should ave, we'd be the backbone of the American middle class," he said, smoke trickling from nostrils and mouth. "Why, hell, it's possible we could even have had a black president 'n, in the process, spare 'r red brothers from the genocidal westward expansion. In short, westward white colonial sprawl! Based on that denial, black folks have become the backbone'a the American underclass, the criminal class—the folly underpinning the hypocrisy on which this country's founded!"

He took a noisily long drag on his cigarette, flicked the fiery ash to the floor and ground it out underfoot. He snorted derisively, snatched off his dark, wire rimmed glasses and his eyes flashed dangerously. He had formerly been War Lord of the notorious South Bronx street gang, the Bishops, before converting, in prison, to the revolutionary doctrine espoused by Malcolm X, Franz Fanon, Che, Mao, Marx, and finally the Black Panther Party quick to recognize his organizational skills. His street name, "Shotgun," was known and feared from South Philly to Harlem, and on all the inner-city streets between. The New York City Police were fully aware of him and, as a result, would contrive to remove him from the streets at their earliest convenience. He leaned forward his forehead creased with concern. He stroked his tawny beard. "We weren't granted the forty acres 'n a mule 'cause the reactionary forces nipped it in the bud; 'n with the assassination of Lincoln, they subverted the political process to their ends. Had America realized that coup, that opportunity, the economics of the country would invariably 'ave swung towards socialism." As he spoke anger knitted his brow, his voice filled with rage, vengeance and love, the Oceanic depth of the American Negro despair. "Up till the end of the Civil War capitalism's enforced slavery 'n it's enforced racism ever since!

"No, not until capitalism, that which brought slavery about 'n the genocide of 'r red brothers, has been rooted out of the socio/political 'n economic life of the country will racism in all its myriad forms vanish. No, not until then! For generations now we've been the sacrificial offering on the altar of American capitalism. It's high time we let 'em know, with fist 'n guns if need be, that it's no longer acceptable, " he argued. "We're now playing by a whole new set of rules; dealing from a whole fresh deck of cards. We're putting the man on notice. We're calling his jive ass bluff. Or, as Eldredge says, 'Stick em up mother fucker this is a showdown!'"

"Right on! Right on!" They clamored in accord, heartened by his fiery oratory.

"While we persist in 'r war with the oppressive pig power structure, we must implement programs that'll improve the day t'day quality of r peoples lives," he pressed forcefully ahead, his teeth gleaming moistly. "We got'a demonstrate how effective socialism can be in solving 'r economic woes, you dig? Now this might seem to 'ave little to do with Lakey, but this is the key: to let the people know what she was really working toward, the bringing of these socialist ideals to fruition for the sake of the community 'n, at the same time, let 'em know how capitalism's been crucifying us, as a people, in the g'd awful name of the American dream.' 'N finally we must, as Che advocates, 'Create three, four 'n five Vietnams.' In a word, we must turn the ghettos of America into breeding grounds for revolution!"

"Uhuru! Uhuru! I hear you! I hear you!" said Rufus loudly, pumping his fist frantically. A deadly smile played on his rude lips; as well he wore a hard pressed, demented cross-eyed stare. Rufus' dementia was not peculiar to himself and would show up, if not so acutely, among other members of the Party. All of these Panthers, including Percival, had been bitten by the rabid dog of racism—an affliction that cut both ways and made for a rancorous culture, "A house divided." However, as Percival saw it he was not so much scarred by racism as he was colored by it. "Let's turn every slum in the land into another Vietnam," said Rufus stoutly. "Off the pig!

"Right on! Right on!" All sang.

We have crossed the line from which there is no retreat," Percival woefully thought, heart racing at a gallop. He suspected he now knew how the American founding fathers must have felt in their struggle for independence as colonist against the British Empire, of which it was said, "The sun never sets!"

The Panthers situation was as hopelessly similar to that of the American revolutionist two centuries earlier in their quest for independence, of whom Benjamin Franklin forewarned, "Gentlemen, we must hang together for surely we shall hang separately." This was indeed revolution!

"While resistance is necessary prudence is, at first, advisable," Joan said in a calm, restraining tone of voice. "Remember, we're not in this for ourselves but for our people. We're here to serve the people. We're servants of the people!"

Then in a sudden burst of enthusiasm, their spirits high, all the other voices in the room, cascading one over the other in a torrent, spoke out at once, each wanting to single-handedly jump start the revolution. The tasks they'd taken to themselves, which in the end would prove their undoing, despite Herculean efforts, was more than revolutionary but Promethean: They had labored under the yoke of oppression all their lives and felt, as such, they had everything to gain and nothing to lose as Marx had written but "their chains." Consequently they would persist in this near fatalistic venture. This, for them, was "The Alamo," a "Dance Macabre," a fateful last stand; the high cost of their shared humanity!

Jamal wiped his brow and raised his voice above the clamor, trying to restore order. Gradually they quieted, then raised their hands at once. Cetewayo was recognized: "Let's face it, the pigs got Lakey dead to right 'n she's bound to do some serious time – no two ways about it. It's not like a conspiracy rap that's as difficult to prove as not. They caught her with the goods. She's a righteous soldier of the people's army, a true revolutionary, 'n should be accorded every privilege of a P.O.W., if not a political prisoner, you know? In other words, we got'a get it across that not only is she a peoples soldier opposing the racist forces of the pig power structure but she's also a servant of the people 'n was working to introduce educational programs; breakfast programs for kids; medical programs; job programs for all the people – follow? That she was striving to help the community help itself, 'n so break the debilitating cycle of dependency on the man!"

"That's tactically sound, especially since it's also true," Clark Squire rejoined, to which the cadre all concurred with a rousing, "Right on!"

"We'd then best get these programs going," said Joan on being recognized by the chair. She also offered to head up the medical program. Percival offered to introduce her to Dr. Osgood, whose reputation as a physician and tactician was equally legendary. "Yes," Joan claimed, "I've heard of her. You know her? I'd very much like to meet her."

Clark Squire offered to put together an educational program, a 'University of The Streets,' as he referred to it. Clark stood. Those ahead turned in their seats to face him. He was tall and lanky with multiple races at play in his features, including native American. "I'll be happy to take that responsibility on," he spoke slowly, melodiously, trying to shed the remnants of a Texas drawl. "I know some rather 'hip' professors from both Columbia 'n City College who'll find it right up their alley. These 'cats' have worked in both the Civil Rights 'n Peace Movement, 'r trying to find an 'in' in the black struggle. It's an idea long in coming. They'll jump at it.

"It'll also be another way of reaching the brothers 'n sisters on the block, too, who'll be glad to share their views with some 'down' professors, cats who can hear where they're coming from. Not home boys but educators who'll take 'em as they come—at face value. I look forward to working on such a project. As an educator, myself, I witness too much of what Tolstoy observed when he said of primary school: 'It's like watching children drown.' But if, as

217

adolescents 'n young adults, they feel free to walk in off the street at any given time, in an open environment, as the idea 'University of the Street' suggest, they'll come.

"It's imperative we get these programs up 'n running; they're the only defense we have against the governmental forces arrayed against us. These programs will, more than anything, explain us better than everything else. Our value to the community will be recognized without 'r having to say too much. The programs will explain themselves, as well as who we 'r 'n what we're trying to accomplish.

"Most of 'r children don't learn by rote—how they're taught in school. Our's is an oral tradition not a written one, as the blues exemplifies; otherwise 'r story would be little known. It is in the blues 'n genius of jazz that we come closest to realizing the truth of our story. What we know best is still orally transmitted: What we primarily learn of ourselves comes from the pulpit of 'r black churches. With few exceptions, however, the preacher-man, more often than not, delivers 'r souls up to Jesus but hands 'r bodies over to the 'man!' Nevertheless, the black-preacher is still very much a part of 'r oral tradition. Whereas the school curricula has nothing to offer in terms of black history, oral or otherwise, except, of course, to say, 'Lincoln freed the slaves.' We 'r all outcasts in this society, 'n share little in common beyond a mutual loss of identity. An identity pitilessly stolen from us. A fate worse than amnesia that bonds us together as surely as shackles on a bondsman's legs! What brings us together if not for 'r shackles? Bonds us as strangers perhaps, but bonds us nonetheless! I mean, I don't know your name any more than you know mine! Bear with me, I know it's been a long meeting," Clark said to effect, revising their waning spirits.

The gathering had proven tedious and the strain was borne out on the brows and faces of all, as they groped to shake the lethargy that had befallen them over the wearying course of hours. They righted themselves in their seats and struggled to remain alert. Clark continued,

"Malcolm X shook off his slave name, 'Little,' in favor of the anonymous 'X,' in his search for identity.' It emasculates—cuts you at the balls 'n brands you as property—their property!" said Clark, decidedly. "Similarly speaking, that's exactly what James Baldwin's essay, 'Nobody knows my name,' is about—loss of 'r historical 'n cultural roots. The engine of one's identity; the steam of one's life. 'N all 'r survival skills have been impaired as a result. Which explains the conditions in which we survive, there is a deep intuitive sense of not belonging that's produced a long 'n jagged scar in 'r collective psyche—as long 'n wide as the Mississippi river 'n Nile combined. It's produced a spiritual gulf that the Christian God, for all his walking on water, can't bridge. There is no 'soul' without 'a manhood;' nor chance for a 'humanity' without the 'man.' Our Minister of Information, Eldredge Cleaver appropriately said, 'We shall have our manhood; we shall have it or the earth will be leveled by our attempts to regain it.' A manhood this country has historically denied us, 'n a womanhood wounded by the loss. Yes, we're struggling for 'r manhood, without which we can't hope to retrieve 'r collective lost 'soul!'

Clark worked the room no less efficiently than had the parish minister worked the conger-grants of his small Baptist Church from the pulpit, with fiery sermons of hellfire come Sunday morning service back home in the Texas Panhandle where he came of age.

"Hence the uselessness of knowledge, of a formal education, it can't restore us 'r souls—'r birthright! 'r heritage! We must find another way to engage the imagination, as Percival said, 'n the 'University of the Streets' in keeping with that ideal.

"For the women among us, I want you to know when I say 'men' I don't mean it as 'a male chauvinist pig' thing; as a guy-on-top-gal-on-bottom, missionary position sorta thing. Before we were brought here, to these accursed shores, before we'd been shackled 'n put to the 'mill stone' under the lash; before we were denied 'r traditional roles in society as men; denied the traditional rights observed all across Africa; of all African peoples 'n cultures, before we were denied the rights of protecting 'r women, providing for 'r families, before we were denied the right to speak out against the wrongs that afflict us, educate 'r children, 'n stand up for 'r community 'n cultural identity. But in this country, ever since, it's been anything but. We've not been allowed to provide for or protect 'r women 'n families. Instead we've been stripped of every vestige of manhood; of dignity or human worth! No, it's not to deny women anything, I say this, but to give black women back their men; their husbands; their sons; their brothers. We've been cajoled by the caprice of the apparatus of the State. There's been a concerted effort these past five hundred years to strip us of every vestige of 'r humanity, 'r identity! In the words of William Cullen Bryant, words Dr. King saw fit to use: 'Truth, crushed to earth, shall rise again.'

"This all starts with the proper education of 'r young, the foundation of 'r humanity; the structure of' r souls. And this system as it stands is a reflection of the emasculating process that governed slavery, 'n 'r lives, in this culture ever since! This is where education fits in; this is why the 4th point in 'r 10-point program reads, 'We want education that teaches us our history. And our role in the present-day society.' That, as much as anything, is why a

'University of the Streets' is necessary. It will not happen without 'r insistence!"

The three women present applauded warmly. And the men hollered, "By any means necessary!" then stamped their feet and clapped simultaneously.

After they'd settled back down, Sekou accepted responsibility for overseeing the children's breakfast program city wide. "We all know," he said, "without my saying, what a breakfast program will mean, particularly for 'r school age children. That's all I 'ave to say, except I'll accept as much help as I can get. Thank you."

"We've got'a beef up surveillance of the police," Rufus interjected, insisting. "No matter, the pigs 'r still the worse problem 'n biggest threat we face. Their brutality is unparalleled 'n increasing, like Huey says 'With America's build up in 'nam.' 'N they're bloody well actin' like we're the Cong!"

"That's who we 'r in their eyes," Bob Collier agreed. "They see our communities as Indian territory."

"You got problems with that?" Rufus glanced at Percival sidewise.

"I never said I had."

"Jus' checking, bro – jus' checking."

Percival smiled wryly.

The captains appointed Zayd to the position of Lt. of Information: his primary function was to keep the channels of communication open between the various branches, as well as help create a favorable image of the Panthers throughout the black community, which would certainly not prove easy. It was also decided that there should be a weekly gathering of the captains that they might bridge gaps and cement bonds between the individual branches, which, again, would not prove easy.

Jamal ventured to say, amidst a lull in the colloquy, "Some of you have trains to catch and for a first meeting this has gone overlong." He glanced at his watch, "If by chance you didn't know who we were before, you certainly can't say you don't know now—'n why we're risking so much."

A date was set for the next meeting. Jamal moved that the meeting be adjourned. It was seconded by Zayd. "All in favor?" Jamal intoned. To which the others chimed "aye," in response. The meeting was brought to a close.

Bob Collier warned, as they prepared to depart, "The pigs 'r out. I've spotted at least three unidentified cars cruising by 'n one standing down the block. 'N strangely enough the avenue's unusually clear of uniform pigs. So be careful as you go. From here on out you can be sure you've been made. 'N I don't mean by the pigs outside. It's not so much the pigs outside but the Judas in our midst who concerns me most!" Seated in the window, overlooking the street below, he scrutinized the faces of those in the room. "'N you can be sure he's with us 'cause the pigs wouldn't 'ave swept down on Lakey with a SWAT team had they not known what the hell they were after."

They eyed each other gravely, suspiciously, and, as if seeing oneself in the other for the first time, they did not feel half so sure. It was as if they had soared skywards only to find victory snatched from out their grasp. The forces arrayed against them, such as the F.B.I. and New York police, were troubling enough without finding oneself in a nest of rattlesnakes,

provocateurs. These were, indeed, the forces the Panthers were up against. As such, it gave the faint of heart an excuse to bolt. And bolt they would. Ergo, the gloves were off.

"We're gonna rely on your cooperation in this matter," Bob stated.

"Run, nigger, run," cried someone from out the ranks.

"To be forewarned is to be forearmed," Cetawayo vehemently spouted.

"A word to the wise!" Sekoue said, out of sorts.

"Be sure, whoever you 'r, that your days 'r numbered. You will be found out," Bob said with rancor, his face empurpled with rage. These Panthers were no schoolboys but revolutionaries. And as Che had made clear, "The only difference between a revolutionary and bandit is that the revolutionary educates!" That is, traitors will be shown no mercy. "You can be sure, Sekou 'n Lumumba know the ghetto scene better than most, 'n have come to analyze it in Marxian dialectical terms, 'n will be sure to smoke your funky ass out 'n deal with you according to the dictates of revolutionary justice! Your fate's as good as sealed," he said with menace. "We will not tolerate provocateurs or informants among us!" He was beside himself, "I'll be damn'd if I'm goin' back to jail or get myself killed on account of some jive-time-punk-ass-sissy motherfuckin' Judas son-of-a-bitch!"

In a calm, more conciliatory tone of voice, he went on to say, "I must say, before we go, Percival Jones', I've seen you fight in the past," he said in open admiration. "Your presence is welcome," he added. "Your work with the Peace 'n Civil Rights Movement is known to us, 'n we look forward to benefiting from your experience."

"I only hope I can be of some benefit," Percival blurted, chagrined. He felt singled out for scrutiny.

The others busied themselves shaking hands, as perchance they may not meet again. Percival shook Rufus' hand at the door. "I'll talk to you later on, bro."

"Ya walkin?"

"I ain't got that far to go."

"Watch yourself, slick."

221

"Say hi ta Lily, okay?"

"Sure thing."

And they went their separate ways.

It was well into the dinner hour and the street was deserted but for a few stragglers. Casting his glance this way and that, hat in hand, Percival took the first corner he came upon. He removed his safari jacket and tucked it under his arm and put on his planters' hat and kept a sharp look out for a tail. He took the next corner, ducked into a nearby doorway to see if anyone was trailing him. Much to his relief, he was not being followed. And with a sigh, he started home.

The meeting had been a grueling affair and had left him drained and scared. Easily more afraid than ever he could recall on having gone south to work for Civil Rights but, in that instance, fate had lent a hand and, as luck would have it, he had met, despite the treachery that lurked behind every unknown crackers scowling face, so many activist, black and white, from across the country and the array of friendships struck with students, professors; socialist; communist; idealist; clergy; atheist; share croppers, etc. And the world of ideas into which he'd entered from Plato to Sartre, Thoreau to Gandhi, Machiavelli to Jefferson, Jesus to Buddha and on and on, causing his head to swim. The spirit of non-violence had flowered, at least among the Civil Rights Workers, and thought became as vital as food. Yes, in the whirlwind activity of the Civil Rights Movement, deep in the heart of Dixie, he had encountered an entire cross section of the social spectrum and had met so many thinkers that he had often felt as if he'd been granted the privilege of having sat at the feet of Socrates – even as he took the hemlock. And those thoughts and ideas had taken possession of him, and he had inculcated them into his belief system, his Soul.

Often afterwards he had wished that it were possible to have lingered longer, in the dreamy south, in a world of ideas in which they had briefly dwelt as kinsmen and friends, even as they struggled to break the strangle hold of segregation over the south. But the cry for "Black Power," alienated white activist and soured that dream.

More so than not, the beginnings of the peace movement in the '60's drew heavily on the store of civil rights workers jaded by the experience and dubious success of integration. "You can't trust anyone over thirty," they'd spouted, and would then turn thirty themselves in turn. Percival had initially scoffed at the notion as an escape clause. An option outside of death black American's did not have. But one many white radicals employed. However, above all else, Percival was a warrior, a fighter, as was his namesake, Parzival, and it was not an option, an escape clause, open to him regardless of race. He was a man "called to action," as Racine had said, quoting from the legend, "who'll out of the welter of things grow slowly wise." A tear slid down his cheek. *If that were only so,* he thought. He missed her, her presence, the warm silken feeling of her body in bed beside his. Their love making.

Meanwhile he had to contend with the law enforcement agencies of the land. The government for which he would once have given his life had laid the foundation for their quarrel. It was bad enough that the military, as it turned out, was a racist arm of the government, but the civil rights Workers who had journeyed south in the firm belief that their cause was just and their country the standard bearer of those ideals, had nevertheless believed that the legal arm of the federal government, the justice department, would, in a pinch, come to their rescue; but they had been sorely mistaken in that assumption. Instead, the justice department, mistaking the cry for "Black Power," no better than a call for race wars, rather than that of self-determination, reacted accordingly. Perhaps it was naive of the activist to have expected otherwise. In any event, the government looked away and left them foundering in their mistaken ideals. Embittered, they left the south, lost faith in their country, their countrymen, and, far worse, one another. Alas, Percival felt cast out, cut adrift, banished, ostracized, his citizenship revoked, an outsider among outsiders, alone on his own, as were all these Panthers outsiders on their own! And for the first time in his life he found himself in full flight—running scared!

***

Percival's first week of work for The Neighborhood Youth Corps found him packed into a lower Manhattan church basement with several hundred others who would be dispersed throughout the five boroughs over the course of the summer to work with ghetto kids as crew leaders. Trying to gain a handle on the job description, they would undergo a week's orientation that would leave them more bewildered than informed.

The Director of The Ecumenical Council Of Churches (the organization through which Federal Funds for the Youth Corps were dispersed), a well-groomed black minister, started off the week with an exhaustive, self-serving oration without word of what the crew leaders, the majority of his audience, were to accomplish, or, for that matter, what was expected of them? He essentially addressed himself to the issues of the programs board, "Who were," as he said with heart felt sincerity, ". grievously underpaid. Consequentially the lack of funds ties our hands and we must often look elsewhere to compensate for the financial loss we suffer as a direct result of our dedication to the poor."

223

Between speakers, Percival addressed Estelle sottovoce: "What the hell was that?"

"He's a typical poverty pimp," she curtly replied, casting up her hands. "But reserve judgment, the weeks only begun," she added sarcastically, a deprecating smile on her lips.

By week's end Estelle's point had been made clear: There had been a catalogue of insubstantial speeches followed by wrangling disputations that went nowhere and finally, toward the closing hours of the week, the Mayor appeared and addressed the assembly but before questioning could ensue, the legendary Jazz xylophonist Lionel Hampton and his octet took center stage and swung out with a rousing rendition of their theme song, "Flying Home."

What Percival had gathered from the slew of speeches over the course of the week – now whirling in a confusion in his head along with the music – was that the Youth Corps had been founded to provide ghetto teens with meaningless summer work in order to keep them from aimlessly roving the streets. Therefore, by default, it was the job of crew leaders to invent projects for them in the neighborhood and thereby steer them clear of explosive situations that might otherwise ignite into costly riots – none of which would profit insurance companies or politicos operating in the ghettos.

When the set was over the crowd rose to its feet in a thunderous roar of approval.

Meanwhile, the mayor had escaped, the day was done and everyone else in attendance turned for the nearest exit.

Monday of the following week Percival met his crew for the first time at the Heritage House on Jersey St., in New Brighton, at the bottom of Carlyle St. above, a solitary bungalow at the top in which Rufus and Lily resided. The Heritage House was a store front that had recently been converted into a meeting hall, library, playhouse and was the only semblance of cultural activity in an otherwise desert landscape. When he'd entered, sixteen young faces rounded on him. He observed them casually from under the brim of his planters' hat, counting heads: There were fourteen boys and two girls. One girl, Katy, was white and the other, her best friend, Inez, was Puerto Rican. All the boys but one, Tzi, who was Chinese and strikingly good looking, were black.

Glancing over her bifocals from a stack of letters and papers on her desk, the receptionist greeted him with a vague smile. "May I help you?"

"I'm a crew leader for the Youth Corps."

"They're yours," she said of the group at her back and carried on with her work.

Most of the kids were seated and talking among themselves while others, leaning idly against a side wall, smoked. One boy picked up his head from out the pages of the Daily News, his lips slack; another, who sat apart, kept his nose buried between the pages of a well-read bible. Straightening listlessly as he approached, they eyed him fitfully, with varying degrees of disinterest, sizing him up. He smiled, searching each face.

"Well everybody," he announced, "I believe we belong to each other for the rest of the summer."

"You're Percival Jones, aren't you?" said Tzi stretching forth his hand, which Percival seized up. "I've seen you fight; for a boxer you're damn good."

"Oh?" Percival responded, eyeing Tzi fixedly along the brim of his hat.

"I'm into Karate myself."

"R you now? You think you can take me, is that it?" said Percival, half-jokingly, loosening Tzi's hand, feeling an immediate kinship with him.

"I don't know I said that," Tzi objected, eyes crinkling.

"Ya had me worried; for a moment there I thought I was gonna 'ave to prove myself."

"No way!"

Percival smiled he liked this guy.

"It's you – you're him!" Katy exulted, drawing Percival's wavering glance. "I knew Racine 'n Dakota," she explained.

"I see." His eyes misted and, dropping his gaze, he felt a constriction in his chest. Then casting off his sudden gloom, he shook hands all round and introduced himself to the others, as well. But none struck him as had Tzi, though one boy, Leroy, the youngest of the pack, would prove his intellectual metal as the summer wore on.

"Well what'a we do," Inez asked?

Rather than admit he didn't know, Percival said, "first we'll get to know one another for a start. We'll walk the streets 'n talk 'n plot a course of action for the summer, dig?"

"Sounds ok I guess," Inez returned with a shrug. "We still get paid, right?"

"That's right, you get paid for hanging out with me," Percival declared. "So let's go."

"I hope it's worth it," someone cracked, as they spilt out the front door of the Heritage House and onto the sidewalk.

Jersey Street and environs looked like a drowsy southern enclave with all its attendant ills. The four busiest spots along the stretch were bars, and both men and women could be seen tumbling out their doors from early on. The back alleys were gathering spots for junkies, drug dealers and crap shooters. It was a penury street that urban renewal had overlooked. It was a poverty-stricken area where the meanest of the poor grappled with the snares and fish hooks of its byways, streets and alleys—a rent in the fabric of the Constitution.

225

The tenement houses along the strip huddled together in a jumble like tinderboxes about to ignite.

Women leaned out windows in their bath robes, breast threatening to plop out, on folded arms and talked back and forth from window to window like magpies while watching their children at play in the gutters below. Every so often a mother would scold a child who'd chased a ball into the street: "Ya best get out'a dat street fore I come down 'n skin your scrawny ass." And the child would race back more grateful for having escaped his mother's wrath than that of being struck by a truck.

It was eighty degrees in the shade and promised to climb higher as the day wore on; the ripened smell of spilt garbage simmered in the rising heat like rancid cheese. Percival had his crew cross to the shady side of the street, whence they began their tour of the locality. Percival started out alongside Katy, and stole an occasional upwards glance. She was tall and leggy, with diminutive breast but a charitable face and expressive brown eyes.

"Sometimes I baby sit Nadia, you know upstairs from where Racine used to live, that is – for Linda's girl, you know?" Percival nodded. "She used to come up with Dakota 'n have tea 'n girl talk – that's how we met. N your name would come up a lot. I mean a lot a lot! She really dug on you, know," Katy said, affecting a black accent. "At the time I was going with Melvin –"

"Melvin?"

"The really cute dude in the back with a bible?"

"In 'r crew, you mean?"

"That's him but he got saved," she said disapprovingly.

Percival glanced over his shoulder and his eyes slid over the faces of his crew on back to Melvin, his head high and eyes other worldly, staying apart, cleaving self-righteously to his bible. Yes, Percival thought, the troubled ones he might hope to reach but he was doubtful of a pious one. After all, he was in the hands of a far higher authority.

"We had a good thing going till he went 'n got religion 'n give me up for the word of God. Said we was sinning. I told him, heck, I don't mind. He say, 'God do.' Said it was to stand with the Satan against the will'a Jehovah! If it was another gal I'd'a know'd what to do – I'd'a tear her clothes offa her back 'n scratch out her eyes. But God!" She plaintively sighed, then broke out in a mournful ditty, "'O dad, poor dad, God loves Melvin 'n I'm so sad.'"

As the walk continued Percival made it a point to talk with each member of the crew and allow them to reveal something of themselves, their likes and dislikes. He also asked, "what do you hope to gain from this program?" Most shrugged but Tzi had replied, "A paycheck."

"Think on it," Percival suggested.

Melvin said, looking round, "to not fall in among the godless," his eyes coming to rest on Katy.

"Amen to that, bro," Percival sang, pushing on without unnecessary delay.

They eventually came to the New Brighton projects and decided to recline beneath shade trees bordering the playground. Leroy began to read his copy of the Daily News. Percival asked, "why not read out loud? You read 'n article from the News 'n I'll read 'n article from the Times, ok?"

"Sure," Leroy said, opening the paper.

"'N you, Melvin, if you like you can read a passage from the bible." Melvin smiled appreciatively. And from then on Percival made it a practice to have them read from the paper first thing in the morning after Melvin had opened with a bible passage.

After the members of his crew were paid and were let loose for the weekend crying, "thank God it's Friday!" it only followed that there would be much to celebrate and some money to do it with, too. As such, they were all excited. Percival was also excited, but for other reasons, when, later on that evening, he joined Rufus at the Heritage House for a meeting with the NAACP, in hopes of obtaining their support for Rufus' congressional campaign. Percival had contacted the President of the local association, Constance Taylor, the week before to inform her of Rufus' run for Congress and, though he seriously doubted that they would grant it, told her that they were seeking to gain the organization's endorsement. Though what he had really hoped for was to incite curiosity and create talk and have the grapevine pick up on it, and, as the NAACP had the most effective grapevine in the black community, come Sunday afternoon every churchgoing black person on the island would know that the Black Panther Party would be opening its doors on Jersey St., as well as running a candidate for congress, which was no less than what Percival had hoped for in the first place.

Most of the seats at the conference table were taken by the time Rufus and Percival arrived and Constance Taylor, shuffling papers, was at the helm. The meeting was about to start. There must have been twenty-five or more friends and members present, including the President of the local community college, Dr. Bromberg; the director of the Mayor's Task Force, Miriam Fisk, along with her curvaceous, ultra-sexy, auburn haired and disarmingly pretty secretary whose hazel eyes, lush mouth and saucy breast Percival had difficulty taking his eyes off. She looked to be ten to fifteen years his senior. *Ten to fifteen year jus' right,* he thought, eyeing her lasciviously. A roseate hue suffused her cheeks, she averted her eyes, reading volumes in his smile. Also present was Nina Koestler who, though seated, clung to a crutch as if it were a staff while her other crutch leaned against the desk. She smiled whimsically at Percival as

227

he sat, blinking articulate eyes. He reached across the table and squeezed her hand fondly.

"How 'r ya gorgeous?"

"I see you haven't lost your roving eye," she needled him.

"Yeah but none 'r half so pretty as you."

"Flattery will absolve you of everything."

They laughed easily.

"Hello, Rufus," Nina said. "How goes it?"

"Same ole, same ole," he curtly said, "as to be expected."

Nina shrugged, facing Percival anew, who also shrugged. Again, Nina addressed Rufus, "My magazine is interested in throwing you our endorsement. Or are you so overwhelmed with endorsements that you're not interested in our meager support?"

"Don't get me wrong," Rufus smiled slyly. "But what makes you want'a endorse me all'a sudden? I mean, what's in it for you?"

"It's obviously because of your scintillating personality, what else?"

He lanced her with his singularly unnerving cross eyes.

"OK, you win," she chortled, rolling her eyes. "We're endorsing all the anti-war candidates."

"That's fair enough. Okay, I can dig it – I'll give you a statement afterwards."

"Thank you, I'd like that," said Nina, casually. Then, catching Percival's eye, "Is he always so irascible?"

"I caught that," Rufus snarled, wagging a forefinger in her direction.

Weary of Rufus' acerbity, Nina turned and said to the woman seated to her left:

"Beverly, you remember Percival, don't you?"

"Of course." She smiled. "How are you?'

"Uhh?" he faltered, scanning his memory, trying to fix the name to the face. "Oh yes," he recalled, his brow clearing, "the reporter for the Advance. Good to see you again."

"Likewise."

They shook hands across the table.

"You here to cover the meeting?"

"More specifically to do an article on Constance Taylor."

"I see."

Constance Taylor was a regal, middle-aged woman with skin the color of old ivory. She had almond shaped eyes and glossy gray streaked black hair worn in a braid that was wrapped in a twirl at the crown of her head. She wore a pink blouse, which her munificent breast filled admirably, and her fleshy arms were decorated with numerous African bracelets. She had a commanding presence. All eyes were turned on her even before, in a contralto voice, she moved to have the meeting called to order.

The secretary, a bespectacled, mahogany-colored woman, struck the table with a gravel.

"I move we now call this meeting to order!"

"A motion has been made. Will anyone second it?" said Constance Taylor.

A crosscurrent of voices chimed in.

"The motion has been seconded. All in favor say 'aye.'"

"Aye," voiced the membership in unison.

"All opposed?" Constance glanced around. "The ayes have it, and this meeting is now in session," she proclaimed. "Madame Secretary, is there any old business on the agenda to be discussed?"

"There's Ruth Morrow's report on the Poor People's Campaign which she is prepared to deliver. But first, with your permission, I'd like to recognize some of our distinguished friends."

"Please do."

Madame Secretary then went on to introduce Dr. Bromberg, who nodded his curly, gray head in response. She introduced Miriam Fisk, and her secretary, Gwen Halsey, from the Mayor's Task Force. They said hello simultaneously. Madame Secretary then went on to say, "With us tonight is Beverly Jordan from the Advance, who is interested in doing a feature article on you, Madame President."

"Thank you for having me," said Beverly, as Constance turned her eyes on her prospective interviewer.

"Then there is our very dear friend in long standing, Nina Koestler."

"My friends," said Nina simply.

"And we have with us tonight our first black candidate for the district congressional seat, Rufus Hinton." Rufus raised an identifying hand. "He will have a few words to say later on. I'm sorry but I don't know your friend," she apologized, speaking of Percival, which caused Rufus to gloat and Percival to grin, hoisting a doubtful eyebrow. "In any case, welcome," she said, looking off.

"Don't feel slighted," Nina whispered across the table grinning, "the rest of us know you, I think."

He leaned back in his seat, as if to guffaw.

"I now wish to turn the floor over to Ruth Morrow who, it should be said, is also co-chairperson of the Welfare Mothers Association and coordinated our efforts on behalf of the Poor Peoples Campaign, and one of Dr. Bromberg's first recruits whose gone on from Community College to Hunter. And at this time we would like to say how proud we are of you – Ruth, please!"

A warm applause greeted her introduction.

Ruth was tall, slim and nattily clad for someone of little means. She sewed much of her own clothes, as well as those of her children. She was so slender, however, that her husband, imprisoned for manslaughter, had laughingly remarked on an early visit, "You're so skinny, gal, you can slip between the bars a' my cell 'n we can get it on. Ay baby, what'a you say?" He'd laughed.

"Caught in a predicament like this and still talking trash!" Ruth shook her head. She was not beautiful but she was suitably made; slightly built, slender as a reed. So too was Diana Ross and that did not hurt her appeal. Ruth was also, as often as not, mistaken for an adolescent, which she cherished. But with her large, slow eyes, bedroom eyes – which gave one the impression of her being lethargic, she was, on the contrary, anything but child-like. Moreover, she was a determined woman who had no qualms with honest work, struggle or sacrifice, particularly where it concerned their daughters. "What about our children?" she'd demanded to know. "How are we to care for them?"

"What of them? I did what I could. See if you can do better," he had said. "It's up to you now!"

His remarks shook her, as if from troubled sleep, and left her trembling like a leaf in mid Autumn's decay. The realization of life on her own, in a void, widening like a chasm at her feet, shackled to an imprisoned convict in a lifelong abyss, sucked the spirit from out of the marrow of her bones. She began to see it for what it was, viewing it from his perspective; the prism of his cell; the ominous clank of the prison gate; the shadow side of the jail house walls. She saw the stark, calculating reality of it. The despair of it, the dark nature of it, the God-awful thing of it, as he bemoaned his ill appointed lot. "Twenty-five years to life is not, as the kids here say, 'a minute.' It's not a minute, it's an eternity, a death watch. I'm not getting out'a here any time soon. I don't know I'll get out'a here alive. There's a thousand ways to die in prison, 'n few of 'em pretty," he groaned, chained by sorrows more ponderous than those of Marley's ghost.

"With all these guards you should be as safe as a gold brick in Fort Knox," she had said, somewhat fatuously.

"Safe? In jail? About as safe as possible in a den of cut throats 'n thieves," he howled with laughter, startling her further. "And I don't mean the inmates either. The guards 'r not called 'goons' for naught!"

"Shhh," she cautioned. "We'll be overheard."

230

He brushed her objection aside and said, "If nothing else I've had time to think. One thing sure. I don't quite know how to ask, to tell you, actually, to seek another life 'cause I don't have much of one to offer –"

Before he could finish she gently pressed her fingers to his lips, and blinking back a hot surge of tears, coaxed him to silence. "I married you for better or worse,'" she said, knowing full well that his fate, his years behind bars, would threaten the ability of their family to survive intact.

"I hate myself for saying this; for having to say this," he uttered, in agony of heart. "I don't want to turn my back on you or 'r daughters, but what can I do? I'm in a dungeon of brick 'n steel, buried behind walls I can't scale—a ruin!" He choked, voice frail, "do what you gotta do. I'm dead to the world, if not to myself as well!"

"No, not to me you're not," she disagreed, lips trembling and chestnut brown eyes welling with sorrow.

He turned away, no less teary eyed than she. "I was never quite able to see my future before but now I see it all too clearly. I can't see anything else. It's all I see. And my past is a distant memory. Sometimes it feels I had no life beyond these walls. Time doesn't bend in prison, it collides 'n robs you of all that came before, everything you once held dear," he said plaintively, off key. "So before I forget and lose all sense of myself, I want you to know how sorry I am for the misery I've caused, the torment I've inflicted on you 'n 'r daughters whose faces I barely remember 'n who I'll not get to raise or see grow to womanhood. My life is slipping me by, 'n memories 'r available to me only in the flashbacks of a drowning man. Moments I can't fully access. Memories no longer mine but belonging to someone I once was," he said, lips quivering. "Another thing, I don't recall having told you that I didn't mind carrying my sharea the load when it was mine to carry for us! 'R family. No matter the weight. The sweat, seeing to 'r needs. A family I love. Daughters I adore 'n sorely miss. A woman who's stood by me, remains by me." Trying to restrain a flow of tears, Ruth folded his hands in hers. "I didn't want this. I never wanted to jeopardize 'r lives this way. I wanted something else; something this country can't offer, not a Blackman anyway. Something a black man can't hope to find; not even in his dreams. Dr. King was wrong. This is not to a world in which to dream," he said, throat constricted with emotion. "It's not given us to dream," he wistfully sighed.

"I was straining under the yoke, as you know, well on the way to being broken in, saddled, beginning to settle down when all this occurred. You were going to save me from myself remember?" he said, reflectively, as if taking a stroll down memory lane.

She squeezed his hands harder, tears leaking down her mocha colored cheeks. "I recall," she simply said. He had had a remarkable, raw intelligence unsullied by street life—an achievement in itself— despite its jaded appeal which, in the long run, undercut his higher aspirations and landed him in jail. Hence she found herself enjoying a most grievous penance for being the wife of a convicted felon.

"I was trying – busting my hump at that fucking hospital swabbing floors, making beds, cleaning up shit after the dead 'n dying; pulling double shifts, popping sweat 'n racing off to classes at night trying to pull my head out'a the toilet long enough to get us out'a that shit hole of a place we call home," he said, tautly.

"Apart from that, I was drowning under the white man's yoke – carrying his fucking burden! trying to measure up; to live up to his unrealistic expectations! his misguided Judeo-Christian ethics! Suffering him 'n his indignities! Swallowing his insufferable crap! Seeing to his needs above my own! Yes sir, Mr. Charlie! Yes sir! The White man! The white man! The White man! He's a burden on a Blackman's back! A law unto himself. He's the real reason I'm here. Why we're all here! Open your eyes, gal, 'n look 'round."

She looked about in a daze and observed, all too sadly, a room full of colored men, Hispanics and Afro-Americans alike, from teenagers to septuagenarians, with a sprinkling of white faces which betokened the racial disparity, a small number of whom were guards circling the vast visiting room, nightsticks at the ready. There were also the unfriendly, scowling faces of black guards, which made her fearful for her husband's sake—and the sake of those poor, young black boys wanting for lack of the milk of human kindness. She knew all too well of the mistreatment many black cops inflict on their own in the ghettos. And she could little imagine it being much different in prison. From then on she would remember to pray for the imprisoned, and all who guard them, in her daily worship.

"The penal system is, as you can see, no more than a rudderless slave ship lost at sea without a moral compass by which to traverse the dangers lurking beneath the waves. As if I should care," he said in a despondent, dying voice. "Except, of course, I'm on board." He regretted his situation and the links in the chain of events which saw him to this pass. "Fear is the governing factor in jail. Fear 'n all its deviant minions. I mean, fear of a brute, faceless justice system dancing us about like puppets on a string!

"You see that guy over there, hanging with a group of friends carrying on like wild Indians at a hoopla?" She swung her eyes in the direction of his outstretched forefinger. "The one wearing the rattlesnake band round his head?"

232

"Yes," she acknowledged, staring. She'd caught sight of a reddish-brown, broad faced man with chiseled features, Mongolian eyes, hawk like nose, and frank expression on his lips; his raven black hair cascaded beneath a speckled band, round strong, broad shoulders. She gasped awe struck. She had never seen anyone so fiercely beautiful in all her life. She was intrigued, fascinated.

"He's native American. I never met one before now, till coming to jail. I use to play cowboys 'n Indians all the time as a kid. I knew a lot of cowboys but never any Indians. Ain't that some shit? And here in jail for the first time I meet one." He shook his head dubiously. "He's everything we think of Indians, too; brave, honest, 'n somewhat naive, as 'r blacks. He's in here for trespassing, believe it or not."

"Trespassing?" She asked, still staring.

"He got caught in some secret government facility searching for evidence to evict white people from this land. 'After we've evicted all the white people,' he told me, 'send 'em back to Europe where they belong, then black folks can apply for citizenship, if they like. Your people come from cultures similar to our own; from civilizations older than time itself. You are of a noble people who, through no fault of your own, have been brought low. You can be noble again. We can help each other to become so.'

"He was attending Cornell at the time and writing a thesis for his Masters on The Effect of The Slave Trade on The Native Peoples of The New World, when he was arrested and carted off to jail, having failed to free his peoples, as was his intention. His court room defense was, 'How can you trespass on your own land? A land cannot be bought or sold. It's not for sale. You can't run off and take it with you. It's for the use of all that live on it. Human and non-human alike. You can love it, tend it and care for it. But you do neither. Instead you despoil it, the sacred land of my people! You have no historical, legal or moral right to be here. Neither your Declaration of Independence or your Constitution makes it so. It legitimizes nothing. Your Christian ethics deny you it, too: 'Thou shalt not kill; thou shalt not steal; thou shalt not covert thy neighbor's wife, thy neighbor's goods, thy neighbor's anything.' Not only are you trespassers, you're transgressors: You violate every principles of human decency, being here, presuming to judge. You are would-be thieves at best! You have no more rights than those of common criminals, and they have no rights besides due punishment. In this case expulsion from these lands, the Americas or, as we native peoples call it, Turtle Island. You've out worn your welcome, it's time you pack up and take leave of our country and return to the dust bins of Europe whence you came.' It didn't wash. They gave him five to ten years. He'll surely end up doing ten because he's such a bother—a thorn in their side. He's as often in the Hole as not. He doesn't mind the Hole. There he seeks visions. 'A vision quest,' he calls it. You can hear him chanting all over Comstock, from cell block to cell block. He claims the spirits of his ancestors join him there in the Hole and counsel him. He's more invigorated when he comes out than when he goes in. It's spooky. The rest of us are terrified of being sent to the Hole. He frustrates the administration to no end. They don't quite know how to discipline him, so they deny him his visits from time to time, which he accepts with forbearance. To top it all off, they're afraid of him too. He's no one you want to go up against. They give him plenty space. He says, 'The reservation is no place a free man calls home; but a free man might call prison home. The reservation represents a loss of freedom; whereas prison represents a blow for it.'

"Unlike anyone else I've ever met, he knows who he is: physically, spiritually, 'n morally. He's of the Delaware, an Iroquois. He's the son of a medicine man, and his mother's advice is highly sought at counsel. His name is Sure-Foot. Everyone here, including guards and white supremacist, treat him with the respect due a chief. Everyone! The brothers love him. As for me, I'm glad to call him my friend. He's one of the few I've made since coming to jail."

"Yes! Of course. I understand." And to her credit, she did. She again faced her husband thoughtfully.

"So maybe now you'll see what I mean when I say all too many of these poor devils don't belong here. They've been railroaded! Shanghaied! Victimized by the system, by their ignorance 'n blind stupidity! Who the hell am I to talk? Three years of college with a 3.5 average, and here I am stuck in prison with them," he said with bitter distaste. "I'd carried that pistol the longest, thinking to shoot a white man someday. Which, I suppose, is every black man's fantasy. Instead I used it to kill a brother, that motherless bastard. My intentions backfired, blew up in my face!" He winced, teary-eyed. "I can't deny it. I turned my face from God and killed him over a trifle, as if he was nothing of value. He cheated me at cards, out'a money I didn't have. But when seen from this angle, what I did was wrong – a merciless, god awful sin! I rejected his plea for mercy even after he'd tossed me all his winnings. 'Take it,' he cried. 'Take it all. Jus' don't shoot me!' It was too late. I was too far gone, 'n I emptied the barrel of my revolver on him. A man I hardly knew. In my rage against the white man I killed a brother. It was wrong of me to want to kill a man, any man, a white man even."

Ruth was stunned at his admission and would have run from him in tears but, despite herself, she couldn't move. He was her man, her spouse, the love of her life, and nothing short of death could sunder them!

234

"Yet in one blind regrettable moment all the self-hatred I'd ingested over the years from the white man poured out of me in a torrent of anger against another black man. I thought of him as a nigger and could kill him as such. I said as much, shooting him, 'die, nigger, die!' Like I was carrying out the white man's trash – his burden; a Blackman's cross. It was no less an act of suicide than it was murder. A thing, until that moment, I would never have thought possible. A simple squeeze of the trigger has since come to signify my worth, or lack thereof. I'm lost to myself, buried alive. What more can I say except, I'm gonna rot here in jail; buried beneath its stones. All of which I'm deserving," his voice broke. *"And my victims blood cries out against me! He visits me in my cell and denounces me to my face. God help me,"* he wailed, covering his hands to his face. *"It's a mistake for which I cry every night before going to bed! You gotta pray for me,"* he urged. *"Resurrect me, redeem me through 'r daughters,"* he beseeched her. *"Promise me,"* he implored. *"Promise me!"*

She wept.

Thereupon, she became a devoted welfare mother of three girls. One of which, her lovely, intelligent eldest daughter of 15, Raschelay, would, with Ruth's consent, be among the first to join the newly formed branch of the Black Panther Party. A former high school dropout, Ruth enrolled in a program inaugurated by Dr. Bromberg where it became possible to obtain a GED while accruing credits toward an associates degree, and she was currently enrolled in Hunter College's continuing adult education program with designs on becoming a child psychologist.

The source of Ruth's ambitions were not solely predicated on the salvation of her husband's soul, but was as much in response to her upbringing, the life she saw around her coming up on the streets, and the lives of many another who had succumbed to the lure of the street, only to be hauled off by the police, overtaken by drugs, death or insanity. Street life is its own church, its own religion, and drugs and alcohol its 'Communion' and crime 'Confirmation.' Hence prison is Salvation. 'If,' as ex-cons say, 'the streets don't kill you prison will save you.' Conversely, Ruth herself had narrowly escaped the streets by clinging to the fabric of her faith. The Catholic Church, the Church of the poor, it gave her the means by which to skirt the appeal of the streets. It gave her to know the value of her soul and challenged her to elevate herself through a life of spirit.

However, the Baptist church, to whom most of the NAACP membership belonged, is the primary faith in the black community through which the spirit of the Holy Ghost descends. Come Sunday morning, following Saturday night's revelry, the black Baptist Church rollicks, in a body with the Holy Ghost in an old-time religious tempo, remarkably similar, by contrast to the orgiastic Dionysian spirit found at 'Rock concerts.' It was a bridge to cross. Thus the NAACP, in the black community is considered common grounds. Otherwise the hollowness of everyday life, a life that colors by its sting, makes one a 'nigger' – someone her husband could kill! Someone too many do kill! Hence, with all her energy she promised herself that she would rise above such self-abnegation, and work to redeem herself, her husband, their children and, by extension, the community. She had longed, as a child, to be a Nun and that longing saved her from the streets. And yet, it did not spare her siblings. All too sadly she could only watch as her husband {for whom she kept a candle lit at Sacred Heart Church along with a second candle for the redemption of the soul of the man he'd killed} came undone – as if every step taken had been preordained.

The father she'd little known—'Gone to the devil,' was the word on the block – and mother downcast by poverty, sick with grief, and, given to despair, had become towards the end 'a basket case.' She also had, out of five siblings, two brothers and a sister succumb to the ravages of drugs and alcohol, bemoaning the loss of their cultural heritage; the roots of their family African identity – possessing no other name but the slave master's, whereupon they were caught in a web of the slavers design! Ruth had no wish to see her daughters share such an ominous fate. Many another would have bowed out, shrunk from the task, as many another had, but she was emboldened. As such she rolled up her sleeves, picked up her cross, and proceeded to climb. It would not prove easy but climb she would.

"I look forward to hearing your report," said Constance, granting Ruth permission to speak.

"Thank you madame secretary for your kind words, and fellow members for your reception. Madame President," she went on, looking over her notes arranged on the table before her, "having missed so much of the Civil Rights Movement, I had hoped that the Poor People's Campaign was going to serve as an epiphany. I had somehow thought that some of what was good, noble and fitting in the American spirit would be found there, despite the Vietnam war. But the great American heart, I'm sorry to say, was conspicuously absent. It was far easier to grant Civil Rights and Voter Rights, than grant the staples of life. While it cost a pittance to bestow our Civil Rights, it would take billions to solve the enigma of poverty while our nation spends billions bombing Vietnam daily!"

This rather oblique reference to the Vietnam war was not received without its share of raised eyebrows by the membership who were in favor of the war and in support of the President and his administration, for their strong stance on Civil Rights and Affirmative Action, of which Ruth was a beneficiary. Initially, she had been in favor of the war, before starting out on the Poor Peoples Campaign where she found, to her dismay, the conditions of squalor equally those of a third world nature. She came to realize that the billions of dollars exploding in bombs over Vietnam could easily erase the ravages of poverty, thus shaming her into a change of heart. Under attack by vastly superior forces, the tears of poor Asian peasants duly salted her cup of sorrow.

"Very little of what we like to think of as fine in the American character appeared," Ruth continued. "It was, for the most part, a show of rank poverty. A living testimony to the ills of poverty at which tourist flocked by to snicker. We were obviously obstructing their view of the Lincoln and Washington monuments. To them we were a circus side show. Shortly after the construction of Resurrection City, built between the shadow of those two monuments, we were back to living 'r lives much as in the same way we had before leaving home. Resurrection City was not a Utopia so much as it was a desperate sea of humanity trying to do what's right given the impoverished conditions we came from. But the opposition to our presence on Capitol Hill was, to say the very least, unfriendly. I don't know what we'd hoped for – I don't know," she recounted. "Whatever it was, what we met instead were tight fisted, fiscal minded politicos who, not interested in our story, only wanted to see our backs.

"Let there be no misunderstanding: there was good, plenty of good, though it did not come from desired quarters. It grew out of a camaraderie developed among the participants; it grew out of the respect, love and regard gained for each other over weeks of struggle – an affection we came to hold dear; held us in its grasp. We'd come by the score from all parts of the country; east, west, north 'n south. We were white, black, yellow, red. We were the multitude, the people. The salt of the earth. We'd come with hope in empty hands 'n prayers on parch'd lips. We'd come 'hungering 'n thirsting for righteousness sake.' And the good there was grew out of a kinship born of trial during those hard days. There was a spirit, a fellowship akin to a revival," she said gleefully, as if testifying. "There was as many tears as laughter, singing as hollering, and much clapping and raising of hands in praise. There was as much liveliness as colored people know," she reassured them, "which the whites among us shared in, too. And Native Americans had us join in their ritualistic ceremonies. It was a wonderful revelation! Yes, there was dancing and music making to lighten our load, 'cause at times 'r burden grew heavy. But, I suppose, I ought to begin at the beginning."

She went on to recall the initial, introductory stages of the campaign: She briefly described the 12-mile symbolic march and rally, followed by a caravan of buses from mid-Manhattan to D.C. She then spoke of the inclement weather which greeted them on arrival. "They'd barely gotten up a number of A-frame shacks when we'd arrived, when sporadic, unseasonable rains began and continued throughout our stay; nor would there be enough shelter for everyone and many more people from all corners of the nation were still on the way.

"As bad as the weather was, and the weather was miserable, opposition in Congress was worse. Vice President Humphrey paid us a brief visit and gave us his unwavering support. He even informed Congress that their fears of violence were unfounded; that our purpose was, hopefully, to alert the American people to the plight of the poor in their midst. That was the upside of it. The downside was soon to follow as the leadership Abernathy, Bevil, Jackson and Rustin in the absence of Dr. King, uncertain of the tactics to employ, began bickering among themselves.

"Despite the dour mood of the leadership, Rev. Abernathy proclaimed that 'the campaign was one of the most impressive demonstrations for freedom and justice in the history of the country.

"All too sadly, however, it had a hollow ring since, at the same time rumors were flying to the effect that Bayard Rustin's role was that of a sellout, which cast a pall over everyone's already sinking spirits. What made matters worse was Bayard retaliated by saying, 'The leaders have produced an air of confusion which could well lead to violence.'

"Maybe not violence but confusion and division among the rank and file. Was it any wonder, with such rumors abounding, that so many who'd come so far on empty stomachs found themselves wavering? Consequently, we spent a considerable amount of time moping about 'n complaining because there was as little action as there was food.

"'It's enough to make a grown man cry,' a man accustomed to hard work but who had not worked in quite a while complained. And the crying of bored, hungry children was as incessant as the whipping rains, often confining us to our A-frame shacks.

"An 87-year-old great-grandmother who'd left the Mississippi cotton fields to be with us 'To bear witness' arrived in our midst with all she had in this world on her back. She was sturdy as an ole pack mule and her joints gnarly like the limbs of a crab apple tree. She was as wrinkled as a crawfish and as dark as the delta Blues, with sorrows deep as the Mississippi, but they didn't hamper nor press her down. She was, however, stooped from a life of working the cotton fields from sun to sun. She would gladly share her portion of food with others. Her only staple, as far as I could tell, was chewing tobacco, which she spat in gobs.

"She came to us out of Neshoba County, Philadelphia, Mississippi. She was caught on camera on CBS news, Our Gran'ma Little Peace, as we came to call her, and we became afraid for her safety once she got home. I would like to have said 'safely home' but that's impossible given Mississippi's history. She assured us that she was far too old for the Klan to bother with. We didn't feel so sure about that ourselves. We were most particularly afraid because she came out of the county where those three civil rights workers, Chaney, Goodman, and Schwerner, were killed by Klansmen back in '64. They were found out, brought to trial but, in good ole southern hospitality fashion, exonerated by their redneck peers," she said, with a pinch of sarcasm.

"She remembered it as the terror that swept through the county and state, chilling the blood of every colored man in the vicinity, and frightening mothers for the safety of their sons, and wives for their husbands. She spoke to us of life in the South, of children, grandchildren and great grandchildren. Many having left the cotton fields and moved on, gone to mill towns and the big city. Some came north to escape Jim Crow. Her husband had died shortly before and had encouraged her to join the march. Her folks had been born into slavery and became sharcroppers afterwards. 'But felt,' she said, 'they'd never know'd a true day'a freedom.' No more than had she. And that's why she came, 'left the cotton fields to spread my wings 'n fly free in the face of the Sun; to be free 'n the eyes a God 'n man,' she shouted, exposing a mouth full of blacken'd teeth. She came to bear witness and testify. She had never voted, was illiterate, but wished to declare her freedom, once and for all, for the world to know and rejoice,

"Hallelujah! Praise the Lord! Glory be, eye's free!' She whooped, clapping her hands as tears of joy washed her parched face. 'eye' s Free!'

"She went on to say, to testify before us, the Citizens of Resurrection City – since Congress would not grant us a hearing – 'Jesus say where they be two or three gathered in my name there eye be also. Well here we is in Jesus' name.' 'Amen,' we said in concert. 'Jesus say, the poor's gonna be with us always,' she said. 'Uh-huh,' the rest of us agreed. 'All he say 'bout the rich is 'it'll be as hard fer 'em to enter the Kingdom a' God as it is fer a camel to climb through the eye of a needle.' 'That he did,' we agreed again. 'We also gotta recall,' she said, 'as say scripture, 'Those who deprive the poor of justice commit a sin that cries out to heaven for punishment.' 'Speak, mother, speak,' we urged: 'All eye know fer sure's we gotta look out for each other. Cloth one another, shelter one another. That's the way'a Christianity, an' eye's a Christian. A good one, eye pray. God knows eye try to be! Christianity was the corner stone a' Dr. King's Dream. It was a good dream. It wasn't a selfish dream but for all God's children – children a' the Kingdom – no matter 'r differences. Ta know God's 'will' is to know God don't know the color'a nobody's skin 'n only know da purity a' dey hearts. God don't know no hate. 'N he sure don't like ugly!'

"Her voice was frail but carried conviction. Grateful for her words, we applauded her roundly. She was full of plenty of home spun good sense. And her quiet presence inspired and served as an example. The native Americans among us were the first to call her 'Gran'ma Little Peace.' They also adopted her into their respective tribes. She was deeply honored and told them, 'Mississippi's'a devil state in sore need'a exorcism,' my husband would say. 'N it sure do, too. But it's where eye call home, where eye cast my lot, good or bad. Eye ain't got much but what eye got's out back'a that broken down Aubry big house looking like a ghost ship riding high on clouds'a cotton pluck'd by da work-worn hands'a former slaves, along with they free born new 'un's," she said without rancor. 'We liv'd in the sun bak'd slave quarters my folks were born; 'n all us young un's born there, too, in that ole cabin, topple head over heels into the world, after the Civil War, one upon the next in'a mad scramble—like'a litter a' pups. Masa didn't turn his ole slaves away after the war. He say 'if y'll got some place to go y'll best go! But if y'll stay y'll 'ave to pay.' He say, 'Ole masa can't care for y'll no more. Y'all can thank the god damn Yanks for that. What the damn Yanks mean by freedom is y'll wage slaves now,' he told his ole slaves. 'Y'll got'a pay! If y'll gonna stay y'll best stop slacken' 'n get to them cotton fields lickety-split.' Most stay'd on cause they got nowhere to go—just like my folks. Eye came later. I was the youngest. The baby. Eye had seven older siblings. All 'em gone now, pass'd on. Ey'm what's left. Them cotton fields got the better'a 'em, work 'em under the ground. My folks work those fields as slaves, then share crop 'em since eye can recall, from sun ta sun, singing work songs as we toil'd for no more than'a leaky roof over 'r heads, a' communal garden, 'n barely enough money to put clothes on 'r bare backs.' From there she went on to say, in a more buoyant voice, 'We also got 'r lil church built in slavery, by slaves, to sing hymns of praise to God on High, in which we got to jump, sing 'n shout with joy in glory to his Holy name. Hallelujah! Amen!' she said, seeming to bring the full measure of her mind and gaze to bear on us. ''N my kinfolk; mother 'n father, brothers 'n sisters, aunts 'n uncles, nieces 'n nephews, by the dozens, far back as eye can reckon, whose graves eye see to, all 'em buried back'a that there church yard. Yes, they gone but they souls linger on, biding they time, waiting for me 'N who am eye, a' frail ole lady, to go off 'n disappoint 'em so? The thing is, ey'm free to come 'n go for the first time in my life. Ey'm free to do so if I please!'

"The native Americans understood her well. Of course she decided to go back home! A Lakota medicine man gave her an amulet to safeguard her from inimical forces; and performed a ritualistic ceremonial dance adopting her into his tribe, as one of them. She was moved to tears. So were all of us who attended the ceremony. It was wonderfully heartwarming and spoke to us of a different way of being and doing.

"She made many friends there. All promised to stay in touch. I know I shall.

"She was inspirational. There were others of similar age and experience but none affected us as deeply as did she, our gran'ma Little Peace. As I said, Congress would not grant us a hearing and only saw us as undesirables. We were all of the opinion that had Dr. King lived to have been there that Congress would not dare deny him the right to have testified on Capitol Hill! Without Dr. King we may as well have been a flock of lost sheep as far as Congress was concerned. Therefore, in Dr. King's absence, we gave testimony among ourselves. Out of which Gran'ma Little Peace's words and spirt won the day.

"The Capitol, other than taking the lead from Bayard's ill-fated remarks about violence, paid us small heed. In fact, the Capitol had turned its back on us as if we were outcasts – told us to get out of town. Even those initially on our side said, 'After June 23rd., it would be time to break camp and go.' The cry roundly heard was, 'where to?'

"'Wherever you came from,' was the crass reply.

'We can jus' as easily die'a starvation here as there,' came a lone response, echoing the sentiments of all. It was disheartening, to say the least.

"I spent much of the month talking to veteran Civil Rights Workers telling me how it used to be, recalling former hopes and dreams. And though they were up against some impossible odds, no matter how downcast they became they held fast to the belief that their countrymen were good at heart and would see them through." Many of the NAACP membership shook their heads and murmured in accord.

"'I guess,' I was told, 'we had grown up on all those cowboy and Indian movies and thought that the cavalry would come to our rescue. But there is no cavalry and we were never the settlers whom they were coming to save!' We were especially disheartened because president Johnson's 'war on poverty' had been the cornerstone of his administration, 'The Great Society.' But he's since turned his back on those promises in favor of waging war in Vietnam, a war he'd declared, in no uncertain terms, was to be fought by 'Asian boys alone!' In our culture, sadly, given the choice between weapons and butter, weapons win the day. Once more the poor are forced onto bread lines, into homeless shelters, and on the state welfare rolls. And the taxpayer begrudges us every penny of it, too. At the same time, Native Americans are among the poorest people in their own country—the richest country in the world! As the

241

saying goes, 'One step forward, two steps back.' I'm sorry to say, but at the Poor People's Campaign all foreseeable hope had been extinguished. And the heart sank out many of us.'

"It was very well revealing to me, too, because I caught on to a spirit I'd only gleaned from the television news watching our colored brothers and sisters down south win their struggle for Civil Rights – a feeling I can now claim to have shared in. Nationally the struggle for the right to work and economic security continues, which moved our quest for justice to D.C. Despite it all, 'n legislators stalling, there was a sense of promise, of thanksgiving for our testimony. We saw one another, recognized ourselves in each other's joys 'n sorrow's, 'n promised we'd never forget. As such, we'd come together to testify 'n bear witnesses before the Throne of Heaven. And we did!"

"Umm-hmm," the membership murmured in accord. "Umm-hmm."

"All that's left for me to say then is that the mule train from the Campaign will continue on to both Republican and Democratic Conventions to see if we can gain any political converts from either side of the aisle. All my prayers go with it."

"Amen to that," sang the membership like the chorus in a Greek drama. "Amen to that!"

"Thank you for so candid a report," said Constance. "It was thoughtfully presented and well serves to remind us that there is still much work to be done. And with God's help we shall prevail." Constance then asked the secretary after a brief pause, "What next?"

"Dr. Bromberg is with us to remind us of the scholarship fund for minority students at the college."

"Of course, Dr. Bromberg would you care to say a few words?"

"Consider it said," Dr. Bromberg rejoined, exuding an air of confidence that was palpable.

"Your presence is encouraging," said Constance, genially. "Next?"

"Next on the agenda is Rufus Hinton, the Peace and Freedom Candidate for Congress, Madame President," the secretary informed her.

"Mr. Hinton," said Constance facing Rufus, "the floor is yours."

Rufus rose slowly, looking critically from face to face, taking immediate offense at the men, their overfed, fat, contented bourgeois corpulence reeking of stale cologne. They irked him. He was not of their class; lawyers, doctors, professors. He viewed them with contempt as if they'd sold their souls for a suit. The same corporate suit at that. They wore ties with which he though they should hang themselves. He was of the streets, 'A field negro,' as Malcolm put it. They were professionals, 'the talented tenth,' as Dubois had called them,

242

and were to have lead the Negro out of bondage by taking up the white man's 'burden,' fashioning themselves in his image, and proving themselves worthy in his sightless eyes. "For those of you who don't know me, I'm Rufus Hinton 'n I live up on Carlyle St. above, " he indicated with a backward jerk of a thumb, directing their gaze beyond the store front window to the lone and poorly lighted hill street house. "I'm a Vietnam Vet who's come out against the war cause it's a death trap 'n a hell hole that drove me half way round the bend before I realized the madness to which my country had committed me," he said uneasily, with an ironic twist to his lips.

The membership sat quietly around the conference table, their eyes fixed on Rufus, taking him in as if he were an upstart species of unknown origins, as were all these young black radicals of the day, daring to challenge them, question their hard-won bourgeois respectability.

There was an unspoken animosity on both sides which when read went, 'You don't live up to expectation. You're an embarrassment.' Thus they viewed each other with equal portions of contempt.

In stark contrast to these men in their Brooks Brothers suits, Rufus wore a faded dungaree suit. And sensing that their disapproval of him was no less caustic than was his of them, Rufus addressed his remarks primarily to the women. Though they too were bourgeois they were also mothers, and he could hope to play on their maternal instincts. And so he played his trump card and recounted with sly sensibility, the story of his having lost his rifle in the jungles of Vietnam and of the young Vietcong who spared his life because he was black and was himself killed in exchange, as a consequence. He also told of his long convalescence in an Army mental facility. Percival had heard the story on numerous occasions and it had not ceased to stir him, to raise goose bumps on his flesh. Indeed, they were all affected. "for these reasons I oppose the Vietnam war," said Rufus witheringly. "Let me also say that I'm as much opposed to it cause'a the disproportionate number of blacks dying at home from hunger 'n neglect, as the sister righteously said. N the immorality of 'r nation's stance does little to offset it." He waved a cautionary hand. "Before someone mistakes me for who I'm not, I'm no pacifist. I'm no Dr. King. Far from it, I'm a child of the streets, better educated in tricknology than technology," he avowed, certain they would shrink from one such as he and look down on him from lofty heights of impotent triumph. He offended them and their effete, snobbish sensibilities; that is to say, he was, "too-too," over the top. He could sense them cringe. He reminded them of who they were, whence they came, of the gutter heritage they shared and, stuck to them like a tar on "Brer rabbit," with unshakable tenacity. One looked away, another's face went sour. Rufus wanted to laugh. "But I know 'r people 'r in need'a the necessities of life; need jobs at a living wage 'n decent housing 'n, yes, protection from an abusive police force," he said, screwing his face like that of a petulant child. "N education – for which I'm glad Dr. Bromberg's here."

Dr. Bromberg lowered his glasses to the tip of his nose and rolled his eyes Rufus' way as if to caution, 'don't involve me in your family squabble.'

"I know I'm not gonna get elected but that's not the point," said Rufus, without misgivings. "I expect to use the platform to air the concerns of 'r community that's been politically narcotized too long. 'N so I seek your support. True, I can't win, but we as a community 'ave yet to obtain any political clout 'n so 'r grievances go unattended. Well let's jus' say I'm here to see that that's corrected. I'm hoping for 'n asking for your support. If I can't promise victory at the polls, what I can promise is to not abandon ship." Rufus whacked the table with the flat of his palm, startling those whose attention had wandered. "In fact, we're gonna build a base here; the Black Panther Party for Self Defense is gonna set up quarters cross the street 'n we're gonna address the underlying issues of 'r people. It's like the sister said 'bout the Poor Peoples March—it's the disillusionments. The constant denials. The stumbling blocks thrown in 'r way. Or Dr. King said, 'America has given the negro people a bad check, a check which has come back marked 'insufficient funds'.' And that, more than anything, is what's given rise to the Black Panther Party! We must be reimbursed." He dropped back into his seat, running a hand over his Afro which was sweaty, and his eyes glistened with feverish brilliancy. "Thanks for hearing me out," he finished, shaking with agitation.

Percival lay an avuncular hand on his arm, and they exchanged looks of deep anxiety.

Rufus sank back in silence, absorbed.

The membership looked back and forth among themselves, speaking in hushed tones.

"He did say Black Panther Party, didn't he? I could have sworn I heard Madame Secretary say Peace and Freedom Candidate," said one tepidly, his hand over his mouth.

"Obviously a come on," said a second, less cautious.

"As if this neighborhood isn't bad enough," whispered a third, riled.

"It was bound to happen," said a fourth, shaking his head doubtfully, his face clouding over.

Constance cleared her throat, silencing the clucking tongues. "I'd like to thank you on behalf of the NAACP for – what shall I say – your informative input," she said, noncommittally. "Once we've reached a decision, I'll notify you."

"As you like," Rufus said, hopelessly, twitching nervously, as if about to commit his first crime.

"You ok," Percival asked?

"You'd think I'd lobbed a handgrenade in on em," Rufus said, bitterly, his hands as shaky as a drunkards.

"Ya ave," said Percival. "This is the N double ACP, after all."

At which Rufus snapped, "I guess I've entertained 'em long enough then."

"Let's jus' play out 'r hand, baby."

"Don't panic, I'll hang." Rufus felt as ill at ease among middle class blacks as he did being downtown Manhattan, lost in a sea of white faces.

When Constance checked her wristwatch, which was concealed among the many bracelets on her arm, she realized the hour was late. "We're running past time," she said. "Before we adjourn for the evening, is there anything anyone might care to add or detract?"

Raising a hand, Nina asked: "May I speak, Madame President?"

"By all means."

"As you all know, the conventions begin in a few weeks' time," Nina said, involuntarily fidgeting with a crutch. "And it looks as if Governor Rockefeller has lingered in the wings far too long to really expect to get the Republican nod. And so, as things stand, the party is beholding to Richard Nixon, though the conservatives would prefer Ronald Regan. Anyway, the underclasses are not going to receive any representation from the Republicans. Not this year! But with the Democrats there is still every possibility that we can, if enough pressure is brought to bear, force the issue of the war, racism and poverty. It's a chance that won't come again in this century I feel certain. I for one plan to be with the Mobilization Against the War and lobby in the streets of Chicago as a private citizen. And I'd be interested to know if anyone of you would care to participate." She searched each closed face in turn. They all returned her entreaty with vacuous expressions, as if to suggest that they didn't have an inkling what it was she expected of them? She encountered nothing but evasive looks. That is, until her eyes caught Percival's.

"Damn Nina," he swore, eyeing her craftily, "why look at me, huh?" He grumbled, "what 'r you up to anyhow? Shoo, woman, I ain't got time for nonsense!" He mumbled on, "yet I'd been thinking maybe I'd go. Bobby Seal's suppose to show so, yeah, maybe. Sh-e-et," he swore under breath. "OK, I'll go, I'm your patsy."

Nina reached across the table and squeezed his hand in fellowship, her bright eyes beaming. There was no one else she'd rather go with. Over time she had come to rely on his solicitude, resolve and steadfastness. "Thanks ole friend," she said, with unfeigned gratitude, tears glistening jewel-like on an eyelid.

Constance then moved to have the meeting adjourned. The motion was passed and the meeting came to a close. Dr. Bromberg was the first to rise and start for the door. Percival intercepted him on his way out.

"It's encouraging to hear of your minority student scholarship package," he said, genially. "It's one of a kind."

"Thanks for saying so," said Dr. Bromberg, scrutinizing Percival's face. "It's our every intention to be innovative."

"Well you've succeeded, as far as I'm concerned. In fact, my sister, Lois, jus' graduated from your school 'n my brother, Sam, is in his second year now, though I'm not sure how well he's faring." He grinned.

"And you might be?"

"Of course, you wouldn't know me, I'm Percival – Percival Jones."

"Yes, I know your brother and sister," said Dr. Bromberg, clasping Percival's hand in his. "I knew your face was familiar. You're the fighter."

"So rumor has it."

"A rather good one too from all I read," said Dr. Bromberg, relaxing his grasp.

"It's my claim to fame."

"And an activist as well. Interesting combination, I'd say. Would you also be a scholar?"

"Not enough of one, although I was enrolled in NYU."

"And?"

"It took back seat to the Olympic trials."

"Ah yes, I recall. too bad about your jaw. They say, you're the next Sugar Ray Robinson?"

"I sure hope they're right," he glibly said.

"I hope they're right for you." Dr. Bromberg then said, "Look, I'm in a bit of a rush but I would like to continue our talk at length sometime. Here," Dr. Bromberg handed Percival his card on which he scribbled his private phone number on the back. "You can reach me at this number most anytime. I must now be off."

"Thank you, sir."

"Be sure to call," said Dr. Bromberg, lolling momentarily in the doorway.

"Shall do," Percival promised, as the door closed. He then faced into the room and, bypassing a group of people discussing various issues of the day, sought out Gwen Halsey who, when he located her, was engaged in a highly animated conversation with Nina and her boss, Miriam Fisk.

Nina asked, "Do you know each other?"

"I don't believe we do," said Miriam, uncertainly?

"Have we met before?" asked Gwen in a curious tone, confronting his appraising eyes with candor.

"I'd recall that," said Percival, waving a clumsy hand.

"Let me introduce you," Nina said, as Miriam stuck out a stiff hand. "Percival this is Miriam Fisk." He accepted her hand. "And this is Gwen Halsey. Ladies, this is my dear friend, Percival Jones. They tell me he is arguably the best fighter in the world."

"Are you really a fighter?" asked Miriam, in wonderment. "You'd not think it to look at you."

"I'll accept that as a compliment."

"Please do," said Miriam, diffidently, and as their hands slipped apart he accepted Gwen's, which he gently crushed to his lips like the petals of a flower.

"It's a pleasure."

"It's kind of you to say so."

"Miriam, if you don't mind," Gwen pleaded, "I must be going if I'm to catch the ten thirty ferry into Manhattan."

"I'll be right with you," Miriam said, collecting her belongings. "Won't you excuse me?"

"By all means – go," said Nina.

"You going to the ferry," Percival asked, glancing quickly between the two women.

"I'm dropping Gwen off," Miriam stated.

"Would you mind if I hitch'a ride with you? I'm headed into the city myself."

"Of course," said both women without hesitation.

Then Miriam asked Nina, "have you a lift?"

"I have, thank you," Nina replied. "Beverly will see me home after talking to Constance and setting up an appointment for an interview."

"Then I'll be saying goodnight."

"Good night," Nina sang out.

Gwen waved.

"Before we go," Percival said, looking about. "Has anyone seen Rufus?"

"I almost forgot," Nina said, trying to keep a straight face. "He told me to tell you that he was beginning to feel claustrophobic, shut in among so many intellectual giants, and he being a Lilliputian, and that he would talk to you later. The funny thing is he said it with such dead pan," she said, chuckling under breath. "And he left."

Percival threw back his head and laughed. "That's Rufus for you. When was that?"

247

"While you were talking to Dr. Bromberg," she informed him. "He tried to catch your eye but you were obviously engrossed."

"Did you get a statement?"

"Not what I expected," she chortled, eyes kindling.

"We'll talk. Good night."

"For certain," she agreed. "Good night."

He waved.

The last bell for the ten-thirty ferry was ringing when they arrived and they had to run to beat the closing doors. They had barely made it through the doors before they shut at their backs. And no sooner had they boarded the vessel and situated themselves on the outside deck facing the Verazanno bridge, illuminated like a diamond necklace strung over the river against an empurpled night sky, then the ferry slipped it's berth with a strenuous tug.

"Do I detect a hint of an accent?" Percival asked.

"I'm a southern girl," Gwen said with a nervous edge, her hazel eyes filled with emotion.

"'R you now?"

"I left the south before my liberal views buried me there."

"Really?"

"It was a long, long time ago. Another lifetime surely."

They lapsed into silence, observing the murky night reflected in the swollen river through which the Ferry plunged and the lone cry of a distant fog horn carried over the waves. He turned and looked at her in the wan deck light as would a man look at a woman he was enamored of. "What'a you say we get to know each other over cocktails 'n dinner some night soon?" he proposed.

"A date you mean?" She broke out in a laugh. "Not that I mind. I'm even flattered. But I'm a bit older than you, don't you think?"

"Old?"

"Old enough."

"For what?"

"I see there's not going to be a gracious way out of this," she said weakly.

"You want'a way out?"

"You're charming but impulsive."

He didn't respond but turned her attention to the city skyline, as it drew near.

"The city looks like a galaxy of stars from here."

She marveled at the skyline, still as a picturesque slide.

"Which is why the whole world's attracted to it like a moth to a flame. It makes it appear possible to reach out and touch a star, become a star if one is so inclined, though too few ever do," she said, tonelessly, her hair blown and face flushed by the salty spray.

Percival reached out as if to grasp a star. "Do you like the city?"

"I do where I live."

"Where's that?"

"The Village."

"I'm rather fond of the Village myself."

She invited him to her place for a drink. "If it's not past your bedtime, that is?" He quickly accepted, dismissing the snipe. She lived in a three-room railroad apartment on Christopher St. The living room was comfortably designed. There were two plush chairs, a love seat, glass coffee table with copies of The New Yorker, Time and Book Review sprawled on its surface. There was a handsome floor to ceiling library on a side wall, and reproductions of Van Gogh, Monet and Picasso decorated the remaining three walls. A small bar was tucked in a front corner near a draped window which overlooked the lighted street below. After she had offered him a seat, she placed an LP on the stereo and the tonal colors of the Miles Davis quintet wafted through the room like a heady balm.

She passed him a drink in short order and proceeded to sit across from him. "Cheers!" She raised her glass.

They talked around issues, trying to size each other up without drawing blood – that would come later. She informed him that she was involved with someone but he retorted, as if to mock her, "I didn't ask." She primly retorted, "You're as brazen as you are impudent." He shrugged it off, amused. They exchanged telephone numbers, made a date for early the following week, and enjoyed a slow groping dance to which, inflamed by desire, she stammered, "You dear, dear man!" Then, before she became overly flustered and asked him to stay the night, she ushered him out the door.

"Good night," she called, as he descended the stairs.

"Good night," he returned, from the hall below.

***

On a day in the middle of the following week, Percival took five of his crew members to a Teach in on the Grimes Hill/ Wagner College Campus where he had been invited by SDS to participate. He allowed those of his crew who weren't interested to have the afternoon off. He warned, "I don't wanta hear you cats started a riot without me, dig?" They cawed in response, "No way, daddy-O," and waved him off. He said in return, "it warms my heart to know you care." The five members of the crew who consented to go were, Tzi,

Katy, Inez, Melvin and Leroy, the boy who used to read the Daily News but had since switched to reading the Times under Percival's influence. Percival had thought that Melvin had joined them because he still had feelings for Katy, although he had said it was because of his religious objections to war.

When they arrived on campus the Teach-In was in progress under cover of lush shade trees besides the campus library, adjacent to the walkway which encircled the greensward on which students tossed Frisbees, sun bathed, and over which a limp flag hung in the sultry air and the main, ivy covered building hovered like a citadel – inimical to forming young minds but not averse to stamping them out like so many license plates. The group was composed of seventy-five to a hundred students, including professors. They joined them in a circle under shade trees.

A sandal foot, shirtless, long haired Hippie-type – an SDS member surely – held up a form for the crowd to read, and said in a sophomoric, college boy tone of voice, "We'll be circulating this bus sign up form for those of you who want to attend the democratic convention in Chicago and protest the war on the streets. Bus schedules, arrivals and departures, will also be posted. Bring crash helmets, it's bound to be a ride," he said, then sat cross legged on the grass, in the sun.

"I don't mean to put a damper on things," said another young man, following the announcement, "but I've decided to leave school, join the Army and volunteer for combat duty," he said explosively. "As much as I dislike this war, there are arguments, personal with me, I can't avoid. We do things we don't necessarily agree with for reasons other than our own. We do them because we're compelled. Anyway, that's how it is with me. I don't know how else to put it."

Suddenly hundreds of eyes rounded on him, confronting him.

"No, don't," a coed stared, fearful for his life.

"What reasons? Give me one reason," said a faceless voice.

He had been hoping to avoid such scrutiny. He grew defensive immediately.

"What's this college to offer outside drugs and boredom?" He vehemently said. "Hell, there are more drugs on this campus than there is coal in all the hills of Pennsylvania, where I come from."

The youth's accusations were not altogether unfounded. Indeed, it had been quietly speculated that Wagner College—a Lutheran college— was one of the major distribution centers for drugs in the North East. While the administration was not found to have connived in it, it wasn't entirely blind to it either. And if they were slow to act it was understandable in that they were afraid of the scandal and loss of revenue the college would incur were they to go to the police and word leaked to the "Press." In addition, the school stood in jeopardy of losing its accreditation. Unlike the administration, however, campus security was not above suspicion.

"School and I are done," he said nervously, wringing his hands in anxious self-absorption. "And the winds of war are calling like the bagpipers 'Danny Boy' off to battle in my ancestral homeland. Only I'll be going to Vietnam, ten thousand miles in the opposite direction of Ireland. A land I know of only in dreams and reverie," he said with a wistful, half-secret, half-remembered longing, the warmth of the soil of Ireland, her multi-colored grasses spiraling out in all directions towards the distant corners of the world like 'Sweet Molly Malone's' twirling skirts—a country he'd concocted from folklore and childhood songs. Songs such as "Danny Boy" and the 'pipes' that had summoned him 'off to war.' Beloved songs much a part of the Pennsylvania Irish hill country, whence he came, as were they part of Ireland itself. "I know many of us stood together in D.C., in front of the White House, at the Pentagon, the U.N shouting 'Hell no we won't go!' It must seem to you as if I'm deserting our cause. It's been heart-wrenching for me." He waggled his head. "And why I'm baring my soul, looking you in the eyes," he said in agony of heart, "rather than simply slipping off."

"Don't tell us," roared a history professor, a lion of a man with tousled hair, his orotund voice descending to a growl, "you've been ensnared as was Danny boy by what Abe Lincoln called, 'The exceeding brightness of military glory—the attractive rainbow that rises in showers of blood—that serpent's eye that charms to destroy'—War!"

"Charmed? No not charmed but ensnared. Yes, professor, as was Lincoln pressed by circumstances beyond his control to wage a war he had no wish to fight," the youth reposted. "I'm no less at a loss than was good ole Abe," he argued, seeking understanding from his schoolmates whose expressions were cold, accusatory and unsympathetic. "There are circumstances, forces beyond my control too," he explained. I'm not to blame. Why fault me? Okay, okay, here's the thing! I have a kid brother, see, an athlete, more deserving than me, who graduated high school last May at the top of his class and joined the Army and is now waiting to be deployed. He had a football Scholarship to Notre Dame and passed it up to not disappoint our dad and go fight for his country," he said, choked with anguish. "The kid's a world beater. You should see him on the grid iron; see him shake a squad of tacklers spread out, fan wise, in a maze across the field, eating his dust. He's as hard to latch onto as a greased pig. It's a wonder how well he handles that ball." He cast his mind's eye back

251

on a not so distant scene in which his kid brother, amidst a sea of roaring fans, won the sectionals near single handedly, and was borne aloft off the field in triumph. "He could have gone on to the NFL – if not for this war. But, no, he's given it up to go fight for his country." With a vast shake of his head, his mind wandered back to the issue at hand, the war in Vietnam. "And here I am at a stinking four-year junior college," he laughed derisively, "and this kid brother of mine has a football Scholarship he turns down, to Notre Dame of all places, to go fight a War nobody would wish on their worst enemy! Jesus Christ, don't you see how that makes me feel? I'm the one who should go. Like I'm only here because I'm scared shitless of having my brains blown out in some stinking far-off out of the way Godforsaken shit hole I can't find on the fucking map without a compass! I can't let my kid brother shame me like that; I've got to know whether I'm a man or not," he said, a tremor in his voice.

"'N if you're not," Percival challenged?

"Not what?"

"A man."

"What kind of question is that?" he said ruefully, uneasy in himself.

"You brought it up," said Percival in response. "If it were a question for which I had doubts, I wouldn't go. And if it were a question in which I had no doubts, I'd most certainly not go!"

"Let me put it to you so," interjected a professor, an anthropologist and known *Buddhist*, from under cover of a shade tree. He knocked ashes from out the bowl of a pipe he'd been smoking against the heel of an upended shoe. "Our current notion of masculinity is part of the package inherited from our distant past – goes back to our primal roots, our brutish ancestral heritage – and, of course, Hollywood's farcical take on war and American manhood. What we're discussing is a question of humanity, that which transcends sex and embraces a global perspective. As the philosopher Martin Buber espouses, *'Moving from an 'It' relation to the other, to a 'Thou' relation.'* That is to say, the interconnectedness of all things down to the sub-human, microscopic world. We are here, in fact, in an attempt to nurture the spirit of our commonality which 'conflicts,' such as the Vietnam war, place us in opposition. In short, the wonder of our nature, the universality of our cosmic belonging."

They all succumbed to a moments silence, broken only by the twitter of songbirds.

A student reluctantly chimed in as if in response to the birds in the overarching branches under which they sprawled, while a few basked in the sun as it stretched towards noon. "It also addresses the question, I should think, of what it is to be a man apart from a patriot."

"A shot in the dark," a coed piped in.

"To say the least," said another.

"The bigger problem is, if that's your point ," said Bob Fischer, local coordinator for SDS, "it's the men who come home in boxes; while the others are burning their draft cards and going to jail." He pushed back his unruly hair, restrained by a bandana like an Apache warrior's, that cascaded about his shoulders in wild profusion. "Why not go to jail. It's really the only manly thing to do. There you get to keep your integrity, and, as the professor said, your humanity. If you think about it the frontline of the war is here at home bringing it to an end!"

"Only I don't see any of you burning your draft cards or giving up your deferments and going to jail," said the other, in sharp rebuke. "In your case, Bob, you're no one to speak! You're always on the Dean's list while me, I'm your Joe Blow average student," he spouted. "You, you're an academician. It's who you are; part of your blood line; your racial identity." He knew he should back off, however, his inflamed, Irish temperament got the better of him, "It's nothing to be ashamed of being a smart-ass Jew boy." Bob bristled, glowered, "huffed" and faced away. "It's not like calling you a fucking nigger—" the unchecked spate of words rolled like a thunderclap off his tongue. He realized much too late what he had said. A shock wave passed through the crowd. They all glowered at him.

He cringed under the scrutiny. "*Since when do we resort to such an abusive misuse of language?*" a professor bellowed.

"Shit," the youth spat, succumbing to a cheerless funk. Percival flinched, concerned less for himself than for Leroy and Melvin, the youngest and eldest of his racially diverse crew, teenagers—as were so many of these college students defying their nations call to arms.

"I'm sorry," the youth said. "I didn't mean it the way it sounds," he said from behind his hands in shame.

"I'm at my wits end and my thoughts are in disarray. I apologize," he muttered, crestfallen.

"I meant to say, Bob, you're a Judge's son born to scholarship. Me? I'm the son of an illiterate Irish coal miner born to a life of drudgery and toil," he groaned.

"I'm lost here on campus. At the rate I'm going I'll soon flunk out anyway. When I first came to college I was looking to find myself. Instead, I find myself mired down. The light I sought has since gone out, and the guns of war beckon. The cry for war, deep in the blood, wins out. When I first got here, I was a Catholic but as I leave I'm an agnostic. A uniform will suit me fine. In the army I'll fit in easily. I can't seem to shake the coal dust. Here I'm just an upstart, a social climber. There I'll be one of the grunts," he bitterly laughed.

"Don't sell yourself short. Neither school nor arms define a man," said a coed, off handedly.

"What does?" he asked.

"Strength of character or lack thereof," she returned. "The 'principles' on which Dr. King, wished his children to be 'judged.'"

He hung his head shamefacedly. "Ummm," he uttered haltingly, trying to explain himself, his outburst of temper, "You don't know how Irish and black history parallel each other."

"You gonna hog the whole show? Give me a break, will ya?" someone shouted from out the crowd.

"I'm trying to find my way out of a hole," the youth voiced, defensively. "Despite it all, everything, I'm flunking out of school. I'm at a loss and have no wish to return home a failure; so the Army is one sure way I have to redeem myself."

"And get yourself killed while at it," a classmate added.

"Carry on," said the Chaplin. "Your story is one of the many stories that go untold; too many of our young men set off to war for reasons unbeknownst to us. And those stories should be heard."

Yes, go ahead," called another. "Your life hangs in the balance."

"It's one thing for the school to fail you," Bob said, "but quite another for you to throw your life away because of it."

"You would say that," said the youth, sourly."

"Needless, I agree with the Chaplin. 'I may disapprove of what you say,' as Voltaire was reputed to have said, 'but I'll defend to the death your right to say it.'"

Reassured, the youth continued, "All too many of us, despite knowing better, act as if the United States was a fait accompli, having sprung fully formed out of the heads of the founding fathers. I hate to disabuse you of that notion but the facts don't fit the fiction," he said, his voice pain filled. "It was War after war after war that brought our nation to prominence. Every household, every family, generation after generation, fanned the flames of those wars!"

"Must you help fan them also?" said another.

"Wars are a luxury we can no longer afford," the Chaplain argued.

"No, padre, it'll not stop," he sobbed, his eyes swollen with tears.

A few Hippie types in the far backfired up a joint they then passed among themselves. There was certainly enough cigarette smoke wafting on the air to mask the smell. Or so they thought. Until, that is, the pungent aroma, caught the keen, olfactory senses of a bearish, history professor who bellowed out, "For God sake, this is a Teach-In not a Happening! You do well, whoever you are, to put that joint out now! This young man is deserving of our undivided attention. The tide of this war depends on what we do here. This is not the battle front but, more importantly, it is the forefront of the peace resistance," he said with conviction. "We must ask ourselves again and again, Why this senseless war? And we must not accept easy answers. Please," he said to the youth, "carry on."

The joint was hastily snuffed out.

And the gathering again refocused its gaze on the distraught youth.

"Thank you," the youth sighed, his face damp with sweat. It was not a light affair with him and weighed heavily on his shoulders. He pondered the question and said, at last, "I admit my slurs were a slip of the tongue. I lost my head in the confusion of the moment— racial epithets conjure up images of wrongs suffered by the aggrieved at the hands of those who wish them ill, wish, in fact, to take us back to the golden age of slavery when cotton was king. I don't long for any such thing any more than I care to revisit the holocaust.

"We Irish, too, lest it be forgotten, were driven from our homelands and forced into servitude and brought to the New World, all but on slave ships and in chains, by the British to work as slaves and indentured servants! We were called 'Black Irish' because, like Africans, we were considered property and, until rather recently, we were treated as harshly and still are by the British in Belfast," he said with rancor. "It's only recently we Irish have made our way 'as white' into the American mainstream. It's a dubious honor. Yet, to be white, considered white, accepted as white, is, more or less, part 'n parcel of the American dream. And the Molly Maguires were as responsible for that as was John Kennedy's election to the White House." He smiled wryly. "It's that shared history, black and Irish alike, that gave rise to the Molly Maguires, who've come to be an integral part of Pennsylvania hill country folklore.

"Accused of being vigilantes by the mine owners, they were thought of as avenging angels by the workers in the pits who were treated no better than beast of burden owing their Souls to company stores. They suffer in the same way sharecroppers. The Molly Maguires were legendary where I grew up and were considered heroes. We were black Irish; no better than 'niggers' and worked bone dry like slaves—wage slaves," he bellowed, lips pursed. "If you doubt me, come see the miners as they emerge from out of the pits covered in coal dust that no amount of soap can wash off. Most spend their lives looking like burlesque actors in black face. It's comically pathetic— sadly so— the poverty of our accursed condition.

"Emerson was to say of us, *'The poor Irishman, the wheelbarrow is his country.'*" He winced uneasily.

"They, the Molly Macguires, were a source of pride. Much like the Panthers are for young blacks. The songs of their deeds are still sung in the hill country of Pennsylvania. They earned some respect for us Irish coal miners, though they were utterly wiped out. They were crushed out as were slave rebellions, and the leaders sent to the gallows. My father's a coal miner among many without much of an education," he bitterly said! "The opportunities were not there; there was no such thing as open enrollment. That's how I got to college, because of open enrollment. My dad continues to, 'Owe his soul to the company store.' But he retains a share of pride. He fought in Korea and was a decorated hero. As a good American he saw it as his sworn duty.

"Despite the hardships miners face they take pride in their work. My dad wanted me to follow him down into the mines and work with him in the pits. It was not for me. I was of a different generation. The generation of which John Kennedy—the first Irish Catholic president— said, 'The torch has been passed.' So when I was accepted here at college I came running," he said. "But two years of college has made me doubt myself, see things differently. All too many other questions surface. And pressing heavily in on me is my kid brother going off to war. The war our generation is called on to fight! Of course it's wrong. How can war be right. It's a Faustian bargain! If my kid brother turns up dead then what does right or wrong mean for me? It strikes me as if I'm only here to hang on to my life, this dumb lump of sod."

"It might well be," someone sang out, "but this dumb lump of sod is more precious than any grave will ever be. It's not the war we're protesting so much as affirming our lives and our right to hold on to them. Besides, if you kill others wrongly doesn't it present you with a dilemma of another sort?"

"Given the history you've just outlined, I'd think that would give you every reason not to go," someone called from the depths of the crowd.

"I feel drawn to this war by forces unbeknownst to me, like Hounds from Hell. Forces such as the Draft board, to start." He laughed dryly, at his own expense. "They'll be on my ass as soon as I'm off campus anyway."

"Another question," Bob Fischer poised in reprisal, ignoring the pun, "knowing the war to be wrong and you go, will you be doing your duty as you see fit?"

The student faltered: "This is sacrifice," he fervently objected. "A sacrifice over and above life's callings. Beyond moral proclivity. Tell me, what if my kid brother gets killed or, worse, comes back a paraplegic and I'd not gone but stayed home safeguarding my ass? Then what? Do I hang myself? Besides, like I said, my father went and fought the war his generation was called on to

256

fight, as did his father and his father before that, and now my kid brother is off to the war our generation is called on to fight. Sacrificing his future – everything! The question I'm forced to ask myself is how do I keep on pretending to a morality I don't necessarily have? And how do I tell my kids, if ever I have any, I didn't go when my country, in its darkest hour, called?"

"How do you tell them you did?"

"Our wars, from the revolutionary to now, have marked our nation's progress step by step."

"A base problem with the concept of progress is that there was no word for it in the ancient world," interjected the bearded history professor, reaching for notes stored in the inner pocket of a rumpled jacket. "It's a relatively modern term. And the difficulty with the use of the word is that it's beholding to no one, knows no peace with the past, is restless in the present, and is ever anxious for the future. It's as unstable as nitroglycerine and equally apt to blow up in your face."

"Like Vietnam you mean?" The youth grimaced, agitated. "Those of you who know me are surprised at what you might call 'a breach of faith.' No more surprised than I am," he choked, near gasping. "But listen, I've come to feel that it's incumbent on our generation just as it was on our fathers to fight in Korea and the Second World War. More a karmic debt than a moral one, kismet, you know? How does one avoid one's duty any more than one's destiny?"

"Sounds like you're talking about Manifest Destiny," someone mockingly observed. "The white man's burden." The student then went on to recite with a touch of wicked sarcasm,

"'Take up the white man's burden –

"'ye dare not stoop to less –

"'nor call to loud on freedom

"'to cloak your weariness,

"'By all ye cry or whisper.

"'By all ye leave or do,

"'The silent, sullen peoples

"'Shall weigh your gods and you.'" He concluded with a sly, self-satisfied grin on his face.

"You quote Kipling's appeal to colonialist powers well," said the youth sourly, casting the other an annoying glance. "No, I wasn't thinking of Manifest Destiny or our carrying the torch of civilization to the dark-skinned peoples of the globe. However, in as much as it's consistent with liberty, the white man can use some help about now. Then again, in Vietnam, it's our black brothers who are carrying the bulk of that burden."

"You're arguing in circles," someone rancorously objected.

"Circles is it?" He said, sagging under the burden of it all. "Is this straight forward enough for you? I go home and I can't face my dad; a fearless man; a man with courage in his hands. He's semiliterate, as are most coal miners, the strong, silent John Wayne type. He was awarded the Distinguished Service Cross, in the Korean War, for bravery above and beyond the call of duty! It's prominently displayed in the front room of our home and the first thing you see on entering. When I was a kid I wanted my dad to be as proud of me as I was of him. But the Vietnam war came along and spoiled it," He said in remorse. "He was more than just a war hero, my dad, much more. When tunnels cave in mines, and they cave in often enough, my father's among the first to take a shovel and crew down into the pits to locate and rescue the miners from the tunnels. In many cases, he extracts the dead and bring them up to the arms of grieving widows. It saddens me we hardly speak anymore. It's just as well, I know what he thinks. He thinks 'college has made me soft and weak.' He thinks my shoulder length, Hippie hair style gives me away. I embarrass him. The neighbors think I'm queer. And coal mining communities don't take kindly to 'gays.' To them I look, at best, like a 'drop out' from a San Francisco 'love In.' In their close mindedness, they've imagined a whole other life for me. And for those reasons my father rather I not come home Holidays. He did ask, however, was I smoking pot. I said 'No!' I doubt he believed me. I look so different than when I first went off to school. My whole attire, love beads, tie dye clothes—everything!

"Other classmates of mine who'd gone off to college refuse to return home for similar reasons. I can't say I fault them. You go off to college to change, to grow up, to become educated in the way of the world but then, when you do, you can't go home again. Not to the mountains. Instead you become lost in the ways of the world. My hope was they'd all be proud of me. Proud of my achievements; proud of my taking a stance. But no, they only see me as avoiding the draft; avoiding my one true obligation—fighting to preserve my country. The American way of life." He tossed his hands up in defeat.

"As you might well imagine, it's soured my relationship with my mother, too. She'd always greeted me warmly whenever I'd gone home in the past, but now it's with tepid indifferent. I've been cut from the bosom of my once close-knit family," he said in a strangled tone of voice, heart sinking. "And my kid brother and I don't know how to look at one another let alone speak; and we use to be such pals. I think he doesn't want to fail our dad as I have. He told me once, he was going to Vietnam to fight for the freedom of those people just as we fought the Civil War for the liberty of Southern slaves. He said that 'global communism is a scourge and should be wiped off the face of the earth.'

I'm no Joe McCarthy but I'm no fan of the communist either. None of us can say they are too young to not recall the Cuban missile crisis, and the edge of destruction to which the world clung. Isn't democracy – that which we're all gathered together here in the name of – worth defending? As I see it, we owe it something other than lip service," he argued forcefully, hands outstretched and eyes large with gravity.

"In the best sense of the word," argued another equally forcefully, "democracy is the willingness to discuss ideas not necessarily consistent with one's own. Such as communism – of which Dr. King accused us of 'being morbidly afraid.' And rightly so. Remember, it was President Eisenhower who said, 'We must not confuse loyal dissent with disloyal subversion.' The question is when and where do you oppose an idea by dint of arms? While it might be said that Cuba is in our backyard, 90 miles off the coast of Florida, Vietnam, a tiny country in Southeast Asia, 10,000 miles from us in the opposite direction. And so, it strikes me, that we have our own sins to account for before throwing long range missiles at others who have no such weapons to defend themselves with."

"Neither was it the Russians," someone else chimed in, "who invented the bomb, nor were they the ones to explode it. That privilege belongs to us. When Winston Churchill first received word of its successful use, he said: 'What was gunpowder? Trivial. What was electricity? Meaningless. But this atomic bomb is the second coming of wrath.' And that, it might be said, is our undoing!"

"This war has created a rift between my family and me that won't heal, least of all if my kid brother comes back home in a body bag!"

"Your trying to convince yourself of something you don't believe in," called another loudly.

"You're going for the worst reason," a girl cried shrilly.

"Tell me, if you know, what are the right reasons," he implored?

"Self-defense and in this instance that's not the case!"

"Self-defense, yes. But am I not my brothers' keeper? His safeguard? I owe my parents as much." A sheen of sweat glistened moistly on his boyish good looks. "And I fail myself if I do less."

"You sell your family short if you think they won't accept you for your convictions."

"They won't, as I've said, and besides it's not my family whose on trial here," he replied fairly bitterly.

"No one's on trial save the war policy of this administration," claimed another.

"Besides," he persisted, "according to my parents, I owe them my life. According to the Bible, I owe God my devotion. According to the government,

I owe it my allegiance. Then there is that I owe myself which is confusingly tied up with the afore said."

"Are you not in the least beholding to yourself?" asked someone else.

"That's the question, isn't it? How much of our lives is truly our own." He sulkily argued, his face clouded, "To avoid my duty – to fail in my family's eyes; to fail my country in its darkest hour in recent memory! I ask, what's become of 'My country right or wrong?'"

"Individual responsibility. The Nuremberg Trials," was the immediate response. "Wasn't it established there that each of us; each soldier in particular is responsible for his own actions? not his commander! not his nation! He and he alone is beholding for his deeds!"

"I know my reasons may sound trite but I'm as filled with apprehension as was Hamlet: 'To be or not to be.' As for me, 'to go or not to go,' amounts to the same thing. I don't see myself in the mirror any more without seeing a coward steering me in the eyes, mocking me. What you all say is true to a point but, it's come to sound to me, true or not, like a coward's lie."

"Are you sure it's not the other way round," a coed asked?

He began to sweat under the strain, subjected, as he was, to scrutiny by his school and classmates. "Maybe but as my father says, 'Peace comes with the surrender of your enemies.' I don't quite agree but I do see his point," he said without conviction.

"I would like to explore the idea of patriotism a bit further," interjected the professor of anthropology, gesturing broadly with a flourish of his pipe. "As I see it— apart from Samuel Johnson having famously declared '*patriotism*' to be '*the last refuge of a scoundrel,*'— the dilemma it presents us is similar to that of masculinity. The notion of muscle flexing, the necessity of proving ourselves more formidable than the ape. Despite the achievements of modern civilization and its offspring science, we've not come one jot closer than the ape to solving the riddle of the Sphinx. That is, recognition of the unity of the family of man. The recognition of our being 'one' or of the same species," he said with sangfroid. "Patriotism limits our horizon and presumes everyone else to be the other or the enemy; then goes about creating that enemy. When, in fact, they are neither 'enemy nor other,' but distant relations, global citizens – the link in the key to the puzzle of our being. We must busy ourselves at mending fences."

The professor paused, scanning the many faces of young adults sprawled fanwise out from under shade trees onto the sun dappled greensward, basking in the glow of a bright Summer's day. He was one of the younger, more popular professors on campus. And they were fully absorbed in the discourse. "As author and psychologist J. D. Lang reminds us, '*What we think is less than what we know; what we know is less than what we love: what we love is so much less than what there is. And to that precise extend we are so much less than what we are.'"* He smiled genially and said, "Victor Hugo, author and statesman, was similarly to have remarked, 'We must be guided by the spirit of the higher law. *The law of laws – The human heart,*'"

The assemblage broke out in wild applause.

The youth, however, felt downcast as a result and spirits dampened.

"I say what I say knowing full well you have grave doubts," the professor continued. "Indeed, you are trying to talk yourself into something that is disagreeable to you. And, needless to say, you are absolutely correct: Our country is passing through one of its more troubled periods. It is one reason these Teach Ins are essential. We are searching, all of us, for a way by which to get our nation back on track. And in the process, spare our young unnecessary hardship. There is a moral imperative in all this: One goes to college not only to further his or her education but to learn how to chart an ethical course by which to live. And if you don't know it now, hopefully you will later on."

"Maybe." The youth sulked, his courage flagging. "Right now I don't have time. My ass is on the line. My brother is off to war 'to stop,' as he says, 'the spread of communism,' while I debate value systems with, as my dad would put it, 'A bunch of Pinko commie finks.' This is not an intellectual exercise. While I might agree with all you say, if my kid brother comes home in a body bag –And, I dare say, I see him dead if I don't go," he said breathlessly. "True enough, I don't see him alive if I go but, on the other hand, I don't see him dead either. And for me, that's good enough. All I know is if something happens to him and I'd not gone, I won't be able to live with myself. All else aside, I owe my family, if not my country, my life to this moment. That's inarguable! Besides, didn't John Kennedy say, and he was one of our more gifted, modern leaders, 'Ask not what your country can do for you but ask what you can do for your country?' Does this or does this not hold true?"

"That's simply an elegant rephrasing of "My country right or wrong," responded a voice from out the crowd. "And isn't he the one who got us in to this war in the first place? Besides, the government, no less than the nation, should be fashioned round the legitimate concerns of its citizens, not the other way round. That's the way the framers of our Constitution meant it."

"It's an evil thing – War," stated another. "General Sherman declared war 'Hell', and he would have known. Indeed, war is the Hell out of which every other evil rears its ugly head."

"If it's an evil I shall have to do penance afterwards." It did not matter right or wrong. The die was cast, his decision made, and the chips left to fall where they may. "If I die I must then suffer the consequences. Either way, I go."

"In the final analysis we're all accountable to God and God isn't going to judge nations but individual souls," a coed sang out! "All too sadly, more people go to hell in the name of patriotism than any other sin known to us. If you must enlist why not join the Army Medical Corp as a conscientious objector," she proposed as an alternative? "That way you can serve your conscience, your country, and prove your manhood without tossing your convictions away?"

"When this is all over I want to still be able talk to my brother," he said, the love for his younger brother apparent in his tone. "Then I'll be able to see his side and maybe he'll be able to see and respect mine. At least we'll be able to talk unlike what we're doing here."

In the long run he would accept the coed's advice and serve in the military as a Medic and conscientious objector, thereby fulfilling his duties to conscience, family, and country. He would not receive the Distinguished Service Cross as did his dad, but he would have proven himself. He remained true to his convictions. And that's how his family remembered him in the epitaph inscribed on his tombstone: "He died as he lived, in defense of his principles."

The discussion carried on briefly along similar lines up until a cat call rend the air, drawing their attention: "Oh shit, jocks!" A coed exclaimed, as if they were a sub species. Percival craned his neck, facing over his shoulder. Five members of the football squad, attired in the team's jersey, approached from the greensward, flinging insults: "Hey guys, look what we got here, the red brigade. All the campus commie finks lined up in a row to be shot down."

"You can smell the lot of em; they can all use a bath!"

"Naw, what they really need is a good stiff dick up the ole kazoo – the faggot sons of bitches!"

"If you don't like it here why the fuck don't you go to Russia where you belong?"

"I say we should kick ass."

"I second it."

"I third it."

"Let's do it!" And a stone was lobbed in, missing it's mark. At that Percival uncrossed his legs, handed Katy his planter' hat, and proceeded to stand with a raw, nervous energy. He took a step forward, raising his hand in a conciliatory gesture:

"What gives, cuz?"

"Who the fuck you calling cuz, spook?" asked one, spitting out the side of his mouth, eyes glowering.

"I'm trying to make nice 'n you're actin like a jerk."

"Swing on it, nigger!"

"Say what you like but it's like this," said Percival, warming. "We're trying to conduct a serious discussion here. If you want'a join in – do! We'll debate the issues with you, one on one, if you like. But if you're thinking of jumping bad 'n kicking ass – Well," said Percival confidently, beckoning them on with both hands, "you can start with me, dig?"

"Woe, the spades got heart. Ha-ha-ha. What'a you say guys, we can kick one lone nigger's ass, don't you think?'

"Shit yeah," they shouted!

"I'm not gonna ask you twice," said Percival, his face devoid of expression.

"We're scared! In fact, we're shaking in our boots, aren't we guys?" They laughed coarsely. Just Then Tzi bounded to his feet with the agility of an acrobat and hurtled himself through the air with a flying kick and shriek that scattered the birds in the trees with a flutter of wings and startled everyone in hearing, save Percival. He landed beside him, light as a cat, assuming a Karate stance, fingers curled like talons. "Count me in," he said fiercely, exhaling through his nostrils, assessing the situation with shrewd eyes.

The football players collided into one another in wide eyed surprise, coming to an abrupt halt.

"I don't know who the chink is, but the spade looks like Percival Jones to me," one of the guys whispered fiercely to the others.

"You mean the fighter?" they asked in concert.

"Now you mention it," said another, "it looks like him to me, too. And let's not overlook the Karate kid."

"Still, it's only two of em."

"Yeah but –"

"Hmmmmmm?"

"Before I ask'd, now I'm telling, give ground," said Percival, staunchly, assuming a casual boxing stance. "Or lets deal!"

One of the professors's, the historian, stepped out from under cover of the trees, his hands on his hips. "Gentlemen," he said, "if you don't immediately desist I'll have you up in front of the disciplinarian board and off the football squad and out of this school so fast your knuckle heads will swim."

Somewhat hesitantly the lead member of the squad finally yielded, with a dismissive wave of the hand, "Fuck it – it can't be worth it!" And with a small amount of quibbling they withdrew. One flipped Percival the finger, as he turned away.

Tzi and Percival embraced triumphantly, like warriors, brothers in arms, as the assembly cheered and the jocks shamefacedly departed. "Righteous," said Percival to Tzi, looping an arm over his shoulder. They then rejoined the group on the grass under cover of the trees. Katy set Percival's hat back on his head, askew: "Ya did good, Charlie Brown," she said with laughter in her playful eyes. "You too, Tzi."

***

First thing next day Katy and Inez recounted the story of the previous day's adventures for the rest of the crew. "Y'all should'a come," Katy began, fully animated. "Percival n Tzi backed down half the fucking football squad."

"No shit?" exclaimed one of the crew excitedly.

"Yeah," Inez swore. "They was about to pop them fay dudes out."

"They was bad," Katy concurred.

"We did nothing," Tzi said, "jus' scared em a little."

"If I was there," said one, "I'd'a whup some ass myself."

"It didn't look to me like they needed your help," said Inez cuttingly, with flashing Spanish eyes, and a hand perched defiantly on an out thrust hip.

"Sounded out!" the rest of the crew busted a gut, slapping five all around. "She blew you away," they taunted.

"That wasn't cool," said the victim. "It ain't that funny either."

"Ya can't take it?" Katy asked.

They bantered playfully back and forth until Percival saw fit to bring it to a head saying, "Inez is right, we didn't need your help," causing the crew to howl the louder.

By mid-morning as they were engaged in clearing out a vacant lot to turn into a playground for the neighborhood kids, Estelle dropped by and started through the debris toward Percival. Two dump trucks had been supplied by the department of Sanitation to help remove the trash. As Percival paused over a shovel of rubble he'd dumped into a wheelbarrow for Tzi to wheel away, Estelle waved. He caught sight of her from the distance. His dark face was covered in sweat under his planters' hat. No one was spared from the heat and humidity of the day. All the boys had stripped to their T-shirts and tried to talk Katy and Inez into doing the same, strip to their bras, at least.

"Yeah, right," Katy responded. "Ya'd like that wouldn't you?"

Inez brazenly unhitched the tails of her blouse and tied them into a knot below her bosom, exposing her bare belly to view; and Katy did likewise.

The boys watched delightedly, exchanging sly grins. Some wolf whistled.

"N that's as much y'll get to see, too," Inez said sharply.

Katy leaned into Inez's ear. "But Melvin can ave all mine," she whispered, and they tittered, getting back to work.

The boys faced away, feeling they were the objects of their scorn.

Melvin did not participate in this play. Ever high minded, he kept apart and busied himself with his workload.

"You're doing a fine job with your crew," Estelle sang, as she watched them rake, haul and shovel with a protective hand shading her eyes. "The newsletter your crew puts out is the envy of the Corps, as the many letters to the editor attest. Katy's column, "Advise to the Lovelorn," is simply priceless!"

Tzi wheeled the barrow off that they might talk freely.

Percival listened, dabbing his face and neck with a handkerchief, curious as to where this was leading.

"How's Rufus' campaign coming?'

"For what it is it's not going badly. The office is opened and a membership is slowly developing n so we ave people out canvassing the area, trying to get a consensus."

"By the way, I heard about the incident at Wagner yesterday from one of my colleagues. She was quite impressed with your handling of a fairly volatile situation. But that's not why I stopped by." She swung back her loose, shoulder length hair, and cast a doleful eye on him. "I have a favor to ask."

"Shoot!"

"I was invited to address the Richmond Club next Thursday and I can't make it. I was wondering if you'd be interested in speaking in my place?"

"Huh?"

"I think you'll do the affair justice. They'll provide you with a gourmet lunch," she appealed to his appetite.

"The Richmond Club, you say?"

"Yes, precisely."

"That's like the business and professional circle, right? I mean, the pillars of society?"

"Some would say that."

"N you want me to talk to em?"

She smiled mischievously. "That's it."

"No holds barred?"

"None whatever."

"In that case you're on."

"I'll let them know to expect you," she said.

The luncheon was held in the banquet hall of an exclusive club and restaurant, "The King's Arms." A sequence of stainglass windows, depicting scenes from the *Age of Chivalry & Grail Quest,* muted the passage of outside light, hence chandeliers illuminated its interior. The room was reserved for such occasions. Percival occupied the guest of honor's char at the head table among the officers. A monsignor opened the occasion with a benediction. After luncheon Percival was introduced by the Club's secretary, who tapped on a water pitcher with a spoon for silence.

"Our guest speaker for today, though speaking on behalf of The Youth Corps, is none other than the up and coming future Middle Weight Champion of The World, Percival Jones!"

Percival gained his feet amidst a welcoming round of applause. A colorful silken bandana adorned his throat. He wore a faded blue jean suit and sandals. He clenched his planters' hat in his hand by his side, prepared to bolt. The meal had been good but the talk was bound to draw sparks. He assessed his audience as if they were spectators at ringside: they were of New York's upper crust, White men of influence, pillars of society—with family names that harken back to *who's who* of the Gilded Age—distributed throughout the spacious dining hall at separate tables, waiting to hear him out. They were cleaver, learned and, like their *Robber Baron ancestors,* ambitious men.

Suffice it to say, Percival's was the only black face to be seen.

"Gentlemen," speaking off the cuff, Percival began, "I appreciate your introduction and warm reception but I'm gonna have to be fairly honest with you, anyhow," he said, causing them to yell with laughter. "The subject of poverty is no more an easy one to address than racism because, as often as not, they're one 'n the same. That is, the greater half of the Negro problem in America. In either case, we're talking about people that the general white population believe to be a burden on the taxpayer, unless there's a war, like the one in Vietnam, then they're expendable! Outside that, they're a burdensome lot: N combine em into one person; one individual; one identity; one isolated human being; one soul n see if that doesn't conjure up a haunting picture of misery – the hated enemy within! It's poverty of spirit that allows for these conditions n not necessarily the afflicted's fault, as is more often suggested than not.

"I was asked by my boss to speak to you t'day about the Neighborhood Youth Corps. Well I don't know what it is I can say. It's an anti-poverty program that little strikes at the heart of the problem; n is mostly geared to bringing about a halt to rioting in ghettos," he said, with an irony more caustic than wit. "N on the surface it's a success. The program pays ghetto youth a weekly stipend to do clean-up work in the slums, etc. It's something like child labor used to be: You don't employ the parents at a living wage, instead you hire the kids out at a subsistence wage n suggest you're fighting poverty. N, by the way, it's only a summer project. This would be comic if it wasn't so tragic. Doesn't it strike you that someone has overlooked Fall, Winter n Spring? Not actually cause riots don't occur during those seasons. Yet they're no less poor the rest of the year, too; n their lives no less stunted. To solve this dilemma I'm telling the kids in my crew that they got'a start rioting in the off seasons, in the middle of winter, n see if the government won't extend these programs throughout the rest of the year.

"That said, I'll now take questions." He smirked, looking out over their stupefied faces.

"We're victims of the system ourselves," one shouted facetiously, while others hooted with laughter. "What do you suggest we do?"

"I'll tell you what," Percival shot back. "You burn downtown while I burn uptown!"

They were aghast and grew numbingly silent and, despite air conditioning, they were all sweating; their eyes were fixed on Percival, bulging with outrage.

"You just revealed yourself!" A florid faced, broad shouldered man in his mid-forties with a crewcut and military air trumpeted at him, rising from a table in the back and slipping on a uniform jacket in the same motion causing Percival's heart to thump as he was taken by surprise at sight of a police captain among the membership.

"You're the other bastard responsible for opening a Black Panther unit in my Precinct, aren't you?"

"N it's because of bastards like you that we do," Percival hurled back.

"I just wanted to meet you face to face on neutral ground first. Be sure, we'll meet again." He spun from the table, placed his cap in the crook of an arm and, his back as wide as a shield, marched from the room.

"I'll look forward to it," Percival defiantly called after him.

The gloves were officially off.

***

Summer was quickly coming to a head. The Republican Convention had come and gone and the Democratic one loomed on the horizon. As expected, the Republican Convention proved memorable only in as much as it was predictable. Richard M. Nixon was, as had been expected, nominated on the first ballot as "A law and order" candidate to no one's great surprise. It had proven a dull affair and the newspaper people, T.V. newscasters, analyst and spin doctors were chomping at the bit to wrap up and head on to Chicago where, rumor had it, history would be made. And in as much as news thrives on rumor, all the world's news gathering agencies would alight on Chicago or, as a poet called it, "The City of the broad shoulders."

Therefore, no one coming to Chicago in late August of '68 came with their eyes entirely closed. It had been anticipated that there would be violent confrontation on the streets with the anti-war people. In anticipation of the horde of protestors expected to arrive in Chicago to disrupt the convention, Mayor Richard J. Daley, not wanting the Republicans to hog the issue of "Law and order," had had his twelve-thousand-man strong police force outfitted, arrayed and galvanized into storm troopers to meet the insurrectionist head on. He also had five thousand of the Illinois National Guard mobilized and put on standby near the downtown area. If any nihilist coming to Chicago did not know who ran the city they would then learn at the hard end of a policeman's nightstick. The situation was such that The Mobilization Against the War had issued a warning, "If you're afraid of violence don't come to Chicago." Indeed, things looked so grave that Nina's husband and friends had tried to talk her out of going.

Her husband begged, "You're a cripple, for God sake! You have two children who rely on you. What will become of them – who knows what could go wrong?" he tossed up his hands in exasperation.

Her friends pleaded, "Nina, we love you. Please, for our sake, don't go. The Chicago police are among the most brutal in the country."

She laughed lightheartedly. "I'll be so far in the back that I'll be lucky if I even see a cop. let's hope I won't need one."

"Oh, Percival," they implored, "you talk her out of it."

"What can I say," he said, "I'll be in the back with her."

"Oh!" they shook their heads in dismay. "You're just as incorrigible as she. You're black and should know better."

Percival was dumbstruck and irritated. He could not quite make the connection.

Chicago's Lincoln Park along the shore of Lake Michigan's plush northeast side was dizzy with activity when Percival and Nina arrived late that Monday morning. The area was cordoned off by heavily armed police wearing Plexiglas face shields, who were being jeered at by irate demonstrators. "Fascist slobs," they shouted, sticking out their necks, the veins distended like cords. "You're turning the country into a fuckin' pig sty!"

"Hell no, we won't go!" Many flashed "V" signs to passing motorist.

Inside the park, a ragtag army of war resisters roved about like routed soldiers in need of a place to drop and lick their wounds and rest their groggy heads after the previous night's skirmishes with the police. Sporting bandaged heads and eyes inflamed from tear gas, some swore like combat hardened troops about the abusive tactics employed by the police in rousting them from the park. "They came at us like the Gestapo," complained one to another. "I never ran so hard in all my life."

"Tell me about it. I was the guy behind you."

It had been Percival's hope that a permit to sleep in the park would have been obtained by the time of their arrival but as yet the city had not seen fit to issue one. A flyer put out by the YIPPIE's read, "Sleeping in Lincoln Park after 11p.m. isn't as important as living out our revolution there the rest of the day (the park opens at 6 a.m.).

At the edge of the woods where demonstrators were sleeping face down in the grass and others rested in the shade, they found a tree under which Nina settled with her back against the trunk. She stretched her withered legs out in front of her, placing her crutches within reach.

"I'll be right back," Percival said, heading off into the meadow among the scattered army of protestors armed with placards and banners denouncing the war, sunning themselves, talking revolution and singing folk songs. He kept his ears open for any news as he strolled about, examining the strength of these young nihilists. On his return, as Nina was massaging her lower limbs, a few flower children paused and asked, "What would possess a cripple to enter this war zone, that's what it is you know."

Nina smiled up at them with a strangely absent air. "And how much more crippled would I be if believing as I do, I'd stayed home?"

"You're here to protest the war?" they asked incredulously.

"That and exercise my constitutional right to assemble."

"Aren't you afraid?"

"Not because I'm crippled."

"Groovy," they exclaimed, flashing her a "V" sign as they departed.

Percival rejoined Nina under the tree. "While you were off searching for news," she said, laughing in his direction, "it found me."

"So I saw," he said, following the flower children with his eyes as they gamboled off into the meadow like gypsies. He continued to look on as they disappeared amidst the scattered throng. There was, for the most part, an overall feeling of All Hallows Eve, youth in vagrant like getups, clad in mortician and grave digger clothes. Young girls were as prettily made up as ladies in a pageant, and their escorts like long haired versions of Tom Sawyer and Huck Finn.

Abbie Hoffman, self-proclaimed mad cap prince of mayhem and co-founder of the YIPPIES, cradled their candidate for president—a suckling pig— in his arms. By his side was their Miss America with rouge stars on her cheeks, garishly painted lips, and plastic tits as big as fun house balloons. Jerry Rubin and other YIPPIES were painted up like Counter-Culture Indians on the war path. And always lurking in the background, the ominous presence of the heavily armed Chicago police. It all made for a macabre setting in which to dance. And dance they would, as if under an atomic cloud burst; under radioactive fallout. As if the world were coming to an end. They danced the hallucinogenic dance of forgetfulness. But Percival, on the other hand, was more inclined to sit it out!

Percival was left with an altogether unsavory taste in his mouth as he looked out over this motley collection of white radicals, these Hippies, Yippies and Flower Power Children. Mainly, he wished that he were somewhere else. Anywhere else, in fact, save here. But when his eyes rounded on Nina— small, helpless, crippled Nina— he realized for the first time how attractive she was and how attracted he was to her. He had never before been able to admit it to himself because of her affliction and he could not allow himself to imagine her as a sexual being because she was an invalid. The thought made him feel odious, unnatural, perverted in his desires, and thus he had to expel it from his brain. Besides, she was a wife and mother of two, so it was well he expel it from his brain. Nevertheless, he was inarguably in love with her— warmly, compassionately, charitably. It was, in fact, why he had come to Chicago, because he could not bear to see any more harm befall her than nature had already visited upon her in one cruel stroke when, as a child, it had inflicted her with polio.

As every other person in the park with a portable radio was listening to the Peace Delegation at the convention call for an open convention and peace platform, a police van bounded over the meadow with three other cars in tandem, scattering angry, fist shaking protestors. A number of policemen leapt from the vehicles as they drew to a halt and with threatening clubs, bullied their way through the horde. They seized Tom Hayden— SDS founder and anti-war activist— clapped him in cuffs, and hauled him off, as demonstrators closed in shouting obscenities and casting stones at the fleeing vehicles.

"What is it?" Nina asked, straining?

"I'm not sure," Percival answered, having been brought to his feet by all the commotion.

The word quickly spread that Tom Hayden had been busted and just as quickly protestors gathered from all over the park to march to the downtown jail. Nina hoisted herself up with Percival's aid, grabbed her crutches, and they trailed the army of protestors to the city jail.

A pattern of intimidation developed as police, over the next few days, harassed and intimidate and arrested known leaders as frequently as possible, thus driving them into hiding or resorting to the use of disguises.

The demonstrators picketed the jail. "Free Tom Hayden, free Tom Hayden," they demanded. And within hours of his arrest Hayden was released on bail. A rousing welcome greeted him when he appeared on the jail house steps. The protestors then turned from the prison in a swirl and took an impromptu march through the streets to Grant Park across from the Conrad Hilton Hotel, which doubled as Democratic and press headquarters, chanting their slogans and blocking traffic in route.

Originally, the organizers of the anti-war forces had only requested a permit to march on the amphitheater, but the city fathers were no more willing to grant them a permit to march on Convention Center than they were willing to grant them permission to sleep in Lincoln Park. Despite the city doing all in its power to curtail the activities of the protestors, impromptu—or guerrilla activities, as they came to be called— were spontaneous outbreaks of the anti-war demonstrators' frustrations.

Committed to non-violent civil disobedience for the most part, the protestors did all they could to thwart the city's fathers. They engaged the Chicago police over possession of the streets as they slogged to Grant Park, which would become one of the many battle grounds over the next few days. Moving in an undulating wave through the streets, they shouted to the world vie T.V. and newspapers, "Hell no, we won't go!" then "1-2-3-4 we don't want your bloody war," and "Dump the Hump," while the Chicago police stood by bridling, waiting their turn.

The protestors rallied at Grant Park and were told what to do if arrested and given a number to call for legal aid. "Moisten a handkerchief and press it to your face," was the rudimentary advise, in case of a tear gas attack. As night descended over Chicago, a city visibly under siege, the protestors returned to Lincoln Park in defiance of the curfew and better judgment of their leaders.

Determined to not be roused from the park as easily as the night before, it was suggested they build a barricade between themselves and the police. Knowing it would prove useless, Percival pitched in anyway. Nina dragged tree limbs while Percival helped stack tables and benches against one another. Meshed garbage cans were added to the mix as the rickety structure went up. They labored ceaselessly until weary and drenched in sweat, and could not find another loose twig in the growing dark.

The barricade ran a distance of a hundred feet and stood six feet high, at least. Perhaps it was only something to do to keep their minds occupied and off the looming danger, and to not lose heart.

Nina hovered bird-like between her crutches, wheezing breathlessly. "That took my mind off things for a while anyway," she said, winded.

"I only feel more disheartened," Percival remarked, breathing soundly. "I mean, the cops can jus' as easily go around."

Police cars finally rolled in over the meadow and came to a stop fifty yards shy of the barricade, their high beams fixed on the makeshift structure, and revolving lights atop squad cars swept the wood line at the protestor's back with menacing regularity, affecting each one's nerves differently. The lights seeped through the gaps and slats of the picnic tables. A company of police in riot gear moved in behind the squad cars.

Nina slumped to the ground slowly and in parts, in the face of insurmountable odds. Percival collapsed to the ground beside her and gazed forlornly at his watch. Someone asked the time. "Seven past ten," he said. Exact time was crucial. Curfew was eleven. The waiting had begun. Time never moved so slow, so fast, so all at once.

They all knew that the structure behind which they hid was useless and that the cops could have them at will. It became increasingly evident with every passing second that the barricade was less a defense and more an ostrich sticking it's head in a hole.

"I feel like a scared kid walking through a graveyard late at night," Nina confessed.

"It's pretty hairy, all right."

"I thought you weren't afraid of anything," she said, tautly.

"That's during the day when I'm not being outflanked by an armed police force," he rejoined, in a distant tone of voice. "Otherwise, I'm with you all the way."

"I'm glad you are, too." She looked him in the face, in the dark. They sat together on the ground under a blanket, a comforting arm about the other.

Other protestors stood anxiously about, fidgeting, making small talk and casting fitful glances on the stream of crisscrossing lights from squad cars, which passed through the gaps of the untested barricade in which they'd put so much effort and placed so little hope. Likewise, their numbers, in the thousands, was no more reassuring.

Again, someone checked the time.

Again, someone asked, "how much longer?"

"Thirty-nine minutes left," was the half-hearted response, followed by an uneasy, sweat inducing silence.

A lookout cried, startling all, "five coming in!"

The five came in, one after the other, causing a stir. Percival was astonished to recognize, among the reinforcements the bespectacled, tall, long haired beat luminary, Allen Ginsberg, with the smaller, bald, pug-faced, French author and saintly convict, Jean Genet. The others he didn't know. Nina told him they were, William Burroughs, Terry Southern, and Richard Seaver. Assuming that the Chicago police were less literary than he was, Percival sneered, suspecting their arrival was too little too late.

But the fuss these literary lights generated among the other protestors caused them to forget their predicament for a moment anyway.

After the initial excitement caused by the new arrivals had died down, Allen Ginsberg sat on the ground under him in the lotus position and invited all, in a beatific voice, to join him. "If you will, I'll lead you in the Hindu Mantra Om. It alleviates tension and clears the butterflies." With these words and a tinkling of finger cymbals, he commenced, "Om –" And bit by bit the mantra was taken up by the multitude, a couple thousand strong. The sound of the mystical syllable permeated the night sky like a racket of crickets in mating season,

"Om – Om –"

The crackling of a bullhorn suddenly rend the air over which the mystic syllable hung like a cadenza, and an amplified voice blared, "You have five minutes to vacate the park. Five minutes. This will be your only warning!" The warning fell on deaf ears, and the hum continued unabated.

"Om – Om – Ommmmmmmm –"

A man said to Percival, "If I were you I'd get her out of here."

"If you're talking about me," said Nina, curtly, "address me directly. I'm an invalid not an infant and neither am I deaf."

"Sorry, excuse me," the man apologized, drawing back into the shadows.

"Care to help me to my feet?" Nina asked, facing Percival, on whose face a spectral light passing through a gap in the barricade, flashed.

"We don't ave to go if you don't like."

"I have no wish to be underfoot."

"Okay, sister, let's go," he said, slowly rising.

They were caught midway between the police cars and barricade when the assault began. Tear gas was lobbed in first, unleashing a choking grayish-white smoke that billowed out into a wafting fog over the area of the barricade. Next, a police wagon smashed a gaping hole in the center of the construct through which club wielding police in gas masks swarmed. Where before the mystical Hindu syllable was so pleasantly chanted, there now arose shrieks and groans of gagging protestors being attacked, as they sought a way out of the sulfuric mist in which they were caught. Slowly they emerged, pitching forward blindly with police in close pursuit, clubbing them savagely. Some toppled over vomiting their guts, while others stumbled on trying to escape the park and the nightsticks.

Horrified by the groans and cries issuing from the direction of the barricade, Nina drew to a standstill, bringing Percival to an abrupt stop with her. She looked frantically between him and the barricade with a ghastly expression on her girlishly pretty face.

"This can't be happening," she uttered, dumbfounded. "This is America, isn't it?"

"I'm the wrong person to ask," said Percival, tonelessly. "There's nothing we can do but go before the gas overtakes us too."

Nina shudderingly acquiesced.

They emerged from the park on LaSalle Drive, as rivulets of protestors raced by with other more cautionary veteran activists shouting after them, "Walk! Don't run! Walk!" The conventional wisdom being cops, like rabid dogs, chase whatever runs. But as the dissidents reached the sidewalk rather than safety, they encountered other police laying for them. So run they did, through parking lots, across lawns, scampering over fences with police close on their heels. Neither were news photographers exempt from attack. Far from it they were singled out. The nihilists flooded the streets snarling traffic and fighting off cops, crying, "The streets belong to the people!" The ragged army split up into guerrilla bands which roamed the streets setting trash cans ablaze, breaking windows, and demolishing a number of patrol cars.

The unsettling pop of gunfire was heard close by.

Trying to stay amidst the shadows, Percival led Nina through the melee. Warning her, "make haste slowly." She moved awkwardly, painstakingly, thrusting her hips forwards in an exaggerated arc, much like Bette Davis, only more so. Percival's hands, from which she drew solace never left her, but steadied her along like a rudder. To their relief, they stumbled upon a subway. Percival scooped Nina up and carried her down the stairs to safety. They discovered a whole encampment of refugees who'd escaped the fray in much the same way.

Nina slumped to the ground along the wall in a cold sweat, exhausted. She lay her crutches across her lap, and felt her heart beat wildly in her frail chest. She wept silently for the country she sorely felt she'd lost; however, she was determined to stay and fight and not surrender the field to the infidels! Percival collapsed along the wall beside her, listening to the outburst of gunfire from overhead, which continued on intermittently for the rest of the night.

There was a tension in the air from the spillover of violence in the park the night before. That tension was felt more acutely later that afternoon with the arrival of Black Panther Party Chairman, Bobby Seale, to address the assembly. The police patrols had been doubled for the occasion and though they kept their distance their high visibility did little to diffuse the explosive situation that existed between them and the war resisters. Many more heads were bloodied and bandaged and eyes sore and watery than the day before and tempers ran high. While no one necessarily expected the cops to move against the black revolutionary, neither did they rule out the possibility. Thus, the white radicals formed an impregnable wall around him with their bodies.

"Power to the people!" Seale began, head cocked to the side at a rakish angle, adorned by a tam. And despite the warmth, he wore a black leather jacket under which one could only guess he bore a concealed weapon.

"Power to the people!" The crowd of white radicals chanted in response.

"Right on! Right on!" Seale said to the enthusiastic crowd through a microphone that squawked. "I'm here today to salute you my revolutionary white brothers and sisters." He gazed out over the sea of white faces, and beyond his own circle of bodyguards, there were only one or two other black faces to be seen. "Until you move against domestic imperialism, growing rampant fascism – right here in America you can't end the war in Vietnam or all other forms of aggressive wars like Vietnam," he claimed, adding it was time to move the struggle to still higher levels of resistance, "where political argument spills over in blood." In addition, "even as 'dialectical materialism' must be taken to the next step, as says our Minister of Defense, Huey P. Newton,' into intercommunalism', which," he suggested, "is the continuum of Marxist development of 'evolution in cycles.'" There were sporadic outbursts of "Right on," from the young nihilists. Seale admonished them, "Throwing stones at a force as well armed as the Chicago police is folly. No doubt you've proven John Brown is not dead, you've proven that."

Being somewhat of an iconoclast, Percival was fundamentally opposed to an ideological doctrine of communism or any other "ism" for that matter. He was no religionist by any means but, given the circumstance, communism was not an entirely unacceptable compromise; that is, it sat easier with him than did capitalism, surely. He also felt that as an individual he could stand with Mao, Fidel, Che, Lumumba, Huey and the Black Panther Party despite their adherence to Marxist-Leninism or, for that matter, Fanon's "revolutionary native" for whom bloodshed was a catharsis. His position was more one of solidarity than ideology; much as in the same way he could embrace Jesus, but not Christianity.

"As we say, Power to the people! All power to the people! And Panther power to the revolution," Seale ejaculated, in conclusion, fist clenched and raised against a sluggish afternoon sky.

"Power to the people!" the protestors sang, rising as one, pumping the air with balled fist, "Power to the people," the cry spread like a contagion through their midst. Even Nina took up the cry, "Power to the people!" Percival tried to make his way through the thicket to shake the chairman's hand but was repulsed at every turn. And the chairman had swiftly been rushed off.

The horde of anti-war protestors streamed from the park and spilled out into the streets in a sprawl, spouting their new mantra, "Power to the people," no less vigorously than they'd chanted "Om" the night before. They took divergent routes through the city to the crumbling Chicago Coliseum to celebrate President Johnson's 60th. birthday in what was billed as an "unbirthday party" and "freak-out of the biggest freak of all, our president, 'A Mephistopheles in cowboy boots.'"

The hope was to depict the "grubby reality of a Texas born politician" in contrast to the image of a world statesman as presented by his supporters, led by his vice, Hubert H. Humphrey, at the convention across town. Therefore, the Mobilization Committee to End the War in Vietnam had hung unbecoming mementos of the Johnson Administration on the brick walls in the form of numerous photographs depicting Vietnamese civilians writhing on the end of American soldiers' bayonets; refugees streaming out of charred villages; and young black American men in ghettos fleeing police in riot torn situations.

Nina moved cautiously among the viewers filing past the display, as if by a corpse in a casket. Meanwhile, Percival hung back as the Holocaust No Dance Band crashed out in an all-time Rock n Roll favorite "Tuttti Frutti," at earsplitting decibels from the stage under throbbing strobe lights that glinted off a dozen mirrors in the drafty, semi-darkened coliseum.

Nina had seen most of these photos before, but now they came home to her, like quivering arrows to the heart. She grasped her crutches with fierce fingers, her knuckles whitening from strain. She felt tempest tossed, and as if she would collapse from vertigo. She moved from photo to photo on seasick legs, unsteady on her crutches. Her eyes grew misty and her nostrils ached with blood. Each photo proved a slap in the face, burning her with shame. And then, taken up short, she found herself in front of a photo of a small, wretched child, a Vietnamese child, more helpless than she, standing naked next to an automatic weapon with the child's hands covering her eyes. Nina was not alone in her sentiments, others, too, clicked their tongues in shame. Nina trembled, assailed by the lyrics of a song, "Master of Hate," dedicated to the president, which reverberated off the walls like the howling of some God unknown prehistoric night creature being eaten alive in four/four time,

"Suicide is an evil thing
But at times it's good
if you've been where the master
lives
I think you surely should."

Ed Sanders of the Rock group, The Fugs, one of the organizers of the event, addressed the crowd afterwards: "This unbirthday party is hopefully to provide you with a little joy in a week otherwise filled with terror."

"Joy?" Nina yelped, facing Percival with stark eyes. "He's being facetious, right?"

"Ya can only hope."

The crowd was then brought to its feet when the folk singer, Phil Oches, sang, "It's always the old who lead us to war. It's always the young who fall." The more than 3,000 youths who packed the cavernous hall held their hands aloft in the V-for-Victory sign and chanted "No, no, we won't go!" While here and there flames shot upwards in the darkened coliseum symbolizing the burning of draft cards in defiance of the law. They all were crying, shaking fist and singing, "Even treason might be worth a try/ the country's too young to die."

The author, William Burroughs followed Phil Oches on to the platform. He carelessly pushed back his fedora on his head and said, "The police acted like vicious dogs attacking everyone in sight. I do not protest. I'm not surprised."

The speaker Percival was most interested to hear was Genet, the French author and convict, who he had only recently discovered. Genet attacked the Chicago police through an interpreter as, "Mad dogs. But," he unsparingly added, "it does not displease me that white Americans find themselves threatened by these dogs who for the past 150 years have done the same thing with greater brutality to blacks."

The final speaker of the night was Comic and Social Activist, Dick Gregory, who quipped, tickling his audiences' funny bone, "I've just heard that Premier Kosygin has sent a telegram to Mayor Daley asking to send 2,000 Chicago cops immediately."

"Back to Lincoln Park," said Nina with dread, as they left the coliseum.

The protestors had resigned themselves to the inevitable and would make no attempt to provide cover for their safety in the park that night. And though many had rocks in their pockets and bricks in their hands and some wore crash helmets, the rest were there on principle. As curfew drew near, a train of three to four hundred members of the cloth and concerned local citizens arrived in the park behind a towering cross borne aloft by three acolytes. They placed the cross in the midst of the protestors under a lamp, to the jeers of skeptics.

Sadly, the cross would prove ineffectual that night. Within the previous few days the Chicago police had developed a taste for blood, which the sameness of their race, religious convictions or symbol of their shared faith could not slake. They had been whipped into a frenzy and were as capable of devouring their own God as Saturn did his children or, for that matter, dragging him down from on high and casting him into a sea of flames. Such was the depravity into which they had sunk.

Certainly many of these young idealists needed something stronger than their politics to sustain them over the coming few days. They were weary, cringing under the brutal blows from the policemen's nightsticks', and exhausted from being hounded from pillow to post until bone weary and in need of spiritual comfort, they found themselves at the foot of an ancient instrument of execution, praying for deliverance.

Then there were the nihilists, self-fed off their own narcissism, the idol bashers who knew no god outside themselves and for whom Chicago was a free-for-all.

His arms outspread as if in benediction, a prelate said to the diverse crowd, "As members of the clergy we join you in vigil and prayer."

"Keep your prayers to yourself you soothsayers, charlatans and peddlers of snake oil," called a voice out of the dark.

"Go peddle ya papers elsewhere," jeered another.

"You opiate of the masses," mouthed yet a third.

"Yours is the vocabulary of those you would oppose," said the cleric, undeterred.

"You detest them but you're willing to resort to their methods so long as you can get your way."

"Save it for your congregation," cried still another. "Or go sell it to the pigs. We came here to petition our government, and the city of Chicago chooses to wage war on us."

"Yes, that's right," muttered a number of dissenters in accord.

"Don't you see," argued the prelate, "that to do as they do is to be no better than they?"

"And to accept your counsel is to follow a Judas goat to the slaughter. You're all over thirty and your counsel is pointlessly irrelevant!"

"Wait, please," interjected a voice of reconciliation, "there are as many of us here who strongly embrace nonviolence, believe in civil disobedience and are driven by our faith. And for those of us who've been out here as long as any of you, spare us the rhetoric that we might prepare ourselves for what's ahead."

The strident voices dwindled to a grumble.

"'Blessed are the peace makers," said Nina under her breath, "'for they shall be called the children of God.'"

Percival focused his eyes musingly in her direction, discovering yet another aspect of her multifaceted personality.

Once more the circling lights atop the police cars washed over the encampment of protestors, while a phalanx of police encircled them like a tightening noose, leaving them no avenue of escape.

A gravelly voice issued out of the dark through a bull horn behind the high beams of a police car. "You have five minutes in which to leave the park."

A shudder passed through the dissidents, as the clerics prayed and Allen Ginsberg chanted "Om" in a now hoarse whisper, surrounded by Burroughs, Genet, Southern and Seaver while others sang "The Battle Hymn Of The Republic, "Mine eyes have seen the glory of the coming of the Lord/ He has trampled out the vintage where the grapes of wrath are stored –"

The stature of the cross under the park lamplight made for a compelling devotional figure, and as the central sign of the majority faith. It also served as a symbol of safety thus, the protestors gathered around and shyly introduced themselves to each other as if afraid to die alone. And from much of the conversations Percival overheard many of these youths came from well-to-do families and attended the better schools and universities. As was the case of one young couple meeting up for the first time, "I'm afraid," the girl said, approaching a guy and taking his hand. He assured her, smiling ruefully, "So am I."

And another, "I'm Jacob Moore, what got you in this fix," one protestor asked another?

"What got me in it? Shit, I'm more concerned with what's gonna get me the fuck out of it," he laughed nervously.

"Touché." The other guffawed.

Thus it went.

Percival placed an arm around Nina and gently prodded her. "Come on," he entreated her, but neither wished to leave their fellow compatriots. "We really must," he insisted, feeling an ache in the pit of his gut, fearful for them all, for what was sure to follow. And they started off, hurting inside, embarrassed and ashamed as if, for the second time, they'd abandoned the higher moral ground. Then the pop, pop, pop of tear gas canisters were heard at their backs and the stabbing smell of mace issued on the air. And those gathered round the cross began to cough and curse, stumbling off, fleeing blindly, as had the Apostles on that dark and terrible day at the foot of another cross two thousand years before.

A cautionary voice cried, "fer Christ sake don't run, don't run!" As police in gas mask chased them, clubbing the stragglers.

The park was awash in tear gas, overreaching Percival and Nina in their flight. Protestors were choking, gagging, writhing on the ground in breathless agony as if they were patients in a tuberculosis ward.

"Don't rub your eyes," Percival warned Nina in a strangled voice.

"You don't either," she gasped.

Percival coughed violently, his oxygen cut off and windpipe seizing up. "Excuse me," he choked, batting his eyes, turning from her he withdrew a pocket handkerchief, unzipped his fly, hoisted out his cock and pissed on the kerchief. Struggling for air, he began to sweat with terror for fear of passing out, of dying on the spot. This was more than he had bargained for friendship or no! Nevertheless, here he was gagging on tear gas and pissing on a rag. He felt like an idiot! He tried to hasten, piss spilling as much over his fingers as on the kerchief. His bladder empty, he restored his cock to his pants, and took the urine drenched cloth and pressed it over Nina's nose and mouth to protect her as much as possible from tear gas.

"Breath slowly through your mouth," he advised her.

Meanwhile, the cross was lowered by three choking acolytes, and carried deliberately, as if in fact it were the corpse of the savior of their faith.

The police were leery of wading indiscriminately into the procession of clerics stumbling from the park behind their cross, gasping for air. Percival steered Nina in among the straggling processionists, thereby effecting their escape.

The hillocks of the park at their backs were dotted with flames and the woods veiled in tear gas, sparklers flared in the darkness and firecrackers exploded randomly.

Percival and Nina spent the night in one of the many churches that opened there doors to provide sanctuary for the beleaguered war resisters, offering them respite from the embattled streets.

Nomination night was Wednesday and thus far the police had managed to keep the demonstrators away from the convention center, the object of their protest. The clock was ticking on the hard-pressed peace organizers who, in order to maintain their leadership credibility, required a victory of sorts. Realizing this fully and wanting Humphrey's ascension to appear no less seamless than was Richard M. Nixon's, the city fathers deigned to toss them a bone and grant The Mobilization to End The War In Vietnam, a police permit to rally at the band shell in Grant's Park – a good four miles short of the convention center. Even if not in good faith, it was nevertheless a concession. That is, the band shell was strategically situated behind the Loop, and caught between the police and National Guard, the protestors, if necessary, could be corralled in the park.

In the mistaken belief that the permit to assemble in Grant's Park represented a victory on their account, the protestors congregated before the band shell to listen to another day of still more speakers.

Percival yawned. Nina elbowed him. He cast a disparaging glance her way. She eyed him in return. They tittered. They were bored.

"They must ave to keep proven they're the organizers of this fiasco, cause they jus' keep blowing hot air at you," said Percival to Nina, incapable of digesting another word.

He looked around and by the vacuous expressions on everyone else's faces noticed that they too were equally bored, but the presence of the police, coiled like a venomous snake at the back of one's mind, kept them all from falling asleep.

Suddenly, a disturbance arose in the rear, between the band shell and the police line. An obviously bored adolescent was climbing the flagpole, to the dismay of some, encouragement of others and offense to the police –, defacing the American flag. The Peace Marshals moved in to keep order, as a column of cops pushed their way through to make an arrest. A few protesters threw stones and booed. The speaker, Carl Oglesby, the national SDS president, asked the youth to come down. "We try to give birth to a new world but there are undertakers in the delivery room. Let's not encourage them."

Though their eyes were set on the youth up the flagpole, the majority of people remained seated as he tried to cut down the American flag and replace it with a rebel one.

Rennie Davis took the megaphone from Oglesby to address the police. "It's under control," he said, trying to quell the commotion. "We have a permit and you do well to pull back to avoid further provocation."

Without warning the police broke ranks and attacked, hacking their way through the marshals on into the startled assembly of seated protesters. People were knocked backwards over their benches like ten pins. Others fled but were struck, staggered and fell. Once again tear gas wafted on the air, drifting over the shrieking, panic-stricken crowd.

The screams were near deafening. Davis was talking but no one was listening, least of all the police. Percival grabbed Nina and they toppled to the ground and rolled under a cluster of benches, flung in a pile in the melee. They lay face down with their hands over their heads quivering, expecting the worst.

A woman ran hysterically by with a child in her arms, confronting every cop she encountered. "Here, beat my baby – beat my baby," she cried. And the mortified infant, more frantic than it's mother, was wailing like a siren, it's cries lost in the overall pandemonium. But the infant's mother, in her hysteria, did not cease to present her child to each policeman as a sacrificial offering: "Beat my baby, beat my baby," she implored, tears streaming down her cheeks while victims of the police clubs fell at her feet but she and the child escaped unmolested.

When at last the melee had come to a halt as abruptly as it had begun, as suddenly as a cloudburst, hundreds of demonstrators had been brutalized and Rennie Davis lie unconscious on the platform. The twelve thousand police, reinforced by six thousand national guard, drew back to their original positions. The overhead sky had darkened with surveillance helicopters. The national guard assumed visible positions on the roof of the Chicago Museum and nearby bridges. Guardsmen with bazookas and machine guns mounted atop jeeps, stretched from the band shell past the loop on back to the Conrad Hilton Hotel. The protesters were corralled.

Surprisingly enough, the rally continued on under these repressive conditions, and an irate, visibly agitated Tom Hayden, addressed the shaken crowd: "We're surrounded," he cried in a tearful, choking voice. "Rennie Davis has been hospitalized and we must avenge him. Whatever you do, don't get trapped in the park, try to find your way back to the Hilton. Let's turn this military machine against itself. Let us make sure that if blood flows, it flows all over the city. Go do what you have to do. I'll see you in the streets," said Hayden, with rancor.

Shortly thereafter, Hayden managed to escape from the park and was not seen again until later on in the streets in front of the Hilton Hotel. A more subdued Dave Dillenger proposed a march to the amphitheater, but no sooner had the march begun than was its progress blocked by an army of police who would not allow them to leave the park. Consequentially, small bands of resisters and individuals, including Nina and Percival, started out along the lakeshore chain of parks searching for a bridge to cross back onto Michigan Avenue and other conduits to the central downtown area. All the crossings, it appeared, were occupied by troops in jeeps with mounted machine guns.

After three weary days of being driven like sheep, Nina had begun to tire. Percival had wanted to drop out but felt it was rightly her call. Yet it was becoming increasingly apparent that she was in little shape to last though she kept up a brave front and never gave voice to any complaint.

"God, Percival," she finally vented, "sometimes I fall so far behind that I simply become an observer. At times like this I most regret being a cripple. I dare not let go my crutches to throw something. And," she frothily said, "for the first time I feel I want to throw something! I'm utterly defenseless without you," she said candidly, brushing her curly brown hair from her copper bright eyes, and pouting in consternation. "We could be in Prague under Soviet tanks and guns," she spouted. "To think that this is America. My God, I'm almost sure that if the vast majority of us were not white, half of us would be dead by now. This situation is more dangerous for you than it is for me. I'm sorry, I shouldn't have involved you. It was selfish of me."

"Not at all," Percival hastened to say. "True, I wouldn't ave come had it not been for you. But I needed to be here, to see this for myself. Let's not say any more 'bout it, okay?"

"Okay," she agreed, sighing.

By some fluke the bridge at Jackson Boulevard, north of the Loop, had been left unattended, and as the word was passed, thousands of protesters wended their way in that direction to make a short hop across the bridge to Michigan Avenue, and there turned north for the Hilton. The crowd was feverishly ebullient, cheering and shaking angry fists.

"Power to the people," "Dump the Hump," they chanted.

Midway across the bridge, Percival and Nina encountered the three flower children who had approached Nina when they first arrived in Lincoln Park that past Monday.

"Hello," said the girl to Nina, "still with us, I see. And what have you to say about your constitutional right to assemble now?"

"Foolish indeed!"

"She's a trooper, walking these days on crutches," said another. "She's been doing double duty. What'a ya say we hoist her up and send her forwards over the shoulders of everyone so she can see it from up front?"

"Let's," they agreed, excitedly! And they seized Nina under her arms, to her surprise, and hoisted her up over their heads. She was as light as a malnourished child, a feather actually, and the congestion of bottlenecked protesters on the bridge passed her forward, easily. She reached the front ranks, eyes sparkling with childlike exuberance, perched on the shoulders of two Yippies. Then, there, before her eyes, causing her to gasp, were the ranks of the Chicago police. Her crutches had been passed to Percival, and he squeezed his way forward. "She needs her crutches; she needs her crutches." Somehow, the crowd made room for him to pass and on reaching Nina he found himself in front of the police force stretched out in front of them up and down the Avenue. "Oh shit," he exclaimed, with a sense of the tragic. Their Plexiglas face masks drawn and badge numbers covered with black tape; they were anonymous, faceless vigilantes, separate, a breed apart, deadly, accountable to no one. He could feel sweat bead his brow and roll in rivulets down his flanks. This was the realization of his worst nightmare. He gazed up at Nina seated on the shoulders of the two Yippies.

She waved timidly.

He smiled mirthlessly.

Then, as if in response to his fears, the three mule drawn wagons from the Poor People's Campaign arrived out of nowhere, with Reverend Abernathy in the lead and two other black drivers bringing up the rear offering a fleeting sense of safety. The mules provided a moment's comic relief. Twilight had set in and the streetlights gave off an incandescent glow. It was close to nomination time. It was learned that the mule team had a permit to travel to the amphitheater. The demonstrators thought that they would simply follow along. Things could not have worked out better. As they made their way toward the Hilton behind the mule drawn wagons, the two Yippies placed Nina on the back of the last cart, her inert limbs dangling. She held onto the sideboard. There was a blank passivity in her expression suggestive of sleep. Percival was pensive, afraid, lest the wagon lurch and spill her face down. He tried to smile, to reassure her. They progressed to Balboa Avenue, before the Hilton. The police held up the mule train, stalling the march. The crowd was growing. The protesters invited passersby to, "Join us –, join us." Many did. Time lagged.

A policeman ordered Nina off the wagon. Percival handed her crutches. She rejoined the demonstrators standing on Michigan Avenue in the thousands. The mule train was sent on its way, and the police immediately cut the protesters off from them.

Once more the battle lines were drawn. The police appeared more menacing than ever. They seemed, in fact, to be snorting. This was the hour of reckoning, the moment of truth. Here in front of the Conrad Hilton Hotel it would be determined, once and for all, who ran Chicago. A paroxysm of fear passed through the swollen ranks of demonstrators like a bolt of electricity. This time they were not so much boxed in as overpowered. Percival knew that a police attack, despite full media coverage, was imminent. Terrified, Nina sucked in her breath.

The stalled march was abruptly tear gassed. The police attacked, fell on them like a brick wall, blocking their passage, and redirecting them into a storm-tossed sea of humanity. They floundered about like a ship in a squall about to break apart and sink. They were savagely beaten, and as they fell back, bled and screamed, unable to escape the bludgeoning, they toppled blindly into one another. The police waded in, hacking a blistering path through the protesters thrown helplessly back on themselves. Their clubs came down again and again, mercilessly.

T.V. reporters and cameramen were beaten in the melee, as America watched the T.V. evening news with horror from the safety of their living rooms; watched the protesters, these young defenders of free speech beaten and pummeled on the streets of Chicago by the police. Their nightsticks would have cracked on the air like baseball bats against balls were it not for the protesters screaming and yelling for their lives. The world watched as the Chicago police went amuck.

Nina searched wildly about for a corridor by which to escape, but everywhere she turned she saw cops. She turned again. And a crutch was kicked out from under her by a panicked protester. She spun about involuntarily and caught sight of a helmeted cop, his club raised to strike. She instinctively threw up her hands, losing use of her other crutch, and slumped to the ground in a heap. Before the club could descend in its arc, Percival threw himself atop her and the blow caught him on the back of the head. And still another came crashing down on his skull, opening a gash in his scalp. He groaned and fell unconscious atop her. "Don't beat him anymore," she begged, "don't beat him!" She cradled his head against her shoulders, in her hands. Blood oozed between her fingers, matting his hair. "Help me," she groaned, crushed under his bulk. "I'm an invalid, for God sake! Won't somebody help us, please?"

Two medics hastily dashed to assist her. They pulled Percival onto a stretcher and carried him off to the McCarthy headquarters in the Hilton, which had been turned into an emergency medical unit. Meanwhile the police had forced innocent bystanders through the plate glass window of the Haymarket restaurant in the lobby of the Hilton. They entered through the shattered window and proceeded to beat the patrons.

Nina sat on Percival's cot after he'd been looked at and bandaged, caressing his unconscious face. "If only I were whole," she wept softly. "If things were only different with me –, if I weren't a cripple, how I'd love you. And despite everything, I do love you. oh Percival," she lamented, tears washing his face.

He eventually stirred, opened his eyes slowly, torpidly. He gazed at Nina for a baffled moment, ears ringing, and head throbbing. He groaned as if from an awful hangover. He said softly, "You ok, beautiful?" fingering his bandaged head. She could not help but cry anew, flinging herself atop him, smothering his face with kisses.

A doctor left the bedside of another victim of the police nightsticks and approached Percival's cot. "You're back with us once again – good! Under proper conditions we'd hold you over for further observation but there's mayhem on those streets and, as you can see, we're running out of cots, as well as space for everyone. And well, your cot is needed. If it's of any consolation, I'm confident you'll be fine. But if you wish, when you get home see your own doctor. In the meantime, I suggest you do not return to those streets. You cannot hope to sustain another such beating without coming to real harm."

"I've seen all I've come ta see," said Percival, soberly, fingering his bandaged skull. "The police won't get'a chance ta beat me again! I promise."

"I leave it to you."

"I think we should go home."

"I think so too," Nina said.

And they caught the next train out of Chicago for New York City, the fingers of their hands interlocked, with Nina's head pressed against his shoulder. All in all they looked like two world weary, star-crossed lovers.

***

"Mama, please, I don't want'a argue. my head hurts enough without it," said Percival, plaintively.

"Ya worry me, boy," his mother said. "You're hard to understand. I mean, jus' look at yourself. What kind'a sense was there for you ta go to Chicago when anyone with any sense would'a stayed clear away?"

"I'd hoped ta have met Bobby Seale," he replied.

"Whose Bobby Seale to you had to meet so bad you went all the way to Chicago to get your head split for?"

"Bobby Seale – Bobby Seale," he repeated in exasperation. "He's Chairman a' the Black Panther Party."

"Lord, Lord," Hattie gasped, leaning back in her chair with stark eyes. "Now them Black Panthers! Boy, your father jus' 'bout put me in the ground 'n you trying to finish the job."

"That's unfair," he said in a strangled voice, seething. Ever since she had told him of his father, Lucius, rather than bring them together, as perhaps she'd hoped, it had served instead to drive a wedge between them. Since then their encounters had become, for reasons unbeknownst to either of them, increasingly contentious.

"If fair only had something to do with it," she said, imperiously, eyeing him severely.

"Fair or not," Percival swung round, staring at her with baleful eyes, "it's unintentional. Ya want us to have a safe life only it's an unsafe world; doubly unsafe for black people, n for black men, impossible. I didn't go in search of this, it found me! It crawled up alongside me at birth like some foul thing 'n has been keeping pace with me ever since."

"Ya got more potential than any chile I got 'n what you doing but squandering it," Hattie railed, shaking her head.

"What should I do, mama? You sure as hell don't want me to box."

"I don't wanna see you banged up like this – first you jaw broken 'n now you head all bandaged up. I mean, what next?"

"It's the times we're living in, ma. It's the times we're living in," he said lamely, pacing restlessly.

"Ya got'a stop wrestling with the devil, son."

"The devil?" he chortled. "It's not the devil ma, it's the fucking Man."

"Don't y'll ever swear under my roof," she scolded. "It's disrespectful to curse in your mother's presence." She pitched forward in her chair, her hands clasped in her lap and head lowered as in prayer.

"I apologize. I meant no disrespect." He sighed knowingly, tossing up his hand in defeat.

"Still you're hiding your light under a bushel," said Hattie, more restrainedly, raising her drooping eyelids.

"N what about Lois 'n Sam?"

"Lois, she's a good, levelheaded girl 'n will do jus' fine. Sam's the youngest 'n somewhat out of his depths as yet 'n needs guidance and relies on you, as his older brother."

"Only he relies a bit too much. I ave a son, Malek, remember? Who I'm not doin' so well with," he spouted. "Your grandson, in fact."

"You can be a coldhearted man, Percival Jones."

"I think I feel a little too much for being in the skin I'm in, if you really want'a know," he said scornfully, looking through her.

"I guess there's nothing I can say, you seem to know it all already. I guess you win. It's your life. I only gave it to yo."

"Don't think I'm not grateful," he said, facing away.

"Ya'd not know it."

"Mama," he implored.

"All right – all right," she retreated, limply, sucking her teeth.

"Where's Lois?" he asked, standing before the living room window, and drawing back the curtain. He looked out over the river toward the city. Gulls sailed low over the white capped waves, barges forged back and forth drawn by pugnacious tugboats.

"She's doing what you should be doing, signing up for school for fall."

"Has she decided to go to Hunter?" he asked, dismissing her rebuke.

"No, she's gonna go to Richmond, here on the island, so she'll be closer ta home n her job n not ave to travel back n forth so much."

"Give her my love."

287

"Yes, you two the closest I suppose."

"Lois is lovable."

"N Sam's not?" Hattie asked with appeal in her tone.

"Sam's Sam," said Percival with a dismissive air, "always underfoot whenever he's around."

"That's to be expected a' the youngest."

"Only he ain't so young anymore." He stared longingly toward the city, shimmering like a mirage in the sultry heat on the far off and, from there, seemingly unattainable shore. "Ma," he asked, "why'd you leave Bed-Stuy –, I mean, why would you ave preferred to live here on Staten Island after living in Bed-Stuy so long?"

She replied musingly, as if having reflected deeply on the subject for some time now and had only been waiting for the question to arise. "Ya'd already left home n Lois 'n Sam would be leaving soon enough n I didn't want'a be coming home every night to a dark house full'a empty rooms with memories collecting like cob webs in darken'd corners."

"I see," he said, absently, gazing on the dark river below, detecting a note of sorrow in her tone.

"N that's why."

He turned slowly from the view out the window and stepped over to where she sat, absorbed in a brown study, "I got'a fly," he said dryly, kissing her tepidly on the brow.

"Where you off to now?"

He paused, resting a hand anxiously on the doorknob, wanting to escape, to be left to go to the devil in his own way. "Ya really don't want'a know," he said, idly, slipping out the door.

'How did we come to this?' they both wondered on either side of the door.

Percival sighted Sam stripped to the waist and shooting hoop by himself in the project playground. He would have passed by but was struck by a pang of conscience for having spoken ill of him to their mother. He sighed resignedly, back tracked and passed through the high gate of the chain-link fence which surrounded the playground. He called out as he neared the court, "Yoo, young blood!"

Sam caught a rebound off the backboard and spun around, planting his feet firmly and palming the ball in one hand. He wiped sweat from his brow with a forearm. Perspiration rolled freely down his chest and gut to the waistband of his soaked shorts.

"What's up, bro," asked Sam, panting.

"It's your world, baby,' n I'm jus' a player in it. So you tell me."

"If only."

"I hear you."

"What the fuck happened to your knot, man?" Sam asked, noticing his brother's bandaged head.

"It's a memento from Chicago."

"No shit –, you went, huh?"

"Stupid me."

"How was that anyhow? I dug it on T.V. 'n it look like some pretty foul shit going down."

"It felt worse to me than it looked to you."

"That bad, huh?"

"That bad."

"Ya seen ma yet?"

"I jus' left her."

"What she say?'

"You know without my repeating it."

"Yeah, I guess so," Sam agreed, tossing Percival the ball. He began to dribble and skirt round Sam, moving toward the basket but Sam effectively blocked him. Percival spun away, fell back and tried to shoot. Sam blocked him, stole the ball; shot and sunk a basket. They played this way awhile, Sam showing Percival up shot after shot, whizzing past his guard and scoring.

Percival threw up his hands to block Sam, to no avail. "You're good, little brother."

"No," Sam countered, "you're good. I'm mediocre. boxing's your sport, at which you're unequaled."

"Naw," Percival claimed, "I can see you're good."

"It's jus' not your game, bro, that's all." Sam sunk another jump shot. "I mean, sure I can smoke these cats round here but elsewhere I'm a little fish in a big pond."

"You're on the college team."

"They ain't but a bunch'a scrubs," Sam sneered, stealing past Percival's guard. "But it got me into college for what the fuck that's worth."

"It's worth something, man, you there," Percival said, sinking a shot.

"For now anyway," Sam retrieved the ball.

"What's on your mind, bro?"

"I'm thinking'a joining the Panther Party."

Percival came to a halt, holding the ball under his arm, and eyeing Sam critically. "What the fuck for?"

"Ta stand for something, like yourself, you know?"

"Geez, g'd, what the fuck, you think I stand for? Forget this crazy Panther shit! Go finish school, get a degree n make mama happy."

"Fuck that shit! You make mama happy," Sam flared. "Wasn't it you tell her that if everybody woke up tomorrow with a Ph.D. the situation would globally prove no better?

So, yeah, why don't you finish college? I mean, what's so special 'bout you?"

Percival lay a hand on Sam's shoulder and, engaging his eyes, said in a desolate voice, "I'm'a die young."

Struck by the ring of sincerity in his brother's tone, Sam gaped at him in stupefaction. "What kind'a crap is that to be talking, man," Sam stammered once he'd found his tongue, his face tingling from loss of blood, as dismay rose in his eyes. "That shit ain't hardly funny," he grumbled, shaking Percival's hand off his shoulder. "Don't talk that crap to me, man, don't!"

Percival shrugged.

"Why would you believe that shit, cause your father did?"

Percival winced. "It's jus' an unshakable feeling, nothing else."

"If that's the case you feel no different than any other young black man." Sam jeered, "She-e-t!"

"Maybe."

"Only more reason I should join the Party. You 'n me, man, together, bro, would be unbeatable, dig?" Sam said, with bravura, trying to conceal a tremolo in his voice.

"Did you not hear what I said? Why don't you jus' go finish college like mama want, 'n forget this Panther stuff."

"You in it ain't you?"

"Not entirely my decision."

"No one drafted you."

"Circumstances drafted me, n sometimes circumstances can be more compelling than a draft board."

"Yeah, well, similar circumstances 'r calling me too."

"I'm serious."

"So am I big brother, 'n I wish the fuck you'd stop treating me like a g'damn kid 'n let me stand with you like a fucking man!"

"If I can't talk you out'a it, then well said."

"It's okay with you then?"

"No, little brother, it's not – but you're right, somewhere along the line you got'a be your own man."

"Right on," said Sam, affirmatively.

"Jus' be sure to let ma know I had nothing to do with your decision, dig?"

"Shit yeah – it's fucking fine with me."

"I'm on my way to the Panther Office now, care to come?"

"Jus' let me grab my shirt."

The Panther Office was two blocks up from the project playground beside a corner bar, The 2nd. Step, and diagonally across the street from The Heritage House.

Percival led the way into the office. The drab store front was illuminated by three bare bulbs which cast gloomy shadows against the side walls. A typist was busily typing away and Rufus, his back to the entrance, was cranking the handle of a manual mimeograph machine while Lily, across the desk from him, was busy collating the materials as they issued out of the mouth of the dispenser. A few others were in the back cleaning their weapons and discussing revolutionary politics.

The typist addressed Rufus: "Would you care to look this over?"

"In a minute," he responded. He wore a .45 under his belt at the base of his spine.

"Power to the people," the duty officer, Skeeter, saluted.

"Panther power to the revolution," Percival returned the salutation and Sam raised a clenched fist.

Lily picked up her head on recognizing Percival's voice. She set her work aside and dashed round the desk and threw her arms about his neck.

"How 'r you?" she asked gleefully. "It's so good to see you, bandaged head 'n all," she exclaimed, examining the gauze and tape round his head. "Nina 'n I spoke 'n she told me. How awful. She said you most probably saved her life."

"I wouldn't go that far," he said, discounting it.

"She thinks the world of you – you know?"

He smiled fleetingly.

"I think she's in love with you," said Lily, scrutinizing his face for a response.

"Come on," he blushed, embarrassed, averting his eyes. "I like her she's my dearest friend, but let's not get carried away," he said, closing the discussion.

"You went to Chicago thinking it was gonna be a 'Happening' 'n the pigs played Be-Bop with your skull," Rufus roared, heartily. "That's what you get for listening to a half-crazy cripple white woman like Nina," he snorted indignantly.

Percival considered Rufus crossly. "You ave a way of saying the wrong thing at the wrong time, man. That half-crazy white woman, as you so inelegantly put it, is a good a friend we'll ever have, got it?"

"I jus' like to tease Nina, no harm intended," said Rufus, clumsily, trying to exculpate himself.

"Ya carry it to extremes. Nina's as close a friend I got. N after Chicago, I'm not much in a laughing mood, dig?"

"It's jus' as well, baby, cause things jumping off here too."

"Such as?"

"I guess you can't know, Jamal's been busted."

"Jamal?"

"Yeah, Jamal!"

"What the fuck for?"

"The only thing I'm sure of is that he was plotting to break Lakey out'a jail. It seems he'd figured out the route of the van from the Women's House of Detention to the court downtown Brooklyn, 'n had set up an ambush which went wrong 'n he was taken with two others. He was snared with guns, grenades 'n all kind'a explosive devices."

"So it's an illegal weapons charge?"

"That 'n more."

"Hmmmm," Percival murmured. "What a shame."

"Ain't it though – that cat's a genius."

"But vastly inexperienced."

"He's only seventeen after all."

"My point exactly. He take this on by himself?"

"N some want'a drum him out'a the ranks for it too."

"That'll be equally a fatal mistake."

"I mean, man, people r fucking paranoid."

"When did this all come down?"

"Let's see, t'days Friday 'n it was two days ago, so it was Wednesday."

"It only makes it next to impossible to spring Lakey," said Percival, resting his chin on his chest. "No, we do better to make Jamal a revolutionary hero since they're gonna bury him in jail we got no need to discipline him by expelling him from the ranks of the party. We begin to appear too harsh if we do, dig? It's better we build him up as courageous rather than a bungler. That way people will gain more confidence in us, especially since we been saying he's a fucking genius all along, dig? I mean, it begins to look like we're talking out'a both sides'a r mouths, you know?"

"Then you should be there tomorrow at the Defense Captains meeting to express that point of view."

"I'll be there."

"Rufus," Sam broke in. "I want'a join up."

Rufus ran an eye over him. "Ya talk to Percival 'bout this?"

"It ain't his call."

"I guess it ain't at that," said Rufus, thoughtfully. "Ya know there's the political Ed program 'n party platform y'll ave to be versed in?"

"I'm hip to it."

"I hope your good at taking orders from your brother," he laughed, "cause I'm having'a devil of a time with it myself." As they spoke the front door creaked open and an out of breath, startle-eyed, sunbaked, raggedy boy appeared in the entranceway. He'd opened the door barely wide enough to squeeze in. They all stopped talking and looked at him with bemused interest and surprise. With ferret like eyes he returned their scrutiny, then scurried behind the duty officer's desk like a rodent. He looked up at Skeeter and lay a finger across his lips. "Shhh," he whispered.

"What gives," Rufus started to say when two cops burst through the door, their eyes roving the room. "Okay, where is he?" the first cop demanded. Rufus stepped forward boldly before they could advance another step.

"Who the fuck invited you in," he shrieked, livid with rage. "Jus' where the fuck you think you 'r?"

"No," said the cop, returning his stare, "the question is who the fuck you think you are interfering with a police officer in the execution of his duty?"

Rufus was irate, lancing him in his cross-eyes. "Y'll mother fuckers best ave'a g'damn warrant cause y'll get your greasy pig asses fried 'n they'll carry two skewed pigs out'a here in bodybags!"

The cops put their hands on their revolvers. Rufus signaled to the four Panthers in the back. They hastily advanced, taking a stand on either side of him, their weapons holstered but in sight. Rufus placed a fidgety hand on his .45, at his back like a pistolier.

"The kid's a thief," said a cop accusatorially, his eyes roving nervously from armed Panther to armed Panther.

Percival waved Sam, who stood mesmerized, out of the field of fire. Then he crouched beside the urchin behind the duty officer's desk and asked, "Is what that cop say true?"

The boy looked Percival over deciding if he could be trusted or not. "What happened to your head?" he chose to ask with the surliness of a street Arab.

"I was beaten by the cops."

"You let em beat you like that?" said the urchin in disgust, shrinking back.

"Not exactly."

"I bet he wouldn't let anybody beat him like that," said the kid of Rufus. "Okay," he then said, wavering.

"Is what that cop say so?"

"Kind'a."

"Kind'a how?"

"Ya could say I took the money out'a Willie's cash register while he was back'a the store doing something else," the kid confessed, unabashed, removing a fist full of bills from his pocket for Percival to see. "He must'a heard the register cause he come yelling 'n screaming like a crazy man. 'N I got in the wind 'n run into them two as I flew out the store 'n they took out after me, so I duck in here cause they say you guys ain't scared a cops, r you?"

"So they say," Percival grimaced. "So they say. But if you want 'r help y'll ave to give back the money."

"How come?" chimed the boy. "Willie's white!"

"We're not against Willie cause he's white or anybody else cause'a their color. Willie's an honest grocer, trying to make it like most folks round here 'n we got'a stick together, see? 'Cause black or white we in the same crap, dig?"

"Kind'a," the urchin relented, handing Percival the crumpled bills, all the while looking at Rufus, eyes widening in admiration.

"What we got here is a Mexican standoff," said Rufus, defiantly, staring into the cops agitated faces.

"Check him out," said the street Arab, open mouthed. "Wow, he's out'a sight! He got them cops psyched out," he went on, directing Percival's gaze with an upraised turn of the head.

"Yeah," Percival confirmed and, realizing Rufus was enjoying himself overly, he swung his eyes on Lily pressed against a side wall, fearing for Rufus who didn't seem to fear for himself.

"N what's your name?" Percival asked, returning his focus on the kid.

"Ricky Bolden."

"N how old 'r you?"

"I'm twelve. I'll be thirteen next month. I should be going into seventh grade but I got left back." He ventured a diffident smile. "I know, I'm small for my age."

"Where do you live?"

"365 Brighton Avenue."

"Is your mother or father home?"

"I got no father," he said, sulkily. "Yeah, my mother'll be home. But you're not gonna tell her 'r you?"

"I got no choice."

Percival regained his feet and leaned into Rufus's ear. "Let em ave the kid for now. It'll be easy enough to spring him. Jus' get these pigs out'a here. N here," he said, pressing the bills into Rufus' shirt pocket, "return this to Willie 'n see he doesn't press charges, dig? I'll get the kid's mother n take her to the

294

precinct house. Lily," he said, facing her, "call the Public Defender's office, Ernie Dodd, 'n see if he can meet me at the 20th. precinct. Tell him it's urgent."

"Right away," she said.

"I don't like it," Rufus fumed.

"Like it or not we got'a diffuse this quick. N when I'm gone get these guns out'a here cause these pigs r gonna get a warrant."

"I'd like to bury the mothers where they stand," Rufus indignantly proposed for all to hear.

"Ya got'a stop flying off the handle at every turn," Percival admonished, in a low voice.

Rufus turned from Percival toward the kid in a huff. "I'm Rufus Hinton, the Defense Captain here, 'n who 'r you?"

"Ricky Bolden," said the street urchin with effort.

"Do ya trust me, Ricky Bolden?"

"Yes, sir. I think your great," said the Arab, standing.

"Good man," Rufus stroked his woolly head, smiling vaguely. "We're gonna get you out'a this. But for now, I want you to go with these pigs. Don't worry, we'll see to it nothing happens to you, ok?"

Ricky paused, tugging at the waistband of his trousers. "Suppose they beat me like they beat him?" he asked, pointing to Percival.

"We'll take care'a that," Rufus assured him, reaching into a desk drawer and retrieving a Polaroid camera. "Remove your shirt," he instructed. Ricky readily complied. Rufus took a half dozen photos of him from every angle, dated them and had the Panther membership initial the back of each photo. For good measure, he snapped a photo of the startled cops, boiling with rage. "Next time we see him," Rufus warned, "we want him to look no worse for wear, got it? Now he's yours for the moment."

"I'm ready," said Ricky, cockily, stretching out his hands to be cuffed.

"Not in here you don't," Rufus commanded. "You got no authority here!"

"You've not heard the last of this," said a cop with malevolence, taking Ricky in hand.

"Get out'a here before I lose it altogether 'n off you mother fuckers where you stand," Rufus snarled, as they hastily departed.

"OK," said Percival urgently, "let's get a move on. Skeeter get the car," he told the duty officer, then turned to Lily but she was already on the phone. "Sam, I want you to come with me."

"Ya got it," said Sam, thrilled.

"Sometimes I wonder who the fuck runs this show," Rufus grumbled, "you or me?"

"Don't give me grief," said Percival, irritably.

"See what I'm saying?" Rufus guffawed, casting Sam a side glance. "Well, y'll heard him," he thundered to the others, "hop to it!"

"The Public Defender will meet you at the precinct," said Lily, ringing off.

Skeeter shortly rolled up to the curb in a blue, '65 Impala. Percival and Sam got in, and the car pulled out. Next they picked up Ricky's mother, then headed for the 20th police precinct located in St. George on Richmond Terrace beside Borough Hall and the County Court, overlooking the ferry terminal and river. The city across the waterway was hazy from that angle but far less mirage like.

Mrs. Bolden flew into the precinct like a cackling goose, wringing her hands and crying. She gasped on seeing her son in handcuffs, being escorted into the back, and threw up her hands in despair and turned to the desk sergeant: "I don't know what to do with him," she sobbed, her hair in disarray. "He's always in trouble. He has no father. I'm only a woman. What can I do? He won't listen to me. He runs wild on the streets. I have three others to care for. I don't have eyes in the back of my head."

"Maybe a judge will be kind enough to put him in a home for delinquent youth," said the desk sergeant, unsympathetically.

"There's no call for that," said Percival sharply, searching desperately round for Ernie Dodd.

"I suppose you're one of those Black Panthers?" the surly desk sergeant rejoined, glowering at him.

"N if I am?"

"I'll handle this," Ernie Dodd interposed, breathlessly. "I'm sorry, I'm running behind," he explained, rolling his eyes in Percival's direction. "I must be in court in another few minutes," he said, checking his watch. He was in his mid-thirties, white, clean shaven, neatly dressed in a summer suit, wing tip shoes, and carried a leather satchel.

"Yes, counselor, and how may I assist you today?" said the desk sergeant, with a patronizing air.

"I believe you're holding my client, a Ricky Bolden?"

"What'a you mean believe?" shrieked Mrs. Bolden, wild-eyed and pointing? "Didn't we jus' see em take him somewhere down the hall back there in cuffs."

"There's your answer, counselor," said the sergeant brusquely.

"And may I ask just what he's being charged with?" Dodd fixed the sergeant with astute eyes.

"You may, but I don't as yet know. They're just now processing him."

"In which case I do well to join my client," said Dodd, turning his tread in the direction in which Mrs. Bolden had pointed.

Mrs. Bolden was sobbing piteously. Dressed with sloppy disregard for her person, she would have been quite pretty had she not become so care worn and burdened down by a life of poverty at such a tender young age. There was a brutal, near savage deadness in her eyes; a deadness similar to that of a fish on ice. As well, was there an odor of poverty about her which seeped through her pores like sweat.

Percival asked Sam to escort her to a side bench on which others were pensively waiting. "Don't worry," Sam said consolingly, leading her off. "It'll all work out. Willie's not gonna press charges. Ricky'll be able to leave with you."

"No," she moaned, "no! they should keep him. Keep him 'n put him in jail! Then he'll see what he's putting me through. Then maybe he'll learn!"

"You don't want that," said Sam. "You're overwrought 'n can't know what you're saying." And as he left her on the bench to rejoin Percival, a few cops had gathered off to the side, staring: "One pointed, "that's them!" Then he said, "burn their faces in your brains!"

"They're dog meat," scowled a second. A third raised an outstretched index finger aimed at Percival's swathed head, cocked his thumb back like the hammer of a gun and said, "Bang! You're dead!"

Percival scowled, gesticulating with an upraised middle finger.

"What's this," Ernie Dodd demanded, coming up on them with Ricky by his side, gloating. "If you have charges to bring against Mr. Jones, do so; then we'll proceed accordingly. If not keep your comments to yourselves or I'll file charges of my own and believe me they'll stick."

The desk sergeant scattered the cops with a wave of the hand, while the precinct captain looked on from the squad room doorway, not without interest.

"How'd it go?" Percival inquired. "You weren't back there very long."

"Apparently they'd called Willie and he refused to press charges, nor were they expecting a lawyer to show so quickly, so they had no alternative but to release him. If I'm correct, this incident's going to stir up a hornet's nest for you."

"If it hasn't already."

"Doubtless," Sam chimed in.

Ricky eschewed his mother's open arms, searching round for Rufus.

"Where's Rufus?" he asked, first off.

"He's at the office. He had other things to do, dig?" Percival winked. "After all, he's Defense Captain 'n he's got'a take care'a business, you know?"

"Shoo," said Ricky, disappointed.

"Mr. Jones, you remember me, don't you?" asked the precinct Captain, supporting his frame against the doorpost, blocking their exit.

"Like a bad smell," said Percival with sangfroid, fixing his gaze on the precinct Captain's clenched face.

"Captain," said Ernie Dodd, trying to diffuse the tension. "Do you mind?"

"Far be it from me to detain an officer of the court, counselor," said the Captain, stepping aside, casting Percival a reproachful glance.

"After you," Dodd invited Percival and the others to go first, while he kept a purposeful eye on the Captain.

"The boy's got no father," said Mrs. Bolden to Percival, as they descended the precinct steps to the waiting car. "He's got no guidance. He admires you guys I can see that. Maybe you can talk to him. He'll listen to you. N maybe you'll drop by some time to say hello," she dolefully suggested. She threw back her shoulders, revealing the full measure of her bosom. "It was awfully nice of you to come get me' n bring me here. You'd think the little wretch would appreciate it, but I do. So please, jus' drop in to say hi sometime, ok? I can always cook you up something. You know how lonely it gets without a man," she appealed, laying a hand on his arm.

"We'll see," said Percival, drawing away and facing Ernie Dodd. "Thanks counselor," he offered his hand. "I appreciate your prompt response. You spared us a lot of grief back there, to say the least."

"I guess you and the captain have met before?"

"We have. I'll tell you about it some other day. For now, thanks."

"Anytime," said Dodd, sauntering off in the direction of the County Court House.

"Can I drive?" Ricky asked, climbing into the back seat of the Impala after Sam.

"Skeeter can handle it," said Percival from the passenger seat up front.

"Don't sweat it, I'm a good driver."

"Why can't you jus' do as you're told?" his mother reprimanded, sliding in beside him.

"But I am a good driver," he insisted.

"When you're old enough 'n have a license, not before," said Percival firmly, as the car leapt forward taking a U turn at the light round a meridian and racing back down Richmond Terrace along the river ledge.

"Be careful how you drive, Skeeter," Percival cautioned. "If the pigs stop us things will go badly, baby."

"Right on," Skeeter acknowledged, slowing to within the speed limits.

***

The city was a hot bed of contention on every front: The fledgling Teachers and Transit Workers Unions were grappling with the new liberal/republican administration in residence at City Hall under the leadership of then Mayor John V. Lindsey; if not a man for all seasons, then surely a man well suited for his times which accounted as much for his successes as for his failures. And the city's ghettos were, in a word, flash points of unrest, tumult and dissent. At the start of school, in the Fall of that turbulent year, the ghettos, principally the Brooklyn Brownsville school district, took on the UFT in a struggle that would paralyze the public-school system citywide.

On what was to have been opening day of school, the United Federation of Teachers, (UFT) called for a citywide teachers strike of the public school system to protest the refusal of the local governing board in the predominantly black and Puerto Rican, experimental Ocean-Hill Brownsville school district in community control, to reinstate 10 teachers accused the previous May of undermining the decentralization plan or doing unsatisfactory work in addition. The Teachers Union were also demanding the district leaders take back 200 other teachers who were locked out after protesting the ouster of the 10 by staying away from work for several days.

Situated at the convergence of East New York and the Bed-Stuy section of Brooklyn, the Brownsville school districts actions opened old wounds and fanned flames of racism and anti-Semitism because of its opposition to the largely Jewish UFT membership. While the issues were not anti-Semitic in content, they were, in fact, Jim Crow.

The UFT felt that its young union had come into existence because of the refusal of the New York Public School system to address teachers concerns, lack of benefits, protection, etc.— while black and Puerto Ricans felt that the school system was archaic and that the teachers did not address their grievances, nor were they particularly sympathetic to their needs. Therefore, as they saw it, decentralization and community control of schools was the only other solution. Hence the Ocean-Hill school board, under the leadership of district administrator, Rhody McCoy, fired these ten teachers because of student and parent complaints. Added to that, the fact that they were also Jewish, helped complicate matters further.

Subsequently, the strike was called off in two days, but the agreement lapsed in three, and so the teachers again staged a walkout of the schools.

"Do you think this strike will go on much longer?" Leroy, who had joined the Panthers under Percival's sway, looked up from the cover of "The New York Times," addressing no one in particular.

"The UFT won't back down n I can't imagine Rhody McCoy giving in unless he's relieved of his duties," Percival answered, nodding.

"You think the strike'll go on awhile?"

"We'll see, won't we?" said Rufus drowsily, his eyes drooping from lack of sleep.

Lily piped in, "It's only been a few days now. Tell the truth, Leroy, you jus' don't wanna go back to school," she teased.

"If he doesn't, I do," sang Raschelay from behind a typewriter where she had been drafting a proposal for a free breakfast program for children. The program was in the initial stages of development and Raschelay, a sophomore at the prestigious Stuyvesant High school in Manhattan, had been placed in charge of organizing it since she was both capable and popular.

Grace in motion, she was a budding Nubian beauty. Her hair encircled her head in a full-blown Afro accentuating her well-formed, honey nut facial features, lush lips, Arabic nose and brooding, large chestnut brown eyes. She was witty, poetic, disturbingly intelligent and deeply committed to the well-being of her race as a people. All the Panther men looked on her solicitously— some lustfully but she knew how to handle them, even at her young age.

On one occasion, Skeeter had playfully swiped her on her rump.

"Dig yourself!" She had scoffed, examining him with merciless eyes. "You're suppose to be a revolutionary black brother respectful of black womanhood and not a reactionary sexist pig!"

All the eyes in the room lifted on them, and Skeeter slinked off with an embarrassed, imbecilic grin on his face.

Sam said to Rufus, "I can't say I much blame him for trying you know? Hell, I'd try myself. It's a pity a girl so young can look so good."

"It's a pity a girl so young gotta ave such an acid tongue in her head," Rufus replied, with a longing glance.

Turning her trenchant wit on the teachers strike with a political acumen beyond her 15 years, Raschelay said: "While I'm as anxious as the next person to get back to my studies, I'm a thousand percent behind the Brownsville school board." She shook her head with disapproval, pursed her lips and said, "The UFT is simply holding up the city of New York to close down the experiment in home rule. And it's awful how most people blame the Brownsville school district for the strike," she said, wryly. "It's no less disturbing how the debate has taken place along ethnic and racial lines, too. No one cares to notice that the Brownsville schools are open, and that it's the teachers strike which has locked our schools down citywide." She added significantly, "it's obvious that the UFT is holding the city's student population hostage to use as a bargaining chip."

As Percival was about to reply the front door to the office swung open and Skeeter rushed into the room stammering breathlessly, "they – they caught em,

300

they took the killers. One of em right next door in my building," he said urgently, his eyes wide and round with alarm. "Mark Hiller, my neighbor, was the trigger man, can you beat that for g'd sakes?" The outside noise of the street dropped off, with the closing of the door.

"Woe, slow down," said Rufus, gruffly, raising a forestalling hand. "What 'r you talking 'bout, man? What murder? Where?" An expression of utter bewilderment touched his depthless face.

"Last night," Skeeter hurried to explain. "You ain't heard? Three brothers did this white dude; jus' cut him down. Shot him dead." He shuddered, as if having witnessed the crime firsthand. "The man's name is Horton. Yeah, Lee Horton. He lives on Westervelt –"

"G'd no!" Lily stared, genuinely horrified. "Poor Willa Horton? That poor wife. My g'd," she gasped, covering her mouth with a hand. "You can't mean it c-can you?"

"They killed him," Skeeter assured her, lowering his voice. "Mark Hiller, he's the one squeeze the trigger. It was a .22. a Saturday night special. They took him with it. I mean, he didn't ditch it. He slept with the damn thing under his pillow. Can you imagine, what dreams he must 'ave had with the blood of a white man on his hands?" he said, hollowly.

Percival wondered, but said with a rueful shake of the head, "Some foul shit, that. A fucking lousy Saturday night special!" He loathed guns; he thought them a coward's weapon, despite the fact that he had qualified as a small arms expert in the army.

"Was there a reason?" Sam asked.

"No reason," said Skeeter carefully. "Horton was on his way home from some grocery shopping, 'n the bloods come up on him 'n blast him in the face like it's funny, n making off with some chump change."

Rufus stood with Ricky who had become his shadow, searching for words. "Maybe we should run n investigation," he suggested, his flexed brows, hooding stalled eyes.

"Maybe we should cut 'r throats, too, while we're at it," Percival quipped. "Let's not go overboard with this. It has a smell to it. A man's dead! Murdered! There's no percentage in sticking 'r necks out. It could taint us unnecessarily. No, we got'a concentrate on ya campaign 'n not allow ourselves to be sidetracked."

"I get your point, but something should be done," said Rufus. "Cause, like you say, a man's dead!"

"A white man's dead," Percival clarified. "It's not for us to do! The only thing that can rightly be done is to call on the grieving widow 'n offer her your condolences. But, believe me, I don't think she'll want'a be seeing any brothers t'day," he said, caustically. "No, let the law take its course this once."

"So the pigs got us over a barrel, do they?" said Sam, slowly.

"That's about the size of it. They got us where we can't do a thing. More to the point," Percival emphasized, "where we don't want'a do a thing."

"I like that, that's good," Rufus exhaled sharply.

"I agree," Lily stated, her voice caught in her throat. "There's something so horribly wrong with murdering another person. It's spiteful; like stealing a coat you can't wear n not allowing anyone else the use of it either – only worse; far worse! It's wrong headed! Wrong! Wrong! Wrong!" she said, face graven, and tears leaking from her eyes. "If we're to sympathize with anyone it's Willa, his widow," said Lily, emotionally. "We should pay her a house call. Only like Percival say's, she wouldn't want'a see any black men t'day." She waved her hand in a gesture of irritability. "So Raschelay 'n I," Raschelay raised her head, "should organize a group of women; perhaps your mother would be willin' ta help us since she's co-head of Welfare Mothers Association, n an active member of the NAACP?"

"I don't see why not," Raschelay voiced. "In fact, I think my mother would be quite interested." She rose and started after Lily for the door. Raschelay was barely out the door when her pert, pretty face reappeared in the doorway. "Can Ricky come with us, just in case?"

Ricky looked up at Rufus beseechingly. He was two years Raschelay's junior, but he was no less in love with her for it. Whenever on the streets in her company, wanting the world to think she was his girl, he would sidle up beside her and preen like a peacock. Rufus gave his consent, and without delay Ricky scooted out the door, leaving the rest of the Panther membership behind, silently ruminating.

Rufus said, breaking the pall of silence which had overtaken them, "the stupidity of it is if school had been in, if the teachers strike hadn't shut down the schools, this probably wouldn't ave happened."

"Could be," said Skeeter, chuckling softly, "but these cats ain't no scholars."

"That's it," Percival exclaimed face alight. "All right, we can't fault the pigs or take the side of these thugs, but we can say that the boredom induced by the overlong vacation as a result of the teachers strike, was the primary cause of this senseless murder. That it was out of idleness and nothing to do but prowl the streets, that created the conditions for this crime." His sharp eyes glinting. "Therefore, we call for the creation of Freedom Schools like they did in Harlem a few years back 'n like the south did. We can use 'r office as a schoolroom 'n get permission to use the Heritage House 'n get as many qualified volunteer teachers as possible. Estelle 'n Morty would surely be willing 'n, perhaps, Dr. Osgood could participate, as could Nina Koestler 'n Ruth Morrow, 'n some SDS 'n BSU members, too. We'll educate em right here!"

"Percival, man," Rufus waggled his head, "that's lovely. I like the way you think, baby," he acknowledged, smiling. "When do we start?"

"We get on the phones, send off a press release, start up the mimeograph machine 'n print up flyers 'n we're off!"

Contacts were made, a press release issued, and, just as Percival had suspected, the volunteers flocked eagerly onboard. Estelle offered her services, though Morty could not due to his editorial obligations. Nina Koestler was only too happy to help in any way she could and there were more than enough college students both white and black. The problem at first, was finding enough for them to do. Doctor Osgood recruited a few other medicos and together they would form the nucleus of what would eventually become the free Panther medical team.

The press release and leaflets distributed throughout the community at large read:

"For the duration of the teachers strike, classes from elementary through high school will be offered by a staff of qualified personnel in both the Heritage House and Black Panther Party Office located at 229 and 232 Jersey Street, respectively. Enrollment starts immediately. Come prepared to learn. Classes are from 9a.m. to 3p.m. Free breakfast will be served. All power to the people!"

Students showed up in larger numbers than anticipated. Indeed, the tedium of the overly long vacation brought them in in excited, babbling droves with shiny, expectant faces—pencils, pens and notebooks in hand – ready to participate. If, as they say, the emerald hills of Ireland boast twenty-seven shades of green, Africa, it might then be said, boasts as many shades of black in its people. And all of those shades that Fall, were represented in the freedom school. In fact, all the students, with the exception of Katy, Inez and Tzi – who came out of allegiance to Percival – were black. Otherwise, white students stayed away. Events were unfolding so quickly that soon there was an overflow of students and more space had to be found to provide for the spillage. The vexing task of providing breakfast for so many mouths fell to Raschelay. It was here where her personality, wit and beauty stood her in good stead. Her charm opened doors and her intelligence acquired much needed foodstuff. Altogether, the effort would provide Rufus with the best news coverage of his campaign. As Beverly, Nina's friend from the local paper, wrote, "While the other congressional candidates scratch their heads over the issue of the teachers strike, the Peace And Freedom candidate, Rufus Hinton, has taken the initiative and, with the aid of parents, teachers, college students, doctors and writers, opened the doors to the Freedom Schools for immediate enrollment."

As time wore on and the teachers strike continued, new accusations of black anti-Semitism arose in the heavily publicized school debate. Hence a group of Jewish teachers, in defiance of the UFT, came out in vigorous support of Rhody McCoy and the Brownsville experiment in school decentralization, stating, "By implication and distortion, black parents asking for a reasonable and realistic role in the public school system have been characterized as gangsters and anti-Semites." The statement further read, "This does not fit with what we see, and as a result a distorted picture has been given to the public and to the Jewish community alike."

In the meantime, Percival had arranged speeches for Rufus to deliver at the island's three colleges, and scheduled rallies for the major black areas—Mariners Harbor, West Brighton, New Brighton, and the Baptist Church in Port Richmond. He was also trying to convince the League of Women Voters to include Rufus in the only debate scheduled for that congressional district. They were less than favorably inclined. He did not threaten a student sit-in, as yet, and would, for the present, hold that tactic in reserve.

The day after Rufus' first talk at Richmond College, he and Percival, along with Bob Fischer, President of the local chapter of SDS, relaxed on fold out chairs around a conference table in front of a blackboard at the Panther Office, analyzing the strengths and weaknesses of his presentation the previous night. The Freedom school had let out for the day. Rufus had sent Ricky off to play because, among other things, he had to give his undivided attention to the discussion at hand. Other Panther members came and went, though Raschelay, trying to secure commitments of staples from independent grocers, supermarket chains, and other charitable organizations, remained behind on the phone, while Sam, like a love sick puppy, pestered her.

"If you can't find something better to do," Percival finally said, "go sell some papers!"

"Do you mind if I listen in? I'm Cultural Liaison 'n if I'm to be effective I got'a be kept in the loop."

"Fine, keep your mind on the business at hand 'n leave Raschelay to hers."

"I'm jus' jivin' man, can ya dig it"

"Don't!" said Percival, returning to the discussion.

Bob Fischer thought Rufus' rage over the Panther Party's Minister of Defense's, Huey P. Newton, recent conviction for involuntary manslaughter of an Oakland cop had been effective in his presentation the night before. "But your comments," he remarked—, *If Huey's not freed, we're gonna put this racist white government up against the wall 'n say, stick em up motherfucker*

304

this is a hold up. And, *the only politics relevant to black people t'day is the politics of revolution. That is, whatever this governments for, we oppose, 'n whatever it opposes, we're for.* While the remarks were both moving and disturbing to many in the audience, they were as titillating as they were frightening."

A shiver passed across Rufus' face. "I couldn give a fuck less," he said, defiantly. He took a perverse satisfaction in needling Bob, a scholar and intellectual.

"I'm just trying to give you a picture of the white students on the college circuit," said Bob amiably, his hands outstretched, unsure of what to make of Rufus. "You can choose to alienate them or bring them over to your cause. But you can't do both."

Percival conceded the point. "The point's well taken."

"Paradoxically," Bob continued, his features inescapably Semitic, "your remarks, *If you help me free Huey, I'll slap the President's face,* and, *You know, if I slap his face I'll have something up my sleeve that'll take his whole head—* were appreciated. Not only for its outlandishness, but, for the most part, because the President is so reviled by America's white youth – more especially since Chicago and this terribly unpopular war in Vietnam."

"They liked that, did they," Rufus chortled, snake eyes rolling, sighting down his nose. He lit a cigarette.

"Politics is never quite what it appears," said Bob, urbanely, with a tauntingly veiled smile on his otherwise broodingly, calf-eyed-boyish face. "You attack the President, who they don't like, and they're with you. Attack the vestments of his authority, the symbols of government for which the nation stands, and they venerate, they're against you. You must separate the man from the Office. It's somewhat like angling, you know?"

"No, I don't," said Rufus, with the slightest suggestion of a sneer.

"He's simply saying," said Percival impatiently, feeling decidedly uneasy, "you don't talk to a child the way you would an adult."

"Is that what you're saying," Rufus asked with a flicker of malice in his tone?

"Precisely."

"Hmph," Rufus snorted, looking off, smoke curling from his nostrils. "Like I don't know the score!" He could little suffer white people instructing him; but for Percival, he would have nothing to do with these brash, young, intellectual white radicals; accusing them of being overly immersed in a metaphysical revolution to be of any value in a real one.

Bob Fischer, the son of a Jurist and stay at home mom, was a sociological major hoping to eventually obtain his PhD in political science. In the spirit of the day, however, he was considered a campus radical. A troublemaker. Even so, he continued to maintain a B+ average. Moreover, he was a mensch, a good fellow and, in as much as he was, he was unafraid of putting his convictions on the line. As a youngster, he had been smitten by the Civil Rights anthem, "We Shall Overcome," and had longed to become a participant in that overcoming. As such he was willing to suffer Rufus's disdain with an extra gram of salt.

"You said something earlier about a guerrilla theatre scheme you're hatching," Percival asked?

"Right – well yes, I was talking to a guerrilla theatre troupe at college and they would be willing to do a series of skits for Rufus' campaign –"

"That so?" said Rufus, intrigued.

"Ah yes," Bob said, smiling, "they were thinking that they might like to do something closer to election at the Ferry Terminal during morning rush hour for full effect."

"Hmmm," Percival murmured, "when you get particulars ironed out, let's talk, ok?"

"You're on."

Just then an angry cluster of community dwellers pushed their way into the office, voices raised, behind two Panthers, Big/Black and Priestus. They tramped in with over five hundred years of grievance on their brows. Big/Black stood out, larger than life, a head taller than the tallest among them—an imposing figure of a man. Rufus swung his head sharply in their direction. They slammed the door shut with a resounding bang. "What the?" Percival blurted over his shoulder. Priestus told the group, "Wait here." Then he and Big/Black saluted the duty officer, "Power!" And tramping by Sam and Raschelay, who looked up abruptly, came to a halt in front of Rufus, Percival, and Bob, seated at the conference table. Priestus broke in,

"Some foul shit's jus' come down the fuckin' pike," said the stout, chocolate colored man with steel rim glasses, panting excitedly, about to break out in a sweat. "The pigs jus' beat up on a seven months pregnant sister on Carson Avenue. They pulled up to arrest some brothers shooting craps on the corner 'n the sister's brother was passing through," he said in a voice hoarse with rage, "she run up to tell 'em her brother wasn't involved 'n two pigs grabbed her 'n a third jabbed her in the belly with his club till she doubled over clutching her gut and they left her writhing on the ground, crying 'Oooo Lord, my baby – my baby, don't let it be dead. Jesus, G'd, don't let my baby be dead. N the pigs left her there 'n drove off with her brother in cuffs, along with the other dudes they'd snared for illicit gambling. A neighbor run her to the hospital." He added and passed Rufus a piece of paper. "But we got the pigs badge numbers. 'N these folks here want'a know what we're gonna do," Priestus said, with a backward yank of a thumb.

Bristling with rage, Big/Black forcefully interjected, "Someone ought'a smoke 'em," he said, catching those within hearing off guard. This was uncharacteristic of the nature of his sentiments—despite the fact that they were "Pigs," as the panthers disparaged them! Although 6'5 and 220lb.'s of brawn, Big/Black was shy, soft spoken, sentimental, and easy going to a fault, and so his remark took all by surprise. Called Big/Black because, as his mother— credited with good common sense— had informed him, on his coming of age, seated at the table in the small, dingy kitchen of a share cropper's shack under an oil lamp casting ghostly shadows on the side walls, "I'm'a tell y'll different than ya pa would'a was he here—God rest his soul— but he was'a man 'n I'm'a woman—ya mother. Ya pa would'a tell ya 'bout da birds 'n da bees but, as a woman, I'm'a tell ya 'bout sowin' 'n reapin. That way y'll know not ta drop'a stitch. Men know da pleasure'a conception', but woman bear da burden'a bringin' y'll in ta dis world'a sin 'n devilry; sometimes at risk'a her own life. Every mother is threatened with the specter'a martyrdom at the birth of'a newborn, 'n must be willin' to sacrifice herse'f fer the hope'a new life she brings into this griefstricken world. That's a woman's cross. F'r womenfolk bringin' chillun in to this ole world is a labor'a love, f'r men folk it's a pleasure f'r which they labor, by the sweat'a they brow, the rest'a they days. It's true a boy should 'ave his pa to talk to at y'll age, but y'll pa work'd his-self into the ground f'r the pleasure'a havin' thirteen chillun to care f'r. So I'm left to talk to y'll instead, 'n what'a man know 'n what'a woman know two different t'ings. I can't tell y'll what y'll pa kno' but I c'n tell y'll what I kno'—w'at'a mother kno'. I'm'a speak heart to heart, mother to son. I'm'a tell y'll how y'll get ya name, get yaself born, enter dis world descendent'a slaves 'n, before dat, Heaven only kno's. But the good book say 'y'll born in the image 'n likeness a' God. 'N who more lofty than dat, I ask? Always remember, then, where y'll come from, 'n that y'll blood is good as any other. Don't y'll squander it or 'spill y'll seed in the sand' like the good book say. They both precious." He looked at her curiously. "'N 'cause y'll my las' I love y'll the more f'r the grief I bore bringin' y'll into this woe begotten world. I'm'a tellin' y'll like I knows it," she said tautly, taking his hands in hers.

"I recollect y'll birth the way I recalls the births'a all my chil'en," she softly began, "with love 'n tears—cause, as Jesus say, on his way to the cross, 'Weep not for me but f'r y'll chil'en!' so on the night y'll born, in dis ole shack wid only'a midwife to catch y'll, a blood curdlin' moon, a witch's moon, was'a ridin' out yonder hills 'n the back, 'n there y'll be'a strainin' 'n a'strainin, strugglin' like the devil to be born." She suddenly broke off, rethought herself and resumed her tale, "I be writhin' on da bed on my back in spasm'a shootin' pain. I be pushin' 'n y'll be'a pushin' 'n together we be a'pushin', 'n with'a mighty thrust y'all head pop out, big 'n black, 'bout ta split me in two." She groaned in agony. A spasm of pain convulsed his face. "I was cryin' like'a lost soul, 'O' Lawd! O' Lawd!" She shook her head back and forth, as the events of that fateful night unfolded before her eyes like a cinematic scene. "I collapsed back onto the bed, lyin' in a pool'a sweat 'n blood, spent, pantin' from exhaustion. The mid wife say 'Try agin.' I do. I try again. Then y'll burst out, thank God, or I'd'a died on the spot. There be no hospital to rush to, no doctor to call on. Jus' the grace'a God. The next t'ing I kno' the midwife done whack y'll bottom 'n y'll' begin'a wailin'. She say 'He da biggest baby y'll done had; the biggest I ever see.' I tell her give y'll to me. She pass'd y'll on 'n y'll latch on to my tit like a hog to a trough. Y'll be twelve pounds easy.

"Y'll pa look down 'n say, 'He big 'n black like my grandpa.' He smiled broadly. 'He my side'a the family sure. We gonna calls 'im Big/black jus' like grandpa.' But me? I was'a worryin' 'bout how I'm'a nurse such a big'a chile like y'll." She would wither into old age nursing him. "The trauma'a birth, da pain a mother bears, is both 'r's, both mother 'n chile's. I brought enough'a y'll into this world to know. All the pain I suffer'd bringin' y'll into this world'a sin 'n woe, was absorbed by the love all mothers 'ave carryin' a'chile in 'er womb goin' on most near'a year. Love be the salve that binds the wound at separation. The whole'a life is but'a healin'. It can't all jus' be sweetness 'n light. Y'll got'a know to forgive in order to be forgiven," she said as she embraced him full heartedly and kissed him fervently on the cheek.

"God bless y'll, my son," she said. He was thirteen.

That Sunday she took him down to the river to be baptized, in the name of the Holy Spirit, by a traveling evangelist.

He was clumsy growing into his body and abysmally shy and was, therefore, perceived as slow. However, in short order he would grow into a tall, lanky, 6ft. 5, muscular, well-coordinated, simple man with a friendly disposition, and languid smile. He was always bigger than the biggest boy, and shy as he was big. And often taunted on account. He seldom reacted out of anger for fear of wrongly hurting another. He was natural in himself and possessed a deep love of life. He likened black folks to kinfolks and white folks to rancorous neighbors who it was necessary to put up with. He'd inherited a gentle spirit, and there was nothing mean about him. He was a country boy, from the Carolinas, on the run from the law, trying to keep a low profile.

"Who say's we won't smoke em?" Rufus snarled, springing to his feet as if about to pounce.

"Slow down," said Percival, sternly, casting Rufus a cautionary glance. "Since we're not gonna 'off' nobody in the next five minutes, let's try this," he proposed, as if about to deliver a coup de gras. "Let's print up a thousand or so "Wanted Dead or Alive" posters on these badge numbers. If they should get themselves offed by some enterprising individual or other, 'r hands 'r clean, dig?"

They all stared momentarily at him, allowing the idea to sink in. Then Rufus burst into laughter, nodding his head. Big/ black smiled shyly.

"I got it," said Preistus, smiling excitedly.

"That's scathingly diabolic," said Bob, slowly, duly impressed.

"Ain't it so," Rufus chortled. "Ain't it so!"

Percival also looked pleased, but not for the same reasons. He continued, "plus, we'll file formal charges of police brutality. We'll get Ernie Dodd to lodge the grievances. But for now we'll flood the streets with "Wanted Dead or Alive" posters. We want the pigs 'n the community to get the idea we're dead serious, 'n these cops removed from 'r streets!"

"Is there anything I can do to help?" Bob asked, looking from Percival to Rufus.

"You can take their statement 'n type it up on'a stencil in'a "Wanted Dead or Alive" flyer to be run off on the mimeograph machine," said Rufus, crushing out his cigarette.

"Shall do." Bob threw back the locks of his shoulder length hair with a dismissive toss of the head, and he began to write.

Rufus started for the front of the office with the shambling gait of an old campaigner about to address his beleaguered forces, with his trusted consigliere, Percival, beside him. "Everything's under control," he assured the group, looking into their strained, angry faces. "We're working on something right now. You can stay 'n see what we're up to or go 'bout you business 'n find out later. Whatever you do, know we're dealing with it."

"This better be good," said some of them, before turning away, grumbling in accord. This querulous band of roughnecks trusted Rufus because they saw themselves in him. They had no way of knowing how far afield they were in their estimation. Rufus was more akin to St. Paul struck blind on his way to Damascus.

On their return, Bob pulled out the stencil from the typewriter and handed it to Rufus. He looked it over, then passed it on to Percival for his approval. It read,

"Wanted Dead or Alive, three police officers, pigs, badge numbers #231, #487, #662, for the savage beating and attempted murder of a pregnant black woman, Margo Rawls, and her unborn child. These pigs cruelly and without provocation held and beat a defenseless sister with nightsticks, then left her helplessly on the street as they sped off, oinking. These three pigs are wanted by the People's Revolutionary Tribunal. If they offer resistance, show them no mercy. KILL them dead on the spot. This is what revolutionary justice demands. This is the People's decision. All Power to the People! Death to the sadistic, fascist pigs!"

"Run it as is," Percival said, handing Sam the stencil.

Annoyed, Sam sucked his teeth, but took the stencil.

The impact of the Wanted Dead or Alive posters, once distributed, was instantaneous. Within days, the three cops were off the streets and reassigned to precincts in another borough. The charges of police brutality were carried forward. Thus, the Panther membership was in a celebratory mood. In the psychological warfare with the police, and without having fired a shot, they had carried the day.

Ricky Bolden, who had become the chapter's mascot, sold "The Panther Speaks" on the street corners stoutly shouting, "Off the pig," at passing patrol cars. The story of the standoff in the office of the Black Panthers between the Panther members and the police, because of Ricky had become legendary. And the police were not taking them at all lightly.

***

In keeping with the spirit of communalism, Rufus and Lily would host weekend suppers at their bungalow from Friday through Sunday for the Panther membership. The entire membership would contribute, and so share in the cost. Lily inevitably took charge.

Inasmuch as she always relied on Raschelay's help, she was also always having to shoo Ricky out from underfoot.

"Rufus would you call Ricky?"

"Ricky!"

And he would respond as quickly as would a devoted dog to its masters voice.

It was on a weekend after the membership had shot up from twelve to eighteen, and the small quarters were flushed to capacity with young revolutionaries, that Raschelay brought Tzi to a communal meal for the first time. It appeared that they were becoming something of an item which did not sit well with Sam. Among this otherwise warm, congenial group, the lilting voice of Gladys Knight wove it's way, "With every beat of my heart there's a beat for you/ With every toast of wine there's a toast for you." Everyone was standing around with a plate of food in their hands eating, talking, and enjoying the music. Percival was engaged in a discussion with a new recruit, Silva Epps, a recent graduate from Brown University who, to his parents dismay, was more interested in revolutionary politics than gainful employment.

"These dinners are a good idea," Silva said, ravenously.

"Ummm, yes, I think so," Percival rejoined, digging in. "Ideally we would like 'r membership to live communally but 'r situation's such it's not yet possible."

"A lot of counterculture groups these days, such as the Hippies, are forming communes in which to live alternate lifestyles."

"Let's not get too hung up on the word, counterculture, for fear of being confused with the Hippies," Percival said with a deprecatory wave of a hand. "They're an anal, prepubescent 'n apolitical group of nobodies. Their social agenda is drugs, sex 'n Rock 'n Roll. They eschew the dialectic 'n avoid the social discourse, while we engage it 'n carry it to its next logical conclusion. In this instance, social revolution! Hippies 'r more like drones in a beehive – useless," he said, his lips turned up in scorn. "As says Cleaver, 'They won't balance two dead flies in the scale of eternity,' baby."

"I hadn't thought of it that way," Silva said, pursuing a solitary pea with his fork round the rim of his plate. "But, ah," he chuckled, "I also think Cleaver was speaking of something else too."

"It's out of context, but you get my drift?"

"I follow, yes."

"Besides," Percival continued, "the word's so bandied about it's become common coin though we try using it in its literal sense. Like 'proletariat,' which comes to us from Latin 'n means 'mass.' 'N 'commune,' common. Here, the dialectic is of the herd or out from the herd." He speared a piece of meat on to his fork and brought it to his mouth. "As used t'day it's become tawdry. It's the fault of the bourgeoisie media, who in applying it to their revisionist ends, sap it of its vitality. What we're really addressing here is more akin to the Israeli Kibbutz, if you follow my drift?"

"I'm with you. It's heady stuff. Deep, man, deep." Silva leveled his fork at Big/black standing beside him. "Did you catch that, man? Did you dig what the brother had to say?"

"Huh?" Big/black gulped a mouth full of food, cowed as a schoolboy ill prepared for his exams. "No. I didn't get it." He agonizingly responded, "'n I don't think anyone else much gets it either. I'll tell ya, y'll talk shit nobody understands, but y'll 'n that's what's wrong. Ya stops poor ole grandma on the street who been call'd dumb all her days 'n y'll talk using words like 'dialectical materialism,' she ain't heard before but she don't want y'll think she's dumb so she jus' go 'n shakes her head 'n say, 'don't y'll know it. ain't

311

that so. Uh, uh, uh, if that don't beat all.' Then she go off down the street apiece 'n someone ask, 'What them Panthers say, ole lady?' N she turn round 'n say, cause she ain't understand 'a word y'll say 'n say, 'they say they gonna burn the whole damn place down.'"

Unable to keep a straight face, Silva turned away. Big/black's barb cut to the quick. Percival blushed and laughed at himself—his pomposity.

"Touché!" he retorted.

"W-what?" Big/black blinked, mystified.

Never mind." Percival said, annoyed with his second faux pas in close succession. He had had no wish to belittle Big/Black any more than had Silva. Big/Black was a lovable, easy going yokel who Percival had liked at first blush, as had everybody else so it seemed. He was tall as a pine tree, and strong as 'John Henry,' that 'steel driving man' of fable and song. He could fell a bull with a single blow of his fist. Yet he'd rather laugh his way out of a fix than resort to fisticuffs. His parents were tenant farmers with "more children than you can shake a stick at," thirteen, of which he was the final, by his count. They had all gone to the same rundown colored school as had their parents before and, no better off for it, they would drop out, one by one, out of boredom and the harsh reality of life. They were going nowhere else than 'the cotton fields of yore'— as would, no doubt, their classmates and friends. The school was inadequate in every detail for want of such things as proper electrical lighting, textbooks, black boards, desks and chairs, as well as competent teachers. In compensation for their inadequacies, the teachers could be cruel and casually sadistic. Big/Black was often the brunt of their ill humor. After years of enduring their incompetence like a friendly dog beaten once too often he turned on his cruel masters in an uncharacteristic act of rage and, one night, burnt the school down in just vindication.

"No one was learning anything anyway," he reasoned.

Hence, he was forced to flee town.

The evening passed as evenings do and everybody slowly left with the exception of Percival, having nowhere to be in particular—Gwen Halsey was out of town and the long trip into Brooklyn was, on such a blustery night and at that hour, daunting— hence, he tarried undecidedly.

"It's raining," Lily announced, closing the front door against the dark, behind Skeeter, the last out. "Perhaps you'd like to spend the night rather than going back home to Brooklyn?"

"If you don't mind," Percival said vaguely.

"Yeah, stay," Rufus implored, raising his head from the arm of the sofa on which he lolled with an open copy of "Time" magazine in hand. Novels such as "Les Miserables," "War & Peace," Ralph Ellison's "Invisible Man," with political tracts from Marx, Lenin and Mao along with pamphlets by Malcolm X were sprawled on the floor by a leg of his couch. He was becoming ever more the Marxian dialectical materialist. '*It might be said that Rufus was emerging as an argument for the often repeated but unproven remark that revolutionaries are furnished by those whom fate has mistreated, the failures in life and love.*' More so than not it would be more rightly said that Rufus was the ill-conceived child of his adolescent nation's cumulative sins.

"There's a spare bedroom upstairs," Rufus casually said.

"Okay," said Percival decidedly, folding himself lazily into an easy chair facing Rufus, as a sudden outbreak of thunder and play of lightening flashed beyond the front room windows.

"You two'll want'a talk, so I'll be off to bed," Lily said as, tired on her feet, she yawned and trundled off. "Good night."

"Sweet dreams," Percival sang out after her.

"Good night, sweetheart," Rufus said, routinely.

For a brief moment all was silent save for the lashing rain pelting the frail cottage, driving autumn leaves from tree branches down to abandoned rain slicked roads.

"What you reading, man?"

"Jus' some jive ass shit 'bout women libbers burning their bras in the court'a public opinion looking to cause a scandal," Rufus said with distaste, casting the magazine aside.

"Don't get me wrong or nothing, I'm for women's rights whatever they may be, g'd knows, but pursuing a separative agenda while their men, husbands, sons' n lovers r dying in an immoral war such as nam strikes me as underhanded 'n no less amoral, especially since we should be pulling together to get em the fuck out'a that hellhole first." He passed a veined hand over his weary dark face. "What this tells me is how far apart men 'n women ave grown in 'r forty-watt, scientific age," he said, then swung his feet to the floor, sitting up.

"Would you suggest we stop the black struggle cause black men 'r dying in Vietnam?"

"It's a far cry from the same thing 'n you know it."

"Let's say I don't."

"Don't get me started, this one's too close for comfort," Rufus said, taking offense. "After all, I was one of those grunts in that fiasco 'n you slipped through the noose. Ya wasn't there, my man. More to the point, we got'a get the bloods outta there n encourage em to join forces with us in r own fucking struggle right here, dig? Cause, like Ali says, 'No Vietcong ever called me no nigger!'" he said, with a look of brute savagery on his face. "But this thing

313

cropping up between men 'n women shouldn't be, 'n should be taken on as codependents, partners in life but, no, women ave become questionable allies. It's not jus' the Vietnam thing," he said in exasperation, fumbling about for a cigarette. At last he found one and lit it in an attempt to calm himself. The cigarette bobbed between his fleshy lips, as he exhaled a plume of smoke. "It's epidemic. No sooner than the bloom's off the rose, women 'r turning out to be tarantulas, black widow spiders who kill their sex partners while copulating or, for that matter a praying mantises who bites his head off in an orgasmic frenzy. At times it feels as if women ave become a stumbling block 'n modernity their ally." He leaned forward, staring malevolently, his expression sad and weary. "Sorry to say, but Freud was right. Women have penis envy 'n technology's become her dildo, her strap on, a woman's prosthesis, which, by no far stretch of the imagination, suggest that a white woman deposed of her pedestal is a whore, 'n a black woman atop it is a bitch!"

Percival listened intently in consternation of soul, fascinated and repulsed, as the rain beat hypnotically against the cottage.

"It's insane, man, I know," Rufus raved. "I mean, there's something so disturbing in wanting to become the despised other – wanting to be someone you both hate 'n love in the same breath, hating yourself to love em the more. The gulf 's wide n the leap deep – yet these chicks want'a be men or, more accurately, not jus' men, but white men – black women 'n white women alike!"

"Black men too, the middle class surely, want'a be white, no doubt, anything to escape 'r plight," Rufus said with contempt.

"Which, I dare say, we too 'r no less trying to escape, but in another fashion," Percival put in, "Trying to attain 'r selfhood, 'r unique, individual identity as men in the historical web of time."

"As black men, you mean?"

"I don't know manhood depends on color."

"You're so fucking sure'a yourself, aren't you?" Rufus accused.

Percival refused to comment.

"How many white men do you know?"

"About as many black men as I know."

Rufus waved a careless hand, reading Percival's mind. "Yeah! Yeah! Ya think what I'm saying's off the wall, don't you?"

"It sounds Loony Tunes to me. I wouldn't repeat it outside present company, if I were you."

"If that don't shoot the shit out'a free speech, then I don't know what the hell does."

"You the one wanting to silence the women's movement, man."

314

"Not silence em, man, recruit em, get em ta understand – create 'n alliance."

"I was worried. For a moment I thought you were about to round up an inquisition to burn a few witches."

Ha-ha, funny," Rufus scoffed. "Think what you like, I know what I know."

"Go on, man, this is fascinating."

"If you don't mind, I was about to say industrialization was the precursor of existentialism or, that is, alienated man; n is responsible for loosening us from 'r cultural 'n mythological roots. They'd have us believe it freed the slaves when, in fact, it served to enslave us more completely. Made us subservient to automation, science 'n the flywheel, especially women, n constantly justifies its existence by throwing em a bone here 'n there, always at the expense of men." He gestured hopelessly. "Yes, science has made us slaves of the technocrats instead'a the clergy. If, my man, religion is the opiate of the masses tell me then what the hell is science? An exchange of one fool's paradise for another," he emitted, as if divulging a little-known secret. "I certainly know this—technology's the new fire 'n we're cavemen standing back in awe of it, ready to go down on 'r weak knees in prayer 'n worship 'r new found God—science. N offer tribute to the High Priest a' this newly found religion – progress.

"G'd help us, we've degenerated into madness, 'n trying to save 'r sanity is now beyond 'r capacities. Oh no, we all may as well resign ourselves to going down with the ship." Seething with rage, Rufus rambled on, following his temper into the labyrinth of speculation. He stared at Percival with a peculiarly unnerving leer. "Yes, the poison of technology has taken root most assuredly through women. Meanwhile, we wonder who the fuck poisoned the well. I'm afraid I'm beginning to feel a growing disenchantment in my breast toward women," Rufus said, clasping his face in his palms. "It sometimes strikes me as if they've succumbed to the least common denominator in their soiled nature as did Eve, 'n 'r all hell bent on unraveling the fabric of 'r mutual existence.

"Women don't get it cause it's all worked out in their favor, 'n nobody sees anything wrong in a situation where it suits their ends. The result being men 'r displaced 'n alienated.

I can't really say I know what's going on between men 'n women but I'm sure, to quote Shakespeare's Weird sisters, 'by the pricking of r thumbs, something wicked this way comes.' It's like we've become locked in a grudge match 'n by definition they defy logic, they jus' go on 'n on like a family feud or some irrational number," he said, with a glassy, cross-eyed, preternatural gaze. "They say Armageddon's gonna be the final conflagration, the ultimate battle between good n evil. I say it's gonna be husbands against wives, wives against husbands, fathers against daughters, daughters against fathers, brothers against sisters, sisters against brothers, a total alienation of the sexes 'n an end to the species. 'The world,' wrote T.S. Elliot, 'won't end with a bang, but with a whimper.' N that, my man, is how I see it." He blew a circlet of smoke, his cross eyes awash in melancholic reflection.

Percival stared at Rufus perplexed, he shook his head, then slumped forward with a sigh, trying to plumb the depths of his thoughts. "What about Lily?" he asked, raising an eyebrow archly. "She's the flower of humanity, a jewel of decency, they don't come any better."

"Why ask me," Rufus said, sulkily. "After all, what the fuck do I know about women."

"Oh g'd," Percival thought, "we're losing Rufus."

Just then another burst of thunder was heard in the near distance, and a cold wind arose and soon sheets of rain came sweeping diagonally across the street.

***

It was a week before the election that the Richmond College guerrilla troupe staged a performance for Rufus' campaign at the Ferry Terminal during morning rush hour. There were fifteen hundred unsuspecting commuters in the terminal at the time waiting like cattle penned in at a depot to be transported to the slaughterhouse. Suddenly, a clamor arose at one end of the terminal. The sound of automatic rifle fire and grenades rend the air, panicking the sleepy-eyed commuters. They reeled back, spilling their coffee, having no place to run but into one another. "What the?" they cried, confused. It sounded like an armed, military skirmish under way. Commuters scrambled atop benches to see what was going on while others sought cover. There were more explosions and the acrid smell of cordite. In an area cleared by the melee, between the men's' room and coffee shop, lay a half dozen infants, their bodies twisted out of joint and bathed in blood while as many women dressed in blood spattered silken pajamas and straw hats, like Vietnamese peasants, were on their knees wailing over the bodies, smoke rising on the air. They beat their breast and threw up their hands in lamentation, as others lay prostrate alongside the bloodied babies for whom they wept.

It was impossible for the crowd to digest, but they watched, mouths agape, horror stricken as the eerie spectacle unfolded. As the crowd stood back in mute astonishment, a squad of American soldiers in combat fatigues and rifles with fixed bayonets forced their way through the thicket of people, knocked the weeping women aside with the butt end of their rifles and proceeded to stab

316

the infants with bayonets, screaming at the top of their voices, "KILL A COMMIE FOR CHRIST." They shouted repeatedly, amidst more rifle fire. Then the women joined the solders as they scurried off into the crowd, tossing leaflets over their heads amidst the commuters which, read, "Stop the war in Vietnam, elect Peace and Freedom candidate, Rufus Hinton, to Congress."

Rufus and Percival had been situated in the doorway of the men's toilet and were no less stunned by the performance than were the unwitting commuters. They cautiously advanced on the bodies of the blood-soaked infants left for dead on the terminal floor. As the crowd surged forwards a man in a business suit and tie turned an infant face up. It cried, "Mama." The shocked man gasped, leapt back, and clasped his stark, gray face in his hands. It was a doll. It's head cracked and eye sockets empty, it's body bathed in pig's blood. The combined smell of blood and cordite on the air was nauseating.

Rufus wavered on his feet, as horror sprang into his eyes and convulsed his face.

"I got'a get out'a here," he said, short of breath, sweating. "I got'a get out'a here." He placed a hand to his woozy, feverish brow, knees caving. Percival caught him by his elbow, steadying him as they departed.

"You ok, bro?" he asked, becoming concerned for Rufus' stability.

"This war's gonna go on killing people long after it's over."

"All I know is it's killing em now."

The bell for the next ferry rang and the sea of commuters, jerked back to the reality of their work-a-day lives, jostled toward the opened doors with no more a thought of what had just passed than dumb driven cattle.

***

That Saturday, following the weekly Defense Captains' meeting, Percival returned to his Crown Heights apartment and Rufus went on to Staten Island and, stopping off at the office, several members under Lily's supervision, were scraping, plastering and painting. Lily was spattered with paint from kerchief to coveralls and looked like a promotional ad for women's suffrage or war bonds. She confronted Rufus with raised paintbrush in hand as the others, including Ricky, worked on.

"That boy's been here all day since we began," Lily told Rufus, wiping her brow with the hand in which she held the brush. "He's breathing these toxic fumes all day 'n he should be out playing. He's jus' a child, though he don't want nobody to say so, especially with Raschelay 'round. He needs his share of sun 'n play jus' like any other growing thing. I tried to shoo him out'a here earlier on but he says he only takes orders from you. I'm telling you to order him to go out 'n play 'n catch a bit'a sun while it's still out to catch."

"N who'll take his place?" Rufus jocularly asked. "He's doing the best job of anybody else far as I can see."

"You," Lily rejoined, sticking her brush in his hand, "that's who!"

"Oh-oh, why'd I ask?" Rufus smiled. "OK, I get it," he said, planting a kiss on her paint spattered face. He then summoned Ricky, complemented him on his work and said, "Now get out'a here 'n get some sun."

"Ya sure captain?"

"Positive."

"Okay." Ricky saluted and dashed out the door as if let out of school.

Rufus went home to change, eat, then returned to the office, took up a paint brush and pitched in. They were in the midst of singing, "The revolution has come/ Off the pig/ The pigs 'r gonna catch hell," when they were startled by the sound of a car careening out of control. They cut off singing as it zoomed by in a squeal of wheels, horn blaring. Leroy craned his neck, looking out the front window, "Who the hell's that?" he asked in a start.

"Some jerk trying to get himself or someone else killed," Silva answered, as a police car sped past in hot pursuit, siren wailing. A few moments later there came the distinct sound of a crash, a sheering of metal, as if a distant roll of thunder followed by a backfire or two. Shortly thereafter, Big/black burst into the office and stood in the doorway like a specter, his eyes searching till they fell on Rufus.

"Rufus," he said, apologetically, "you better come quick!"

"What gives? Rufus asked, looking up.

"Jus' let's go," Big/black urged, glancing up the street over his shoulder. "It's Ricky."

Rufus dropped his paint brush and sprang to his feet and leapt out the door after Big/black.

"I think we should tag along," Lily said. The others all set aside their brushes and hastened after her. A crowd was gathering on the sidewalk further on up the street and mingling in the roadway. A cop was trying to keep the crowd at bay while his partner was on the car radio frantically explaining the potentially explosive situation in which they found themselves. "An angry mob's forming," he relayed.

"What happened?" asked one man of another, joining the crowd.

"They say he stole a car," the man explained.

"Who stole a car?"

"That boy, Ricky Bolden."

"That's no reason to shoot nobody," said the other. "Specially no kid."

"They say he had a gun," said the other.

"He ain't had no gun. He jus' shook his fist at em 'n holler, 'Off the pigs,' when he got out'a the car 'n run. I saw the whole thing," said a third man.

"Ain't he one of them Black Panthers?"

"Yeah, It's little Ricky Bolden."

"What'a shame."

"So young."

"Was he alone?"

"Two got away."

"Who was the driver?"

"Ricky. The boy they shot."

"Someone ought'a fetch his mama."

"Not me. I ain't telling nobody that boy dead."

"Here come them Panthers," someone noted, sighting Rufus' advance. "They'll tell her."

"Yeah, they'll tell her!"

As Rufus approached all eyes turned on him and the others coming up the road behind him. Rufus sighted the body face down in the gutter about thirty-five feet off, a bullet hole in the back from which blood seeped. A car was rolled on its side a few feet further on, its wheels turning. The car off which it had caromed was on the sidewalk, car horn honking. Rufus' pace slackened, his lips became dry and his stomach queasy. There was something all too overwhelmingly familiar about this, something he could not quite put his finger on, something he recognized from another life, deja vu, or was it a dream? There was a growing hesitance in his tread, as each step became increasingly labored and his advance slowed to a crawl. The faces in the crowd all merged into one large angry mouth. He smacked his dry lips and soon hard tears wormed their way into his eyes.

A police officer confronted him, trying to halt his advance. "Get back," he ordered, but Rufus neither heard nor saw him. "Get back," he repeated, going for his gun. Big/black stepped between them and lay his large, bear like paw atop the cop's hand and held it fast, staring fiercely down on him. He shook his head, indicating the rapid approach of the others.

"I don't think you want any more trouble than you got," said Big/black. The cop whitened, his hand paralyzed under Big/black's vice like grip. He sighed audibly, giving ground.

Rufus drew to an uneasy halt over the body, cast in the gutter at his feet like a hollow-eyed doll, and, as he slowly recognized with chilling certainty Ricky's lifeless form (he was "only a chile," Lily had lovingly said), his heart leapt in his chest with thunderous violence, knocking him senseless. Tears

319

fogged his eyes. He collapsed in boneless despair over the body of the boy he had come to love as his own. He clasped the boy tenderly in his arms. He felt a scream welling up inside him as if a fuse had blown in his brain and the light went out of his eyes. Suddenly he was back in the far away war-torn jungles of South east Asia, screaming in mad despair, losing hold of his otherwise fragile sanity.

***

Lily waited anxiously for a cab, facing Percival in the small living room, suitcase packed and ready to fly. The shades were drawn and the room in shadow with all the appearances of an apartment to let. His hands were deep in his trouser pockets and he seemed to devour her with his eyes as her's, in turn, were afraid. They spoke softly. It was four days since Rufus had been recommitted to a psychiatric unit in a Veterans Hospital on Long Island. It was the day after the elections, as was it the day following Ricky's funeral and, filled with trepidation, Lily's eyes were run red from crying.

"So Nixon's 'r next President," said Percival in disgust.

"It seems so." She paused, exasperated, "Too bad."

"Like they say, you get the leaders you deserve."

"Who's to say what another deserves."

"Surely, not the electorate."

"This country fills me with dread," Lily announced with a shudder, folding her arms about herself for warmth. "I-I feel like everything's coming apart," she said. "Like my G'd has forsaken me."

"Do you believe in God?"

"With all my heart," she said firmly, staring at him with an air of sad reproach. "I believe in G'd, his judgment 'n divine retribution."

"No reward?"

"Not in this world, evidently." She rolled her sparkling, wet eyes. "For whatever reason, justification if you will, the best part of me, the part I love most, Rufus, is catatonic 'n confined, more dead than alive, in an Army mental ward," she said tremulously. "He's such a good man, really. If he's gone sour, it's their fault. You didn't know him before he got out the Army, before Vietnam, did you?"

"Unfortunately not."

"He was so different – you got'a believe. He used to be a whole person before that unholy war sent him back home in dissimilar, unrecognizable parts, fragments of his ole self," she recalled. "He came back sick. more sick at heart, which sickened him in the head more surely than not, you know?"

"But you married him anyway."

"Yes, I married him anyway," she said, fidgeting. "What was I to do, abandon him? Desert him?" she asked, pacing. "Where's that cab," she demanded impatiently and drew back a window curtain to look out on the empty street.

"It'll get here."

She again began to pace. "You didn't go to Nam, did you?"

"No."

"Then you can't understand," she said in a strangled tone of voice.

"I understand enough."

"Yes – yes, you do. but it was like I was there with him night after night. I spent sleepless nights holding Rufus against my bosom as he wept in my arms, 'n the terrible dreams, which became my dreams, from which I'd waken him screaming. I-I can't begin to tell you the long, tearful nights I spent nursing him. Yes, nursing my husband like a sick child," she whimpered, "when I needed a man 'n not a truncated one, either. Oh g'd," she wailed, squeezing her eyes shut. "And then when Ricky came into 'r lives he miraculously improved 'n became the glimmer of the man I fell in love with in high school."

Percival's thoughts were cast precipitously back on the graveyard scene of the previous day, the day of Ricky's burial and his mother being escorted stumbling from the open grave while her toddlers tugged at the hem of her skirt, weeping piteously.

"Oh g'd," Lily sobbed, wiping a tear aside. "I-I can't do this!" She moaned, "I'd always thought that had I given him a son, a baby," she said wounded, holding her stomach, "but those wretched doctors – those butchers – those racist white bastards stole that chance from me, from us. Oh dear g'd, those black-hearted white bastards," she caterwauled, striking her barren womb with angry, balled fist. "Why?"

Percival stretched out his hands to embrace her, but she threw up her arms reflexively, to ward off any untoward advances.

"I didn't mean," he faltered, catching a glimmer of her face in profile amidst the shadows.

"Of course," she apologized, averting her gaze. "What must I be thinking?" She spun her lithe body round till her back was to him and her arms crossed under her teacup breasts. "At any rate," she said, flustered, "you'll be taking over command of the chapter – that's good. Rufus would approve."

"I wish it were otherwise."

"Well Rufus appreciated you 'n thought of you as his best friend. You can't help him now so why stick?"

321

"We started something for which I'm much responsible," he stated. "N besides, I owe it to Rufus, to Ricky 'n you, as well as 'r membership."

Lily faced him with unblinking, teary eyes. "You don't owe anybody anything except yourself! This cancels all debts," she said throatily, laying a hand on his chest, which she just as suddenly withdrew. "But you'll stick, stubborn pride I guess. Anyway, I think Rufus would'a want you to have this place," she went on, looking aimlessly about. "And since I won't be here 'n surely you'll need it. Well, it's something I can do. It's rent free. Rufus' military stipend will cover it for us till he gets out, but I don't know when that'll be –"

"What about you, Lily?"

"I'll stay with my mother in Brooklyn for as long as we can stand each other, then who knows," she said, casually, smiling wryly.

"In that case," he proposed, "this place is easily big enough for two. Why not stay, I can certainly use your help."

"It'll create gossip."

"To hell with the gossip."

"Believe me, Rufus wouldn't understand 'n in his place, neither could I."

"I'm simply trying to help."

"If only you could. My concern isn't for the party; isn't for the movement; it's for the well-being of my husband, Rufus," she said, frankly. "As for me, I must appear no less chaste than Caesar's wife."

"I see," said Percival, meekly, relieved to hear the honk of a car horn from outside. "It must be your cab."

"So it is," she confirmed, peering out the window.

He hoisted her two heaviest suitcases and carried them out to the waiting cab. After the trunk was packed, he held the back door open for her. Before she entered the cab, she considered him with weepy eyes, fixing his face in her memory, then embraced him in farewell.

"Oh Percival, do be careful. Don't let them hurt you, harm you, break you, kill you," Lily implored. "They'll do their damnedest to destroy you, you can be sure."

"I'll do my best," he promised, as she settled into the back seat of the taxi.

"N they'll do their worst," she swore.

"Let's keep in touch."

"We'll see." She smiled wistfully and hung her head. "Goodbye," she piped, closing the cab door. The cabbie put the car in gear and drove off. Percival felt that he would not see Rufus nor Lily again. The feeling became more acute after he had reentered the house and was by himself in the vacant living room.

***

Shortly after there came a sharp knock at the door. Percival opened it to allow passage to Raschelay, Silva, Priestus, Skeeter and Big/black. They mumbled "Power," as they entered the living room and waited until Percival sat and invited them to do likewise. He gazed into their eyes to plumb the depths of the dour expressions that clouded their otherwise conflicted faces. They were morose and clearly angry over the mindless slaying of little Ricky Bolden and the unexpected mental collapse of Rufus which they, with the exception of Percival, had not foreseen. Percival leaned forward ruefully, his hands clasped, and his thoughts tumbled one upon the other. The air was charged with a leaden solemnity. It was up to him to take charge, allay their doubts, win their loyalty, command their obedience and earn their trust. Their respect was a foregone conclusion.

"It looks like we've suffered 'r first major setback n, as you've no doubt heard, I've been asked to take charge for the present. If it's agreeable with you, that is."

"Why wouldn't it be," said Raschelay, "you're the best person for the job."

Silva teasingly said, "I'd always thought you were in charge."

"Only question I got," Priestus interposed, "is why ain't everybody else here?"

"The Party's not a democracy. It's a socialist vehicle, a paramilitary organization, a chain of command, as well you ought'a know, n I think you're the nucleus of this chapter 'n where you go the others will follow."

"What about Sam?"

"What about him?" Percival asked, irked.

"He's cultural liaison, shouldn't he be here?"

"If he's not," Percival fenced, eyeing Priestus, disdainfully, "consider that there might be a reason."

"As you like."

"Thank you. Okay, now that that's off your chest," said Percival heatedly. "First thing on the agenda is how in light of Ricky's death do we respond to his senselessly cruel murder by the pigs."

"Well, the two pigs are on suspension pending a determination of the case," Silva said. "Meanwhile, the community is up in arms and demanding a response."

"As rightly they should," said Skeeter flatly.

"Yeah, there's a mood of expectancy among the students in the Freedom School," Priestus added. "They're angry 'n confused n wanting to know why we ain't burn the whole place down yet."

"I hope you've explained to em it's cause it's their home, their community, 'n as diseased as it might be we're not trying to destroy it, but to transform it," Percival responded, his eyes sharpening.

"Gotcha," Priestus mumbled, adjusting his glasses.

"Still, they're justified in asking," Skeeter said. "I for one am damn well furious."

"N they expect us to act," said Big/black tersely.

"They tore out a piece of my soul when they killed Ricky like that," Raschelay said in a thorny voice filled with emotion. "But at the same time, they've also galvanized my revolutionary resolve."

Percival smiled, grateful for Raschelay.

"You couldn't have said it better," Silva agreed.

"Right on, sister," chanted the others.

"I'm glad you all feel that way cause I've a plan. Skeeter," Percival asked, facing him. "Tell us something 'bout those neighbors of yours you say the cops always being called on to stop from killing one another."

"What about em?"

"How often you say it occurs?"

"Once a month, anyway."

"N the pigs always respond?"

"Like clockwork."

"The point I'm making is that they show."

"They show all right. That guy really pounds the hell out'a her. He's hospitalized her more than once, 'n though the pigs treat it like it's funny, it's no joke. One day that cat's gonna land her ass in the morgue. Thing is, she won't press charges."

"N the row of flats 'r all laid out the same?"

"Jus' like cookie cutouts."

"That's what I needed to know," said Percival, frankly. "Here's my idea " He took the next few minutes to explain his plan and outline the part each would play in its execution and, as he spoke, a nascent spark flickered into flame in their faces lightening their eyes. More than any other, Big/black was the most fearless, though languorous. Accused of being a hick, he was far from a bore and whatever he lacked in finesse was more than made up for in courage. Priestus was his closest friend and that, for Percival, was recommendation enough. Then there was Skeeter who, having lived in the area all his life, was streetwise, resourceful, and only to be trusted up to a point. In this instance, his marked hatred of the local police stood him in good stead. Percival was not as yet so sure of Silva, but it was a risk, among others, that he would have to take. He reasoned that Silva, being from an upper middle-class background going back generations who was willing to buck his parents and forego graduate school to organize with the Panthers might then prove more than useful in their stance against the police. Finally, there was Raschelay, although the youngest and only female among them, Percival had absolutely no reservations about her. In fact, he felt certain that she was as well-equipped as anyone, including himself, to run the chapter. Whereas he was admired, respected and even feared, she was loved, respected and revered. Apart from his maturity, civil rights experience and innate cunning, he had little else over her save of course, the fact that he was a man. But she, in the near future, would prove, like Nina, to be devoted, idealistic and irrepressible. In a word, august. It was because of these attributes that he had wanted her in on the scheme. He knew that each one of them would die in her defense and to assure the success of the operation she would prove invaluable. Whereas they might betray him they would not betray Raschelay.

They were all stunned to silence by the time he got through.

Silva said with trepidation, "That'll give em something to consider."

"That it will," said Skeeter, edgily.

Priestus gulped, dumbfounded.

"It'll stir up a hornets nest," Big/black said, unperturbed.

Raschlay's heart stalled in her chest, and she stared at Percival with fearful, unflinching, chestnut brown eyes, torn. His face was unyielding, set with granite-like determination. He was not to be denied, far less crossed. She had wanted to get up and run out but she was petrified, unable to move, caught in a nightmare situation from which she could not easily escape. Her mother would be horrified at what he proposed to involve her lovely, elder 15-year-old daughter in. A chill ran down her spine. She girded herself summoning all the courage at her disposal to shake the dread that had taken hold of her. "May God preserve us," she prayed, exhaled exhaustively. She nodded her head in ascent then nipped her bloodless lower lip. "All right," she said, "I'm in!"

"I'll have the only loaded weapon. The others 'r jus' for convincing," Percival said.

"It'll work. If the trigger's got'a be pulled, then it'll fall on me. I don't want'a see anyone needlessly killed, least of all any of us. Lily was right, 'Murder is wrong. It's stealing' something you can't use.' They'll serve us better alive anyway. It'll humiliate em, send'a chill through the cops unlike anything else."

They mutely nodded their heads.

"I want no spare parts left lying about," Percival stressed. "I want'a strike terror in em 'n send a message to the community that we're in control even to the point of dispensing mercy, got it? Though that's not the way the cops'll see it. I want there to be no doubt about it, we're revolutionaries, not assassins, hear me?"

"Well, you know," Skeeter said, falteringly, "if it was Rufus he'd ice em."

"Lucky I'm not Rufus then, aren't we?" Percival said.

"If you say so," Skeeter complained.

Percival simply cast a deprecatory glance Skeeter's way.

"Won't the cops figure it's us?" Priestus asked.

"That's the beauty of it," Silva interjected. "Knowing it and proving it are two different things. Specifically, who of us?" He smiled gloatingly.

"I want you all to swear it'll go down as I say."

A brooding silence took hold of them and no one hastened to respond.

Percival eyed them keenly, sternly.

"What if—" Skeeter started to object.

"There's no margin for error, so there can't be no 'what if's'," Percival said resolutely.

"But what if there is?" Priestus insisted unhappily, a scared frown on his face.

"We'll deal with it then. Now swear," Percival demanded.

They tepidly complied. "I swear," they grumbled in unison.

"I mean it!"

"I swear," they growled together.

"This also swears you to complete secrecy. I want no wagging tongues. Now, I want you all to swear individually. Raschelay, you start," Percival said, knowing that once she had sworn, the others could do no less.

"I swear," said Raschelay resolutely, starting off. Then Silva swore, followed by Big/black, Priestus and finally Skeeter. They then all joined hands in fealty, one upon the other, with Percival's hand on top. And jointly pledged, "Panther power to the revolution!"

The fact that Percival was able to elicit an oath of such proportion from them was no small feat, and, as he well knew, to be able to command it was to be assured of their future loyalty. That is to say once sworn twice bound.

Percival thought it best to strike while the iron was hot and passions at fever pitch. Therefore, that Friday night round eleven pm, when the police would be busiest and backup not so readily available, Raschelay dialed the 20th police precinct from the apartment Skeeter shared with his dad, a roustabout out for the evening with his drinking buddy from the floor above.

The phone at the other end didn't ring long: "20th precinct, Sergeant Mann speaking, how may I help you?"

Breathlessly hysterical, Raschelay shrieked into the mouthpiece, "Send someone fast," as Skeeter carried on noisily in the outside hall, "I'll kill you this time bitch," he shouted.

"They're at it again, killing each other. You've got'a hurry, come quick or there'll be a murder tonight!"

"Calm yourself ma'am and tell me where you are?" said the disinterested voice.

"It's 337 Carson Avenue, upstairs."

"OK, we know the location –"

"Oh hurry – dear god, hell's breaking loose up there," she said in a theatrical, near panicky voice.

"And you are?" he asked but Raschelay had already hung up. She then proceeded from the apartment building, leaving Skeeter in the vestibule watching the deserted, ill-lit road, and started for the building two doors over. She bypassed Big/black, crouched out of sight under cover of the darkened porch steps. She entered the building and proceeded down the first-floor hall turning through the basement door off the hallway where Priestus stood watch a stocking mask drawn over his face. She descended the steps without a word between them, located the fuse box and identified the hall fuse. She could see Preistus on the upper most step behind the door, peering down the hall, double barrel shotgun in his gloved fist with a heavy-duty flashlight duct taped to its barrel. She wore surgical gloves. She was fearful, the surface of her skin crawled with it. Sweat poured down her lovely face and beneath her arms. She wondered, what would Lily have done under similar circumstance?

Meanwhile, Percival and Silva waited in anticipation for the police, faces masked and posted on the second floor down the hall from the apartment door. They held shotguns also with heavy duty flashlights duct taped to the barrels. The barrels jut out just beyond the flashlights so they would blind those on whom the lights were aimed, and they were thereby made unable to see those holding the weapons. They hoped no one would step out into the hall and find them pressed against the wall in the shadows, shotguns at the ready. Silva was tense and though his breathing was irregular it, unlike his heart which throbbed painfully, was silent. He gave Percival a sidelong look, but he was impassive, revealing nothing, and his steady, hooded eyes, under the mask, were like those of a man swallowed in thought.

Though it was late, the occupants of both apartments upstairs and down were up and the noise from within was like that of revelers, which was exactly what they had hoped for. They wanted the police to be totally distracted and not the least bit suspicious.

The waiting was interminable. Silva's hands had begun to sweat inside the surgical gloves Percival had provided them lifted from Dr. Osgood's clinic, when the dying growl of a siren reached their ears and a car skidded to a stop outside and the simultaneous closing of its doors followed. The shuffle of feet on the outside steps carried upstairs, then the faces of two white cops appeared in the oval entranceway window as they stepped through the double row of doors and into the lighted hall. They started upstairs towards the bickering voices emerging from the second-floor apartment, without hesitation.

"We should jus' let these fool niggers kill themselves," said the elder of the two cops, crassly.

The younger cop gave no reply.

Meanwhile, Big/black had emerged from under cover of the porch and padded stealthily up the stairs behind them and slithered, wraith like, between the closing doors, raising his shotgun as he entered the hall.

The instant Big/black hoisted his shotgun, Priestus signaled Raschelay to unscrew the fuse, plunging them all in utter darkness. Before the cops could react, a voice barked overhead from the top of the stairs, "Freeze!" as flashlights went on, striking the cops fully in the face with blinding intensity, causing them to lose their footing. Panic-stricken, they were flooded in light, blinded by it. Instinctively, they went for their guns.

"Do it 'n ye dead men," Percival shouted, chambering a bullet in the barrel of his pump action shotgun. "Keep your head's 'n nobody'll die here t'night," he cautioned.

"We got you covered from every angle," Big/black shouted from behind, as Priestus aimed his shotgun up on them through the rail posts from below, and Silva leaned over the second-floor rail with his shotgun, snaring the two cops in a stream of light from the attached lamps.

They twisted their heads slightly, squinting into the glare, trying to see the faces in the dark behind the light from the landing above. They were caught, more terrified than escapees frozen in the flood lights of a prison yard, their cringing eyes screwed down. "W-who the devil?" uttered the elder of the two cops, aware of the fact that they had been ambushed and that it was too late to go for their guns.

"No, not the devil," Percival snarled. "Not the devil at all." Doubtlessly, they had stumbled into a well sprung trap and so found themselves at the mercy of their unknown captors? For a brief moment a fog of doubt lifted in their minds and a tidal wave of uncertainty followed.

"Can't you get those lights out of our eyes?"

Percival shouted in response, "Lace your hands behind your heads!" The cops could only see the vaguest details beyond the glare of lights reflected off their stark white faces, and they did as told. "Get on your knees," insisted the faceless voice at the top of the stairs behind the stream of light emitted by his torch. They dropped to their knees without protest, the blinding light trailing after.

"You gonna kill us?" the younger cop yelped fearing an execution, a sheen of sweat covering his pale face.

"Don't beg em," said the elder cop.

"I won't," he said. "I just want'a chance to pray."

"Ah gee," uttered the elder cop in dismay.

"Jus' do as you're told," said Percival, brutally, a base ugliness in his tone. "Now splay yourselves on the stairs. Do it!" he ordered.

The fit on the narrow staircase between the two cops was tight, but manageable. They gripped the steps over their heads with their fingers and supported themselves from below on the balls of their feet. Then Big/Black, the beam of his light fixed on the backs of the cops heads, mounted the stairs and stripped them of all vestiges of authority. He removed their badges, guns, handcuffs, keys, nightsticks and belts, then pulled their pants down and left them to dangle round their ankles leaving them laughing stocks at which the community would point with derision. He took a set of handcuffs and first running the links through the rail post, shackled the two together.

"Keep your heads down," advised the overhead voice.

Just then someone opened the apartment door.

"What the fuck's going on in this hall," he cursed with an inside light at his back, threatening to expose them.

Silva swung round sharply, the flashlight gleaming in the startled man's oval brown face. "Get back inside," he shouted, "and mind your fucking business!" The man faded, and the door slammed behind him. Again Silva pointed the barrel of his shotgun on the two cops.

Outside, Skeeter had cut the police car radio wire, punctured the tires and poured sugar down the gas tank. He then made his way down alleys and across back yards to the getaway car located on a desolate back road.

Stepping gingerly over the cops, Percival and Silva made their way down the stairs. They doused their lights and proceeded along the darkened hall joining the others in the basement from where they effected their escape.

They met up with Skeeter on the gloomy back road in the middle of the block. He started up the engine immediately as they piled into the car. Big/Black carried the items expropriated from the cops while the shotguns were put in a duffle bag and placed in Silva's trust.

"You're the least known of us," Percival said to Silva. "You live in Grimes Hill. The pigs'll not look there. From your place we'll move the guns elsewhere," he said morosely, almost downcast, as if having lost a fight with himself. While he was certainly no pacifist, he loathed guns as having nothing to do with the man and all too much to do with the weapon.

"No problem," Silva said, breathing an audible sigh of relief now that it was over. "I'll just put them in the gun case in the basement. How can they trace them? No bullets were expelled, so there's no identifying them. Besides, my father and I have a splendid gun collection, so they'll virtually go unnoticed."

"Before dropping me off," Percival told Skeeter, "let's stop by a mail box so Big/Black can post that sack."

Pulling up to the first mailbox they came upon, Big/black posted the bag containing the articles taken from the cops and then, as he peeled the surgical gloves off his hands, Skeeter pointed the Impala down Jersey Street, illuminated like a honky-tonk. The noise of the street was shrill and the language obscene. There was a spillover from the bars of drunken men pursuing equally drunken, slatternly women, and, moreover, offering them the moon. At which the women howled with laughter, having been offered it before – long before. Some remembered having possessed it, too. Nevertheless, they would, in any case, be delighted for a chance to embrace it once again.

"If the pigs move against us they'll probably start with you," Silva said, as Percival climbed out of the car in front of his new address.

"If they come, they'll start with Skeeter cause he's the one closest to the scene of the incident," Percival replied.

"Don't worry 'bout me, I've danced with the man more than once before."

"Then they might jus' play coy," Priestus said.

"Yes, they still might be too nervous 'bout the death of Ricky 'n the aftershock it caused in the community to home in on us jus' yet," Percival agreed. "I think they'll be walking on tenterhooks for awhile. They got no support, especially with all the unfavorable press they've received since the shooting."

"I hope you're right," Silva said.

"It's a fair assumption."

"Could be."

"Good night," Raschelay chirruped in her soft voice. "I should be getting home myself."

"Skeeter will see to it. You did good t'night," Percival said in praise, squeezing her cold tremulous hand reassuringly. "You were all as good as your word t'night, so from now on we jus' got'a keep 'r mouths shut!"

"Nobody gonna talk," said Big/black, menacingly.

"Ain't nothing to talk 'bout," Priestus gruffly confirmed.

Raschelay bleated, "And have my mother know?" She shuddered at the thought. "No way!"

"My folks didn't raise no fool," Silva stated, offended by the suggestion that he might break his vow and talk.

"I ain't sure what my parents raised me for," Skeeter mouthed, "but spending the rest'a my life in jail ain't it."

"Well jus' carry on as usual, nothing's happened. It's same ole same ole, dig? Well, good night," Percival said, gravely concerned.

"I'll join you after I've dropped everyone else off," Skeeter said.

"Okay." Then Percival waved them off.

Early next morning Percival put the second phase of his plan in motion, starting with a call to Nina Koestler,

"Nina," he explained, "I need a favor."

"Anything, just name it."

"Your friend Beverly, would she still be interested in doing a series of articles on the Panthers?" he asked, aware that if a number of favorable articles were to hit the local newsstands in the very near future that it would make it that more difficult for the police to wage an effective counter campaign against them. Therefore, while he recognized what a fickle ally the media made, it was no less his intentions to cultivate a relationship with the press.

"More so now you're in charge," Nina assured him.

"Will you contact her 'n have her reach me at the Panther Officer later on t'day? I have a Defense Captains meeting to attend this morning 'n I'll be back in the Office this afternoon."

"I'll see to it."

"Thanks beautiful. I appreciate it."

"Anytime," she said in farewell.

As the Impala drew up to the curb on their returning from the Defense Captains meeting, much to Percival's and Skeeter's surprise, an excited gaggle of people were gathered on the sidewalk outside the Panther Office—and not just the usual spill over from The 2nd. Step, bar next door. "I wonder what gives," Percival said as he got out the car on the passenger side, well knowing it was to be expected. "I know what gives," Skeeter said, gruffly, pretentiously, full of himself. The crowd made room for their passage, their eyes smiling. Many slapped their backs as they passed, all cheered. "Y'll all right," they spouted. Percival considered them as if perplexed and shrugged indifferently while glowing inwardly. They entered the office and were greeted by a similar round of applause from the membership, all rising to their feet.

Percival scanned their faces, his brows furrowed. "What gives?" he asked, filled with dread that the cat was out of the bag. His eyes sought out Big/Black, Priestus and Silva. They shrugged and shook their heads imperceptibly. His eyes then took in Rascelay, lovely as an orchid, and glimpsed, in passing, Tzi's strikingly handsome, moon lit, porcelain face among the darker, earthen hued faces of the cadre on either side of them. He took a lingering gaze at the gorgeous pair and smiled with approval dismissing any possibility of complicity from that direction. They were one of the most handsome couples he'd ever seen. "OK," he said, breaking off his stare, "what's what?"

"Like you don't know?" said Leroy incredulously. "You really don't know?"

"Know? Know what, little brother?"

"Last night. 'bout them two cops ambushed 'n stripped butt naked that's what," Leroy blurted, his voice colored by disappointment, "They guns 'n everything stole 'n they was left shackled to the stairway banister with their pants pulled down to they ankles – jus' a few doors over from Skeeter's place, don't you know 'bout it Skeeter?"

"It's news to me. I stayed at Percival's las night."

"Ya mean to say you didn't do it?" Leroy yelped? "Then who the fuck did."

"Is what Leroy say true?" Percival asked.

"As far as I can tell," Silva replied. "All I know for sure is that the cops are scared and are riding heavy, shotguns at the ready, giving a show of armed force. I didn't have time to do much of anything. The cops picked up Sam and Justin for questioning. I had my hands full trying to get them out of the clutches of the cops. It's been a hectic morning. And the people have been out there on the street long before the bar opened. They've been crediting us with it. I keep telling them we don't know nothing about it, but they hold firm to the conviction that we must. They think it's fucking funny and that we're heroes."

"It is funny," Sam interposed.

"You mean to say you didn't get an investigation going?" Percival asked.

"Investigate what?" Silver inquired.

"This, that's what," Percival snarled.

"I didn't see the need."

"Don't see the need? Get on this right away. If the cops think we did it, they'll try anything to hang it on us. I want to know who did this, so we're not put on the spot," Percival said, for the benefit of any informant or listening device concealed in the office.

"I'll get on it right away," Silva conceded.

"Do," said Percival. "And take as many Panther members as you need. I want'a get to the bottom of this before the cops pin it on us. It's one thing for the community to believe we did it, but it's entirely another thing for the cops to prove we did it."

Afterwards Sam sidled up to Percival and, laying a hand on his shoulder, said.

"You're not gonna try tell me you don't know nothing 'bout this, 'r you?"

"If I am?'

"I know you a lot better than these other cats."

"N jus' what do you think you know?"

"Ya can't deny it, it's your style, bro," Sam said, feeling Percival's shoulder stiffen under his accusation. "Had those pigs been fried I'd of had my doubts, but you the only cat I know with guts enough to pull off such a crazy stunt as that – let the evidence walk. All I ask is to not be left out next time."

Staving off his anger, Percival observed Sam warily, every muscle in his body taut, impressed at how well Sam seemed to know him. However, he had been unaware of Sam watching him from the sideline over the years with a mixture of pride and envy as he grew in stature first as a fighter and then as a man with a chivalrous code of conduct.

"G'd knows I hope the cops give me less credit for this than you cause if not I'm in deep trouble when, in fact, I know nothing 'bout last night," he said with concern. It troubled him. What else did Sam know that he was not saying?

"If you should need an alibi, you know where to look," said Sam cagily.

"I'll keep that in mind."

"You do that, big brother."

Just then the telephone rang distantly in the background.

"It's for you, Percival," Raschelay shouted, calling him to the phone.

Percival regained his composure and walked over and took the call. "'ello," he yelled into the mouthpiece, palming his ear with a free hand to block the crosscurrent of voices in the room.

"Hello Percival? This is Beverly, I got your message. When can we meet?"

"When would be best for you?"

"Anytime you say."

"How 'bout t'night at Rufus' ole place on Carlyle Street, only house on the block. We'll be sharing a communal meal, so we'll all be there along with a few allies 'n friends. Come join us for supper."

"I'd be delighted."

"I'll look for you round six."

"Till then," she affirmed.

After Percival hung up, he turned to Tzi and shook his hand warmly. "I see you've stolen 'r favorite gal?"

"If only. No, she's devoted, 'n between you two I'm being radicalized."

"Glad to have you," said Percival. "We can use friends of your caliber."

"Glad to be a part."

"Raschelay," Percival said, winking at her, "bring Tzi ta supper this evening."

"Can you make it?" Raschelay asked, facing Tzi.

"I think so, yes."

"Good," said Percival with a rapturous smile, taking them in. They delighted him, these two, fired his spirit and gave him to believe in the possibility of redemption, of a new Adam and Eve, a new world if only there were more people like them who would be fruitful and multiply. He was admiring, speechless, wholly inadequate in the face of such young love. He slapped Tzi on the shoulder and left.

After supper that evening when everybody else began to depart, Percival was finally able to relax, sit back and join Beverly. "You've surrounded yourself with a rather impressive group of people," she observed. "You have doctors, scholars, students, professionals, blue collar workers, and a smattering of street people – some of whom I'd cross the street to avoid. Overall I'm favorably impressed, more so because this area is better known for its criminal element. Yet you've somehow managed to gather together a body of rather highly principled people from all I can tell."

"I think so too," he agreed.

"Tell me then," she challenged, her sharp, lucent eyes fixed on his, "and I hope you choose to be truthful with me."

Percival smiled evocatively. "Ya know Caesar Augustus had prudently said, 'I like the truth but I like it with discretion.'"

"Does that mean you won't answer me about last night's incident with the police?"

"You must mean the ambush of those two unfortunate cops? Frankly I'm as much in the dark on that score as are the police. The people seem to be running ahead of us 'n bringing about justice on their own."

"Am I suppose to believe that?"

"You don't necessarily have to believe it to print it, do you?"

"It helps if I do."

"Then no. We didn't do it."

She looked him in the face searchingly, but he chose to exhibit a perfectly inscrutable poker face. "Nina tells me I can trust you."

"At least Nina can."

334

"You play it close to the chest."

"You're a reporter not a confessor."

"We know where we stand then, don't we?"

"We've known all along, now haven't we?"

She laughed, warming to him.

They talked for hours while Beverly took notes. She conducted an exhaustive interview. She found Percival, as Nina had described, forthright, intelligent, disarming and, above all, shrewd. She liked him. It wasn't before the mingling light of day pierced the rooms through the blinds that Beverly noticed the lateness of the hour. "Would you look at the time," she yawned, rising. "I best be going." She had become so engrossed in the conversation that she had lost all sense of time, but, to her satisfaction and despite the hour, her assignment was off to a colorful start. From here she would take to the streets with the Panther membership, eat breakfast with the students before school, monitor the Freedom School classes, and make house calls with various physicians as they visited the ranks of the impoverished sick. In a tour of the community with Dr. Osgood among the sick, Beverly's gaze was directed toward the startling number of malnourished children as well as the mentally infirm. "Which is," Dr. Osgood remarked, "as much a symptom of poverty as not, and no less preventable." At one point, Beverly had to flee a bleak, rundown, rancid and vermin infested apartment for fear of losing her stomach.

She apologized to Dr. Osgood afterwards, then asked with revulsion in her voice,

"How do you do this?"

"I'm a doctor! How do I not?"

***

Percival was engaged in a conversation with Beverly over the thrum of a hand operated mimeograph machine cranking out a community newsletter. Big/Black leaned comfortably back in a chair behind the Duty Officer's desk with his feet up. Dr. Osgood sat at another desk filling out prescriptions for patients who could not afford them without assistance which, from their limited store of funds, the Panthers provided. Dr. Osgood was worn down after a hard day on the go and, at that hour ten-thirty pm, ready to fold. Suddenly a burst of gun fire rend the air, and the whine of bullets ripped through the front plate glass window, as a sedan sped off in a roar.

Dr. Osgood sought cover under the desk on which Beverly was writing. Percival hit the floor as if a trap door had sprung open beneath his feet and yanked Beverly down with him. In the same instant, Big/black struck the ground, a .45 in his fist and writhing on his belly like a snake, he crawled to the front door. Scarcely had he opened the door than Percival was beside him, signaling to the two women to keep low. They looked up and down the gloomily lit street back to back in a crouch, but the road was as desolate as it was silent and all that remained of the vandals was a faint trace of cordite. They returned inside, examined the holes in the window and found bullets lodged in the back wall. Somewhat ruffled but unscathed, Dr. Osgood climbed out from under the desk.

Though shaken, Beverly, too, regained her feet.

"I thought I'd safely escaped the night riders back when I was burnt out of my clinic and home down south years back," Dr. Osgood moaned. "But one can't escape the south entirely, not in this country anyway."

Big/black swung his eyes to Dr. Osgood, with a look of stark terror on his face. "I hope like hell you're wrong, Doc," he uttered.

"If tonight's any indication, Big/black, you're out of luck," Dr. Osgood said grimly.

She slipped a coat on over her frock as a few locals, dressed against the chill entered the office looking circumspectly about.

"Y'll okay?" an unkempt, scruffily little man with alcohol laced breath slurred. "They was plain clothes cops. We seen em as they pass." The others shook their heads in accord, "dat so, bro," they echoed. The man continued, "saw em out the barroom window, plain as day." He winked and the others readily concurred, "sure enough so, boss." He further said, "saw em as they race by shooting wild. They meant to hurt somebody. One'a y'll sure enough."

"Can't say that idea didn't cross my mind," Percival said, staring out in dark dejection. "I guess it's time we sandbag this place good 'n properly like a bunker. We got'a realize that from now on we're gonna be subject to random attacks from the police." He winced involuntarily. "It's fortunate no one was hurt jus' now 'n it's not cause they were shooting high, but driving fast 'n shooting blind."

"I've not been so shaken before in all my life," Beverly confessed, her face drained of color. "I'm not accustomed to being shot at."

"Stick round," Big/black scoffed, sticking his .45 back in his belt.

"I hope I'm up to it," Beverly exclaimed, with a look of bewilderment on her bloodless face.

"So do I," said Percival irritably, realizing she was, after all, only a local, small town reporter and, come what may, he had no choice but to count on her. "So do I."

"I'm exhausted," Dr. Osgood yawned. "It's time for me to go home and get some rest."

"I'll see you to your car," Percival offered, grabbing his jacket off the back of a chair.

"Wait for me," Beverly called, pulling her coat tightly about her.

"There's not much more we can do t'nigh," Percival said to Big/black from the doorway. If you don't mind locking up, we'll call it quits."

"I'm with you," Big/black remarked, and shooed the collection of curious locals out the door to the sidewalk.

Two armed Panthers stood sentinel outside the office as students arrived for classes early the following day. The incident of the previous night was the topic of discussion on the streets. As the students arrived, they took close notice of the bullet holes in the storefront window and marveled at the two guards standing watch on either side of the doorway as they entered the makeshift classroom.

The first class of the day—creative art history— was given by Nina Koestler. She combined it into a hands-on study of the technique and style of a given period. In this instance, her focus was on African Art and Sculpture. She loved to teach and the students, in turn, responded favorably to her. It was her courage, her willingness to face them unafraid and hobble about on crutches that endeared her to them. It allowed their hearts to go out to her, to pity her even with her clumsiness, in a way that the world, despite its handicapping them because of their color, refused to see them. She was, moreover, an able teacher. She used humor where suitable, self-criticism and, on occasion, her handicap, allowing the students to intercede on her behalf where her disability proved a drawback. She held up a mirror by which they might see themselves, and thereby nurtured in them a wholesome regard for the physically disabled, and, by extension, an innate appreciation of themselves.

Percival was at the duty officer's desk up front. He enjoyed many of the classes offered by the Freedom School. And though his thoughts kept racing back to the incident of the previous night, in many ways these were good days, exciting days, high anxiety days. The phone at his elbow rang, distracting him. He answered it, "Panther Party office. All power to the people!"

"Is Percival Jones there?" a brusque, insinuating voice demanded.

"Speaking."

"This is a friend. You don't know me yet. I'm calling to inform you of a secret meeting called by the police to take place at the Mayor's Task Force Office with the local black leaders in the next few minutes. The object of the meeting is to enlist their support in eliminating the Black Panther Party. That is, you. If I were you I'd get there fast."

"Who is this?"

337

"Someone who knows what they're saying," said the voice. Then the phone went dead. More out of curiosity than not, Percival dialed the Mayor's Task Force Office. The phone rang shrilly.

"Task Force Office. Gwen Halsey speaking. How may I help you?"

"It's me Percival."

A moment's silence followed in which he half suspected that she would hang up. Sucking her breath in noisily as if compromised she exhaled in a whisper. "You're the last person I expected to hear from right now." He detected a note of apprehension in her tone. "Do you have any idea what's going on?"

"I do now."

"I only found out just now myself. You weren't to know. No one was. Are you coming?"

"Keep it to yourself," he said, icily and without waiting for a response he crashed the receiver back in its cradle and left the office in a whirlwind.

"I'll be gone awhile," he informed the guards with a backward swing of the head, sauntering off. "In the meantime stay alert."

"Shall do," they retorted.

"Skeeter 'n Sam will relieve you shortly," Percival added, and checking the time darted across the heavily trafficked street for the Heritage House where Silva was engaged as an assistant teacher. He beckoned to Silva from the doorway with a crooked finger. Silva joined him on the sidewalk outside. He bade Silva come with him. They took Silva's Mustang and as he explained matters Silva's foot bore down with increasing pressure on the gas. He sped manically through the streets weaving in and out of traffic, ignoring stop signs and running red lights.

"You drive more recklessly than Skeeter," Percival commented.

"I'll accept that as a compliment," Silva said, pulling over to the curb outside the Task Force Office in a squeal of wheels. They hopped out of the car and hastened into the building. On entering the reception area, Gwen sent them straight on into the community meeting room. Miriam Fisk's eyes widened delightfully as they burst through the door, although the Precinct Captain was anything but pleased at this unexpected turn.

The room was filled to capacity. The front row seats consisted of the borough's District Attorney, the Assistant Police Commissioner, the Precinct Captain, the Community Liaison Officer and, lastly, the Mayor's Representative, Miriam Fisk. The back rows were taken up by the community dwellers, all of whom were black.

After Miriam had greeted Percival and Silva, she asked that they join the others from the community. Among those present was the President of the

NAACP, Constance Taylor, Raschelay's mother, VP of the Welfare Mother's Association, Ruth Morrow, the representative of the Colored Businessmen's Club, a Dickensian character not unlike Fagan, Anthony Howe. Also present was the founder and Executive Director of the Heritage House, Julius Mims, Esquire. All the others Percival knew only by sight if not name. They were all respected members of the black community; pillars of society more conservative than liberal, and more inclined to cast lots with the prevailing status quo, than not.

Percival greeted each of them with a nod as he passed on his way to the back row where he and Silva found seats in a corner and positioned themselves at an angle where they might observe everyone without being observed.

"It looks as if everyone is here so we may begin," Miriam Fisk said, looking gleefully excited at Percival's arrival. She was fashionably attired in a red blazer, purple scarf and pleated black slacks. She clasped her bejeweled hands in front of her. "It's a privilege to have with us today the District Attorney, the Assistant Police Commissioner, and our own Precinct Captain, along with the Community Liaison Officer." She bowed slightly, tilting her head birdlike. "And you, distinguished members of the community, it's an honor," she proclaimed, with outspread hands. "This is to be as I understand it, an informal gathering to update us all on the status of your embroiled community. I will have more to say later. For now, I would like to turn the floor over to our Precinct Captain who requested your presence here today. Thank you all for showing up on such short notice. Captain," she announced, with a flourish of the hand, "the floor is yours."

Impressively arrayed in all the splendor of his rank and honors bestowed over the long years of an outstanding career, the Captain stood up in his dress blues, glittering with brass buttons and golden shield; tall, erect, and broad in the shoulders. He carried himself proudly, as if a Spartan on review. He clasped his cap in the crook of his left arm.

He regarded the assembly of black faces pensively, at a loss. "When last we met it was due to the brutal murder of one of your neighbors, Lee Horton, and while we should have gathered after the tragic but accidental slaying of Ricky Bolden, it did not occur because my office had been swamped sorting out the facts," he said, evasively, disturbed by Percival's presence. "And that's essentially why this meeting was called, to clarify some widely held misconceptions and find out what's on your minds," he stated, cautiously, reluctant to reveal himself further. "If any of you wish to say something, please do." He paused, his eyes flitting anxiously from face to face for a response. When none came, he was forced to say, "maybe you'll think of something as the meeting wears on."

"I have something to say," Percival declared. All heads turned in his direction. He then stood and started forwards, fist clenched and eyes steadfastly on the floor. He was deeply conflicted, chancing that what he had to say would not ring the death knell on the chapter; knowing that the people whom he had to win over were conservative and that they, the upholders of the status quo, had stacked the deck mightily against him. He recalled with bile Rufus' brilliant faux pas on asking the NAACP to endorse his candidacy – to no avail. True, he and Rufus were different people and things had somewhat changed since then. For one, little Ricky Bolden was dead, killed by a reckless, gun happy cop and Rufus, as a result, had lost his reason and was again back in an Army mental hospital. And tragic though that was, the agony of a similar community meeting back in the south following the lynching of a fellow civil rights worker flashed across his mind the way life flashes across the mind's eye of a drowning man. He reached the front of the room, raised his head, and scanned the faces of the populace as if coming out of a trance.

He smiled wanly at Miriam and she, in turn, smiled back. After he'd cast a searching glance over the others in the front row, he looked beyond the row of white faces to the rows of blacks seated behind; faces upturned, they looked on gravely, like a cluster of Baptists in the amen corner.

"Mr. District Attorney," Percival began. The DA leaned toward him, with a pontifical nod of his silver white head. "Captain." The Captain glowered at him. "Assistant Police Commissioner." The Assistant Police Commissioner rolled his eyes away. "And Sergeant Keel, Community Relations Officer, how 'r you?"

"We'll soon find out, won't we?" he said, enigmatically.

"N last, ladies n gentlemen, community leaders. But I swear you look more like lackeys to me, boot lickers rather than community leaders. Don't take offense," he chided, raising a forestalling hand. As they began to feel self-conscious, there came an uneasy scraping of chair legs. "But you've got'a consider it. Here in the front row 'r nothing but white faces. White leaders. The Man! 'N in the back rows, back'a the bus, all black faces, community leaders of a sort. It looks to me like you're not part of the decisionmaking body, at least not by the way it's presented here. I'll be more specific: When was the last time you saw such an array of city officials n it wasn't the St. Patrick's day parade? I mean, the DA himself, now this is an occasion 'n he's not campaigning, not running for office. What the hell's then so urgent about an informal community meeting to drag him away from locking up felons?" His chin grazing his chest, the DA barely raised an eyebrow. "N the Assistant Police Commissioner comes from Manhattan – it's beyond belief. 'N, of course, 'r Precinct Captain 'n the Community Relations Officer. When was the last time you saw so much brass in the same room at the same time? I mean, so much political clout. Not after the death of Lee Horton. 'N not after the death of little Ricky Bolden, a killing committed by one of their own.

"Not then, so why now? So how do you explain it?" Percival said. "We have with us the DA 'n, after that, everybody else falls in line like servitors, flunkies, lackeys. Here's how it works, the Assistant Police Commissioner kisses the DA's ass or else. N the Precinct Captain kisses both their asses – n what a good job he must do too. 'N god only knows all the asses Sergeant Keel must kiss." At that, an involuntary cackle erupted from the body of community leaders while the faces of the white officials whitened, save that of the DA who sat back in his chair as if waiting his turn to cross examine the witness. "Don't y'll laugh jus' yet," Percival said, sternly. "Not jus' yet. If they're all ass kisses 'n flunkies then who 'r you suppose to be but flunkies 'n ass kisses yourselves? Oh, you don't think so, do you? In that case, why the hell none of you know why the fuck you were all summoned here on such short notice in the first place? 'N still you think you not their flunkies? That is, their niggers? 'N if you don't watch out they'll waltz y'll right back on the plantation where they think you rightly belong!"

Percival swung his accusatory gaze over the group of black faces and, confronted with such burning accusations, they shrunk from his confrontational gaze.

"You were summoned here because you're their puppets 'n they got y'll dancing on a string to any tune they wish to play, help them pull off some foul shit! Yes, they called you here in secret to enlist your aid against us, against the Black Panther Party," he accused. He leaned acutely as if trying to grasp something. "Why do they want us off the streets so badly? Why? Cause they're scared. Oh, yes, they're afraid. 'N that fear grows out'a the fact that jus' retribution was visited upon em the other week when, as you all know, two cops got waylaid 'n stripped of all insignia of authority 'n shackled to a stair rail. 'N though no harm befell em, no injury inflicted on em other than that of humiliation," he said with a wayward grin. "It's my understanding that the perpetrators used flashlights to blind em with so they couldn't identify em." He chortled under breath. "Now if the cops want'a give the Panthers credit for it, fine. In that case, they're only strengthening 'r hand against em, 'n that's ok by me. If the cops want'a bestow undeserving credit on us, well 'n good, cause the deed was deserving of applause. I mean, doesn't it jus' make em look like the Keystone cops? I'll take it further 'n say, it makes em look like the precinct's run by the bungling Inspector Clouseau 'n his inept manservant, Cato. 'N it's fucking hard to tell whether the Captain's the bungling Clouseau or his hapless manservant, Cato."

The Precinct Captain, livid with rage, bristled. The Assistant Police Commissioner, sensing the captain's fury, laid a restraining hand on his arm.

""N if I knew who the perpetrators were I'd congratulate em myself," said Percival with an imperious ring to his voice. "So, lacking credible evidence, they want'a fix blame on us, but they got nothing. Whereas last night, the Panther Office was shot up by unknown vandals, but we can pretty much guess who they were, can't we Captain? Much as in the same way you guess we ambushed those two cops. Maybe both of us 'r right. Then maybe both of us 'r wrong," he teased. "I'll say this though, we got eyewitnesses who can identify the cops 'n the unmarked car from which they fired the shots." He paused for effect, and Constance Taylor's unruffled face floated out of the assembly at him. Garbed in African attire and arms laden with bracelets, and throat adorned with exotic necklaces, she looked as if she were a mambu, a ju ju woman, at whom he stared as if from a long way off, through a rent in the veil of time.

"Yes, they're scared," he went on, removing his gaze from hers. "They're afraid that they've lost control of the community, 'n they'll say, as a result, anarchy reigns. Let me set the record straight: since 'r arrival on the scene the rampant abuse of blacks by the cops has declined considerably, 'n they're the second biggest problem we face as a people in this country. The first being this wretched economic system of dog eat dog. In a word, Capitalism," he said reprovingly. "N, as y'll know, we've got a free breakfast program which feeds over a hundred 'n fifty kids a day. We've got a free medical program going 'n, while the teachers 'r on strike, we've got a school program going as well with an attendance rate that could be the envy of any school district in the nation. If that's anarchy, then we can use a bit more of it!

"You're here cause the cops got no more cards to play 'n you're the ace up their otherwise empty sleeve. They can't get rid of us without your help, it's that simple. Which means you must be willing to do their dirty work for em 'n find a way by which to discredit us, 'n so help em destroy us in the process. In short, sell us out. 'N that, in a nutshell, is why you're here."

Percival relinquished the floor and as he resumed his seat the Precinct Captain leapt to his feet, his face empurpled with rage, eyes bulging. He leveled a threatening finger at Percival which served as a warning to all others as well. "I've got a prison cell waiting for you, Percival Jones," he bellowed. "I'm hardly intimidated by a bunch of hooligans masquerading as revolutionaries, and don't think for a moment that I require the consent of the community to do my job – their help is incidental." He roared, "We'll flush you out with or without them. Who the hell are they –" The District Attorney coughed, caught the captain's eye, and signaled him to cut it. The Captain's voice sputtered and trailed off. The sentence was left dangling as he sat in a huff, like a bully who'd received his comeuppance.

A stunned silence blanketed the assembly. The community leaders began to whisper back and forth among themselves. They were outraged by the Captain's dismissing them as incidental. Percival's rebuking them was as an insider, like it or not, whereas the Captain's dismissive handling of them was, on the contrary, a slap in the face.

Percival smiled. The Captain had delivered the community leadership into his hands.

"Ladies and gentlemen, ladies and gentlemen," Sgt. Keel, the Community Liaison Officer called for quiet, gesturing with outspread hands. "Percival said some rather harsh, irresponsible and inflammatory things," he waded in with restraint, gaining their attention, "but painted a glowing picture of the Black Panthers. They will, in the long run, prove less effective than described. First off, you must remember that we, the police, are upholders of the decisions passed down to us by our elected legislators. The people you elect. We are, after all, a society governed by laws and if a law is wrong then we, as voters, adjust them through the democratic process, through elections, but we don't take it upon ourselves, because then we fall outside the protection of the law," he argued, trying to mollify them, lest he lose them altogether. "In any case, we as police are sworn to uphold the laws as they stand. That is our sworn duty. We are not the enemy as Percival paints, though there are abuses. For the most part, given the nature of the job we –" his voice faltered and all eyes swung toward the squeak of the opening door, as Damion Meeks, Director of The Urban League, slowly entered. He shook off his coat, every gesture apologetic like a parishioner late for Sunday service. He closed the door and stood off to the side trying to ascertain the gist of the subject under discussion from the little he'd overheard on his way in.

Inflamed to passion, and before Sergeant Keel could resume, Silva rose, saying, "Those laws you're sworn to uphold are laws against property – impersonal, brutal laws— and no one of color in our community with the exception of Anthony Howe, here," he said, with a dismissive wave of the hand, "own property. And he doesn't live in the community either. The law's you're talking about enforcing are opposed to the safety and wellbeing of the community inhabitants. It's easy for you to speak of responsibility, but responsibility for whom and to whom? Absentee landlords? The legislators of whom you speak are theirs; you're hired and paid for by them which makes you an occupying, mercenary army paid for in blood money. Our blood," he said, fiercely, his ruddy face brimming with color. "And you damn well know we have no representative in neither state or national legislature, either side of the aisle. Adam Clayton Powell, the one we had, has effectively been censured. On racial grounds I might add," Silva said with acrimony directed at Sergeant Keel. "Don't jive us, man!"

Damion Meeks cut in with his deep, suave, baritone voice, "I know I've only just barely arrived and my suggestion may even prove out of place, but wouldn't it make sense if the police and the Black Panthers were to put aside their differences and work together for the overall good of the community?"

"You're right," Ruth Morrow, hauntingly sad but elegantly clad in fall colors, spoke, holding her shoulders back. "You are off the mark – way off. Had you been here earlier you would have seen the Precinct Captain point his finger directly at Percival and tell him in no uncertain terms that he has a prison cell waiting for him! Now how do you expect him to work with someone intent on locking him up? That would be like asking Martin Luther King to work with Bull Connors. The only way that's possible is to throw away one's principles," she asserted, as the Community Liaison Officer fell back in his chair defeated by this new assault. "I'd like to clarify something for all of you, because I get the feeling you think we're just a bunch of unrefined ignoramuses. For your information, we're all well versed on the issues which concern us, and are just as politically astute, and fully understand how you'd wish to play us. Percival is justifiably mistrustful. His immediate survival and that of his rank and file is at stake. The Panthers are under attack nationally. The death of little Ricky Bolden is more than a tragedy, it's a citywide disgrace and considering his close association with the Panthers, gives one reason to pause," The chords in her slender throat distended like ropes and a nervous irritability in her tone gave immediacy to her words. "The motives of the police are, at best, to be suspected. Given the fact that no one has been brought up on charges so far, is an insult to all of us gathered here. I thought sure this meeting was called on that account – to update us on the disposition of the case. But no, instead, it's about the humiliation you think your department suffered on account of those two cops who you suspect were waylaid by the Panthers, and not the senseless slaying of one of our black children at the hands of that very same department. How callous can you be? Frankly, we're not interested in who ambushed those cops, but we know who killed Ricky Bolden and we're much more interested in what you're going to do about that."

"Tell it, sister," the black leadership chimed in, nodding. "Tell it!"

"Yes," Ruth continued, "the Panthers are under attack. I know little Ricky Bolden – knew him, that is," she said, a crack in her throat. "What more terrible a thing to say of someone so young is than you *knew* him. But it's being said more and more frequently these days, with this war. And I know his mother: She's going out of her head with grief. She goes through the rooms of her house

344

searching for him, expecting him to return any minute. She'll tell you, 'he'll be back.' You don't know the misery you've inflicted on her. And neither do you care. She'll never recover," she rasped, raking the fingers of a hand through her tight, springy hair. "But her wellbeing is not your concern. Oh no, you're concerned for your department's image; for your officers. Well, they're alive, and despite their humiliation, they return home to their families, nightly. They're alive! And has the police department apologized to poor Ms. Bolden or acknowledged her loss? No, not at all – not a blessed word!

"I speak as a mother, not a community leader when I say the ethics of this disturbs me to no end. I'm disappointed that the police could not be forthright with us and tell us what this meeting was about. Instead, at the sight of Percival, they hemmed and hawed like kids caught with their fingers in the jelly jar. Times are not what they once were when you might hope to divide us, and thereby conquer us. No, I for one, stand behind the Panthers, not because I approve of their methods, but because they've brought a sense of purpose to the youth of our community and have given them something of worth to struggle for. Yes, we represent the old guard and would undertake the struggle at a different pace, but it's not surprising to any of us that our youth have grown impatient –"

Percival whispered to Silva, "I've heard all I need – they'll fare far better without us now."

They rose, squeezed past Damion Meeks, and quietly withdrew.

Percival paused at Gwen's desk.

"How'd it go in there?" she asked.

"Favorably, I'd say."

"Will you call?"

"Things 'r jumping off the roof, but yes," he promised, blowing her a kiss as he and Silva turned out the door. No sooner had they hit the sidewalk than the repeated beep of a car horn across the street caught their attention. "Jones!" Percival was somewhat startled at hearing his name shouted out by a stranger in a pale green sedan parked outside the Tompkinsville Bowling Alley. "Can I talk to you?" he called.

"You know this guy? "Silva asked.

"I don't think so."

"How you think he knew you were here?"

"I think I'll jus' go over 'n find out."

"Want me along?"

"I'll see to it myself," Percival said, checking the traffic before dashing across the street. He placed his hands against the car and leaned into the window. "Well," he said, scrutinizing the man's beardless, angular face, and taking notice of the surrounding interior of the car, but more specifically the police band radio mounted under the dashboard.

"To whom am I speaking?" he asked, meeting the stranger's cobalt blue eyes.

"Is the meeting over or did you leave early?"

Percival eyed the stranger quizzically. "What you say? Who 'r you?" he demanded irritably.

"I'm FBI. My name is Bianco. Special Agent Lawrence Bianco," he claimed. He reached for his wallet and flipped it open for Percival to examine his credentials.

Again, Percival cast his gaze on the agent's face in wary suspicion. "OK, now what?"

"Get in I want to talk to you. Not here, there are too many people I'd rather not have see us together."

"Like the police?'

"Like the police."

"Is this official or something?"

"Just a request. I think it'll prove beneficial."

"How so?"

"For instance, the friend who informed you of the meeting?"

"You?" uttered Percival, incredulously.

"That's how I knew where to find you."

"Now I'm interested," Percival stated. Then turning to Silva, he called, "follow us," and entered the car on the passenger side.

"I'm right behind you," Silva trumpeted back from out of the driver's window of his glossy red Mustang. As the light green car pulled out, Silva made a quick U-turn into the stream of traffic in hasty pursuit.

"I've been wanting to meet you for some time now," said Agent Bianco. "I'm a fan. I've seen you fight, oh, five times or more. You're impressive. Very impressive, as was, I might add, the ambush of those two police officers."

"You don't really expect me to fall for that do you?"

"No more than you would a feint," Agent Bianco laconically said, cruising Bay St. toward St. George and the Ferry. "You know they were seeking permission in there from the community heads to allow them to kill you on the streets in hopes that they would quell any riots that might follow." Bianco cast a quick glance Percival's way, searching for a reaction.

"Probably," said Percival stiffly, shifting uncomfortably.

"You'll need my help if you want to stay alive."

"You say."

"I say."

"Look, I'm sort'a pressed for time, so can we get on with it?"

"Of course. It's like this: the FBI is an information gathering agency, and right now we're in the process of obtaining information on the Black Panthers, and I thought we could be of some help to each other."

"How you figure that," Percival asked, suspicious.

"Well, that meeting was one good example now, wasn't it?"

" I owe you, that's what you're saying?" said Percival in forbearance.

"I thought you might be grateful."

"Not that grateful," said Percival, curtly, checking the rearview mirror to see if Silva was behind them.

"Silva's with us, don't worry. I won't lose him," said the Agent, smugly.

Taken aback, Percival swung his head and eyes on Agent Bianco, lifting an eyebrow in surprise.

"Surprised?" Bianco smiled, his smile having the appearance of being tacked on.

"If you care to know more, he comes from one of the oldest and most prosperous black families hereabouts. Graduated Brown last May with honors and, of late, his parents haven't been exactly pleased with his newly acquired playmates," the Agent said, enjoying himself at Percival's expense.

"Very interesting but what's that to do with me," said Percival, morosely, starting to sweat?

"As I was about to say, I know your chapter can't meet its daily operation expenses, for instance."

"You know too much, it strikes me."

"I'm not talking to you without having certain, should I say, privileged information."

"If that's so, then why do you need me?"

"I don't need you," Bianco smiled. "You need me."

"There's a frightening thought. 'N why, out of curiosity, would you be interested in helping me," Percival asked, his expression verging on the bemused?

"There are certain advantages shall we say, to be gained by seeing to it that your organization is not entirely undermined by the police."

"Now that's curious."

"I'm commissioned to offer you certain cash rewards for your providing me with information, not injurious to the Party or yourself, mind you, but public information. It's just that I'd like to have it in advance of the police."

"You want it first, that's it?"

"That's it."

"What kind'a money we talking 'bout?" Percival said, wistfully.

347

"Enough to keep you afloat."

"N I'm not obligated in any other way"?

"Only in that."

"Then why do I get the feeling I'm being set up. We're enemies, Hoover has made that perfectly clear; so why would you want'a enter into a silent partnership with the Panthers?"

"Let's just say there are certain advantages to be gained by keeping one's common enemies afloat."

"Such as?"

"Playing them off another enemy for example."

"Like who?"

"That's not important for you to know. You have your secrets and I have mine –, fair?"

"I didn't say I was in, did I?"

"No, I guess you didn't. Here's the Ferry Terminal. I'll leave you off at the taxi drop," said Agent Bianco, rounding the long terminal ramp to the depot. "This is my card. You think about it. Call me if you become interested. You've nothing to lose."

Percival accepted the card and placed it in his pocket without looking at it. Then he was deposited at the Ferry Terminal where Silva picked him up.

"Who was that?" Silva asked.

"Of all people, the FBI. It appears he was the friend who informed me of the meeting jus' now."

"No shit," Silva blurted, swerving.

"Watch out, man," Percival bellowed.

Coming out of the swerve, Silva asked, "What he want?"

"Not too much, jus' for me to put my soul in hock."

"Oh," Silva exclaimed, raising an eyebrow? "How so?"

"I think he wants to play us off against the cops."

"To what avail?"

"Beats me."

"Cute," Silva remarked.

"Ain't it though."

The fucking FBI."

After Silva had turned off Richmond Terrace onto Jersey Street and the car had passed the projects and playground, Percival sighted, as they came upon the Panther office, a commotion in front of the bar next door. There was a small crowd from both the bar and students from the Panther office. Then Percival recognized Sam and a local, off duty black cop, Homer Johnson, arguing fiercely while Skeeter was trying to keep the students at bay. Homer stuck a finger in Sam's chest, which Sam knocked away.

"Stop 'n let me out," said Percival sharply.

"What the hell?" Silva wondered aloud, breaking to a stop.

Percival leapt from the car onto the sidewalk and stepped between the two disputants. "What's this about?" he demanded, swinging his eyes back and forth between the two.

"Fuck you," Homer barked, shoving Percival aside. "The big bad Percival Jones is here to protect his little brother. Well, protect him from this, motherfucker," he said in a drunk, slovenly drawl, brandishing his service revolver.

At sight of the weapon, Percival froze. He stared transfixed by the gun, then looked into Homer's eyes, grinned wryly, and shook his head, not saying a word.

"Nothing to say, huh, nigger? Jus' like I thought. The big, fierce Panther leader is speechless," he growled, with the glowering eyes of a mad dog.

"He's got a gun," someone said in awe. The crowd drew back, but their curiosity was that much more wetted as a result.

Homer shoved the gun into Percival's face. "I want you to open you mouth motherfucker. I want you to suck on the barrel like you sucked my big black cock the other night. I want you to show these people whose woman you are." He laughed maliciously.

"Get those students back inside," said Percival, almost casually. He didn't feel as calm as he sounded.

"I'm the one giving orders here. N I want em to see Mr. Percival Jones, the big bad boxer, the tough revolutionary leader, suck on the end of this gun," Homer shouted, "jus' like he sucks dick. Now go on," he bade, pressing the gun against Percival's tightly closed lips. Suddenly, Percival was conscious of a nameless chill, a chill that took possession of his blood, body and brain, nearly buckling him in the knees. A glow of perspiration glossed his stolid face and gleamed in the sunlight.

Silva had difficulty finding a parking spot, and, in his frantic search, saw Big/black walking towards the Heritage House. He honked, drawing Big/Black's attention, alerting him to the situation. Big/Black picked up his pace, moving stealthily from car to car, on the other side of the road, trying to avoid being seen. Fortunately, Homer's back was to the street, giving him his one advantage. The instant he was close enough and traffic slow, Big/Black strode across the street, approaching Homer on his blind side.

" – you don't suck it nigger 'n I'll take you out, I swear it! You won't be the first nigger I kill! Now suck!" Homer forced his gun against Percival's lips, his finger itchy on the trigger. "You know how to do it cause you've done it before." He laughed obscenely.

Big/Black pulled his .45 as he came up on Homer and shoved the barrel hard against his temple. "Put it down," he said gently but forcefully, "nice 'n easy 'n nobody gets hurt."

Homer rolled his eyes toward Big/black and laughed crazily, stiffening. "If I go, I take Jones with me," he said edgily.

Big/black sneered. "Percival expects to be killed. He's ready to go. The question is 'r you? Hell, he'll be a martyr. But you, what will you be? Jus' another dead nigger," said Big/black abrasively, pressing the gun barrel firmly against Homer's temple, cocking it. "Now, like I say, lower your weapon real easy – real easy."

Homer's arm twitched, grew limp and sunk to his side as if the weight of the weapon had sapped his strength. Big/black quickly grabbed the gun from his loose fingers and removed the shells.

Percival did not move his eyes from Homer's, but locked on them, boring into them. Grinning meekly, as if to say, 'it was only a prank,' Homer looked strangely pathetic and woebegone. Eyes still locked, Percival slipped into a crouch, moving in a blur beneath Homer's gaze, left fist balled, then recoiled with the propulsive force of a jack hammer, driving his fist into Homer's gut, emptying his lungs like a deflated pinpricked balloon. The air gushed out of Homer's lips in an explosive gasp. He grasped his belly and toppled over in sections and lay like a curled-up caterpillar, on the sidewalk crippled in agony at Percival's feet.

Big/black lowered himself to one knee and put the gun on the ground under Homer. "Here," he said, pitilessly, "I left one round in the chamber in case you want'a go home 'n play Russian roulette."

"Did y'll see that? Did y'll see that? Them Panther's don't play," said one person to the other gleefully, slapping hands. "Woe, they something else!"

Percival sought out Sam, laced an arm around his neck and gruffly said, "let's talk." Rounding the corner, out of sight of all others as Homer's drinking buddies helped him to his feet, Percival slammed Sam against the side of a stucco wall. "What the hell were you thinking caught up in a brawl with that jive ass nigger?"

Sam stirred, uncomfortably. "Well, he was ranking on us 'bout last night 'n shit—"

"You're Liaison Office, Joe College, a smart cat, you suppose to keep shit from flaring up not add fuel to the fucking blaze. That mother's insane. He's a fucking vice cop. He's in the process of a bad divorce. He's on the bottle, the dude's life is on the skids 'n working vice has jaded the son of a bitch miserably. Besides, he's a member of the community, it's his home. All these people know him from jump. They're drinking buddies 'n ole school pals, they got history, they may not necessarily like him but there's no percentage in getting yourself killed in a brawl with him."

"You done shaming me?" Sam asked, his face grimaced in puckered woe. He lapsed into silence and turned away dejectedly.

Percival then sought out Big/Black. "You hauled my ashes out'a the fire sure."

"Hell, I trusted you'd taken that gun from him yourself," said Big/black half-jokingly.

"Sure," said Percival smiling, lopsidedly, casting him a blank stare. "It was my plan all along."

They laughed, without humor. There was no escaping it, the pressure was on.

***

Ruth Morrow was right, the Panther Party leadership was under attack by the nation's top law enforcement agencies. It was their intention to disrupt, infiltrate, undermine and eliminate them, one at a time if need be. The most notable, convict and celebrated author, Eldridge Cleaver, the Black Panther Party's Minister of Information and former Peace and Freedom Party presidential candidate had gone underground and fled the country to avoid criminal prosecution. He hopped from one socialist port to another in pursuit of his utopian fantasy. Meanwhile, back home in the U.S., the Black Panther Party's cofounder, Huey P. Newton, Minister of Defense, remained on death row, where more and more Panthers were joining him behind bars on a day-to-day basis. The Panthers had captured the attention of the media and, moreover, the imagination of ghetto youths, but for all the fanfare it was an example more envied than emulated.

These concerns were uppermost in Percival's mind when one such youth, Frank Jenkins, approached him on the street one windy afternoon.

Frank engaged him, confidentially, "My big brother wants to talk with you. He says it's important."

"So why isn't he telling me himself?"

"Joel's a cop 'n can't afford to be seen with you."

"He could call."

"It's jus' as risky. Ya phone's bugged."

"N how would you know that?"

"My brother, he's a cop – he knows."

"How convenient."

"He says to tell you a few other black cops will be there with him so don't worry, ok?"

"N did he say down what dark alley we should meet?"

"The meeting's to take place at 'r folks crib. He says cause y'll know nothing's gonna come down there. He wants to know if you'll show 'n if eight t'night's ok?'

"Eight'll do fine if it's got'a be."

"He says if you'll feel more comfortable with it you can bring two others. He says, no guns."

"Is that an ultimatum?"

"It's a request since it's 'r folks place."

"Out'a respect for your folks, no guns."

Percival took Sam and Raschelay with him. Sam because he felt that he had unwittingly misjudged, slighted and accused him unfairly for what, perhaps, was not entirely his fault. After all, Sam was his brother whom he was obligated to by blood. He brought Raschelay along because, as he saw it, *When off to meet a potential threat you do well to have someone with you who can tip the balance in your favor,* and Raschelay was easily that someone.

Similarly, out of deference to Mr. and Mrs. Jenkins, who Percival both knew and liked, they came as requested, unarmed. Mrs. Jenkins welcomed them and escorted them to the living room. She left them to join her husband in the back kitchen.

The house was typical of most working-class Negro homes in the area. Religious as well as political symbols adorned the walls amidst gaudy paintings purchased from the local five-and-dime to, for more than aesthetic reasons, conceal cracks in the walls. The living room was cluttered with musty furniture and a brand-new console T.V. looking like a central altar piece topped with a vase of plastic flowers. A cluster of ceiling lights bathed the room in a brassy glow.

There were five men standing about in a haze of cigarette smoke and talking among themselves. Two were armed and in uniform. They quieted as the Panthers entered and sighed on seeing Raschelay. "E-l-l-o, mama," one uttered, heartened by the sight of this lusty teenage beauty, despite her panther uniform.

"Let's get to it," Joel said shortly, disengaging his eyes. His blue-black face glinted in the light of the hazy, smoke filled room. "Names are not so important since this is not a social call —"

"Sorry to say," lamented a sepia colored cop, devouring Raschelay with greedy eyes. "Now there's a Panther I'd like to tame," he whispered into the ear of a fellow cop beside him.

"You 'n me both," the other returned.

"The point is we all know who Percival Jones is," Joel continued with a mixture of caution and arrogance. "You can sit or stand, as you like."

Percival sunk into the cushions of an old armchair with loose springs and looked up in discomfort.

After they were all seated, Joel said, "First off, this has nothing to do with the incident the other day with Homer, if that's what you're thinking. As far as we're concerned he got what was coming. He's a rogue cop, on the take. A loose cannon. As much an embarrassment to the force as he is to his race. They keep him on the force because they know, he's an embarrassment to us. So you're taking him down a peg is no skin off our noses."

"That was hardly my concern," said Percival, stiffly.

"Secondly, we invited you here because you're a Brother. No other reason," Joel persisted, with a look of repugnance. "We realize you think of us as sellouts, Uncle Toms when, in truth, that's hardly the case. We're responsible family men trying to get by and take care of business," he smiled as he spoke, his voice had no inflection. "The truth is, being on the force is no more easy for a Brother than it is anywhere else in this society for blacks. In many ways, it's more difficult. We're up against a system within a system inside the force, the 'Police-Benevolent-Association,' which is all white, racist and firmly entrenched. They're an institution unto themselves and constitute the single most powerful political block in city politics. They have the backing and money to enforce their political will. We black cops, Johnny-come-latelies, have been at their mercy from jump. But we're smartening up and have formed a counter organization, the Guardians, of which we're all members. We're a group of conscientious black cops motivated to bring down the racist glass ceiling, which separates us from real political clout. You following this?"

"I hear your pain, brother, but I don't feel it," Percival said.

"Well as I've said, we're black family men and understand your struggle in a way you can't appreciate ours –"

"You make the mistake of thinking that we're addressing the issues based solely on race," Raschelay said, smiling. "That's only partially true. We realize that our plight is an unusual one, but our situation can't be properly addressed unless the whole social order is turned topsy-turvy, reconstructed from top to bottom." She intertwined her fingers for emphasis.

"Be that as it may, sister girl," Joel said with strained patience, rolling his eyes. Beauty or no, she was only an adolescent and presuming to address him as an equal was, to put it mildly, irksome. "It's risky enough having you here without being sidetracked by a discourse on polemics by a teenager."

"I didn't bring the sister along for light or frivolous reasons, man," Percival said, flatly. I expect her to be respected for her views, not her age."

"Excuse me if the sister has to run the risk of hearing this, cause I don't think she should have to."

"You think I should be playing with dolls, no doubt?" Raschelay said.

"Certainly not guns."

"I'm trying to feed starving kids," she said. "Guns notwithstanding."

"I apologize."

Raschelay accepted the dubious apology with a doubtful nod of her head.

"If I may say," Joel ventured, wearily, "it's kind'a cold, but it's like this, bro: after you've lost the fight – and lose it you shall. There'll come a time when nobody'll remember just what you were fighting for. Then it'll be us, we'll be the ones' in the foreground, the one's to carry the ball. That is, if we've not been the ones' carrying it all along and you and your crew have just been dead weight."

"That's what I was afraid of. You've been carrying the man's balls for him all along."

"That was uncalled for," bristled a cop to Percival's left.

"Let him mind his manners, then."

"Forget it," Joel said, with a contemptuous wave of the hand. "I didn't invite you here to argue. We invited you here to let you know that the 20th. precinct has a contract floating among the PBA membership on you. They don't want to arrest you, they want to see you dead. So much so, they have a bounty on your head and they all want to collect. They want to mount your head in their trophy room." Sam and Raschelay started to their feet, mouths agape. "We got wind of it, and despite our obvious differences we couldn't let the man gun you down without warning you. In any case, Jones, unless you flee the scene you're dog meat."

"Don't count me out so easily," Percival said, rising slowly. "I'm not dead yet, nor am I running scared."

"You look dead to me."

"So that's what this was about?"

''That's it, baby."

You could'a spared yourselves the grief," Percival replied. "I'd figured as much." His lips were bloodless and cold, as were the fingers of his hands. He felt as if he'd caught a chill.

"Now you know for sure. We don't want your blood on our conscience."

"Only you'll move against us when the man says to, no matter your organization, the Guardians or your consciences," Sam said, angrily. "Then you'll come down on us jus' as hard as the resta the man's pack of wolves; forget your fucking conscience. R blood will be on your heads."

"That time is yet to come, bro."

"Consider me informed," said Percival, throwing up his hands. "You say you informed me cause I'm a Brother? My question then is, if you were in tight with the PB, would I ave received this warning?"

"Whose to know."

"That's what I thought," Percival mocked, staring off. " You want'a play me for a pawn, do you?" He turned to go and Sam and Raschelay followed him out.

"If that's how you want to take it, bro, no sweat off our noses, dig?" Joel called as they tramped down the hall. "Just remember, this conversation never happened!"

Without a backward glance they saw themselves out.

As they made their way along dimly lit streets, past tenements and single-family dwellings, where sallow lights kindled wanly in windows, Raschelay asked with poignancy,

"You believe them?"

"They said nothing I didn't suspect," said Percival in a disembodied voice.

"There's a difference – now we know you're targeted," Sam said.

Percival was in a fog. He didn't know his own mind. "I suppose," he groaned, every nerve ending strung to the breaking point. He felt like a condemned man awaiting his hour in the shadow of the gallows. The light from the street made him too visible, and so he avoided them in favor of the shadows. Every passing vehicle was viewed with suspicion. Sam looped an arm over Percival's shoulder like when they were boys back in Bed-Stuy and would stroll home in the glooming, the best of pals.

There were tears in Raschelay's eyes –in all their eyes.

***

Considering the Panther's growing popularity Percival had come to expect some reaction by the police possible. They had virtually crippled the 20th. precinct. Thus, it was impossible to think otherwise. Though ominously close, this proximity to death was not new. It had stalked him before back in the south, in the Civil Rights Movement, and now it was back breathing down his back. Then again, hadn't Malcolm warned, "South of the Canadian border is south?"

As luck would have it, the first article, by Beverly, in a series of five on the local Panther chapter hit the newsstands on Sunday, November 17th., and was well received by the readership. It sparked an interest in the branch beyond the community and from the most unexpected quarters. As a result, Percival became widely sought out as a speaker and was invited to address civic groups, church groups, anti-war rallies and, of course, the college crowd. While the articles most immediate effect was to stay the assassin's hand, they also served to bring pressure on the powers that be to create an independent fact-finding commission in the slaying of little Ricky Bolden. A cover-up had been suggested, causing the precinct much embarrassment. Hence another such shooting was, for the moment, out of the question.

Percival took to carrying a .45 at all times. He could kill easily, too easily, he thought, and with little or no remorse. It was the loss of self which he feared most. He practiced as religiously with his .45 as he'd trained for a fight, leaving no margin for error; reclaiming his expert status with small arms in the bargain, though not liking guns any more for it. In fact, he became more confirmed in the belief that guns were an odious weapon, a coward's weapon, a murderer's weapon of choice. The more he was forced into handling them, the more he realized that America, the bane of his ancestors, was turning him into a brute, stamping out in him any and all finer fellow feelings, all refinement and sensibilities, turning him into an abstraction. It was reducing him by degrees into becoming a base and vulgar person. He would forever resent what it had done to his forefathers and what it was doing to him, forcing him to become. It was an ailment, an infirmity in the national character, a demoralizing aspect of the American dream. This was not the revenge for which he craved, to become one of them, the opposed other, thus locking him in mortal combat with himself.

Sam came to refer to him, in awe as, "Billy the Kid."

It irked Percival. He'd retort, "Billy the Kid died for your sins."

He had become as paranoid as any outlaw with a bounty on his hea and took to stretching a string of piano wire six inches above the floor across his bedroom doorway, as well as laying crumpled newspapers on the ground in case an assassin should bypass the tripwire. He slept with a proverbial eye open and a pair of .45's close at hand. Yet in his reverie, he longed to be a Gandhi, King, Thoreau, a Malcolm X even.

Then, too, he had come face to face with the sad, but incontrovertible fact, that in America, the gun had taken on the symbolic proportions of an icon. The gun in the hands of the invading European horde was itself America; more so, the land stolen at gun point. Without the gun they had, and have, no claim to the land, certainly none they dare plead before the Throne of Heaven.

Moreover, the gun remains their only right to the land. Hence, the gun retains an exalted status in American life, above God, conscience and the rights of humanity at large. He did well to recall that the birth of a nation, no less than its demise, is a godawful, ugly affair.

At the same time, Percival could not escape the sad fact that in his willingness to rely on use of the gun he was no less American than the likes of Al Capone or any other similar type on the lower end of the food chain. One do well to keep his K-9's razor sharp.

It wasn't that he had changed his mind and decided against the futility of dying young, but it had become more imperative than ever that he not succumb to the nagging sense of fatality haunting the land, much like the ghost of his own unrevenged father. Was he to avenge Lucius, and if so, must he then also succumb to his father's fate when life had so much more to offer? "Longevity has its place," Dr. King had said on the eve of his assassination. Though Percival clearly understood that blood sacrifice was always required in the liberation of a people, he had also come to realize that he had only scratched life's surface and had not yet glimpsed its kaleidoscopic, multifaceted possibilities. Unlike Dr. King, he could not claim to have "been to the mountain top." As such he was not half so sure that if he did not reach the promised land himself that anyone else would get there either. No, death would only prove a waste. The good fight was yet to be won!

The prolonged citywide teachers strike was finally resolved. On Monday, November 18th., a proposal put forward by the Council of Supervisory Associations was accepted by the rank and file of teachers in secret ballot. Albert Shanker, the teachers union president, said, "Ours is not a victory with a capital v, but the big fight has been won."

Once a rallying cry for free determination, the bitterly crushed experiment in home rule in the black and Puerto Rican district of Brownsville was now set aside to fester.

All the teachers who had been released by the Brownsville district school were reinstated, although three principals in the demonstration school district were relieved of their duties. The reverend C. Herbert Oliver, chairman of the local school board decried, "It's obvious that the black and Puerto Rican people of the city are not going to be allowed to determine the future of their children. It is equally obvious that this may be the beginning of the end of Ocean Hill Brownsville."

Autumn was short lived that year. Suddenly, the trees were divested of their fiery, mottled colored leaves. The first snow of the season fell soon after Thanksgiving, following which a bitter winter's chill set in for the duration.

Fully aware that his unemployment benefits were about to expire, Percival became increasingly concerned over financial matters and the fact that all there was to sustain the chapter were paltry sales from the Panther Speaks, occasional honorariums for speaking engagements, donations from employed members from time to time, and a small stipend, they enjoyed, from the FBI. It was barely enough to keep their doors open and keep the broad array of programs afloat.

Percival had initially refused the FBI's offer of financial assistance in exchange for trivial information, but that Saturday at the Defense Captains' meeting, he was persuaded by Lumumba, Zayd, and Chairman Bishop, not to look a gift horse in the mouth.

Bishop had said, almost flippantly, "You can't deny your chapter can use the cash. N since you're only providing em with useless information—where's the harm?"

"Besides," Lumumba added, "Huey's ok'd such practices in the past. You're on solid ground. This is revolution, baby, 'n we got's to finance it somehow. If the pigs want'a contribute to their own downfall, all the better."

The advice disturbed Percival, but he could not argue the fact that his chapter was in dire need of money, and he was at a loss as to where it might otherwise be obtained.

"It doesn't sit easy with me," he argued.

"You have other sources?" Zayd asked.

If any of the other defense captains had any objections they weren't stated.

Therefore, with the financial mess he found his chapter in, he went in search of seasonal employment. At first he thought he might find work in MOMA's gift shop, but, under the circumstance he dare not apply. Too many people knew him there and he longed for anonymity. He was becoming isolated, a lone wolf, and the increased pressure of always having to watch his back had turned him into a dangerous, sanguinary man, more Hyde than Jekyll. Fortunately, he found work in Gimbals Department store on 34th. St. & 5th. Ave. in the stockroom, where he hoped to keep to himself and stay unobserved.

The stockroom was a veritable warehouse, taking up the whole tenth floor and half of the ninth. It was about the most confused situation into which he had ever entered. It made him smile. It was exactly what he'd wanted. No one had time to know anyone else. Supervisors didn't know their staff, and to be sent off on a job for a department was to disappear for half the day. The only inconvenience was having to punch in and out, but Percival took it in stride and went to work.

To conceal his .45, packed at the base of his spine, he wore an overlarge, woolen Navy shirt with tails out and baggy trousers.

Every morning, along with his fellow co-workers, he would be assigned a department to help keep stocked for the day. Each department had its own regular stock boy, as well, who then assumed the duties of supervisor over the extra help.

With work orders issued for the day, he would load up a hand truck, then wait with the horde of other stock boys for one of the only two freight elevators. The wait could take up to forty-five minutes, since an elevator could only accommodate four stock boys and their load at any one time. Meanwhile, it was simply a matter of keeping the precariously stacked boxes from tipping over. Also, personnel came from every floor to put in additional orders for their departments. It often appeared as if these two floors were among the most harried in the store and became more so once it's doors were opened for business.

While waiting for the elevators, the cluster of stock boys smoked and indulged in trivial conversation but, having no appetite for small talk, Percival kept apart and to himself. He simply wanted to be left alone. He began to notice one of the stock boys staring his way. When he'd catch his eye, the stock boy would look away. One morning as Percival stood waiting on the elevator this fellow sidled up to him.

"Aren't you Percival Jones?"

"What of it?"

"I'm Grady – Grady Heart, recall?"

Percival shook his head, scowling.

"I fought you a few years back."

"I fought a lot'a cats a few years back."

"Ya still at it, or what?"

"Hey, look man, I don't want'a be rude, but I got'a lot on my plate, you know? Forget me, man, who I am; who I was, ok?"

"Sure, bro, sure.?" Grady observed Percival with a peculiar intentness, backing off. "I'm cool, it's jus' I figured you'd be on your way to the top 'bout now, is all."

"As you can see, I'm not," Percival said, rankled.

"I jus' wanted to say you the best, man, that's all."

Percival cringed and his face reddened as if slapped. It wasn't the last time he was to be recognized, but he would curtly rebuff any advances and say, "later," and walk on. Although he could not place the face, Grady's remark struck home, "Ya the best, man, that's all." Causing him to wonder, "What the fuck am I doing with my life?"

While the tension on the streets between the Panthers and the police was more palpable than ever, Percival was laughing while the community cheered them on. He thought the whole damn thing a joke. The bastards were at bay. Beverly's articles were mostly responsible for it, but then she had seen fit to tell the story from the Panther's perspective, rather than the usual other way round. Hence, ever disdainful of the cops, he continued to tread a perilous course. But the cruel reality of his stance came crashing in on him early one morning before work when his phone rang, waking him abruptly.

"Percival," came the anxious voice on the other end, "Zayd here – Kinshasha's been killed in Philly by the pigs, early this morning."

"W-What?" Percival responded, uncomprehendingly.

"Kinshasha, man, Kinshasha's been iced by the Philly pigs. I don't have all the details yet. As it comes in I'll pass it on."

"Kinshasha? Kinshasha?" Percival wondered, clinging to the phone in stupefaction. "'n Leon Oaks with him, man. Some foul shit! You see the pigs 'r starting to come down heavy. Watch your assets, baby."

"Yeah," Percival yawned, fully awake now. "You too." He hung up, trying to place Kinshasha and Leon Oaks' names, trying to put faces to them, attribute lives to them. 'But damn a lot'a Panthers 'r turning up dead,' he thought, sweating. He'd been waking up in a cold sweat a lot lately. He wasn't so much afraid of dying, as of losing. Having his efforts scrambled and account for naught as Joel had said and, in the end, becoming a broken or embittered man haunted by the ghost of what might have been, worse off by far than a punch-drunk fighter.

He sighed, struck by another thought, "how many others on a day to day basis were left unaccounted for? How much carnage? How much human waste?" He felt he might be sick, but he urged himself on anyway. He had to remember who the devil Kinshasha was in the hierarchy of the party, outside of being it's latest martyr. 'But I'm not cut from a martyr's cloth,' he consoled himself, as if it would deflect an assassin's bullet. Boxing had disciplined his body in accordance with his spirit, but a martyr's spirit must be pure, a spark able to ignite other sparks, a conflagration of sparks.

At such times, he knew himself to be a confused jumble of parts. He knew that what was at bottom had surfaced to the top like scum on a pond, and that he, a born savage, schooled and civilized for all intents and purposes, was confronting himself out of time and place – at odds with his environment and all else. It's not that he didn't understand. To the contrary, he understood all too well. After all, he was civilized, wasn't he? Yes. Had he remained a savage? No. Therefore, the most immediate problem facing him was how to exorcise the carnivore in him that saw civilization as a sacrificial offering. Here is where he felt himself falling to pieces. He was over civilized and civilization was, at best, a God-awful, interminable affair.

He turned to Gwen asleep beside him in bed. Her face shone palely, as in moonlight, against the pillows on which her auburn hair cascaded round her head. The appearance of crow's feet at the corner of her eyes and tiny, pitying lines about her mouth revealed her years. An occasional snore escaped her lips. He would have to waken her. She would have to leave for work shortly. He decided to forgo work that day. As he called her she murmured like a rill, opening her eyes, looking out balefully on the darkened room.

She yanked herself up like a petulant child, and, discarding the covers, threw her legs over the side of the bed in defiance of the world she was to go out and meet. The crumpled newspapers underfoot sent a shiver up her spine. "Are these guns and scattered newspapers and tripwire really necessary?" she asked, stifling a yawn.

"More now than ever," he assured her, examining one of the .45's.

"You'll have to pardon my not sleeping over more often," she said, sarcastically.

"It's safer by far at your place."

"Don't you have a drink or anything?" she asked, switching on the bedside light and rifling through the draw in the bedside table. She found a cigarette, lit it, and blew a cloud of smoke. "I can sure use a drink."

He ignored her. "Tell me, you know the name Kinshasha?"

"Kinshasha?" she reacted. "It sounds vaguely familiar. Why, is it important?"

"I jus' got a call from Zayd. This Kinshasha's been killed by the Philly police," Percival said, grinding his teeth, astonished at himself for the relief he felt at being alive.

She gave her head a fervent shake, chilled by the news. "Oh my God," she emitted, "you guys are dropping like flies. I'm sorry," she caught herself. "But yes, I remember. He was the Defense Captain who spoke before Cleaver at the NYU student forum last October."

"That's it. The guy you thought overly antagonistic – Yes." he nodded knowingly. "I remember now. Well," he uttered, "the Philly cops offed him along with some other cat name'a Oaks."

"You tell me the most God-awful shit first thing in the morning without offering anything to wash it down?" She shivered. "I've had my fling with danger in the past and that's exactly where I wish to keep it." She broke off in a huff "Where's my purse?" Finding it, she retrieved the remains of a pint of vodka from which she took several gulps before offering him the bottle.

He turned it down. "I got'a be razor sharp."

"I got to get to work," she said, finishing off the bottle.

"I'll call you."

"Let's meet at my place from here on in."

"It'll be less frequent."

"It can't be much less than it is already," she said, struggling into her clothes.

"As you like."

"It's not what I like. I just don't want this," she said, with a sweep of her hand. "The whole damn thing rattles me. I can't deny it, if you're not scared I'm scared for you. I don't know, I suppose this might make a coward of me, but I don't want to be around when the shooting starts. Maybe it's best we don't see each other for a while."

"I would argue with you, but I can't," he said resignedly, .45 cradled in his lap.

She drew to a standstill at the tripwire on her way out. "Call me," she said, with a penitent sigh, glancing back over her shoulder in appeal.

He inclined his head in accord.

***

The reaction from the others on hearing of Kinshsha's death was one of mute surprise, cold terror and embarrassed relief. "Who's next," was uppermost in all their thoughts. Among this small band of Panthers it was expected Percival would be next despite their not knowing of his meeting with the black police, the Guardians. Percival had no wish for it to be known that there was a price on his head, so they were kept in the dark. It had been assumed, however, that since the ambush of those two cops his head was all but in a noose. Sam embraced him impulsively, to his chagrin. He mistrusted such overt displays of affection. Coming from Sam, the insincerity of it was grating. He felt a pang of betrayal. Half-brothers, they could from time to time read each other's soul, but as often as not, it was as difficult and cloudy as a cesspool. Percival was irritable. "Let's not get too choked up. Jus' remember, Kinshasha lives so long as we fight!"

"Right on," the group responded, looking at him as if he were a ghost. Then again, the Black Panther Party was a revolutionary party with a compelling social agenda which, given the bleak circumstances of their everyday lives, was well worth the sacrifice. With that in mind, they would persevere.

"Okay," said Percival, breaking the dour mood, "let's not jus' stand round like we're waiting on the second coming. We've work to do, got'a revolution to win!"

They scurried off to their appointed tasks.

Silva and Percival sat down at the office for a considerable time going over the ledgers. Afterwards, Percival exclaimed, "I guess I should'a gone to work after all." Then he asked, visually sweeping the room, "Anyone seen Skeeter?"

"Not since this morning," Sam said, frowning, "when you first told us 'bout Kinshasha up at the house."

"Well he's suppose to be here 'n he's not."

"Sundown 'n Priestus took off with him earlier," Sam voiced. "They'll show."

"Timing is everything."

"There he is, now," Silva said, watching Skeeter saunter down the other side of the street with a walk that was half prowl and half dance. Percival was surprised to see him on foot, without his car. He hated walking, though he walked like a preening peacock. A measure of urgency seemed to prod him on. "I wonder what gives," Percival asked, as Skeeter crossed the street oblivious to oncoming traffic. Silva opened the door. Skeeter rushed in, a look of consternation marred his sullenly handsome face, covered in a sheen of sweat. He looked unblinkingly between Percival and Silva, who stared curiously back at him, waiting.

"What gives?" Percival asked. "Where's Big/black 'n Priestus, aren't they with you?"

Skeeter responded in near hysterics, "The pigs got em." His face was drained of color and his eyes were unusually stark. "They got em, man, they took em—Big/black 'n Priestus."

It took a moment for the impact of Skeeter's words to sink in. Unable to conceal the incredulity in his face, Percival seized Skeeter by the shoulders, breathing harshly in his face, "What'a you mean the pigs got em?"

"Jus' that – took em, man, busted em," Skeeter said, near tears. "There was nothing I could do."

The shock of it held them all in thrall.

"No," Percival murmured, loosening his grip of Skeeter, and falling back. "It can't be!" He could not recall having ever been so jolted by anything outside the blow that fractured his jaw and cancelled his Olympic dreams. Or was it when Martin was killed? Or no, Bobby? Or when the Chicago police turned their nightsticks on the Peace Protestor. "It can't be," he whispered huskily, shaken to the core. "It can't be!"

"I'm sorry, really sorry, but that's the way it jumped off," said Skeeter, contritely. "They jus' got em."

"What the fuck brought it on?"

"I don't know. I can't say, I wasn't there. That's how I got away. It's all a kind'a blur. I had a bunch'a errands to run then I was to scoot over to my ole man's cause he ain't been feeling himself of late. Priestus 'n Big/black wanted to hang so they come along for the ride, you know? Then when I finally stop off at my crib, 'n since I was only gonna be a minute, I left em in the car with the ignition on, listening to sounds, the heat up so they could keep warm.

"I wasn't gone but'a minute when I hear a commotion out front 'n look outside to see Big/black 'n Priestus up against the car 'n these pigs patting em down. Then when I saw one pull a piece off'a Big/black, which I can't figure, cause it was Priestus who had the gun. I'm thinking they gonna come look for me next, so I split out'a my ole man's back door 'n made my way across backyards 'n down alleys till I hit Jersey St., 'n that's 'bout as much as I know."

"Ya did right," Percival said.

"I sure hope they didn't impound my fucking wheels," Skeeter muttered, sucking his teeth. "'N I hope they had sense to cut the ignition, too."

Percival collapsed in a nearby chair in dark despair. He lowered his face in his hands, lightheaded. He had ventured far a field and there was no turning back. If only he could withstand the pressure, the continual assault on his nervous system. He could little afford to fold, not for all concerned. God knows it wasn't suppose to be this way. He felt like he was between the rounds of a fight he wasn't half sure he could win. He had to rely on the solitary sentinel at the back of his brain urging him on.

"I know how you must feel," Silva intoned. "We all feel the same way."

"No, you can't know," Percival rasped, his voice strangled. "I'm not too worried 'bout Priestus, he'll walk away okay. It's Big/Black. There's a warrant out for him back in his home state. It's hard for me to be objective. The man hauled my ashes out'a the fire," he said, feelingly. "He's one hell of a cat, one of a kind."

After a brief silence Sam—embarrassed by the memory of which Percival referred— said, with a pang of envy, "if you say so."

Percival eyed Sam, murderously. "If I say so? Meaning what?" he asked, explosively.

"Nothing, bro," Sam said, defensively, "but, ah, people 'r saying Homer was only jiving."

Percival rounded on Sam. "What kind of'a fucking fool 'r you anyway? Jive all you want but sticking a gun in my face is no laughing matter! Besides, I know the talk on the street 'n as usual it ain't worth shit." At times, Percival had the gravest difficulty reconciling himself with the fact that Sam was, indeed, his brother, no less his mother's son, blood of his blood, if only by half, a distinction he'd begun to make on being told by their mother of his real father, Lucius, distancing them from each other.

"I wasn't trying to take anything from Big/black," Sam argued. "All I'm trying to say is what is, dig?"

"Don't!" Percival signaled Sam to silence.

"Forgive me fer being alive, shit!"

"Please!" Percival begged.

"You going to be ok with this?" Silva asked, placing a hand on Percival's shoulder.

"As soon as everybody leaves me alone." This new development had taken him aback in a way that he could not have anticipated. He considered Big/black his strongest ally. The phone jangled at his elbow and he picked it up. "Panther Party office," he snarled into the mouthpiece.

It was Ernest Dodd.

"Yes counselor," Percival hedged, eyes roving. "I understand." Pause. "Big/black told me as much." Pause. "Yes, I know it doesn't look good." Pause. "Night court?" Pause. "Targee Street, we'll see you there. We'll all be there." He thrust the phone back on its rest, gazing at it, awash in thought. He could little remember when all had been right with the world; had it ever been alright? and when had it become his responsibility to correct it?

True to his word, the entire branch membership, eighteen strong, turned out for court in full Panther regalia, doffed of berets. They filed into court only after the judge had been seated so that they would not have to rise on the occasion of his entering. Having no charges on which to hold Priestus, the police had released him shortly before night court when he joined his comrades.

The judge loomed over his bench from a high back leather chair like an ancient bird of prey, staring disapprovingly down his nose at them through rimless glasses. He summoned the bailiff with a crooked finger. "Who are those people in my courtroom?" he asked.

The bailiff replied softly, "They're Black Panthers, your Honor."

With a sour expression on his face, the judge observed them critically, not knowing what to make of them, then firmly said, feeling it his duty, "You're well advised to behave yourselves accordingly in my court."

Big/black was hauled before the bench like the others before him, escorted through a side door by uniformed officers of the court. Unlike the others, his hands were cuffed and links of chain ran through a belt ring, rendering his hands useless. His legs were clapped in irons. He moved slowly, unsurely, like a captive slave with a clanking sound trailing his every footfall. Looking absently ahead he wore an ironic, hurt expression on his dusky face.

Right hands raised and clenched in the Black Power salute, the Panthers rose in a body when Big/black entered the court. And though they were deferentially silent, Raschelay's eyes welled with tears.

Big/black paused long enough to acknowledge their tribute, then continued round with a clank of chains, like finger cymbals, and faced the bench, head high, a noble brought low.

The judge's gavel came down with a bang that resounded through the courtroom like a shot. "Any further such demonstrations," said the irate jurist, "and you'll all be removed from my court or charged with contempt. Let there be no misunderstanding!"

The arraignment was as swift and brief. The judge, as expected, denied and remanded him pending extradition procedures. Then as Big/black was lead off dazed like an ox about to face the butchers knife, the rest of the Panthers solemnly rose and marched out of court.

Not having had the chance to speak to Priestus earlier, Percival spoke to him on the courthouse steps. "What happened, bro? What went down?"

"It all happened outta the fucking blue. I mean, the man was on us before we knew what was up. Well, he wasn't on us that fast, but fast enough, especially since we weren't looking for it, you know?" Priestus adjusted his glasses, eyes glazed. "It was a matter of us being in the wrong place at the wrong time," he said, as they waited for a car at of the bottom of the court house steps under a street light. They were surrounded by the others all wanting to hear the story too. "Anyway, you know, we was out with Skeeter kind'a enjoying ourselves; jus' hanging while Skeeter took care'a some business.' We was waiting for him with the radio going, fingers popping to the tunes 'n jus' jivin' feelin' mellow. We was passing the time, digging ourselves 'n talking trash, when these pigs must'a spot us – 'n saw us enjoying ourselves, n you know how they jus' want'a crackdown on some Brothers having a good time. They hoping ta catch us with weed, or smack or whatever else to bust us on, ya know? When I see the mothers pulling up 'long side us, 'n recognize us, I know we knee deep in shit. So I go for my rod to ditch it under the seat. But Big/Black reach over 'n say, 'No,' grabbing the piece from me. Because I see he's ready to go down, to smoke these pigs— Oh man, was he ready— I say, 'There ain't no shells in the clip.' He takes the gun 'n looks at me 'n curses, then shoves it down his boot 'n pulls his sock up over it 'n pulls down his pant leg 'n mumbles, 'Better one'a us go down than two or three'a us, dig?' He told me he got outstanding charges of arson against him back home."

"I know," Percival said. "He told me he burnt down his school."

"That's it, that's what he say," Priestus confirmed. "He say, 'Hell, I know once they got us here they gonna find out I'm wanted for arson. So shit, if

I'm'a do twenty-five to life any fucking way, why not even the score 'n take out some pigs for Kinshasha 'n Leon Oaks, while I'm at it.' He say, 'It's better this way, at least you 'n Skeeter can continue on in the struggle.'"

"That's Big/black," Percival said, his chest welling with sorrow.

"I'll tell you what, man, the thing them pigs talk 'bout most is how they wish it was you they had back'a they car. They say you'd never get to the precinct alive. They say they'd ice your black ass on the fucking spot! The way them Philly cops did Kinshasha. Then they laugh 'bout it. I tell you they had me going. 'N one of em put his gun to my head. N man was my heart pumping 'n I shut my eyes tight as a fist. He say, 'Bang!' n it's over jus' like that.' I mean, I gasped, every nerve in my body twitching. They laugh some more. Then he say, 'Boy, you ain't shit yourself back there, ave you? Cause I sure as hell smell it up here.' Big/black was looking out the side window like he's not hearing, but he turn 'n say, 'Jus' like a pig to smell itself 'n not know what the fuck it's smelling!' That made em furious, but it shut em up, too." Priestus chortled with a lazy shake of the head. "I admit I wasn't sure we was gonna get to the precinct alive, ourselves. Let me tell you, I was scared for my life back'a that squad car."

At the sight of Big/black trussed up in chains back in the courtroom, Percival's mind had become hell bent on vengeance. And so now he rest his hand on the hilt of his .45, fingering the trigger under his full-length black leather coat, and clapped Priestus firmly on the shoulder with the other hand. "Good, you've made it through."

It wasn't until that weekend a tense few days later, that Percival was able to visit Big/black at the prison on Rikers Island. It was congested, no less noisy than a zoo, and reeked of a similar odor. Percival found himself yelling in frustration to be heard. Despite his trials, Big/black appeared in reasonably good spirits, though his eyes were empty and his facial expression taut.

Suddenly tears sprang to Percival's eyes.

"Ya not crying for me, man, I know."

"I can't help but think you don't belong in jail."

"Nobody belongs in jail," said Big/black, gloomily, "any more than they belong slaves."

"I guess it's jus' that I thought it was gonna be me."

"It might yet, but not alive."

"That's comforting."

"To think I ran north to hide out. I guess the Panthers wasn't such a good hiding place after all."

"It's so damn'd unfair, so stinking unjust!"

"Justice," Big/black howled. "Ain't no such thing as justice on stolen land!" His words faded amidst the cacophony of other raised voices in the visiting room.

"Yes." Percival shook his head, sadly. It was like a zoo – a human zoo. He wore a somber, expression on his face, a sadness that was in contrast to his usual self, which betrayed an underlying fear and sickness of heart. He eyed Big/black with remorse. "I got'a get out'a here," he said, flustered, standing awkwardly as a pang of grief knifed its way through his gut. "I can't stand to see you here. I got'a go. We'll keep in touch."

"If you say so, man."

"No, I mean it. I'll write."

"Don't bother. I can't write 'n I can't read worth a damn, that's why I burnt that fucking school down in the first place. I spent twelve years in it 'n can hardly add 'n subtract on both fingers 'n hands."

Percival strolled from the prison, his head spinning, eyes cast on the sunless sky with snow-bearing clouds accumulating against the distant city skyline.

"Snow's coming." He sighed."

***

The Johnson years were now a thing of the past. Promises of "The Great Society" had all but faded with the cost of prosecuting the war in Vietnam. Nixon's call to unity, to "Bring us together," became the watchword of the day as he ascended to the presidency in January of '69. Within the first months of his presidency, he proved more cautious than a fakir walking on a hot bed of coals. The Paris peace talks, begun by former president, Lyndon B. Johnson, continued, despite evidence that the Vietcong were deploying for an all-out offensive against various cities in the south. Nevertheless, the new president, feeling the pulse of his war wary countrymen, promised to "reduce American forces by 50,000 soldiers." He retracted that offer shortly afterwards, saying, "In light of the current enemy offensive, there can be no reduction of American forces in south Vietnam in the foreseeable future." Along with a credibility breakdown there developed an emerging sense among the populace that, once again as of old, the war would escalate, which came as no surprise to the new president's detractors.

Hence, his campaign promise to "Bring Us Together" was made impossible for a man as suspicious of political dissent as Richard M. Nixon was. Consequently, the nation's schism deepened. Wishing to rule quietly, his law and order agenda, which suited his temperament, was pursued with characteristic disregard for the constitutional rights of dissenters and political opponents, especially black militants operating in the ghettos, singling out the Black Panther Party for special handling. Again proving Black Panther Party, Minister of Defense, Huey P. Newton, was right when he warned, "As the aggressions of the racist American government escalates in Vietnam, the police agencies of America escalate the repression of black people throughout the ghettos of America."

Because of the escalation against the Black Panthers Percival was growing accustomed to being wakened first thing in the morning by the urgent ring of the telephone. Usually it didn't amount to much, but on the off chance that it might, he invariably answered it. And so he did that morning too.

"'Ello," he said with a smoky, sleep filled voice, lifting the receiver to his ear.

"Percival?"

"Yeah?"

"That you?"

"Zade?"

"Thank God you wasn't netted in that raid las night," Zayd said with relief.

"Raid?"

"I guess you don't know. So far this morning, the pigs ave busted something like seventeen Panthers in a citywide sweep, counting my brother, Lumumba, 'n his ole lady, Afeni."

"No!" Percival bolted up right, grabbing a .45 from the nightstand, feeling a certain security in its heft.

"Some dark shit, ain't it?"

Percival didn't reply.

"If I'm right, they ain't collect all they're after. I know Sekou's gone underground. Anyway, we'll 'ave to call'a pow-wow."

"Sure. Sure."

"Cat's ave got'a get down from upstate, so let's say one-thirty this afternoon at the Harlem office?"

"Okay, sure, you're on."

"Power," said Zayd, hanging up.

"Yeah," said Percival, diffidently, stretching back out on the bed and contemplating the cracks in the ceiling, spreading out from the light fixture like diverging paths, and listening to every sound in the sleeping house, every groan and crack of its joints, agonizing over his life and wondering where all those other roads might have lead had he not broken his jaw; had Rufus not gone insane; had he the will to have gone his own way when he had the chance to do so. "When was that?" he asked aloud. "Given the color of my skin, the

369

circumstances of my life, walking away was not an option." Had he been a man of faith, it would have been said that he had lost his way.

His attention shifted, drawn to the stirrings of other household members rising from various corners of the small, two-story dwelling. He listened to the creaking of floorboards and groaning of stairs as they descended. Gruff, curt morning greetings in the kitchen were part of the morning mix.

Slowly, Percival rose, threw back the covers and climbed out of bed, slipped on his slippers and stepped over the trip wire into the darkened living room. Drawn toward the illuminated kitchen beyond, he crossed the carpeted floor, leaned a shoulder against the kitchen doorjamb, and peered in on its occupants as would a sleepwalker wakened from a bad dream.

Silva was at the stove. Priestus was waiting impatiently for the use of the toilet. Skeeter was seated at the kitchen table with a cigarette dangling from his full lips, eyes closed, chin cupped in a palm, dreamily waiting for the coffee to perk.

The toilet in the bathroom flushed, and shortly after Sam emerged.

"I've something to say," Percival announced.

"Can it wait?" Priestus asked, pleadingly. "I got'a go."

"Make it quick," Percival said.

When Priestus rejoined them Percival began to speak, and, raising a hand, he found, to his dumb surprise that along with a .45 clutched in his fist, he was also sporting a raging hard-on. He wondered at his rude nature, at the heat of the fight rising in his loins.

None of the others were startled, they had grown accustomed to the constant presence of a gun in Percival's possession over the long winter months, naked or clothed. No one commented. They, too, had little to nothing on but towels, as if they were in a men's locker room.

Disregarding gun and hard-on, Percival went on to relay the disconcerting news, which Zayd had passed on to him. Shoulders sagging, stricken with disbelief, they groaned as one. Unlike Kinshasha or Leon Oaks, they knew these people, had on occasion rubbed shoulders with them, hence, they were invested. The news was more than disturbing to them and those who ate did so without appetite.

Percival had Skeeter call the other members to inform them; and to have them stay in close contact over the next number of days in case of any unforeseen developments and, in the meantime, keep a low profile.

The radio was on to catch the latest news update, and the dial set to WBLS, a station which originated out of Harlem. The D.A.'s office had issued a statement: "A Twelve count indictment has been brought by a grand jury this morning at 1a.m., charging twenty-one members of the Black Panther Party

370

with plotting to plant bombs in midtown stores of Macy's, Alexander's, Bloomingdales, E.J. Korvette's, and Abercrombie & Fitch at the height of the Easter shopping season."

The Panthers were advocating there be no violence in response to the arrests. "Acts of random violence won't help," Chairman Bishop was reported to have said. It appeared Harlem had been taken off guard as much as they and were in a state of shock. "They're trying to railroad our revolutionary brothers and sisters," said an irate deejay before turning the microphone over to listener call-ins: "It's deja vu," one said. "It's the Scottsboro Boys all over again," said another. "I'll tell you, the shit's gonna hit the fan!"

The deejay cautioned, "Ya can't swear on the air."

The next caller said, "I won't swear but your first caller's right. This has gone on long enough?" There were more, "Have you noticed it's almost a year to the day Dr. King was shot 'n killed? Get outta the way, all hell's 'bout to break loose." Then the deejay played Billie Holliday singing, "Black buttocks swinging in the southern breeze/ strange fruit hanging from a poplar tree."

That afternoon Percival had Silva accompany him to the emergency meeting up in Harlem. They took Silver's Mustang, crossing into Manhattan by way of the Staten Island Ferry. They took the West Side Highway up to Harlem along the Drive and turned off at 125th. Street. & 12th. Avenue. He found parking on 7th. Avenue within walking distance of the Panther Office. The avenue was congested, flowing with a bustling pedestrian traffic and vehicles moving in both directions. Harlem was similar to Bedford Stuyvesant only in that they shared a vast black population, but there the similarities ceased. This was Harlem, the black capitol of the United States, a flawed African jewel in the midst of white America. Harlem gave the United States the only cultural renaissance it's had. And though Jazz was not born there— like so many other African American art forms (belles-lettres, theatre, music, dance)— it took root and flowered there, offering it's gifts to the world. Since its renaissance, Harlem had fallen into disrepute and was increasingly considered more a ghetto than a Mecca or an intellectual and cultural heartland which every black American felt a spiritual kinship to. Though the arts no longer flourished there as they once had, there still remained pockets of culture. There was still theatre, dance, music, literature, the Schaumburg Library and City College, the poor man's Harvard. Harlem still had much to offer the connoisseur.

Percival could not help but smile recalling when, as a boy, the only thing he knew about Harlem was that it was the baddest place on earth and grew the baddest niggers as a matter of course. Rumor had it that if you were a Harlemite you could hit harder and cut deeper than anyone else. It wasn't until he first heard Benny King sing, "A Rose in Spanish Harlem," that he was finally disabused of that notion. And he was already in his adolescence when he himself was becoming recognized as one of New York's topflight amateur fighters, having already captured the nationals in his weight class.

There was an angry, youthful crowd gathered outside the Panther office, spoiling for a fight and making it difficult to pass. "Who you?' they challenged as Percival and Silva tried to force their way through. "Let 'em by," Zayd shouted from inside, "they're one of us." And so they grudgingly gave ground, disappointed in their attempt to pick a quarrel.

The last of what remained of the decimated ranks of the New York Panther defense captains after the police raid against them the previous night, Rasheed Hill arrived forty-five minutes late from upstate Peekskill. Rasheed was a lab technician on staff at Vassar College. Profusely apologetic, he explained, "Sorry I'm late. I had to catalogue specimens and file some slides before I could break away. It couldn't be postponed. My apologies for holding things up," he said, taking a back seat.

The Harlem office was a large nondescript store front and the meeting was held in the back quarters. The room had been carefully swept for bugs and two armed guards stood watch up front.

The meeting was finally called to order.

"Power to the people," Chairman Bishop saluted, facing the Captains and Lieutenants. He sat up front between Zayde Shakur and Rosemary Bird—cousin to Joan Bird— taken in the raid earlier that night.

"Panther Power to the revolution," came the dispirited reply flung back from the wrecked ranks of Captains and Lieutenants.

Chairman Bishop was a lanky, good looking, mocha colored man in his mid-forties with grizzled hair and sentimental eyes, which betrayed an underlying, middling intellect. He was droll, unlettered and of the streets. He was senior member of the New York Panthers and, therefore, in deference to his age, not because of any outstanding leadership quality, the post of chairman was conferred upon him. His duties were ceremonial in function only. The post was by way of honoring him as an elder brother. The problem was, with so many of the Panther leadership incarcerated, including its spokesman, Bishop became, by default, both spokesperson and leader.

The fact that there was no one else in the Panther hierarchy with the combined intellectual and moral stature of Malcolm X was a burden under which the rank and file groaned. Having served in both civil rights and peace movements, it was a fact that had not escaped Percival's notice. He was ambivalent, feeling he couldn't explain himself, his carrying a gun, a weapon he abhorred, to his former associates, none of whom would have expected him to do so. Nevertheless, he came to see them less and less. This included Nina which he saw as a safeguard. He was beginning to nurse a growing disenchantment in his breast.

"Yall know the score…all yall been informed," Bishop began in an undercurrent of fury. "So yall know the deal. Hell, the whole world knows the deal. It's been on the fucking news since early this morning 'n in the afternoon papers. She-e-t, it can't get more widespread. But what yall ain't heard is the insane amount'a bail they asking. They asking a hundred thousand dollars a head," he said with a leaden, southern drawl. "Can you dig it? That's over two million we ain't got!"

Eyes rolled with incredulity, the Defense Captains and Lieutenants straightened, others whistled or gasped in disbelief.

"I'll be damned," one uttered.

"My sentiments exactly," Bishop groaned.

"So how we gonna deal with it?" someone piped up.

"That's why we're here," said Bishop, uneasily, smoke eddying from his lips.

"My question," asked another, "is why didn't they defend themselves?"

"They were taken separately, caught off guard in the middle of the night, early morning, anyway," Zayde supplied. "They was damn well sleeping!"

"Yeah, I see, the pigs couldn't explain that much blood on they hands."

"Not at all."

"What's stopping us? Why don't we do it, take it to the streets, bust em out?" said a volatile Lieutenant, speaking out of frustration, his brow knitted in consternation.

"Hell, for as difficult as it would be to break em out of the Tombs we may as well knock off Fort Knox," Silva resorted to humor, trying to crack the nerve wracking, tension filled air. "Then we can liberate more than enough to ransom the twenty-one and still have money left over to finance our community programs, that will otherwise suffer as we try to raise that obscene amount of bail. We can even have a few bucks left over to party awhile," he said, snapping his fingers, eliciting a modicum of nervous laughter from the remnants of the disheartened band.

"Seriously," Zayd interposed, quelling the laughter, casting a baleful eye over the decimated ranks. "Not that the humor's lost on me, but, under the circumstance it's absolutely unfunny. My brother's in jail, as is Rosemary's cousin, Joan, as are 'r comrades," he said, his forehead creased, eyes deep as twin, infant graves. Though small in stature, no more than a bantamweight, he was recognized by all as embodying the heart of a Zulu warrior. "N now that we've had 'r laugh perhaps y'all want'a get down to business, eh? Ya can be sure that what y'all laughing at, breaking em out'a jail or robbing Fort Knox, is exactly the kind'a jive ass charges they holding the twenty-one on. Conspiracy to blow up the Botanical Gardens', blow up Penn Station 'n Macy's 'n other mindless crap like that that's got em jailed! What I'm saying is, what you saying could land the rest'a us in jail on conspiracy charges if overheard by the wrong persons, dig? Let's scrap the jive 'n get down to what's really brewing."

"Right on," they tinily uttered, one after the other. "Right on!"

"Percival, you ain't said nothing 'n you got as much organizational experience as any of us – more even. What'a you think," Zayde pressed, stroking his wispy Fu-Manchu like beard. "What'a you make'a this?"

Percival shifted uncomfortably and slumped forwards, resting his forearms across his thighs. He hung his head in thought, then slowly replied, "I've been turning this over in my mind since your call earlier t'day, as well as catching the news updates as they've been coming in, 'n the best I can come up with is what Lakey Sako said, following the death of Bobby Kennedy, 'New York's got the most sophisticated politicians in the country.' 'N looking at it from that angle, I agree. 'N, of course, there's the District Attorney's office with all the apparatus of the state's machinery at its disposal to throw at us," he said, sourly. "No one was killed 'n that's significant. The police 'ave been itching for a gun battle with us from jump. The fact that there was none, was a political decision, not a police one. That, in a nutshell, baby, is what we're up against. Furthermore, unlike the Free Huey movement, which galvanized the radical community round a single, charismatic figure, they're making sure no such fate befalls em here in New York. Which is why they didn't jus' bust one Panther but twenty-one, cause it's impossible to make a cause celebre of that many people. One you can personalize, but twenty-one's like a class photo, which has no meaning for anyone outside the class.

"Mostly, though, it's this insane bail, like Bishop said, 'One hundred thousand dollars a head.' They know we don't got that kind'a money, 'n, more than likely, trying to raise it will occupy, if not exhaust all 'r energies or cause us to do something rash, like trying to break em out'a jail or rob Fort Knox," he said. "N they know that at the same time we're gonna ave to put a lot'a 'r programs on hold while tryin' to raise a fraction of the monies, 'n try we must. Where once we were championing the people's cause, striving to serve their needs, we got'a turnaround 'n ask em to help us come up with two million plus 'n, in their suspicious minds, it's gonna sort'a resemble a shake down. Which means we got'a turn to a dwindling white radical community for support. In short, we, the vanguard party, 'r on the defensive 'n got'a go begging. It's somethin' like Robin Hood shakin' down the poor rather than stealin' from the rich to give to the poor. Since you ask'd, I got'a say, depending on who the twenty-one defense team turns out to be, they damn well got us the fuck in check!"

Bishop considered Percival with rueful eyes.

"Thanks for that analysis," said Zayd, dispiritedly.

"I'd say that's a fair assessment of our current predicament," Rasheed Hill interjected. "The question is, how do we proceed?"

"I guess it's time we call Oakland in 'n see what they got'a say," said Zayd.

"That's an idea," agreed Queens Defense Captain, Ali Khan, commander of a near three-hundred-man strong Panther unit, the largest in New York.

Percival grimaced at the thought. "East is east 'n west is west."

"Meaning what?" said Zayd.

"They're Hollywood. We're Broadway. They're cinema. We're theater. We're culture. They're ersatz."

"I don't catch your drift."

"After you've invited Dracula into your home how do you get rid of him."

"Go on?"

"We know each other, we trust each other, but they don't know us and we don't know them. They'll be suspicious of us, fault finding and looking to place blame," Percival explained.

"It wouldn't be my first choice either," Zayd agreed. "Only there's no getting round it. It's international news by now. They got'a know, anyway. They're just waiting for us to call. Besides, they're Central Committee. It's 'r duty 'n their due.

"Which can prove fatal," Percival said.

"How so?"

"We need the community's backing more than ever now 'n introducing a foreign element into 'r ranks can only foster a belief that we're not capable of solving 'r own difficulties. 'N if that's true, how can they trust 'r leadership?"

"Hell with it then," Ali Khan growled. "Let the flood gates open 'n set the dogs of War loose!"

"We need not set them loose," said Percival. "They are loose."

"The pigs' 'ave seen to that," Rasheed stated, matter-of-factly.

***

The arrest of the Panther 21 reverberated throughout the ranks of the New York Panthers like a seismological tremor in the bowels of the earth, as the powers that be had intended. Within days membership fell off sharply. Members vanished and were not heard from again. Percival miraculously managed to hold his small band intact. He rallied them. He contacted each and every one who was not attached to the Panther house. He visited them, cajoled them. He always brought Raschelay along. Her presence alone; her youth, beauty, intelligence and charm, coupled with her devotion, gave heart to the more timorous.

"We've got to decided," she would say, "do we stand back and give into fear? Do we believe less than our southern brothers and sisters who, unarmed, walk into the lion's den day after day singing, 'Before I'll be a slave, I'll be buried in my grave.' Have we less resolve than they do?" she'd prod them, shaming them. "Are their lives less precious than our own?"

"The sister's right, you know," Percival would add. "So long as we hang together, things will work out. It was not only the membership that required reassurance, but the communities in which they operated, as well. This was made even more apparent when, with the increased hardships imposed on them, the provocateurs and infiltrators in the ranks busily planted seeds of division, both among panther members and community dwellers alike. In a heightened state of paranoia Percival recognized that if he had not been picked up in that last sweep it was because he had been earmarked for special consideration – the likes of which God alone might know. To relieve the pressure somewhat, he would alternate between staying at the Panther house, and with Gwen at her Greenwich Village apartment, and would return to the island by alternate routes.

The next few months proved treacherous. Everyone was under suspicion and not to be trusted. Percival found it necessary to carry on as if everything was as it should be. For the benefit of all concerned, he had to appear as if he were unaffected. He insisted on doing the field work, being at every Defense Captain's meeting, and at the mind-numbing repetitious demonstrations outside the lower Manhattan Court House in support of the 21. On more than one occasion, Chairman Bishop demonstrated his ineptitude as city newscasters from various networks stuck microphones in his face and asked glib questions, to which he blurted inane answers. Such as,

"How long y'all think the people gonna tolerate this crap, this frame up against the people's revolutionary party?" Chairman Bishop spoke as if from a pulpit. "The people 'r gonna rise up against this imperialist mad dog empire, this pig power structure, 'n put a stop to all they oinking in the faces'a the people. This is gonna prove, as 'r Minister of Defense, Huey P. Newton, say 'The negation of the negation,' can y'all dig it?"

The phrase, "negation of the negation," that is, was borrowed by Huey Newton, from the American Zen scholar, Allen Watts, but in the mouth of Bishop it sounded trite and out of place.

Nevertheless, it appealed to the anti-intellectuals, the lumpen in the ranks, those who'd come into the party solely because of the gun. They thought it profound. As for the others, they were stretched to the limits of their endurance. They bore up under it even as the party became more and more directionless, with so many of its more capable leaders behind bars. Given the circumstance, it was not surprising that a crude, brutish element – a criminal element encouraged by agent provocateurs – insinuated its way into the top echelons of the New York Panther hierarchy.

Hence, it was something of a relief when the Defense Captains entered the Bed-Stuy branch of the Black Panther Party office in mid-July for their usual weekly meeting, to find themselves face to face with an utter stranger casually ensconced between Zayd and Rosemary, in Chairman Bishop's stead, with a guard on either side of him. Chairman Bishop, wearing a crestfallen, hangdog expression, had been shunted off to the side and set on display as if an object of ridicule. The bewildered Captains, along with their Lieutenants, filed noiselessly into the room. They kept a steady eye on the central figure. When they were all seated Zayd made the necessary introductions,

"I want yall to meet Field Marshall E.J. McKay, he's in from Oakland with his staff ta help us resolve some internal contradictions that ave cropped up since the 21 bust in April; 'n to see if they can shed some light on 'r more pressing problems."

'How the hell's he gonna do that?' Percival wondered, scrutinizing McKay closely.

Field Marshall McKay, or E.J., as he preferred to be called, sat back in his chair like a war lord, one arm slung over the back of the chairs and the other at rest on the thigh of his outstretched, booted leg. All he required was a bandolier. With his open safari jacket and hairless bare chest and paunch, all he needed was a bandolier. He could easily have passed for a "B" rated, mustachioed, Hollywood bandito with a toneless Clint Eastwood voice. His green eyes crinkled at the far corners from constantly squinting against a glaring California sun, which also left him with a golden, honey colored complexion. The Lieutenants to either side of him, stood like leashed dogs while he gave the New York Defense Captains an audience. Half of what they had to say went unheard and the other half was dismissed. The New York Panthers were to be regarded as renegades who had to be whipped into line, and the Panther 21 were superfluous collateral. Thus, the New York Panthers would have lost their organizational integrity by the time they discovered that the leadership from the West Coast was in no position to direct their course. And by then, a number of their members would lay dead on the streets as a result. But for now, they would stay the course charted by the West Coast.

"I'll take it from here," said McKay curtly, bringing Zayd to silence with an imperious wave of the hand. "My people will be visiting each branch 'n scrutinizing operations firsthand to see where theory 'n practice are in conflict," he said, facing the captains with a detached air. "N where we find contradictions we'll eradicate em; too many'a you ave been in bed with the pig, otherwise, twenty-one of your numbers wouldn't be sleeping in jail," he said dryly. "I want your complete cooperation in this process. I want ledgers 'n bank accounts made available to my investigative staff. Yall get to meet the rest of my people Monday night. We're gonna start off with a week of political education classes in Harlem at P.S. 225. Zayd's made all arrangements. I expect to see everybody there without fail. Understood? Make that clear to your cadre. 'n if you're a Panther y'll be there. We won't tolerate slackers," he said.

His face wreathed in a cloud of smoke McKay went on to explain why Bishop had been stripped of his Chairmanship. "The Party has but one Chairman, 'n that's Bobby Seale," he said, coolly. Not that the loss of Bishop's Chairmanship constituted a hardship, but it did undermine the authority of the Captains. They were the ones who had assigned him to the post and to remove him without their consent was a monumental slight.

Ali Khan rose to his feet, cleared his throat, and said with all the confidence of a man with a 300 strong dedicated and disciplined Panther unit at his command, "Excuse me, but do I understand you correctly? You say you have the right to remove our chairman without first consulting us, the captains who assigned him the post?"

"It's my right as a field marshal, yes."

"We captains invited you here to advise, not run the show," Ali Khan said, in rebuke. "I can't speak for the others, but for myself I'll go along only in as much as it fits in with the Ten Point Program!"

Field marshal McKay's face reflected his displeasure at having his authority challenged. "Don't tell me why I'm here. I know precisely why I'm here. I'm here as a field marshal with full authority from Central, committed to investigate the situation at hand and use whatever corrective measures I deem fit. And, brand you a renegade if you don't cooperate. Ten-point program or no ten-point program. Removing Bishop is within my authority. As I've said, the party has but one chairman." McKay eyes swept the faces of those in attendance, finally resting balefully on Ali Khan. "I've come here to find myself in a battle zone strewn with the remnants of some of your best men, 'n the rest of your ranks demoralized. Twenty-one of your members 'r locked up with a two-million-dollar ransom on their heads, while a quarter of the others 'ave fled underground. You're in a near state of collapse 'n you dare question

378

my authority? You're in shambles, 'n barely able to function. You're falling apart. That's why I'm here. I insist on your full co-operation. So yes, you're damn right I have the authority. And let there be no bones about it, if heads must roll, I'll roll 'em. Anything else?" McKay said, challenging Ali Khan to defy him further.

"Which means you can remove any of us captains as you feel fit?"

"With due cause."

The captains looked back and forth among themselves faces stark, their hearts crashing in concert, like cymbals.

"Anything else?"

"Not for now," said Ali Khan, drawing his chair up under him. "Not for now," he repeated as he sat, assessing what had just transpired.

"Carry on with your meeting as if I wasn't here," McKay said. He folded his arms at his chest, leaned back in his seat, staring evasively off.

'Not likely,' Percival thought, uneasy, not able to imagine any other defense captain feeling much different.

After the captains gave their reports, the meeting was adjourned. With his guards, Zayd and Rosemary, McKay was out the door and back on the road to Harlem. The Defense Captains took their cue from McKay and, without further discussion, were back on their way to their respective branches, fearing what was to follow.

On reaching their office, Percival and Silva found numerous members present along with Dr. Osgood and several locals among them.

"Listen up," Percival shouted, calling them to attention. "Things 'r shaking 'n I don't mean the bacon. I want you to hear me good 'n clear! A field marshal from California's in town, coming to straighten out inconsistencies, do a little house cleaning, 'n, I suspect, create some conflict," he said. "Anyway it's only a guess, but we all got'a go to Harlem next week for political indoctrination classes 'n stand muster, as it were. Hang on. We're in for a bumpy ride."

When Percival was through, Dr. Osgood drew him aside. "Take it from one who has run the gauntlet and bears the scars to prove it," she cautioned. "I smell a purge in the making. I think you're right that you are in for a bumpy ride. While I hate to say this, hate to disillusion you, your most trusted allies can quickly turn out to be your worst enemies. Be careful. For a guy already watching his back I suppose it's superfluous to tell you to be careful. But do watch your back. To be on the safe side, quote Marx and Lenin. And if they expect you to be versed in Stalin too, and they might, consider yourself lost."

"Thanks for the tip, Doc."

"It's the least I can do."

***

The assembly hall in Harlem's P.S. 225 was filled to capacity the following week, with Panthers from all across the state, both anxious and expectant. The air that first night crackled with excitement as a massive Chicano woman mounted the auditorium's stage. She was quite impressive, Amazonian. She was dressed in fatigues and combat boots and wore a black beret with a button of a springing Panther between the words "Free Huey."

"Power to the people," she shouted, pumping the air with a clenched fist.

"Panther Power to the revolution!" they responded in deafening tones, fists pummeling the air like angry strikers threatening scabs.

"People are not made for safe havens," she went on, striding back and forth, keeping her audience off balance and hanging on her every word. "An urban guerrilla," she informed them, "initiates acts of terrorism that'll make the government prefer withdrawal from our communities rather than continued occupation." The assembly went wild. She had to insist on their quieting down so she might proceed. Then she said, "The problem with the French Revolution was they didn't lop off enough heads." Again the crowd rose in applause. "You can be sure," she shouted above the hullabaloo, "that plenty heads will roll this time. We'll be knee deep in blood; swimming in blood. There'll be blood to the horse's neck," she promised, rousing her audience to thunderous applause of approval. "Whose gonna survive America?" she chanted.

Spirits soaring, they sang in one voice, "Very few people, no Pigs at all!"

Tuesday was a rehash of the previous night, but that Wednesday she read from Fanon's "The Wretched of the Earth," and called on various others to read. Bishop was deliberately called upon. He read badly, enunciating his words poorly. To his dismay, she coached him from the stage as he staunchly labored over unfamiliar syllables like a tongue-tied schoolboy. The stunned Panther membership whispered back and forth among themselves, embarrassed in front of the California leadership, because they had unknowingly been led by an illiterate, uncouth dolt until Oakland intervened. They had conveniently forgotten that Bishop's chair was solely symbolic—that of an elder brother. With this shameless exhibition, this sideshow, it became clear to Percival what Oakland was up to, what, E.J. McKay, was about. They were establishing the supremacy of the West Coast leadership over the East Coast leadership which, as it turned out, would prove to be at the expense of all concerned.

Without question, the young Chicano Amazonian sister was right, 'heads will roll!'

380

Thursday saw another of McKay's staff singing the praises of Minister of Defense, Huey P. Newton. "He's the baddest motherfucker to ave strapped on boots," proclaimed tall, gangly, Sam Napier, searching the faces of his audience. "Without Huey there'd be no ten point program to relate to," he informed his listeners and, going over the program together point-by-point, they concluded in a crescendo, "'We want land, bread, housing, education, clothing, justice 'n peace.'" The assembly then rose to its feet, rocking the building with applause.

That Friday McKay surmounted the stage in full Panther regalia with the aegis of authority, dressed in field marshal khakis, combat boots and beret, as if all that had gone before had only been a prelude to his presentation. He took the mike from its stem and addressed the crowd. "As y'll now know, Stokely Carmichael's resigned his office as Prime Minister. Like we give a fuck. This cat's been over the edge, so awful in representing 'r position from jump, that, like 'r Minister of Information, Eldridge Cleaver says, 'It's come a year too late.' Since the day of his appointment to the office, that is."

"Right on," the assembly roared, laughing.

"Since then his vile attempts to denounce the Party has made him a cohort of the running dog imperialist," McKay continued. "His lame clinging to black nationalism, pork chop nationalism, like it's a crutch, 'n denouncing us as 'dogmatic.' Then he condemns 'r revolutionary alliances with white radicals. It made him unfit to be Prime Minister of the Black Panther Party. 'N we want'a send a message back to his jive time reactionary little ass which says kiss off, 'n let him know he's become an enemy of the people."

Again there followed a rousing "Right on" from the assembly, causing Percival to cringe.

"Well, I got a tape recorder here, 'n I want y'll to raise your voice on the count of three 'n give Stokely this little message: 'Keep your jive ass, pork chop nationalist self in the reactionary pig sty in which you find yourself or be ready to face revolutionary justice!'" He then asked, "y'll got it?"

"We got it," they echoed him.

"All together on the count of three. One. Two."

And as the assembly raised their voices in condemnation of Stokely, Percival was mute, aghast as he watched ashamed of them all, of himself. His mind whirled at how they had been whipped into a feeding frenzy over the course of the past five days and now, salivating like Pavlov's dogs, Stokely was thrown to them like a piece of raw meat in which to sink their fangs. Moreover, he could not recall having seen such a demonstration of unleashed fury since the bitter days of desegregation in the deep south when racist whites turned out in masses to stop black children from integrating their schools, despite the protective of Federal Marshals. Stokely was often the only one with presence of mind and courage to escort those terrified black kids through howling mobs of rednecks clamoring for blood.

Before he had time to think, Percival was on his feet and as the voices quieted he cried out, "I object!" A dead hush engulfed the auditorium. He could feel their eyes crawling over him like a swarm of flies on rotted meat. He flushed and raced on before losing heart, "While I don't agree with Stokely's more recent position on issues, I still recall his finer hours. I say it does us no good to get caught up in a war of words with him since, dialectically speaking, without him we would not have arrived at this hour; 'n for that we're beholding. At the same time, let's not forget that the Central Committee, knowing Stokely's views, ask'd him to be Prime Minister, hoping to seize his heroism for ourselves," he stated. "This is more their error than Stokely's. That he turned out to be no more than he claimed shouldn't surprise anyone. If we judge Stokely by these terms, we'll soon claim Malcolm X is a reactionary, cause of his religious convictions— 'Religion being the opiate of the masses'— remember? No, what we're doing is beneath us. Stokely's gone— fine. But for us to get caught up in a shouting match with him is bad form. We'll only be sidetracked by airing 'r differences publicly, as Malcolm warned us against, all too often."

"Boo," the assembly jeered, 'boo!'"

"No applause," he said, sarcastically.

"Keep it down – keep it down," McKay intruded, motioning for silence with a raised hand. "Let's cut the brother some slack." He favored Percival with a less than cordial glance. "The brother's entitled to his say; he's not said anything counterrevolutionary. It's sentimental, but not necessarily reactionary. So far anyway." There was a hint of menace in McKay's tone. "You're Percival Jones, aren't you?" he asked, storing Percival's face away in his memory bank for future reference.

"Yes, I am."

"We can't fault the brother's loyalty – it's commendable, the stuff on which we rely – it's just that one should remember who one should remain loyal to." McKay's smile was blatantly misleading.

"Right on," cheered the ravenous crowd. "Right on!"

Percival felt that he had won the battle but lost the war. Now it was a matter of trying to stay the course. Percival folded himself in his chair fully aware of the fact that he had won no friends that evening.

After the meeting, which didn't last much beyond that point, various individuals, including Ali Khan, accosted him on the street and told him, "I liked what you said." Others offered their hand. "You're right, we shouldn't be denouncing one another." It had come as a surprise and Percival thought about it, as Skeeter guided the car through the congested uptown traffic with Raschelay, Sam, Leroy and Priestus, packed together for the journey home. Other members had come in two separate cars: one driven by Silva and the other by a new member, a sister, Nora Delaney. They drove cross-town and swung onto the West Side Highway, going south. It was a sultry night and the distant lights along the shore of the Jersey Palisades was reflected on the dark, turgid face of the Hudson. The car windows were rolled down and they caught a welcomed breeze as the car sped down the highway.

"If you'd not said something back there in defense'a Stokley, I was gonna," said Sam, with false bravado, smiling. "I don't believe those cats. Don't they realize where they at? This is New York City, the Big Apple, not Disneyland. I mean, they act like some misled country cousin, coming to the Apple to teach their poor city cousins how the fuck to farm! These cats 'r way off base, you know?"

"I'm afraid you might ave something there," Percival agreed, not feeling good about any of it.

"They say Huey made McKay Field Marshall cause he brought home the lion's head," Leroy said, admiringly.

"Is that what it is?" Percival said, thoughtfully.

"The what?" Raschelay asked.

"Yeah, you know – he did a cop," Priestus explained.

"Oh, I see." Raschelay was seated up front between Skeeter and Percival.

"Why don't we let em know how you engineered the ambush'a they two cops?" Skeeter asked.

"No," Percival insisted, holding them to their oath of silence. "That was not to ave been mentioned again but locked away to decay. I have no wish to play into their hands. I refuse to play the game. On this I stand firm."

"Is there any particular reason why not?" Priestus wanted to know.

"Because there 'r some things which 'r jus' not meant to be made public."

"I understand," said Raschelay.

Unable to believe his ears, Sam couldn't restrain himself. "Ya – you," he started, eyes blinking, nostrils flared, his eyes burning with unbidden tears. "H – how? I can't believe it – I knew you'd done it – Oh, I knew. kn-knew it, but didn't, c-couldn't think. I mean, why h-her 'n not me?" he said, resentfully. "Ya chose her over me. n y-you two, Skeeter n Priestus, y-yall in on it t-too, d-don't deny it," his voice was strangled. "All in on it, but me." He felt cheated, diminished in their eyes and, therefore, humiliated. "I-I d-don't get it. I-I jus' d-don't!"

"It's not what you think," Percival barked, facing Sam over his shoulder in the back of the car.

"Not what I think?" Sam yelped. "Now you want'a tell me what I think."

"It was us – Hot damn," Leroy cried exultantly, face alight.

"This goes no further than this car," Percival demanded, giving Skeeter a withering glance. "Damn," Skeeter cursed, annoyed with himself for having carelessly opened his mouth.

"Not a word from me. I swear," Leroy promised, "I'm jus' glad it was us who did it – Wow!"

"Hear me?" Percival asked Sam.

"I'm not deaf, am I?"

"I'll make it up to you, bro."

"I can't believe you would include her 'n leave me out. Me, your own brother. I can't believe it."

"This is not the time."

"Of course not. It's never the time with you."

"I wasn't in on it either," Leroy said, sheepishly.

"Will you let it go?"

"Yeah, okay man, it's gone," Sam said, sullenly, folding his arms across his chest and lowering his face, scowling.

Percival gazed out the window at the rolling dark river as they rode along in funereal silence.

***

The next day at the Defense Captains meeting while everybody was congratulating themselves on how well the week's political orientation had gone, Percival, on the other hand, was deciding to up the ante, drop the other shoe and tell McKay that he was in contact with the FBI, let the chips fall where they may. When called upon to give his report, he began by saying, "I think it well you know upfront that I've been in contact with the FBI over the past seven months."

McKay's jaw clenched, his eyes narrowed, and he tugged at his earlobe, digesting the announcement uneasily. His lips receded, exposing his teeth so that his face had the hideous look of a death skull. "Anyone know anything 'bout this?" he asked, sharply.

"We all know," said Zayd unhesitatingly. "Lumumba, Bishop 'n I told him to take the pig's money 'n put it to revolutionary use."

"Go on," said McKay, nostrils flaring.

"That's it. I jus' thought you should know," Percival said to McKay's displeasure.

"This has to be looked into," said McKay, wryly. "It presents us with a new set of difficulties."

"The brother's always been up front," Zayd came to Percival's defense. "He's always included any encounters he's had in his weekly report. Ask anyone, they'll tell you."

"That's right," the other defense captains concurred, nodding their heads.

"Jones has been up front every step of the way," Ali Khan said, forthrightly. "He's a righteous brother!"

"That may well be, but until I find out for myself, the brother's under suspicion; though he'll continue to function in his capacity as Defense Captain, or until informed otherwise."

"As you say." Zayd shrugged.

"If I'm correct, we're all under suspicion," said Percival, defiantly. "Otherwise there'd be no need for your presence here."

"R you trying to sow dissension here?" McKay eyed him, with a mixture of threat and appeal.

"There's no dissension here. I'm jus' trying to set the record straight. Correct me if I'm wrong, but isn't it Huey's policy to rip off the man to further 'r advantage?"

"I don't need to be reminded of our Minister of Defenses policies," McKay said, irately, lips compressed, his brows drawn tight.

The Defense Captains eyes looked from one to the other as if observing a fencing match.

"As I said, I jus' want'a set the record straight."

"I'll bear that in mind."

"Please do."

"You're boxing yourself into a corner bit by bit," Silva cautioned Percival on the return drive. "You're leaving yourself exposed."

"Something stinks, man, can't you smell it? I don't know who Huey is, all's I know is I don't trust McKay worth a fuck. He's not here for New York's benefit you can be sure'a that, he's here for Oakland."

"How you figure?"

"It's like this. This cat's in command 'n he don't know shit 'bout 'r fucking situation – now how the hell's that possible? McKay seems to be operating under the assumption, 'If you've seen one ghetto you've seen 'em all,' like Spiro Agnew said. You catch what he said 'bout Harlem having the largest black population nationwide but the least members in the party for its size?"

"So?"

"Hell, man, come on, Harlem's seen it all – seen it come 'n seen it go. Harlem's got history, man. It's got style 'n creates style, 'n is not easily influenced by a style not of its own design. Harlem's a trendsetter, the pacemaker, not the other way round. What I'm saying is, the man knows nothing 'bout New York 'n far less 'bout Harlem. Let's face it, bro, there 'r probably more blacks on the corner of 145th. Street 'n Lenox Avenue than there 'r in alla Oakland," he spat.

"Probably."

"I rest my case."

"If all that's so, where does that leave us?" Silva asked. "What about all that we've been struggling for; all that we've put our time and energy into? Put our lives on the line for? What about the revolution?"

"I'm gonna tell you. The Panther 21 bust flattened us. Until they're released, 'n that's not gonna be anytime soon, everything else is fronting."

"You think McKay and his staff are just an encumbrance?"

"That, 'n the only reason left to stay in the party is to keep faith with the 21."

"What about Huey?"

"What about him? I don't know Huey, do you?"

"No, I can't say I do."

"But we do know the 21."

"I don't know who else will agree with you but, no doubt, your point is valid."

Silva drew up to the curb outside the branch office. A noisy spillover of revelers from the The 2nd. Step, stood on the corner talking and catching the afternoon sun. They saluted sloppily and shouted, "Power," as Percival and Silva emerged from the car. Percival returned the salutation and continued toward the office, but Silva hung back to say "hello."

Trying the latch, Percival found the door locked and, despite the fact that the lights were on inside, he could see little else beyond his own reflection in the doorway window and that of the street at his back.

"What's up?" Silva asked, coming up behind him.

"Door's locked."

"It's not like Raschelay to leave her post unattended."

"Maybe an emergency came up."

"I don't know," Silva said, hesitantly, "these guys just finished telling me there was a ruckus earlier inside, but they say they didn't check it out for fear they'd see something they wasn't suppose to. Then they said Sam split in a heat soon after. One said he tried to look in after Sam cut, but the door was locked and he couldn't see much."

"Ya got your keys?"

Silva retrieved his keys and opened the door. No sooner had they entered the office than their eyes were assailed by the disheveled state in which they found the room. Chairs were tossed, tables askew, a typewriter lay on its side on the floor, the telephone dangled off its hook, papers were scattered about and, in the center of it all, lay a woman's shoe.

Percival sucked his breath in sharply, fearing the worst. "What the hell happened here?"

"I think I'd rather not know," Silva replied.

Percival called out, heart pulsing, "Raschelay, it's me 'n Silva, you here?"

Then as if in response to his appeal, a faint whimper came from the direction of the toilet in the far corner of the room. Percival and Silva caught each other's eye. They hastened to the back and found Raschelay in the toilet, face down and squeezed between toilet and wall. She lay helplessly, crying soundlessly, blood seeping down her exposed thighs.

"Ah, geez," Percival emitted, kneeling beside her.

The toilet was too small for three people, so Silva stood awkwardly in the doorway, peering over Percival's shoulder. "Jesus God," he swore.

"Ra-Raschelay," Percival stammered, both ashamed and repulsed by the brutal deflowering of this wonderful child; this beautiful black rose. He wanted to look away, close his eyes, and he did as much as was possible as he gently pulled her skirt over her plump buttocks and slim, boyish hips. At the same time, he rolled her over, raised her slightly unwedging her, and cradled her in his arms. Her blouse was torn open, bra straps broken, her breasts tumbled free. Her chestnut brown eyes were two raw, unseeing tear-filled wounds; her lips bloodless, bruised and slack. She trembled all over, whimpering, her voice fragile, like crystal breaking. A haunting picture of a broken angel.

"What happened?" Percival calmly asked. "Where's Sam?"

Her breath came short and raspy, each drawn with considerable difficulty. "I fought him," she moaned. "I-I fought h-him." She was, no doubt, in shock.

"I know you did."

"H-he hurt me. He h-hurt me bad." A fresh stream of tears cascaded down her coffee colored cheeks to her trembling lips. "Why?" Percival. W-why?" she pleaded, looking him in the face with luminous eyes, spilling tears.

"Was it Sam who did this to you?" Percival swallowed hard.

She covered her mouth with her hand and lowered her eyes. "H-he wa-wanted to k-know ab-about the ambush n-n I w-wouldn't ta-talk about it n h-he w-went c-cr-crazy." A tidal wave of memory washed over her in a flood and she collapsed in a swoon.

"Shhh," Percival comforted her, folding her against his chest. "It's all over now. it's all over." He braced his back against the toilet bowl, in a cold sweat, trying to fight back tears of rage to no avail.

Silva could not keep from crying either.

Percival picked her up. She was light but solid, earthy and voluptuous. His nostrils filled with a cloying, musty after smell of sex. A cold terror rent his heart as he handed her to Silva. She lay inertly in his arms, sobbing quietly.

Percival took off his shirt and covered her bare breasts. "Get her home," he said, standing in his undershirt. "I'll call Doctor Osgood 'n ave her meet you there."

"What are you going to do?"

"I'm gonna find Sam 'n place him under house arrest for the moment."

"You better notify McKay while you're at it."

"Yes, you're probably right."

"You should also get Skeeter and Preistus to back your play."

"Shall do. Meantime get her home. See to her welfare. Tell her mother, I'm doing all I can from this end. Tell her, tell her – No, it'd be best coming from me."

A number of the men from the street had entered the office after Percival and Silva and, as Silva carried Raschelay out, they stood aside to make room.

"Can we help?" they asked, looking hopelessly deficient.

"When you damn well might ave done something you were too damn scared you'd see something you wasn't suppose to," Percival scolded them. "Now that there's nothing for you to help with, your all so fucking eager – Go to Hell. Go on, get out'a here! Beat it! I've things to do." They scurried out the door like tossed leaves in a storm.

He watched solemnly from the doorway as they retreated to their corner haunt under the neon sign. Silva set a sobbing, semi-conscious Raschelay in the front passenger seat of his car, and buckled her in while one of the men, who had rushed forward held the car door. When Silva drove off Percival flung the office door shut and took one more look at the tossed room. 'She must'a put up one hell of 'a fight,' he thought, shaking his head sadly.

He picked the phone up from the floor. He listened for a dial tone, then called Dr. Osgood's clinic. "She's busy," the receptionist said when Percival asked to speak to the doctor.

"Tell her it's Percival Jones, will you? It's 'n emergency."

In a moment Dr. Osgood was on the line. "Percival, how may I help you?'

"It's Raschelay Doctor, she's been violated. She's at home. She can use some medical attention."

"Violated, how?"

"I don't know how to say over a tapped line –"

"Don't! I'll be right there."

"I hope to see you there." Then he called the house and Leroy answered. "Leroy, I want you to get down to the office right away 'n bring Skeeter 'n Priestus if they're there with you, okay?"

"They're here."

"Good. Tell em I'll need some muscle."

"I'll tell em."

Percival waited in front of the office. Leroy, Skeeter and Priestus rounded the corner.

"What gives?" Skeeter asked.

Percival addressed himself to Leroy. "I want you to stay 'n watch the office. Clean up the mess, 'n call the others 'n ave em here pronto, dig?"

"Got ya."

"Skeeter, Priestus," Percival gestured with a wave of the hand, "come with me."

They fell into step. Along the way he explained the situation, omitting the gory details, and informed them of his suspicions. "It all points ta Sam."

"Raped Raschelay?" Skeeter asked, incredulously. "Raped her? You joking?"

"Ya sure?" Priestus prodded.

"Jus' as sure as can be without a corroborating witness."

"Did Raschelay identify him?"

"Indirectly."

"What we gonna do with him?"

"That's to be decided. Right now we're gonna put him under house arrest."

"Ya know where he is, I guess?"

"At 'r mother's place, most likely."

"In the projects?"

"Where else."

Skeeter and Priestus grew quiet. No one noticed the squalor or the people they encountered in route. When they reached the projects they took the elevator and got off on the 5th. floor. "Stay here," Percival said, "while I go collect Sam."

They stayed readily behind.

Percival knocked at the apartment door gingerly at first, then more insistently. The door was finally opened the width of the chain lock. His mother peered out through the crack.

"Ta what do we owe the honor?" she asked peevishly.

"Come on, ma, don't be like that."

"Don't be like what? I can't remember the las time I saw you at this door."

"I know you don't approve of what I'm doing, so I've been avoiding the argument."

"What brings you now?"

"I'm looking for Sam. Have ya seen him?"

"N if I ave?"

"I need to find out something from him."

"He swept in a while ago face all scratched up 'n hardly say boo, looking like something the cat drag in. When I ask, 'What got hold'a you,' he tell me some foolishness 'bout tripping in a bush."

"I jus' bet." Percival snorted.

"Something wrong?"

"Not that I know of."

"Something's wrong all right, that's the mood he come in when something's wrong. I know, he my youngest. A mother's got a special bond to her las born. N you coming in behind looking for him ain't good."

"There's nothing wrong I know of, Ma. Maybe if you let me in I can find out."

She apologized, then opened the door. He went straight to Sam's room and entered unannounced. Sam raised his head off the pillow. "Oh, it's you," he said, then rolled over and faced the wall. "Close the door on your way out will you?"

"Get up, man. Let's go!"

"I ain't going nowhere with you," Sam said in a truculent tone of voice. "I quit!"

"If only it were that easy, pal. You committed a terrible crime, a cardinal offense 'n left me holding the bag."

"I told you I'm not going."

"Look, fool, get your ass up out'a that fucking bed 'n don't make me sweat any more than I got'a," Percival said, jabbing Sam in the back with the fingers of his hand.

"What you gonna do, beat me up?" Sam laughed, his body twitching.

"That's too easy. No, man, I'll walk outta this room 'n tell ma why I'm here 'n jus' exactly how you got your face all scratched up."

"I didn't mean it," Sam yelped, turning and rising on his elbows with a start, his eyes fixed steadfastly on Percival's. "I don't know what t-took over of me – I must'a jus' gone off, I felt I couldn't face Raschelay after las night I-I felt useless."

"I tried to tell you it wasn't what you thought," Percival raised his voice. "I needed you for other things. If, for instance, something had gone wrong I'd need someone outside I could count on. Someone who could'a carried on."

"Why didn't you say so?"

"Why didn't you trust me?"

"I-Is she gonna be okay?"

"Raschelay you mean? You raped her! Brutalized her! Stole her right of choice from her 'n now you ask is she gonna be okay? Come on, man," Percival insisted, voice cracking. "I don't got all day."

"No, man, wait, don't. It ain't right, man. It ain't right. I'm your brother."

"No one's denying that. But Raschelay's a kind'a sister too 'n, for that, there's no one I want'a hurt as much as I want'a hurt you now. But cause you're my brother I got'a take ma 'n Lois into account. I've no wish to hurt Ma any more than need be. Let's try to handle this end of it without saying more than we have too, huh? Let me tell you, man, I love that girl – love her like I love Lois, you dig? 'N I love Tzi like I love my son, Malek, but I've always loved you like you were Cain 'n I was Able or I was Cain 'n you was Able. It's bothersome cause I do so want'a love you but, to tell the truth, I could kill you right now with my own two hands, but for the mother between us. Silva 'n I found Raschelay 'n what you did to her was so base; so loathsome; so foul," he snarled. "N if I didn't bring a gun with me it's cause I was afraid I'd use it on you right here in this house under Mama's roof, know what I'm saying? Now get the fuck up 'n let's go!"

Sam gained his feet with some difficulty, wiping his eyes with the back of his hand. "What you gonna do to me?"

Percival sighed, clenching clammy fists. "Don't make me think about it."

"Do you know?"

"All's I know is we're not gonna do what I'd like to do to you, right now."

"N w-what's that?"

"I'd rather not say."

"Is everybody else mad at me t-too?"

"Everybody else don't know yet."

"R ya gon'a tell em?"

"What the hell do you think?"

"Does everybody have ta know?"

"The Panther membership must, yeah."

"Ya not gon'a tell Lois 'n Ma, 'r ya?"

"Not if I can help it."

"Ya not gonna let em hurt me 'r you? I'm still your little brother, d-don't forget. remember how you used to look out for me 'n Lois when we was jus' kids. I r-really didn't mean it you got'a believe me. I don't know what g-got into me–"

Percival studied Sam's face briefly; it had been savagely raked, the flesh peeled back and seeping blood. "I see she put up a hell of a struggle."

"She's a she devil," Sam declared, covering his face with both hands, then let out a muffled, strangled gasp of uncontrollable sorrow. "I'm so ashamed of myself. I-I don't want to be seen. to show myself."

"Come on, man, wipe those eyes. We got'a get past Ma without her suspecting more than she does already."

"OK, ok," Sam sniffled, trying to brush tears from his cheeks. "You think they'll want'a k-kill me?" he asked, the life having left his voice. "I t-think that's what I'd want'a d-do."

"I don't know what everybody's gonna want," said Percival. "I only know I wish it hadn't happened." He took Sam by the arm and proceeded to accompany him as would a bouncer escort an undesirable out the door.

"Where y'll off to?" Hattie called after them from the kitchen on their way out.

"We got unfinished business to settle," Percival said.

"Y'all welcome to stay for dinner. Lois'll be home shortly."

"Another time, Ma, we're in a rush," Percival answered. "We got people waiting."

"Everything's okay, ain't it?"

"Sure, Ma, sure," said Sam feebly, without conviction.

"Give Lois my regards," Percival added, as he rushed Sam out the door ahead of him and closed it tightly at his back, his face sweaty, heart racing.

"Keep going!" He prodded a reluctant Sam along.

Skeeter and Priestus started toward them, passing a tenant on his way out.

At first sight of the two, Sam drew back with a sharp hiss of breath. He wore a fearful, hunted look on his surly face and, seeking an escape route, his bloodshot eyes roved furtively about. Percival laid a hand on Sam's shoulder and he wince, wilting like a spent flower.

"H-Hi f-f-fellas," Sam said, looking timidly from one to the other as they closed in on him.

"If Percival wasn't your brother –" Skeeter started with raised fist but broke off in disgust. He and Priestus stood on either side of Sam, their hearts bitter. They escorted him back to the office with Percival following behind.

"I'm going to talk to Raschelay's mother. Hopefully, there'll be news of some sort by now." Percival got his gun and stuck it in his boot. "I want y'll to keep an eye on him," he instructed. "If he tries anything, restrain him. Forcibly, if need be."

"Want me to drive you?" Skeeter asked.

"No. It'll be best if you stay 'n help keep an eye on 'r prisoner here."

"If you say."

It was perfectly obvious that no one felt comfortable being saddled with such odious an undertaking.

"Besides," said Percival, "the walk'll do me good. I can use the time to clear my head."

To the contrary, the walk did little to resolve his misgivings. In fact, by the time he finally reached his destination, little if anything had been resolved. Thus encumbered, he dragged himself up the stairs, to the second floor landing.

He knocked at the door. Ruth was quick to respond. He was hardly through the door before she accosted him,

"If you're here, I guess it's because you've taken Sam?"

"We got him, yes," Percival said grimly, lips tight. "How is she?"

"Dr. Osgood's still with her."

"She'll be okay, won't she?"

"Only time will tell," said Ruth, scrutinizing him.

Percival was nervous, uneasy. "I see."

"You know she wasn't deserving of this, Percival. She didn't deserve this!" She emitted a long, low and sad moan, "My chile!" She wagged her head, sorrowfully. "I tell you this much, Percival Jones, if her father wasn't in jail right now for manslaughter he'd be headed there tonight for murder, you understand me?"

He blanched. "I do. I understand." He felt hot tears at the back of his eyes. "This is not going to go unpunished, take my word for it. Sam will pay for this!"

"See to it he does."

"You've got my word on it."

"You care to wait for Dr. Osgood?"

"If you don't mind."

They stepped into the living room where Silva sat on the couch with a cup of coffee in his hand. Percival asked if he could use the phone?

"Help yourself." Ruth waved a hand toward a table on which the telephone sat next to a vinyl covered armchair. He sat on the arm of the chair and dialed.

"May I speak to E.J. McKay, please? It's Percival Jones calling."

"Speaking," said the voice on the other end.

"I've a situation on my hands," Percival said tremulously.

"That is?" McKay eventually responded.

"The only thing it might be advisable for me to say under the circumstance is it's the rape of one member by another."

393

There was no response for a long minute. "If you're half 'a who they tell me you 'r, you'll handle it, won't you?"

"I'm not a field marshal, you 'r."

"Jus' keep that in mind no matter the shit!"

"It's why I called, bro," said Percival, bristling.

"Then deal with it," McKay snapped, and hung up.

Percival held the phone for a moment before putting it back in its cradle. If the truth be known he had no idea what to do. He had never faced such a crisis of conscience before. Never been of two minds on any one score before. Never! This was growing ugly. He had to admit, if only to himself, that he was out of his depth. This would be the most crucial judgment of his life.

He leaned forward to confer with Silva. "I jus' had McKay on the line."

"So I figured. What he say?"

"Not much. He wants me to handle it."

"How so?"

"He wouldn't say."

"That could only mean kill him."

"What else?"

"Damn!"

Ruth stood, distracted, waiting by the bedroom door. Her seven-year-old daughter tugged at her skirt, wanting attention. "Mama," she asked, "what's wrong with Rasch?"

"Not now," Ruth coaxed. "Be a good girl and go play with your sister in your room."

When Dr. Osgood finally emerged, Ruth fastened herself to her like a burr. "How is my child?" she implored. "Will she be ok?" She fired off a dozen more questions in quick succession. Silva stood and Percival started to rise as she and Dr. Osgood conferred. Afterwards, Ruth went in the bedroom to hold her ailing child's hand.

Dr. Osgood was an extraordinary woman whose waters ran to sea, with whom he could confer. "I guess you wish to be filled in?" she said to Percival.

"If you don't mind."

"She's been sedated. I've done as much as possible for the moment. There's been extreme trauma to her genital area. She's suffered multiple contusions. It's more the psychological aspect of it which concerns me now. But I have a psychiatrist friend who I'm certain can be of help. I assure you, we'll get her through this."

Percival wrung her hand. "That's good to know."

"Goodbye," she said, "I have other patients to see."

He saw her to the door. "Doctor," he asked, "I can use some advice."

"If it's what I think it is, I've none to offer."

"Doctor, people will want'a see Sam killed," he said gloomily, as if she were his last hope.

Dr. Osgood fixed him in her gaze. "I've just left the bedside of one of the most lovely girl I've ever known. I feel toward her as one of my own. When I think of what Sam did to her, I realize that people are killed for far less, all the time."

She walked off and left him teetering in the doorway. He turned inside as she descended the stairs. He summoned Silva and they returned to the office under cover of a darkling sky.

***

The membership had assembled and was waiting for Percival and Silva to arrive. Some stood. Some sat. Some smoked. Some engaged in small talk. The mood was such that it did not invite conversation. The pressure was on, the atmosphere bleak. A lone, slowly revolving, ceiling fan pushed the languid air around. Every so often someone would cast Sam a secretive, though deprecatory glance. He had been bound and left seated on the floor against the wall in the back of the room.

Face contorted in anguish, Percival burst in through the front door, looking like a man possessed by devils. Then Silva joined him and the others in the office.

They gathered round a makeshift conference table. The prisoner was then brought before the ad hoc revolutionary tribunal. Sam's face was puffy with flecks of dried blood, his tired eyes, swollen. He was terrified, too afraid to cry out or to whom he might appeal. His comrades wished to disown him. Percival, who should have presided as counsel head opposite him, could not stomach the sight of him and chose to sit alongside with other members, to avoid eye contact. Indeed, Sam was on his own. He sighed, lowered his eyes in defeat, and gazed helplessly at his bound wrists.

Skeeter and Priestus stood guard on either side of him.

Not knowing where any of this might lead, Percival was no less afraid than Sam. Thus, divided in himself, he reluctantly opened procedures. "I guess everybody knows by now what this is about? Anyway, let me acquaint you with the facts. Simply put, Sam raped Raschelay. These proceedings 'r no more than exploratory," he explained, his head aching behind sore eyes. "No decision will necessarily be made based on anything we discuss, but I want your honest feedback. It could prove crucial to making a right decision rather than a wrong one. The question on the table is how is Sam to be punished?

Before we proceed," he said wearily, addressing his clasped hands atop the desk, "if at any time, Sam, you have something to say for yourself, speak up, understood?"

"Y-Yes," Sam murmured, tonelessly.

"Did you do this or not?" Percival asked, refusing to look at him.

Sam gave no reply, seeming not to have heard the question.

"Well, did you?"

"I-I d-did; I told you I did. By God I swear, I didn't mean to. What more can I say?"

Sam raised his bound hands in appeal. "I swear to God to you, I didn't mean it," he lamented, then lowered his eyes, tears sliding along the side of his nose.

Percival deferred to Silva. "I suppose if you've something to say you should go first since, we're the ones to ave found her."

"This won't be easy," Silva began slowly, gathering his thoughts. "I don't dislike Sam enough for this to be easy. I only wish I disliked him more, so I could seek vengeance. But, no, I don't dislike him, so I must compromise and seek justice. Ironically, in this instance it looks as if vengeance and justice are not mutually exclusive, but very much alike. I hate it! But I love Raschelay," he said hoarsely. "We all do, including Sam I suspect. And that's the rub. As Percival said, we found her and let me tell you," he fumbled, searching for the right words, "I felt ashamed at finding her so cruelly mishandled: her body stuffed like rubbish between a smelly ole toilet and a dank wall. Before that, she was always so pleasurable to be around. But there, in that toilet, I found myself ashamed of my sexuality; my manhood: One, because I had not been there to protect her; and two, because I was revolted by what can become of passion gone blindly awry. I just wanted to hide my face and cry as did the biblical Adam when he found himself naked before God. But now that I've had a little time to reflect, I know that as revolutionaries we have little choice. In other words, we have no means of incarcerating someone for an extended period and, therefore, have few options available to us. Historically speaking, Sam would be taken out and summarily shot. Then again, like the rest of you, I didn't join the Panther Party for this," he waved a hand dismissively, in pained annoyance. "It was the last thing on my mind. I joined the party, like all of us, to contribute to the welfare of our community; to help our black brothers and sisters. Nevertheless, this must be dealt with; this too is our duty, sadly enough. It's part of our responsibility to protect our own and discipline our own, to meter out justice when the occasion arises. The only other choice available to us is to hand Sam over to the police, the courts, which is not a choice at all. Even if we could turn it over to the justice system, with their

396

cultural attitudes towards rape – in such a male dominated, chauvinist society as this –, there is, indeed, small likelihood that justice would be done."

Not a word was uttered as the seriousness of the offense sunk in, and punishment proposed, digested. No one wished to speak; to break the slender thread of silence. In short, no one wanted to compromise themselves. Then Skeeter broke the spell of silence. "If this was the south 'n it had been a white chick, he would'a already been taken out 'n lynched!"

"Ain't that the truth," someone said.

"But," Leroy reminded them, "if it was a black girl like Raschelay, they'd'a ave a shotgun wedding instead."

"That doesn't cut it," Percival said, brusquely, quelling the titters. "'N in any event, that's not an option in this case."

Wardell, who seldom ventured an opinion, spoke out to everyone's' surprise, "I know if Big/black was here he'd ice Sam in a minute; snap his neck like'a used matchstick. I know we all know how he felt 'bout Raschelay. Like we all feel 'bout her. She's every woman we've ever loved. Anyway, Skeeter's right, if this be the south 'n she was white, Sam'd swing from an ole tree limb."

"I understand what's being asked of me, don't think I don't," said Percival dryly. "But you may as well ask me to kill my own mother because, in the end, that's what I'll be doing," he said, defensively.

"Sam's your brother, true, but you're telling us cause y'all share a mother he should go unpunished?" said a guy who Percival suspected of being an agent provocateur. "Uh-uh, I don't see it that way. He's the one won the lottery 'n the prize is a bullet to the backa his motherfucking skull!"

"N you'll be willing to pull the trigger, no doubt," Percival hurled back, glowering at him?

"Wouldn't you?" he said, returning Percival's scowl.

"That's what I thought," said Percival smugly, turning away. "I need to know what justice demands, not vengeance," he boomed. "It's Raschelay's place to seek vengeance. It's for her mother to want vengeance. It's for us to determine justice!"

"What if, as Silva say, in this instance, they're one n the same?'" said the provocateur. "Seems to me you got one of two choices."

"Which are?'

"Cut off his fucking dick, lynch him, or off him yourself!"

Percival started from his seat. "What kind'a fucking obscene proposal is that?"

"N why not? It's what justice demands."

"Justice?"

"I-I'd rather be d-dead," Sam screamed.

"You better watch what you wish for," Silva retorted.

Sam's knees buckled and Priestus helped him recover his balance.

A torturous silence followed much like that of spectators before the guillotine drops. If many did not offer an opinion it was because the gravity of the situation was such that they feared the consequences of making a rash decision. No matter Sam's transgressions, he was, nevertheless, one of them. Indeed, Percival had never seen them so closed mouthed on any subject, so reticent. No doubt, if released from their charge they would scramble over one another to the door. Not that he could fault them. After all, no one wished to have their soul besotted with the stain of Cain.

"Since when 'r we the K-K-K?" asked Nora Delaney, reproachfully, startling them out of their hypnotic silence. Having captured their attention, she pressed on. "You should hear yourselves. Since when have their tactics served as 'r guiding principles? Let me know now, so I can quit! I know how unspeakably foul an act Sam is accused of committing. My heart goes out ta Raschelay 'n I'm sure I speak for my other sisters here as well." She inclined her head in the direction of two women seated across from her. "But if we put 'r hands to Sam's death what becomes of us as a group? On this score, Leroy's right, a shot gun wedding's more appropriate than a hangman's noose. There 'r enough human catastrophes out there already, without my proposing yet another. No, I simply oppose kissing my black brother as did Judas kiss his Jewish one. Maybe this is not exactly the right allegory but I think y'all catch my drift. Ask me to blow up the 20th. precinct 'n I'm your gal; ask me to hijack the Staten Island Ferry to Cuba 'n I'm on board. But killing Sam? Uh-uh, I'm sorry, this must be what they call men's' business cause, baby, I can't see the point of it 'n I don't want'a be any part of it!"

Nora pushed back her chair, stood, and gazed on the faces of those nearby, then turned and walked out. The two other Panther women hastened to catch up to her, causing Percival much distress. He glanced at Leroy, curious to see what he would do. Leroy, however, had evidently decided, no matter the cost, to stick with the men.

The men grew morosely silent, duly chastened by the women's departure.

"There's nothing more we can accomplish here t'night," Percival said, shortly. "Anyway, I'm tired as sin 'n can use some sleep. Let's call it a day, huh? We'll lock Sam in the cellar up at the house for now, 'n put a guard on him," he said wearily.

The office quickly emptied out onto the noisy street. Silva locked the office door. While everyone else went their separate ways those who lived in the Panther house surrounded the prisoner and climbed the hill to the isolated, dark residence at the top. There, Leroy switched on the lights, and the prisoner was escorted to the cellar.

"Percival," Sam pleaded over his shoulder, as he was being forced down the cellar steps. "Percival," he repeated with greater urgency as the door was closed and locked.

Having had his fill for one day, Percival turned a deaf ear to Sam's plea. It had been a long day. It had been a long and difficult day. He sighed with despair, turned and went off to bed. He stumbled over his bedroom tripwire, forgetting it was there, and plunged headlong into bed fully clothed, staring up at the darkened ceiling as if into a void – which, he felt certain, his life was becoming or, as Silva had earlier warned, "You're boxing yourself into a corner." His eyes drooped shut and he succumbed to an unrewarding, fitful sleep. He woke up abruptly, and sat upright, reaching for his gun. His heart raced at a gallop and a cold sweat broke out on his brow. His body became covered in sweat, distilled from ice. The mattress under him was damp. He looked anxiously about. For a moment he wasn't quite sure where he was. In a panic, thinking Sam had been taken out and executed, he climbed out of bed, stepped over the trip wire and crossed the living room to the lighted corridor where a guard sat in front of the cellar door, half asleep.

"Is he down there?" Percival asked.

"Yes, of course."

So how goes it?"

"Okay so far, I guess."

"I'm sorry, man, but your name escapes me for the moment."

"It's Luther Olds."

"Of course. Luther, would you open the door, I'd like to see my brother."

"The prisoner?"

"Him too," said Percival, a moment of humor easing his fears.

Luther unlocked the cellar door and Percival descended into its dimly lighted bowels; the steps creaking under his weight. It was not much larger than a cramped, musty dungeon with rodents nesting in its rafters. Its two small windows were no bigger than gun slits. It was, for all intents and purposes, inescapable.

Sam was seated on the edge of a cot like a lost kid on a street corner, his face cupped in his hands. He looked up slowly, his eyes red-rimmed from sleeplessness and tears. "If it ain't my big brother," he scoffed, then sank back with a groan, clasping his head.

"I thought you might be up. I can't much sleep myself. Ya got us in one hell of a spot, bro," said Percival, pacing back and forth.

"Easy enough for you to say. You're not the one everybody wants to see d-dead."

"Leroy doesn't, Nora doesn't, 'n I sure as hell don't!"

"That's mighty white'a y'all too."

"That was damn well uncalled for," Percival snapped back.

"Well I hope y'all get your way."

"Something I want'a ask you, something been bothering me all night," said Percival, an expression of bewilderment on his soulful face. "What'a you mean you didn't know what come over you? That you didn't mean it? How's that possible, man?"

Sam was silent for a moment. "Jus' what I say. All's I know is w-what I said," he said irritably. "At first I was jus' talking to her, kidding her, sorta, you know? Jus' trying to get some digs in for las night 'n feeling left out." He shrugged, wearing the smile of an imbecile. "Then I ask her 'bout that night, 'n she put me off like I'm some fucking junior flip or something, telling me to fucking ask you," he flared, irate. "Then we get to arguing real bad, 'n I got mad – mad not in my head but in my heart, in my soul. Then she became everything I ever hated, 'n I snapped, I broke, I went over the edge – I guess I r-raped her. I mean, I knew, but I didn't want'a believe it. I didn't believe it. That is until you come looking for me. Till then it was somebody else's dream I was trying to waken out of. Cause if I'd done it, I'd lost control, lost control when all I really w-wanted was for her to yield, t-to give me my propers, like Aretha say, you know?" he said in a torrent. "I g-got no pleasure out'a it, if that's what you asking," he said, guiltily. "When I think a-about it, I d-did no more than half these c-cats wanted to do, including Silva," he spat.

"I wouldn't go that route if I was you," said Percival, sternly. "That's a line of defense you don't wanta pursue."

"I'm n-not fucking crazy, but this thing's gotten me crazy c-cause I sure as hell can't recall doing it. M-maybe I went temporarily out'a my mind, t-that's possible, ain't it?" Sam said, clasping Percival's arm and looking beseechingly into his brothers sad eyes. "I l-lost my head, but I d-don't want'a l-lose my life," he wailed. "I d-don't wanta die. I beg you, p-please, d-don't let em d-do it!" Tears glittered in his eyes. "I'll do anything. I'm t-too young t-to die."

Percival removed his arm from Sam's grasp. "For both of us, for all of us, I hope there's some other way. I swear to God I do!" He mounted the stairs and departed hastily. The cellar door was locked again behind him.

***

Later that morning Percival went to the office. It was a glorious Sunday morning. The streets were deserted, except for the people going to church. The Saturday night revelers were home sleeping it off. The church would be filled, no doubt, with a few husbands roused from bed to attend services with their families, despite not having fully recovered from the previous night's debauchee, the boys, antsy in their Sunday's best and the girls, angelic besides their mothers who, despite life's perversities, were intent on shepherding their flock through Salvation's pearly gates.

Shortly before noon Tzi ventured into the office looking like he'd entered the wrong door.

Percival raised his head at the sound of the door. Seeing Tzi, his heart lurched, his eyes widened and his mouth fell open. "What brings you this way?" he asked.

"To tell the truth, I don't know," Tzi said, diffidently. "I went to pick up Raschelay for a picnic we were going on with a bunch of friends to Clove Lake, 'n her moms answered the door 'n told me I need to come talk to you. So, here I am. What's up?"

Percival sighed. This could prove more difficult than he cared for. He loved Tzi, loved him the way he wished he could love Sam. To inform Tzi that Sam had raped Raschelay, that Percival's brother had raped Tzi's girlfriend, might well prove more than their friendship could endure. He sighed again and said, I" didn't expect this, but ya'll need to sit."

Tzi drew up a chair.

"What Ruth couldn't tell you is that Raschelay's been raped 'n is incapacitated, I'm sorry to say," he said, flushing darkly.

"R-Raschelay r-raped," Tzi dumbly spluttered with a shake of the head, his eyes starting out?

"I'm afraid so."

"R-raped? Raped?" Tzi leered, paling. "By w-who?" he asked owl like. "Who?"

"Of all people, my brother, Sam," said Percival, deeply ashamed.

"You can't be serious."

"If only," Percival said, splaying his hands.

Tzi kicked back his chair and sprang to his feet like a confused, wounded animal looking to strike out at its tormentor. "He's mine," he said, furiously, leaning forward, hands pressed atop the desk, holding Percival's eyes in his own.

"Can't do! Life's full of tragedies 'n ya'll ave to accept this as one of em, dig? Besides, by the time this is all over more than a few hands will ave been soiled, 'n yours need not be one of em. I owe you that much," Percival said, reluctantly.

"Only she's my girl!"

"I appreciate your dilemma, but ya'll ave to see mine," Percival said, feelingly, trying to calm him. "He's my brother."

"What's that suppose to mean?"

"Jus' that."

Tzi scrutinized his face, searching for any deceit, then shrugged resignedly. "Okay for you but not Sam, I'm gonna trust you to deal with it." His voice shook with passion as he fell back in his chair, the wind knocked out of him.

Percival sighed more heavily, with relief.

"Ah – well you know – ah – she was a virgin." Tzi confided, embarrassed.

"I imagined as much."

"She was saving herself for her wedding night," he explained. "She saw it as a sacred act. 'A sacrament,' she called it. She wanted the occasion to be immaculate – pure. 'N since she wanted it that way, I wanted it that way too – for her."

"I understand."

"Other than children, she thought it would be the greatest gift she could offer her future husband – her virtue, now it's stolen!"

"No-no-no," said Percival, vehemently. "Never."

"But her virginity was proof of it –"

"Her character is proof of it. Never forget that 'n never think otherwise – Never. She fought him like a she wolf."

"Did you know she's Catholic?" he said, his thoughts wandering. "She goes to church every Sunday morning."

"I had no idea."

"She went to early Mass so no one would suspect. She thought you had to be an atheist to be a revolutionary."

"I guess it helps," Percival affirmed.

"That's why she didn't want anyone to know." Tzi's eyes blinked, then he asked, "Do you believe in God?"

"It's all according to the daya the week you ask me, I suppose. T'day's not such a good day."

Tzi pursed his lips glumly, looking out the window at the traffic of returning church goers. He was classically handsome, his skin the color of porcelain or moon glow, his lanky hair more blue than black. His and Raschelay's children would be stunning. Percival watched Tzi watch the late Sunday morning worshipers pass by the office window. An expression of pathos and deep despair intruded on his good looks. "I know you're not in my place, but if you were, what would you do?" he asked, nostrils flaring.

"You don't need to ask me that, man. Tell me, what will you do?"

"I kind'a thought you might say that," Tzi said softly. "She's stunning, isn't she?"

"In more ways than one. You're one lucky cat."

"I am, aren't I?"

"Ya know you 'r."

"So, what am I doing sitting here talking to you feeling sorry for myself for?" He clapped Percival affectionately on the shoulder in farewell. "Thanks, man, I'll be seeing you."

"Good luck to both'a you," Percival called after him.

No sooner had Tzi left than his sister, Lois, on her way home from church, stepped through the door. Had she been a moment sooner, she and Tzi would have collided. *'What now?'* Percival wondered, wanting to bury his face in his hands and sob. Smiling broadly, he said, "What a happy surprise."

"I'll just bet," Lois said, dispensing with pleasantries. "Tell me, is what I've been hearing true?"

"It's all according to what you've been hearing, I guess."

"Don't patronize me," she said. "I'm not a little girl anymore."

"That you're not." Percival was genuinely amused for the first time that day. "Tell me what it is you're hearing then."

"That our baby brother, Sam, raped that beautiful young girl, Raschelay."

Percival winced. "I hoped you'd not get to hear that on the grapevine. Does Maw know?"

"Not yet."

"Let's try 'n spare her as long as possible."

"She knows something's wrong."

"How's that?"

"By the way you came and fetched Sam yesterday."

"Umm," he murmured, studying how pretty she was in her print summer's dress. Her hair was piled atop her head, African style with pearls woven through it that shimmered in the room's jaundiced light. He wondered if their mother had been as attractive in her youth. When he was small he recalled thinking her the most lovely of women. He further thought that if his father, Lucius loved her, she would had to have been.

Lois shifted uncomfortably under his scrutiny.

"Well we got'a keep it from her, somehow," he said frankly.

"How do you propose we do that? The whole neighborhood's been talking."

"Jus' deny it."

"Where's Sam, now?"

"Some place safe I can assure you," he said impatiently.

"What are you going to do to him?"

"Who says we're gonna do anything to him?"

"Don't play me for a fool."

"I don't know," he confessed. "I really don't know."

"Tread carefully, big brother."

"Keep this to yourself, please."

"You mean not tell Ma?"

"Something like that."

"I'll leave it to you to do the right thing."

"You're a good sister, Lois," he said fondly, "but I don't mind telling you I'm up to my neck in it."

"How so?"

"A field marshal's in from Oakland 'n he's all gung-ho."

"Meaning?"

"He'd jus' as well see Sam's head impaled on a spear as not."

She gasped, horrified. "My God," she exclaimed, cupping her mouth with her hand. "What are you going to do?"

"I'm trying to work something out, but it's not fool proof."

"Well, you're a sly one. If anyone can pull it off, you can."

Percival raised an eyebrow, his face impassive; a mask, keeping his unholy plans to himself. He might well have already said more to Lois than he had intended. He wondered.

***

By Thursday Percival had finally ironed out most of the difficulties in a plan to punish Sam sufficiently, without necessarily having to take his life. The only immediate drawback was in securing the cooperation of the people best able to help bring it about, and that might prove a bit tricky. In any event, it would certainly be risky for all involved. He would have to make an all-important telephone call. He chose to use a local candy store from which to place the call. He closed the door of the booth and dialed in St. George. The phone rang several times on the far end.

"Federal Bureau of Investigation, Special Agent, Harrison speaking. How may I help you?"

"Can I talk to Lawrence Bianco?"

"One moment, please."

The call was taken on another line. "Agent Bianco speaking."

"This is you know who."

"Yes, I do. I've been expecting your call."

"Oh?"

"I understand you've got troubles?"

"Wall to wall."

"The blood related one must really complicate it, I imagine?"

"Ya've got damn good sources."

"We're professionals."

"I'm gonna need to speak with you right away.

"Okay. It's ten past eleven now, why don't we meet on the Staten Island Rapid, let's say about twelve thirty? The train should be virtually empty then, so we can talk. I'll catch it in St. George and you can pick it up, oh say, in Stapleton a few stations down the line? If I'm not reading a paper, join me. If I am we'll have to make other arrangements. But I expect at that hour it should be fine. I'll be in the second car from the front."

"That'll give me plenty time to get to Stapleton. I'll see you then."

On hanging up, Percival again checked his watch. It was a quarter past eleven. If he caught a bus now he would arrive in Stapleton in ample time. Sucking the life out of a bottle of Coca-Cola, he waited for the bus in the air-conditioned candy store away from the sun. When the bus arrived, he stepped outside and boarded the bus behind another passenger. He paid his fare and took a seat in the back corner, protecting his back. He looked out the window and observing the quickly retreating landmarks: the dilapidated tenements slowly becoming middle class, black faces becoming white, the area opening up and becoming less congested, the long, sloping hills, the sharp, treacherous corners which threatened to tilt the bus. The old familiar route made him think of the words to a song— "a sentimental journey." His tail bone recognized every bump in the road along the way.

He got off at Beach Street in front of a popular coffee shop, "The Missing Link," walked to the corner of Water Street across from Stapleton Park. The air was sultry, perfumed with assorted fragrances that triggered memories of by gone days; yesterdays; days when he was far less troubled, safe and capable of trust. He loved this small park, an island of joy he had shared briefly with Racine in happier times. For the first time in a long time he allowed himself to lower his guard.

He had a few moments to spare so he strolled the park's shady, tree lined, cobble stone paths. Then left crossing Bay and continuing down Canal. In the distance, he thought he saw, Racine waving to him with Dakota straddling an

405

out thrust hip, but when he blinked, she was gone; the product of an overworked, fanciful imagination, and the oppressive, midday's heat.

He reached the bottom of the station under the trestle and clambered up the stairs. The view from the station was expansive. His eyes took in the abandoned piers and moved across the river to Brooklyn; his home; his spiritual abode.

He didn't have long to wait for the train.

As luck would have it, Agent Bianco was the only other passenger in the second car. It was hard not to notice a man in a suit on such a hot, torpid day. His tie was loose and his jacket unbuttoned. But still he looked uncomfortable. His suit was off the rack and of an inferior quality. Although athletic and attractive a man in his early thirties, there was something about him that made you overlook him. And yet, he was a decent enough person to deal with. Not so surprisingly, however, Percival viewed him with grave apprehension. He suspected his decency was only a ploy, a means by which to disarm and place you in his confidence. Plus, he had no alternative. The traffic ran both ways. His antennas went out and his guard was raised.

They shook hands as Percival sat across from Special Agent, Bianco.

The conductor approached and asked for Percival's destination.

"All the way."

The conductor accepted the fare, punched a ticket, and handed it to Percival. He went on about his business as the train rolled rapidly through the southernmost tip of the island's townships and lush, verdant countryside.

"I can use your help," said Percival, nervously, leaning forward, kneading his hands, his elbows resting on his thighs.

"How's that?"

"I'm trying to save my brother's worthless life."

"Things are that bad, are they?"

"Couldn't get much worse."

"Go on."

"Well, as you may or may not know, my brother raped one of the Panther women."

"Yes, so I'm aware."

"N something short of involving the police must be done. That means punishing him is up to me or, more precisely, my branch of the party," he said in a raspy voice. "In any case I can't involve the police. We must deal with it and we ave no alternative short of killing him at 'r disposal. No matter how stupid he may be he's still my baby brother. He must be punished, deserves to be punished, no doubt; but killing him only complicates things."

Agent Bianco considered Percival with amazement. "I see your dilemma," he said. "And so?"

"This is where you come in. Look, I've figured it out. We need guns 'n rifles 'n stuff. Everybody'll go for a deal, if say, I can convince em that after delivering a supply of stolen weapons Sam'll be exiled to Cuba 'n, hopefully, redeem himself there." Agent Bianco looked puzzled? "The way I see it, you can arrange for him to get a case of guns from Fort Wardsworth, 'n then inform the police of some place where they can intercept him and charge him with possession of weapons stolen from a military installation. Knowing my brother as I do, he'll offer no resistance. That should get him twenty-five years to life, 'n the burden of having to punish him would ave been lifted from my shoulders. What'a you think?"

Agent Bianco rubbed his chin, thoughtfully. "It's an intriguing scheme. It's diabolical in every sense of the word. It's a damn good idea from your standpoint but I don't see the benefit to the FBI?"

"Look," Percival said, with a cynical leer, "I'm no fool. I'm on your payroll. Don't you think I've not figured it out? While you've deposited everything in the Panther account 'n I've not endorsed any checks, still the nature of 'r association is such that I've been compromised. That being the case, you've accomplished your purpose. Now I'll tell you what you can do for me. You can have the decency of sparing me the burden of having to kill my own brother! Because I'd be the one who'd have to do it," he said, his voice trembling with emotion.

Considering Percival with cobalt eyes, Agent Bianco sucked his breath in slowly.

"What you're asking is risky. It leaves too long a trail. It's going to involve the Army's base commander and his Quarter Master, for a start. If I understand your plan correctly you'll need about five grand, front money."

"I guess," Percival agreed.

"Do you have that kind of money?"

Percival grinned faintly. "No!"

"Which means I'll have to requisition those funds. I'll have to sign for the money, explain its use, etc. I don't know if I can do that."

Percival pleaded silently with his eyes.

While the train wheels sang, the train cars swayed like cradles to and fro, Agent Bianco considered Percival for a good long time. His face was the color of putty, his eyes bloodshot and sockets darkened from lack of sleep. "Damn, Jones, it would be easier if you just kill your brother," he said, casually as if the words held no significance. "Then we'd be rid of our bigger problem, which is you."

Percival smiled, awkwardly. "I believe you're capable of other things but I'm convinced that you won't leave me in such a damnable spot."

"I don't know why not," said Agent Bianco cheerlessly. "But you know I really did see you fight," he said reminiscently, shifting gears. "I've seen you fight on several occasions. I was a fan. I'd like to see you fight again, someday."

"I'm fighting now, t'day, for my brother's life!"

"Okay, so you are, I'll see what I can do. But don't get your hopes up, we're not out of the woods just yet; the FBI is not a charitable institution. This is no decision I can make on my own. First, I'll have to convince a lot of bureaucrats that it's in our best interest."

Agent Bianco and Percival continued their talk: They dissected the particulars of his plan, considering it from every angle, filling in the gaps, assuring themselves that there were no glaring oversights.

Before disembarking at the New Dorp station, Agent Bianco turned to face Percival. "If all goes well I'll call your office next Thursday morning at ten o'clock. You must be ready to move. If I've got the go ahead, I'll simply say, 'Sorry, wrong number,' and hang up. The money would have been deposited and the rest you know. In the meantime, let's keep our fingers crossed." As the train rolled into the depot and came to a halt, Bianco looked around cautiously from force of habit, then stepped off.

Percival continued on to Tottenville, the last stop on the line. The station was at the bottom of a sleepy hamlet nestled in woodlands and overlooked a murky swamp alive with the sounds of insects and frogs.

***

That night, for the first time in a long time, Percival slept the sleep of the just.

Based on no more than he felt prudent, Percival informed the branch members of his plan. He said, "The mission had its hazards, but if Sam should choose to accept it and brought it off, it would serve as a precondition for exile, as opposed to any other form of punishment." Some grumbled dissatisfied, "Yeah, Sam's your fucking brother, so you find him an easy out, but what if it was one of us?" Nevertheless, Sam would go away and perish somewhere out of mind, leaving their hands clean. Besides, he would leave them a stockpile of arms which was only fair since you can't run a revolution without guns.

Percival presented the proposal to Sam. He described the banishment as more of a reward for the securing a large quantity of weaponry than

408

punishment. Sam responded favorably, without hesitation, "it's above ground breathing air, ain't it? I'll do it!"

The following Thursday at precisely ten O'clock a.m., the office phone rang. Percival grabbed it straight off. "Hello," he said clearly, "Black Panther Party for Self Defense."

"Sorry, wrong number."

Percival hung up, elated. "Wrong number," he said aloud to everyone's befuddlement. But within seconds, the phone rang again. He picked it up reluctantly, his ears tingling and his heart plunging. "You should know," said the voice on the other end, "the cops were told you would be the one transporting the weapons. Believe me, it got their attention, for what it's worth."

Percival cupped the mouthpiece and said, "They want me dead!"

"Have your brother play it smart," said Agent Bianco. Then the line went dead.

Percival would slowly tramp back to the house. He descended the cellar steps in a pensive, uneasy state of mind; ready to dash the whole thing. But he recalled Raschelay's mother's words, "If her father wasn't in jail right now for manslaughter he'd be there tonight for murder." Slim as it was, it was Sam's only chance. He found Sam unusually talkative, reflective, and wouldn't let Percival get a word in edgewise. "Remember that time when we was kids' n I woke you up cause a rat got in 'r room 'n how scared I was?"

"Yeah, sure," said Percival, impatiently.

"It was Christmas time, recall? 'N you got your Boy Scout knife 'n a stick to kill it, but it escaped 'n you thought I'd only dreamt it up?"

"Sure, sure. I recall."

"Then we came home from school next day to see this big ole dead rat out front on the pavement in 'r yard 'n it turn out mama kill'd it 'n left it for you to throw down the gutter," Sam said, eyes dilated. "She'd cornered it in the bathtub 'n backhanded it a few times— whack, whack, whack— then held it down with a plunger 'n filled the tub with hot water 'n drown'd it – remember?"

"How can I forget?" Percival said, his dark eyes sparked with amusement. "But Hattie comes from a sturdy stock of tenant farmers."

"I don't rightly know what made me think'a that right now," said Sam, warily. "Maybe it's cause you've pulled me out'a a number'a tight spots when we was kids coming up in Bed-Stuy. I guess you kinda doing it still," he said, gravely. "N I wouldn't want you to think I'm not grateful, cause I am."

Percival looked hard pressed, not at all pleased with the world. "Actually, it's mama who deserves credit, not me. I mean, I've come to realize that had I cornered that rat that night as I'd hope to things would not ave gone so well as I would'a liked." He laughed. "I mean, bro, after all, I was what, all of twelve years old?"

"It's not so much you didn't do it," Sam insisted, "but that you would'a cause you my big brother. It says something, something bigger. That's all I'm saying."

"There's no need to," Percival said, reflexively.

"I won't let you down on this one, bro. I swear. I'll show you. I'll hold up my end or die trying."

"Come on now, let's not get all melodramatic, huh?"

"No, I mean it. I've been doing a bit'a soul-searching down here in this cellar these past days, 'n I realize I owe you big time."

"Don't, it's no big deal. 'N now that we've survived 'r trip down memory lane," Percival said, with a rueful grin. "I think we best get on to the business at hand, dig? I came by to say I jus' got the word 'n the deal's to go down t'day at two o'clock."

"I guess I'd figured as much," Sam said, solemnly. "I've had this funny feeling, something like esp., you know?"

"I don't wanta bore you with details, but like I said, I've been negotiating this deal for some time now 'n a lot depends on it. A lot of effort's been expended 'n groundwork to set it up 'n yours is the last leg of what for me's been a very trying ordeal. 'N now it's up to you to not fuck it up 'n to bring it off without a hitch."

Sam nodded his head eagerly.

"I jus' want everything straight, okay?"

"I hear you, brother man."

"So long as you do. Now when you get to the post you go to Headquarters Company. A black staff sergeant will be waiting for you. He'll recognize the car's license plate number. He'll get in the car on the passenger side. He'll say, 'all's in order' 'n you'll say, 'lead on.' He'll direct you to the pick-up point. You won't give him the rest of the money till everything's been checked off 'n loaded in the trunk of the car, dig?" Again Sam nodded enthusiastically. "Here's a list of what's involved." He passed Sam a checklist. "As you can see, it's some pretty heavy firepower we're talking 'bout."

Sam's eyes widened as they went down the list. He whistled under his breath in disbelief. "Grenades 'n grenade launchers, M-16's, .45's, heavy-fucking-duty, baby!" He looked up at Percival admiringly, but Percival looked away, checking his watch, refusing to meet Sam's eyes.

"As you can see, this is big time," he said, deceitfully. "Remember, you're Joe College 'n this should come off without a hitch; but if for some reason it don't it's better you err on the side of caution 'n we'll take the loss, dig? Don't be reckless. I want you to walk away from this in one piece."

"I hear you."

"Be sure you do."

"Don't worry 'bout me big brother, I'm on."

"Right now I've got'a leave 'n take care of some business: rent a car, get the rest of the funds up, make a call, see a cat etcetera. I'll be back shortly."

Percival left Sam seated on his cot, the thrill of fear written all over him.

When Percival returned he was running late, and quickly gave Sam final instructions. "I know you know what to do," he said as he pressed a loaded .38 in Sam's palm. "But," he cautioned, "if, by chance, you got'a use it you're almost certain to come out the loser." He paused for effect. "This job requires smarts above all else. Remember discretion is, by far, the better part of valor."

"Yeah! Yeah! Yeah!" said Sam edgily, "I hear you," having heard nothing, spellbound as he was by the lure of the loaded pistol in his grip. "I'm hip."

"Ya'll need to be."

"Anything else?"

"The money's in the glove compartment of the car."

"Okay."

"Any questions?"

"Jus' this, had I not, you k-know, n-not R-Raschelay would y-you ave picked me for this job?"

Percival studied Sam, debating how to reply. "No," he said, firmly. "Simply because of the amount of preparation I put into it, the value of the weapons, 'n the danger involved, I thought I'd take the run myself," he said with guile, unflinching. "But this was the only way I had to pull your ashes out'a the fire – so I took it."

"I appreciate your being straight with me. I'll do you proud." He paced restlessly, caressing the handle of the .38, his eyes dilated, shining like lamps. "I'm ready," he said giddily, excited, like a man with a new lease on life. "I'm looking forward to going to Cuba, getting outta this backwater." He stuck the gun under his belt and tugged at his trousers like a truculent delinquent. "I can't wait to be in the land of all those lovely senoritas. Ooh-la-la." He smiled superciliously and snapped his fingers like they were castanets.

"The car's outside. You should be back round three-thirty latest. Everyone'll be here to help unload the car."

Sam shook his head. He was anxious, rubbing his sweaty palms. "This is gonna be a piece of cake," he said, mounting the steps. "I'll come through for you, big brother. Yes, I will."

"I'm sure you will," said Percival, climbing the stairs after him. "Just be sure to come through in one piece."

As they emerged from the house into the scorching light of a summer's day, Sam raised a hand to his eyes. "It takes you off guard, you don't see the sun for two weeks." He squinted, a look of fear on his face. "One more question before I take off."

"That is?"

"What if I take the money 'n split?"

"You won't do that."

"How do you know?"

"We were raised under the same roof."

Sam drew a meditative breath, paused, then nodded to himself. "I guess I owe you," he said. Let's do it."

Percival embraced Sam clumsily, half-heartedly, trying to drum up an ounce of sympathy for the damned. Then Sam climbed in behind the wheel of the car. He revved up the engine. "Good luck," Percival called, waving nonchalantly, as the other members, excited about a new supply of arms, saluted with closed fists. The car crawled down the hill at a slow pace and, no sooner had it made a right-hand turn onto Jersey Street, too late to turn back the clock, Percival felt the inexorable hand of fate clap him soundly on the shoulder. He would not rest easy until he'd received word that Sam was apprehended, and safely locked behind prison bars.

The Panther members waited excitedly expecting Sam to pull up outside the house with a fresh supply of guns and lord only knew what else, any minute now. They were thinking that they could launch an all-out assault on any police precinct in the city. They would be the best armed branch of Panthers in New York. The wait for Percival, on the other hand, was an interminable one. He paced back and forth looking at his watch every few minutes waiting for the phone to ring. The pressure was such that he feared his nose would bleed. Then when the phone did ring, he grabbed it with grave apprehension. "'Ello," he said, with a tremolo in his voice. "Uh-um," he cleared his throat, steadying himself, "hello?"

"Percival is that you?" asked a frantic female on the other end.

"Y-yes," he stammered, perplexed.

"You've got to come. right now. it's me, your sister, Lois. the police are here. they say Sam's d-dead," she yelped. "I-is that s-so? K-killed in a s-shoot out?"

"W-what" w-what 'r you saying?" he gulped, thunderstruck, blood seeming to drain from his face, disquiet filling his breast. "K-killed? "

"Mama's not home," she peeped, faintly. "She won't be back till late t-tonight. They say they need us to go to the morgue a-and identify h-his remains," she said in a choking, little girl's voice. "They want t-to take me, but I'm not getting in a c-car with any of them. Will y-you come g get me, please?" she implored.

"I'll pick you up outside your building in five minutes," he said, filled with a poison that sapped his strength he almost collapsed as he lay the phone back on its hook. He faced the others, his color drained. "Something's gone horribly wrong," he murmured. He looked about vacantly his hand clasped to his forehead.

"What is it," they all cried? "What is it?"

"Skeeter," he called, "I'll need you to drive me."

They looked back and forth among themselves, then Leroy asked, "What is it, Percival?"

Percival eyed each one of them accusatorially, angrily, then his gaze fell on Leroy and he broke. "He's d-dead, little brother," he said, voice cracking, "S-Sam's been k-killed in a shoot o-out."

Silence filled the room. A dreadful silence. A look of unspeakable horror on their faces. "My g'd," they gasped. They had gotten their wish; the bargain struck with ole Nick was complete. They shrunk from Percival as if he were Faust. It was his idea, his plan, his fault. Maybe he had concocted it in secret as a way to rid himself of Sam. It wasn't entirely inconceivable. Was he Cain, cursed among men to be shunned? All they knew for sure was that they wouldn't be getting in a new supply of guns any time soon. They turned away, their hearts cold, not knowing what to say.

Percival started for the door.

"Can I go with you?" Leroy asked with a pitiful look on his face.

"There's nothing you can do, little brother." A smile crept over Percival's serious face. "But thanks." Then he turned away.

"I'm damn sorry 'bout Sam," Skeeter said in the car, starting the engine.

"I know you 'r," said Percival. "I know you 'r, you've been a good comrade."

"That's saying something coming from you, especially since I –"

"Ya don't ave to say it, man. It wasn't your doing."

Skeeter jockeyed the car down the hill and swinging left on Jersey he pulled up in front of the projects a half mile away.

Lois stood in the entranceway her arms folded at her bosom as if she were cold. Skeeter honked. She ran awkwardly to the car. Percival opened the back door for her.

"Oh, Percival," she wept.

"I know. I know."

Skeeter made a U-turn and pointed the car in the direction of Staten Island Hospital. Lois clung to Percival's hand as would a frightened child; and he looked at her, half turned in his front seat, bereft of all facial expression.

"I asked them – the cops – how'd it happen," she cried. "They told me, they bragged, that they got a call from the military base's Provost Marshall's office. They were given the description of a car suspected of possessing firearms that were stolen from that base. The car Sam was driving fit the description," she whimpered, her voice reflecting the misery in her face. "When they tried to pull him over, he e-engaged them in a high-speed chase. And when he found himself cut off he jumped out from the car and opened fire on them and they returned the fire. In the exchange he was k-killed. They say evidently he was the culprit cause they found all the missing weaponry in the trunk of his car." She sobbed uncontrollably, tears and mascara streaming down her cheeks. "I t-thought y-you had him under l-lock 'n key. S-so, so how'd this happen?"

"Not now," he put her off, delaying the inevitable. "We're here."

Skeeter let them out in front of the emergency room entrance then drove on to find a parking spot and wait.

Lois squeezed Percival's hand so hard it felt numb. The emergency room was hectic, swarmed with people needing medical attention. Doctors flew in and out of rooms while patients groaned, and nurses dashed about like track stars. Two uniformed policemen emerged from out the welter of activity with a plain clothes detective.

"Percival," said the detective with suppressed hostility. "This way." He led them down a long corridor. The antiseptic smell permeated the air. They took an elevator to the sub-basement. The detective led the way with the two cops bringing up the rear. The sound of their footsteps echoed menacingly in the silent hall. The detective pushed his way through a pair of swinging doors and they followed. The detective signaled to an attendant who walked over to a set of cabinets set in the wall and pulled out, with some energy a long draw on which a covered body laid. Then the attendant rolled back the sheet from the face of the corpse.

Percival approached, apprehensively, afraid his stomach would bolt. Lois knees sagged. He gazed hypnotically at the still, lifeless face. The empty face; its mouth slack and eyes on the verge of opening. There was little that was recognizable about it. It was as if he had dredged it up from a harrowing dream. The spectacle was Narcissus drowned, face up, in the pool of his own vanity. Sickened, Percival broke out in a feverish sweat. He noticed where three blood stains the size of half dollars, in the area of the chest and abdomen, had seeped through the sheet. He drew the sheet back further, holding his breath, and, gazed down at the puncture wounds in Sam's slight, athletic body through which his life had run out. He fell back, appalled, numb, his breath shallow. "Damn you," he cursed Sam, "it wasn't suppose to be this way!" An icy chill gripped his heart and spiraled outward to his extremities, his lips trembled. His mind reeled, overwhelmed. He staggered, and the celestial light from a thousand suns turned to darkness in his soul. He pressed his hand against his eye, fighting for the next breath, trying desperately to feel the course of life in his veins.

"Is that your brother?" asked the detective.

"You know it is, you son of 'a bitch," Percival managed to say. "Yes, it's our brother, Sam."

Inconsolable, Lois dashed her face against his chest. Adrift in his own misery, he could little respond to hers.

"We could of taken him down without killing him, but we thought it was you." Then a cop whispered in Percival's ear, "Next time it will be."

Percival spun around, his face stark, but Lois held him, having overheard the remark. "What kind of people are you anyhow?" she wept. "You vile, wretched creatures. You bastards, you. May God not forgive you your sins, ever!" She spat at a policeman's foot. He drew back, clamping his fist, his lips tight. "You've killed one brother and now you want to kill the other? May you never be forgiven. Not now, not tomorrow, not ever!" She threw back her head defiantly. "God damn you all to hell!" she swore with a vehemence she had never felt before.

***

"The earth is the Lord's and the fullness thereof, the earth and everything that dwelt therein. O Lord hear our prayers and grant our young brother, Samuel Mathew Jones, eternal peace and may perpetual light shine on him forever." After pronouncing these words, the aged, dark preacher, attired in ministerial robes, milky, bespectacled eyes clouded with grief from having put too many young black boys in the ground, scattered sod on the coffin that was suspended over the open grave like a sea fairing vessel. "Ashes to ashes and dust to dust," he concluded. Then the small, dispirited band of mourners trudged solemnly back through a wilderness of headstones and numerous other burials taking place. It was an old, sprawling Brooklyn cemetery, as overcrowded as an urban slum. The Panthers, except for Nora and Leroy, stayed away at Percival's insistence. Hattie, utterly despondent lagged behind. She leaned on Lois' arm in a stupor, as if sun struck, having refused Percival's offer of assistance. They had quarreled bitterly on her return home late that previous Thursday after she had been informed of Sam's death. She had been stunned out of her wits and had to sit down. When she was able to compose herself, she said in a low, shaky voice, "Y-you was t-to look o-out for him. Y-you was to protect h-him. He was your b-baby brother."

"No, ma, he was your baby, not mine," Percival said, defensively.

"Who put him u-up to stealing them guns in the first place, I ask?" she accused, her throat and chest knotted into a deep, painful sob. "He wouldn't'a done it had you not put him up to it. Your fingerprints 'r all over it!"

"Mama," Lois broke in, "you don't know what you're saying."

"Don't I?" Hattie's eyes were wide and unblinking, like an astonished child's.

"I d-didn't mean –" Lois turned away.

"What don't you mean, girl?" Hattie wanted to know. "Well, what?" she blazed, fixing her long-suffering eyes on Percival.

"I knew I shouldn't'a been here," he exploded. "It always comes to this. Ain't it bad enough Sam's dead? Ain't it?"

"Boy, you be running," said Hattie, coldly, "but you not running to d'Lord you be running from the Devil!"

Lois swung round. "Mama you're going to have to let this go. You have to stop faulting Percival for Sam's failings. If you don't know certain things it's because you chose not to know," she said, trying to control her rising voice. "It's been the neighborhood gossip for days now, Ma. Sam raped a girl! A young girl, a teenager!"

"No!" Hattie bellowed. "No, don't tell me that. I won't hear it. That's no way to talk 'bout the dead," she sobbed. "We got'a think to pick out'a suit'a clothing from the closet 'n go find a casket to bury him in." She moaned, crossing her arms over her womb as if suffering from excruciating labor pains. "He was my las born, the youngest a' my children. He had no father to raise him, only me, his mother, a woman."

"That's no excuse, ma," Lois retorted.

"He needed more than ya'll two."

"Now maybe that's an excuse," Lois added.

"N I was your first born," Percival reminded her.

"As such you was to look after him, see to him. Steer him in the right direction."

Hattie railed, striking Percival feebly on the chest with balled fists. "My baby," she wailed, staggering off to her bedroom and throwing herself across the bed, weeping. She realized she had faulted Percival unduly. Tragically, her anger sprang from the long-ago subconscious fact that she had steeled herself against the day when she would receive word of Percival's death, not Sam's. Never for a single moment had she thought that it might turn out to be Sam. Never. It shook her to her core.

She wept, profusely. She cried for all the mothers who'd ever lost a son; for all the daughters someday bound to lose one. She cried with the Biblical Rachel weeping for her children; she cried for all the ages when it was said, "Let the day perish wherein I was born/ and the night in which it was said/ there is a man child born." She cried herself to sleep.

She had not forgiven Percival and had not spoken to him since that fateful day, that god awful night. He was too much his father's son, and in as much as she was still mad at Lucius, so too, was she mad at him; but, being a God-fearing woman she would forgive him, eventually. She bore this cross with unbearable difficulty. All the men closest to her in her life had died violently, badly, and, yes, some of the blame rested with her. In her tortured state of mind, she thought she had been unlucky for them and therefore, if Percival were to be safeguarded, she knew she could be of no use which grieved her further still. She felt as if she would give in and just die. She cleaved ever more closely to Lois, as Lois guided their footsteps through the graveyard's gates to a waiting car.

Closing the car door after them, Percival said, "I'm dreadfully sorry, ma," but the car pulled out without Hattie responding.

Percival got into a waiting car with Nora and Leroy and Silva behind the wheel. They said very little and Silva sped off all too glad to distance himself from the cemetery.

"When we reach the Island I want you to drop me off at Nina Koestler's," Percival said wearily, rubbing his tired eyes.

"Should I wait for you?"

"No, man, I'll walk."

"Do you think that's smart?" Nora asked.

"I'll risk it."

"We can't afford to lose you," said Leroy.

"It's probably better I wait," Silva decided.

"I won't argue," Percival said, as they continued driving.

Percival had not slept for days. He hadn't wept neither. He dabbed his face with a handkerchief as rivulets of sweat rolled down his back. Succumbing to the futility of it all, he groaned, folded his arms across his chest, and slumped down in his seat, hoping to catnap before reaching Nina's. As things were, she was the only person left he trusted enough to confide in. Nina lived in Stapleton, on St. Paul's Place, diagonally across the road from St. Paul's

Episcopal church. Her house was an old, prepossessing antebellum house with a large yard, shade trees and well-tended flower gardens.

On their arrival, he exited the car and crossed the path to the porch. He climbed the steps and rang the doorbell, as he waited. Music from the car radio wafted toward him, noticeable amid the otherwise quiet street; in the white, upper middle-class sanctuary.

Percival recalled the similar circumstances in which Big/Black was arrested and called to the occupants of the car, "Better play it safe 'n pull into the drive."

Silva responded as if to a race flag. He'd fancied himself a race driver since adolescence. He pulled his mustang up the driveway with a squeal of wheels.

From inside, there came a fumbling at the doorknob. Then the door opened slightly. A shirtless, pug nosed, freckled-faced boy, not much taller than the height of the doorknob, peered out. His frail body blocked the entrance. His ears stuck out between tufts of tousled hair.

"'Ello, Terry," Percival fondly said.

Terry leapt from the ground into Percival's arms, shouting, "Mama, Mama, it's Percival! It's Percival!" Terry's sister appeared, jumping up and down excitedly, also wanting to climb up into his arms. He shifted Terry onto his back and picked up Lenore. She clung to his neck. Nina hobbled out of a back room on crutches, like a wind-up mechanical doll. She smiled anxiously, holding back as if vexed.

"Well, hello, stranger," she said, affectedly. They had not crossed paths since the previous fall. "And what, may I ask, brings you so far out of your way?" She looked at him with curiosity.

"I guess I deserve that," he said.

"I think you do."

"I'd apologize, but it couldn't be helped," he said in a feeble attempt at an excuse. "I need someone I can talk too, 'n you're probably the only friend I got left or, that is, the only one I can trust – which amounts to the same thing."

She laughed nervously, ill at ease.

"I mean, Nina, ave you not heard?"

She smiled sadly, relenting. "Yes, all too tragically, I have," she said with a chastened look, afraid. "I read about it in Friday's papers. I saw in the obituary column that the burial was today. I can't be more sorry about Sam – for your loss." She sighed. "I tried calling you, but you've been unavailable."

"I've been running, as my mother said. I've been running hard 'n I've been running fast; running from myself faster than I've ever run from the man. Now I find myself knocking at your door," he said, breathing strenuously hard as if, indeed, he had been running." He had become that hounded black boy running to escape the Furies pursuing him—swirling in a maelstrom about to suck him under. "This is jus' the tip of the iceberg," he said, with a certain appeal in his eyes.

She was startled, unable to imagine him running from anything.

"Children," she called. "Children, I don't think Percival's quite up to all that at the moment."

"It's okay," he said, pressing Lenore to him, as Terry rode him piggyback. "It's jus' what the doctor called for."

"Come join me in the kitchen and I'll put on some tea."

While waiting for the water to boil, he rolled around on the floor with the children who were ecstatic. Nina announced tea was ready and they scrambled to the table while she served cookies and poured tea for the four of them.

"O' boy, "Terry sang, "it's a Mad Hatter's tea party." Waving a cookie as if it were a conductor's baton, he broke out in song, "'A very merry unbirthday to me, to me –'"

"I've been reading 'Alice In Wonderland' to them over the summer and the song is from a record I found in the attic," Nina explained, laughing lightheartedly, running her fingers through her curly, light brown hair, her eyes sparkling like crystals in a stream.

"How many freckles you think I have?" Terry turned his face up to Percival, biting into his cookie. "Do you want to count them?"

"No, Terry, not now," Nina said, casually.

"I've got a lot of them."

"Yes, Terry, the whole world can see that," said Nina, in exasperation.

"Stop showing off," Lenore scolded. "Nobody wants to see your ugly ole freckles, anyway."

"I'm not ugly."

"You are, too."

"Now children, let's not fight," Nina interceded.

"She started it," Terry trumpeted, taking offense.

"Did not," Lenore denied.

"Did too!"

"OK, that's it, finish your tea and go outside to play so Percival and I can talk."

"I'm done," Lenore sang, departing the table.

"Wait for me, wait for me," Terry called after her, slipping off his seat, racing to catch up.

"I get first ride on the swing," Lenore announced on the way out the kitchen door.

"I'm never first," Terry pouted, swaggering behind.

"I'll let you be first all day tomorrow," Lenore promised, very grown up.

"Sometimes those kids are just too much. They certainly give me a run for my money." Nina shook her head wonderingly. "Now, where were we?"

"Down the rabbit's hole," said Percival, gloomily.

"Yes, the Mad Hatter's tea party."

"It's a far more welcoming place than I've been in quite awhile," he said, a sly twinkle in his eye.

"Don't be too sure," said Nina less than cheerily. "Often I end up down the rabbit hole myself. So be mindful of what you ask for."

Percival was silent, sunk in thought.

She reached across the table and clasped his hands in hers, her eyes wide with concern. "Tell me, ole friend, what's eating you?"

Percival leaned forward. "I'd tell you, but I don't know where to start."

"At the beginning."

"The beginning is inexplicable, as pretty much is the end."

"You know the end, do you?"

"I know the odds well enough – yes."

"Well, you need a place to begin so if you can't start at either the beginning or the end you have no choice but to start in the middle."

"It's the middle that's falling out," he said sourly.

"Never mind," she said, squeezing his hands, reassuringly. "It doesn't matter."

"It's well you say that, but I need to talk."

"Whenever you're ready."

"You know, Sam's been killed by the cops."

"Yes and I was so sorry to hear it," she said, plaintively.

"What you can't know 'n we're trying to keep it secret, is that he'd raped Raschelay."

"For God sake, no!" She dropped his hands with a start and clapped them to her face, aghast. "Tell me it's not true!"

"I wish I could, but I can't."

"Oh merciful heavens," she groaned. "How awful."

"That's the easy part," Percival said. "When it happened there was a lot'a pressure on me to ave Sam taken out."

"Oh!" Nina started with raised brows. "I guess that's not all that surprising, either."

Percival was tortured by remorse. His anguish at recalling his treachery was far worse than any physical pain he could possibly suffer. "It's all gone badly," he told her, throwing up his hands and sinking back in his chair. "I feel like I'm coming apart. Raschelay was raped by my brother 'n something had to be done. N, whatever it was, I was expected to do it – everybody else was wishing to pass it off, wanting to wash their hands of it. So, ultimately, the blame falls on me. Hell, I'm the defense captain, aren't I? My God, I was at my wits end as to how I was gonna keep Sam alive 'n still do right by Raschelay. You know how much everybody thinks of her. How much I depend on her. She's the heart of the branch. So yes, I set up a situation with the FBI's help in which Sam was to be taken with a stockpile of weapons by the local cops 'n do some heavy jail time. But no, he gets himself killed in a shootout, in a scheme gone wrong, which I set up." He sighed heavily. "Anyway, no one wants to believe I wasn't instrumental in his death including my own mother." He smiled sickly.

Nina sat very still their eyes locked. Then a shudder ran through her body. "Jesus God," she exclaimed, "make it hard on me why don't you."

"Forget it. I thought this might be a mistake. Maybe I should go." He started to rise.

"How dare you." She seized him by the arm, stopping him short. "I don't deserve that from you," she said, her eyes hot and gleaming. "You come here, drop this bomb on me from out the blue, and I'm not supposed to react. Maybe I can't help you in this, but I have every reason to believe in you. In any case, I owe you every consideration. I can't begin to imagine the hell you're going through. I couldn't do what you did but, if it's any consolation, you certainly didn't betray Sam in the true sense. What Sam did to Raschelay was dreadful beyond belief, unspeakable!" She hesitated again. The corners of her mouth sagged as if she were about to cry. "Sam made your decision for you. Whatever you did, under the circumstance, you had little choice. Sam endangered all of you. In fact, if you didn't feel guilty I'd be surprised. After all, he's your brother and despite your differences, and I know of a few, you've loved him. You sheltered him against the storm for as long as you could, and when you couldn't hold him safely anymore he fell of his own weight. If you'd had the instincts of an animal you'd not mourn one second, but you're far more complicated than that and loss is a dear – the dear price we pay for our humanity."

"I don't know how much more I can endure," Percival said, exhaustedly. "In any case, McKay, the field Marshall in from Oakland is using this to put me on a back burner for a while. He told me the other day I'm under too much pressure at the moment 'n I should take a few weeks to collect myself. Hell, I don't disagree but I know it's not being done out'a concern for my welfare. But I can't argue. I can use the rest. I've been under attack too long. I mean, he really wants me outta the way to ave one less obstacle to contend with while they solidify their hold over the New York leadership 'n give it more of a western flavor, destroying its New York characteristics." Percival's eyes were red, eyelids heavy. "The price we've paid for this," he ruminated, "the ongoing sacrifices, 'n for what?"

"All of what you say may be true but, correct me if I'm wrong, you entered the Panthers to help Rufus and Rufus is now long gone and you're still playing nursemaid to something you never really wanted in the first place. It wasn't your cause it was Rufus. It may have been right for him but it was myopic for you. What you sacrificed was your personal vision. You suspended your conscience to follow the dictates of the Black Panther Party. You may not have clearly seen your way into this, but no doubt, you'll have to clearly see your way out." Nina tossed her hair.

Nina toyed nervously with the handle of her teacup, eyes downcast. "This was not your thing. It was Rufus' thing. You just got caught up in it." She looked at him again. "You were on your way to the Olympics and disaster struck. King was killed and your jaw was broken. It wasn't in your future; it wasn't your design; you lost control of your destiny. You joined the Panthers under duress – against your better judgment, and now that better judgment has been borne out." She shrugged her petite shoulders. "You drifted from your higher aim and lost your way and your moral purpose."

Percival grasped Nina's hands across the table and tears filled his eyes. He dropped his head, sobbing, his body wracked with grief. Nina gripped his hands fervently, allowing him to cry, to let it all out. "It's okay," she encouraged in a soft, level voice. "It's okay."

The children had silently reentered the kitchen. "Mommy, why is Percival crying?" they asked.

"Some bad people hurt him," Nina explained.

"Don't cry," said Terry, cuddling up to him.

"Don't cry," said Lenore, climbing into his lap, putting her arms about his neck. "We love you."

"Yes," Terry echoed his sister. "We do."

"You say you have a few weeks to kill." Nina snapped her fingers, struck by an idea. "It's time you meet my aunt Amelia. I've been telling her about you, forever. We can get you up to her farm in Saratoga County by tomorrow, I'm sure."

"Wait," Percival hedged, feeling pressured, one arm around Lenore and a hand on Terry's messy head of hair.

"No ifs ands or buts," Nina insisted with a pontifical wave of her hand. "There's nothing to stop you. You say you can use a rest. It'll be ideal. She'll love to have you for as long as you can stay. I'll make the call right now."

Percival gave Silva final instructions before boarding the train at Grand Central Station the next day, Tuesday, for Saratoga. "I'll be gone a week or two, depending. Nina will know how to reach me if anything should come up. I'm not deserting you, though I'm concerned for the chapter's morale. You know I'll be back. This was forced on me. I wouldn't be going otherwise. It's the wrong time."

"I know that, Percival. We all know it. You just come back rested, okay?"

"Be careful. I suspect McKay's up to no good."

"I kind'a figured as much."

"In any case, I'm leaving 'r branch in your capable hands."

"I'll do my best not to disappoint."

"I've no doubt."

They seized each other's hands and solemnly went through the black power handshake, as if they would not see each other alive again.

"Power!" they said, fists clenched. Then Percival turned and boarded the train so he would not have to meet Silva's eyes. He took Nina's suggestion and sat on the left side of the car, the river view side. It was almost hypnotic it was so idyllic, and he drifted in and out of sleep. The ride was restful and the scenic view absorbing, sailing past his window. By the time the conductor called, "Next stop, Saratoga," three hours later, he had become a stranger in his skin, and felt as if he had shaken a burden for every mile of track traversed.

The Saratoga depot was a quaint little station house on the outskirts of town. The platform was vacant but for the lone figure of a woman in a straw hat, print dress and sandals. She was nut brown, of average height, in her mid-fifties, with an open face and serene eyes that drew you in. She approached him as if she knew him.

"Percival Jones. I would know you anywhere," her voice was lilting. "Welcome." He accepted her hand. It was warm like bread fresh from the oven. He liked her instantly. She, like Nina, exuded charm. "I'm Amelia," she introduced herself, leading him out to the farm truck. He tossed his suitcase in the back, then climbed up to join her in the cab. She switched on the ignition. "I was sorry to hear about your brother's death."

"Yes, thank you," he said.

"I have a few errands to run in town before we head back to the farm, okay?" She pointed the truck away from the depot toward the center of town.

"I'm only along for the ride," he said, swept up in the expansiveness of the sky, the sweep of the land, the town as freshly made up as a movie set, hearkening back to the turn of the century.

423

After Amelia made her stops and they were on the way again, Percival commented, "That's a lovely little town you have."

"We like it," she responded, steering the truck over the blacktop undulating between fields of golden-tasseled corn and fenced off pastures. Cows lolled in the sunlight as far off field hands bent to their tasks. It had been years since Percival had been outside the five boroughs and he had not seen anything to surpass the beauty of upstate New York. He felt as if there was room to breathe, to shrug one's shoulders, without breaking all the china in the shop.

"It's good to finally meet you," Amelia said, glancing his way. "It seems you're a dear friend of my niece."

"Yes, she's special."

"Well I'm glad you can stay with us awhile."

"I appreciate your having me, especially on so short'a notice."

"Happy to have you. This is my place coming up," Amelia said, as the truck barreled down a stretch of road. "The surrounding land on either side of the road is mine."

Percival observed wheat fields, corn fields, apple and cherry orchards, cows and migrant workers. He could not help but notice that they were all black, which caught him off guard – though he thought no more of it.

"How much land do you have?"

"Enough on which to exercise."

"N you run it by yourself?"

"My foreman would take exception to that," she laughed. "No, I have considerable help. My foreman, Renal Poincare, actually runs it – with a bit of interference from me, of course. But I do little enough farm work anymore with my hundred 'n one other tasks to perform."

"Such as, if you don't mind my asking?"

"I wouldn't want to bore you so early on in your visit," she riposted. "Some other time, perhaps."

She swung the truck ably off the road into the driveway which wound round to the back of the old farmhouse under cover of leafy, widespread branches of maple trees. The house was not too far off from the barnyard with chickens clucking and scratching in the dirt. The house was freshly painted. Three dogs of dubious origin greeted Amelia as she climbed down from the cab of the truck.

"These are Buck, She-she and Fell. You're good dogs, aren't you?" After she had scratched their heads, they wandered over to sniff Percival. Fell gave a low, menacing growl.

"That's enough," Amelia warned.

"I'm ok with it," Percival assured her. "We're ok, aren't we Fell?" He stuck out the back of his hand for the cur to sniff.

Amelia led the way into the house through the back entrance. She neglected to turn on the lights. Having a southern exposure, the room fairly dazzled in a dance of light.

"Come, let me show you to your room." He followed her down the hall. She opened a door off the hallway and said, "This will be your room. Beyond is a living room off which you'll find a library and my study. Please feel free to use it. I'm certain you'll be able to find something to your liking.'

"Thanks, I'll take you up on that."

"While you acquaint yourself with the room I'll go fix us some lunch." She disappeared down the hall, leaving him alone.

He set his suitcase down and considered the tidy little space. A single bed occupied a side wall. A bureau with a statuette of Mother and Child stood next to the doorway. A sweet, milky fragrance entered the room through a wide-open window, along with the melody of birds. Under the window there was a writing table with a clock and small number of books. He picked a book up at random. It was Tolstoy's "Resurrection." He considered it carefully and put it back down, smiled and collapsed on the bed with a gentle sigh. He brought his hands up under his head and gazed at the ceiling, lost in thought, daydreaming.

He soon lost track of time and was startled out of his reverie when, from the kitchen, Amelia called, "Soup's ready."

"Coming," he called. He yawned, scratched his unshaven chin, and went and joined Amelia at the kitchen table over a bowl of barley soup and black bread. They had almost finished lunch when a sharp rap was heard and the back screened door opened and a young woman, in full length-skirt entered. She was in shadow, the outside light at her back.

"Aunt Amelia," she trilled, and, on sighting Percival's back, apologized, "Sorry if I'm intruding. I'd no idea you had company. But I'd finished your correspondence and thought you'd like to have them to go over."

"Come in, my dear. It's quite alright," Amelia coaxed. "I want you to meet my houseguest." Percival turned in his seat, his eyes dilating. "Lisette, I want you to meet Percival. Percival, this is my niece, Lisette."

"Hello," she said in a throaty, melodic voice.

Percival rose from his chair and taking her hand, raised it to his lips. "Charmed," he said.

She blushed to her eyes —at a loss for words. The silence ensued. He smiled, looking into her generous, dark eyes. She was a rich palette of tones, a blend of differing nationalities, a harmony of parts. She was substantially attractive, in her early twenties, with an aristocratic bearing. She was lovely to behold, carrying her beauty without artifice.

"It's a pleasure," he added, finding his tongue. With some embarrassment they realized they were still clinging to each other's hand. They laughed as their hands slipped apart, her shoulders bouncing with laughter.

"Here is your correspondence," said Lisette to Amelia, turning from Percival for the moment. "You should only have to sign them." She set a stack of letters on the table before her aunt.

"Thank you. I'll go over them later. I trust you've seen to everything, as always."

"How long will you be staying?" Lisette asked, again facing Percival.

"A couple days to a week or two. If it's ok with your aunt."

"He's one of Nina's dearest friends," Amelia explained, "and is welcome to stay for as long as he likes."

"You know Nina," Lisette said, animated.

"As your aunt says, we're tight, the best of friends. Yes."

"How is she?"

"She's great – the best, you know?" said Percival, playing it cool.

"She is isn't she. She's not been up this year at all, so far."

"And my flower garden's suffered as a consequence," Amelia said. "But she promises to come for Thanksgiving."

"It'll be too late for your garden," Lisette said, musingly.

"But she's always the loveliest flower of the bunch anyway. So Thanksgiving will have to be soon enough."

"At least I'll be home from school. Maybe I'll call her just to say hello," said Lisette in a soft, unhurried voice. "To let her know we're thinking of her."

"That's a fine idea," Amelia approved. Then, by way of an explanation she said to Percival, "From the time Nina was small she used to visit us every summer. But because of her handicap, she could not work the fields, as she so longed. So my mother used to let her tend the flower garden and she developed a splendid green thumb over the years. We always boasted the most beautiful flower garden. The varieties were breathtakingly spectacular."

"Yes, of course," said Percival, casually, "she has one or two in her own yard."

"That's wonderful," Lisette chirped, pleased. "Oh well, I've got to run. My ride is waiting. And if I know Julius he'll be growing impatient. Yes," she cocked her head as if listening, "I can hear him revving the engine now."

"Before you run off," Amelia said, "there are two favors I wish of you. One, can you still get tickets for Saturday's ballet? I've promised to take a few of the girls."

"I'll see what I can do."

"And two, would you mind terribly while Percival's here, showing him about?"

"How can I say no to a friend of Nina's?" she said, eyes aglow. "I'll also bring him a calendar of events at SPAC in case there's something that suits his fancy."

"SPAC?" Percival asked, casting her a covetous glance, pained by the rapture of his heart.

"It's where I work for the summer. It's the performing arts center, and summer home of the New York City Ballet Company."

"I see."

"We passed it on our way in," Amelia reminded him.

"Ummm," he murmured. "Where the racetrack is?"

"That's the place," Lisette chimed, avoiding his eyes. "Oh well I should get going, I suppose. My chariot awaits me," she said in a puff of laughter, turning to leave, her skirt sweeping the floor. "I'll do my best to show you a nice time while you're here," she promised. "Goodbye, Aunt Amelia," she called, as she flew down the outside steps.

"Goodbye, my dear."

"Next time," said Percival, watching as she crossed the farmyard, scattering clucking hens in her way, skirt billowing at her heels. A good looking, fair-skinned young man in dark glasses awaited her in a '69 Corvette convertible. He drummed restlessly on the steering wheel. She slipped into the seat beside him folding her skirt under her and closed the car door. She cast a back-ward glance at the house. Percival took it as a sign. She pulled a kerchief from her head, and tossed her hair, black as a raven's wings which spread fanwise against a sunlit sky. The car eased out of the drive. He found himself wondering who the guy was? The type of man she likes. Was he her beau? He hoped not, for his own selfish ends.

"She's a wonderful girl," said Amelia, matter-of-factly, joining him at the doorway as the Corvette dipped over the hill where, an orchard blurred at the horizon, like a mirage in sunlight.

"I assumed as much."

"She's my foreman's daughter."

"Oh? I'd not realized you were related."

"You mean Lisette referring to me as aunt? No, we're not related by blood, but by affection, which can be just as strong as blood. She was born here. In my house. I was the midwife. And she has lived here all her life. Her family is my family."

"I see," said Percival, tonelessly.

"I must join my farm hands in the fields," Amelia said, stepping out onto the back porch, adjusting her sun hat. "Feel free to venture as you like. There's a lake over yonder." She pointed with an outstretched forefinger. "It's a lovely spot. A few mothers and their children are usually there this time of day."

They strolled off in different directions, he to the lake and she to the fields; the dogs trailing lazily after her.

The lake was expansive. On one side a forest rose, lush and dark, on the other a beach where children frolicked under the watchful eyes of their mothers. There was a dock on the lake where one could fish or dive back into the clear water.

He signaled to the women with a wave of the hand. One squinted in his direction as he neared. He sauntered up casually. There were seven women in all and a dozen or more children. They greeted him coolly, viewing him with mild suspicion until, he introduced himself. "I'm Amelia's houseguest," he told them, not giving his name. He quickly learned that they were island people, Jamaicans and Haitians mostly, content with having cast their lot in with Amelia. They told him that, 'With the exception of a few island workers, the big machinery was operated by local white hands, along with the foreman, Mr. Poincare, Lisette's father. 'They lived in the hillside house, overlooking the farm, up there amidst the red maple trees. The same ones as in the boss ladies yard.'

"Ameli's a' fine woman," said a mother holding an umbrella over her head and shoulders.

"Ya've known her awhile," he asked?

"Ya, mahn," she said. "Goin'n ten ye'rs. "We be comin' up, oh, jus' af'er 'er daddy pass 'n she m'ke et 'n organic farm."

"Natural, you mean?"

"No posins, mahn."

A Haitian woman interjected in patois, "W'ere ya kno' Amelia fr'm, chile?"

"I don't. I jus' got here. She's the aunt of a friend of mine."

"Ya n't gonna w'rk f'r 'er?" asked another.

"No, I'm not."

"Cuz I wus gonna say ya w'n't finda be't'r boss lady, chile." Another grunted, "dat so," in concurrence." Others chimed in, "Dat's so." "Dat's rite, She da bes'." "We more kin da he'p."

"She's a saint," said the woman with the umbrella, crossing herself with her free hand. The others nodded their heads, "Dat' so."

Percival shrugged, he couldn't say what a Saint was or wasn't. Then a mother broke from the pack, snatching a little boy from the lake and striking him soundly on the rump sending him howling like a banshee.

"Boy, w'at et is I say 'bout goin' 'n da wat'r aft'r ya jus' fill ya belly full'a food!" she scolded.

"Well," Percival said, casting his gaze across the lake, "it certainly looks like a fine enough spot."

"Mo' 'n dat, mahn, 'cause ya can't eat da scen'ry or ra'se'a fam'ly on'a view, 'n is 'y I lef' da i'lands 'n da f'rst pl'ce, Amelia pay 'r mehn'a livin' wage, union sc'le wid 'ealth ben'fits. N da housi'g's fine, mahn." She told Percival that they were treated with respect. That in bumper crop years, they shared in the proceeds. "She looks out f'r us, lyke we blood. W'en da other farmers 'cuse er'a incitin' unres' 'mong da workers 'cause she pay union sc'le, she tell em, 'ya'll 'ncite em by treatin' em like serf; unlyke chil'ren'a God,'" she said in a sing-song peculiar to Caribbean people. "'W'at's rite's rite 'n w'at's 'rong's 'rong, no arguin' dat,' she tell 'em."

"Dat's God's trut'," said one.

"Ain't et doe," piped another.

"W'en da l'cal farmers a'cused her a' incitin' unres' 'mong dey w'rkers cause she pay union s'ale, she say, 'y'll incite em yarself's by treatin' em lyke serf; unlyke chil'ren a God,'" she said in a sing-song peculiar to Caribbean peoples. "'W'at's right's right 'n w'at's 'rong's 'rong ain't no arguin' dat,' she told em."

"All da migr'nt w'kers 'ere 'bouts com' fr'm da i'lands 'n ta'ks, so we kn'w w'at go on fr'm fa'm ta fa'm," another woman broke in.

"I see. N 'r you farmers, too?"

"R 'usbands dey da fa'mers we runs da road sidestan' dere." She inclined her head toward the road.

The women were obviously devoted to Amelia. They considered her a benefactress, a family matriarch and friend. She sounded, to his ears, too good to be true.

But then, seeing everything now through the lens of Sam's death, he had to acknowledge that he was becoming cynical, skeptical of the powers of human decency to be of much use. Then he was forced to recall that it was Nina who had arranged for this encounter, had wanted him and her aunt to meet for what must be reasons known only to herself. Thus, he'd do well to observe, listen, and not play devil's advocate.

Eventually the women went back to talking among themselves as if he were not there. He strayed from their midst and ventured out onto the dock where a rowboat was tied, and a young boy sat fishing, his bare feet dangling above the water.

"Fish biting?" he asked.

"They okay. See, I caught'a bunch," said the boy, hauling up a line of fish strung together from out of the water for Percival to admire.

"Very nice," said Percival. He looked across the lake at the forest. He had a desire to step foot on the other side, to enter that forest. The lake flashed silver in the sun and was sentineled by pines. There was a mystery hidden in those woods; a mystery whose depths he was intent on plumbing.

He climbed into the craft, untied it and started across the glittering, sun-speckled water. With every stroke of the oar he felt compelled by the beckoning forest beyond. He rowed harder and harder until he reached the distant shore, breathless and sweaty.

He pulled the boat ashore. Then hardly having taken a dozen steps into the woods, he came upon a clearing. There was a woodland church with a dome as high as a Gothic cathedral with sunlight streaming through leafy branches and dappling the mossy forest floor in a filigree of light and shade.

He could not have been any more awestruck if he had found himself at the Vatican in St. Peter's Basilica, in the Sistine chapel admiring Michelangelo's famous ceiling. A harmonic silence which welled from out of the depths of the woods filled the forest church like the dying strains of an organ. Seven trees on either side of him bore roughly hewn carvings of the passion of Christ, his trial and journey to Golgotha, the Stations of the Cross. The fallen trunk of a heavy log lay on a carpet of moss like an altar with a crude crucifix and votive candles. A blue jay far off in the depths, shrieked; a sparrow sang softly. The liquid song of birds called back and forth.

Struck by a profound sense of the sacred, he emerged from out of a brown study with a confused start. He found that he could not press on, as if to do so would rend the veil of the Holy of Holies. Thus fearfully, reverentially, he withdrew back to the shore and rowboat, feeling like the ancient poet, Omah, "Having left by way of the door he'd entered," though he would return a few more times before he was to leave for good.

***

That evening after a light supper, the children of the migrant workers came to the big house for dessert. Amelia served up bowls of blackberries in heavy cream with a sprinkling of sugar. Afterwards they played croquet on the lawn, inviting Percival to team up with one of the older boys, the young fisherman from the dock.

Amelia had been enlisted on the side of the children, who clung to the hem of her skirt, and crowded her generally, helped her strike the ball, cheating on her behalf, and then applauding themselves roundly for having been so cleaver.

"Why is it children so like to cheat?" she asked of the sky.

As the game progressed and Percival's side was down by two games, his partner suddenly looked up over the hedge which enclosed the front lawn, as a Corvette convertible turned into the driveway across the road, leading up a hill to a house concealed among red maples. Again, Lisette was seated in the passenger seat and the voice of her companion carried on the dusky night air.

A young urchin with a bold grin said, "I'm'a marry her when I grow up. He won't scare me off like he do them older other guys. They jus' sissies. Shoo, I ain't scared'a that turkey."

"He scares off the competition, ah?" asked Percival.

"He's always bullying people, pushing em round, remindin' em'a they place, actin big 'n bad cause his daddy's a hotshot lawyer 'n he be in law school, but he ain't but a blowhard."

"Is that the story?"

"Dat's it."

"I owe you," said Percival, with a wink. "If she has a younger sister, she's all yours. I promise."

"I ain't gonna ave trouble with you, too," said the scamp, eyeing him suspiciously.

Percival smiled.

After the game of croquet, the children followed Amelia onto the porch bathed in the glow of a yellow bulb. As she settled back in a chair to read them the story of Blessed Martin de Porres from a book on "The Lives of the Saints," a few birds descended from out the branches of trees and settled on the porch rail. A small bird landed on the head of a young child who had climbed up in her lap. The dogs lay at her feet, and all the other children clustered eagerly about. It was an idyllic scene. Percival leaned against a stanchion, gazing intently at a distant light in the window from the house across the way – Lisette's house, enshrined among maples and a lullaby of crickets.

The children quieted as Amelia started reading.

"Martin was born on December 5, 1579 in Lima, Peru. His father, Juan de Pores, was a noble Spaniard. His mother, Ana Velasquez, was a free Negro. When his father saw that his son was black, he wanted nothing to do with him," Amelia read, catching Percival's interest. He listened more closely. He had no more than a superficial knowledge of the Catholic faith and it's pantheon of saints, and so to hear that one was black came as a surprise.

The children listened in rapt attention, looking up at Amelia with expressions of enchantment on their faces. She read of Martin's many miracles, of his "powers of bi-location" and his abilities to heal the sick by a touch of the hand. She read of his devotion to the poor and how he would plant fruit trees on public grounds so the poor would not have to trespass and steal from private property and go to jail. They were told of his great love for God and how, rapt in prayer, saints would visit him in his monastic cell and that he would be levitated in their divine presence.

No less enchanted than the children, Percival wondered if there was any truth to the tale, or was it just an opiate, as Marx said? By the end of the story he was seated on the porch, legs crossed at his ankles, wondering if divine intervention were remotely possible, and if he could by some act of mercy, ever be rid of this pain eating at his heart. But the distant stars to whom he addressed himself remained stoically silent. They offered no more a reply than when he had wished upon them back when he was a boy, a lifetime ago. "Damn," he swore under his breath.

Eventually, the lights from the Corvette blazoned descending the drive, skimmed the tree lined darkness like ghostly fingers. Then the car swung onto the country road and sped off.

"What you gonna read us tomorrow?" the children were curious to know.

"The story of Saint Catherine of Siena," said Amelia.

"Who she?" asked a girl.

"You'll find out tomorrow," Amelia promised. "If you behave."

"We'll behave! We'll behave!" they yelped, jumping with glee.

Then the voices of mothers calling to their flock were heard in the dewy, uncertain dark, like varying notes on a scale, some more in key than others.

Each child quickly kissed Amelia "good night," then started off up the road fleet of foot, racing home.

"Last one home's a rotten egg," one boy shouted, challenging the others.

They all ran, darting shadows on a lightless, country road.

Percival sat silently for a while, looking out at the dark sky, watching fireflies mate and listening to a racket of crickets. He did not talk, he did not want to move, for to do so would stir a hornet's nest of thought and he just wanted to be still and drink it all in.

Amelia rose and said, "I have things to attend to. Good night." The dogs slunk off as she entered the house.

"I'll see you in the morning," he said, not stirring. Shortly after she shut the door behind her, he was struck by a pang of conscience. Outlined amidst the constellation of stars, he could have sworn he saw Sam's face. In a panic, he started to his feet, but caught himself. He slumped back down, breaking out

432

in a sweat. He missed Sam, missed him terribly, and though he could not recall Sam having a single quality he admired, he missed him nonetheless. He experienced Sam's absence as one would a missing, phantom limb. His insides screamed of loss, threatening his sanity. He cupped his face in his hands. He was alive and Sam wasn't. Emotion yanked at him and tears slid down his cheeks. He stayed out a moment longer, then collecting himself he went in for the evening.

***

Percival arose early with the coming dawn. He was wakened by the sound of something snorting below his window. He threw off his covers and peered outside. In the pale, pre-dawn light, before the rooster had wakened to crow, he saw Amelia stroking the head of a deer with three fawns close by eating apples, the dogs watching, incuriously. The doe nestled it's head against Amelia. Percival was surprised because he had always thought that they avoided human contact. Since he was already up, he decided to take a stroll in the crisp air. He donned a pair of sweats and sneakers and left by way of the front door, so as not to intrude upon Amelia. He started to walk but the chain of nagging thoughts, of recent events began to assail him. He picked up his pace and began to jog, trying to outstrip his demons. The fields and woodlands emerged from out of the gloom, as somewhere a rooster began to crow. The fog was gradually being burnt off the by the rising sun. A distinct pearly haze of dawn suffused the skyline. He was puffing up a long grade of road when the engine of a vehicle slowed and a truck came to a crawl alongside him.

Lisette spoke out of the rolled down window on the driver's side, "What are you doing?"

"Getting some well needed exercise," he panted.

"Join us in the fields, you'll get plenty exercise there."

"Maybe I'll do that," he said. "Where 'r you off to?"

"Delivering some eggs to various outlets in Saratoga. Care to join me?"

"I guess no harm will come of it." He shrugged, coming to a standstill. He joined her in the cab of the truck and, shifting gears, she accelerated.

"Any first major impressions you care to share?" Lisette asked, her eyes on the road swept by high beams.

"A few of no account, 'n hardly worth the mention."

"Go ahead, try me."

"Well, you know, it's too soon to say," he began, with an indecisive frown. "I miss'd the noise of the city streets last night. The silence here makes everything echo like a guilty conscience. There's nothing more somber than laying awake in the dead of night listening to the beat of your own heart, as you would the sound of a leaky faucet, or the house beams yawning, creaking the night away. I'm outta my element. For instance, there 'r no friendly stray cats or dogs in the city, everyone is rabid, 'n you best cross the street before coming in contact with an unleashed animal of any species. But I was awakened this morning to see Amelia caressing a deer 'n feeding it's young apples, 'n the dogs lying about like it's nothing. Well let me tell you, it's something where I come from."

Lisette laughed good-naturedly. Her gentle laugh in the small, dark enclosure was heartwarming.

"Actually that deer thinks Amelia's its mother. A few years ago she was struck by a car and left in a ditch by the road. Amelia found her, brought her into her house and called in a veterinarian who told her to destroy it, that it was beyond healing. Amelia refused to take his advice. And between her and my elder brother who was then in Medical school, they nursed it back to health. She cared for the animal both night and day, never being away from it long. She set up her bed in the kitchen so as to be by it throughout the night. And bit by bit, the animal came round. And once it recovered, it was so funny to see her follow Amelia about like a toddler." Lisette laughed, reflectively. "It stayed through the winter then ventured off one spring day and did not return for almost a year. But the following spring she showed up in Amelia's backyard with a family, and just about every day since she comes by first thing on her migratory rounds." Lisette's profile was suddenly illuminated by a splash of sunlight on the windshield. Her features were Latin, her neck slender as a reed. She wore coveralls, and a kerchief covered her hair. She smelled of hay and soap. Then the road swooped and her profile was cast into shadow once again. "I'm sorry I sidetracked you, you were telling me of your first impressions?"

"This may sound harsh but I'm usually skeptical of the motives of good white people, for this reason 'n that," he confessed openly, not holding back. "If it wasn't for knowing Nina as I do, I'd ave my doubts 'bout your aunt. N still I don't get her disarming the children'a these migrant workers, these impoverished kids, by telling em such fantastical stories of Saints – such fiction. Someday they got'a know there's no more a God than there is Santa Claus."

"What venomous serpent got it's fangs into you?"

"Maybe I overstated my case," he said, smarting.

"Poor baby," she said, as if she could cradle him in her arms and exorcise his devils. "Didn't your mother ever read stories from the Bible to you when you were a boy? Would you prefer she read them Uncle Remus than the lives of Saints? Who better to emulate, Brear Rabbit or King David?"

Percival peered out the window at the darkened line of woods as the truck's headlights searched the lonely road ahead.

"Amelia read those very stories to us, my two older brothers and me from as far back as I can recall," she said. "I still love those stories. In fact, one of my brothers loved those stories so much he became a priest. And Amelia is the one who paid for his education, as well as sending my eldest brother, now serving as a field doctor in Vietnam, through Medical School. He's a pacifist, refuses to carry a gun, caring for the enemies wounded with the same dedication as he does our soldiers. My younger brother is a parish priest in Bedford Stuyvesant Brooklyn."

"Bed-Stuy," said Percival, mouthing the words, "that's my stomping ground, my home turf."

"Oh really? Then you might know him, Father Dominick – Father Dominick Poincare."

"I doubt it. I'm not Catholic."

"He's a priest at Our Lady of Victory Church."

"Can't say I do."

"Before I go on, I should also say aunt Amelia's sending me through college as well. Let me tell you something else about Amelia. I'm almost certain you've not been in her study as yet. No, you misjudge Amelia if you simply take her for a good white, Christian country farm girl – that would certainly be a terrible oversimplification. Amelia's not your typical anything, not at all. Not by a long shot. Aunt Amelia's an original – one of a kind; an intellectual of stature. In fact, she holds a bachelor's degree in sociology, a masters in psychology and a doctorate in philosophy. She's an Augustinian scholar, professor and chair of humanities at SUNY, author, renowned lecturer and agronomist. She's in correspondence with the likes of Coretta Scott King, Cesar Chavez— the farm workers union organizer— Thomas Merton— author and Trappist Monk—, and Andri Sakharov, the Russian physicist and dissident, to name but a few. She's also in close contact with Dorothy Day the activist and co-founder of The Catholic Worker Movement. In case you're interested, those letters I brought for her to sign yesterday when we first met were to those very people. Lest I forget, to the best of anyone's knowledge, she was the first white person to successfully exchange correspondence with Malcolm X on his return from Mecca in the brief interval before his death."

Contrite, Percival apologized. "My error. I see, for the first time, why Nina wanted us to meet."

"She even had Betty Shabazz stay with her daughters up here for a few weeks afterwards."

"That's really astonishing." He flushed darkly, feeling quite foolish.

"Isn't it though?"

"Did you meet them?"

"Of course."

"How fortunate."

"You'll be equally surprised by who else has occupied the room in which you sleep; the people who've passed through Amelia's doors."

"I'm speechless."

"After salaries are paid the lion share of the profit from the farm is donated to what's left of the Iroquois confederacy," she said, further. "This farm, Amelia's farm—which has been in her family for generations— rightly, as she sees it, belongs to them and their people and so she pays them for its use."

"That's one hell of'a gesture," Percival said, as much surprised as impressed. "That'll teach me to keep my mouth shut won't it."

"The lesser sum of monies goes to her expenses, upkeep of the farm and, as I've said, she's a professor and chair of humanities at SUNY. By no means is she impoverishing herself. We don't live in a vacuum here. No one's avoiding the realities of American life but, by the same token, there is work and there is prayer."

He felt the measured beat of the arteries in his temples. This woman, this Lisette, was proving to be more savvy than he'd bargained for. He'd do well to stay awake.

"All of her workers think she's a saint and all her neighbors fear or revere her for very much the same reason. They understand her as being a secular saint. A woman in touch with her spiritual depth, swimming not treading the bottomless sea of humanity."

"And you?"

"She's my aunt. I was raised with her. It's who she is."

"For myself I wouldn't know the difference between being possessed by devils, or angels. It's not an area of which I'm familiar."

"You've mentioned only the deer. But you'll come to see that birds and other animals come to her, eat out her hands and perch on her. This place might not be Shangri-La, but Amelia runs it with a heavenly intention. Taking it seriously, the words from the Lord's prayer, 'On earth as it is in Heaven.' Enough of this, what about yourself," she asked?

"There's not much to tell," he claimed, with a shrug. "I'm jus' up to catch the air 'n clear my head."

"You're the first man I've met who's not taken the opportunity to reveal how charming he is and tell me why I should be impressed."

"You see that many men this way?"

"You'd be surprised."

"I'm the new kid on the block, recall? I've been told I'd do best to learn the ropes rather than shoot my mouth off, exposing my Achilles' heel."

"You're trying to hide something, aren't you? Are you in some kind of trouble?" she asked, then answered herself without waiting for a reply. "Yes, of course. I should have known."

"If you're asking if I'm hiding out or running from the police, no. But t'day, every man worth his salt is, more or less, in some small measure of difficulty," he said ruefully. "But I shouldn't lose any sleep over it, if I were you. Besides, trouble is a matter of choosing who your gonna share it with or not."

"Is that a hint?"

"Not necessarily." He laughed.

"Then I'm not politely being told to mind my own business?"

"Far be it from me." The sheer joy of being in her company was sadly overshadowed by the proximity of Sam's death.

"We're here," she announced, "so it gets you off the hook for the moment, anyway," she cautioned, swinging the truck off the road into the parking lot of a grocery store, and backing it up to the loading dock.

They dropped off four cases of eggs then went on to other stores, diners, restaurants and nightclubs. Lisette was quite popular among the men. They wouldn't permit her to lift a box, and despite Percival's presence, flirted with her shamelessly. She had grown accustomed to this play and laughed it off as little more than good-natured, boyish clowning.

"That your new boyfriend?" asked a cook.

"That's yet to be seen," she said, coquettishly glancing back at Percival standing off to the side with a devil-may-care look. "Maybe. I don't see it's any of your affair."

"Curiosity."

"Well I'll keep you posted, then," she said, sashaying off.

She considered Percival again for a moment after they'd climbed back in the truck. She smiled indulgently. She liked what she saw.

"Everything okay?"

"Just fine," she said, out of voice, smiling to herself, and turning the key in the ignition. "Just fine."

Percival caught the advertisement in the window of a club announcing the coming appearance of Jazz great, McCoy Tyner.

"Wow, I'll have to catch that if I'm still here."

"What's the fuss?" asked Lisette.

"Ya don't know McCoy Tyner?"

"Jazz is only a word to me."

"What music do you listen to then?"

"I hear too much country 'n western, rock 'n roll, of course, but in my home growing up there was always a smattering of classical music. And of course at SPAC, it's mostly classical. It's a fine bonus for working there."

"The best way for me to explain it, is to bring you – you up for a night out on the town?"

"I thought you'd never ask. It would be my pleasure."

***

When Lisette dropped him off at Amelia's, he entered the house and immediately found the study. The room was cozy, bright, and easy on the eye. It had four windows and ceiling lights. Three walls were lined from floor to ceiling with shelves of books alphabetized and categorized. A good size mahogany desk with lamp, manual typewriter, and family photographs neatly arranged atop the desk, occupied the last wall. Above the desk's plush, oxblood leather chair and between two windows hung Amelia's diplomas along with graduation pictures and fine etchings of those hallowed corridors of learning.

Percival sat in the plush fold of the swivel chair, at the desk and considered the photographs. The closest one was of Amelia as a young woman in the arms of a beau. Then there was an equally old photo, Amelia later explained was her father, mother, two brothers and an elder sister, all in their Sunday best. Percival thought there was an element of despair about the photo, as if they'd just received bad news. In fact, he learned, they had gathered for what would prove to be a last family photo because war had just broken out with Japan. Lastly, there was a photo of Amelia, by herself, in a nun's habit. This was as unexpected as it was intriguing. He studied it, hoping for it to reveal itself, but he met with little success. Amelia was or had been a nun? This he found curious. If that were so, then why hadn't Lisette mentioned it? It certainly would explain the absence of a man around the house.

It was a well-used room and every book on which he lay a finger had been read through. Indeed, after spending her early mornings in the fields, Amelia would retire to her library and spend the rest of her workday in the study. Usually, one of the wives of a farm hand would prepare supper and she and her family would join Amelia for dinner. This way Amelia came to know her workers and kept a direct line of communication between them. She reserved her evenings for the children, serving them desserts, joining them in croquet and reading The Lives of the Saints to them. Then, as often as not, after the children had gone home for the night, she would return to the study for a few more hours before bed.

One night when they were in the study together, she leaned back in her chair, wanting to talk. It was then she told him about the photos on her desk. The one with her and the young man was taken back in '35, before he went to Spain to fight with the anti-fascists against Franco, where he met his death.

"In my grief," she revealed, "I entered the convent, but fled before taking final vows. He was the love of my life." She sighed, casting a tender eye back on the past. "It's not easy to love again unless one first learns to love God, otherwise it might be impossible, as the sad story of my younger brother proves. But I'm jumping ahead of myself. Coming to love God, I fell in love with, of all things, mankind, and became a bride of humanity – though, for some reason, I could not face it as a nun."

The final photo, the family photo, was painful. Her older brother had been killed in the big war, and her younger brother came home from the Korean conflict criminally insane.

"He had always been a quiet boy, a sensitive boy, a good boy," she said, fingering the frame delicately on which she gazed. "We were all shocked at how changed he was on his return. He had seen too much death; had seen too many young men die before their time; had himself participated in too much bloodletting. He had his fill of war and could not get the stench of it out of his nostrils, nor wipe the blood off his hands. He had seen the ugliest side of life and life had lost its savor. War had debased him utterly, had left him a moral lech: a vulgar, coarse and godless man. He stayed home only long enough for the sheriff to run him off.

"The terrible surprise of it, the pain inflicted on our parents, was incalculable. For many years afterwards we knew nothing of his whereabouts until my father was contacted through an attorney in Texas, requesting money in a last-ditch effort to save him from the gallows, on appeal. It seems he was on death row for having killed a man in a barroom brawl over a woman they'd just met. Well, the lawyer lost the appeal, and my brother met his end on the gallows," she said, forcing back tears. "He himself never contacted us. And though he was five years my junior we had been close as children, so it made a certain sense that I go see him before his execution and return with the remains afterwards, for burial. So I took myself in hand and went to see him. He was never moved, never contrite, faulting no one save that of being born. That's hardest of all to accept from a Catholic woman's point of view, considering a Catholic mother would be expected, as an article of faith, to sacrifice her own life in childbirth, if necessary, for the sake of the newborn."

She sighed explosively. "I, for one, was not the same afterwards. He wouldn't own me or, should I say, refused to acknowledge me unless I agreed to witness his execution and somehow be included in his death, to shame me

439

for living on, in face of his dying. I reluctantly agreed, but only if he would not mind my praying for him in his cell. He only laughed at my attempts to save his worthless soul by prayer. His final words to me were, 'I've been leading a debased life all these years. I've only now been caught up to. I'm not damned because I killed that worthless cuss. Hell, I'd been itching to stick it to somebody since leaving New York, and that unlucky bastard found himself on the wrong side of my ice pick. And so I stuck him like a pig. You remember how we used to kill pigs back home, on the farm?" She had borne the pain of it for years in stoical silence, and breaking that silence wrung her out emotionally like a wet rag hung up to dry. She said, solemnly, eyes cast low, "I then decided to give up eating meat. 'Yes, I stuck him for old time sake,' he said, 'for the boys back in my ole military unit, like saluting them for past favors, for who I've become, for what that war made me. I can't entirely blame it on the war. Hell no, the war was just a trigger. It didn't unhinge me as such, it just introduced me to myself, my nature, no more. There is a brute satisfaction, a fiendish delight in taking another's life. It's not exactly the Last Supper ritual, but it is a ritual. Like snuffing out the life of all mankind – eclipsing the sun.' He blew on me, on my face, as if blowing out a candle. And I could almost feel the ice pick go through me. I was aghast, horrified, and drew back. He laughed all the more. I dared not cringe for fear of him taking delight in my frailty. 'True, I deserve this death no less than hell but not for why they're hanging me but for my having been born a moral leper.' I reminded him that he had been a model child.

"'Spare me,' he said, disgustedly. 'Spare me!' To see a man hanged. Your own brother killed on the gallows before your eyes at the end of a rope. Not only is it his neck they break, but all else within you as well. He had been such an impressionable boy, far too sensitive to have fought in a war. And yet, having done so, it doomed him – turned him into a monster. And then for me to travel back by train with his remains. It was like three days in the tomb, a dark night of the soul. It was a death to all I had been before. You either condemn the world or become more determined to mend it. I only hope that I've chosen correctly."

"You'll get no argument from me," Percival remarked.

She closed her eyes against the pain. "My sister, Nina's mother, was the fortunate one, if you care to couch it in such terms. She wanted a large family and her husband had gladly accommodated her. Sometimes, I guess, that's the best you can hope for. I, for one, miss not having had children."

***

Later that evening Lisette took Percival to a Boston Pops concert at SPAC featuring, guest singer, Dionne Warwick. She had to work but he was able to bring a blanket, beach umbrella, folding chair, and virtually camp out on the grounds. He set himself up out on the lawn among hundreds of other listeners. After a while as the music washed over the sprawl of people, Dionne Warwick came out on stage and was greeted with thunderous applause. Then with the first full note from her bell tone throat, the crowd grew silent, transfixed. Captivated by the seductive sway of the songstress's voice, they were held enthralled. Soon Lisette appeared and joined him while Dionne regaled them, "The moment I wake up before I put on my makeup/ I say a little prayer for you." Percival had not been this relaxed for some time nor this happy. Thrilled! Lisette slipped away back to work as Dionne brought the house down and the audience came to its feet in rousing applause, crying "More! More! More!" as the diva departed the stage.

Lisette met Percival after work and they roamed the streets of Saratoga, dined and listened to a lesser jazz band in a side street cafe but, high off each other, didn't hear the music.

"If you care to help me pick eggs," Lisette proposed on leaving him off in sight of the back porch light by which to navigate his way, "meet me at daybreak in the hen house."

"I'd be delighted." He was there the next morning as the cock crowed. She introduced him to the routine of collecting eggs. The chickens clucked furiously at them, squatting stubbornly on their nests or strutting worrisomely at their heels. "Pay them no mind," she told him. "You learn fast for a city slicker," she said, after he filled his first basket.

"Look who I've got for a teacher," he commented, in mock reply.

On concluding their chore, Lisette balanced a basket of eggs on her head while carrying a basket in either hand, besides.

"Aren't you afraid you'll drop those eggs," he asked, as they crossed the barnyard to the storage room.

"Oh, no," she said, reassuringly, "I've been carrying baskets like this for as far back as I can recall."

Hence, he came to know the secret of her carriage. She moved with such easy grace, despite the bulk of her coveralls. Her spine was so well poised on the counter sway of her lovely derriere and splendidly, up thrusted breast. She could easily have been an island woman on way to market.

***

Supper was taken under a tiffany lamp at an oblong oak table covered in linen with a bouquet of flowers set in crystal. It was a spacious dining area off from the kitchen with two windows that looked out over flower beds. The curtains billowed from a gust of wind like spectral wings, beyond which a soft, balmy fragrance entered the room. Against the far wall there was a mahogany cabinet filled with ceramic china. At his back a grandfather clock struck the time with minute to minute accuracy. When it tolled its chimes echoed throughout the rooms of the spacious house.

"Thank you for dinner, Cora," said Amelia to the svelte, coca-colored wife of a farm hand, Henri, after dinner was served and grace said.

"'N t'anks ya f'r 'avin' us,'" Cora responded with a sidelong gaze at Amelia, before she too began to eat. Cora was no great beauty, but she was not unpleasant to look at. She reminded Percival of other lands and distant places, eliciting a smile. She was a child of the Caribbean sun, Haitian, of African/French descent. She was as rare a sight as a sea nymph, with a wondrous smile punctuated by dimples. Her handsomely cast head was held aloft on a slender swan's neck. Her raven hair was drawn back and parted in the center and fell midway down her back in a single rope like braid. She wore a sleeveless West African print dress and African jewelry, such as a shimmering, copper hammered necklace that graced her throat, a copper snake like bracelet twined her left arm, and matching earrings hung from her earlobes, accentuating her chestnut brown complexion. She went bare foot and wore a gold ring on her big, right toe. The plain gold cross she wore at her breast was surprising, and out of keeping with the rest of her attire. She was dressed in all her finery to cook and dine with the mistress of the house.

She was presently distracted by the antics of her two small boys. "Y'll want'ya'r fad'a ta take'a strap ta ya do ya?" she asked, in annoyance.

The two shook their heads, vigorously, settling down.

"W'at's fer des'ert?" said the younger boy, with a lisp.

"You'll have to wait and see," Amelia chirped.

"Dey m' boys," their father boasted.

Percival measured men by weight class and took Henri, at 6ft. 2' and 175 to 180lbs of rippling muscles, for a light heavyweight. He was a crudely handsome man with distinct onyx eyes, who wore his hair in a decorative maze of corn rows. He was genial and his smile revealed fine, even teeth, beneath a thick mustache. In addition, he had a brazil nut skin color with an engaging, singsong, musical accent. He was a spokesperson for the field hands. His English was barely tolerable, but Amelia spoke French and understood Haitian patois like a native. Communication was fluid. He had freshened up after work and was scrubbed to a gloss from his flat black face to his calloused hands. He was older than Percival by a few years, 26, perhaps, and Cora, his wife, 23. He was ravenous and ate without delicacy. His sons sat across and beside him and were also scrubbed to a gloss, shirtless, shoeless, and wearing short pants.

Percival picked at his food.

"N't h'ngry," Cora asked? Her English was far better than her husband's.

"Sorry," he apologized. "My mind was wandering."

"I see Lisette's taken you under her wing," Amelia said, draping a napkin across her lap.

"Umm," he gulped, his heart pounding. He dared not look at Amelia, but he was, non the less, conscious of her eyes. "I've been helping her deliver eggs in the morning. She's shown me the milking operation, too. She even had me try my hand at it, but the cow was disagreeable 'n kicked the bucket 'n milk all over me." He laughed.

"Dey do dat," said Henri. "Dey gro' s'rly w'en ya dunno ya stuff," he grinned, easily.

"I don't," Percival confessed. "I met Lisette's father for a moment. At any rate, long enough to shake hands. It's quite an operation you've got," he said, directing the conversation away from Lisette, the real object of his fancy. "But her father seemed preoccupied."

"He's a capable fellow, that Renaldo. I can rely on him, utterly. He sees to every detail of the farm, especially while I'm away performing my function as chair of the Dept. of Humanities at SUNY, Albany, for the school year," said Amelia. "It's not that far away, true; and I come home often enough, but my workload is such I can't take on the farm as well. Besides, Renaldo's more than competent. He knows the operation of the farm as well as I. He was something of an adventurer in his day," she said, off-handily. "He's done many things in his past. In that sense, he puts me in mind of my one and only, lost to me in the final days of the Spanish Civil War," she said with heartfelt longing for a boy she once knew and a girl grown old remembering. "Yes, I suppose that's why I hired him. He had that dashing, carefree air about him like the swashbuckling Errol Flynn." She jabbed the air playfully with her knife as in fencing. All laughed but the boys—who considered her curiously. "Renaldo and his wife, Felicia, along with their two sons, Renaldo Jr. and Dominick, had already been with me a while before Lisette was born. Dominick was also born here now I think of it. Yes, he was. They're precious to me. We're family. He's a good man, Renaldo. If I'm not mistaken, you two have much in common."

His daughter for one," thought Percival, shamelessly.

"I should tell you, I'm aware of your secret," she informed him. "Nina felt she had no right to conceal it from me." If she were expecting a reaction she didn't get one.

"I didn't know I had a secret," he said.

"No secret?" Amelia returned. "An Olympic hopeful, Civil Rights Activist, defense captain for the Black Panther Party, your providing safety for Nina at last year's tumultuous Democratic National Convention in Chicago? For which I'm thankful. Then, too, the more recent loss of your brother? For which I'm sorry." She observed a tear form in the corners of his eyes. "You've been under a cloud. I agree. And now here you are holed up in an out of the way upstate farm, and that information is not passed on— and you say that's no secret?"

He felt cornered, as if found out. Sly as a fox however, he showed no inkling of discomfiture. "I wouldn't expect Nina to have withheld much from you. I'm a stranger, after all trying to keep a low profile; lose myself for a while," he said.

"Is that at all possible?" she asked.

"You can run but you can't hide, aye?" he said, quoting the great Joe Louis. "I don't mean to hide, but I must process this on my own. That's why I'm here. I need time with my thoughts. That's all."

"You were made welcome based on my niece's word and I really have no right to question you. I should not have brought it up. It's yours to share, if and when you please."

"That's reassuring."

"Anyway, Nina thinks the world of you, and that's good enough for me."

Percival grimaced, changing the subjects, "The field work's left me stiff with back pain. I'm not accustomed to spending so much time in the sun. I never had a sunburn before, but I have one now. And Lisette's been kind enough to apply aloe for me." He pressed a hand to his stiffened, sun burnt back. "I'm sore all over." He groaned.

"I appreciate your efforts," Amelia said.

"Da chil'en' say y'll two l've b'rds," Cora laughed heartily.

"The children," Percival exclaimed, "they're always spying."

"They b' 'r eyes 'n ears," Cora chuckled, taking his profile in. "They always on da look out; 'n quick ta tell w'at they see. "N they ain't not'in they don't see."

"No," Percival said, evasively. "She's just doing what Amelia asked, giving me the grand tour."

"To'r?" Cora gave him a cutting glance. "I l'ke da way da chillun's tell et bet'er."

"Am I missing something?" Amelia asked.

"Cora seems to know more about it than me," Percival said, averting his eyes.

"As I said before, it's yours to tell," Amelia conceded. "As for farm work," she hurried on, "I believe, as did Peter Maurin, that 'there is no unemployment on the land.' And in the daily operation of this, farm that concept – 'work should ennoble a man, not degrade him' – is my credo."

"I realize that from reading your book, 'Seeds of Change and Fruits of Love,' which I borrowed from your library. And no, field work is not degrading, it's back breaking."

"Ah yes, my paean to God."

"I'm enjoying it," he said. "You draw from so many sources. You're quite eclectic. You reach across cultural, historical 'n national divides to make your case. I'd almost mistaken you for a traditional Christian, I'm sorry to say."

"You mean narrowminded and hypocritical?" she asked, causing him to blush.

"No, I'm a catholic, small "c," or so I like to think," she said, voice rippling with laughter. "It's a common error. We become enmeshed in the habit mind and tend to think solely along cultural lines. And culturally speaking, we fall prey to the childish notion that God, in his infinite wisdom, wrote a bible where, in fact, he created a universe. A book, by the way, of which Christianity is a lesser part. And yet the Jewish faith goes unrecognized."

"Yes, you make a strong case for compiling the world bibles into one that people might read as such. That'll be fine with me, especially since I've not read any as yet," Percival said, fork at the ready.

"It's just as well," said Amelia. "As badly as most people read the daily papers they also read the bible, except they read it over and over and still arrive at the same mistaken conclusions. If you're going to read one Bible and not all the others, you're probably better off not reading any at all. They are all but scattered pages of the same book. I for one no longer subscribe to a single creed, particularly since in my capacity as Chair of Humanities at S.U.N.Y., where there is a growing number of Asian, African, and Middle Eastern students, of every religious persuasion under the Sun, with whom I must interact. I do well to know more than a little of their culture and faith. I do not deny my faith but neither can I deny theirs. And so you'll find a well-read copy of the world bible in my library, if you care to take a look."

"Maybe I'll take a look."

The boys grew antsy once again, defiant as elves. They cast monkey faces back 'n forth at each other. The elder sat beside his father and the younger alongside his mother. Cora elbowed him and gave the other a withering glance. "Chil'n out'a b' seen 'n n't 'eard," she upbraided them under her breath. "Ya'' bes' hush yaselves!"

"This is scrumptious," said Amelia, savoring her meal.

"Et's fr'm me co'ntry, Haiti" Cora said, with a dimpled cherubic smile.

"Umm, yes, I think I know it," Amelia responded. "It's Fungi, no?"

"Wom'n, ya sure c'n co'k," Henri praised, eyeing her favorably.

"Go on wid yarself," she said, tittering.

The boys exchanged doubtful glances.

"I found your chapter on education most fascinating, 'specially since on so many levels, while in the course of pursuing an education myself, I found that I was doing it like so many'a youth today, out of panic, and in a mad scramble to catch up to the March Hare." Percival felt self-conscious, unsure of his footing. "But, all 'n all, 'r national priorities have been so screwed up that there is this tragic underlying feeling that nobody knew where they were going, or why. We believed in the country, 'r national destiny, but found it morally bankrupt. Which is why so many of us took Tim Leary's advice to heart 'n 'Turn'd on, tune'd in 'n drop'd out' and the man was a Harvard professor. More so, the American system of education underscores our national dilemma. The educational scene having been sounded to its depths, proved hollow, a cultural wasteland, a barren, mindless affair for which LSD proved a nostrum."

"As an educator myself, I know all too well the shortcomings of the system," Amelia said, tersely.

"You discuss many of them in your book and that's why I admire it and feel free to express myself openly."

"As rightly you should," said Amelia, shrewdly.

"However," Percival persisted, "many blacks continue to view conventional education, after civil rights, a means by which to obtain full enfranchisement—as if a college degree will whitewash 'r history." He comically smiled. "But when you've ceased, as I 'ave, to be in awe of the white man 'n his world, his institutions, when you no longer care to be like him in any guise, then what else has he to offer? After you've 'peeped his hold card,' so to speak, why would you want'a continue on to become a man you absolutely revile?" Saying what he had previously refrained from saying, he became irked at himself that it had inadvertently slipped out. And that if he had ever believed otherwise it was because it is the province of youth to believe in the good and the beautiful, despite all evidence to the contrary.

Henri considered Percival, skeptically. He felt his remarks rude and inappropriate for a house guest: issues taboo in polite society. Yet he found no rancor, nor disturbance in Amelia's countenance. She was as poised and sanguine as ever.

Amelia was mistakenly perceived by her workers as either childishly naive or devilishly shrewd. In other words, a saint. Be that as it may, she ran her farm with an "iron hand in a mink glove."

The grandfather clock struck the hour. The two boys paused in their meal and listended with childish delight to the resonant, tintinnabulation of bells.

Percival forged on, indifferent to the peal of chimes, "I just want the white man off my back," he said, voice choked, raspy. "But when I stand, 'n stand I will, I don't want'a follow in his footsteps either. I simply have no wish to be menaced by him. I want to be free of him —his God awful history. I mean, freedom is a form of expression well in keeping with the ideals of one's father, 'n one's father's fathers, 'n not somebody else's father no matter how well meaning they may be. 'N by no means 'r the founding fathers my forefathers, they 'r my forefathers oppressors. (The chimes echoed throughout the rooms and corridors of the old house with a haunting refrain as the clock struck the 6th and final note. The boys clapped gleefully). As such, they 'r my oppressors too. I must gain for myself a better grasp of the word freedom since there is no mention of honor, indispensable to liberty, to be found in the Constitution save for the honor among thieves; a theft of which I, as 'r they, byproducts of a kidnapping," he grievously said, eyes misting as his glance passed from one member to the other of the young Haitian family. "That theft, this act of piracy took 'r identity (Henri seemed puzzled, unsure of Percival's assertion). Stole from all black Americans a sense of self and constitutes an act of psychical genocide that reverberates, till today, throughout the race mind." Assailed as he was by a whirlwind of emotions, Percival turned to Amelia and said in anguish, "They may just as well have lobotomized the entire race! In fact, that's exactly what they did! They violently eradicated all remnants of our entire collective cultural memory! And for the nature of its perversity, the American system of slavery, like non other, is aptly described as, The peculiar institution," he said with rancor. "To turn a Supreme Court ruling on its head,'The oppressor has no rights that the oppressed 'r bound to respect.' This is where I take my stand; regain my honor 'n redeem myself: The unsullied majesty of my misappropriated humanity. No one has the right to tamper with another's destiny —No one! But tamper they do! I for one would simply like to find my own way unmolested. Otherwise what's the use?" The words seemed to have lain coiled in ambush at the tip of his tongue, waiting to strike. Then, with a shake of the head, he added, mindful of Amelia, "No offense intended."

"None taken, I assure you." She gave him a firm but gentle glance. She could not deny his take on the eclipse of the cultural norm. Hence, she murmured, lips taut, "I fear, however, in starting this conversation – I think I started this conversation?" She laughed, as did he. "I seem to have opened a can of worms."

Henri breathed a sigh of relief.

"No, not that so much as the hard lessons learned early on as a child growing up poor in ghettos!"

"You state your case most convincingly. I fear I know exactly what you mean," she said. "Without a doubt, our country has much to atone for. I know the country in which I live, and I am fearful for my soul and those of our forebears on account."

The younger of the two boys, bored with his meal and with an axe to grind, said of his brother: "Ray win me marbles 'n I got none ta play wid." He pouted.

"So?" Ray objected, fearing rebuke. "I ain't steal 'em."

"Ya did."

"I win em."

"Ya ain't—"

"Ya not to cheat ya lil brother ya 'ear?" said Cora mindfully, trying to quell the outburst.

"I was only funnin'," said the other in self-defense. "I give em back."

"N y'll two be'ter b'ave at Miss Amelia's t'ble," she said. "Ain't I tol' ya, chil'en 'r ta b' seen 'n n't 'eard? Shush 'n finish ya supp'r."

The elder boy wriggled in place, then stuck his tongue out at his brother.

The younger boy wailed, "Ma, he stick 'is tongue at me."

"If ya won't b'ave y'selves y'll go ta bed widout des'ert, ya 'ear?"

"Lis'en ta ya mud'r'r or I'll pull me str'p off!" said their father sternly. "I'm so'ry f'r da fuss," he apologized to both Amelia and Percival.

"Small thing," said Percival.

"You mustn't strike them on our account," said Amelia, in appeal. "Remember their bodies are the temples of God."

"Dat's aft'r da devil be'n driv'n out'a 'em," said the father, defensively. "Da b'ble say, 'Spare da rod 'n spoil da chile.'"

"Dat so, Miss Amelia. Dat so," Cora hastily agreed. They were a family of Sanctified Christians and this was one of the few times that they had shared supper with Amelia – eventually she got around to sharing supper with all her workers. And, as always, they were doing their best to impress. Percival's opinions rankled. His views were subversive, ungodly, foreign to their own. He made them uneasy. "We raise 'r sons by the good book, by the word'a God 'n 'and when need b.'" Cora regarded Percival apprehensively. What Amelia saw, however, were two antsy, bored and playful boys, vying for attention. She relented. "The old Testament, of course," she uttered. "Pardon me if I've spoken out of turn?"

"Ya mean no 'arm," said Cora, agreeably.

Amelia gave the boys a consoling smile.

Henri said, "Y's ma'am, no 'arm don'." He pushed his plate aside and, facing Percival, asked, "'Scuse me Mr. Percival sence I d'n't 'no ya st'ry no better dan ya kno' myne; I g'ess I jus' c'n't see ya case."

Percival turned his gaze on Henri. "Oh?" he said, searching the man's face with ruthless curiosity. He had tried talking to Henri before, in the fields, and found his patois difficult to decipher, his accent thick and barely comprehensible. He smiled, though reddening slightly with anger.

"Please continue."

Alight with purpose, Henri began, "I ain't got m'ch scoolin' ta spe'k'a, dat's tru' b't I re'ds me b'ble fatally, 'n t'ks cumfert 'n Afr'can wisd'm; n't dispisin' wid me B'ble any." A coverall strap slipped off his shoulder under which he wore his Sunday best T-shirt. He wore no ornaments save his wedding band. As for "time" he relied solely on the sun. "Et' ge'ts me in'a bit'a tro'ble wid Cora," he said, as he replaced the strap, then wiped his mustache of any bits of food. "She say et's 'eresy b't Afr'ca, mahn, w'ere et all st'rt, all'a et b'gin, mahn."

Cora gave him a solicitous glance.

"'N me 'inglis," he grimaced, "ah—ain't dat gud."

"And my French is nonexistent," Percival replied. Amelia, on the other hand, having studied at the Sorbonne, in Paris in her youth, spoke French fluently; and had come to visit Haiti on several occasions following catastrophic earthquakes and hurricanes that devastated the island – time and again—with humanitarian relief aid groups offering emergency medical assistance, building materials, and necessary food stuff. As such, she had come to know its people, their heritage, patois, culture and social graces. She found them an extraordinary proud but decent people. An admirable people even. A good people, sure.

"I wuz a'boy'a t'irteen w'en I lef' Port-au-Prince ta cum' 'ere, mer'ly 'a bag'a bon's,'" Henri said with an on running laugh. "I lef' 'ome 'cause dey b' no food ta stay f'r, jus' rocks f'r bre'd 'n notin' 'lse m'ch, mahn," he voiced, casting a backwards glance on the specter of an impoverished youth which presaged his daring the swollen depths of the Atlantic with its mountainous range of overlapping foam capped waves, threatening to upend the makeshift sea fairing craft on which he and a few other dare devil cohorts sailed. "The States or bust," was their aim and hunger their compass. "I fi'st saw ya co'ntry as'a str'nge, cur'us 'n f'rbidd'n pl'ce dat fill me wid fe'r 'n 'ope'.

"I wuz'a boy 'n da sp'tacle'a da States 'ntrall'd me so, 'n me sp'rit shr'nk b'sides da 'anormity 'a et all 'n me legs b'ckle. 'N I fe'r'd me 'opes w'uld b' crus'd b't 'oped me fe'rs won't b' realiz'd," he said, recounting the hazards they encountered in route. "I wan'ed ta t'rn 'n go b'ck 'ome, I wuz so a'fra'd'a

449

da un'knon' b'fore me, b't cho'se ta face da fears 'a dat b'fore me dan face da fe'rs 'a da kno'n b'hind me. I wuz more a'fra'd'a drownin' or, wo'se, starvin' ta debt b'ck 'n Port-au-Prince. No, sir, I wuz 'n no r'sh ta tempt da h'nds 'a fate ag'in. If I dr'wn'd I'd b' f'rgot'en lyke I n'ver wuz 'n ther'd b' no cryin', no fune'al, no eul'gy—no not'in'. I b' wash'd a'way wid da t'de 'n dat wou'd b' da end'a dat— lyke I wuz n'ver b'rn!

"I w'rk'd me way up fr'm Florida, t'ru da delta, a'long da narrow spine'a da migr'nt tra'l ta da nort/e'st, le'vin' da d'mp 'n s'lty sea 'n tropics b'hin'," he voiced. "Et w's e'rly spring, 'n da sap w's runnin' fr'e d'wn da trunk'a ev'ry fr'it 'n m'ple tree, fr'sh on da air, sweet, sweet, sweet!" Henri leaned back and closed his eyes savoring the diffuse fragrance wafting into the room through the open windows, along with the distant cry of a mourning dove. "Et far diff'rent dan da smell'a da s'lt sea," he said, recalling the tumultuous windswept waves threatening to up end the makeshift craft upon which he and his cronies braved the Atlantic.

The briny smell of the perilous sea remained with him, in his nostrils— roiled in his blood and brain and in the erratic heartbeat of his dreams, in which he would toss and turn as if cast about on the waves of a stormy sea.

"The cities of destruction," the streets on which Percival grew up, Henri would never know; no more than would Percival know the disconsolate conditions under which Henri struggled in the slums of Port-au-Prince. A disjunction of cultures to be sure. Contrarily, however, Henri would only see the States as a cornucopia, a land of 'milk 'n honey,' since all he would ever see of it were its ripen fields of grain and orchards in which he labored, fertile farmlands, stretching from horizon to horizon in all directions from Sun to Sun. As such he could not fathom Percival's complaint. How could he? After all, he only knew, saw, and worked with other islanders and they only concerned themselves with the day to day difficulties of survival back home.

"Y'll liv' n'a'dev'leped furst w'rld contry. I com' fr'm Haiti, a'undev'lep'd t'ird w'rld nasion. Y'll c'n say it's a'retched pl'ce, bar'en as an ole crones w'mb. Y'll c'n say dat b't et's also'a beaut'ful tr'pical i'land l'cat'd at da g'teway ta Afr'ca in da Caribbean Sea, 'n lookin' out ov'r er 'er wav's ya c'n send'a' mes'age by Conga's 'n get'a r'ply fr'm mud'er Afr'ca on da incomin' tyde. 'N 'er g'fts com' rollin' in; g'fts fr'm 'r anceste's: fo'klore, culsur', tr'dition—w've on w've top'el a'sure in'a'tumult, mahn; cr'sh a'sure wid songs a' da Congo; Nairobi; Uganda; Mali, a'f'ver 'n 'r blood." His head swam with images of ancient African civilizations and glory days of black Gods and Kings; of empires that bestrode the world like colossi from the dawning of time. "W'en we beat'd Napoleon's army 'n 1804, ole slav' masa sob 'n say,''da D'vil w'n us 'r fre'dom.'" Henri snorted in derision. "''Ow da

D'vil w'n us 'r fr'dom, mahn? 'e w'n 'nyb'dy dey fre'dom. Da D'vil'a slav'r 'isse'f! 'N so w'at if we use Voodoo? dey Afr'can G'ds, Tino G'ds, Gods'a 'r fore-fad'ers. B't nob'dy d' c'n say any dif'rent, mahn, we w'n 'r fre'dom 'rsef! W'n 'r anc'ent pr'de 'n se'f r'spect wit' a'mighty blo'a 'r fist," he boast, hands as lively as a Conga player's. "Haiti's a'force'a natcha, mahn; a'force a'mud'er love! A'force to b' re'kon'd wit'. She gimme l'fe; she gimme bre'th; she gimme a'sense a' wort'; a' sense'a b'uty. A'sense'a G'd!" He paused, then abruptly said, "She gimme relig'on too." He spoke of Haiti as would a son usually reserve for the affection he feels for his mother. "I gr'w up on Voodoo, Afr'can 'n Tino In'ian rit'als, b't b'come'a Sanctifi'd Christian un'er Cora's infl'nce. I b'rn ag'in. Hallelujah," he yelped! "Haiti's a'lan' a'g'ost, w'ere gud 'n ev'l wa'k's h'nd 'n h'nd. She ma'b' poor 'n everyt'in' 'lse b't she r'ch 'n da g'ft'a da Spi'it."

"There is that to be said of Haiti for sure," Amelia affirmed.

Despite the fact that Percival found the singsong cadence of Henri's patios melodic, the words, for the most part, fell unintelligibly on his ears, yet he was able to eke out a hazy understanding but didn't quite know what to say in reply. He feared Henri understood him far better than he understood Henri.

Henri lingered, then said, "'R ya mar'id, Mr. Percival?" taking Percival by surprise.

"Not that anyone might know of," Percival replied.

"Don't play the cad," Amelia reproached him.

"You have someone in mind?" Percival chortled.

"Lisette!" Cora chided, causing Percival to blush from his throat up through the strong, ruddy features of his face. He sputtered with laughter.

"I won't lie," he confessed, "it's a tempting idea."

"Isn't that rather presumptuous?" Amelia asked. "You barely know each other."

"Miss. Amelia," Cora sang, with a twist of her head, "w'at y'll f'rget 'bout love? Et's got no rhyme, 'n kno's no reason. Love's lyke'a hon'y bee, et stings ya w'en ya least s'pect. Ain't et so, hon'y?" she asked, reaching for Henri's hand.

Cora saw Henri as "a man in full" from the crown of his corn-rowed head to the bottom of his bare, calloused feet.

He folded her hand in his.

Smitten by the young couple and their sons, Amelia embraced them with a blissful glance, while reserving a more sober eye for Percival.

Henri said, "D'spite 'ow I fe'l 'bout me co'ntry, Haiti, a mahn mus' prov'de f'r 'is fam'ly 'n will undert'ke ev'ry 'ardship ta do et; crawl on 'is belly 'cross da burnin' sands'a da Sahara!" he asserted, unnerving Percival,

451

forcing him to recall, with much anguish, the bitter quarrels he'd had with Joleen over his refusal to pay child support for their son, Malek, while under her mother's roof and influence.

Henri reminded Percival of Big/Black, the one person who could intimidate him by the mere strength of his presence.

He found himself shaken, unable to break the spell Henri had cast over him with his mocking, onyx eyes. This man, Henri, was from one of the poorest corners of the globe, and Percival from one of the richer; nevertheless, he envied him—particularly his simplicity and childlike innocence; his masculine, self-assurance. Percival felt his mask slipping, as if he had been seen through, to a place of pain and sorrow. And wavered uncertainly. It was unsettling. He was transported on the wings of Henri's view of the world that contrasted sharply with his own.

Similarly, he was being transformed by Lisette and Amelia, working in the fields under the hot summer sun, in the fresh air, alongside island migrant workers. Indeed, he was beginning to feel a pang of envy towards this Haitian farm hand and the world he inhabited. Unlike Henri, however, whose veins coursed with the blood of both Africa and Haiti, Percival felt neither Africa nor America in his. With the death of his brother, Sam, and his dream of the Olympics shattered, he felt, dislocated. Lately he'd awaken heart sick, confused by who and what he was becoming? Racine, Dakota, and Sam were gone and he had to shoulder much of the blame. His innocence was gone, and the last of his youth gone with it, filling him with a nameless urge, lost in a in a weakness of passion to which he gave himself entirely.

He yearned for redemption.

"I b' comin' back 'n fort' I see ya plite wid str'nge ey's,'" Henri persisted. "B't f'r d'rk w'isperin's I d'n't 'no ya story a'tall. Em 'ere'a few mont's out'a da year, den em 'ome ag'in till next ye'rs plantin'. Till I c'me 'ere da color'a mahn's skin wuz no of'ense ta nob'dy b't it's 'n of'ense ta y'll. I w'rk 'ere, dats all. I w'rk 'ard, b't ets n't fer me. Et's n't me 'ome, ya kno'?" Henri measured himself by his abilities as a worker and prided himself on how well he provided for his family; nothing else. His psyche and world view were aligned. Color was a non sequitur. It did not fit into his calculus. "They b' class str'fe in Haiti, y's. Sum f'lks I've high off'a da hog, wh'le da res'a us I've off'a dry b'nes 'n stones. Haiti 'as'a hist'ry a' tro'bles f'r shur b't one of 'em ain't cul'a. Lyke da song say,' 'All God chillun got tro'bil's.' Still ev'ryb'dy's da col'r' da Sun m'ke 'em, mahn. It's nothin' ta b' pro'd or a'shame'a. God wills it so, 'n there ain't no nay sayin' dat. I pity da ey's dat c'n't see da be'uty 'n bla'k."

"I pity the eyes," Amelia echoed. "I pity them."

"I can't pretend to understand all you say, but If I hear you right I can't know your story any better than you know mine," said Percival, his voice constrained. "Despite it all, you don't know your name any more than I know mine. Therein lies the rub," he scoffed. "Yes, you can go back home to your Island nation where the sun made you the color it has. No fault there—"

Amelia recalled Dr. King having once said, "There comes a time when silence is betrayal." As such she cut in and said, "Whites don't know themselves well either. Certainly no better than 'we' know blacks. And 'we' have created, as a result, a historical and cultural divide based on what 'we' don't know of each other, least of all ourselves."

"Who was it that said, 'I'm white because you're black?'" Percival asked.

"Faulkner," Amelia replied.

"It's aptly put."

"Aptly," she reposted.

"Anyway, what you say about whites is also true of blacks, particularly since losing our names and cultural identity," Percival said. "Obviously, from what Henri says, there are strong remnants of cultural identity in Haiti, but that's not so in the States where our identity only surfaces in our music. Otherwise, I agree with you entirely."

"The mystery of race is that it bedevils us," Amelia said in her firm, quiet way. "Racism is no less than any other mortal sin. It is, in many ways, akin to murder, in that it denies another their rightful place of being. And to deny another their right of being is to deny the free expression of life itself. In a sense, that's what happened in slavery, isn't it?"

"America bedevils us all too sadly and seems unable to move beyond the sins of its patriarchs," said Percival, reflecting on Amelia's words. "Mores the pity, we've been traumatized by the convergence of our historical past. I mean, America has no real claim to a past. Yes, one gets to start anew, but without a cultural reference."

"We all chillun'a da same God; born 'n raise'd 'n His self-image," Cora joined in, smiling broadly. "We da color da sun's blite rays m'ke us un'er c'ver of'a 'avenly sky."

"Hallelujah," Henri hollered.

"Glory be," said Amelia in praise.

"Sing-the-song y'all," Percival chanted, joining in.

Eyes roving back and forth, from face to face. The boys sat quietly listening to the adults, their meals unfinished.

"Your struggle, as you say, is with the harsh realities of nature." Percival picked up the thread of his unfinished response, "Whereas ours, in the States, is a racial one. In my eyes, my color is not a problem. After all, as you say, it is the color the sun made me. However, it is a problem in the eyes of my countrymen who are indifferent to, as Cora suggests, 'the sun's blithe rays,' its efficacy." He smiled wanly, "With, of course, the exception of our hostess." Amelia nodded her silver head in accord. She was nut brown from working the fields alongside her farm hands—for which they held her in esteem. "Otherwise, as I see it, I am no more black than my white countrymen are white. The only thing they know of 'us,' both of 'us together,' white or black, is what their base ignorance allows which, sad to say, is not much. And that's what makes this color thing rancorous."

"Ya c'n de'l wid ya contri-mahn, b't ya c'n't de'l wid mud'er na'cha'."

"It's a devil's bargain to be sure," said Percival.

"Ya'a gud mahn; ev'n a' sma't un, b't ya d'n't kno' ya roots."

Percival smiled, sadly. "Maybe not so well as I may like, but perhaps far better than you think."

Henri set his elbows on the table and laced his fingers of his hands together on which he rested his chin and cocked an eye at Percival's, unable to fathom the troubling depths in which "this" black American "man" swam?

Henri was as at ease in his skin as any black man Percival had ever known besides Punchy, who was as composed a man he knew.

A brooding, uneasy silence settled in.

The idea of "race" not occupying a central place in the political, social, economic and cultural landscape of a nation gave Percival cause to wonder. Without the constraints of Voodoo, witchcraft, superstition, and black magic, it could produce, an enlightened citizenry, and veritable Utopia; exactly what Amelia was attempting on her farm from all he could tell. But, on the other hand, "What if it took black magic to accomplish it?"

Percival's gaze then wandered out a side window behind and to the left of Amelia when, by chance, his eyes came to light upon a hummingbird, hovering silently over a day lily in the scented flower grden, eliciting a smile.

Amelia smiled in return, assuming his smile was for her.

"Despite all we just shared," she was moved to say, intruding on his reverie." Huh?" he uttered, startled back to himself. She went on, "It's been my long held view that self-love, 'amour-propre', is, above all else, the true genesis of one's identity. It is those who hate their neighbors or any other person outside themselves, as they do, and for loss of self-project their hatred on to those they see as other than themselves. No one hates another more than he who does not love himself. I assure you I've never known anyone who truly love themselves to harbor an iota of hatred in their hearts for another. Identity is to be found in the light of self-love. And self-love is indispensable to all other expressions of love.

"If we are to live we are to live from the heart of the world; and the world has but a single heart."

"I do believe I love myself, if that's the question," he said, wryly.

"I don't doubt for a moment you love yourself," Amelia said reassuringly, holding Percival steadfastly in her gaze. "But presently you're under a cloud."

"Thank you for the vote of confidence," he said, pleased. "And yes while I may be of two minds I am at one with my spirit."

"I see that also."

"Frankly, however, there are some people I don't like very much, but I can't think of anyone I especially hate," he said.

"It's the people you dislike you learn most from," said Amelia with mirth.

"That's possibly true! I dare say, however, I think I'd rather be hated than hate based solely on the superficiality of someone's complexion," Percival claimed. "No matter, I still want the white man off my back! I don't want to be fighting him, or anybody else for that matter, every inch of the way for the rest of my life."

"I can't fault you there," said Amelia, tautly.

"I fully understand now why Nina wanted us to meet." He knowingly laughed. "Yes," he said, "I now have a better grasp of what's going on in your book 'Fruits of Labor: A Child of Love, too. I'm now on chapter 7 where you say, in 'Fruits of Love, "This is where the chapter 'Fruits of Labor: A Child of Love,' that education must be sought for itself alone, for the development of the inner being who 'hungers 'n thirsts for righteousness sake.' That love alone is the reason one should wish to be educated. That is love of humankind. Or, as you say, 'To deepen one's cup of fellowship. Education, like travel, should broaden one's horizon, and open one up to a wider view of our human experience.' You also say that education was in its original form, the province of the priesthood, and that candidates seeking initiation were found fit based on moral rectitude as much as scholastic aptitude and not, as now, solely on scholastic aptitude. That's a fact I'd not considered.

You use the ancient Pythagorean school where one of the prerequisites for initiation was the observance of a seven-year silence. You say we must go that far back if we are to truly appreciate the value of education in the life of a soul, because it should not simply be for the maintenance of the corporeal being, but more the sustenance of the whole person, which the word "paideia" personifies in the scholastic tradition. You go on to explain the derivation of the word "education," from the Latin, *drawing out from within,* if I remember correctly, *a leading forth.* Then from Plato's Meno, you use the example of Socrates coaxing answers on geometry from a slave boy who had no previous knowledge of the subject. You quote Rousseau saying, *education comes from* to us from three sources; from nature, from men and from things, since all do something for us.'

"But you also say that nature, the most neglected of the three methods in our current system of education, should rightly be the first and primary teacher, imparting the questions of life on the consciousness of the young, rather than dead pages of textbooks. You imply nature is unbiased and what she teaches is indispensable. If, as you say, students attend school after such a preparation, after they have had the opportunity to engage nature in her realm and on her terms, to have questioned her firsthand, then their schooling would prove much more beneficial. They would bring to the classroom situation questions for which they require answers, and not the other way around. 'No one,' you say, 'should simply be a receptacle. Have I left anything out?" he asked.

"Not much," said Amelia, patiently, "You've absorbed a lot. You have a remarkable memory for details, surely. I'm impressed, but Nina said I would be."

"The only problem I 'ave with that picture is that in the cities there is not enough of nature left for it to engage the mind. The only thing that grows on concrete is crime."

"Yes, I'm sure, but I try making the point Plato does in 'The Republic,' *The city, of its very nature, corrupts.'* Which is why St. Augustine, almost in direct response to Plato's city, wrote the 'City of God' in which he says, *'The divine dispensation of grace gives hope to a man and makes it possible for him to attain his eternal beatitude in the City of God after his pilgrimage in the earthly one.'"*

"Another work I don't know I'm afraid. In fact, I don't know who St. Augustine is," Percival admitted. Amelia lifted her eyes from her meal, with a start.

"You must get to know him," she said in affectionate rebuke. "You must. It's so very sad that as well-read, astute young man like you don't know Augustine. It goes to the heart of the American educational dilemma. We live in a culture that pretends to a knowledge it doesn't possess. It's shameful because St. Augustine is one of the pillars of Christianity, a foremost thinker and architect of the faith. And perhaps even more important to you he is was, black. North African. As Jesus was undoubtedly brown. But race back then had no meaning to the ancients. Augustine was a great man, a towering example of the powers of faith and intelligence. You must read him. His Confessions. Do."

"I'll put him at the top of my must-read list of books."

"Do that." Amelia smiled, pleased.

"So what's the solution?" Percival asked.

456

"Excuse us won't you?' Amelia apologized, turning to Henri and Cora. "We don't mean to be impolite or exclude you –"

"No, y'll talk. L'me lis'en. Mayb' I le'rn somethin'," said Henri, setting his empty plate aside.

"We talks 'bout education 'rselves," said Cora agreeably, in singsong, fiercely proud. "We wants 'r boys educated. We don't want 'em ta be farm h'nds. Dat's ok f'r us 'cause it's all we kno'." She cast Percival a reproachful side glance. "We wants 'r boys ta do bet'er dan us. We wants em to be like da Poincares', Renaldo 'n Dominick, ministers 'n doctors. We want em ta succeed!"

The boys squirmed, eyeing each other.

"Of course," said Amelia, graciously. "You couldn't pick two finer examples for your sons to emulate." She flushed with pride, as if it were her sons of whom they spoke. And before she could return to Percival's question the other children had started to collect outside the screened door.

"Come in," Amelia called, and they tramped in like a gaggle of vagabonds, scampering for empty seats as if in a game of musical chairs and, in places, squeezing in two at a seat. A little minx climbed onto Amelia's lap and beamed precociously up into her face.

"All weady f'r dessert," she lisped, palms face up and fingers open wide in appeal.

"We shall have to continue our discussion at another time," said Amelia, as the children waited with impatient eyes.

***

Savoring each other's company, Percival and Lisette sought each other out, becoming something of an item and cause for gossip among the farm hands, as less and less was seen of the Corvette. The children would spy on them and report back to the adults. At first sight it would appear as if they could not have much in common. She, for all her sophistication, was a farm girl and he a boxer, an urban guerrilla, a revolutionary. Yet, together, in each other's company, the world became new, wondrous and full of sparks, sweetness and light. They would steal off nightly and take long strolls as the sun set. That evening they met by the lake and went rowing, away from all prying eyes. Far off to the southwest a brilliant sun was steadily descending beyond distant fields of hay aflame in the slanting light, its rays striking a golden band across the still lake, highlighting the boat and its occupants against a darker sky beyond. They ceased to row as they reached the center of the lake and allowed the boat to drift. Curious about his rival, Julius, he raised the subject.

"Ya've told me little 'bout Julius?"

She cast a fretful glance his way, and began with baited breath, "There's nothing much to tell. We were childhood friends and high school sweethearts, briefly. He escorted me to my prom. Julius is the eldest of three children and the only son. He is wealthy, well-educated, and suffers from all the mania of it, meaning, he expects everything to fall into his lap. And he courts me incessantly because I have yet to fall into his lap. He expects that I shall eventually be won over by his many charms and money. Julius is charming but, all too regrettably, charm, like wit, can easily be a coverup for lack of substance. Mostly among his store of charms is his father's wealth. Not that I'm opposed to it, but money does not make the man. It should be the other way round. I imagine you're penniless."

"N without prospects," he confirmed.

"And yet a man after my own heart." Lisette laughed, a silvery ripple of laughter that bubbled naturally like a sun dappled stream. "You're pure potential, all possibility. I can sense, taste, and touch, so much in you that I know you are trying to conceal from me as if for my own good. You think I would be intimidated if you were to reveal yourself to me all at once when the opposite is more likely true, than not. What I do know about you is that you're the most splendid man I've ever met. As for the rest, I won't mind taking a lifetime to discover.

"I know you want to hear about Julius. Like I said, we have been friends since childhood and our parents wish that we would marry. They take it for granted that we shall. I've told my mother otherwise in the past, but she says, 'You only say that now.' It wasn't serious enough to pursue till now, even though I'd brought other young men home in the past." Her voice was rapturous, convincing. "Julius is of the black upper crust and is upwardly mobile bound. I can only be window dressing in such a fanciful world; to be worn on his arm for show like an expensive trophy – which I'm not – at social affairs, soirees, political functions, and opening day at the track. Don't get me wrong, he'd be an attentive husband, which would not be half bad if that were my desire or if I truly loved him, but it's not, and I don't. I want to share in a dream of love, not one of ambition." She sighed, a fleeting, quizzical look came into her lustrous eyes. "In any case we've been friends since first communion."

"I take it he doesn't share your conviction?"

"No, he thinks I'll come round but I can't," she said, securing Percival's hand, "especially now."

"You know so little 'bout me," he said, with emotion, as if brought to life.

"I know all I need know. Some people live whole lives together not knowing one another but loving one another for it all the same. More so,

458

perhaps, for not knowing one another," she said petulantly. "And if I could know you, did know you, maybe I would grow bored with you, too. Certainly it's that way with Julius. Not only do I know him but I know what he desires, a dead end in which nothing fresh can flower. His father is, as he puts it, 'A fat cat corporate lawyer.' And it's Julius' intention to become, as he also puts it, 'The big head. New York's first black senator.' That's his ambition." She shivered, "Brrrr! It's all so crass." She then said with hesitant coquetry, "No, I couldn't thrive in such a climate. I would wither under the confused, sterile limbo that underlies such a facade."

"It's ambitious," Percival acknowledged.

There was a radiant wistful look about her. Her raven black hair was tightly bound in a knot at the nape of her neck revealing the contours of her sculpted, Latin, taffy-colored face, her onyx eyes deeper than the body of water on which they floated, her fruity, quivering lips, soliciting a kiss. "God," he thought as he leaned in and kissed her fully on the mouth, "is she ever lovely."

The sparks between them were fiercer than ever.

Eyeing her speculatively, he ran a hand through his wooly hair believing there was merit in what she'd said. He seemed to be holding something back, in check, even while thinking of what to say. "You think love is akin to the state of an atom? That if you know where it is you can't tell it's speed 'n if you know its speed you can't fix its location. If you love a person you need not know em, 'n if you know em, you may not necessarily love em, is that it?" He laughed in spite of himself.

She was deeply touched, musing it over: "Oh I don't know what I'm saying," she said impulsively, with quiet intensity. "I'm just saying it because it sounds clever, because I'm giddy in love and I hardly know you, so I say that's why I love you and if I knew you I'd probably say that's why I love you, too." She grew silent and their eyes searched each other's out as the sun plunged below the horizon and the stars came out one at a time blinking distantly in the bluish twilight. "I can't rightly say why I love you. Love is the only time when in all your life the only answer is, 'Yes! Yes! Yes!'"

"I'm convinced you're right," said Percival, solemnly. "But, of course, you know I'll be leaving shortly." He felt as if they were strangers, moving in different worlds. "I return to that life of which you know so little."

"You mean that life which gave you to me, like the sea casting up its bounty?" She burst into an amusing little laugh, picturing it in her mind's eye. "I might know more of that world than you think. I spoke to Nina the other night. She asked me how you were. I told her about us. She was delighted. She knew we'd meet and hoped we'd fall in love."

"I might'a known," he said, glibly.

459

"Although I had not called her for that reason you can guess I couldn't resist but ask her about you. She told me it was your story to tell and that you'll tell it in your own time and way. 'And that,' Nina added, 'is how it should be.' I agreed, thanked her and left it at that. She did tell me to take good care of you, as there are few such men as you about." She faced him suddenly with startling eyes. "I was left with the strange impression that she's in love with you herself. But it didn't make sense so I thought I must be mistaken."

"We're best friends," Percival said, softly. Taking Lisette in his arms, they slipped down into the shell of the craft. He rested his head on the seat, and she lay her head on his shoulder, his arm enfolding her. His heart sunk in a kind of despair.

The rising night wind rippled the waters on the face of the lake on which their craft rocked and wound its way through the leaf laden trees of the forest beyond.

"It's time I invite you to my home to formally meet my parents," said Lisette in an undertone of intimacy. "What about Friday? It's my day to cook."

Cocking an eye in her direction he had a sensation of something like panic and almost thrust her from him. Instead he hesitantly said, shrinking, "I can't refuse that now, can I?"

"Believe me, I can cook," she said, as a matter of fact. "My mother and these island women have been teaching me how forever."

"I see."

She burst out into an all-knowing laugh.

"Hush, you vixen," he admonished her, flushing a deep, wine-red to the roots of his hair. He drew her firmly to him and they gazed off into the firmament at the distant Milky Way splashed across the depthless vault of night, their hearts melting and summer dissolving in starlight.

***

Having returned from delivering eggs and finding the house meditatively silent, Percival went to his room and folded himself comfortably in the chair before the writing table in front of the open window. Before he turned to his reading, he gazed out on the motionless day as the sun, in its eternal arc, inched its way toward noon. The trees in the farmyard were ghostly still. A copy of "The Confessions of St. Augustine" lay open in his lap. He was fairly relaxed, enjoying his reading but only slightly. He found Augustine's prose archaic, stilted, but expressively beautiful. All in all, he had been reluctant to review his own irreligious practices, his alienation from God, his lack of awareness of a divine presence. The only thing of late that had come anywhere close to being such a presence was the chill felt on viewing Sam's remains in the city morgue, that fateful day. The cold, overpowering terror which wrenched his heart, breezed through him and left him a tattered rag blowing in the wind, a substanceless wraith.

He closed his eyes. In these days and weeks, he had come as close to a religious experience as he'd ever known. An atmosphere of serenity surrounded Amelia despite her busy life. She was easy to be around. He breathed easily here under her roof away from it all. He was glad for the past two weeks. It was exactly what he'd needed, to feel other emotions. To remember that not everyone was caught up in this dogfight. It was good to know Amelia. She was wonderful. One of those saints of whom she loved to read. Her workers had observed it. It also distanced him somewhat from the entangled emotions which had swamped him as a result of Sam's death.

Then there was Lisette. His mind grew hazy thinking of her which, of late, was often. She had become a fever in his veins; kindling for a bonfire which smoldered in his brain, fogging his perceptions. That evening he was to have supper with her and her parents as she had reminded him on dropping him off. He was not sure that he was prepared for such an encounter but, for Lisette, he would run any risk. He had little choice.

Lisette had been easy. She was easy to talk to or, for that matter, be silent with. She had been favorably impressed by the fact that he could hold his tongue and did not have to speak endlessly about himself as so many of the college Joe's trying to win her over. She found him mature, self-assured— "nothing but a man" – though she had intuited that beneath his cool there lurked an inner turmoil, a ferocity, a rage the likes of which she couldn't fathom. It would have frightened her had she been someone else or had he not been secure in his identity. But his self-confidence, the coiled, taut poise of the fighter peeked through. Though he had been badly shaken by the death of Sam, the loss of his son, and the current madness which infected the Black Panther Party he had had to single handedly scrape his guts off the floor, stuff them back in place and stitch himself up with needle and thread, much like Dr. Frankenstein's monster. Lisette still found his confidence reassuring. What she couldn't know, what he didn't tell her, what he wouldn't admit even to himself, was that his was the confidence of a wounded she-lion backed into a corner fighting for her life. He knew it on occasion when it wakened him in the fall of night in cold despair; knew it at odd moments during the day. But all his apprehensions dissolved into mist whenever she was in view.

Before Percival could resume with *"The Confessions,"* he caught a glimpse of an indiscernible fleeting shadow pass under his window. He turned to look but too late, it was gone. He then heard the opening cry of the backscreen door. He was suddenly brought up short, struck to the heart by an agonizing cry which fixed him in place. Stiffening, he listened. A wrenching sob followed. It was Amelia. She sounded so much like his mother, Hattie, on the night she learned of Sam's death. He rose to his feet on sea legs and walked from the room as if on a ship tossed by rough seas. He felt, in fact, seasick.

Sobbing piteously and body shaking violently, Amelia sat on the edge of a chair at the kitchen table, her face in her hands. Dumbstruck, Percival watched helplessly, both embarrassed and confused. He felt like an intruder, an interloper. Yet he did not know how to extricate himself and, therefore, chose to advance. He lowered himself to his haunches besides her. He placed his hands on her shoulders, turning her his way. He asked softly, "Amelia, what's wrong?"

She raised her head slowly, dejectedly, her face as bloodless as a corpse. Her white hair was in disarray about her face and eyes, and she looked at him as if he were unknown to her, a stranger. She did not seem to recognize him.

"It's me – Percival," he reminded her, shyly.

"Yes," she said, bitterly, eyeing him as if resenting his presence. He had never felt more vulnerable.

"R you ok?" he asked.

"I'm sorry," she blinked. "I was somewhere else. You must pardon me." She brushed a hand across her brow, dazed. "I'm afraid I'm not myself, as you can see." She sniffled. "Renaldo, R-Renadlo Jr., Lisette's older brother," she whispered hoarsely, "is d-dead! H-he, he's been killed in that insane war in Vietnam," she wept, lowering her head on his shoulder.

"Oh my God," he gasped, with a start, "Lisette." He embraced Amelia, the hairs bristling like electricity on the nape of his neck.

"He was such a beautiful soul," she lamented, her voice muffled in his shoulder. "Did Lisette tell you about him?"

"The doctor, a pacifist? Yes, she mentioned him several times."

"I can't believe, he's gone," she said, withdrawing from his clumsy embrace. He straightened up. "The day had promised to be a lovely one, too, then Renaldo Sr. was summoned from the field by his wife, Felicia, and, shortly afterwards, I was sent for. But I saw the military car as it left their drive, so I had a fairly good notion as to what it was about. And when I reached the house, no one had to say a word. It was so apparent on all their faces. I was stunned, practically paralyzed. I spent a brief period collecting myself then left to be alone with my thoughts."

She wiped her eyes, then blew into a napkin. A fleeting smile crossed her lips. "Renaldo had the soul of an Albert Schweitzer. He was born to be a healer. As his younger brother, Dominick, a priest, is a physician of the soul, so too was Renaldo a priest of the body. You should have known him, Percival. You should have met him." She threw up her hands imploringly, her eyes round and filled with tears. "But he's gone! He was and he is no more! What a waste! Oh, God, it's such a waste, such a pointless waste," she lamented. "I know, who am I to question God's will? But I loved him so," she said in her own defense. "He was dear to my heart.

"He was on his way to South Africa to open a clinic in one of the poorest townships because they were in such dire need of medical care when he received his draft notice. Many people had counseled him not to go, to flee the draft."

He asked me and I asked him in return. 'What do you want to do?'

"And he said, ' Go to Africa – but, I'm a doctor, a healer. True, I could flee the draft and go to South Africa easily enough. This draft means nothing to me. Yet, on the other hand, the misery of war, the special needs of men in combat, no matter the politics, are far greater than those of the poorest, because, indeed, they are the poorest in spirit, at any rate. Their need for medical attention does not, of course, outweigh the needs of others, but the horrors that attend such needs is as much what a doctor would have to address on the battlefield as not. Because their souls, as much as their lives, are in constant jeopardy they, more than others, need to have their lives sustained so they may have a chance in which to eventually atone. That failing, often the doctor would serve as a dying soldier's confessor, his last attendant in this life. If I go into the military, I do not go to serve a country, but my fellow man. And South Africa, no doubt, shall still be there after the war,'" Amelia said, throatily, reminiscent. "And off he went and now he's dead." She shook her head, bewildered. "It seems like a field hospital in which he was working came under mortar attack and, while attempting to evacuate the wounded he was killed in a direct hit," she said with horror in her voice.

Percival wondered if she knew what that meant? If she knew that he, in all probability, had been blown to bits with numerous others and all that would be left for burial would be boots and dog tags?

"He wouldn't abandon them to save himself," she said savagely, lips tightening in a grimace, to Percival's surprise. "I don't know. It's all so unclear. What else do you hear after they tell you the one you expected so much from, the one with so much more to offer has been cut down in the prime of life?"

She fell silent and an air of grief filled the room with its baleful influence.

"I should go over 'n express my condolences," Percival said, girding himself for the ordeal. He left a teary-eyed Amelia seated at the kitchen table and strolled gravely for the house across the road, realizing how nervous he had been about meeting Lisette's folks. And now that this awful tragedy had befallen them, granting him a reprieve (the dinner would have to wait), he felt no better for it. In fact, he felt far worse. It sunk into his system like a virus, dredging up sediments of old which had presaged Sam's early death, sickening him.

Set back out of sight on a hill, the house was a considerable distance from the road. He approached it under the maple trees along the winding driveway. He rang the front doorbell, observing the inside through a stainedglass cluster set in the door at eye level. The door was answered by a lovely, middle-age woman who appeared more Spanish than not. It was more apparent that she had been crying.

Surprised by the unexpected presence of a stranger, she considered him with pathos and suspicion in her moist, black eyes. She saw him vaguely. He could see that she was deeply upset. She forced her dim, tear-stained eyes to focus and saw that he was tall, roguishly attractive, muscular with strong, underlying animal magnetism.

She looked about for a car but saw none.

"Can I help you?" she finally asked, certain that he was not a farm hand. Indeed, he carried himself with authority, as if beholden to no one other than himself.

"Mrs. Poincare?"

"Of course!" She whacked herself on the forehead with the heel of a palm, and dimly realized that this must be Percival, the fellow with whom her daughter, Lisette—to her father's dismay— was obviously smitten. "You must be Amelia's house guest. Come in, won't you? My daughter's told me about you." She stepped aside, suppressing a sob.

"Who is it, Felicia?" her husband cried, entering the living room. "Oh, it's you," he said curtly, considering Percival with a cold, discouraging glance.

It was easy to see that Lisette had come about her beauty honestly, both parents were exceedingly good looking. Her father, Renaldo Sr., was fair skinned and his hair, a bundle of curls, crowned his handsome, well-formed head. He was strong, broad-shouldered, and as bull-headed a man as ever bent his back in servitude to the land. He was Jamaican, of French and African ancestry, whereas her mother, Felicia, was comely and demure, Dominican, of Spanish, Indian and African heritage. And though her dignity was flagging, at the moment, she carried herself with no less poise than her daughter, Lisette.

Suddenly, to Percival's relief, Lisette appeared at the top of the stairs, drying her eyes. She descended and, bypassing her parents, took his hand. "Thanks for coming," she said weakly, tonelessly, full of sorrow. She was tremulous and looked as if she had received a frightful scare. It took her another moment to collect herself. Then said, "This is Percival."

Mrs. Poincare accepted his hand.

"Daddy, you remember Percival."

"Yes, I recall," said Mr. Poincare, stiffly, shaking his hand halfheartedly, his face a ghastly hue. He appeared to be fighting back a rush of tears.

"I only came to offer my condolences," said Percival, humbly, ill at ease. "Amelia told me of your loss – 'n so, well, if there's anything I can do. let me know. I won't stay. I'll be begging off from supper t'night, too, if that's okay. I don't want'a intrude on your grief. It's difficult enough without trying to entertain or make small talk."

"Thank you for understanding," said Felicia, charmed.

"Yes," said Mr. Poincare gruffly.

"I said what I came to say, I guess," said Percival dryly. "Well then, I'll be off. Again I'm terribly sorry," he repeated as he backed out the door.

"I'll talk to you later," said Lisette, closing the door after him.

After he'd left Lisette's father turned to her. "You've been seeing quite a bit of that boy since he arrived," he said bluntly.

"I don't know I'd call him a boy by any means," said Lisette in reply with a little nervous run of laughter.

"You know what I mean," he said, peevishly.

"He's certainly no kid," added Felicia.

"I like him," Lisette blushed. "I like him a lot," she said, decidedly.

"There's something suspicious about that boy," said Renaldo bitterly.

"Could it just be that he's a man and not a boy?"

"And what's that suppose to mean?" her father asked, eyeing her with hostility.

"You know." She returned his gaze with a look of defiance.

"How much longer is he going to be here? A week or more?" Felicia asked.

"I don't think he's leaving planet earth, he's only going back to New York City."

"What about Julius?" Felicia asked.

"What about him?'

"He thinks you're going to marry him," said her mother.

"I never put that idea in his head."

"He thinks it anyway."

"I never encouraged it."

"You've been friends since childhood."

"We're still friends, I hope."

"And what do you know about this man, this Percival?" her father demanded.

"I know he's a close friend of Nina's and Aunt Amelia's opened her door to him."

"Now I love and respect your Aunt Amelia, but she'd as soon let the devil in if he were thirsty and in need of rest," said Lisette's father.

"And that makes Percival the devil?"

"Don't twist my words. I didn't say that."

"You can't you don't know him."

"And you do?"

"What I know is what my heart tells me."

"Rubbish," said her father forthrightly. "Rubbish!"

"Stop it! Stop it this minute," Felicia interjected, scornfully. "This boy— excuse me— this man, Percival, is not what you're arguing here. Our son, Renaldo, your brother, Lisette, our Renee is dead, k-k-killed," she bleated, "blown to pieces and you stand here arguing over, o-over –" she spluttered, and fled the room in an outburst of tears.

Lisette came to herself with a gasp and pressed the tips of her fingers to her bloodless lips. Her father, Renaldo, lapsed into silence, coming to his senses, ashamed of himself. The shock, the cold horror of Renaldo Jr.'s death washed over him anew.

"Oh daddy," Lisette moaned, flinging herself into his open arms.

"All I've ever asked is to be able to provide for my family." He wept, holding her close.

"I love him, daddy, I do. And all I know about him is that he's a beautiful man and won't come again in my life."

"Go, go," said her father, releasing her. "I've got to see to your mother."

She hurried out the door and, calling to Percival, raced down the drive after him. Turning to face her, he drew to a halt, as she overtook him. She threw her arms about his neck. He raised her off the ground. Her voice was tearful but beneath her sense of grief, her spirits soared. "I'm a bundle of conflicting emotions right now," she said, tears streaking her face. "But, oh, I so want you to know I love you."

"I sort'a guess'd," he rejoined, smiling. "I love you, too."

She pecked him affectionately on the forehead. "Put me down, please. I've got to help my parents through this."

"Of course."

He lowered her. She clasped his hands in hers, kissing them fervently. "I'll see you," she said, lifting her eyes to his. Then she turned back for the house, and he continued on his way.

***

Lisette informed Percival that her brother, Dominick, was home and would offer Sunday Service in memory of Renaldo in the woodland chapel. She was wondering if he would want to attend and meet him afterwards. He had never attended Mass before, hence he was amenable. She picked him up the next day, Sunday, shortly before 9 a.m., and they joined the others on the path round the lake, across the bridge, to the chapel. All the farm hands had known Renaldo— better known to them as Renee and were deeply grieved by the loss. Thus, they joined the family of the bereaved under the shade trees of the woodland church where sunlight poured in through a deep cover of leaves like balm onto their sorrow.

Arms folded under his sacerdotal vestments, Father Poincare stood before the altar in front of the chapel and watched as the supplicants sat and crossed their legs under them, Indian style. Percival's jaw slackened, and he did a double take. He recognized the handsome priest and in all probability the priest would, if he had not already, recognize him. There was no convenient avenue of escape.

"Is that your brother?" he asked Lisette in consternation, breaking out in sweat.

"Yes, that's Dominick."

"I know him!"

She gazed at him inquisitorially, surprised. "Really? How interesting."

At any rate he didn't think so.

Father Poincare greeted the attendance with a short benediction then commenced with service: "Introibe ad altare dei," he said, joining his hands. "Ad deum qui laetificat juventutem mean," the altar boy, the boy in love with Lisette, responded. "Oremus," said the priest, and, extending his hands, he approached the altar. Despite himself, Percival was struck by the majesty of the Mass, the solemnity of the ritual, the incomprehensible beauty and mystery of it. His soul took flight and for the moment his burdens were few.

The Altar boy rang the bell for the Gloria. It chimed harmoniously among the song of the birds flitting back and forth among the leafy branches of the overhanging trees. Then facing the bible set on the altar, the priest read, "dominus vobiscum."

Dominick faced the mourners. "The Gospel for this morning is from Luke." After he had read the gospel he folded the bible in his hands and held it at his waist.

Searching the faces of the mourners, his eyes coming to rest on Percival, he said, "I wish to say a few words about Lisette's, and my brother, Renee. Our parent's first born, your friend and doctor, who we all knew and loved. Excuse me, love is forever, and therefore we love him still even as he loves us.

Before I forget, the memorial service will be held in Saratoga tomorrow morning at ten a.m., so if any of you need a ride please let my father know."

He paused as if unable to continue. The Missal slipped his grasp. The altar boy quickly retrieved it. Dominick faltered on, "I was about to say, all of you have your own personal memories of him. I know he touched each of us in his own inimitable way. That was Renee. There are those of you who recall his binding a wound, setting a broken bone, nursing a fever, and so on. In fact, one or two of you younger ones, he'd even delivered into this world." He smiled wanly at a toddler nestled in its mothers arms.

"He went out of his way to be of service. These are your experiences of him. The young man striving to become a physician. His nose always in some medical text or other. Researching plant life, examining bugs, seeing to the domestic livestock. This was the person we knew and loved. This man, all six feet two of him, as physically powerful as a bull, and yet the most gentle human being I've ever known. No one, to my knowledge, ever saw him raise a hand in anger. Yet many saw him mediating disputes." Dominick sighed, closing his eyes briefly, and then, on opening them again, sought the comforting assurance of his mother's face. But she was falling to pieces, collapsing in sections in her husband's embrace. Stunned to see her so, he shifted his gaze to Amelia. She was drained of color and wavered as if from vertigo. Birds would, no less, swoop down and rest on her, and once again fly off. Squirrels too approached her, seeking her attention. Children, as always, surrounded her, leaned on her, wept with her, tried to comfort her. The dogs were not far off. Dominick, as a child, once lisped, "Animals luv 'er, critters luv 'er jus' like we do." Dominick blinked. As difficult as it was, it was his sacred obligation to continue: "This was my big brother. And though we were three years apart, he three years my senior, we were the best of friends.

"This woodland chapel, for example, would not have been without Renee. This glade, in our youth, our boyhood was our campsite, our bivouac. It was here where we decided to become priest and doctor, under these trees, in this glade, this forest. After I had decided to become a priest—I was merely thirteen. Renee, it seems, had always known that he was going to be a doctor. It was his idea that we commemorate this spot by dedicating it, consecrating it, and turning it into a sacred place, a shrine. With that in mind we gained permission from Aunt Amelia to do so. With her help we turned this little spot into a place of worship in which we now remember Renee. I recall our clumsily carving the crosses for The Stations of the Cross, and daddy cutting down the tree and hewing the trunk into an altar, and Amelia making candles from bees wax and mama sewing an altar cloth and Lisette contributing the first flowers. In fact, my last memories of Renee take place here.

"It was a little over a year now when he got word that he was to go to Vietnam, and we came here to talk. In that discussion he spoke of the real possibility of dying. As a priest and a doctor death is a part of our everyday reality. He was under no illusion. He knew that this could happen, and did not shrink from it, though he strongly disapproved of this war. He told me before he left, *'All is in God's hands.' I only pray that I'm doing his will.'* I'm sure he was as there is no other will. Afterwards, I heard his confession and we shared a prayer together as in days past. If I am the least bit comforted it is because my dear brother is with us still, here, in this place, I share a special connection with him and feel his presence ever more deeply. So, in our remembering Renee, remember too that he is a living presence with us this day and forever."

Dominic did a gracious about-face and went on with the Mass, faltering slightly as he did, tears glistening in his eyes rolled upwards, arms extended in supplication.

Everyone had been affected, including Percival, and crying profusely, Lisette cleaved to him as if he were a pillar of strength.

"Suscipe, sancte Pater, omnipotens aeterne Deus, hanc immaculatam histiam, quam ego indignus famulus," said the priest in adoration, raising the Host heavenward. He poured water and wine in a chalice, then blessed it and drank. He next took the remains of the Sacrament and faced the congregation. "Ecce agnus Dei, ecci qui tollit peccota mundi," he said, calling the faithful to communion. They came forward and knelt at the foot of the altar. He passed among them, saying to each recipient of the Host: "Corpus Domini nostr Jesu Christi custodiat animam tuam in vitam aeternam. Amen." Each in turn rose as if levitated, transformed in body and spirit, and returned to their respective places.

As the drama of the Mass, the bloodless sacrifice, drew to a close, the priest again faced the worshipers. "Dominus vobiscum," he chanted.

"Et cum spiritu tuo," sang the altar boy in response.

"Ito, missa est," said the priest in conclusion, hands outstretched. "Arise and go in Peace."

The congregation rose to its numbed feet, stretching and brushing themselves off. A soft breeze issued in through the trees off the lake, rustling the leaves. The children darted about, playing tag, while the adults mingled.

Dominick rushed from the altar towards Percival. "It is. It's you. I thought so, Percival Jones! What are you doing here?" asked the priest, seizing his hand and smiling through his grief.

His parents and Amelia looked at each other with raised brows. "You two know each other?" Renaldo Sr. asked.

Catching the expression on their faces Dominick quickly put two and two together. "Know him? You mean to say you don't know who you've been entertaining?"

"Do tell," said Lisette, markedly curious.

"He's Bed-Stuy's first citizen, arguably the best fighter to have laced on gloves since Sugar Ray Robinson."

"Not the fighter who got his jaw broken in the finals of the Olympic Trials and still won?" Renaldo, Sr. exclaimed.

"The very same," said Dominick, boastfully.

"You're Percival Jones?" said Renaldo, looking at him anew.

Percival grimaced, a hot wave of blood flushed across his body.

"Why didn't you say something?" Renaldo asked.

"What was I to say? I was trying to lay low, trying to come to terms with some personal stuff, 'n needed to distance myself from myself. Trying to see things differently."

"Oh, yes, I'm sorry," Dominick broke in, face downcast. "I was terribly saddened to hear of your brother's death a few weeks back."

"His brother?" said Lisette, startled.

"You didn't know? Yes, he was killed by the police while supposedly transferring a cache of arms, wasn't it? The inner city is a roaring inferno these days," said Dominick, lapsing into a conversational tone of voice. "There's a war going on for the hearts and minds of it's young. It's a fearsome battle. Viewing it from the pulpit is my only safeguard, though I precious little like to use it as such. And in certain instances, its entirely of no avail. No doubt, the police are small respecters of any person of color wearing a collar. I fear for so many of my young parishioners daily. I pray for you black men trying to develop breakfast and medical programs in these ghetto communities."

Percival kept a poised, thoughtful silence.

"That explains a lot," said Lisette, pensive, hand on her hip. "And what else is there about Mr. Percival Jones that I ought to know but don't?"

"Aside from being a great fighter and social activist, he's considered somewhat an intellectual, which makes him quite a role model. And in the ghetto, they're few and far between."

"Interesting combination," said Renaldo, stroking his chin with a callous, sun brown hand.

Percival blushed, laughing uneasily. "Ya've blown my cover, man."

"No need for one here," Dominick assured him.

"I thought you said you didn't know my brother," said Lisette, catching his eye.

"Sounds to me you know each other remarkably well."

"Not really," he responded, holding her gaze.

"In all honesty, I would know him far better than he would me," said Dominick in Percival's defense. "I'm a fan. I used to bring a group of boys to watch him work out at the gym. And, of course, take them to see him fight. He would only know me by sight, at best."

"I see," Lisette intoned, gazing at her father with a look of vindication.

With a quizzical, wondering expression on his set, leathery face, Renaldo stood with the folded arm of a hand supporting the elbow of the arm under the hand which cupped his cleanly shaven jaw.

Lisette, no less than Felicia, had always been able to read her father and she knew that he had dug in for the final phase in which he would melt like butter in her hands.

"Come Felicia, let's go prepare breakfast," said Amelia, inviting all to the main house to dine.

***

A reception after the Monday memorial service was held at the home of the Poincares. The driveway was backed up with cars to, and along, the road, the overflow spilling on to Amelia's driveway. The church had been filled to capacity with mourners, and it appeared as if as many had come to the reception as well. Obviously, Renaldo Jr. had been as loved as he was popular. The Dean of his alma mater had come as had his high school teachers, professors, fraternity brothers and colleagues. The Bishop, rector and mayor were also present. Rumor had it that he was to be awarded the Medal of Honor posthumously. In any event, Percival realized that Renaldo had indeed touched many people's lives and that they all sincerely grieved his passing. "G'd," he thought, "had I only been able to grieve Sam's death half so earnestly." He wondered who this man was in life to have been deserving of so many friends. And guessed he would never know.

Lisette emerged from out of the crush of people with Julius on her arm. Percival recognized the caramel-colored pretty boy by how nattily attired he was. He disliked him impulsively, and, suspecting he would prove a colossal bore, he stifled a yawn in advance. Julius wore a brown on brown shirt with matching wide tie, brown pleated trousers and Gucci shoes. He looked as if he were just in off a shoot and was laying about to be made over.

"Percival, I want you to meet somebody," said Lisette by way of opening. "This is Julius, the childhood friend I told you about. Julius, this is Percival – my beau," she said, beaming effusively, taking Percival by the other arm. They shook hands across her, eyeing each other contentiously. She looked from one

471

to the other archly. "I want you two to get along. I've got to help out. I'll leave you two to get acquainted," she said, with a reedy trill and left, glissading gracefully across the lawn.

"I've heard a good deal about you these past days," said Julius shortly, affecting a bonhomie he didn't feel.

"N I've heard 'bout you too."

"It's hot as a pistol," Julius remarked, casting a glance skyward through the overhead cover of leaves under which they stood. "It's so sad about Renee. But you didn't know him did you? I guess there's a lot you can't know. Oh well, he was doing his duty."

"Vietnam, you mean?"

"Yes, he died in service to his country."

"Is that what he did?"

"The greatest country in the world."

"So they say."

"You're from Harlem, aren't you?"

"No, Bed-Stuy."

"One back alley or another what's it matter," said Julius, indifferently. "Lisette's been carrying strays home since childhood."

"There best be somebody over my shoulder to whom you're talking," said Percival, with a backward yank of a thumb, holding his temper.

"You think you can just waltz in here from wherever you're from and walk off with my girl?" said Julius, sharply, dismissing Percival out of hand. "You'd better think again. I'm not going to roll over for anyone. You can be sure of that! I'm going to consider her fair game until she says, 'I do,'" Julius said, with injured, youthful pride. "And I'm betting it won't be to you!"

Percival bristled. "Look, man, do what you got'a okay? Cause if you've not been able to pull it off till now, you'll pardon me if I don't sweat it, dig?" Smiling mirthlessly, Percival clapped Julius lightly on the cheek, then straightened his tie. "Besides, I don't think you want any part of me," he said menacingly. Julius blushed visibly to his ears. "Jus' you stay out'a my way." Then Percival pursed his lips and blew Julius a kiss. "Kiss off, sweet-cakes," laughing with contempt as he departed.

Cut to the quick, Julius left without a word to Lisette.

Shaking his head, Percival went in search of Lisette. It took him awhile to locate her amidst the crowd. She had gone inside and was seated with her brother and a few close family friends round the living room coffee table, pouring through old family photo albums. Lisette and Dominick made perfect hosts, attentive and congenial. The family resemblance was so strikingly obvious between them that Percival could not understand how he had not seen

472

it previously. In any case, he saw it now. They were unmistakably brother and sister, hauntingly so. He liked Dominick, had always liked him, that is, what he had known of him, which wasn't all that much. He was simply a neighborhood priest who used to bring a group of boys to the gym with him to watch the fighters work out. Perhaps, they had exchanged a few passing remarked on occasion, but nothing more.

He beckoned to Lisette. She excused herself and joined him.

"I'm off," he said.

"Are we on for tonight?" she asked.

"If you're up for it."

"Dominick says I shouldn't grieve overly it's too self-indulgent, he says. And I know your time here is short. Reservations are set and I'm looking forward to hearing some great jazz with you.

They kissed in parting.

"Tonight then."

"I'll pick you up."

The day gave way to dusk and a burnished rubescent sun hung low in the evening sky on a long day spent in mourning. The vast outpouring of love and sympathy from the community of friends and neighbors was no doubt of great comfort to the Poincare's. A still grievous Lisette picked Percival up well into the dinner hour in her father's new Eldorado, and they started out for Saratoga.

Simply elegant in a backless blue dress, hair drawn in a knot at the nape of her neck, Lisette appeared poised behind the wheel of the car. Her eyes were dried from bouts of crying.

"We're traveling in style," Percival said. "Not jus' the ole pickup truck, I see."

"My father must like you," she said, removing her eyes from the road. "He doesn't usually let me use his car."

Percival grabbed the steering wheel, as the car swerved. "Let's get it back ta him in one piece then."

"Ooops," she gulped, fastening her eyes once more on the road.

"You okay?"

"I'm fine," she said, stoutly. "I'm looking forward to this."

The drive was brief. She parked and they stepped onto a little side street where lamps poured pools of golden light onto the sidewalk.

Lisette chatted frivolously, laughing the while. They entered the nightclub and were shown to a table up front. The room was cozy and filled quickly. The first set was soon to begin. A waiter took their order.

Percival took in Lisette across the table. She looked healthy, a woman who'd come into her own and was sufficiently proud. Her dark animal eyes took in the plush room. "I'm excited," she said, folding her shoulders like wings, and taking his hands into hers. A tender look came into her eyes. Her sensuous lips pouted in anticipation. The musicians mounted the stage, McCoy Tyner taking his place at the keyboard. The music began with a crash of cymbals.

The music stole its way into Lisette. She removed her hands from Percival's, set her elbows on the table, folded her hands and placed her chin atop them in an attitude of intense listening. She proceeded to forget her sorrow in the music. She found herself transported, in a state of rapture, enchanted. She said to Percival between sets, "This music gets me home in a way I can't explain, as if I've not heard music before."

"I know, it's all so very fresh."

They stayed through to the third and final set of the night.

"So that's jazz, is it?"

"That's McCoy Tyner, anyway."

"Wow."

They were silent on the drive back, afraid to say anything that would break the spell.

"I don't know how to thank you enough for tonight, the music," said Lisette for something to say, well into the homeward drive. She pulled off the road onto the lakeshore in distant view of the farmhouse's back porch light. "I don't want the night to end," she said, stepping out of the car.

"I can't agree more," said Percival, following her out onto the dock.

Again they lapsed into silence, observing the shadowy forest across the way under the starry dynamo of night, feeling the darkness wondrously alive all around them.

"I know," said Lisette, suddenly, "let's take a midnight swim."

"I've no bathing suit."

She laughed, wickedly. "You are a city boy, aren't you?" she teased, and, slipping out of her clothes, plunged headlong into the lake. He raced out of his clothes and plashed into the water after her in quick pursuit. They found one another through the blinding water by the strong pull of their shoulders. He reached for her as she reached for him. She raised her head and met his mouth in a kiss. Their lips locked, their bodies cleaved, their breath intermingled. She laced a leg round his buttocks and drew him to her, drawing him closer, inwards. He penetrated her slowly, gradually, and her body gave in with a convulsive sigh. She gasped and gave a full-throated cry, "Oh yes!" She made a small moaning noise, afraid, and cleaved to him like a trembling vine. He felt her heart leap into his. He stood, buoyed by the water, clasping her tight, smothering her terror. They remained still for what felt like an eternity. And then slowly, ever so slowly, he followed her, countered her, swept along in their passion by the rising tide of their blood, drawing her life into his as she drew his into hers. He felt himself, felt her, felt the pull of the overhead stars as the whole lake instantly trembled and they became one. The whole world beat with the throb of their unrestrained, bursting bodies. The water rippled out in concentric circles about them, lapping the shore, making them the center of the lake, the center of an ever-expanding universe over which the stars ruled, wheeling like a children's carousel in the milky air of night, wheeling until they were thrown apart like sun and moon by an explosive rapture that spent them.

Catching his breath as his wits returned, his heart beating violently, Percival uttered, "I didn't know, I didn't think. You should have said something."

"It was beautiful, my love, my darling," she whispered, kissing him to silence, her recent sorrow subsumed in her newly found joy. "You're beautiful."

"My love," he said, with a sincerity that astonished him. He was in love and it was disconcerting.

They waded back to shore hand in hand, dripping wet. Using his undershirt as a towel, they dried each other off. Then they dressed and she slowly drove him home. She parked behind the main house in the wan glow of the backporch light and they lingered, scheming as lovers do over kisses and caresses. She snuggled up to him, cooing, "Oh, Percival, I'm so in love with you. You make me complete, so blissfully happy."

She further asked, in passing, "When do you leave?"

He did not reply for quite some time: "Any day now, I'm afraid."

"I see," she said, dismayed. Then she blithely chirped, "At least we had this before you left. We'll write. Call. Stay in close contact. You'll come visit me on campus and I'll come to the city. We'll find a way," she said staunchly, determined. "Now I've found you I'm not going to let you get away so easily."

"There's not much chance of that," he said, trying to see beyond the veil. If the future was in anyway a reflection of the past then it held little promise for them, yet he clung to the thread of hope this love had to offer. He could not see his way to letting Lisette go without a fight.

A surreal, pale light appeared in the eastern sky, along the horizon, as day was about to break, and they could hold their eyes open no longer. They were finally forced, more from exhaustion than any desire to part, to say "goodnight."

***

He had barely climbed into bed when the cock crowed. He drew the covers over his head but, like a child on Christmas Eve with its head full of fancies, he was much too excited to drop off. He passed in and out of sleep for the remainder of the night, his dreams filled with symbols of love, loving, and the source of it all, Lisette. That was the first night since Sam's death that he had not been startled awake in a cold sweat by a bad conscience.

A faint knock at the door caused him to stir, but he was too lethargic to respond. A sharper, second knock followed. "Yeah," he responded, lifting his head off the pillows and yawning.

"Telephone," Amelia called through the door.

"Telephone?" he uttered, surprised.

"It's Nina."

"Oh," he said. It couldn't be good. "I'll be right there." He took the call in the library, "'ello?"

"Percival?" He recognized Nina's voice. "I've got Silva here. He says he needs to speak with you."

"Put him on," he said, with a sinking feeling.

In a moment Silva was on the line: "Percival, I'm afraid you've got'a get back pronto, man. Some foul shit is brewing and there's no hope of my dealing with it alone." He said in a single breath. "It's my guess you're pretty much caught in a squeeze play. I've checked the train schedule. The next train out of Saratoga is twelve-thirty, which gets you here about three-thirty. Will that give you time? It's now ten o'clock." As always, Silva was thorough.

"That should give me sufficient time," said Percival, sighing.

"I'll pick you up at Grand Central."

"We'll talk then."

"Right on."

"Power!" And the line went dead. Percival cradled the receiver. He grew hot and cold by turns from the urgency of the unexpected summons. He could only imagine the worst. These weeks had relaxed him, had given him time to think and feel and now all of a sudden, he had to strap on his .45 again, call all his defense mechanisms back into play and if possible, bury Sam once and for all. He could not afford any more than could Hamlet, to enter the fray encumbered by the presence of a ghost.

He left the library in a cold sweat and strolled stiffly to the kitchen as if he were an amnesiac dazed into remembrance. His gaze was distant and abstracted. His face grim, and jaw set.

"Well," said Amelia, "you're up late this morning. Did you have a good time last night?"

He did not readily reply but said at length, "I'm sorry, I was distracted, what did you say?"

"Never mind. Would you care for a cup of coffee?"

"I got'a get back to New York City," he mouthed emptily, as if talking to himself. "The train leaves at twelve-thirty. Can you possibly get me there?"

"I've things to do in town. I'll be leaving shortly. It'll be a bit early for the train, I know, but that's the best I can do," Amelia said, scrutinizing him closely.

"I've got'a say goodbye to Lisette, do we ave time?"

"Have yourself a cup of coffee and you can say goodbye on the way out. We'll make the time."

"Thanks," he said, tonelessly, pouring himself a cup of fresh coffee. It would not be easy to say goodbye to Lisette so suddenly after last night, he thought, taking a seat. He felt like a scoundrel. What had he done? He had committed the most grievous offense a revolutionary could, that is, falling in love.

He threw his things into a suitcase and had a second cup of coffee. Amelia drove him up to the Poincare's door. She waited in the idling truck while he rang the bell. Felicia answered the door after a brief interval.

"Good morning," she said, quietly, flashing a smile and waving to Amelia.

"Good morning, Mrs. Poincare, is Lisette in?"

"Lisette and Dominick went for a walk in the woods, I'm afraid. There's no telling when they'll get back."

"I see," he said, looking off anxiously. "I've got'a get back to New York City right away," he started, flummoxed, despair in his tone. "It's urgent. Something's come up 'n I can't wait. Damn it!" He stamped a foot impulsively, frustrated. "Tell her. tell her," he uttered clumsily, "I came by to say goodbye."

"I'll see she gets the message."

"Tell her. tell her. I'll call as soon as possible," he said, stalling for time, encountering Felicia's eyes, Lisette's eyes. "Tell her I'm sorry to be leaving like this, without a chance to say goodbye."

"I'll tell her."

"Tell her – tell her, for me, I love her."

"I'll be sure to tell her that."

He turned back for the truck, hands thrust in his pockets, shoulders hunched.

Amelia guided the truck out of the driveway and along a stretch of country road bordered on either side by woodlands. The horizon shimmered unsteadily in the sunlight as if in a pool of water.

Percival wallowed in a gloomy, tragic silence.

"I know you came from difficulty, and with the urgency with which you're leaving, it's my guess you've been called back by those difficulties," said Amelia, breaking the thread of silence between them. "I'm fairly certain from all Nina's told me about you that there is a certain amount of personal danger involved, as well. I can also see that you and Lisette have fallen in love. It may not have been avoidable, but such as it is, it was unfair to have involved her in your life. Your path is froth with uncertainties and your life is not exactly your own. It belongs as much to the wind as to yourself, from all I can see."

Seized with panic, Percival's heartbeat like a trapped bird beat its wings in a furious attempt to be free. "I'm going back to make my life my own," he said, in a feverish undertone. "But you're right, when I'm with Lisette I'm in another world from which I cannot pull myself long enough to say, 'no,' this can't be.'"

"Then it must be, mustn't it?" Amelia said, musingly. "This is where you get out," she said, pulling up in front of the train station. "I have nothing more to say other than may your guardian angel succor you throughout your comings and goings and may you find what you seek so desperately waiting for you at the other end. My prayers go with you."

They embraced each other with unutterable regard. Percival grabbed his suitcase from the back of the truck and entered the train depot.

He sat outside the station on a bench in the shade of an overhang. He watched the run of tracks narrow in the distance, heart sick at not having seen Lisette before he left, although, after the conversation with Amelia, he felt unsure and edgy. Going back was deliberately tossing himself into the breach. It meant throwing away all possibilities with Lisette. He wished he had seen her, had spoken to her before leaving. It would prove heartrending no matter the cause, when she found out he was gone. He was altogether angry with himself, but then he had promises to keep, even if he must deliver himself into the devil's own hands. So be it. He had danced and the piper would be paid.

In the middle of his thoughts the station door flew open and Lisette stepped out, trailed by Dominick with a suitcase in his hand. She was lovely in a strapless summer dress. He hair was held back from her face by a scarf, its ends trailing over a bare shoulder. She looked fleetingly around. Their eyes locked. His pulse quickened.

She took his breath away. He sprang to his feet. "Lisette," he cried out joyously.

"Percival!" she shouted in response, racing into his arms. "Am I ever glad to find you still here. Mama told me you had dropped in to say goodbye. Had I known you could have rode in with us, Dominick is due back in his parish today. I'm so glad I got the chance to see you before you left. I would have been distraught had I not."

Percival sat, and Lisette joined him on the bench. Dominick strolled on and stood at the edge of the platform, looking down the tracks.

"What's wrong?" Lisette asked, observing the troubled expression on Percival's face.

He replied, considering her with sad eyes. "I had a talk with Amelia on the way in 'n I was given to realize that I have little to offer."

"I can hardly believe that. I'm a big girl. Aunt Amelia knows I'm independent minded enough to make my own decisions. Anyway I didn't ask you for anything. And everything's good enough so long as we share it," she responded, hopefully.

"I guess I was only dreaming," he said.

"In that case, let me dream with you."

"As much as I love you, 'n love you I do," Percival said, his brows tight, his eyes filled with apprehension and conflicting emotions, "I can't ask you to wait, to put your life on hold till the forces that be determine my fate. I know I should have told you before, but I'm a Black Panther Defense Captain 'n I'm returning to a much more treacherous situation than your brother's described. For all I know, I may well be going to my death."

"Then I'll die too. God, Percival, I've spoken to Nina and Dominick's told me no less about you. Don't you think I know what I'm letting myself in for?"

"Why didn't you say?"

"Now you sound like my father."

He laughed. "I don't mean too."

"They both simply confirm that you're the fabulous person I know you are."

"I have promises to keep."

"I understand. Go! Keep your promises, then return safely to me."

"If it's in my power, that's a promise I'd gladly keep," he said, feeling his temples throb.

She lay a hand gently on the side of his face. "My heart is in your keeping."

"What ave I done to deserve you?"

"You've transformed me overnight into a woman. Not just any woman, but your woman," she said, with a rapturous smile, eyes aglow. "And I don't mean only as a result of last night, either. That was a confirmation of my love and trust."

"A love I share 'n trust 'n hope I'm worthy of."

"I believe in you. Will you believe in me? You can ask me anything, including asking me to wait. I return to school shortly and in the meantime,

I've enough to occupy me without my drying up. Besides, 'They too serve who stand and wait,' so the saying goes." She gave a soft, sorrowful laugh of empathy.

"In that case," he said, giving her a look of brooding affection, "I promise to do all I can to not make your wait overlong."

"That's all I ask," said Lisette, flinging her arms about his neck. "You can do this. We can do this. We can make it happen."

"Thanks for being you," he said, clasping her to him.

"And you for being you," she said softly.

"Sorry, you two lovers will have to hasten, the train is coming," said Dominick, interrupting them.

Lisette smiled and quietly took Percival's hand. They rose and walked to meet the oncoming train.

Lisette hugged Dominick fiercely before he boarded the train then kissed Percival passionately, sealing their bargain.

Percival mounted the train steps once again heartened and strangely in love.

"Goodbye for now," Lisette called after him from the platform.

"For now," he said, waving.

Percival took a seat opposite Dominick on the river side of the train.

"Well," said the priest, as the train pulled out of the station.

"Well, padre," said Percival, ironically.

"Call me Dominick. For one, you're not Catholic, and for another you're almost family."

"Am I?"

"Lisette thinks so," Dominick smiled. "My sister's a woman, a real woman, a Catholic woman, and that means something, I can assure you," the priest said, leaning forward, his voice increasing in resonance. "She's intelligent. She knows her heart and knows her mind. She's not fickle and her loyalties run deep."

"Yes, I think I know that. But why do you raise the point?"

"I've never known my sister to be as serious about a man as she apparently is about you."

Percival dropped his eyes appreciatively.

"She is my sister, my baby sister at that," the priest went on. "Renaldo and I used to look out for her. Now it's left to me. I hope your intentions are honorable."

"You're a priest, right?"

"Obviously."

"And what I tell you is strictly confidential, right?"

"You're not Catholic. This is not the confessional, but if that's what you want, consider it so."

"I'd appreciate it."

"As you wish."

"The truth is, Dominick, I don't know where I'm going. I mean I know why. But all I know for sure is that the New York cops want me dead, 'n I'm not sure jus' what the Panther's want of me, anymore. In fact, for all I know, I may be of more use to em dead than alive."

"And yet you're going back?"

"I don't know how to run, 'n even if I did I wouldn't know where to run."

"You can run but you can't hide, uh?"

"Something like that." Percival went on to explain to the priest as much as was prudent for him to reveal. Without naming names, he told the cleric about the purges being conducted on behalf of the Central Committee trying to unify the party nationally and gain an ironclad grip on it. He told him as much as was necessary, and no more, of the story surrounding the circumstances of Sam's death.

Three hours later, they disembarked at Grand Central station. Dominick said to Percival in parting, "If you need me for anything at any time you know where I can be reached. Until we meet again, may God be with you."

***

The commodious station was busy, alive with a diverse pedestrian traffic. Redcaps hawking their services, recklessly maneuvered hand trucks through the congestion like surly cab drivers. Silver met Percival at one of the many arrival gates as he was saying farewell to Dominick. Silva considered the priest diffidently as he headed through the confused swirl of people, for a nearby subway. "Good to see you, man," said Silva, sizing Percival up in his gaze. Clasping hands, they went through the black power handshake. "Power," they ejaculated in exchange. Silva said as they Crossed the station, "You look rested," weaving in and out the cross current of traffic. "You'll need to be for what I've got to say. You're not going to much like what's been coming down in your absence, man," he said, gravely.

A shadow passed over Percival's face.

"I was put on the defensive almost immediately on your departure," said Silva, expressionlessly.

"We can talk at Stouffer's," said Percival, sidling off in that direction, feeling as if the ground were rolling under his feet like the speed of the train. There was also a sense of coming out of a trance as if and those weeks in the country had only been a dream. It was almost a shock to find himself back in the city coping with the tumult and noxious smells assailing him all at once. His internal compass was fluctuating wildly, trying to regain its bearing. "You can fill me in over a cup of coffee," said Percival, sullenly.

"Only I've left Nora and Leroy waiting in the car in case it has to be moved. They'll be expecting us."

"We won't be all that long. Besides, I first want'a know what the hell I'm walking int'a, dig?"

Silva hung back indecisively, then quickly caught up.

They occupied a window booth where they could watch the stream of commuters come and go. A waitress took their order, and shortly returned with two cups of coffee and a Danish for Percival.

"It's like this, man," Silva began, his hands outthrust as if to show he had nothing up his sleeves, "within less than a week of your departure McKay sent in a member of his staff to inquire into our branches 'internal contradictions,' as he put it. Well the dude he sent in, a cat named Scratch, was himself a contradiction. He's a coarse vulgar and petty hood not averse to coercion or twisting arms; he's as ugly and illiterate a wretch as any street nigger you can find. One of McKay's henchmen. He's got more in common with the drunks who hang out in front of 'The 2nd. Step' than not." Silva laughed. "He calls himself 'a field nigga. When he found out I was a college grad he began to razz me for it. Accused me of bourgeois tendencies. Despised my parents for being professionals and was jealous of the fact that I drove a new Mustang, and wouldn't let him get close to it. He asked me, as obnoxiously as you please, if I was out slumming. I told him if I were I'd not choose his company in which to do it. He said, 'So we know where we stand?' I assured him, if he didn't, I did." Silva's his expression was grim, his eyes fixed steadfastly on Percival.

Percival gave Silva a bewildered look over the rim of his coffee cup.

"Although he dislikes me as much as I dislike him, he dislikes you even more,.." There was a note of despair in Silva's tone. "He thinks you made McKay look bad during political education week and he has it in for you. He's going about getting you in the most underhanded sort of way. First off, he's buddied up with the most disgruntled among us. Hanging out with them and introducing them to a drink from Oakland of cheap wine and lemon juice. He's constantly nosing into Sam's death, trying to drum up suspicion, trying to find a connection to a preconceived notion he harbors. Failing that, he let fall the bombshell that you, by your own admission, were in contact with the FBI. He got a hell of a rise from the cadre out of that one. I tried to point out, tried to explain, the rationale behind your actions, but the seed of doubt had been sown. While at it, he lead many of the cadre into thinking that you had deliberately

482

set Sam up, and not because of any felony on Sam's part, but that you probably had personal reasons for wanting him out of the way, and used this 'sham rape charge,' as he called it, as an excuse to be rid of your brother. He went so far as to say it couldn't have been rape because part of a true revolutionary sister's role, and I quote, 'is on her back, rewarding the warriors for putting their lives on the line against the repressive forces of the pig power structure.' Then he was so bold as to quote some jive ass remark attributed to Cleaver about "pussy power 'n free love being' the motive force of the revolutionary' and that Panthers don't hold petty bourgeois hang-ups about sex. And what's worse, I could tell by the sly smiles that some male members wanted to side with him on that point and would have, too, had Nora not blown up and shot back, 'You're the only fucking pig here, as far as I can see.' I nearly had to pull Nora off him. She was outraged. She called him every form of lowlife there was, and walked out swearing not to return. I had to calm her down and remind her that we were obligated to you.

"She railed, 'If they think I'm going to screw every Tom, Dick 'n Harry, they got another think coming. What the hell happened to our high ideals, our principles, when did we sink so low?'

"I had to remind her that that was never the way it was under your leadership. Then she came round. She said, 'I'll only stay to see what Percival does when he gets back.'"

Percival shriveled inwardly, swayed by the terrible truth of Sam's conviction that despite Raschelay's youth, or because of it, men were irresistibly attracted to her and were covetous of her.

"Well the fucking pressure's on, is it?"

"Yes, the heat is up!"

"Damn it."

"It's been hard, man. I mean, really hard, with the effort of trying to raise money for the Panther 21 defense fund and keeping all the other programs alive and dealing with the likes of Scratch on top of it, too. I had no choice but to approach McKay and complain. He told me that he had every reason to trust Scratch since they go back together. It was us who were under investigation, especially you." He said I'd well to make myself useful by cooperating in the inquiry, instead of trying to hinder it. That's when I decided to contact you, because things are spinning out of control. I mean, the Defense Captains aren't talking to one another; everybody's paranoid. Things are bad. You can't look for allies in that direction. You've returned to a nest full of riled hornets. And I think they're out to nail you."

"This is fucking disappointing news. Then, treachery always is. Sh-e-e-t," Percival spat, with a sickening feeling and a look of dumb anguish on his face.

"Where does Skeeter 'n Priestus stand in all this? Do I have the core of our groups confidence, or not?"

"It's hard to gauge, exactly. I've not seen Skeeter for days. He says this isn't why he became a Panther. And Priestus, well, he's playing it cool waiting for you to return before he decides."

"I was afraid of this." Percival sighed and closed his eyes. He was tired – bone weary. He had had no more than three hours sleep in all and it was beginning to tell on him. He could little recall what had passed the previous night between him and Lisette to have fatigued him so. Then Lisette's face, like so many broken promises, came to mind and, in light of the many new developments confronting him, she was slipping deeper into the past.

"I don't know if this means anything but "The Tribune" is doing an in-depth series of articles on the party and a reporter has been round to visit our branch. He was especially interested in our medical program. He spoke to Dr. Osgood at length."

Percival shrugged absently, his mind on other things. The two sat silently opposite each other for a few minutes. Percival's Danish remained uneaten. His hands flat on the tabletop, he stared at them with absent, uneasy eyes, trying to gather himself. "I was sent away so they could more easily apply the screws," he said suddenly, furiously, slamming the table with his fist. "Son of a bitch!"

Customers jumped and a waitress spun round, startled, as if a gun had gone off.

Speechless, Silva threw up his hands and stirred, uncomfortably.

"There was more than one good thing about the Civil Rights Movement," Percival said, on reflection, "but one thing in particular was we reserved our fire for the enemy, not one another. But here we don't even know who the fucking enemy is 'n we're creating one among ourselves. In the Civil Rights Movement we didn't sic dogs on one another, it was the opposition who did that to us, instead we did all in our power to keep faith with one another," he said abjectly. His voice harbored the far-off ring of hollow pain. Sweat broke out on his troubled brow despite the coolness of the air-conditioned room. He could neither dispel nor shake the ghost of Sam hovering over his shoulder. "If ever I had any scruples I've sacrificed em all in becoming a Panther," he said, dabbing his brow with a napkin. "'N I don't know it's been worth it."

"I realize how costly it's been for you."

"I've not much else to lose."

"What do you propose we do, go back to our branch and see to putting our affairs in order?"

"You say this cat Scratch has fabricated more than enough false charges against me by which to hang me, then it'll only be a waste of time going back to the branch. As they say in the fight game, 'the best defense is a good offense.' So we'll turn a page from Cleaver's book 'n enter the den 'n see if I can't seize my balls from the jaws of a paper tiger," Percival whispered fiercely, his eyes dilating wildly from lack of sleep. "Did you bring my gun?"

"Leroy's got it in the car."

"Let's do it then."

"It's your call."

"Waitress," Percival barked. They left the diner and exited Grand Central Station onto the bustling city street. Forty-second Street was heavy with traffic, cars, trucks, and the horrific crush of people. The tall, stately buildings narrowed in their skyward climb where silver daylight only touched the very tops, but the sun's shy, bashful rays never reached the street below. The air at ground level was stultifying, and the late August heat radiated from the street and beat like congas off the brick buildings.

Silva was on the lookout for his car. A horn honked, the sound of which he recognized among the many, and a Mustang pulled out from the curb and drew up alongside them.

After setting his suitcase in the trunk, Percival climbed in the back of the coup and lowered himself tiredly beside Leroy, who seized his hand, glad to see him. Nora slid out of the driver's seat to the passenger side, and Silver took the wheel.

"Good to ave you back," said Nora irritably, sounding put out, much like a woman carrying on despite undue provocation.

"From what I hear it might not be so good but, never mind, it's good to see you three anyway."

Silva guided the car from the curb into the current of traffic and turned uptown on Park Avenue.

"Silva told you what's been going on in your absence, huh?" said Nora, bleakly, over her shoulder.

"He has."

"He tell you about Scratch?"

"He sounds delightful," said Percival, wearily.

"About as charming as a rabid dog. I don't know where they found his sorry ass but I wouldn't be surprised if it wasn't under a prehistoric rock. The first thing he tried after we'd met was to get me in the sack. I told him to 'dig himself.' I mean, there's nothing remotely desirable about the crud. And he has jus' about all the finesse of a leech," said Nora, scornfully.

Leroy chimed in, "He must'a thought he could break me down cause I'm the youngest 'n get to you, but I told him, 'You the best, ain't nobody badder. I said, you taught me everything I know," Leroy spoke with bravura, pleased with himself.

"I knew I could count on you, little brother," Percival said, folding the youth to his bosom in affection, then releasing him.

"You my ace," said Leroy, handing Percival his .45, which he stuck under his safari jacket, beneath his belt at the base of his spine.

"You thought about how you're going to go about this?" Nora asked "I guess you've not had much time, huh?"

Percival shrugged. "I've been expecting something of the sort, I suppose all along. When you're caught in a squeeze play, such as this, you can't come at it from a blindside, so you must confront it head-on." He sunk back in the seat. He felt a deep, welling loneliness coming on. He closed his eyes. Silva turned on the radio. They arrived uptown at the Harlem branch of the Black Panther Party. Silva found parking out front of the office. They swept into the office like a gust of wind.

The office was lively. Percival recognized most of the faces. E.J. McKay sat at the main desk, dressed in fatigues, cigarette in hand, quite the revolutionary and very much in command. He was giving an interview to a reporter, the one Silva had mentioned, Percival surmised.

An oscillating fan offered a pretense of relief from the hot, sultry dog days of August, under which the rooms occupants were wilting.

"Percival," said McKay, gruffly, not overly surprised at this unannounced visit. He uncrossed his booted feet and lowered them to the floor, sitting up. "What brings you this way?"

The reporter turned his florid face over his shoulder.

"We got'a talk," said Percival, between his teeth.

"I'm busy right now. If you want an audience you'll have to go through channels."

"Channels be damned!"

"Don't be impolite. Can't you see we've a guest from the press?"

Percival didn't bother to look but gazed steadfastly at the field marshal. "More reason we conduct this in private."

"As you like," said McKay, annoyed. "I guess I can spare a few minutes."

"Or more," Percival insisted.

McKay shook his head in wonderment, then chortled unpleasantly, glowering at Percival. "I must say you got guts." He rose abruptly to his feet and proceeded into the back room with Percival and two guards following.

"We'll be right outside the door," Silva said, reassuringly, but Percival had not heard him. The reporter, seemingly quite innocent, approached Silva and offered him a cigarette which he accepted, edgy, listening intently over the room noise – as did the reporter.

"What's this about," McKay asked, after the door was closed and he had ensconced himself in an armchair. The fingers of his hands were steepled and he assumed an expression of pious respectability. Percival remained standing while the guards approached to search him.

"No need to frisk me," he said, frankly. "I'm packing."

"Care to hand it over?" McKay asked.

"Not particularly. I'm not here for anything other than what I'm here for. 'N that, in a word, is to talk. But I won't submit to being handled either, dig?"

"And the reason you want'a talk would be?"

"You know damn well what it is, sending your man to investigate my branch in my absence."

"You needed a rest. You'd been under a lot of stress with the death of your brother, and I had to get on with the business I was sent here by Central Committee to perform. As it happened, you fell under investigation."

"For what, may I ask?" Percival looked at McKay, his eyes grave and taunting, spoiling for a fight.

"Counter revolutionary activities."

"Such as?"

"Right now you're under suspicion for collaborating with enemy agents. Official charges have yet to be made."

"There 'r none to be made 'cause none can stick."

"We can clear that up right away then."

"How so?"

"You can submit to a scopolamine test."

"A what?"

"Truth serum."

"I know what it is. 'R you joking?" Percival considered McKay's unsmiling face with suspicion.

"Do I look like I'm joking?" McKay's gray cat's eyes were remorseless. "No, it's one sure way of getting rid of all doubts. We've a doctor who can administer the dosage."

"I doubt, you. I doubt you, sincerely. Do I get the opportunity to test you, too?"

"Let's not get ridiculous, now."

"Whose being ridiculous here, you or me? What kind'a fucking ultimatum is that? The father of the dialectic, Plato, Socrates, says 'The unexamined life isn't livable,' n your suppose to be a dialectician 'n would subject me to a scopolamine test, render me unconscious so you can ferret the truth out of me?" Percival's voice was calm, quiet, but incisive. "How the hell you figure that? I've already told you the truth! Hell, they at least gave Socrates a trial."

A slow mocking smile dawned on McKay's lips. "What kind'a trial did you give your brother, Sam?"

Percival flushed with rage. He was infuriated but reined in his anger else it spill uncontrollably, "I'm not going to dignify that with a fucking reply! If you've charges to make against me, make em in front of a tribunal. You've got nothing on me."

"More than enough for my satisfaction. As for a tribunal, that's not the way it's going to work. You're going to submit to the test or you're out!"

Percival gazed at the floor, raised his head and turned aside. After a brief silence, he asked, "Jus' on your say so?"

"Just on my say so," said McKay, impatiently. His face was set in hard, bitter lines and he gave the impression that his anger was barely under control. "You've been nothing but trouble since we met. I'm fed up with you and you're out unless you submit to the test, period!"

"When I was in SNCC –"

"That's one of your problems, perhaps, you have divided allegiances. You still harbor allegiances for SNCC, for Stokley, which makes you a reactionary."

"You're putting words in my mouth."

"You're the one brought up SNCC, weren't you?"

"Well, what allegiances to Stokley? Because I won't denounce him, because I won't put his head on a political chopping block for you without due process does not make me a reactionary. The reverse is more likely true. If we're seeking justice, 'n we certainly demand it in our party platform, then how have I abandoned our aims? No, what I was about to say was, had you done your homework you'd know I've been involved in one part of the movement or another for years 'n never has my loyalty been questioned until now." Percival stood his ground defiantly, "Never."

"Never, ah? Have you ever had a brother turn up dead on your doorstep before?" McKay countered, salting the wound. "Or ever found so deep in bed with the pigs? Cause you sure couldn't pull off his execution without their participation."

"That's assuming I had him killed, which I didn't!" Percival declared, emphatically, feeling himself grow hot all over, and his heart sink in despair. A haunted expression crossed his face. He felt nauseous, woozy, but held on with a fighter's resolve. "That was uncalled for," he said at length. "A cheap shot! I called, I called 'n asked your advice 'n you as much as suggested –"

McKay cut him off, "don't say that! Don't you ever say that! You misunderstood me. The point is your brother's dead at your hands."

"Not as a result of my desiring it, no! It's bad enough it's so," said Percival colorlessly, his voice a drifting murmur. "But what I've done is nobody's concern. Certainly not yours. It's between me 'n my conscience. N I'll not have you, of all people, question my integrity. It's your behavior here, since you arrived, that's questionable," he said, irate. "You're no more than a petty tyrant!"

"Get him out'a here," said McKay, disgustedly, waving Percival away.

The guards hastened forward. He threw up his right hand, index finger upraised, head cocked and every muscle in his body flexed, poised for action, in marked defiance. "Don't touch me," he warned. "I walked in on my own 'n I'll walk out on my own!"

The guards held fast. His reputation was well-known and for a moment they were tense. Percival turned and walked out of the room seething with rage.

"You think about that offer," McKay called after him.

"There's nothing to think about," Percival shot back, without breaking stride.

"I'd take it if I were you, it's the only one you'll get."

Percival flipped him off and tramped out of the office. Covering his retreat, Silva, Nora and Leroy cautiously withdrew after him.

The reporter, having left the office before them, accosted Percival as he was about to enter the car: "You're Percival Jones, aren't you?"

"What of it?"

"You're now a Black Panther. What I overheard inside would make for interesting copy."

"Who the fuck 'r you anyway?"

"I'm a reporter from the Tribune and I know you fairly well. I'm a fight fan. I'm presently doing a series of articles on the Panthers and I'd love to interview you."

"Well, you're too late. I've jus' been expelled."

"More reason to get your story in print."

"Let's get the hell out'a here," said Percival to Silva, turning his back on the reporter, but Silva could not pull out before the reporter had thrust his card into Percival's hand.

"Call me if you change your mind," the reporter shouted after the departing vehicle.

As the car raced south along the West Side Drive, fronting the river, Silva asked,

"What went down in there that you left in such a heat?"

"McKay wanted me to submit to a truth serum test," Percival replied.

"Dear God," Nora exclaimed.

"He wanted you to what?" Silva asked, explosively.

"I didn't stutter."

"A bunch'a nice people they sent in from Oakland," Nora said, critically.

"We'll be scattered like marbles in a shoot," Silva lamented.

"This summer's going all too fast for me," Nora said, gazing absently at the turgid river.

"I-it's over?" asked Leroy, dumbfounded.

"It is for me," Percival answered.

Leroy gasped and stiffened against the back seat of the car, eyes stark, with disbelief.

A daunting silence overcame them. It was one of those silences which wore on and on, filled with gloomy significance. *"I guess I'm back,"* Percival thought, miserably, looking out the car window. The city blocks flew past, quickly receding in the distance. Sail boats bobbed on the murky river and the ripe smell of garbage laden barges drawn by tugboats, wafted on the air.

It wasn't until passing through the Battery Tunnel into Brooklyn on way to the Verazzano bridge that Percival spoke, breaking the dreary run of silence: "Listen Leroy, my little brother, I want you to promise me you'll return to school come fall 'n stop dodging the truant officer."

"Why, man, they ain't got nothing to offer me there."

"Probably not but you got something to offer them."

"I'll think about it."

"I don't want you to think 'bout this one, I want you to do it as a favor to me."

"Ah man."

"I want ya ta promise."

"I promise I'll hate it."

"That's okay so long as you do it." Percival sighed, "I mean, little brother, what the schools ave to offer may be dismal, but what the streets ave to offer is far worse." He smiled. Leroy returned that smile with a sad, puppy dog look of acquiescence. "If you want me to."

Percival roughed the boy's head with a hand as if to say, "good man!"

"You just did a really good thing, Percival Jones." Nora choked back tears.

"If you'll excuse me, I'm gonna catch up on some Z's," Percival yawned, folded his arms across his chest, slouched in the corner of the back seat, and fell asleep.

***

They found everything in the house a little chaotic on arrival and everyone in attendance slightly uncomfortable in Percival's presence. Wasting no time, E.J. McKay had obviously called ahead and informed the branch members that Percival was out and that Scratch would be assuming the reins of authority, until further notice. Percival had been branded a reactionary and, therefore, a traitor, and though none of them could quite believe it, they accepted it as one would an article of faith. Since the house was on loan to Percival he could not be cast out, but he made arrangements to stay with Gwen in her Village apartment, until he could get back on his feet. Initially, he had asked Priestus to call Lily and update her on the status of the house and see how she wanted to handle it but he changed his mind and called himself. He explained the situation to her. She decided since he would be leaving the house that she would reclaim it for herself. She and her mother were wearing on each other. In addition, Rufus had not improved much, his mind was still very much in abeyance. She was glad to hear that he was out. No matter how. He was alive and intact. That was an accomplishment in and of itself, she said. He thanked her for her many kindness' and they said farewell.

Recalling his and Lisette's last evening together, which was only the previous night (how long ago it all seemed now), Percival went to bed wishing he were back upstate in her loving embrace. As he fell asleep, this idyllic fantasy soon turned to fear, uncertainty, suspicion and paranoia. One moment he was taking revenge on McKay, the next he was concerned with where he might find work. He was tortured by accusations of being his brother's assassin, pronounced a "Cain" by unseen, condemning, and faceless voices. He broke out in an agony of sweat, tormented by the fact that he would be betraying Lisette's trust staying with another woman with whom he was sexually involved. Thus, he passed the night in a turbulence of mind and heart, wrestling with demons.

The next morning he went to see his mother. He walked the few blocks to the projects and shortly found himself outside her apartment door. He had not seen her or his sister since Sam's funeral. He was apprehensive before ringing the bell; their last encounter was no recommendation, but he hoped to find the pain had subsided and that the grief was somewhat in remission and that he, like the prodigal, had been forgiven.

491

His mother cracked the door, blocking his entrance and eyed him suspiciously. She looked wretched, lines of fatigue cut deep into her face, and dark circles ringed droopy, sleepless eyes. "What'a you want?" she asked wearisomely as if trying to discourage a door to door salesman.

"I thought I'd drop by to say hello," he said, awkwardly, "n let you know I'm outta the party – the Panthers, that is."

"Oh?"

"Since yesterday. Actually, I was kicked out." He colored at the admission.

"It ain't gonna bring your brother back from the grave."

"You're not gonna go on holding me responsible 'r you?"

"N who else? That girl, that really pretty girl you say Sam raped, that Raschelay? She was here, came to see me, 'n from all she say I put two 'n two together. It wasn't that hard. Ya think you so smart. Ya had the cops do it for you. Never mind how you done it, your brother's blood is on your head," she raved. "You darkened my door with the curse'a Cain. You brought death under my roof 'n had Sam killed. You brought confusion into my life, confusion like I've not known; so much so I spend sleepless nights pulling my hair in grief. Yes, you my son but, no, I don't think I want you under my roof – not anymore."

Percival looked dumbly about.

"We're not gonna ave this discussion in the hall 'r we?"

"Here or nowhere else," she responded. "It's a wicked world 'n it takes a wicked man to kill his very own brother the way you did, Percival Jones! In the south white men kill us but in the north we conspire to kill r'selves. I don't know what kind'a people we've become. You was to look out for your brother but instead you got him killed."

"You don't believe that do you?" Percival asked. "You know better than that."

"I don't know any such thing."

"You know me."

"No, I don't know you – I don't know you at all. Like I done told you, that girl, Raschelay, she was here. She told me as much. She came to tell me after Sam raped her, she'd thought her life was ruined. She weeped hysterically, wishing Sam dead, wishing she could kill him, claw him to death with her fingernails. But her mother assured her that you had promised to see to it yourself. And when Sam was killed, though no one said anything, they knew you'd done what you'd promised, that you was the avenging angel, that you had done the devil's work that day. Then, she said, when she found out she was pregnant with Sam's child –"

492

The news struck Percival like a bolt and he fell back, stunned, as if about to drop. "Pregnant? Raschelay, pregnant?"

"You didn't know did you? Well, she is," Hattie scowled, then went on with what she had to say. "She thought God had made her pregnant for praying for Sam's death, that the burden of his death was rightly on her head. But as she prayed night 'n day, she came to realize she could not have an abortion, she could not kill this child, that it was God's way of giving Sam back the life he'd lost. The life stolen from him. She could not kill Sam twice, she said. N, in any case, it's against her religion. She wanted me to know that I was going to be a grandma. That she was going to have Sam's baby, 'n she was terribly, terribly sorry that the child won't ever get to know it's father but she wants it to know it's grandma. Now, goodbye!"

"Mama, don't shut me out; don't turn me away."

Tears sprang to Hattie's eyes as she shut the door with finality. Percival shuddered at the door's abrupt closing. He stood there, empty, as the sound of the slamming door tugged at his innards, reverberated through him. He hesitated, no longer than that of a stalled heartbeat, then, in a daze stumbled down the hall to the elevator.

He had just pushed the button for the elevator and pressed his brow to the wire covered pane window when the closing of a door and footfall echoed along the corridor at his back. His name rung out, calling him to his senses. He swung round slowly as in a dream and leaned heavily against the elevator door as he observed Lois, through blurry eyes, as she approached in slippered feet, bath robe, and hair net.

She dashed into his arms and clung to him with unbearable aching, trying to absorb the burden of his suffering. "Oh Percival," she wept, "I'm sorry. I overheard the last of what mama said to you. I'm so ashamed, but she's been overwrought by the news of Raschelay's pregnancy, as well as coming to grips with the fact that Sam had really raped her. It's been too much for her to handle all at once. And so she struck out at you."

Percival raised a hand to his brow and closed his eyes. He could barely look at Lois, she so resembled their mother, Hattie. His mother who had done what McKay could not, what no one else could—she had taken the starch out of him— and he would have collapsed in a heap had the door not been at his back for support.

"Don't worry, Mama will come round in time."

He looked at her starkly. "I don't know I ave that time."

"You didn't have Sam killed did you?"

He laughed. "Yesterday, McKay, the field marshal, accused me of much the same thing, which is what he'd tacitly hinted I do in the first place. He wanted to know so badly that he asked me to subject myself to a scopolamine test, which I refused – 'n for which, among other things, I was expelled." A wisp of a smile played on his lips. "Hell, it's gotten so I'm beginning to doubt myself." He gazed off distantly, eyes tearing, "Ya know I went upstate for a couple of weeks. I visited a farm. I met a girl – Lisette. I was never more happy. We fell in love, can you imagine? It was almost religious; as religious as I've ever felt." He sighed longingly, holding Lois in his gaze. "Ever since I got back I feel my soul's been in hock 'n I got'a find a way to redeem myself, to buy myself out'a pawn. But I don't know which way to turn." He recalled with a pang, Amelia's parting words, *"Your life belongs as much to the wind as to yourself."* He felt a sudden, cold chill pass over him.

"You met a girl? Good! You're in love? Great!"

"No, Lois," he said, his mind back on track, "I didn't have Sam killed. Still there 'r things you jus' can't fight. If I'd kill'd him, perhaps – but I'm not so cold as to think I could face ma with that on my conscience. But I've been accused of it so often of late, I may as well have done it."

"No, Percival. You're my big brother. I know you better than that. Don't let them destroy you. No, not you too!" She looked at him pitifully, appealingly.

"It's not them, it's mama." He grimaced, turning to keep the disappointment out of his voice.

"Mama's inconsolable. She's to be pitied. From your father on, her life has been a sorrow with too few joys. But you, you scare her. She fears you go where black men dare not tread without suffering the gravest of consequences. She's afraid for you."

"She's got a strange way of showing it."

"Mama's not terribly sophisticated, you know that. She's toiled these many years in the homes of rich white folks by the sweat of her brow for a meager living. She relies more on instinct than reason for a guide. And so far, but for you, all the men in her life have ended up badly, destroyed by the mechanics of racism."

"It's not my intention to become one of em." He blushed, embarrassed at being caught off guard, in a weak moment. "But thanks, sis, you've saved me from despair."

"Mama will come round. Just give her time. I'll work on her."

Percival rolled his eyes, searching for words. The elevator arrived. "I got'a cut," he said, backing into the empty conveyance. "I got'a see Raschelay."

The elevator descended and rattled on its chain to the lobby. Percival was issued out of its maw out into the lobby. He struggled to contain himself. He fought back anger and an onrush of tears before hitting the street. He had been numbed, stultified, by the bitter accusations cast by his mother. He started up Jersey Street as skittishly as a one-eyed alley cat, his shame pronounced, radiating electrically from his nerve endings. He began to sweat. He felt naked, vulnerable, without any forces to cover his ass, stripped to the depths of his soul. He wondered whether word of his expulsion had hit the streets, that all might bear witness to his brute nakedness. After all, how could he expect more sympathy from the fickle mob than from his own mother? A rabble always on the prowl for wounded prey on which to glut themselves.

He arrived at Raschelay's home without incident. Her mother, Ruth Morrow, answered his knock. She gaped at him in momentary confusion, mistaking him at first for Sam.

Irritably, he asked, "Expecting someone else?"

"No, not at all," she replied clumsily. "Come in, won't you?" She escorted him to the living room. "It's just that for a moment I thought," she began to explain, looking everywhere but at him, afraid to meet his eyes, to know the sin of their complicity. It was well they not speak. It may have suited her purposes far better had he been a ghost. A ghost could only accuse so loudly, not being flesh and blood. "I'll fetch Raschelay for you," she said, and hastened out the room.

A moment later Raschelay entered the living room, and though her pregnancy was not yet noticeably advanced, she wore a loose-fitting summer smock. Outside of appearing a little nervous she looked—but for an expression of timidity and lack of customary panache – like her usual self. "It's good to see you," she said. Her chestnut eyes were skeptical and less confident than usual. "I'm glad you're here. I owe you much. I understand you were away." She took his hand, led him to the couch and had him sit by her.

"Can I get you something?" she asked.

"Nothing, no."

"Are you sure?"

"Yes, quite."

"Some tea, maybe?" she asked, looking at him for what seemed like an intolerably long time.

"I'm good," he assured her.

"Well of course," she said, dropping her eyes and placing her hands in her lap.

Her two younger sisters burst in upon them, one behind the other, to see who was there.

"You remember Percival, don't you? He's my friend," Raschelay said, warmly.

"Uh-hu," the girls acknowledged, shyly.

495

"Say hello, then run off and play, ok? We need to talk, Percival and I."

"Hi Percival," the girls chirruped in unison.

"Hello," said Percival in response.

"Now go play," Raschelay said to her sisters.

"What should we play?" the girls asked.

"Why not play pickup sticks?" Raschelay suggested.

"That sounds fun," sang the girls, bouncing joyously off down the hall to their room.

"You first," said Raschelay.

"No, you," Percival insisted.

"I was only going to ask how you were."

"That's not so easy a question to answer."

"Yes. Some days I'm better than others. I don't know if you know I'm pregnant. I'm going to have your brother's child. Sam's child. I'll be a mother soon," she blurted, crying. "I want to do the right thing, but I'm scared."

"Yes, I know. My mother told me."

"I'm scared, Percival. I'm really scared. Whenever in the past I'd thought of having a child it was with romantic eyes. I thought my child's father would be my husband, the man of my dreams, the man I love. Not that of a. a predator. a. a rapist!" She cradled herself with her arms, trembling like a cowed dog. "The day I spoke to your mother, I wasn't faring so well. I may have said things that were better left unsaid."

Percival gestured helplessly, as if to say "alas."

"Was she disagreeable to you?'

"Brutal would be putting it mildly."

"I'm sorry. I've been losing my head a lot lately." She collapsed against him, her eyes swimming in tears. He embraced her with sympathy, stroking her back, trying to ease her pain, her grief no less than his own.

"It's not your fault. Have you spoken to Tzi?"

"I don't want to talk about him. I can't face him. I've got too much else on my mind," she said, pushing away from him. "I'm seeing an analyst and she assures me it's probably too early and understandable that I'd be apprehensive. I don't quite know how it'll work itself out. I've got so much else to think about. To do. I've got to finish school somehow. I've got to consider the well-being of my unborn child and see to my own mental stability too."

"Of course. You're right."

She touched him lightly on the arm and smiled sorrowfully.

He covered her hand with his own.

"I was desperate. I wanted to throw myself into the river, wash myself clean, drown my sins. I couldn't imagine what it was I'd done to make Sam want to hurt me, you know? My analyst keeps telling me it wasn't my fault. She says I shouldn't blame myself, that I wasn't deserving of it. She says I'm distraught over it because of how helpless it left me feeling, for the loss of control over my person. All I know is that it was this pregnancy which finally lifted me out of myself. If I couldn't live for myself then I'd live for my unborn child. Sam stole something from me that the bringing of this child into the world must restore – it must!"

"Or else?"

"I don't know." She raked her fingers through the tight, springy curls of her hair. "I need to recover a sense of myself, I know that."

"Do you want this baby?"

"More than I wanted Sam dead."

"N if he were alive?"

"He's not, and besides, it's against all I believe."

"How old 'r you?"

"I'll be sixteen when the baby comes."

Percival grimaced. "My heart goes out to you."

"You're a good man, Percival Jones," she said, a smile breaking through her sobs.

"If only."

"You're the best man I know, white or black."

"I've been kicked outa the party," he said, as if to contradict her.

"Oh?"

"Yesterday, I think it was. I've lost all track of time."

"I'm sorry to hear that. It doesn't bode well for the party. Certainly not our branch."

"I'm sorry to say."

"Though it doesn't come as a surprise."

"No, I can't say it does."

"You tried."

"I've something else I need to clear up."

"That is?"

"Well, while I did ave Sam set up, like you think, it wasn't to be killed, but apprehended with a stockpile of stolen military weapons. He would ave received a sentence similar to that of aggravated rape, if convicted. I know what I told your mother, but I couldn't see it through though it worked its way contrary to my arrangements."

"It's not that I'm not glad you didn't have Sam set up to be killed, I am, but how does that pardon me for wanting him dead? I did, you know? I wanted him punished. I'm not proud of myself for saying it but, oh, if it were only

497

possible, I would have killed him myself." The fingers of her hands curled into talons. "With all my heart I wanted him dead!" Conflicted, she hid her face behind her hands in shame.

"I'd be surprised if you'd not."

She parted her hands from her face and looked at him as if all the crying were out of her. "Before you go, I want to ask a favor of you."

"Anything," he promised, without hesitation.

She paused, drawing her breath. "I want you to be my baby's godfather."

Percival's heart bounded in his chest, and he spluttered, "G-godfather? Who me?"

"Yes, you."

"B-but why? W-why me, of all people? I've a son of my own I've not been able to see let alone care for," he said with an ironic, coarse grin on his handsome mouth. "So why pick me to be the child's godfather?"

"Because you're it's uncle, and because we both owe this baby something. This could be a way to repay him. Besides, you've always kept faith with me. I could always rely on you. You stood behind our branch of the party like a rock. We all took heart from your leadership. I also know about your son, Malek. Lily mentioned him to me and from all she said, it's his misfortune his mother won't allow you visitation rights. I for one, want you in my child's life, be it a boy or a girl."

"Can I think on it?"

"You've already promised."

A brief pause followed.

"Yes I have," he said, pressing the fingers thoughtfully to his brow, and rising. "I should be honored. If one can say that under the circumstance."

She rose with him from the couch and saw him to the door. She embraced him with a kiss on the cheek before he departed. "You're the first man I've kissed since, you know, my incident." She blushed. "I want you in my life. I want you in my child's life. We're family now."

"Inarguably," he agreed, then descended the stairs.

***

Percival had packed the sum of his earthly belongings into two suitcases, but fearing that he had forgotten something he held back and took mental inventory: He had said his "goodbyes" to all the branch members, with the exception of Skeeter who had not been seen since Scratch's arrival, though most did so charily. They were afraid of being tarred with similar a brush and so distanced themselves from him. Only Nora, Leroy, and Silva, unafraid of contamination, remained with him. This was a dark hour of hell on which heaven turned its eyes. Along with everything else, to be falsely accused and condemned without a trial was, for him, a slip into the abyss of a more personal kind – a hell out of which he was unable to climb.

While Nora, Silva, and Leroy sat around talking, Percival took a second look about the house but could find no trace of his ever having been there. It was haunting it was so ghostly: He felt as if someone had died, and he was of a mind to leave flowers. Percival was ready to go when the phone rang, jarring everyone. Percival answered it. A voice on the far end said, "I hear you're out, that's the best I can wish for you – now try to stay alive." As the line went dead, Percival recognized the voice as having been that of Special Agent, Bianco.

"I'm out," he overheard Nora declare as he cradled the phone. "I think I'm jus' gonna drop out'a sight like Skeeter. I was only staying round for Percival to get back anyway 'n now he's out I'm out with him. When Scratch gets back from whatever errand McKay's got him running, I'll ave been in the wind."

Silva gazed at her noncommittally, sucking in his under lip.

"It ain't right! It jus' ain't right," repeated Leroy, intermittently, with a bleak expression on his raw, boyish face.

"You ever meet Scratch?" Silva looked at Percival with a long, slow look.

"If it's who I'm thinking of, yeah, briefly. I'd met him at one or two meeting's in the past."

"A heartwarming sort'a fella," said Nora, with a touch of mockery.

"If you're ready," Percival started to say when the front door flew open and Skeeter burst in on unsteady legs. Everything else came to a standstill. "It's true, after all," he slurred. "Ya out, blowing town, hatting up, getting in the wind." He sniggered, derisively, waving a copy of The Tribune. "Bet you ain't seen this." He thrust the copy at Percival. "It says you been expelled, fucking kicked outta the party for being a God damn informant. Well, maybe not in those words," his voice trailed off. His eyes were bleary and a foul smell of decay was on his alcohol breath. He plucked a cigarette from his lips, blowing smoke.

Percival looked at him, annoyed, then gazed at the article with intensity, particularly the paragraph in which he was mentioned. His nostrils flared angrily as he read. It began, "Former Olympic hopeful, Percival Jones, who has not been seen in the ring since the '68 trials, has resurfaced in the ranks of the Black Panther Party as a defense captain caught up in its fractious politics." The article went on to say that he had been expelled by the West Coast leadership for suspicion of having been an FBI informant.

"You believe this crap?" he asked, dashing the paper aside in a burst of rage. Silva retrieved it. "Well, do you?"

"I never said I believed anything!"

"What's it say?" Nora asked.

Silva passed her the paper. "They're out to crucify you," she exclaimed after a moments scrutiny, doubt in her voice.

"I know you didn't sell us out. Like I knew what was up when McKay's man, Scratch, the grand inquisitor, show'd up at 'r door in your absence,' n so I cut out. I knew he was up to no good. But what I want'a know, want you to tell me is, did we do any good?" Skeeter had a sly, street smart, underworld look about him. "I mean, man, we lost people, good people, people believed in you – in us. We put 'r lives on the line cause'a you." Skeeter averted his face, his eyes fixed on infinity. "N this God damn community's still the same ole shit hole in which I was born 'n looks like the one in which I'm'a die, sooner than later most likely. What I want'a know from you is, did we do any good? Cause if you say so I'll believe you since I can't see it for myself. Tell me, did we?",

They all waited on Percival's reply.

"We did what we could," said Percival, his heart strained with anxiety.

"To what end? Does that answer satisfy you? No, man, it wasn't enough. Not for what we gave. People ave been damaged. You yourself give it your all 'n look at you. This is the thanks you get you've been tainted.

"You stoned, man."

What of it?"

"Jus' curious."

"Goodbye."

"Stay, join us, let's rap awhile."

"What for, man? I ain't much into funerals, 'n it looks like y'll holding a wake," Skeeter looked about searchingly. "Naw, I'd rather remember us as we was. I ain't gonna mourn what we've become. No way. See you. No, I guess I won't be seeing you." He turned and stumbled out the door.

Silva stood up and began to pace.

There grew a pause, while each considered their separate fate. Recognizing the mood swing, Percival hoisted his bags and said, "If you're ready to roll, I'm set to go."

They all stepped outside without further delay into the late, brassy morning light. The sun, hemmed in by clouds, splashed a little light on the sidewalk. Percival threw his luggage in the car trunk and climbed into the front passenger seat beside Silva. Nora perched an elbow against the open window and peered in.

"You got my number," she said, sighing sadly. "Don't go being no stranger." Stepping back she laced an arm about Leroy. "Don't worry 'bout the scamp, I'll keep tight rein on him for you."

"I owe you," said Percival, the words sticking in his throat. "I'll not forget you, either of you."

"Goodbye," said Leroy, teary eyed.

Percival waved and Silva drove off. They reached the ferry terminal in a matter of minutes. Silva let Percival out, parked the car, then joined him in the terminal snack bar. Over a cup of coffee they waited for the next boat out. They addressed each other, as would comrades, knowing full well that their paths were diverging and that, in all probability they would not meet again. They spoke to the point.

"It was good knowing you, man," said Silva, restrainedly. "Working with you was worth the cost. I want you to know."

"Thanks for saying so."

"You know the thing I'm most grateful for?"

"What's that?"

"That we didn't off those two cops when it would have been so easy to do. That is what gives me the most satisfaction. You preserved our integrity, man. I'll always be beholding to you for not having to bear that burden."

"Thank Lily, she's the one who gave me to see right. 'Taking a life is stealing something you can't rightly use' she'd said. It made me pause. But Sam is another story. I tried. God knows I tried. At least I hope he knows. The thing I find most disheartening about Sam's death, for me anyway, is that he was a blank slate. He'd yet to find his footing. "

"I agree, his life was short changed and, as you say Lily said, 'a theft.''

"In the final analysis I think Sam took on those cops out'a blind attempt at Self redemption. Still I can't shake my share of blame."

"Don't take that bit of nonsense into your head, it was Sam's fault entirely."

"Some people won't agree with you on that."

"Since when did you start to care about what others may think?"

"I never thought the price of doing the right thing would prove so costly."

"It's a wicked world."

"Thanks for the vote of confidence," said Percival. "But I'll harbor doubts the rest of my life, if only because subconsciously, I may have desired it."

"You got a raw deal, man."

"I suppose the Panther's 'r as much entitled to their mistakes as anyone," Percival said to Silva's surprise.

"That's generous."

"If Sam could only say as much for me," he muttered. "Tell me. You gonna stick?"

"I think I'm out. In fact, I know it. There's nothing left in it to hold me anymore. It's all too problematic. Scratch has it in for me. No, I dare not stick around. Besides, as Skeeter said, 'a lot of people have been damaged' and, frankly, I don't care to add my name to that list. Big/black's in jail for God knows, the rest of his life; Raschelay's incapacitated, Nora's out, looks like Skeeter's back to using, Sam's dead, as is little Ricky Bolden. Rufus has checked out, something vitals gone out Priestus. And without you it's a crap shoot. I guess, like you say, 'the army's a boy's last hurrah.' And since I didn't go into the military I suppose that this was my 'last hurrah.' It's now time I put away childish things. I must say, Skeeter's asking 'did we do any good,' caught me cold. It was the question I dared not ask myself. I was all too afraid of the answer. I still am. All too often I feared that we were doing nothing more than spinning our wheels. I think I'll accept my parents offer and enroll in grad school. I mean, I may as well, right?" Silva said, unconvinced. "This was so much breaking free from the bonds of my parents, now I have nowhere else to turn."

"If only I had as much."

"And you, Percival, what about you?'

"Me? For now I'm gonna worry 'bout a lot less folks wanting to see me dead."

The bell for the next boat sounded.

"You're one of the few real revolutionaries I know. I mean, that is, not wanting to do it you did it for the right reason."

"I wish to God that were of some small comfort."

"Goodbye," said Silva, misty eyed, incapable of masking his sorrow.

Percival smiled wryly, his eyes glazed, and as the final bell rang, he raised a clenched fist and said, "Power!" then turned and raced for the departing boat.

"Look for me in the Whirlwind," Silva called after him, the doors rolling to a close, speeding them off in different directions.

Percival stood outside on the ferry's upper deck and cast his eyes over the depthless expanse of the rolling river, toward the Verazanno bridge and horizon beyond. The water's turgid dark face reflected his mood, no less than it did the overcast sky.

And for a moment, fighting tears, his thoughts ventured back over the years of active participation in the movement. Then, sick at heart, he gazed with longing into the fathomless reaches of the black foam topped waves, trying to conjure up Lisette's face. He could have sworn that had he the fortune to have encountered her there, that he would have been no less at a loss. As deeply in love as he was, he felt more alone than an abandoned child. Only two days before his heart was rhapsodic, complete, and he was one with himself and all of life, now it had all come undone and once more his spirit was plunged in utter darkness. Overcome with unbearable sadness, he reached for his gun, his .45. He gazed at it reflectively, felt it's heft in his sweaty palm, fondled it's trigger, then seized it by the barrel and with a mighty toss, flung it aft. It struck the water in a plash and was quickly swallowed up by the rolling river.

*****

Percival spent the first week at Gwen's physically and emotionally drained. Barely rising before noon he'd sit up in bed like a frightened child wakened from a bad dream, cowed by his mother's saddling him with the curse of Cain and the ever-present specter of Sam. He wondered how it had come to this, how it had all gone so wrong so fast as if he had been inattentive. He would wonder about Rufus locked away in an asylum, staring off in a catatonic void, lost to himself and a world that could no longer threaten him. A world contrived in the image and likeness of the white man from which escape, by any means – including insanity – was justifiable. The quote, *"I saw the best minds of my generation destroyed by madness,"* flitted across his mind. He could see Rufus now, smiling secretly, like Mona Lisa. He had made it, flown the coop, *Free at last.*

He would then turn his speculations in on himself and wonder about his own prospects which, in his limited view, were scant. He was battle weary, heartsick, and tempted to cry for no reason. Then he thought about Lisette, despite the fact that this love, as he had known, as had Julius known, was ill-fated. However, it was the only possibility to which he held fast. Lisette was the only ray of hope in an otherwise bleak landscape. He would sit in bed and brood and mull things over in the darkened room until it began to grow in him like something unnatural, a malignant force. He would shake his sloth, climb from bed on shaky legs, dress and stagger outdoors and wander the streets like a man recovering from a grave illness. Ever on the alert, he saw the city through furtive eyes, the accused eyes of the damned.

Washington Square Park, across from NYU, became his favorite haunt during that period, as was it for so many others. The sweet, cloying aroma of marijuana wafted on the air, clung to the leaves of trees, and hung over the park in a haze as everyone lit up. It was the final days of summer and the hippies reveling in the park were out in force, holding an ongoing love in, singing bawdy rock songs and frolicking, semi-nude, in the vast fountain. The Flower Children had disappeared as if their season had passed, and hippies were sprouting up everywhere, in their place like weeds. Their antics put him in mind of the comments made by southern whites about their darkies, as they used to think of blacks. "Wish I could be like em. Nothing bothering 'em. Living for t'day."

But Percival was aware of the pent up, underlying fury of these desperate off-springs of the American dream, these lost children of Hamlin seeking an escape, seeking a Pied Piper to whisk them away. They were not, as the media often portrayed and despite doing their own thing, grandly happy, but, moreover, they were no less miserably disillusioned than were blacks, but for different reasons.

Percival spared them his sympathy because, despite knowing what they knew, they had chosen to take their guru, Tim Leary, to heart and *"Turn on, tune in and drop out."* Narcissistic, self-absorbed, they had chosen to close ranks in a conspiracy of silence, to stop their ears from hearing and shut their eyes against the suffering around them. They escaped into a hallucinogenic fog which, given the temper of the times, was almost pardonable. Their motto, which launched the now legendary Woodstock music festival, was *"Sex, drugs 'n rock 'n roll.* "They were, as the Panthers' had put it, *"part of the problem."*

Despite his grievances against them, he would grant them alms when asked, as often he was, *"Say man can you spare some coins?"*

Fully aware of what his argument with his countrymen was, he could not fathom what the disagreement of these young white hippies was were with their parents that they would prefer to remain on the streets begging for shelter and food, rather than return to the sanctuary of their suburban homes? It was for a similar a reason, he assumed, that Racine could not return to the bosom of her family.

Percival had no particular desire to return to Gwen's apartment either. He was uncomfortable there, with the hypocrisy of his role. He had not yet told her about Lisette, which he knew would not go over well. He was going through a difficult patch and wished to be alone. He was simply there because he required shelter, a place to crash, to rest his weary head, sort out his troubles – no more; for he had received a shattering blow to the ego, his self-esteem, and was, as a result, left floundering in the dark with only instincts to rely on. His sexual fantasy of carrying on an affair with an older, more experienced woman had long since run its course. Gwen was womanly, voluptuous, and sexually alluring. She exuded sex. It enveloped her like the scent of a heady perfume. But he was in love and fully aware that to have sex with anyone other than the object of that desire could prove disastrous in more ways than one. Nevertheless, since they were sharing the same bed it was becoming unavoidable. As unavoidable as not having a friendly drink with her before dinner when, night after night, she would arrive home from work and head for the liquor cabinet pouring herself a tumbler or two of vodka martinis, sure to ask if he wouldn't care for one. But he was despondent enough without it and thought it best he not indulge and refused her.

He knew that she liked her drink, but she carried it off with such aplomb that he had little suspected her of being a lush until one evening at the turn of the second week, having evaded her sexual overtures by one ruse and another, she again tried coaxing him into joining her in a customary evening drink.

"Sure you won't have one?" she asked. "I don't mind drinking alone, but two's a party."

"I'll ave a beer if you got one," he relented.

"Come on, join a gal in a real drink," she pressed. "Don't be such a spoilsport."

He gave her a lingering glance. "I'd prefer a beer if you don't mind."

"I'd not realized you had such a proletariat streak. I thought you had more style than the circle of people in which you moved," she scoffed and, holding an empty martini glass aloft, flounced over to the liquor cabinet with the disdain of a sophisticate, throwing her hips suggestively. "Don't get me wrong, I have nothing against the Panthers, obviously, I just never thought that they were you."

"I don't wanta hear it," he said, icily, casting a gaze over the room's decor. "I'm out of it."

The alto saxophone of Charlie Parker playing "Old Folks," issued from the stereo. A graduate of Tampa U, she had all the sensibilities of a cultivated southern belle. Consequentially, it surprised him how little an accent she'd retained for coming from the deep south.

"But you're not out of it."

"Says who?"

Her face took on a look of melting sympathy as she slowly turned and faced him.

"I'm sorry for what's become of, well, your world, if it's any consolation."

"But it's not. It comes too late. Let's jus' drop it, ok?"

She pouted. "You can at least be pleasant."

"Don't," he added.

She stood before a print of Picasso's, Three Musicians. "It seems I'm fresh out of beer, so if it's all the same with you,"—she said, pouring the contents for martinis in a jigger.

He felt put out, annoyed at her insistence. "You drink too much," he accused. He thought about adding, "I never knew you drank till I saw you sober," but thought better of it and changed his mind.

She looked at him sunk in a lounge chair with incredulity. "How dare you! Just where do you get off telling me how much I can or can't drink?" Her voice cracked like a whip, her eyes were hard as flint. Though they made love that night, or an approximation thereof, that exchange was the start of hostilities between them.

He had no wish to join the hippies on the street, although Abby Hoffman had declared, "The streets belong to the people." He had no wish to join Abby Hoffman there either.

"Alright! Alright!" he threw up his hands and gave in and after a few drinks, as his body conspired against him, he found he was unable to resist. He caved into her munificence. Even better than he had remembered, she was consummate, fearless, an uninhibited lover. When she was through seducing him, playing him like a lute, he was hers for the picking. The world outside the cradle of her beach white thighs ceased to exist. Everything else was nestled between the columnar dunes leading to the smoldering tropics of her cunt, which she lavished on him until he wailed, "baby, baby, Oh, sweet baby," as if singing a lullaby.

Afterwards, he lay in the dark beside her like a limp sot, half asleep, never more ashamed of himself. He knew that he was losing his grip and had to do something. His dignity had slipped by degrees, and he could have killed her for it; killed the white temptress where she so peacefully slept beside him. Without clear grasp of his predicament he was despondent and a solitary tear slid from his eye for the loss he felt, the loss of Lisette, for his betraying her. He was disconcerted, this should not have been. All that he had previously found alluring in Gwen had turned into a corpulent, flaccid and aging white woman who sickened him, turned his stomach with her lechery and lust. But if this were she then who was he? He dare not consider it too closely. He was now more determined than ever to get on track, get a job and get out before he did something rash.

The next day as Gwen rose to the alarm with what he was beginning to recognize as a ritualistic hangover, she grunted and groaned, uncertain of her whereabouts slowly regaining consciousness. She reached over searchingly and turned off the alarm with a clumsy stroke of the hand. She rolled to the edge of the bed, clasping her head in her hands and flung her feet over the side to the floor, moaning. She sat there momentarily, scarcely breathing, ossified, stricken by the blind panic she felt on awakening. She reached for the bottle of vodka tucked away in a bureau draw. She took a good, long swig, screwed her face miserably, and waited for the burning to subside and the alcohol to take effect. She shuddered, returned the bottle to the draw, then roamed the lightless room in a daze, collecting her discarded clothes and taking them into the bathroom. He listened to the running water. She visited the room a few more times, completed her toilet in phases, donned dark glasses to mask her red-laced eyes and said sotto voce, "I'm off, my sweet, don't expect me after work. I've a mayor's conference to attend this evening, so make do without me."

"Don't worry 'bout me," he stifled a yawn, anxious for her to go. He wanted to confide in her as little as possible. When she left, his skin crawled. She'd called him "my sweet," then it wasn't a wet dream. They'd made love. The memory of it flooded his consciousness and caused the sap to rise in his loins. What the devil was he thinking? He threw back the bed sheets and stood up, his head throbbing with regret. Filled with self-loathing he went about his morning, disgusted that he had allowed himself to become dependent on Gwen's hospitality, and sickened that he had to pay for the dubious privilege with his flesh. He was determined to find work, to get out from under. His reflection, in the mirror, stared back at him with glazed, stunned eyes as he shaved. After he had finished up in the bathroom and was on his way out he took a second look at himself in the hall closet's full-length mirror. He made the obvious concessions to custom by wearing a white shirt with button-down collar, sport jacket and slacks. Having no wish to hang himself from the tree of cultural acquiescence, he refused to wear a tie. It was galling enough, to say the least, for, as Che had said, "a revolutionary wins or dies!" And he could not say that he had won. In fact, he had been compromised. Whereas Sam, foolhardy Sam, no matter his offense, had redeemed himself and had died an unsung revolutionary. While here he was, insofar as McKay was concerned, "a reactionary," on his way to finding work. Moreover, he had been expelled, driven from the folds of the vanguard party into the ranks of the struggling unemployed. He had gone from being a desperado, a revolutionary, from creating social upheaval, to a cog, a non-player, in a society from which he was utterly estranged.

He had never taken such a dark, self-accusatory look at himself before. He was irked, chagrined, out of sorts with himself and dissatisfied with his looks. His Afro was too wild, too intimidating. He hadn't had a hair cut in weeks. He couldn't see himself under it. It was like a helmet. It may have worked in his revolutionary guise, but it was out of sync in his present attire. He didn't know himself. Maybe it was just as well if nobody else recognized him either. That, at any rate, left him hopeful. He smiled slyly, turned from the mirror and walked out, tripping light footed down the stairs.

He walked along Christopher Street to a local coffee shop. The side booths were occupied so he took the first available counter stool. It was a tight squeeze and, smiling benignly at the people flanking him, he tucked his elbows in like clipped wings, constraining them as much as possible. The counterman took

507

his order and shouted it out to the short order cook, sweating over a hot grill in the back. He wolfed down his breakfast without tasting it and called for another cup of coffee. He paid the tab and left.

He paused outside the coffee shop and glanced at the overhead slice of sky. Tenants trickled out of the nearby buildings to join the ceaseless flow of villagers on the way to bus stops, subways and work or school. He took a deep breath, threw back his shoulders, and joined the parade. He caught the 7th. Ave. Subway downtown and emerged on Fulton and Broadway, immediately swallowed up in a forest of people, coming and going. The office buildings which lined the streets allowed for very little passage of daylight, thus everything took on a gloomy aspect. The streets were snarled with vehicular traffic, and passage by foot was no less difficult. It was necessary to keep up or risk being trampled.

This was, by no means, an area for sightseers, but neither could it be struck from the tour bus route, to wade through this sea of humanity in a double-decker tour bus was as breathtaking as a view of Niagara Falls—more so, it was the financial investment capital of the world.

It was impossible to navigate through the pedestrian traffic with facility. He was jostled, pushed and prodded along at a snail's pace. He reached John Street, in short order, where office windows carried signs, five-foot-high, which shouted, "Jobs! Jobs! Jobs!" The block was ablaze with such signs, and the street cluttered with such agencies. He had no doubt that one of those jobs, despite his limited qualifications, was his.

He entered the first office he came upon. The agency was located on the congested second floor and an excess of applicants spilt down the stairway. The noise of the office, no less than that of the street, was near deafening. The agency's staff manned phones and conducted business over the general noise level.

After a considerable wait Percival finally made it upstairs and was summoned by a personnel official, with a telephone between his ear and shoulder, to whom he presented his application. The official gestured for him to sit, while he simultaneously went over the forms and conducted a conversation on the phone.

"Well, Mr. Jones, is it?" said the official, on hanging up, and extending a hand.

"Yes," said Percival, accepting the proffered hand out of courtesy.

"I see here you've been in the military, have over two years college, and worked at the Museum of Modern Art. Good, all good. But I notice you've nothing down for the past year. Would you care to tell me about that?"

"It's nothing much to tell," said Percival evasively. "I've been traveling."

508

"You've worked as a guard at the Museum. Outside that you have no other work experience."

"I guess not."

"Are you looking for work specifically in the area of security?"

"Not necessarily."

"I'm reasonably sure we can find something for you, Mr. Jones. You're the type of person our office likes to get jobs for. You're well-spoken and present yourself favorably. So, if your references check out, and I don't see why they shouldn't, then I'll be in touch with you. This is your telephone number, right?"

"It is for now, yes."

"You left the Museum to travel, is that it?" asked the official, making notations.

"Yes, as a matter of furthering my education."

"Very good. Let me run down these references, and I'll be in touch. If you'll accept a small piece of advice," said the official directly, "you might want to consider wearing a tie at these interviews and cutting your hair. It gives a more favorable impression."

Percival smiled though put off at the suggestion, and bade the official "good day," then went on to the other agencies and filled out similar job applications for the remainder of the morning and a good portion of the afternoon. Much like the first agency, they all said the same thing, "if your references check out.," and having no cause to doubt they would not, he concluded that he would be employed in a relatively short period of time. Chancing nothing, he spent the following days, which melted into weeks, beating the pavement in search of work. None of the employment agencies to which he'd placed applications had called him back. When he had contacted them they were evasive. He was perplexed, they had initially been so encouraging, and now they were anything but reassuring. He continued to tramp the streets. He was determined to find a job. At a low point, verging on despair, he once more made the observation, "The only thing to grow on concrete is crime." His spirits in decline, he longed for the tranquility of the country, for Lisette, Amelia, and company of Caribbean farm hands; he longed for something other, as when he had joined SNCC, the peace movement, and the Black Panther Party. He longed to fly away, embrace the sun, and to be "excused", along with Jimi Hendrix, "while they kissed the sky." He longed for something else despite being earthbound and fettered. He longed to contact Lisette, to tell her everything, explain himself. And though she, along with Sam, was always uppermost in his thoughts he dare not. Besides, he couldn't explain himself, his circumstance, and not simply out of obstinacy for, at bottom, it would only amount to a pack of lies. Not that he was averse to lying, but not on this score, and certainly not to Lisette. Moreover, he was bewildered and had been experiencing, much of late, the blind panic of being trapped in a world he little understood. He was also exhausted and had been or so it felt, for a long time.

Neither were things going well with Gwen. Things were in stasis. Moreover he didn't know what was going on. With her busy work schedule and his comings and goings, they were constantly missing one another in passing. Early one morning she had reached across the cold divide of their bed, searching for a warm body to cling to, to help dispel her fears, but aside from the empty space he was not there or anywhere to be found in the apartment.

That night she faultingly asked, "Where were you last night?"

"I'd been looking for work on the docks. That failing, I found myself wandering the streets of the waterfront contemplating my situation," he said gloomily.

"Rather than come home?"

"I needed the air. 'N anyway, since when 'r you my keeper?" he said abrasively, cutting her short. Once burnt she would not inquire into his affairs uninvited again. The tension between them, though minimal, was palpable. She ceased to believe that he was not deliberately trying to avoid her, though that was not the impression he had wanted to impart. It galled her, casting her sexual prowess in doubt and bringing her female wiles into question. He was easily ten years her junior, and the thought was unsettling enough without thinking he was trying to avoid her. But in all fairness, she had to admit that he was not himself; had not been himself since his brother's death. The trip upstate had only made things worse as far as she could tell. In any event, he refused to discuss it. Added to that, his expulsion from the Black Panther Party had made him morose, ill-tempered and withdrawn. She could therefore afford to be charitable, under the circumstance.

While it was true that he had indeed been avoiding her, he had not wanted their relationship to deteriorate into incivility. Hence, one evening after she had poured herself a cocktail, he asked to speak with her.

She was amenable and turned towards him. She was dressed impeccably, as usual. Divested of her blazer, she wore a silk pink blouse opened at her ivory throat, tails tucked in at the waist into crisply creased slacks, which favorably accentuated her voluptuous form. She stepped out of her shoes and crossed the carpeted floor in her stocking feet. She took a seat on the sofa under a reading lamp which gave off a soft light. She flicked her auburn hair from her face with a languid toss of the hand, took a sip of her drink and leaned back. She crossed her legs and gazed at him with hazel colored eyes, as if to say "Do tell."

The strains of Beethoven's fourth piano concerto served as background music. She was eclectic in her taste.

Percival gazed at the curled fingers of his upturned hands at rest in his lap, searching his empty palms as would a down 'n out Gypsy fortune teller. "I feel empty," he said, shifting his eyes from his hands and the potential for evil he saw there, balling into fist. "I shouldn't ave come here. God knows I'd been ready for death or prison, but not much else. I shouldn't of involved you. It's unfair. Hell, it's not fair to anyone. I shouldn't be anywhere other than by myself right now. I ask'd could I stay cause I had nowhere else to turn. I still don't. It's not that I'd wanted to intrude on your life this way," he said sadly. "I jus' needed to catch my breath. If I'd gone on the streets, I'd surely ave gone to jail, but I don't wantta be locked up for craziness, stick ups 'n that jive ass sort'a crap. I'm no G'd damn hoodlum, but they're driving me to the brink." He stopped short and the sudden silence rend the air like a shot.

"My dear man," said Gwen graciously, starting forwards. "It's not you, your style –"

"Please!" he implored, shrinking back. "I don't know what my style is anymore. I don't even know who I am. I've so much stuff to work through, get outa my system, 'n I shouldn't be exorcising my demons in public. I feel like I'm about to come apart." He was, in fact, succumbing to depression.

"Would you care to talk to my analyst?"

He looked at her crossly as if to say, "for all the good it's done you."

"This is no time for you to be alone," she argued. "I'm glad to be able to do the little I can. Don't worry about it, you'll soon be back on your feet. Right now you're going through a difficult, but transitional phase."

"Amen to that," he said, tonelessly. "I'm bound in a knot, waiting for the ax to fall."

"I'm sure it's hard for you right now. Your background is questionable, to say the least," she said, arching her brows. "You're pretty much a misfit."

"A misfit?"

"A rebel then."

"It doesn't seem to bother you."

"Me? I'm pretty much one myself. That makes us kindred spirits. Besides, I've always preferred to walk on the wild side. I like my men with stamina, with blood in their veins, not afraid to run risks. And if they have a little larceny in their hearts, all the better." She smiled mischievously, moistening her lips with the tip of her tongue.

"You're clearly very much a woman 'n I'm a man sleeping in your bed under false pretenses, with unresolved issues on my plate – N I jus' can't cut it," he said, with dismay, pulse racing. "I'm jus' not up to it, any of it."

She laughed, lightheartedly, relieved, as if a burden had been lifted from her. "Is that what's bothering you? My dear man, it's only tension, anxiety, post-traumatic stress. Let me and I'll have you cured in no time," she offered, leaning far enough in his direction for him to see down her blouse, her bra, to the swell of her plump bosom.

He blushed, riding wave on wave of guilt, and then broke out with a cry from the very depths of his soul, "That's jus' it, I don't want'a be bothered!" He covered his eyes with his hands as if to blot out the image of an undesired scene, or to conceal the grief etched in his face. "I jus' want'a be left alone."

"If that's what you want," she said tartly. Feeling rebuffed, an arctic chill wreathed her heart. She swallowed the last of her martini in a gulp along with her pride, then lowered the empty glass abruptly to the coffee table between them.

"If only what I want had something to do with it," he said. She didn't understand. She didn't want to understand. It wasn't in her interest to understand any more than it was in his to be forthright.

"I care for you – I do, but you're not making this easy. You used to excite me, arouse me; be happy to be around me. Make me feel vital. Alive. You're closing me out. I want to stand by you, but you keep pushing me away. I think I understand some of your heartache, what you're going through. I know it can't be easy to have been expelled from the Panthers after all you've sacrificed. But the fact that you're alive should give you something to celebrate, not mourn. I don't understand. Is there something you're not telling me? Cause it sure feels that way." He shrugged indifferently, shifting uneasily in his chair. "Ok, if that's the way you want it, you can sleep on the couch again tonight. You know how it's done. You've chosen to do it enough on your own these past days, coming in late. I need to turn this over in my head." She got to her feet and said stiffly, "There's nothing in this for me. I don't know I can deal with you under these conditions."

He slept restively on the sofa again that night, awakening earlier than usual determined that if he was going to tramp the streets that he was going to get paid for it, therefore deciding to seek day work. He had discovered that finding employment would not be easy for, despite the many job leads he'd followed up on, all eventually led down a blind alley. Meanwhile, he was out on a ledge, and his prospects for finding gainful employment were growing slim. "Your life belongs as much to the wind as to yourself," he could hear Amelia say. If he hadn't known it then he knew it now, he had nothing to offer Lisette. She would say, had indeed said, "I didn't ask you for anything." No, it wasn't her so much as it was him. He had required it of himself. Insisted upon it, in fact. He had noticed an agency, ManPower, providing manual day labor, crosstown on the Lower East Side. Their motto, "A day's pay for a day's work." At that point. he was ready for most anything, including robbery. He was out the door before Gwen had awakened and they had had the chance to pick up the thread of the previous night's quarrel which, he had assumed, could only grow ugly.

The gloom of night which had arrested the city, had since passed like a ghost ship in the mist before the rising sun. Streetlights had gone out all over town and, shaking off the lethargy of sleep, people had begun to emerge, slowly at first and then with increasing regularity, from out the shelter of their homes. The city's conduits—thoroughfares, highways, streets, bridges, all its trade routes, the arteries of commerce and industry – the city's life's blood were once again alive with the rumble of early morning traffic. Like a genie let loose from its bottle, the city that "never sleeps'" shook off its sloth, yawned and stretched itself, reaching to the sky, awakening on a new day.

However, it wasn't such a new day for Percival, plagued as he was by conflict and circumstance. Nor was it particularly new for the men queuing round the block in front of the ManPower office longing for its doors to open. Many had arrived before the streetlights were out, in hopes of obtaining the first available jobs. Percival was late by comparison, arriving at seven-thirty. It was a long line of men, borderline cases, men in need, hard pressed, down on their luck, out on the streets, cut off from the world, livelihood and family. They were bedraggled, cast out specimens of humanity seeking a day's pay. Some were alcoholics craving the price of a drink, some were gamblers in need of front money for a high stakes game of chance. All had their story. There were some strong, healthy men struck down by ill luck, trying to assess their misfortune, perusing their horoscope in the daily papers, trying to figure out what they'd lacked in the cosmic scheme of things to have sunk so low. The majority, husks of their former selves, were men who had long ago slipped through the cracks. Percival was the lone exception, denounced by his comrades for a treason he hadn't committed, and having lost all faith in the system. "A system that eats it's children for breakfast," as Abby Hoffman had put it. His lot was the most wretched, by far.

They queued round the corner of the block like a shiftless caravan of vagabonds, with grim epithets stuck in their mouths, waiting impatiently for the agency to open its doors. When a light finally went on in the office, and movement was detected inside, the men surged forward, crushing those upfront. The crowding was excessive, causing the men to almost break out in fisticuffs.

"Quit it back there you fucking oafs," a man swore. "What y'll trying to do, kill somebody?"

The doors were opened, and the men charged in like ruffians scrambling for seats in a game of musical chairs, leaving many standing about no less dumbfounded than Ole Dan Tucker of folklore fame. Percival had managed to edge out another man, and so had secured a seat for himself.

The room was fairly large, similar in size to a state employment office with fluorescent lights. There was a counter towards the front behind which the staff were at work, taking calls. A heavy set, mustachioed man with sleeves rolled up and tie askew, leaned heavily on the counter. Chewing a corner of his mustache, he cast a beady-eyed glance over the room of men.

The usual employment forms were passed to the new applicants. Percival felt qualified to fill them out blind, at this point, even carrying his own pen for the purpose. Upon completion, the forms were returned to the man behind the counter, who didn't look any of the applicants in the face. Percival certainly didn't look him in the face either.

Within the next forty-five minutes more than half the men were sent out on various job assignments for the day. As calls came in the men went out. Within the next half hour, the stout man stentoriously announced, "Sorry fellas, tomorrow's another day."

Percival swallowed his disappointment hard, as did the others. He found it difficult to stand. His eyes were dry and his lips parched. He had hoped to be thrown a bone, a lifeline, a semblance of something by which to cling. But it had not materialized. He hung his head abjectly. He heard the last of the men groan as they, too, struggled to gain their feet, and, searching empty pockets to no avail, they shuffled aimlessly out the door. Percival broke out in a sweat, recognizing himself in these men in the not too distant future. At present he still had money in his pockets. He felt a cold chill enter his bowels. He climbed to his feet and started in a zigzag toward the door. He was feverish, afraid of losing his sanity under the strain. The awful fear of losing his mind, which in Rufus' case, as he saw it, was freedom, would, in his, amount to capitulation, even shame. It would mean, in effect, that the man had won, had neutralized him, deprived him of his self-worth and packed him off to the reservation.

Once again on the street he breathed easier, but the anxiety lingered. His mood was downcast. He was in a quandary and undecided as to what direction he should take, hence he decided it was time to set aside his pride and go reapply for his old job at the Museum of Modern Art. He had left the museum on good terms and had been considerably well liked. No one, to his knowledge, should have any major objections to his returning. It was the only thing to do under the circumstance. Get his old job back.

He caught the Lexington Avenue subway uptown and was disgorged at 53rd. Street. Mid-Manhattan was less congested than was the Lower East Side, the financial district, and was a more leisurely part of town in which to get around. It was the shopping district, the high fashion district. The theater district, a tourist area. There was much to see. And the Museum of Modern Art, located on 53rd. Street west of 5th. Avenue was a major attraction. The Museum's office building entrance was modern only in as much as it was minimalist in design, as compared to its gallery entrance.

"Hello, Percival, long time no see," said the fair-haired receptionist.

"'ello, Diane," he returned her greeting, smiling, taking her in at a glance. She was blond with deep set blue eyes, and elongated nose, and small, but pretty, mouth. She was tastefully attired and attractive as befits a front desk representative of such a prestigious institution. They had been friends in the past when he had worked there and would often take lunch together in the museum's sculpture garden, weather permitting. They had gotten on well. He was moved to see her again, as she was to see him.

"How've you been?" she asked.

"You know how that goes. Keeping the faith; holding the fort; lying through my teeth; keeping it real."

"Isn't that the way it is."

They laughed.

"Actually, Diane, I don't mind telling you, I dare not look back for fear of something catching up to me."

"Yet here you are."

"Yet here I am."

"And what brings you this way?"

"I'm hard up for work."

"If I'm right, there should be a few openings in security. You might be able to get your old job back."

"Wish me luck."

"I'll keep my fingers crossed."

"I'll see you on the way out."

She checked her watch. "I'll be going to lunch soon. Would you care to join me? We can catch up."

He smiled, broadly. "I'd like that."

"Break a leg," she said, cheerily, raising and crossing her fingers tightly.

He winked at her, nodded to the lobby guard, who he also knew, and boarded the elevator along with other passengers going up. He selected his floor, and within a few idle moments he'd reached his destination. He disembarked and turned straight for the Personnel Office. A small number of applicants were seated in the hallway, waiting to be interviewed. He stood at the entrance to the outer office, trying to catch the attention of Yuki Ahoshi, the assistant personnel manager. When by chance she finally looked up, she paused, catching his eyes. "Will you excuse me. I'll only be a moment," she said to the young woman across the desk from her.

She wore a suit and white blouse with ruffles at the throat, which gave her a sedate appearance.

"Percival," she greeted him in a tone of apprehension, taking him aside. "I'm surprised to see you here." She didn't seem terribly happy to see him. "Is there something I can do for you?"

"I'm looking for work," he said, gravelly voiced.

Her expression fell. She looked stealthily about, then drew him further away from the office door. She looked at him with entreaty. "I don't quite know how to tell you this, but you're not welcome here. It's like this, the FBI over the past year has been here several times on your account. They've threatened and intimidated. There was a meeting with the director, personnel and security. In short, we pulled your file at the FBI's insistence. That way, any time anyone calls seeking a reference for you we simply say, 'We have no such person listed in our files.' And when possible, we take the name of the interested parties, and that information is passed on. I don't know to whom. All I know is, it is.

"Then the article in the Tribune didn't help. It just gave reason where one was previously lacking. It was nothing anyone necessarily believed, but neither do they care to bother. I for one didn't believe any of it. If it were true, then why was the FBI working so hard to discredit you and have you blacklisted? But, on that score, my opinion doesn't carry any weight. And under pressure from the FBI, the museum would never consider taking you back.

"This place, despite it's being the Museum of Modern Art, is a rather conservative institution. All you have to do to confirm that is take a look at the names of the board of trustees cut into the wall of the first-floor gallery. It would be pointless for you to use us as a reference in the future. I wish there were something I could do, but my hands are tied. I'm sorry, I have to go. I've someone waiting," she said, and she beat a hasty retreat back to her office.

He wavered, stunned. Indeed, had it been a fight he would have been counted out on his feet. They had been friends, or so he'd thought, he and Yuki, and now she couldn't wait to be rid of him. The earth could as easily have opened and swallowed him whole. He was in shock. He flushed and his heart beat so he could hardly breathe. For the first time in his life, he knew complete fear.

He left the museum in a daze, shaken to the marrow. He passed Diane at the first-floor reception desk, blind with rage. She called to him, but in his fury he'd forgotten all about her. He brushed past Moon dog, the blind poet, arrayed

516

in Viking garb and leaning on his staff, on 6th. Avenue, practically bowling him over to the horror of passersby. He raced on to the 7th. Avenue subway as if sun struck, trying to put as much distance between himself and the museum as possible. His brain was in overdrive and his thoughts bubbled furiously, as in a cauldron.

He felt inept, stupid, regretting having thrown his .45 in the river. God, but could he ever use it now. He could stick up a liquor store, rob a bank, resupply his dwindling store of funds. Without capital or a gun, his future was circumscribed, hemmed in. It appeared to him, in all likelihood, as if the FBI were trying to push him out of existence, drive him crazy, drive him to self-destruction— *"Keep that nigger running."* He sighed. Is that what agent Bianco had in mind when he had said to him that fateful day, six weeks ago, "Try to stay alive?" Were they toying with him? If so, then why shouldn't he go ahead and throw himself on the subway tracks before the next oncoming train? And just why he didn't, he would not quite ever know. However, if the truth be known, he couldn't justify killing himself with money remaining in his pockets.

That evening, when Gwen got home and entered the darkened apartment, she switched on the lights and was startled to find Percival staring off absently, slumped in a lounge chair.

"You almost scared the hell out of me," she said, as if talking to a sick child. "What are you doing anyway, sitting in the dark?"

"Jus' blending in," he said, languidly, following her with his eyes. She was uneasy, he could see. She evidently had something of consequence on her mind. But she didn't say anymore until she'd finished her first drink. Then, when she finally looked at him, in the process of pouring herself a second, she said, "My God, what's become of you? You look dreadful, like something the cat's dragged in."

"I've had a revelatory day of it."

"Would you care for a drink?"

"Please," he said, blankly.

She mixed, poured and passed him a drink, all without looking at him. She did not turn the radio on or put on a record, as was her custom. She instead paced restlessly back and forth, sipping her drink.

"What gives?" he asked, irritated by her pacing.

"I've had a day of it myself," she said, with a sigh. "I even called my analyst. He suggested I re-enter group, of course. We talked for a considerable time." She paused and faced him, a look of tragedy on her face. "I can't handle this."

"If you can't handle it, can we skip it, cause I've had one hell of an awful day of it as it is."

She lowered herself to the sofa across from him, crossed her legs casually, and said with an undercurrent of anxiety in her voice, "My day has been no bed of roses either, primarily because of you." He sat up, alert. This had been one of the many reasons he had been hiding like a child in the dark, trying to return to the embryonic seclusion of the womb. "The problem is I have an emotional investment in our relationship that you don't share. I love you, but I have to face up to the fact that you don't love me. And you make me ashamed of myself, ashamed to express my feelings like some gangly adolescent girl caught with her head in the wrong door." She pressed the fingers of her hand to her brow, her lips tight, fighting tears. "Only I'm every bit a woman and your rejecting me, rejecting the love I offer you is humiliating. It wouldn't be so bad if, say, you weren't here, but your presence permeates everything, including my sleep. When I roll over in bed and catch your scent, my body longs to absorb you, open like a flower and absorb you. But instead, I'm left climbing the walls in frustration. And I'm afraid that the longer you remain the more difficult it's going to be for me. I don't mean to put you out but you must let me in or make other arrangements. I'm not a cold fish, I'm simply foolishly in love, as absurd as that must sound to you."

He gazed at her with a look of disbelief. Then he dryly said, "I had no wish to lay a trip on you. It was a matter of survival for me that I ask'd you could I stay. I only wanted a place to lay till I could put something more permanent together, then I was gonna split. That was to ave been understood. It was not to be a love affair, but more an affair of convenience."

"I'm a woman, not just a means to an end," she yelped. "I trusted you, damn it!" She wore the sadness that an invisible hand had inscribed on her face.

"I betrayed your trust?" he asked, incredulous "Woman, I've been running on empty here 'n miss your meaning?"

"You're using me."

"You've got me mistaken for someone else. I'm jus' trying to make my way through troubled waters."

"You're no different. You're just like all the others."

"Others? What others?"

"Men," she scoffed. "I know about you – you can't fool me; there's nothing I don't know about men – for the most you all grow up to be unfeeling, heartless boys."

"I said nothing 'bout men. I was trying to say something 'bout me, one man in particular; n you don't know half'a it, half'a what you're saying, half'a what I'm going through."

"Is it some secret black thing, like a Masonic ritual or something?" she said sarcastically.

Glowering at her in a squall of rage, he started from his chair. But catching himself, he wagged a finger at her. "Naughty, naughty," he warned, settling back in his seat. "You seem to ave concocted some fairy-tale notion of love. Ours was anything but love. You're twelve, fifteen years older than me, for G'd sake; 'n you're clinging to me outta some fairy tale notion of romance. What you're looking for is a knight in shining armor to come along 'n rescue you, but you're a little too late. In fact, you're a few centuries too late. It now requires that we both be able to rescue each other. 'N the truth is, we're ill-equipped to rescue each other but, as friends, we might be able to help one another. That's all I ask'd of you, a helping hand, not a hand in marriage. There's a considerable difference between the two!"

"Obviously, you're holding something back. It's not so much what you say, as how you say it. There's another woman, isn't there?" she shrieked.

"It's my life we're talking 'bout here," he said, with panic in his tone, sensing his youth slipping wastefully through his grasp. "Cut me some slack, will you? Throw me a lifeline? I'm grasping at straw. No, there's no other anybody. Where is she, in my pocket?" Even at risk of being put on the streets he would not give her the satisfaction of admitting to there being another. "N if there is, so what? But, alas, you're wrong." He threw up his hands in defeat.

"How'd you manage to change the conversation back to you? It's always about you, isn't it? Well this time it's not about you. It's about you frustrating my life. And I'm going to have to re-enter therapy because of it. Because of what you've put me through these past weeks."

Percival looked steadily at her for a minute. "Like the standup comics say on a bad night," he said, "'I'm dying on my feet.'"

"You must take me for a real fool."

"No, I take you for a frustrated, middle-aged woman indulging her fantasy."

She flushed, her anger welling, "You insensitive little prick! I'm hardly middle-aged."

"You once told me you were ole enough to be my –"

"Liar," she broke in. "I never told you any such thing. And if I did, it would have been gallant of you to have not brought it up."

"So now you're a babe in arms, eh?"

"You're being snide."

"N you're being damn well catty."

"And you're insolent."

"You're a fucking lush. You need the bottle far more than a lover."

"You dirty no good nigger!" She was horrified, taken aback at herself, her response, her words, but they had spilt out in the heat of the moment and she was unable to recall them. She glared at him with affright, her eyes strained in their sockets, in mindless panic.

"That's all you had to say," he said, growing a dark wine red with anger. He clamored to his feet, knocking his unfinished drink over. He reached into a pant pocket. "Here 'r your keys." He flung them at her. "I'm gone," he spat, snatched his pea coat off a hook on the back of the door and stormed out of the apartment before he killed her.

Gwen finished her drink in a gulp, gaining her feet and ran after him in a drunken haze. "Percival," she bleated, feeling the swell of a cold, lonely place in her breast. But he had already departed, gone out to face the demons of his own underworld. "I'm sorry," she apologized to the empty hallway, the word "nigger" resounding accusatorially in her ears. "I didn't mean it," she called, distraught, her brows drawn down like a visor over glazed eyes. As a neighbor trudged upstairs, she went back into her flat and poured herself another drink, a stiffer one this time.

***

Percival stepped out into the veil of night. The misty streetlights cast circular splotches of yellow light onto the sidewalk. He didn't know how he had gotten out of Gwen's apartment without injuring her. He had been seized by an overwhelming urge to take her by the throat and squeeze the life out of her. "I could still go back 'n do it," he thought as his fingers itched with murderous rage, but his feet led him away in the opposite direction.

He was in turmoil and didn't know where he was headed or where he would spend the night. There appeared to be nothing else but to wander the streets. He walked aimlessly among the faceless mass of people until the numbers began to dwindle, leaving only the after-hours crowd—the nightclub set, hipsters, high rollers, the winners and losers, players—people of the night who eschew the day, crawling back in their holes like night owls before dawn. As a teenager when he had felt downcast, he would go to Coney Island. And he decided that, no, he would not go to Coney Island, which tempted him only it would be far too cold to be by the water. But, yes, he could still go to Brooklyn. He descended the subway station at St. Marks & 8th. Street, Cooper Square, and took the Lexington Avenue line. The nearer the train came to

Brooklyn the less anxious he became, as if he were traveling back in time to a more carefree day, a happier time. A time before the web of disillusionments had ensnared him and left him without an exit. Yes, he was going back to Brooklyn. He could hear it in the roar of the train, in the spinning of its wheels, the way he'd heard the roar of the crowd at Ebbets Field when Jackie Robinson stole home plate. He was returning to the Brooklyn of the Brooklyn Dodgers, the Brooklyn of his rough-n-tumble youth. The Brooklyn of his first love and heartbreak. "A Tree Grows in Brooklyn," The Brooklyn of humanity. The Brooklyn he loved. His heart welled with emotion as he tried to hurry the train along. "Faster, faster," he urged, as if encouraging a derby horse across the finish line. He was impatient and could hardly wait. Then the train pulled into Grand Army Plaza & Park Row – a good a spot as any to get off. He bolted from the train and raced up the steps, as though he had been suffocating and Brooklyn was the only place on earth where he could draw breath. "Ahhh," he exhaled. There before him was the great bronze statue of Neptune rising majestically from a fountain, and across from the Plaza, illuminated by street lamps, was the Brooklyn Public Library, Prospect Park and the Botanical Gardens. As he cast his misty gaze over the shadows of familiar landmarks, a melancholic feeling of loss swept over him.

He gazed up and down Eastern Parkway. The streets were empty, save for a few lone Taxis. He felt as if he were alone on the most valuable piece of property in all the world.

He crossed the street and took a seat on the library steps under a lamp and set his face between his palms, marveling at the darkened street in a kind of euphoria. He didn't know how long he had remained there, basking in the overhead light, absorbing by a process of osmosis, all the learning stored in that great repository of knowledge. A cop walking his beat approached him.

"Nice night," said the cop genially, swinging his nightstick.

Percival looked up at the sky beyond the streetlamps, hardly a star perceptible, not a cloud in sight. "Yes," he agreed, "it is."

"You're up late," added the cop.

"Couldn't sleep," Percival rejoined. He did not experience the usual malice, the instinctual inner panic on confronting a cop, but enjoyed the courtesy of two men bidding each other the complements of the day. They passed a few more pleasantries before the cop was off. Percival observed him as he left and thought, "How civil," then thought,

"Nothing in Brooklyn could ever be evil." Until, that is, he remembered Joleen and how she would not allow him to see their son, Malek, and her mother and what a viperous shrew she was. Then it occurred to him that even the Dodgers had left Brooklyn, scared out most likely on account of those two

Harpies. As these thoughts crowded his mind, he got up and started along Eastern Parkway, trying to juggle his thoughts and the blinding series of events which had brought him to this fateful, dark hour. When he was about to despair even of Brooklyn, he took a seat on a bench near another on which someone lay curled up, their coat collar raised against the brisk autumn night.

Percival inspected the body casually from the distance, when it stirred and yawned. "Huh," uttered the man with a start, realizing he was not entirely alone. "Got a cigarette?" he asked.

"Don't smoke."

"Just my dumb luck."

The man swung his legs off the bench and sat up, staring at Percival who was gazing absently over the street. "Percival, is that you?"

Percival turned and when he saw the face his heart leapt. He blinked. The last time he saw that face it was one of fearless youth, of strength and determination, but it had since changed and not for the better. The face had aged beyond it's years and soured.

"Jamal," he said, in a strangled voice.

"It is you, then," Jamal said, distantly. "What you doing here on Eastern Parkway this God-awful time of night?"

"I could ask the same of you."

"You could, but I ask'd first."

"I'm homeless as of t'night. Can't finda job 'n I'm pretty much down to my last dollar. Anything else you want'a know?"

"That makes no sense. You're the best fucking fighter in the world with the possible exception of Ali."

"What's that?" he asked, startled. Then it all came flooding back to him, a remembrance of himself in bits and pieces, like the recollections of an amnesiac. "Doesn't make sense, does it. I only remember now thanks to you." A frown crossed his face. "I'm gonna do it! I'm gonna return to the ring. I'm gonna make a comeback," he sang, leaping to his feet. "My first love, second only to Brooklyn!" He laughed, ebulliently. "You just hold on," he said, glancing back at Jamal. "I'm gonna be right back."

"I got no place else to go."

Percival dashed across the parkway without caution for the nearest phone booth. He dropped in the required change and dialed. He was more excited than he had been in quite a while. The phone on the other end rang repeatedly, still he did not hang up. Eventually it was answered by a gruff, sleepy voice.

"Who's this?"

"Punchy, it's me –"

"I don't care who it is, don't you know it's past three in the morning?"

"It's Percival, Punchy, it's me!"

"Percival?" said Punchy with roused curiosity, then more excitedly asked, "Is that you? talk to me."

"I want'a go pro 'n I want you in my corner."

"Where else would I be?"

"Let's meet t'morrow, I mean t'day, at the Gramercy Park Gym to talk 'bout it, say four o'clock?"

"I'll be there."

"Hey, Punchy."

"Yeah?"

"I'm looking forward to seeing you."

"Me too, kid. This promises to be an exciting ride."

"Later then."

"Later it is."

"Thanks, man."

"Thank you. It's the realization of an ole man's dreams. I've had fighters who've gotten close, but you can take it if your heart's still in it."

"I'm hungry, hungrier than ever; hungrier than a lone, starving wolf!"

"You'll need to be!"

"I need this."

"I didn't think you'd return to the ring otherwise."

"It's all I 'ave left."

"This afternoon then."

"This afternoon."

"Gotcha."

"Good night."

Percival hung up, then rejoined Jamal on the bench.

"I don't know what I've been thinking these past weeks." Percival shook his head, lazily, smiling to himself. "I've jus' been somewhere else, I guess, cause I sure as hell ain't been thinking straight."

"It's easy to become disorientated, given the many betrayals of trust."

"N you, Jamal. What about you?"

"Me? I just got out of jail the other day and haven't figured how I'm going to go home and face my father. So while the weather holds I figure, what the hell. I've been warehoused this past year in a six by eight cell with the barnyard odor of men caged like animals filling my nostrils to the point of nausea, amidst the ceaseless monkey house chatter up and down the cell block intruding on my sanity from lights on to lights out. It won't hurt too much for me to remain outdoors awhile and stretch my limbs and catch the air. I'll stay out till winter anyway, then I'll consider facing my father's frosty gaze."

"I had a parting of the ways with my mother, too," Percival sighed, looking off. "She couldn't understand."

"They seldom do."

"Hell, I don't understand."

"I heard by way of the grapevine, which is very accurate in jail, that your brother, Sam had been killed by the pigs under very suspicious circumstances and that you were implicated somehow and expelled from the party as a result. I'm sure your mother couldn't understand if that's the case."

"There's only a vague semblance of truth to that story." said Percival, up in arms, as if his veracity were under attack.

"There usually is," Jamal acknowledged, almost indifferently. "If the cops would tap into the prison grapevine they'd solve more crimes than they do. No, the rift between my father and myself was of a religious nature. My father thought I'd ceased to honor him in his home. Which wasn't quite true. I just differed with him. My father's a Black Muslim. A devoted follower of The Honorable Elijah Muhammad, as I was raised to be, and was, until Malcolm broke ranks. Though I was only thirteen at the time, he struck a resonant chord in me, and I chose to follow in his footsteps. Malcolm had put aside racial hatred, racial animosity, at that point, which is at the heart of The Black Muslims belief system. But my father thought Malcolm ungrateful, an apostate. I tried to argue that, no, Malcolm had outgrown Elijah, had opened his eyes, but my father thought I was being disrespectful, rebellious, that I was only a boy, no better than a man-child, that "I," as he put it, "had grown too big for my britches." And we ceased to speak.

"Not once while I was in jail did he visit me whereas my mother came frequently, even against his objections. If he hadn't kicked me out of the house it was because he would have had to reckon with my mother and despite the fact that after Malcolm's death I joined the Panthers, I was also in college and on the Dean's list, as well, with a full scholarship to MIT pending. And though he felt that I'd dishonored him, he was fiercely proud of my academic achievements, always holding my grades up to the Islamic community and to my other brothers and sisters, who despised me for it.

"It was unfair, no doubt. They were average students and I have, as you know, a genius IQ, and is why my father was on unsure footing with me, whereas my mother accepted it in me as if it were an infirmity, a clubfoot or something," he said with indifference. "And' coming out of a ghetto environment, she was fairly right. My teachers, who were all white, backed off from me, skipping me to higher and higher grades until I found myself in Brooklyn College. I'd always felt out of place and had wanted to hang out with the brothers, be one of the guys, but no one would let me until the Panthers became a vehicle for my intelligence and rage. A rage that had been brewing in me for years, evidently. A rage at being different, at being an anomaly, being victimized for not only being black but intelligent, too, in a society in which it was unacceptable. I could as easily have been retarded. In the Panthers I'd found a place. And in prison I became an anomaly all over again.

"And though my mother visited me frequently, my father had come to consider me a closed book. When all charges against me were finally dropped, I was ready to get out, but I was not ready to go back home. The funny thing is, I love 'n respect my dad and would do almost anything to be in his good graces but I can't deny myself, my intelligence, my experience. Still, the fact that my father didn't visit me, not once while I was in jail, hurts more than I can say; n now I can't face him. It's not so much facing him either, it's what's bound to follow. You can't know how heart rending it all is. I honestly needed him, if only to say 'I told you so,' to validate my existence, my being. And God, let me tell you, if there's anything you need validated in jail it's your existence, cause it's so easy to lose track of reality. I would at least have known he cared. But he never showed, 'n consequently I don't exist. Jail erases you or blurs the margins of your existence."

"But, Jamal, you're a brilliant cat on your way to MIT, for goodness sake."

He turned to Percival without expression and said, "Since I've been busted, that's now a lifetime ago, I'll be lucky if I can get through the back door of some second-rate college let alone MIT. No, man, I've lost my dreams, my ambitions. I've hung em up with my hat, as you've hung up your gloves, evidently. I'm burnt out, man. I'm empty of content 'n don't want anyone strumming my nerves. I spent the last year with people plucking my strings to a point where I'm a near fucking basket case.

"Let me tell you, you go to jail 'n your priorities shift, as do you. Oh boy, do you change. Shortly after my incarceration in the Tombs, I came to discover that my association with the Panthers was not going to be of much use because, there are cats in there, predators, who are no respecters of a heightened revolutionary perspective. They feed on anything that they perceive as weak or alone. I met no one in jail I'd care to encounter again. It was an unhappy experience, to say the least. And that's putting it mildly. It taught me nothing of value, absolutely nothing. Except that if faced with the possibility of prison run like hell. Run until you drop. Run until your heart bursts. I guess I'm running now, only I'm not too sure from what."

Jamal stared off into the dark night, observing the streetlamps, glitter like votive candles in a darkened cathedral with the fragrant hint of flowers wafting gently on the air from the Botanical gardens behind them.

"It was damn well hard for me. I was alone 'n the party had cooled toward me, because I'd acted without its approval in trying to bust Lakay out of jail. Then came prison," he said, stiffly, "like nothing I'd ever known nor prepared for. It could be worse than slavery, cause in slavery you're of value to the master, if not yourself, but in prison you're of value to no one, including yourself. I was young, trying to hold onto the very scraps of my dignity while day by day the forces that be—the guards n predators, working in collusion— were gnawing at it, eating me away, heart 'n soul. The Panther 21, on the other hand, though in the Tombs, were isolated. They didn't want them to contaminate the general prison population with their revolutionary rhetoric.

"In jail, man, you lose faith in people. What I learned in jail, what I saw in the faces of guards, the faces of inmates 'n gradually in my own reflection, was the absence of God. The loss of spirit. In jail plenty of guys say they find religion, but I assure you, no one finds God – no one –, they find their fears 'n fall to their knees 'n worship them. Even with Malcolm, it took years after jail and going to Mecca before he found Allah. I mean, what he found in jail wasn't God but Elijah Muhammad and The Nation of Islam. It took going to Mecca for that. And what he preached for years was founded on our fears, if you follow the gist of what I'm saying, dig?"

"I think I can agree with you on that."

"In jail, man, there are only the scared and the sadistic. Predators 'n prey. I may have lost faith in God, but jail restored my belief in the devil or, that is, the existence of evil. It was easily found in the faces of sadistic guards, both white 'n black, who encouraged the predatory practices of fiendish inmates who were no respecters of anything outside their bestial nature. I'd come to hate those guards, especially the white guards, who would turn their backs and allow those fiends to indulge their appetites at the expense of the weak. I fought hard with myself to not hate those brother's who'd allowed the man, those sadistic racist pigs, to turn them into something less than human. And yet, in the face of it all, I had to believe, must believe, that there are still a few good white people in the world, despite the guards, the society," he said, surveying the depths of his soul.

"I mean, I don't know too many white people – who of us does? We only know the man, Mr. Charlie, the police, slumlords, grocers, and sometimes an occasional classmate, if we're lucky. And that's not usually on intimate grounds either. I mean, no one invites you to dinner. As such, there is no love lost. In fact, as a Black Muslim I was raised to think of em as devils."

"That's as safe a way of thinking of em as any. That way you don't ave to risk yourself," Percival said.

"Or trust. My mother brought me a collection of essays by James Baldwin in jail 'n he says in one of em, 'When the white man learns to love himself, he'll no longer have a need to hate us.' And I think I believe that. At any rate, I want to believe it. We must believe it, mustn't we?"

"If you put it that way." Percival laughed, inoffensively, at Jamal's seeming naiveté. "I agree, the white man doesn't like himself very much and he has said, along with Milton's Lucifer, from "Paradise Lost," 'It's better to reign in Hell than serve in Heaven.' All too tragically, though, we've caught his disease – which is self-loathing. 'N have said, with Milton's Satin, 'Evil be thou my good.' The mistake we as Panthers made, all too sadly, was losing sight of that. 'N in our taking up the gun, we sealed 'r fate 'n caught the disease. 'N all 'r subsequent mistakes were based on that initial folly. But, then again, you're right, we must believe in the few, as we believe in the exception to the rule. I don't know I believe in God any more than you do, but I do believe in the exception to the rule. Then yes, it's the few to whom we're obligated. But, on the other hand, if the truth be told, there aren't enough good white people to make a shade of difference. That said, I hope the fate of the world isn't cast in 'r hands either, for the world has a way of turning everything topsy-turvy."

"It sounds hopeless on one hand and, on the other, it sounds like you've become a pacifist."

"We've buried too many of 'r innocent for me to feel optimistic. But no, I'm not a pacifist. I'm simply convinced that violence only creates more problems than it solves."

"As I recall, you were trying to balance the ledgers. Have you met with any success?"

"I'm deeper in debt than ever."

"Still, I like the way you think, no less than the way you fight."

"I had my doubts."

"Under the circumstance we all had, and with good reason, too. I mean, take these internecine, gangland style slayings, for example, which have left Panthers from both camps, east 'n west coast, dead on the streets of New York. Over internal party conflicts, which served to weaken my resolve when I needed both strength of mind and body to cope with the everyday ordeals of prison life. Granted, the Panthers had distanced themselves from me. I admit, I made a costly mistake. Still, I very much felt a strong kinship to the party and the nobility of spirit which had informed it but has since been reduced to the least common denominator," he said, rankled. "We deserved better from our leadership."

"That's saying they had it to offer," Percival said. "We mistakenly endowed them with more integrity than we ourselves have. As it turned out, they were, at best, poor reflections of ourselves."

"That's a detached observation if ever I heard one."

"It would have been nice, as in precise, but we had no right to expect different. I mean, look at the culture out of which we come."

Jamal shook his head and, lips pursed, ruefully added, "Well it didn't leave such a good impression on the overall prison population, either. Instead, it looked like the man had us once again where he wanted us, horns locked 'n killing ourselves."

"I'm afraid I've not been following the news much of late. I've been too busy trying to keep myself intact."

"In prison, my man, keeping up with the news, breaking events of the day, is half of keeping yourself intact."

"Speaking of doubts, Jamal, how'd you ever get out'a jail?"

"The charges were tossed because entrapment had been proven. It was a police set up an agent provocateur instigated the breakout, and supplied me with materials for explosives."

"I see. Well we can talk freely now out on the streets, stripped of 'r illusions 'n licking 'r wounds, thoroughly disenchanted 'n not jus' with the party. As they say, 'This might not be hell, but I can see it from here.'"

"All too sadly," Jamal agreed, as he curled back up on the bench, crowding Percival. "Or as someone said, 'The silence of God is a long, long awful thing and the whole world is lost because of it.'"

"And it is," Percival said. Then after a moment's pause, he asked, "You must be what, twenty-two, twenty-three now?"

"I've aged, I know. I'll be nineteen late next month."

A youthful fervor had passed from Jamal's face, and in the harsh light of the street lamps it appeared somewhat jaded.

Percival winced, turning up the collar of his pea coat. "It could be the streetlights," he said, apologetically.

"Only it's not."

"So then, Jamal, you didn't say got any plans?"

"It'll suit me just fine if I only have a rock for a pillow, a park bench for a bed, and the next thousand years or so to sleep it all off."

***

"Kill him!" they shouted. "Kill the bum!" The fans were on their feet in a frenzy, as Percival sent Kincade reeling from ring post to ring post. He had built his fight over the rounds, moving from strength to strength, and, as his opponent's fight peaked, he turned up the pressure. Kincaid, the number two middleweight contender, his face puffy, a crimson splotch with a glazed, wanderlust look in his eyes, was in trouble. Though Percival had bled the starch out of him and he was in peril of losing his feet, no less than his rating, the fight was not over. Kincade fought back gamely, weathering Percival's assault, striking back with a defensive number of blows. Percival shook them off and snuck in two quick, cobra like jabs. Kincaid lobbed in a wild overhang right, which Percival slipped, digging in with a right of his own, to the ribs. Kincaid shut his eyes in pain and spat his mouthpiece.

Sensing the kill, the fans were howling themselves hoarse. Percival crossed his lead left foot over his right, inciting Kincaid to follow, then dropped him all of a sudden, with a sucker right – the blow Jersey Joe used to drop Joe Louis. The difference was, Louis would rise from the canvas, beat the count, and go on to retain his title – whereas Kincaid was counted out on his back. The crowd was jubilant No one had seen that maneuver since Jersey Joe left the ring. It was classic. Punchy smiled, as did Percival, savoring the moment. He was at the height of his game, of his powers, and had been promised a championship match if he should dispose of Kincaid, and with that last blow he had done just that and now only the signing of contracts was in order.

They were on the way once again!

"The winner, by knock out, in one minute thirty-seven seconds of the seventh round, Jones!" It was his 23rd. K.O. in 27 straight wins in as many months. He was being hailed as "incomparable," though there he differed with his proponents and said, "Ali's incomparable. I'm to be compared to Sugar Ray Robinson," which always raise a laugh among the sports writers in attendance. He was receiving much press. His rise had been meteoric, though not surprising, certainly not for Punchy who had shaped his progress step by step. He was just grateful that Percival had returned to the ring to fulfill his potential following that long layoff, long in that it was, from his perspective, heedless. However, as Percival had explained, that day at the Gramercy Park gym, after that surprising late-night call over two years ago, as they sat in the viewers gallery, watching fighters work out on the floor, "I'd been hopelessly blindsided by events, 'n couldn't find'a avenue of escape."

"So now you want'a go pro?" Punchy asked, stroking his grizzled chin. "Well, I guess from what you say you've had'a time of it. 'N the death of Sam coming as it did must'a caused you some grief. I'd heard 'bout it, of course. It's not surprising he would end up badly. Sam was always out'a control 'n underfoot. It was almost predictable. He was foolhardy. That's not surprising of itself, growing up in your shadow.

"I fought for this country. I saw a lot of good colored men die for this country, for 'r second-class status. I don't know if you 'n your generation's right or wrong. That's beside the point. That's not what we're here for. We're here to box, to see if we can't take it to the top, to place your name among the pantheon of champions where it belongs."

"Amen to that!"

"For now, I'd like to see what you got."

"Fine," said Percival, his lips compressed in resolution. "Anyone in particular?"

"How 'bout that light heavyweight warming up in the ring?"

"Your pick," said Percival, flatly, giving the fighter the once-over. He descended from the viewers gallery and bypassed the other fighters working out on the floor on his way to the locker room. He changed into a borrowed pair of sweats, reemerged from the locker room and climbed into the ring with a tautness in his gut. He hadn't fought in over a year and a half – or had he? he was out of shape and, as a consequence, on edge. Punchy gloved him up." I want'a see what you got, how sharp you 'r, but don't spend yourself, either."

"Got ya."

At the bell, Punchy set Percival's mouthpiece in place. Percival swung out of his corner sure of foot and after snapping off a few lethargic punches, he began to feel himself back on home turf – at ease in his skin for the first time in a long while.

He had started off stiffly, a little rusty, but warmed up quickly, and by the second round his competitive edge had returned. His punches began to sizzle with razor like accuracy and he caught the slower fighter, again and again, with lancing blows. In due course, when they became embroiled in a grueling exchange, Percival dropped the surprised heavier man to a knee with a terrific left hook. And though he quickly regained his feet, he backed off with a newfound respect for Percival's abilities.

Punchy was no less taken aback, and his eyes widened in delight. He had not expected such a heavy exchange between fighters, and what he saw in Percival was not so much a changed fighter or an improved one, but a more purposeful, calculating one – cold, deliberate and efficient. He wore the look of a seasoned assassin. His face an inscrutable mask, even to Punchy, who'd known him like a book. Punchy was intrigued. It gave him to pause: He saw in Percival a changed man, capable of murder, capable of setting up his brother. He shook the thought away. Whatever it was, Percival was focused with the sanguinary intensity of life's bitter uncertainty. He had gained something from hard won gutter politics. His eyes were fixed like a stalker. He was the hunted, turned hunter.

They later agreed that Percival would stay with him until other, more adequate housing arrangements could be made. In the meantime he moved in with Punchy on Hancock St., in Bed-Stuy. "It'll be good having you," Punchy said. "It'll be like having the son I never had." Percival gave him an ingratiating smile. "I'll contact Derrick Rafkin 'n ask him to handle you," Punchy went on. "He's handled other fighters for me in the past and I trust him. He's a good man. I've played poker with him, 'n you can tell a good man by the way he handles his cards. So yeah, I trust him. After all, we've been partners in one scheme 'n another now since the big one. He's white, but as you know that ain't entirely his fault. In this game colored managers don't rate," Punchy said, cogently. "I'll train. He'll manage. He's always been interested in the possibility of handling you in the event of your turning pro. It'll be a handshake only. That's another reason I trust him. He likes handling good fighters, 'n he's good to em in turn."

A few days later they all met at the gym. Percival remembered that when he was a kid Derrick would drop by the gym to scout out new prospects and confer with Punchy. On one occasion, Punchy had summoned Percival off the floor to make the introductions. If he remembered correctly, he was 17 and had won the nationals for the first time.

Derrick Rafkin was a tall, lanky, gentleman gambler in his late fifties with graying hair and full mustache. He was meticulously kept, with a faint smell of cologne about him. He carried a pocket watch on a fob tucked in a vest pocket, and wore a diamond encrusted pinky ring, a college ring on the finger next to that. He liked a good cigar which need not necessarily be li but rolled speculatively in his mouth. He was a soft-spoken man and could easily have been mistaken for an investment banker. He was a graduate of City College and had met Punchy in the war.

He had been an Officer in a Negro unit and would fraternize with the men, gamble with them in defiance of Army regulations to the contrary. He was known among his fellow officers, particularly southern ones, as a nigger lover; a name to which he attached no significance. He had seen, firsthand, the trials and tribulations of every ethnic group who had come to Ellis Island, passed through the grubby streets of alphabet city—as the Lower East Side was commonly known— and into the greater American mainstream. As a result, he had become inured to the derogatory name calling. Besides, he was a gambler, and black life in white America was, at best, a crap shoot.

He liked the ponies as well as fighters, but preferred cards as the more reliable, although he had a strong suspicion that Percival was going to be the best bet he'd ever placed.

He lived out of a suitcase in a room at a mid-Manhattan hotel, The Commodore. He was a globe trotter and would travel the world to wherever a high stakes game of chance might take him. He had played cards and roulette in every major casino in the world from Europe to Hong Kong. But fortunately enough, a high stakes game of chance could always be found in New York City.

He was a cultured man, a man of refinement, as one would expect of a world traveler. He liked fine art, music, food, the theater and literature. It was not so surprising, considering that Punchy was the consummate sportsman and would only work with people of similar a cloth. Percival liked him, and if Punchy could trust him, then so would Percival.

Their agreement would consist, just as Punchy had said, solely of a handshake.

"I don't want to move you too fast; but I want to move you steadily. I want to keep you active. If I can get you a match, a four rounder, would you be ready in a month's time?"

"Easily," Percival assured him.

"Good! I'll arrange it. Punchy, any objections?"

"None. I ave all the confidence in the world in Percival."

"So do I."

"I told Percival you might 'ave some available digs for him in the area."

"The deal is this," said Derrick, facing Percival. "I have a few buildings on 7th. Street. between B & C, within walking distance. You can do your road work along the East River walkway or Tompkins Park, as you like. In any case, I'll need a superintendent for two of those buildings. If you want the job it's yours. It'll start at the end of the month. The responsibilities are minimal, and there's a stipend to go with it. It'll free you to concentrate on your boxing. What do you say?"

"I can use the apartment 'n some pocket change can't hurt. What 'ave I to lose?"

"The maintenance is simple. Whenever anything comes up you can't handle on your own my agent will attend to it. I'll give you his number and so forth."

Derrick walked Percival around that evening after his workout to show him the location:

"The neighborhood's changing," he noted as they walked, observing the disparate throng of pedestrians moving somnolently along. "It's drawing a lot more students, artist types, hippies and runaways. They're not setting down roots, it's more like they're hiding out from fear of turning into their parents. The turnover of tenants is considerable. Anyway, it keeps me afloat."

The buildings Percival was to attend were across from each other. They were six-story walkups, and his apartment was a first floor walk through – a railroad apartment. There was a small back yard on which the light of day seldom shone, but there was good cross ventilation, there were two bedrooms, a kitchen, dining area, bath and living room, more space than he required. Hence, it would suffice. He accepted the position.

"I'm your man."

"Glad to have you on board," Derrick said. Again, they shook hands.

***

Since he would be leaving Bed-Stuy at the end of the month, and since Punchy's place was well within walking distance of Our Lady Of Victory, Percival thought that before he moved into his new apartment on the Lower East Side, it would be inexcusable not to drop by the rectory to see Dominick and say "Hello." He knew the whereabouts of the church, but only in passing. He had never gone inside. He did not know the majestic structure was as ornate inside as its exterior suggested, adorned with murals that were replicas of some of the greatest religious printings. There were stained glass windows intricately patterned with saints, angels and cherubim, which admitted beams of light. There were three altars, a central one and two side chapels, and, on occasion, three masses would be offered, simultaneously. A school and convent were also cloistered on the grounds.

Percival dropped by the rectory. He asked to see Father Poincare. The housekeeper, a thin, matronly black woman, showed him to the study, it's windows overlooking the front and side gardens of the rectory in which priests often read their breviary. Through the window Percival watched as a priest, deep in contemplation, paced the dying autumnal gardens awash in the brassy, mid-afternoon glow of late October.

Father Poincare swept into the study, as if in a rush, his cassock brushing the floor. Percival had forgotten what a handsome man he was. When Dominick smiled, it cast his thoughts back to the priest's sister, Lisette, and how lovely she was.

"I'm glad you've dropped by. My sister's been half out of her wits with concern. Of course, she saw the article in The Tribune. Julius made sure of that," Dominick said, accepting Percival's hand. "I told her not to worry. That you can take care of yourself. Sit. Sit, please," the priest insisted, taking a chair and facing Percival, rather than ensconcing himself royally, in the monsignor's plush leather chair, behind the cumbersome teak desk. "I've heard that you've

533

returned to the ring and that you were here in Bed-Stuy, but I withheld saying anything to Lisette. I was waiting for this visit."

"Where do you get your information, man?" Percival's face wrinkled in curiosity.

"It's one of the small perquisites of being a confessor; people are always confiding in you for this reason or that. There's not much that goes on within this parish that I don't know of. I'm one of the more popular priests primarily because I'm also black."

"I see. Well, I'll be leaving Bed-Stuy again, shortly."

"Good. Bed-Stuy is like a small town in so many ways."

"I'm beginning to realize."

"I can't talk long. I'm afraid you caught me as I was on my way out on my rounds," said Dominick, drawing back his sleeve and glancing ruefully at the time on his watch. "I've a few hospital calls to make and stops at homes of various parishioners who can't get to church to receive the Eucharist, as well as a wake to attend later. Please come again when I can make time for us to have a proper visit. I'm sorry for the rush."

"Don't apologize Father, I mean, Dominick. I know I dropped by unannounced," Percival said, starting to rise. "But, I'm curious, and I mean, no disrespect," he said glibly. "And ya don't ave to answer me if you'd rather not. I mean you're still a man, a celibate, yes, but a man nonetheless. A good-looking man at that. Tell me, if you don't mind, don't the women come on to you? You must ave urges. In the black Baptist church the minister's usually the biggest cock in the barnyard. Is that so in your church, too?"

Dominick smiled. He did not appear at all offended. "I wish I had more time to answer that," he paused at his seat. "I guess another five minutes can't hurt." With a thoughtful expression on his sculpted face, he said, "You and I *are* bound to be brothers. You and I are brothers. What I now tell you is in the strictest confidence. I've only told my confessors."

"If you'd rather not," said Percival, suddenly embarrassed by the inappropriate nature of his question. He was surprised Dominick would care to respond when, obviously, Percival was only being flip.

"In your case I don't mind. I don't often get the chance to speak outside the functions of my ministerial duties, not since my brother, Rennie. We were able to have such talks. He understood so much. I miss him sorely. His compassion and understanding was a thing on which I often relied. I feel a similar kinship with you, Percival. My sister's intuition speaks volumes, but your spirit recommends you, too. And as you have trusted me, I shall trust that I too can speak to you no less man-to-man.

"I suspect something more to your question than meets the eye. Not being Catholic, and suspicious of men who would sacrifice their sexuality in the service of a remote God, you think it unnatural. Civilization is also unnatural, if you think about it, but we're all invested in it. No, your question cuts to the very core of my manhood and, ultimately, my search for God – my raison d'etre.

"It's a hazard of the work, a condition of being a member of the clergy. In truth, I'm always being tempted by both men and women," he said, soberly. "All parishioners, both men and women, feel free to approach me with all their demons, and so elicit mine in response. I'm afraid I'd realized back in high school that I was as much attracted to boys as to girls. By the time I reached college, and after a handful of failed experiments, I was spurred on in my earlier decision to become a priest because I realized that if I pursued my appetites, a lot of people would be cruelly hurt, both men and women. That included me as well. I'd need to be promiscuous, dissolute and sordid to fulfill my cravings. Therefore, I chose the greater good, and that was to remove myself from the playing field entirely and make my life an offering to God as I had promised myself when a boy. '*And a little child shall lead them,*' is that not what they say?

"If I may anticipate your next question—*have I ever suffered a lapse?* My answer would be no, I've not.' And I have the necessary tenacity, the grain of faith, the faith of a mustard seed, that assures me that I shall not. I think my nature is the way by which God chose to call me to his service. The way might be straight, but the gate less so.

"This priesthood, this service, this cloth, is my way of sublimation. It has always been my life's ambition, falling short of sainthood, to be a decent man. That is something I should, in this brief life span, be capable of. The point is, for me anyway, to be no less honorable. That's the least I can do for all concerned. And this collar is a constant reminder of that to me. It is a vow I intend to keep. For me, this is the way by which I hold my manhood intact. And that's what we're talking here, isn't it?" Dominick said, stoutly. "More so for a man in a cassock, behind a collar.

Percival wavered, shaken that a man, a priest no less, would dare be so frank, so open. He had been moved, in a near religious sense, and, in any event, he'd glimpsed a possible other value for religion. The encounter would leave him with much to consider. He would never be able to say again, with any certitude, what it takes to be a man – a thing of which he had once felt certain. They embraced fiercely, passionately, as would brothers reunited after a long separation.

***

The sun was descending over the tenement rooftops in an incandescent glory, as Percival trudged back to Punchy's brownstone on Hancock Street late that mid-Autumn day. Later that evening he sat at a table to write a long overdue letter of apology to Lisette now away at college. The bitter quarrel and departure that he had had with Gwen had shaken his confidence more than he cared to admit and had left him feeling morally inadequate. His inability to be honest with Gwen when the chips were down had led him to believe he was unworthy of someone with Lisette's character. He felt his involvement with Gwen had sullied him and that his moral precepts, if he had ever had any, were dangling like disemboweled entrails in the sawdust on the floor of a slaughterhouse. But his brief visit with Dominick had convinced him that despite everything, Lisette had remained steadfast in her devotion, clinging to their promise of love that she had not forsaken him and was anxiously waiting word of his well-being. He began,

"Percival Jones

432 E. 7th. St.

NY, NY 10021

Tel# 212-255-0431

"Lisette, my love—if I'm still entitled to call you that— I hold the grains of your memory in my hands fearful lest they slip through my fingers like so much sand in an hourglass. Each grain bespeaks an aspect of you, and while I hope time has not run its course, I don't know why you should still be waiting. These weeks since we've been apart have been traumatic for me; for fear of losing you, but also for the loss of so much else I'd held close, and for which so many have paid highly. I've paid. Paid more than once. And I'm sure, the price is such that, in all probability, I'll pay again.

"If I didn't write sooner it's because I didn't want to upset you. Besides, I didn't know what to say. I would have been trying to say things beyond my capacity. I was grievously heartsick. I had been drummed out of the Panther Party; was trying to find work and to stay off the streets, which means staying with a friend. Something which became overly complicated. The less of which is said the better. Suffice it to say I've been stretched at both ends. If I did not yell uncle it's because the vision of your loveliness sustained me. My silence was not intended to reflect upon my feelings for you. Quite the contrary. My situation was such that I was running gauntlets. I have gained cover for now, if not exactly safe harbor. You can't begin to imagine the pitfalls I encountered on way to writing you this overdue letter of apology.

536

"In any case, I'm back to boxing, doing what few others do so well. In fact, my first professional 'bout will be held a few days after Thanksgiving on November 29th., at Sunny-side Arena. In the meantime, my manager, Derrick Rafkin, who also owns some apartment buildings, has hired me on as a superintendent. I start next Saturday. I'm staying with my trainer, Punchy, for now. I spoke to your brother, Dominick, earlier today. We had a short but revealing visit. He's a surprising fellow. He gave me more than a little to think about. I'll know to appreciate him better from now on. I like him. I like him a lot. He's quite a man. I wish someday to be able to say as much for myself. And, may I ask, how are you? How is school? I look forward to hearing your news.

"If you care to contact me, I can be reached at the above address starting next Saturday, Oct. 29th. I so look to hearing from you.

All my love,

Percival."

The following Saturday, shortly after he had settled into his new rooms he was stretched comfortably on his bed, hands under his head, gazing dreamily off. He was savoring the prospects of a future go at a championship bout when the telephone rang echoing through the near empty rooms, shaking him from his reverie. He climbed lazily out of bed and answered the insistent ring, "'ello?"

"Percival is it you"? asked the sultry voice on the far end.

"Lisette," he sang, "your jus' the person I wanted to hear from."

"Oh, I'm so glad because I was certainly happy to hear from you. I knew you'd write and I looked for your letter every day, twice a day, without fail. How my heart would sink day by day, but when your letter came how it soared. I literally jumped for joy. My friends couldn't believe me I'd been so down till then waiting to hear from you. I just got it the other day and I've been calling this number all day and now you're there and it's oh so good to hear your voice," she prattled on, gleefully. "Am I making any sense? If not tell me, won't you?"

"You're making as much sense as there's sense to be made," he said, feasting on her voice.

"Oh, Percival, I've missed you so much."

"As I've missed you. But tell me about school. How r things?"

"It's been a little shaky, but that's because I've been concerned about you, especially after I'd read that terrible article. Julius sent me a copy thinking I'd have second thoughts, no doubt. Well I did and realized just what a louse he really is. I never thought he'd stoop so low. I know he thought he'd destroy us and that I'd run into his arms, but what it did was frighten me dreadfully and gave me to know how deeply bound I am to you. I could just detest him for it."

"Well don't brood over it."

"I won't now."

"Good."

"But he was a longtime friend," Lisette added. Percival bit his lip. "Dominick figured you'd gone underground for a spell; that you would be all right and resurface in due course, and here you are."

"I'm not fully over it, but it's in the past."

"Tell me, Percival, what are you doing for Thanksgiving?"

"I've no plans as yet."

"Why not join me and my family upstate for the holiday weekend?"

"I don't think I can swing it being so close to my fight 'n all."

"Oh," she sounded disappointed.

"Is there any way I can talk you into coming here?"

"Is there," she yelped, gleefully. "I'd like that even more."

They talked awhile longer, then Lisette had to go to surrender the phone to a roommate. "Let's stay in touch over the next few weeks."

"'N months 'n years," he said, laughing.

"Remember I love you," she whispered, confidentially.

"It'll rock me to sleep nights," he replied. "Till next time."

"Next time it is," she concurred, ringing off.

**

Slowly Percival adjusted to his new environment and came to know the problems of the two apartment buildings he was tending, along with their occupants. The Lower East Side was legendary, of course, but he was a Brooklyn boy and had only ventured into this area at night to go dancing at "The Electric Circus" or "Fillmore East" for Rock music. "The Five Spot" and "Rafakies," were two favorite Jazz haunts. He had never taken time before to prowl the narrow corridors and ferret out the unseemly treasures, which were embodied in the diversity of the areas dark ethnicity. There were more than five tongues spoken on the streets of Alphabet City. It was easy to feel as if one had become lost in an exotic hellhole with an occasional oasis strewn here and there. The building's older tenants— Russians, Ukrainians, Lithuanians and Polish Jews— were among the most abrasive and demanding. The students, artists, hippies and runaways, were of a different breed. Because they were usually late with the rent, they seldom complained, but the old tenants felt they had, over their thirty or forty years of residency, paid for the building a few times over, and were therefore deserving of deferential treatment.

The job of stacking the garbage, keeping the halls clean, sweeping the walk, attending to the small problems that came up was not terribly time consuming and left him with a good amount of time on his hands before going to the gym, much of which he occupied by reading. Therefore, to help fill the remainder of his day, he bought a heavy bag and as he was taking it to the basement a young boy, a tenant's kid's, asked if he could he help. Percival accepted the offer and together they lugged the bag down the cellar steps to the basement.

"You a boxer or something?" the boy asked.

"Yes, I am."

"Are you any good."

"The best!"

"Why ain't I heard of you, then?"

"Don't worry, you will."

"So, that's why you run in the morning, huh?"

"That's why."

"Can you show me how to box?"

"Would you like to learn?"

"Sure would. Would you teach me? I want'a beat someone up bad."

"Oh? N who might that be?"

"My father," said the unkempt boy, openly, his black, cow like eyes filled with despair.

"Really?"

The boy shook his head fervently.

"Why? He's never around far as I can see."

"That's why. And when he comes home he always makes my mom cry. He takes her money and leaves us hungry."

"What's ya name?"

"Jonas Sapistano."

"You're Italian?"

"My father is, but my mother's Jewish."

"All right, Jonas. If your mother says so, I'll teach you to box. The manly art of self-defense," Percival agreed, ruffing the boy's hair.

Happy that someone would take an interest in Jonas, Mrs. Sapistano agreed and Percival began teaching him the fundamentals of boxing. In turn, Jonas became devoted to him and, bit by bit, Percival came to learn the family's story. They were on welfare assistance. Mrs. Sapistano, the former Riva Horowitz, a tarnished beauty, was still quite lovely. But for the thread of

539

religious convictions to which she cleaved life had played her cheap. She wore a brooding, racial melancholia like a shroud. And the light, which had once shone in her proud young face, her onyx eyes, had since cowed and faded with so many dreams and schemes. Younger by far than Gwen, she was in her prime, 33, but not half so well-tended.

As the saying goes, "Out from the fire and into the flames."

She had been a child bride, as her husband, Tony Sapistano had, been a child groom. She was of Russian/Jewish extraction and he, Italian/Catholic. Neither side of the two families had wanted the union but since she was pregnant the grooms side relented. Riva's side, particularly her father, was intransigent and would not yield, and when she went ahead and married against his wishes, he disowned her. He cut her from the clan like blood grudgingly given. He told her she was dead to them. Although knowing full well who their grandparents on their mother's side were, the children had never been formally introduced, despite the fact they would encounter them on the streets and in the neighborhood ethnic shops. Eventually Riva had a child, a son, Tony Jr., and now, at seventeen, as nattily clad as a well turned out pimp, he ran wild. He didn't like Percival or the influence he was having on Jonas and would glower at him in passing.

Mrs. Sapistano was weepy over her eldest son, always pleading with him to stay off the streets, to not follow after his father's example. When that failed, she'd beg, "Don't stay out too late, you hear?"

"OK, ok, ok," he'd say, edging his way out the door, scrambling down the stairs, not to slow down again until he was on the street and well out of range of her voice.

All the girls thought him "fly" as he pranced by – well on the way of becoming a ladies man.

Percival had encountered Jonas' father, Mr. Sapistano, on several occasions. He was a surly but good-looking man— definitely a ladies man—, well kept, if only in a seedy sort of way, and though he didn't appear drunk exactly, his eyes always had a vengeful glassiness to them. He was a bookie, a pimp, an overall smalltime hustler, and was rumored to have had a second family. Blind to his faults, Riva would hear nothing against him— her beloved Tonio. She would welcome his infrequent visits with caresses and kisses, like a new love. She would sit him down, remove his shoes, scatter the children, run into the bathroom to comb and brush her hair and make herself as alluring as when he had seduced her at age fifteen. The last of her three children had been conceived on such a visit. If she were lucky he would remain a few days grow restless, ask if she had any money, take what little she had left of her welfare check, and leave. During these visits, Jonas had come to ask Percival if he could stay with him, since no one seemed to care where he was.

Thanksgiving was quickly approaching and Percival was getting the apartment ready for Lisette's arrival as well as preparing for his first professional fight. Derick frequented the gym more often of late. He enjoyed watching Percival work as did the whole gym.

"He looks damn good," Derrick said. "He looks ready for a championship go."

"No doubt when the time comes," said Punchy coyly, smiling. "He will be."

"That's all I meant."

"I know what you meant. I've played cards with you."

"I was only saying –"

"I know what you're saying, but do you see what I'm saying?" Punchy asked, observing in Percival's near flawless fight the wrinkles, which needed be ironing out before a championship bid was conceivable.

Derrick yielded the point.

One of Percival's neighbors, Ashton Croft, from across the hall, was a freelance journalist. He had escaped induction into the military because of a debilitating disease from which he had not fully recovered and the pallor of which suffused his gaunt, boyish face and wan, gray eyes. He had traveled extensively in Europe for a few years hoping to facilitate his recovery, spending time at a Swiss sanatorium, and trying to retrace the footsteps of Hemingway's Movable Feast as well as other such notables of the "Lost Generation." He had fallen in and out of love and finally, homesick, packed it in and returned to the states to pursue the migrating herd to the Lower East Side. Though he was not a runaway, Hippie, student or artist, he was a lost soul and, at present, floundering.

"I'm all of twenty-eight, but here I am, a graduate of Stanford, among all these misfits, trying to put the pieces of my life together," Ashton said theatrically. "I suppose as romantic as Europe is, it was like looking through a glass darkly.

"I eventually became lost in Europe, estranged, disenchanted even. Coming back to the states, I feel no more welcome than any of the many soldiers who go without thanks on returning home from that godless war they fight in Vietnam. While I oppose the war, I do sympathize with the soldiers, their plight, their blind patriotism."

"You're not alone in that," Percival agreed.

"And still Europe burns in my imagination like a mirage on the Sahara."

541

"I know the feeling," Percival said, as they visited in his sparsely furnished rooms. "I was in Europe, too, stationed there in the Army."

"You're also black. I should think you'd have an entirely different relationship to Europe?"

"I suppose. Yet there's that unsettling feeling of crumbling splendor. If you think about it percentage wise anyway, as many black American artists, as white, set sail for Europe more than any other single port of call. What might the attraction be?"

"Apart from the fact that all roads lead to Rome? I wouldn't know."

"That 'n the sad fact that we're all lost on the yellow brick road. Europeans 'r at home in Europe, as Africans 'r at home in Africa, but here in the United States, both blacks 'n whites 'r restless in their skin—itching to get out."

"Well if the truth be told," Ashton went on, "I went to Europe to find something of myself, some missing part of my being, the vital-élan. Innocence, maybe? With ill health came a desire for repentance. I confess, it's much like Nietzsche says: 'The world must be empty for him who has never been unhealthy enough for this infernal voluptuousness. Indeed, it is imperative to employ a mystic formula for the purpose.' And so, you see, I was sick and I'm still in recovery. This alone allows me my insight. At times my illness illuminates my mind like a lamp at full heat. Its only drawback is I can't see beyond the veil of love, the density of which love is too thick for mortal eyes to behold.

"Anyway, I wished to make contact with the source from which my ancestors were uprooted. The leaves of the pages from which my life was torn. I'm sure you understand having lost so much of your inheritance in the worst possible way. And the loss we Whites feel as a result of our having left Europe, uprooted, then rudely transplanted, outweighs the gains. It may be because, unlike blacks, we retain more than a vestigial memory of our homelands. I've heard it said, 'I have no people, as if I came from nowhere and nowhere is where I am.' Europe calls like a Siren's song. Many Europeans caught up in the intolerance of the reformation and inquisition came here to get away, escape their tormentors, distance themselves from their past, their heritage, believing it to be of no great value. All too sadly, the loss was immeasurable. Their culture was as rich as it was stifling—"

"In turning from their homelands," Percival cut in, "'n crossing the Atlantic, they lost their identities, too, 'n became 'white'?"

"In that crossing they ceased to be Europeans and became a 'color.' Much as in the same way Africans became 'black' and were forced into slavery. Yes, so it was, Africans became 'black' in order for European emigres to become 'white.' You know, of course, this all comes out of Calvinist, Puritan, fundamentalism, out of which Manifest Destiny sprang."

"In that crossing, color was born, 'n turned their religious problems into a racial thing," said Percival casually. "'Black' and 'white' came to mean a loss of cultural 'n historical identity—the former stolen, 'n the latter abandoned."

"Cultures are like perishable goods they don't travel well."

"And the worst elements in them turn up when they do."

"Comme ci comme ca." Ashton shrugged.

"The oppression they fled they soon inflicted on those who had had no hand in their infelicity."

"That's the tragedy of the story."

"As such, the Americas became a safety valve for the crown heads of Europe; a means by which they could get rid of their undesirables."

"That's why the revolution took place here, and not there."

"You've considered this, I see."

"I'm an American, a white American, and given the present cultural milieu, how could I not? In fact, I'd thought of becoming part of the civil rights movement before heading for Europe, but my health was such I couldn't handle it."

Percival said, "For yourself, however, you make it sound like an orphan mourning the loss of his surrogate grandmother more than that of his birth mother?"

"Well said," Ashton conceded, chagrinned. "But when all is said and done, America is more a foster home for foundlings than a home in which we have roots. Indeed, we have barely scratched the surface."

"That's because blacks were the one's tilling the soil 'n whites the ones reaping the harvest! So, as you can imagine, I'm of two minds on that score."

"Yes, America owes you more than it can easily repay. In that your plight is similar to the Jews pursuant to the fall of the Roman Empire and ascent of Christendom which, in our 20th century, resulted in the holocaust."

"You've raised two separate points. But if by that you mean, 'Me thinks my lady protest too much?' Yes, I catch your drift," Percival voiced. "Patriotism makes fools of the best of us 'n, no doubt, the end result can be catastrophic."

Ashton smiled wanly. "Somehow I thought you might see my point. It goes to the heart of what I've borne witness in feverish states of delirium –"

"Go on, " Percival urged.

"We think patriotically of America as our nation. A nation we would kill and die for, murder for. Native peoples, on the other hand, think of it as their homeland—the soil out of which they sprang, belong, and are anchored. A land that at our hands they have mostly died for. The question is, how do you build a nation worthy of trust on another people's land, then presume to call it a republic of virtue? Small wonder we are, as a nation, in such difficult straits," he added with a shake of his head. "Such unwarranted a theft complicates the matter utterly. And tramples every word of decency uttered in our constitution. It makes liars of us. And our lives a fraud. 'The Odyssey,' marks the origins of civilized man, of whom Odysseus, 'a liar, trickster and self-deceiver,' is the archetype. In a word, an egotist, and is the hero of Homer's epic poem. It's the equivalent of our 'New Testament,' if you will, and the 'Iliad' our old. It makes for a great read. Along with my health I've suffered a loss of faith; not in God but in politics; not in man, but his reason. There's a moral declivity off which we've slipped. I for one feel adrift, not so unlike the hapless Flying Dutchman without a port at which to drop anchor."

"Which Hitler referred to as 'The Big Lie!'"

"And which he put to the most diabolical use."

"America having set the standard."

"As James Joyce put it, 'History is a nightmare from which we're all trying to waken.'" Ashton then hastily added.

"Sounds to me like you're up a tree."

Ashton threw up his hands in exasperation. "I'm up in the air with it all, anyway. 'Trying,' as the hippies say, 'to find myself,'" he said. "The past is relived in the present. For that reason it's well we revisit it from time to time, as one would visit the grave of a loved one to place flowers. As an investigative journalist history is both my occupation and avocation. I'm of the opinion that our revolution should have been fought on European soil, and there, the rights of man established. We evolved out of the soil of Europe; its cultural milieu. It was ours to call home. To fight for. To live, love or die for. It is the location of our belonging. We have no roots here of which to boast. We're off kilter here, and the world's thrown off course." To emphasize his point, he broke into a popular Neil Young song, "'Look at mother nature on the run in the nineteen seventies –' Percival was surprised at Ashton's good singing voice. "The consequent result of the French revolution, despite its mishaps, was to bring us into 'the modern age,' as Goethe observed. The age of Man. Man as an individual.

"We know the ' individual' is the corner stone of Christianity and yet it took the Church and crown Heads of Europe another millennia and a half, after the death of Christ, to acknowledge it; afraid, no doubt, of losing their heads, sans crowns. And lose their heads they did – long after so many had defected, fled Europe to escape a life of mindless subjugation to both Church and State. As a result of the Age of Reason, the wheels of the state were brought to a grinding halt by the revolutionary fervor of the masses, weighted down by a feudal system that had chained them to a life of drudgery. Cast aside the age-old faith-based doctrine of the Divine Right of Kings – the distant father as opposed to God, the absent father – they chose, to establish direct rule by law.

"We recognize the tragic results of the French revolution in relative contrast to the success of our American one. Anyway, we like to think so," Ashton said, drily. "The mistakes the French made are forgivable because it was on their land and did not destroy an innocent, whole other people in the process. At the end of the day, there are just not enough apologies to go around. For every stone in the temple of civilization, the blood and brains of the younger generation, particularly it's son's, is required sacrifice." Ashton was adrift in thought. "Sadly, in not having our revolution there – and the wrongful bloodletting of this country's native peoples here – we lost stock in our Christian heritage, a map of ourselves, our psyche, thus, we suffer from a collective national guilt. It was a crime of unpardonable proportion. And our city skyscrapers, which Freud mistook for phallic symbols are, in fact, headstones, monuments to the crimes committed against its native peoples in our obtaining this misbegotten land. A feeble, subconscious attempt at atonement on our part to recognize the sins committed against these luckless first nation people at our hands."

"You suggest this country of ours was born of the blood of Abel, 'n bears the mark of Cane?"

"You look like I'm raving?" Ashton blushed.

"Not so much as you might think," Percival responded. "It's just that I'm unaccustomed to a white person, particularly a white man, being so candid." He smiled, bemused. "In fact, I'd thought the truth to be a well-kept secret from white people; but here you turn out to be the honest man for whom Diogiones spent his life searching the streets of ancient Athens."

"I'm happy to be able to amuse you," Ashton retorted.

"No! Quite frankly, I find it refreshing. An honest white man." Percival laughed. "How quaint." He was experiencing the truth as he'd not known it, and found it disturbing, especially when considering its unlikely source.

"It's not for me to apologize," Ashton stated.

"Far be it for me to expect you to," Percival said.

"I mean, I can't apologize even for myself."

"It's far too late anyway, I'm sure."

"And far too much water under the bridge," said Ashton, his face crimson.

"Besides, people embrace their faults much the same way they secretly enjoy their own farts, but not those of others," Percival said.

"A crude but apt observation, if ever I heard one."

"It's a frightful thought."

"Perhaps," Ashton said with a dismissive toss of his hand. "I'm made more aware of it because of my ill health – and the ongoing fevers to which I succumb, which affords me a crystal gaze. Yet, ongoing to Europe, I found that the Europeans don't have it certainly not to give – a spirit of belonging; of self. A baptism. The epiphany I sought, the spirit of which I speak, the Apollonian spirit, is a Greek world view passed on to Europe, but could not survive passage across the Atlantic, no more than has the fabled Spirit of Christianity. A delusion under which the Church labors. And spiritual life is, I found, of absolute necessity. It's all that saved me from myself and a solitary game of Russian roulette. I'd considered it seriously, gun in hand, in Paris, after a love affair gone sour with a married woman of prominence. She fondly called me, 'My sweet gigolo.' I was no such thing. I was her lover, not her gigolo – sweet or otherwise," he said, rankled. "That was her way of putting me off. I would have died for her. Well, in fact, I almost did. I've heard said, and my experiences verify it, that 'through one's wounds the soul enters the body.'"

"Yes. I can see that."

"Before leaving for Europe the sports editor of The Herald Tribune, for whom I'd done some copy, wrote glowing letters of introduction on my behalf to numerous persons in various European capitals in which I'd planned to stay. As it was, the affair of which I speak occurred in Paris. Where else? I presented one of the letters of introduction to an editor of a Paris daily, "Le Figaro," and I was immediately admitted into some of the city's finer circles. The women were kind, especially Francoise, to whom I was immediately drawn. She dazzled me with her charm and sophistication. And over time we became lovers. She sympathized with me, nursed me, toyed with me. She intoxicated me. Enchanted me. I became lost in her. She was a woman of vast experience. Until Francoise, I'd only known girls. She was sagacious, sanguinary, and hungry in a way I'd never known a woman to be hungry before. When she'd leave our bed, she took my soul with her. And I would follow her to the toilet, or wherever, for fear I might otherwise perish.

"It's only fair to say, in Francoise's defense, that she had warned me. In not so many words, you see, as in ways, that she would break my heart. She reminded me often that she was a married woman of standing and had her husband's reputation to consider. I paid little heed to her warnings, however. I've mentioned that on occasion I attain a crystal gaze, but love is a corner round which you can't see, Cupid aims his arrow, hits his mark and the poison seeps into one's blood with fatal remorse. Or so the Greeks thought. Anyway, I'm still sucking out poison left in me from the affair, but I'd gladly drink from that cup of sorrow again if allowed. I took no precaution and in time she did as she said she would. She left me, unannounced, stranded, and all the doors formerly opened to me, shut. I felt myself the gay fool, used and dashed aside – brokenhearted and never more callow. I could not have felt more stupid. A young, ignorant American, heart bitten with lust. I was young. I was never more young if twenty-six can be called young." He grimaced.

"Put me down for a hopeless romantic. Europe creates a climate for ill-fated lovers and suicides alike with its many gothic cathedrals, ancient graveyards and ruins wherever you turn. The promise of romance. It has, as you remember, a mausoleum like quality. And for one as susceptible as I, at the time, it called like a song of mandolins, which were played on the streets by Gypsies everywhere. I was melancholic to begin with – sick as I was and lost. And Francois' rejection of me was the final straw. I withdrew into myself, gun in hand, trying to work out my last thoughts when I turned to Plato, The Republic. A particular thought struck me, caught my eye, and resonates with me still, 'Care of the Soul is more important than the care of the body.' It gave me pause and I recalled the words of Jesus: 'What profits it a man to gain the whole world and to lose his soul?' I was swayed to drop the gun, to take another look. Socrates' willingness to down the hemlock, and Jesus going to the cross on that score was, for me, the turn around. Why could I not try and see if, as in the words of Emily Dickinson,

"My life closed twice before it close; it yet remains to see if immortality unveil a third event to me, so huge, so hopeless to conceive as these that twice befell parting is all we know of heaven and all we need of hell.'"

Ashton's story telling powers were not lost on Percival and, much like a child spellbound by a good campfire tale, he was delighted, seated on the edge of his chair – transfixed.

"Why should I abdicate my life so easily, so early on?" Ashton went on. "On what account? The throw of the dice? The spin of a wheel? Yes, I'm sick but I'm in recovery. I opted to return to the States and see where it all leads. You can say I gained an awakening, a baptism of a kind, as did Hemingway when Gertrude Stein told him he was among a lost generation of Americans who'd come back to Europe far too late. There, too, I came to discover, as did he, no doubt, the face of the *Ugly American* as my own. That was the only revelation Europe had to offer.

"Is it any wonder that on my return I chose to lose myself on the Lower East Side among a disparate pool of immigrants, social rejects, hippies, misfits, and run-a-ways? A vain attempt to forget the 'Sins of our fathers,' rather than go straight home on return. When going down on your knees in prayer you first have to know what to ask God forgiveness for; in this instance, the crimes of our forefathers under the shadow of whose sins we live." He sighed heavily. "What's that song Bob Dylan sing?" 'How does it feel to be on your own scrounging for your next meal; to be without a home, a complete unknown, like a rolling stone?' Here on the Lower East Side that feeling is up for grabs on every corner of every street you pass." He rolled his eyes. "'The son of Man,' as Jesus put it, 'has no place to rest his head,'" Ashton said, tonelessly, the jaundice pallor of his face a sickly hue in the room's pale light. "It's a tragedy that we've ceased to trust our experience, ourselves, and rely solely on what we read in the papers.

"In any case, I was reluctant to look over my shoulder for fear of turning into a pillar of salt – hence our nation's restlessness. An uneasiness with our identity. And while I was homesick, it was not so much for the States as for the grave. Death haunts me. I carry it everywhere I go. It's become my constant companion. What I found in Europe, I confess, was a weariness of spirit. It having been bled white with one war after the other over the centuries till it's become anemic, if not spiritually barren, and is only now crawling its way out from the ashes. Ergo Sartre's bleak play, 'No Exit.' On the other hand, we, here in America, may not have bled ourselves bone white, but our souls are no less sullied as a consequence of the crimes committed in obtaining this misbegotten land."

"Yet, here you are."

"Here I am."

"Despite it all we must forge ahead," Percival said, archly.

"Whatever it was, it no more exists for Europeans than it does for us. As such they've come to see us as the new world; the promise of things to come – while we suffer, differently."

"Sad but true," Percival said, bleakly.

"All too sad," Ashton remarked. "I realize as we speak that, I would not have spoken to a black person, or anyone else for that matter, as I speak to you now. I had neither distance nor perspective by which to do so before going to Europe. And I could not have had it had it not been for both my illness, which colored my frame of mind, and my having toured Europe. The combination of the two gave me an uncommon view of the world and, more particularly, our country. I can safely say I came to know myself for an ugly American gone to Europe in hopes of a redemption that's not to be found."

"Now you're back."

"Yes, I'm back. When the chips were down, I had nowhere else to turn."

"'The streets of America 'r paved with gold,'" Percival said. "For us too, I suppose. I recall so many Europeans saying as much."

"Well, they got part of it right. The streets are paved," said Ashton. "All but a few want to come here while the others see us as l'enfant terrible." He sighed. "In any case, I'm going home for the holidays," he said, holding Percival's gaze. "Would you keep an eye on my apartment while I'm gone?"

"Sure enough. But you've not told me, Ashton, where 'r you from? I mean, where do you call home?"

"I was raised in South Dakota, Indian country, Sioux territory, near the foot of the Black hills. The Sioux's sacred burial ground, with which they're in contention with our government, still," Ashton stated. "I was raised to view Indians as relics from the past, the disappeared –"

"Yes, I know, I feel them all around," Percival interjected.

"You sense their presence, also?"

"Yes. Their Spirit's haunting. It overshadows us like a curse – the nation as a whole."

"As a child I'd see them in town and view them like lost spirits, damned by fate," Ashton continued. "I'm now ashamed to say I knew a few by name, but none to speak to. Only a begrudging "Hi" would pass my lips from time to time. Sometimes, in bed, I'd hear them from the reservation chanting their ghost song as they danced all night. Their chants would drift over the land, for miles, like the wail of coyotes; calling their Gods down, The Great Spirit down, their ancestors to revenge the wrongs done them. Their Ghost/Dance is a counter theme to our "God Bless America," he laughed. "There is no more eerie a mournful song you can imagine. It often unsettled me, in my bones, as a boy growing up."

"You have an unusual sympathy for native American people," Percival said.

"We do not talk about them, and they need to be spoken of. If we are to know ourselves, we must speak of them and what we did to them; to know our past if ever we are to become whole again. Their story is our story, there is no escaping it. You can't hope to understand American history if you don't know the part Native Americans played in that story. The price they paid. It's pivotal! Much like an old refrain, they haunt my reverie." He sighed. "They have no reason to love us. And, needless to say, they don't. Who dare fault them? And so they will continue to dance and sing that way until the edifice of our existence crumbles at their feet."

"Do you believe that?" asked Percival.

"Look at us. Poised to blow ourselves off the face of the earth. How can I not?"

"You sound disillusioned."

"Disillusioned? No, it's the nature of the beast. Much too much of our culture has, all too sadly, proven itself a cul-de-sac. The human condition. We've grown our brains to fill our craniums, yet we use less than 3% of it –"

"It's embarrassing when seen that way," Percival conceded.

"– and the other 97% is a void – a wasteland."

"Are you going to South Dakota, then?" he asked."

"No. My parents came to see the light and relocated to Cape Cod where we will gather for the holidays. From Indian territory to Puritan New England – the founders of the feast, so to speak." Ashton laughed, unaccustomed to the practice of late.

"Yet people stay."

"And they are why we fight in Vietnam."

"How so?"

"They sincerely believe God would not have given them superior arms by which to defeat the Indians had he not intended them to hold on to the land."

"Is that so?"

"To be sure."

"Alas!"

Ashton then went on to say, "Every time I go home of late I feel more lost, as if I'm a black sheep and they're all judging me for not measuring up – they have, so why haven't I?" He splayed his hands sadly, and there appeared a faint gleam in his eyes, a distant sorrow. He was, as a consequence of his long illness, given to a morbid, melancholic turn of mind. "They treat me like it's my own fault; as if my disease had nothing to do with it. My sister's a tenured professor. My brother's VP of a corporation, and my folks have their own ad agency," he lamented. "While, at best, I'm only a wandering journalist, which, in their eyes, is worse than a wandering Jew. They feel a certain insecurity around me, like I'm contagious."

"I can dig it, bro. But, in that case, why bother going home?"

"Identity," Ashton explained. "Something to substantiate my existence before the grave. Often while in Europe I'd felt romantically close to death, especially as I'd stroll those haunted old cobbled back streets alone. It's family. They call to me like salmon bucking up stream. It's who you are when all else fails, where you turn when the chips are down."

"I see."

"Of course, it might be like stagnant water— it reflects poorly but it's the only view available."

Percival was silent, a pang of remorse tweaked his heart. "Or drown you," he said, bitterly.

"Enough of that," said Ashton, changing subjects. "I'm looking forward to seeing you fight."

"I'm growing anxious myself."

"Your girl comes tomorrow, doesn't she?"

"I'll pick her up at Grand Central round one o'clock."

"I'm off tonight so I won't have a chance to meet her this time."

"In the near future, then."

"Well, I have to go and pack."

***

The train was late. Percival was becoming anxious. He had spoken to Lisette the previous night, shortly after Ashton had dropped his keys off and left for Nantucket. She was looking forward to being with him in the city. "So, where is the train?" he asked at the information desk. The arrival gate was flooded with an influx of disembarking passengers. He breathlessly scanned all the faces searching among them for Lisette's. As she came into view through the gate in a cluster of new arrivals, he waved and called, "Lisette!" never more glad to see anyone.

She, in turn, saw him, gasped, and, eyes stalling, dropped her luggage and dashed into his arms. They clung to one another swaying, fearful lest some mishap tear them apart. "Oh, Percival," she murmured, near tears.

"You're here," he said, choking with emotion.

Their lips found each other's and then, in a swoon, they drank each other in with their eyes. She was dressed in earth tones, her hair was drawn back from her toffy colored face by a scarf — just as he had last seen her, but it struck him that she was even more lovely, if that were possible. Her eyes were as bright as dew drops, and her face was flush with the bloom of youth and love.

She looked at him with her dark, luminous eyes, eyes that roused him, drawing him out of himself, as from his inner core. Her smile widened, and a flame pierced his heart.

He blinked, breaking the spell, remembering where they were and the crowd that swirled around them. "Let's not jus' stand round holding traffic up. Let's grab your bags 'n catch a cab."

"It's your town. Lead on."

She took his hand, their lips brushing in a light kiss. They then collected her things and went out to flag a cab.

"This is the Big Apple, is it?" she mused, gazing out on the city, as the cab raced down Lexington Avenue navigating the heavy stream of traffic.

"You've not been to the city before?"

"No, I've not."

"You've not seen Dominick's church either?"

"Never. But, if you don't mind, I'd like to go for Sunday mass. I spoke with him and mentioned that I'd be in town with you and he hopes to see us both."

"That's fine by me. It'll be a pleasure to see your brother again."

"Then that's settled."

Jonas was waiting on the front stoop when they arrived. "Hi, Percival's girl," he called, as she stepped out of the cab.

Lisette spun around. "Well, hello," she said, liltingly, her eyes emitting a liquid light. "And who are you, may I ask?" She set a petite foot on the steps and, blithely sizing him up, stretched out a hand.

"I'm Jonas, Percival's running buddy. He's my trainer," the boy claimed, taking her hand and shaking it stiffly, surprised at how firm a grip she had.

"Is that so?" said Lisette. "Well it's a pleasure to make your acquaintance, Jonas. I'm Lisette."

"I know. Percival told me. You're real pretty," he observed.

"It's kind of you to say so."

"Ya got a strong grip for a girl."

"I'm a farm girl."

"Yes, Jonas is my main man," said Percival, starting up the steps, baggage in hand. "How r you, dude?"

"I'm ok, coach. Need a hand?"

"Can you get the door?"

"Sure thing." Jonas raced to hold the door.

Lisette entered the foyer. "Thanks, Jonas," she said.

Percival entered the building behind her, lowered the luggage and unlocked the apartment door to his left. He escorted her in. She slowly scanned the freshly painted, sparsely furnished front room. The blinds were drawn not so much to stanch the flow of light, which was nil, as to conceal the ugly, protective burglar gates that covered the windows fronting the street.

She raised her eyes to his. "Mind if I look around?" He lifted his eyes in compliance. She ventured through the other rooms, peered out a window onto the noise filled airshaft where an array of conflicting radio and T.V. broadcasts seems to air their differences. Next she stepped out in the back yard, where she could barely stretch her arms without touching the neighboring buildings. She said, "So this is the Lower East Side?" she said. "It has a certain seedy allure— a dark influence. I'll bet, this apartment is a story in itself. Do you know anything about it?" Percival felt as if it were a condemnation. "But it definitely has possibilities." She shrugged, 'Which is our bedroom?" she said, gaily.

552

"The one with the bed," he said, wistfully. "We'll ave to share it or I can sleep on the floor in the other room, if you like."

She looked at him in rebuke. "Don't be silly," she said, "of course we'll share the same bed." She threw her arms about his neck and kissed him on the mouth. "You do want me, don't you?"

"More than anything," he acknowledged. "But I wanted no misunderstandings either."

"If there were, you'd have brought me down here under false pretenses," she said, as an amused look crept over her face. "There's no misunderstanding. Now, where exactly is our bedroom?" she said with buoyancy, in full possession of her womanhood.

After she had unpacked her belongings, perfuming the bedroom with the essence of her femininity, Percival invited her to go with him to the gym. She was as excited to see him train as she was to take a second look at the city from the street. She had not come to New York City to sit alone in a drab apartment. She had come to the city to be with him, her man, Percival, and she had every intention of spending as much time in his company as the next few days would allow. Her mind was set on that score.

The only thing wrong with his place she thought, casting a backward glance over the rooms as they left, was that they required a woman's touch – her touch, more specifically. She had been afraid on coming to the city to find that he was sufficient unto himself. She was greatly relieved to find that, as competent as he was, he needed her; needed and loved her as much as she loved and wanted him.

They strolled hand in hand through the grim, narrow, cheerless confines of the Lower East Side and wended their way through its side streets to the busy, wider corridor of 14th. Street where the afternoon sun came down the crosstown roadway, exposing to view much that lurked beneath the City's underbelly. They passed a glut of bargain basement stores strung together end to end like the redlight district of a trailer park, competing with the avenue streetwalkers. On occasion, a garishly clad prostitute would approach a car that had slowed to a stop, negotiate with the driver, then climb into the car. Lisette found it all fascinating in a bizarre way. It was nothing she'd ever seen in Saratoga. There was a perverse element where, at bottom, lurked the grotesque.

The street was as filthy as a banquet hall left in squalor after a night of debauchery. People were dressed as if entire wardrobes had been obtained off the back of a truck. The word "Tinsel Town" could easily have been coined for many a Manhattan street, including 14th. Street.

Lisette was glad she had come along.

"This bears scrutiny," she said, gawked, utterly fascinated, taken in by the street. "It's absolutely fantastical," she exclaimed, thrilled.

"You ain't seen the half'a it," he chortled.

Secure in his company and proud to be on the streets of New York City with him, she was undismayed.

"It's quite a spectacle."

"Not so much as you might think," Percival said, reflecting on 42nd. Street, midtown. "Though you're right, it bears scrutiny. Here we 'r," he announced, pushing in the door to the Gramercy Park Gym.

Lisette's jaw slackened when she saw the daunting flight of stairs confronting them, appearing as if to go up and up, into the void of a darkened attic above. "My god," she uttered, "climbing these stairs must be a workout in itself."

"That was my response on first seeing em, too," Percival laughed. "Since there's no elevator, there's no way past it."

They climbed the steep flight of stairs to the gym: The gym was as noisy as a city street under construction. The staccato rat-tat-tat of speed bags, the repetitive slap of twirling jump ropes striking the floor, and the rancid smell of pugs laboring under the watchful eyes of their trainers, assaulted her. The trainers barked, "Stick! Stick! Stick!" And heavy bags sagged under a barrage of blows by sweaty men and boys in pursuit of a payday, a championship, a near impossible dream. Then at one- and three-minute intervals, a bell tolled the rounds.

If she had been disoriented on the streets, she was even more so now: Not so unlike a gladiatorial school, it was a world apart. A world of men. The cruel, often vicious expressions on savage, sweat covered faces startled her, left her queasy.

He escorted her to the viewers stand overlooking the street below, and introduced her to Punchy and Derrick, who had been awaiting his arrival. He left Lisette in their care while he went to the locker room to change.

"Are you a fight fan?" Punchy asked.

"Not till now. In fact, this is my first visit to a gym," she said, her eyes flitting over the gym, taking in every detail. "Though my father and brother are fans."

When Percival emerged from out the locker room, Punchy joined him on the floor and Derrick moved over to sit beside Lisette. He ran his eyes slowly up her tapered, well-made legs to her bare knees and followed the lap of her skirt up to the imperceptible rising and falling of her full breast beneath her blouse. He drank in the sharp, Latin features of her profile and caught his breath. She was startlingly pretty. She could be devil or angel and he wanted to know which of the two she was.

She barely noticed Derrick. She focused solely on Percival. He was shaking out, warming up, and conversing with Punchy. After working up a sweat he climbed into the ring. Punchy gloved him up, adjusted his headgear, rinsed out his mouthpiece and set it in place. Then an-up-and-coming light heavyweight, Johnny James, entered the ring from the opposite corner.

"Why is that guy so much bigger?" she asked Derrick, near panicked.

"Watch and see," said Derrick, rolling his cigar from one side of his mouth to the other.

The bell rang and the two fighters faced off at center ring. Percival laced into James, setting the pace, forcing the fight. He moved with the agility of a big cat. His every movement calculated to surprise. Lisette sat amazed and deeply impressed. He was spectacular, magnificent, she couldn't believe her eyes and, swept away, she looked on trancelike, a schoolgirl charmed by the antics of her boyfriend. Still, a ripple of concern crossed her brow, and she bit her bottom lip.

"What do you think of your boyfriend?" Derrick asked between rounds.

"My fiancé," she corrected.

"Oh? And when is the happy event to occur?"

"We've talked about sometime after I finish school. We don't know. I mean it won't interfere with my schooling. I know we're meant for each other."

"You'll be well off. Percival's bound to make big money."

Nostrils flared, indignant, she gave Derrick a cutting glance. "Excuse me, is your interest in Percival solely monetary?" she said, curtly. "The idea of money never crossed my mind. And I'm a practical girl. When I met Percival, when I fell in love with him, that is, I had no idea he was who he is." She gestured with an outstretched hand toward the ring. "If money were my object, I could easily have married a former beau who has all the money a girl could possibly want."

She winced at a blow that glanced off Percival's head. He rallied with a double hook— one to the body the other to the jaw— followed by a right cross that rocked James on his heels. "I've never seen Percival do this before," she exhaled. "As I was about to say, when I first met Percival – rather, I should say, when I first saw Percival, really saw him for who he is, there was this mischievous, devil may care attitude about him. A certain 'je ne said quoi.'" She kissed the fingers of her hand in an expressive gesture of delight— a rapturous smile alighting her face. "I, at first, found him impudent but charming. With a look all the frat boys were going for with various degrees of success; but Percival carried it off with a nonchalance that proved intriguing, causing me to take a closer, second look. And as I saw the man beyond the trappings, I realized that, for the most part, I'd been looking at boys these many years.

"Percival's doesn't pretend to be anyone other than himself." She went on, "Beneath that devil-may-care veneer was someone of substance. A deep and troubled soul lay bare before me, but he bore his pain, his cup of sorrow, with an uncompromising integrity. Like a moth drawn to a flame, his grief, though not mentioned, drew me dangerously close and pierced my defenses. Before I knew it, I'd fallen in love." She brought her hands to her face, aglow with love. "He may not be my ideal, but he is my man for all time to come," she said, emphatically. She blushed, her eyes riveted on Percival as he moved deftly about the ring, using his superior speed and agility to keep the heavier, slower fighter off guard.

"You speak well for yourself."

"Am I under scrutiny?" she asked, sharply.

"In a manner of speaking," Derrick replied. "I was just thinking you seem to know your mind."

She laughed. "On that score, anyway," she agreed. "It's also obvious Percival's been around the block, but it hasn't jaded him or made him unnecessarily bitter. I may sound sentimental and childish, but that's how it is for me."

"Far be it for me to find fault," Derrick said.

"That said, you tell me, is your interest in Percival solely monetary?"

"Now who's cross-examining?" Derrick smiled. "Though we're all in it for the glory, as Percival's manager, I'm also about making money for all concerned. After all, boxing is a business."

"So I hear. Percival says you're a professional gambler. From all appearances a prosperous one, too," she noted, looking the nattily attired gambler up and down.

Yes I am. Are you a business major by chance?"

"No, I'm a Social Anthropologist."

"And where do you attend school?"

"Skidmore College."

"Saratoga Springs."

"You know Saratoga?"

"I go every summer for racing season. It's a lovely little town. Is it your home?"

"My family lives on a farm where my father is foreman."

"Then you know the value of thrift."

"Among other things."

"I'm glad we had this little chat."

"It's been revealing."

"For both of us."

"Thank you."

When the bell to end the sparring rang, Derrick joined Punchy on the floor by the heavy bag on which Percival was starting to work. He removed the stub of a dead cigar from his mouth. "She's okay. She's the real McCoy. Percival's lucked out with this young lady," Derrick said, with admiration in his tone, looking back at her. "If only I were younger."

"If only you wasn't senile," Punchy quipped.

"That too." Derrick chortled.

"If only you're right," said Punchy, stubbornly. "We sure don't want women troubles. They can destroy a good fighter faster than junk. N let me tell you, Percival's had his share."

"She's the genuine article. I'd make book on it."

"I hope you're right. We've got a lot at stake," said Punchy soberly, tossing a towel over his shoulder. "Finish up on the bag 'n exercise out," he called to Percival. "Let's call it a day. Have a good Thanksgiving 'n we'll see you Friday. Don't overindulge yourself. Next Wednesday's fight night don't forget."

"I'll keep tabs on my weight," Percival promised.

"N your other appetites as well," Punchy said, casting a disparaging eye Lisette's way.

Derrick slapped Percival on the shoulder on his way to the locker room. "You and your lady should enjoy yourselves. Have a good holiday. You deserve it. She's as lovely as a rose."

"Thanks Derrick. You ave one yourself."

***

On the way home from the gym Percival and Lisette stopped off to shop for some well needed staples at a few old style East European country stores located on 1st. Avenue. A strong, rich aroma, redolent of herbs, meats and spices, wafted fragrantly on the air throughout the stores. Lisette found the shops delightfully quaint. She was especially struck by the older women's simple, cultural garb, their accents and the multiplicity of tongues, which enriched the neighborhood. Suddenly, she found the East Side less drab and hostile, but made more colorful by the makeup and ethnicity of its parts. She was unaccustomed to seeing such a rich array of people, even on campus – especially not on campus. She exchanged recipes with some of the older

557

women who found her charming and wished to mother her. The grocers went out of their way to be helpful. The butcher would only sell her his best cuts of meat, and the produce man dug fresh fruits and vegetables from cold storage for her sampling. The shopkeepers cordially invited her to return. She was made to feel welcome, for which she was appreciative. As a result, the whole atmosphere took on a less severe aspect.

They had no sooner gotten home and put away the groceries, than Lisette threw her arms about his neck and said with a come-hither coo, "I've been waiting to do this since forever." She kissed him with a hunger that stirred him. She coaxed him into the bedroom, without much difficulty, her body melding itself into his, her nails sinking into his flesh. "The while I watched you sparring, watched the rivulets of sweat run along the contours of your muscles, down the gully of your back, glistening all over your beautiful body, I pictures this— our coming together in a crescendo of love and lust." The back of her knees struck the bed and she toppled backwards onto the mattress, and he fell on top of her.

They dined by candlelight, then stretched out in bed and watched T.V. late into the morning. They made love intermittently and fell asleep only after the network had closed down for the night and the station's test patterns filled the screen.

"You best marry me and make an honest woman of me," Lisette said, coyly before falling asleep.

"I've married you a couple'a times already t'night," he teased. "One more time won't much matter."

"And each and every time was sweeter than the last." She cuddled up to him. "No, I want you to marry me in church, in the sight of God and man, then marry me again in bed afterwards," she impishly urged. "I want us well married and to someday have children."

He turned in her arms and faced her, his brow restless in the light of the T.V. screen. "I'll be happy to, anytime, anywhere." He felt troubled as he had yet to tell her about, Malek, his son.

***

Percival had been invited to Raschelay's for Thanksgiving dinner and was told that he could bring a guest along. Thus, he and Lisette arrived forty-five minutes in advance of the meal, shortly after the other guests had arrived. Raschelay answered the knock. "Percival," she exclaimed, flinging her arms about his neck, taking small notice of Lisette. "It's so good to see you."

He embraced her in turn. "It's good seeing you too."

Then Raschelay looked at Lisette and fell silent. She was instantly jealous. Not so much at Lisette's remarkable beauty which, no doubt rivaled her own, but at her unsullied freshness, a freshness that emanated from her like that of a young child. Lisette's freshness was also Rashelay's a few short months ago, before the rape, the assault that had left her pregnant. In Lisette, she saw all that had been denied her. Contrariwise, and for all those reasons, Raschelay was also irresistibly attracted to her.

Lisette came forward. "You must be Raschelay. I'm Lisette, Percival's fiancée. The way he goes on about you is enough to make a girl jealous. Now I see what he means." They embraced. "We must become good friends."

"I think I'd like that," Rschelay said, impulsively, blushing, absorbed by Lisette's warmth and beauty.

"You have a lot to tell me about Percival."

"Now," said Percival warily, "don't you two go getting too chummy."

Raschelay escorted them into the living room where the others were gathered. Otis Redding's "Dock of the Bay" emanated from the stereo system, filling the room with his romantic, bluesy voice, "Looks like nothin's gon'a change/ everything still remains the same –." Nora was seated in an armchair as was his sister, Lois. Leroy was sprawled on the couch. He leapt to his feet on Percival's entrance with a broad grin on his face, but the women held fast. "Hey," he yelped, then saw Lisette and came to an abrupt halt. "Wow," he gulped, observantly, as she removed her coat and passed it to Raschelay. "Nice," he said to Percival, clasping his hand and embracing him with the other.

"I'm so glad you approve."

"She's as pretty as they get."

"She'll be happy to hear you think so."

"And I thought Raschelay was pretty."

"She's no less so than the bloom on a rose."

"Do I get a hug?" Lois asked, standing.

Percival embraced his sister. "I want you to meet Lisette."

While Lisette and Lois embraced, Percival hugged Nora. On the verge of tears, they considered one another with heartfelt emotion. In a choked voice, Percival broke the silence to introduce Nora and Leroy to Lisette.

Raschelay's two younger sisters entered the living room to see what all the fuss was about and met Lisette, to whom they took a fancy and abducted on the spot, spiriting her off to their room, their secret clubhouse.

"Don't you two hog Lisette," Raschelay admonished, as they scurried off tugging a laughing Lisette by the hand.

"We won't," the girls sang, closing the door to their bedroom.

"I thought Paul would be with you?" Percival said to Lois.

"He had to work. We're going to need the money to start a family, he says. I see him less and less."

"Let me go say hi to your moms," said Percival to Raschelay, heading for the kitchen. There were pots simmering on the stove, a turkey and sweet potatoes baking in the oven, and pies were cooling on the windowsill. The aroma was amazing.

"'Ello, Mrs. Morrow," said Percival, stepping gingerly into her domain.

She twirled around from the hot stove at the sound of his voice, the back of a hand to her brow and an expectant look on her gaunt, fretful face. "Oh Percival," she said, tonelessly, at a loss for words at the sight of him. She had liked him considerably, but their complicity in the death of his brother made looking at him, at the ghost of Sam, unbearable.

"Please Percival, to you I'm Ruth. Or was, before all this terribleness happened."

"Yes," he said. "Suddenly, I know you differently."

"And I you. It's been awhile."

"It has."

"How are you?"

"I'm coming along."

She dried her hands on her apron and drew back a chair from the kitchen table on which she invited him to sit.

He straddled the chair unceremoniously. The accumulated smells from the kitchen, which lulled him, were reminiscent of when he was a boy and would sit in the kitchen as his mother prepared the holiday meals. She used to impart all her love into her cooking. And she would let him lick the spoon and eat the pot cake.

"Can I get you something?"

"I'm fine, thank you. I jus' wanted to drop in 'n say hi 'n pay my respects to the chef."

"That's mighty decent of you."

"N how's Raschelay, if you don't mind my asking?"

She folded her lips in consternation and lowered her eyes. "Some days are better than others," she said, her tension slackening. "I hope she can bear up under today, but she wanted to do it. I mean, see you, Nora 'n Leroy, all at once. Lily was invited, but she couldn't come cause she had to go see Rufus. Nina and Dr Osgood were also invited but, for different reasons, they can't make it either." She shrugged dismissively.

"It would'a been nice to have seen them to say 'ello'." His eyes narrowed. "Any word on Rufus?"

"He's pretty much the same far as Lily can tell."

His eyes darkened his face deeply pained.

"The memories," she said. "I hope it's not all too much for Raschelay to endure."

"I came especially for her."

"You've been a good friend," she paused and pursed her lips pensively. "I don't know how to thank you enough, nor how to apologize for the grief I must have caused your family. I wish I could take it back, but it's done, and no one's better off for it. I'm not. I've been made miserable as a result. I hope that's some comfort to you."

"I don't fault you, Ruth. We were under extraordinary pressure. We were under the gun. We were making life 'n death decisions, decisions which we had no right making, but making em we were 'n given the climate there were no other choices for us to ave made."

"You're one of the good ones, Percival Jones."

"In that case I've paid royally for it."

"Well, it's true."

"It's good of you to say."

"My pleasure."

"Have you seen Tzi?"

"He's seldom mentioned round here anymore."

"How sad," said Percival, glumly. "They made such a lovely pair."

"Yes, they did," Ruth concurred. "Why don't you go join your friends while I finish up in the kitchen. I'm only recently back from visiting my husband in Comstock, and it's hard for me to talk after that ordeal."

"Yes, of course. But may I ask, how is he doing?"

"He's trying with all his energy to hold on to himself. However, he slips time and again. And often when I get there, after I've traveled seven hours to see him, he's loathes to see me. And yesterday was such a day. The visits are seldom pleasant and never easy. And dealing with the authorities, the guards, is like abasing yourself. It's the plantation system all over again, anything other than 'yessa massa,' won't do, it's utterly degrading. Then, after pleasing these cretins, I get to see my husband who is a remnant of the man I once knew and loved. I donknow to say how my husband feels, but I want to break out in tears every time.

"The holidays are the worst. They are the hardest on the cellblock. There are always a rash of suicide attempts and the inmates are more prone to violence. My husband also becomes restless and uneasy. The bus ride for me is seven hours one way. That makes it fourteen hours both ways. I left yesterday morning at 2a.m. and returned late this morning, so it's an overnight commute. The visit left me exhausted. It's not pleasant, but it's for him, my husband, the father of my children, the one man in my life. I tremble for him every second of every day and pray he survives this with some semblance of humanity intact. God knows I love him as only a wife can. We did not part well this visit. And the time on the bus is never restful with a busload of prisoner wives, girlfriends and family members somber and pitiful as if they, too, were inmates on a cell block.

"Excuse me will you?" She said, tears in her eyes. "In the state I'm in I can't talk just now?"

"Certainly," he said, rising, sensing her grief.

"Would you be so kind as to tell Raschelay I can use a helping hand?"

Percival rejoined the others and told Raschelay she was wanted in the kitchen.

Lisette and the girls had not yet resurfaced. but the laughter and noise from the bedroom spilled beyond its confines, and when they finally did emerge they were giggling and the girls were clinging tenaciously to Lisette.

Lisette leaned over the back of the couch on which Percival sat beside Leroy and kissed Percival on the crown of the head.

"Hello, darling," she said, placing her hands on his shoulders.

"Welcome back," he murmured, rolling his eyes upwards.

Lois gained her feet. "It's my time to steal Lisette away," she said. "I guess there must be things you want to discuss in private and Lisette and I would simply be in the way; so why don't I borrow her awhile and we'll be back shortly."

"No need to rush," Raschelay called from the kitchen, "everything's behind schedule."

"We'll be back in plenty of time," Lois promised.

The girls wanted to go with Lisette. "Can we go? Can we go?" they implored.

"I'll be right back," Lisette said and departed with Percival's sister.

"So what's going on with the chapter?" Percival asked Nora and Leroy.

"The wind could'a just up 'n blew it away. Nobody knows it was ever there. It's now just an empty shop with a for rent sign on the door," Nora replied.

"You mean it shut down?"

"Jus' like that."

"My God, tell me about it."

"You really want'a open ole wounds? Suffice it to say, we're alive; struggling, but alive."

Percival felt a gnawing, melancholic ache in the pit of his belly." How's Skeeter?" he asked.

"Then you don't know?"

"Know what?"

"Skeeter's dead; he died from a drug overdose."

"Geese God!" Percival winced, he was not overly surprised, the greater surprise by far was that any of them were alive and they all well knew it. "If you recall Skeeter had said to me last I saw him, 'This God damn community's still the same ole hell hole in which I was born 'n looks like the one in which I'm'a die, sooner than later.'"

"I recall," Nora said, sadly. "The Party was the only thing holding him together for the longest."

"N Priestus?" he dared ask.

"Priestus 'n Skeeter were rooming together awhile," Nora continued. "Priestus got himself hooked. Beyond that nobody knows what become'a him after Skeeter's death. It seems he jus' vanished like the rest'a em, jus' blew away in a gust'a wind."

"No word from Silva?"

"I called his house the other day to invite him, but his mother told me we'd done enough harm to their family 'n ask'd I not call back."

"N you, Nora, what about you?"

"I'm working for the hospital, in maintenance, the housekeeping department. A few of us have been trying to form a union but they've been trying to ferret us out. So far, I've been able to maintain a low profile. But these workers like to talk. You know how that goes. Other than that the bills keep coming in n the money goes out."

"No love interest?"

"I had my eyes on Silva."

"That I didn't know."

"Neither did he, evidently."

"I'm sorry," he said.

"Never mind. I got my man Leroy here to keep me occupied 'n out of mischief."

She smiled at the scamp seated alongside Percival. "He comes over my place faithfully 'n does his homework 'n we talk stuff. He's an "A" student, I'm proud to say."

"I'm glad to hear it."

"I'm only doing it cause you made me promise but I still don't like it," Leroy grumbled.

"No one said you was suppose to like it," Percival chuckled.

"Well I don't. But since I'm doing it I'm'a make the best of it."

"Ya got my approval, man."

"Oh, he's enjoying it," said Nora. "In fact, he's trying to talk me into going to night school."

"That might be an idea."

"I'm toying with it, believe me. I mean, even in her condition, Raschelay's going. I guess I ain't got much of an excuse."

"I've decided to return next semester myself."

"Along with the boxing?" Leroy asked.

"I need to fill in some gaps, if you catch my drift. I've been fighting too long, every step of the way. I need something to smooth out my rough edges."

"And your lady doesn't do it?" Leroy asked.

"She's not suppose to. She's the flint that strikes the spark. I have a rage in me still that needs to be checked somewhere along the way; not that I expect an education to do it but the effort might temper it 'n the boxing take care of the rest."

"She's certainly lovely," said Nora, offhandedly.

"I should 'ave to agree. In more ways than one."

True to her word Lois had Lisette back before dinner. On the way to the dining room table Lois sidled up to Percival. "You'd be crazy to not marry that one," she said. "She had mama eating out of her hands within five minutes after we were in the apartment. Ma would forgive you just for bringing her into the family. When Lisette spoke to Ma about you, I saw something of how she must have felt about your father, Lucius. Tears were in her eyes. She asked Lisette to come again soon. Which I take means bring you."

"She is winning, isn't she?"

"She's as sweet as she is lovely," said Lois, frankly, watching the girls as they scrambled for seats on either side of her and the others found places round the sumptuously spread table.

"Percival," Mrs. Morrow said, indicating with a gesture of the hand for him to sit at the head of the table, opposite herself. He turned from Lois and whispered to Lisette, in passing, "Save the last dance for me." She reached back and clasped his hand and squeezed it reassuringly, then gave him a look with a spark of love that lit her face from within.

"Looks like you've gained a couple fans," said Mrs. Morrow to Lisette.

"And they're perfectly adorable too. I only wish I could keep them."

"Oh, we might be able to arrange that if they don't start behaving themselves," Mrs. Morrow said, looking playfully stern at the girls who smiled up at her, into her love.

"Meanwhile," Lois persisted, "take a sister's advice, don't wait too long, as have Paul and I."

"Something's wrong between you two?"

"It's the waiting, the waiting, it's not conducive to romance. I want romance and instead I get prudence. Waiting to accumulate a nest egg, waiting for a raise, waiting for a promotion, all this waiting grows old fast. I don't have a schoolgirl crush anymore. We're like an old settled couple, terribly predictable. It's the planning of it and not doing it. It's the interminable waiting. If we were married we'd at least be together, and that could be romantic; certainly more romantic than what we have now. But no, it's more like waiting to be taken from the shelf and dusted off."

"Why not call it off, then?"

"I've too much invested. Anyway, I'm much too fond of him; we're compatible, and that is almost as difficult to find as love."

"You've never said anything before."

"I'd not known Lisette before. She's the first of your girlfriends I sincerely like. She made me aware of something I'd lost – romance. She's in love with you, romantically so, and I envy her for it. Believe me, I never for a moment cared for Joleen, not even when we were schoolgirls playing double Dutch on the sidewalks of Bed-Stuy."

"Please," said Percival, sourly, turning a cutting eye on Lois. "She never liked anyone either, including herself."

"It doesn't much surprise."

They took their seats.

They all folded their hands and Mrs. Morrow said grace: "We thank thee Lord for thy bounty and friends and family with us today and we add a special thought for those who are not. In Jesus' name we pray. Amen." She then carved the turkey and the meal commenced. Conversation erupted spontaneously as plates of food were passed round the table, and a diverse number of opinions rendered on several topics. Dessert was served shortly after the meal along with coffee or tea. There were three kinds of pie: apple, pumpkin and pecan. Lisette helped clear the table and offered to assist Raschelay with the dishes. "No," Raschelay refused, "you're our guest."

"I know of no better way to get acquainted than doing routine chores together," Lisette rejoined. "This way we can enjoy each other's company and be rid of the dirty dishes at the same time."

"If you insist."

"I do."

For Percival the time passed about as pleasantly as a slow heartbreak, although he felt less on the verge of desolation than when they had last parted.

Though he loved each and every one of them, the spirit had grown tepid, passion absorbed by the daily grind. But it was better than visiting Sam's grave, another task awaiting him for which he had no taste. At any rate, it had grown late and he and Lisette needed to explore the power and the depths of their relationship, which required privacy.

Percival offered Leroy a complementary ticket to his upcoming fight. He promised.

Nora he'd stay in touch and made his apologies to Mrs. Morrow for having to leave so soon. The girls embraced Lisette fiercely in parting. "Don't worry, we'll see each other again," she promised. As they bade Raschelay farewell at the door, Lisette confronted Percival, "Would you mind terribly if, say, instead of my going to the gym with you Saturday I invited Raschelay over for a visit?"

"As you like," said Percival, accommodatingly. "Then later we can have dinner out or something'a the kind."

Lisette faced Raschelay. "Well, what do you say, care to visit us?"

"I'd like that," said Raschelay, enthusiastically. "I'd like that a lot. I can use an outing. I've been hiding behind schoolbooks and these walls all too long. Yes, I can use a change of scenery. Saturday will suit me fine."

"Good. I'll look forward to it."

"See you then."

"Then it is."

Lois dropped them off at the ferry terminal. They found seats on the upper deck facing the island from which they were departing. The boat slipped it's berth and plunged into the choppy river under an empurple sky.

"Aren't Raschelay's sisters adorable? They're so sweet. They make you just want to eat them up."

"That they do."

"It's so sad about Raschelay, though. She's too young and beautiful to be so encumbered."

"It's tragic, I agree. But if anyone can see their way out of such a tangle it's she."

"You say that so easily."

"Not so. Not at all. I share her grief, but there is little else I can do but sympathize."

"It'll take considerable time for her to heal, and she'll need the patience of all her friends."

"It was considerate of you to invite her over."

She looked out at the brooding river. "Darling, don't those girls give you ideas? Such as, how many children you suppose we'll have?"

"I've not given it much thought," he said brusquely, taken by surprise.

"Oh, I know," she insisted, "I've heard it said you shouldn't have more children than you can educate and I would almost agree but –." She fell silent, having felt Percival stiffen beside her. She gave him a long stare as a strange look came into his eyes.

"I should ave told you sooner," he said, slowly. "It's something you should ave known right off, 'n as such I have no claim on you." She listened, her heart thrumming. "Ours was a promise made before you knew me, really. 'N god knows, at the time I didn't know if I'd live long enough for it to matter, 'n besides I was too distracted by other things 'n it was the least of my concerns back then. But now it's of the moment –"

"Before you go on," she interjected, afraid to hear him out, afraid for their love, "I knew you were enormously burdened when we first met. Though I didn't know the details or depths of your troubles, I recognized there was this nobility of spirit; a strength I could not resist. The combination was irresistible. And, there was the physical," she said, warming. "Then during the weeks when I'd not heard from you – after that dreadful article –, I promised myself that if you emerged, when you emerged, I would stand by you no matter your cross; that I'm in it for better or worse unless you can say you don't love me."

"My tongue would have long rotted in my mouth before that day arrives."

"That's all that matters, then." She leaned against his shoulder, closing her eyes dreamily. There was a radiant, wistful look about her. "Now tell me, what were you about to say?"

"I'd like to agree 'n say, yes, that's all that matters but, no, it's not. I have a child, a son; his name is Malek." Lisette's eyes flew open and a surge of envy rose like bile in her. She took his hand and clasped it in panic. "I've not been able to see him for all the wrong reasons. But I'm gonna fix that. I'll be able to. That is, I'll ave the money to. I guess what I'm saying is, yes, I want'a marry you." She squeezed his hand softly. "But until this thing with Malek is resolved I dare not think of having another child, even with you. 'N I want everything with you."

"I didn't think love would be entirely pain free but now I've suffered my first prick of disappointment," she said, her voice breaking. "I mean, I'm jealous that some other woman has borne you our first child."
"I'm the one at fault," he proclaimed. He hung his head solemnly, then looked at her steadfastly. "If there's anything else I may regret, anything for which I'm most sorry, would be the only apology I feel I owe anyone, any woman certainly, would be Racine, but I can't apologize … She's gone."
"Yes," Lisette acknowledged. "You've mentioned her in the past along with the sad loss of her child, Dakota I believe it was? which precipitated her death. You've mentioned them several times in the past."

567

"I just want you to understand."

"I assure you I'll try."

He kissed her hand, and she stroked his head. "If, however, you want out— "

"No, not ever, not unless you have a wife stashed away somewhere as well."

He looked at her carefully, with searching eyes. "No, I promise. No more surprises."

"I knew you'd been around, of course." She shook her head, determined not to give into despair. "You've only proven yourself a man. The man who holds the key to my heart; the temple of my universe." She secured his arm in hers as the boat neared the city, a city crouched in the harbor like a thousand-eyed mythical beast over which the Statue of Liberty kept watch.

"One more thing," he added, as they disembarked. "There is my father, but that's a story for another occasion."

***

That Saturday following a leisurely afternoon together, Lisette and Raschelay met Percival downstairs in front of the 14th. Street Gramercy Park gym. From there they went uptown by bus to Central Park where they hired a horse drawn carriage and took a scenic tour through the park, despite the late Autumn chill. As night blanketed the city the streetlights cast their glow and the park became enchanted. The clop, clop, clop of the horse's hooves was hypnotic. Outside of the park, yellow lights spilled from windows and doorways as they rode past the Plaza Hotel on Fifth Avenue and the Dakota on 72nd Street and Central Park West, both winking through the trees that lined the avenue. They returned downtown by subway and ate at Sweet Basil's in Greenwich Village. They went to listen to the great Jazz bassist/composer, Charles Mingus, at the Village Vanguard, a few doors over.

"Does he ever stretch the range of one's listening experience," Lisette commented between sets.

"That's Mingus for you," Percival acknowledged.

"It's my first-time hearing Jazz," Raschelay confessed, sounding somewhat baffled. "I have to admit, I felt left out."

"I'd not heard jazz before Percival turned me on to it, either," Lisette said. "Now I can't get enough of it."

"Mingus is Mingus," said Percival. "The devil himself, the Wagner of black American music.'

"You know Wagner's music?" Lisette asked.

"Enough to know Mingus to be his American counterpart. Mingus, in his way, has done for black American music what Wagner did for German folk music."

"I'm impressed you would know to say that," Lisette said.

Percival looked amused.

They remained through a second set. When he realized how late it had become, Percival thought it unwise to send Raschelay home alone so he invited her to stay over. She was hesitant, but not reluctant,

"I would have to call my mother."

"Ya can call when we get home," Percival suggested.

They left the club and returned to his apartment crosstown by foot. Raschelay contacted her mother and told her 'not to expect her.' Due to her delicate condition, Percival surrendered his side of the bed to Raschelay, thus having to sleep on the floor in the spare bedroom. Lisette had come to look upon Raschelay as would an elder sister and was equally glad to accommodate her.

While Raschelay prepared for bed Percival and Lisette lingered in the hall, pawing each other playfully, needing only their eyes by which to speak, and, before parting, they feverishly kissed. Lisette waited by the doorway and waved with an affected play of the hand as he entered his room.

"Good night, my love," she whispered. "It was a glorious night."

He blew her a kiss, then closed the door. He stripped to his briefs and curled up on the floor under blankets ready for sleep. He was certainly tired enough, but found himself restless, unable to fall off. He didn't know how long he lay awake, his mind racing. The street noises intruded on his thoughts. The sound of Saturday night revelers floated into the room as did the nearby sound of someone crying. He tossed and turned sighing longingly. He turned on his side facing the door, wishing Lisette were beside him when the door creaked open and she hovered ghost like in the doorway, the light from the hall spilling in around her. She closed the door gently and was swallowed up in the gloom. She called out gently, apprehensively, "are you asleep?"

"No," he said, his voice scarcely a breath. "I've been up waiting for you."

She came to him anxiously and stretched out under the covers alongside him.

"Hold me. Hold me, tight," she urged, nestling against him. He enfolded her in his embrace. He sensed she was close to tears. "Raschelay's asleep. I needed to be with you. I hope you don't mind?"

"Not at all. I've jus' been lying here missing you."

"Do you mind if I talk?"

"Feel free."

569

"Raschelay told me she cries herself to sleep every night since, as she put it, her incident and resultant pregnancy. It just about scares her witless." Her voice was choked with emotion. "She cried herself to sleep again tonight. I couldn't help but cry along with her."

"So that's the crying I heard."

"I was unprepared for what she had to say. It sunk my heart. In trying to stand by her religious convictions she was left vulnerable. She lost the love of her life along with the wonder of sharing her first sexual encounter with the man of her dreams. And she doesn't know what she's going to do with this child once it comes. She thinks she's lost the ability to care, to feel; she's been numbed, she says, from inside out. She's lost everything. She was quite in love with this fellow, your friend, Tzi, evidently, but she said she could no longer look at him, because of the shame she felt. Even more, she was afraid of the loathing she feared she'd see in his face. She couldn't bear to see hatred and contempt in his eyes, the eyes of the one she loves. She knew it would be there despite all his efforts to conceal it. She can't escape the feeling of degradation. So, she'd rather not face him, as much as she loves him. It is the only feeling she has left – one of loss."

For a fleeting moment, as Lisette was describing Raschelay's distraught state of mind, Percival did not regret Sam's death, but wished that he had played a more active role in its execution.

"How awfully sad," he said. "I don't think Tzi's that way, not at all. He's an exceptional person for his age. I hope she'll be able to face him, though it might already be too late." He yawned, sleepily. "He's a proud cat, no two ways about it."

"Listening to her and trying, at the same time, to comfort her, I suddenly grew afraid, more afraid than I'd ever been. I was afraid of losing you. Suddenly my world felt empty, the more I listened. I wanted to leave and fly to you, into your arms, be certain you were safe, that we were safe – our love was safe." They cleaved to each other, breath hot on each other's cheek. "I know we spoke of getting married after I graduated, but just now talking to Raschelay, I wondered about its soundness. She made me think about how pointless things can quickly become. She'd held herself back from Tzi on religious grounds. She felt much obligated to her future husband even as much as she loved and wanted it to be Tzi. She was determined to preserve the flower of womanhood for her husband alone. I understand that. We are both Catholic, she and I. She'd often wanted to give in to Tzi, but her sense of honor held her back. She wished to hold her virtue intact.

"I admit I too held out until I was sure my prince had come, my husband to be, and then the flood waters washed over me despite my upbringing, and I was swept away in a tidal wave of longing. I knew as certainly as if a veil had been lifted from my eyes that you were the man for me, my consort to be, the future father of all my children. So why should we have to wait? What is there to prove by waiting? For who, may I ask?"

"Strangely enough, my sister Lois said as much. I'm all for it," he said, exultant. Yes, he would marry Lisette, the sooner the better: Her love had proven a cleansing fire, a baptism in which he had been resurrected.

She kissed him passionately. "Oh Percival, I adore you! I can finish out my junior year at Skidmore then transfer down here to a local college for my last year."

They talked through the night into the wee hours of the morning and before falling off briefly, they decided that they would ask Dominick to bless their union that day.

At first Dominick was reluctant, although not entirely surprised by the request. He leaned back in the Monsignor's high back chair and surveyed Percival and Lisette, his fingers steepled. He was fully aware of the fact that Percival was a non-conformist, a radical, a non-Catholic – a potentially dangerous mix. All in all, in the argot of the street, he was "a bad nigger." It was his sister, Lisette, who he had to be concerned about; and in as much as he admired Percival, he knew that he could not surrender his sister over to his agnosticism. As much in love with him as she was, she would bolt the Church, marry outside the faith and become lost to the religion. He had seen it happen all too often in the past with people less in love. He asked nevertheless, "Would you wait to marry, if I thought it the wiser?"

"We had planned to wait until I had graduated," said Lisette. "Then I met Rschelay and became all too aware of the hazards of waiting too long."

"Yes, there is that too," Dominick agreed. "And Raschelay's the young woman seated in the hall? The one you told me about on the train?" He swung his gaze to Percival.

"So she is."

"I see." Dominick nodded. "And how is she?"

"I can't rightly say."

"She's hopelessly tormented," Lisette interjected, drawing her brother's gaze.

Dominic leaned forward on the desk, and sighed. He knew that his position as a priest was compromised and that he would have to make his decision as Lisette's older brother and not her confessor; which, no doubt, was why he had been asked. Besides, he could not refuse her anything within his power to grant. He loved her more than life and had faith in her good sense. Despite his concerns about Percival he felt that he had as much a capacity for greatness as had any debased sinner turned saint before finding God, and if anyone could help him find his way it would surely be Lisette.

"I have the utmost confidence in the two of you." He put his hands on the edge of the desk as if to stand. His deep-set eyes thoughtful. "Therefore, I shall put aside convention and bless your union, as you ask after, Mass is said."

The Church was cavernous and dark, but for the votive candles that flickered in the gloom, and beams of sunlight entering through stained glass windows like arrows through the body of a martyred Saint. There was also a lighted side Chapel in which a small group of elderly worshipers gathered for noon Mass. The choir was conspicuously silent in the rear of the Church, and the scent of frankincense lingered on from an earlier mass.

Dominick performed the ceremony reverently, as if it were a magical ritual, an invocation of the most high. It was clear in the response of those in attendance that they had come to this mass to worship specifically with this priest, their beloved Father Poincare. As such, the prayers of these supplicants ascended heavenwards like a balm, pleasing to the nostrils of God. Raschelay found herself drawn in by the ritual; absorbed, caught in the magnetic current of the service. She had not been to church since, "her incident." She did not know whether it was because she'd lost faith in the efficacy of religion, or because she was too ashamed to approach the throne of God in less than a state of grace. But, here in this Church, in this dimly lighted chapel, with this young priest officiating, she thought she could hear in his voice the words of the founder of the faith,

"Blessed are they that mourn for they shall be comforted."

After reading the gospel and delivering an inspirational sermon, Dominick invited the small congregation to remain for the nuptials and asked that they, along with him, offer their prayers as a blessing and safeguard on the union. The members of the congregation looked searchingly about until their eyes fell on the couple for whom they were to pray. Raschelay squeezed Lisette's hand gently and smiled.

At the conclusion of the mass Dominick invited the intended couple to approach the altar. Casually attired and insouciant, Percival was roguishly handsome beside Lisette. She was bewitchingly attractive, sparkling eyes reflecting her raven black hair, her Mexicali complexion shining faintly in the Chapel's off light. She fixed her betrothed steadfastly in her gaze.

"Do you in the sight of God take this woman?" asked the priest.

"I do," said Percival, resolutely, gazing fixedly at Lisette, her wonderfully kind face, a face he could easily look on all his days. She returned his look with rapture and a shy pensive smile aching with love, her cheeks aflame. She softly repeated, "to have and to hold from this day forward –"

They had no rings to exchange. An elderly couple stepped up and offered the loan of their bands for the occasion. "It'll bring you luck," the woman promised, beaming. "We've been married fifty years." The old man nodded in accord. Percival and Lisette pledged their troth, exchanged rings, and the ceremony was brought to a close. "I give you, for the first time, Mr. & Mrs. Percival & Lisette Jones!" the priest announced, his hands raised in blessing over both their heads, and they were received by the congregation with applause.

Raschelay had been affected in a way she would otherwise not have expected. She hugged them warmly, crying openly, spiritually uplifted. She loved them, loved them deeply, as she loved the new life stirring in her. She gazed on the radiant faces of these newlyweds who she'd come to adore, and, in that instant, knew she would live again, love again, if only for her child. She would heal and become whole again. She smiled through her tears, wiping her eyes with a handkerchief passed to her by Dominick who introduced himself.

"I'm Father Dominick Poincare, Lisette's brother."

"It's good to meet you, Father. I'm Raschelay. I loved your sermon. I felt it spoke to me directly," she said softly, as the assembly came forward to greet the newlyweds. "Would you be so kind as to hear my confession?"

***

The first of Percival's eleven professional bouts were no contests. He had simply gone through the motions as a matter of course and then disposed of each opponent with the ease of a careless lover. He had used them for a workout, toyed with them shamelessly, then, in the final rounds, knocked them out as if an afterthought. He was averaging one and a half fights per month, right on track. He had racked up eleven straight knockouts and the boxing world was beginning to take notice; more so following his previous night's win, a preliminary at Madison Square Garden. It was an eight rounder, which he had won, coming from behind, explosively, and with a dazzling display of courage, skill and stamina, against a seasoned journeyman. The papers claimed that he had stolen the show and that the fans were still on their feet howling long after he had left the ring and the main event was being introduced from ringside. The consensus among sports writers in attendance was, as said one, "Percival Jones, easily the best fighter this writer has seen in years, promises to fill the vacancy left by Sugar Ray Robinson." Another writer went so far as to dub him "incomparable," an adjective that would stick.

Ashton and a few other tenants were milling about on the sidewalk in front of the apartment building discussing Percival's latest win when, towards the end of his daily five mile morning run, he came racing down the block, at breakneck speed, in pursuit of Jonas who had been lying for him as he did every day, about a quarter mile before their stoop, and, with a block and a half lead, raced him back to the building. Within a few doors of their own Percival overtook the boy and came to a winded, heart pumping stop before the tenants. He collapsed forward, panting, throwing sweat like a wet dog shaking itself. He straightened up he strolled about hoisting his legs jauntily as would a stallion, his chest heaving. Sweat ran freely down his flanks, along his legs and arms and glistened on his dark face in the early morning heat which, the sun not yet having scaled the tenement roofs, promised to become more fierce as the day wore on.

Jonas caught up to him. "I'll beat you yet, you'll see," he said, winded.

"Maybe," Percival smiled, puffing fiercely, "but not t'day." He ruffled Jonas' hair with a gentle hand. "Fill the buckets up for me to clean the halls, 'n then hose down the stoop 'n sidewalk 'n I'll see you after I shower off, okay?"

"Sure thing, coach." The boy saluted smartly.

"You're gaining on him," said Ashton encouragingly.

"Yes," one of the tenants, a paint spattered artist, up early in order to catch the ascending light, agreed.

The student, another tenant, accustomed to this rivalry, smiled at the boy as he descended the basement steps. "Don't give up," he called to Jonas. "I can see you're wearing him down."

"I won't," Jonas assured him, looking back as he descended the basement steps.

"Have you seen the morning news," Ashton asked Percival, passing him a copy of the day's paper.

"Not yet," he panted, gazing on the sports page.

"Ashton's been telling us about your fight last night and from what the sports writers are saying it looks like I'll have to go see you for myself," said the printer, who lived on the third floor. "I've seen some good fighters in my day. The best, including Sugar Ray, more than once. I'll reserve judgment, if you don't mind."

"I'll try not to disappoint."

"Ashton was impressed anyway."

"And for good reason," Ashton remarked.

A wiry old codger, a former German seaman, who also lived in the building, barged through the circle of men with spiteful disregard, swinging his cane back and forth. "Go congregate somewhere else," he snarled.

"Watch where you swing your stick, ole man," said the student, angrily.

As the codger mounted the stoop he drew to a standstill and rounded on Percival, gazing fiercely, under craggy brows. "When are you going to get around to fixing my faucet?" he asked, leaning on his walking stick. "When?" he stared, wildly, giving off a rank, offensive odor in his worn-out, shapeless clothes. "Well?" he demanded, striking his cane impatiently.

"It'll be easier if you leave me your keys like I told you a dozen times already."

"And trust you? Why would I do that. So you can rob me blind? It'll be a cold day in hell when you catch me napping, sonny."

"What ave you got I can possibly want?" Percival asked.

"Mr. Kruger," the printer attempted to intercede, "didn't you hear Percival won again last night?"

"Won? Won what?" asked the old man, acerbically.

"His fight, man! His fight!"

"Should I care he won a fight and not fix my faucet?" He raised his cane and shook it, menacingly. "You get my faucet fixed or I'll call the cops."

"You do that," said Percival.

"All you young people are just alike. You got no respect for anything," said the old sailor, his eyes searching for someone else on whom to vent his spleen. His eyes found the printer. "You should be ashamed of yourself, encouraging these hooligans."

"Bah!" spat the printer. "That's nonsense and you know it. You're just being an old bully."

"You're defending them are you?"

"They need no defense from me."

The old man shook his walking stick at no one in particular then scrambled up the stairs like a crab in flight.

"There's a mean-spirited coot," claimed the student, brushing a lock of hair from his eyes. "He growls at me just about every day. I hate living next door to him. I don't want to grow so old I become miserable like that."

"He's just lonely," said the printer, sympathetically.

Percival wiped his sweaty face with the tail of his shirt.

"You're dripping like a leaky faucet," the artist said, laughing.

"Very funny," Percival replied. Then facing Ashton, he asked, "What 'r you up to for t'day, man?"

"I got a bread 'n butter gig for The Voice I gotta see to. It should cove my bills for the month."

"Oh well," said the artist, gazing skyward beyond the tenement roof's. "I better be off before I lose any more of this light." He took up his easel and sauntered off.

"Let me go shower off," said Percival, starting up the stairs. "I'll catch you later on." He entered the building and let himself into his flat. He threw the light switch and the front room became bright and inviting. It had been tastefully transformed; furnished, decorated with a few impressionist paintings, African sculpture and books displayed a decidedly woman's touch. That touch became more evident as one made one's way through the apartment. Lisette's hand was apparent everywhere and he liked it that way. She had come down at the end of the school year in early June to join him, transferred for her last year to NYU and found employment at the Henry Street Settlement as a Community Coordinator. It was mid-July and summer, despite their not as yet having had a honeymoon was proving to be a honeymoon. Intoxicated by the mere presence of the other, they were blissfully happy.

He found her in the kitchen, freshly made up for work in a white halter dress encircled at the waist by a thin black belt; her bare shoulders and back were exquisite, a perfection of her being that filled him with ecstasy. Her hair was twirled into a bun. She was seated sedately at the kitchen table drinking coffee and enjoying a solitary moment, a silent moment of pleasure alone. He crept up on her from behind, flung the paper on the table in front of her, then laced his arms about her and kissed her on the nape of the neck.

"Ummmm," she swooned, in response. She smiled dreamily and stroked his unshaven face with slender fingers. "And how is my love today?" she asked softly, her heart palpitating at his nearness.

"Hankering for you."

"You're a dream boat," she said wistfully.

"I best go shower off," he said, starting to go.

"Oh dear," she cried with a start, noticing a substantial sweat mark left on her dress from his amorous embrace. "You've soiled my dress. I'll have to change," she said, without reproach.

"I'm sorry but you look so irresistible sitting there that I forgot myself," he explained, at her mercy.

"So long as you keep on finding me so," she trilled, dabbing the spot with a napkin. "Never mind, it'll dry. I'll just have to go to work smelling of you, like some exotic perfume." She laughed as would a songbird if it could. "Go shower off so we can have a bit of breakfast before I go."

"Your wish is my command, fair lady," he said with a flourish of his hand, bowing out the door. He whistled in the shower, lathering himself with soap, then showered off. He toweled off leisurely, wrapped himself in a white terry cloth robe, and rejoined Lisette across the table from her.

"Aren't you hot in that?" she asked. "You make me sweat looking at you."

"I'll be switching into something more comfortable shortly."

"It's building to a scorcher," she observed, fanning herself. "And between flashbacks of your fight and the sweltering heat last night, I could barely sleep."

"We're heading into the dog days of summer all right. N here in the city tempers run short fast. Speaking of which, I ran into ole Mr. Kruger after my run n he was already fuming."

"Is he still after you to get his faucet fixed?"

"With a vengeance! Only he won't give me the key to let myself in."

"It's his way of controlling the situation."

"I think I know that."

"It's only a leaky faucet."

"Not to hear him tell it."

"Anyway, I read the write up on your fight last night," said Lisette, passing the paper across the table. "You seem to have smitten them." She sighed. "But, I must say, as much as I love you – because I love you –, and don't want to disappoint you or have you take what I say the wrong way, I just can't make it through another of your fights," she said in a strained voice. "I've seen you fight twice now and I can't do it anymore. Last night I thought I'd lose my stomach right there at ringside."

She paused and stared stonily at her hands folded atop the table before proceeding. She felt as if a switch had been thrown putting her heart in darkness. She had no wish to betray him with her feelings. Then said, "In all honesty, it's more than I can handle. I can't bare seeing you punched!" She waited with bated breath for his response.

Percival's eyes were veiled. "Listen, kid, frankly I'm glad you made it to as many as two. I didn't expect it. I mean if I were in your place I don't think I'd want'a see me fight either, though I think it can be beautiful. Yes, violence can be beautiful. Much in the same way something of beauty, like sex, for example, can be made ugly, cruel 'n demeaning." He thought of Raschelay who had given birth back in May to a baby girl, Samantha. She named her for Sam, of all people. He and Lisette were godparents. "I know the nature of violence all too well to be overly disappointed. Your prayers 'n best wishes will suffice in your stead," he said then winked. "Jus' so you save the last dance for me."

She felt as if he had thrown the lights back on and the room in her heart had grown brighter, more receptive. She was not sure she could bare to love anyone so much but love him the more she did. "You can have all the dances, including the last, if you so wish." She grasped his hands. "For the rest of our lives."

"Fair enough."

She smiled. "I don't want to disappoint you ever."

"Let's not dwell on it," he said. "I suffer enough for both of us."

"I trust you do."

He took a sip of coffee. Her eyes ventured to the clock overhead on the wall at his back.

"I'm afraid I must run."

He saw her to the door. She kissed him, yanked herself away with reluctance, and passed out the door, gone for the day. He closed the apartment door, took a moment's notice, considered the weight of her absence, then got into gear. He dressed quickly and went to the basement where Jonas was working out on the heavy bag. He came to a halt, threw his hair back from his face with a shake of his head, and stood by the bag as if posing for a photo.

"I washed the sidewalk 'n stoop 'n your buckets 'r full, just like you asked."

"Good! You stay on the bag 'n I'll take care of the halls, then I'll return 'n give you a few pointers."

"Sure you can't use a hand?"

"You jus' do what you're doing."

"Okay, coach, I got you."

***

By the time Percival left for the gym that afternoon the sun had been baking the city for hours, and its insufferable rays had wilted the inhabitants by progression, leaving them listless, irritable, and short tempered. But the street urchins, to the contrary, had stripped to the waist and were frolicking in the gush of water from the city's many fire hydrants.

Percival wore his planters hat, safari jacket, neck-a-chief, khaki shorts and sandals. He was surprised to encounter Punchy standing idly on the sidewalk, outside the gym, fanning himself leisurely with a shade hat.

"Hey, Punchy, what gives?"

"I jus' wanted to let you know Joleen's upstairs with your son. Derrick's with her. If you want'a duck out now's your chance," he said, beads of sweat forming on his balding pate.

"No let's go up."

"It's your call," said Punchy, following. "I jus' hope you know what you're in for."

"I'm not comfortable with it but I can't escape it either."

"I'd let Derrick handle it."

"I can't. I need to see my son."

"I can't argue that."

Percival scanned the viewers gallery on entering the noisy gym and saw Joleen and Malek right off, seated among a cluster of fight buffs. Derrick stood off to the side, leaning on the apron of the ring, in which two fighters were sparring. Percival strolled over. Constrained. He accepted Joleen's hand reluctantly and without sentiment. There was nothing left between them but a cold and heartless dynamic. He eyed her bitterly. She was no less beautiful – unnervingly so: She held herself back, aloof, as if tightly wound, however. And those sexless Barbie doll attributes, attributes which she had cultivated in order to safeguard herself from men, were fully intact, and her beckoning, come hither smile, a smile that used to enchant him so, lingered disturbingly on her petulant mouth, and her almond, almost Asian eyes that used to cut to his soul, no longer moved him. There was no warmth to her beauty. No spirit to animate it. She could easily have been an ice statue. She had the power to possess him, body and soul, but all his former feelings for her had long since spoiled, and all she stirred in him now was revulsion.

But the boy, looking up at him curiously, mystified, was a different matter. Percival wanted to know him – love him as one would love the blood from which one is woefully estranged – but they were strangers nonetheless, and all he could feel was a helplessness, a kind of self-pity, an unutterable agony of mind and heart, an abyss over which he could not cross. Yet, the face of the child insisted he try. He was bedeviled and uncertain as to how to proceed.

He took the boy up in his arms, but he soon squirmed, wanting his mother.

"I got'a workout. I'll talk to you after, if you like."

"That's why I came," she said, nestling the child against her breast.

He looked at her, felt a sharp pang of envy, and hastened off. Punchy and Derrick followed him to the locker room. Punchy strode restlessly back and forth, and Derrick sat alongside him on a bench, anomalous among the bare assed pugilists, dressed, as he was, like a landlocked riverboat gambler, in a white silk suit, red tie and pocket handkerchief with three points showing, alligator shoes, and a Cuban cigar dangling from his lips. His face looked cool, fresh, even in the extraordinary humidity of the lockers, thought he had slipped off his jacket, then pushed his hat back off his forehead.

"Okay, what gives?" asked Percival, looking from one to the other?

"I know it's not our place but watch yourself," said Punchy, finally. "I think I know what I'm saying. Take an ole fool's advice. She jus' wants a chance to ruin you. I know her, remember?"

"I don't see how she can do that?"

"Your son's her weapon against you," Derrick intruded, half pleading. "I tried to talk to her. But she had nothing to say. She was more intent in listening. She was trying to play me. She's mistrustful. I'm sure she can be devious."

"I've got'a face it eventually."

"Let Derrick handle it!"

"You have a history that's best kept under wraps. You don't need this kind of exposure. Right now the news boys are focused on your boxing. We don't want to direct them elsewhere."

"I agree," Punchy broke in. "Reporters do what they have to do to sell papers 'n that means they'll sell you to sell papers. And don't feel flattered cause they're favoring you t'day cause t'morrow they'll jus' as gladly turn round 'n sell you down river. Nothing or no one's a more fickle lover than the newsboys."

"Then what am to do?" asked Percival, rattled.

Derrick pouted. "Concentrate on your fighting. I know the right people, topnotch lawyers. We can handle this any way you choose, but we need to keep it under wraps, like I say. We'll quickly make arrangements that are both amicable and legally binding, deal?"

"I'll tell you after I've spoken to her."

"That's fair enough, I suppose," Derrick said, dead set against it.

"Thing's r gonna get tough after last night's win," Punchy said, sunk in thought. "We won't be able to pick 'n choose 'r opponents much anymore. We've got'a stay focused."

"Bring em on," said Percival.

"I've been on the phone all morning," Derrick said, groping about in a mental fog. "After last night everyone wants a piece of you, a piece of the action." He smiled stiffly. "You're a hot item. You're a draw; an attraction. I've a number of offers from all over the place. I'm working on a deal to get you a European tour. You can bring that lovely wife of yours, Lisette. Punchy and I will look these offers over then present them to you for approval. As for the other difficulty, let me know, sooner than later, how you want it handled." He clapped Percival fondly on the shoulder, pretending to a confidence he didn't quite share. "Okay?"

"Let's get to work," said Punchy, as Percival finished taping his hands.

"Yeah, I've promises to keep, don't I?" he breathed, exhaustively, flinging himself to his feet.

"This gal's bad news," Derrick warned Punchy, "This gal's bad news."

"Don't I know it," Punchy agreed. "She's a witch, 'n I mean that literally."

"Bitch is what I was thinking."

"She's a witch who practices bitch craft."

"I can't argue that. She's potentially fatal."

"Thank God fer Lisette."

"I thought I'd never hear you say that."

"A persons got'a right to change his mind once proven wrong," Punchy said, defensively.

Unable to focus, Percival's performance was, at best, lackluster. Punchy sent him to the showers early.

"Talk to her if you must. Talk to Lisette, too. Do what you got'a but get it outta your system fast. N show up tomorrow ready to go."

That moment – that terrible, unexpected moment – had been hanging over him forever now like the Sword of Damocles. And as inconvenient as it was, it was a chapter in his life which he needed to face.

He took a cold, brisk shower, thinking, as icy needles of water struck him forcibly, dissolving his lassitude, *"Isn't it ironic, Racine used to compare me to the legendary, medieval hero Parzival in his quest for the Holy Grail. But, in fact, here in America, it's the Sword of Damocles that hangs threateningly over the head of every Blackman— every Blackman, that is, who would be a man! As has Dominick staked out his ground, drawn a line in the sand, 'n said to the world, 'Here as a priest, as a man, I make my stand I can do no other!' 'N that, in America, being a man, is the challenge, the quest we're on at 'r ever lovin' peril."* It was strange that he had not thought of Racine for quite a while now. While he had not loved Racine as she would have liked he had cared for her, for her child, Dakota, both gone. Then he remembered who was waiting for him, Joleen, and his ire was raised. He toweled off, got dressed, left the locker room and crossed the gym with vague apprehension. The din of activity on the floor raced with the tumultuous roar of blood to his brain. He recalled their argument in full, like a drowning man reviewing his life, and, on reaching the viewers gallery, he asked her.

"Care for a cup of coffee?"

"As you like."

They found a little coffee shop on 15th. Street., overlooking Union Square Park. They took a window seat in the back, from which they could see the vacant park. Malek's forehead barely reached the top of the table, and his startling, animal like eyes seemed to rest precariously on the table's edge.

The waitress took their order and returned shortly after with a glass of milk, two cups of coffee, and three English muffins with butter and jelly on the side.

Joleen took out a cigarette lit a match to it and exhaled from out of the side of her mouth. Then she held the cigarette daintily aside. "I see you're wearing a wedding band," she observed. "I take it you're married?"

"Yes."

"Does she know about me?"

"What there is to know."

"Have you any children?"

"One son. R son, Malek," he responded, gritting his teeth at this line of inquiry.

"I mean, don't you have any children with her?"

"Lisette, my wife? No, not yet."

"I don't mean to be nosey."

"But you do."

"I'm sorry, maybe this isn't a good idea," she said, sulkily.

"Don't play me. Ya want something, what is it?"

"If you're going to be like that."

"I'm sorry, but I didn't expect this visit. If I'm apprehensive it's cause we come with baggage."

"I owe you an apology."

"Big time."

"Let's start again, shall we? I know this may sound strange, but I came looking for you because your son is going to need you. Maybe it's shortsighted of me to only see it now but I've had my ups and downs these years and I've learned some hard lessons in between. One of them is that you've been right about so much and I've just been stubbornly blind, listening to my mother's closedminded opinions on almost everything."

"I wish I could say I find some satisfaction in that, but I don't."

"I know how difficult I must have made it for you these years, but it's not been a bed of roses for me either, in case you're interested."

"The suffering of others is cold comfort, indeed."

"I tracked you down from an article in today's paper. Don't think I've only come for money, because you'll be wrong. I came, like I said, for Malek's sake and, well, I'd hoped you'd still have some feelings for me, too. But, of course, that was silly of me. You're a prize catch, after all. I hope the lucky gal appreciates what she's got the way I never did."

"I think she does."

"Is she very pretty?"

"No one's prettier than you, if that's what you're asking," he said, generously. "No one."

She took another pull on her cigarette. "Well, I wouldn't know that," she said. "But if you say so."

"I say so."

"But no chance for us?"

"None that I can see."

"I was being just a little unrealistic, I guess."

"Not so unrealistic as you might think," Percival said, playing her along.

"You're kind," she said, arresting him in her gaze.

"If I'm right we want the same thing for Malek. I'm making some money 'n can offer to pay support."

"I want you to know, Percival, that I left my mother's. Well, frankly, she kicked me and Malek out after my father's death, a year and a half ago," she said gravely. "I'd started drinking quite heavily. Me and my father would get drunk together and pass out routinely in the front room. I guess alcohol became my way of coping with the sexless, loveless life I was living under my mother's roof, as well as a way of getting back at her; to lay dead drunk in the living room before her eyes, along with my father, her husband," she spoke with an undercurrent of malice. "Although, I admit I didn't see it then. After all, I'd started drinking when you and I were first together, and it just got progressively worse. It was left to my mother and sister to care for Malek. It's nothing of which I'm proud. Then when my father died suddenly mama told me straight out that if I didn't change my ways she'd kick me and Malek out into the street. It's not that I didn't believe he I did but the bottle had a hold on me. And well, true to her word, she put us out, despite my pleading. I even held Malek up to her, but her mind was set against us.

"She said to me 'I didn't raise any child of mine to act like no nigger. If you're going to drink like one you can go out on the street and live like one.' I must have been hysterical, but she was unrelenting. 'I'd had it with your father for years, but at least he paid his freight.' I cried and cried. 'My son, mama, not my son. Your grandson.' She only said, 'He's his son too!' And she flung the door shut in our faces. I collapsed and laid in the hall beating on her door, crying for her to let us back in, give me another chance, but she didn't. Finally, a neighbor took pity on us and took us in for a few days. She was a neighbor my mother wouldn't speak to because she was too black. She was kind. She found room for us at a woman's shelter. There I met another woman from The Welfare Mother's Association. She got me on the welfare rolls and helped me find an apartment in the Park Slope section of Brooklyn. We were in the shelter for three months. I was also encouraged to join Alcoholics Anonymous. Well, I've been sober going on a year now."

"Congratulations," he said, stiffly.

"Thank you," she said, taking a drag on her cigarette. "I guess I'll have to give these up next." She laughed faintly, a trickle of smoke spiraling from her nostrils. "I want your son to know you. I've told him good things about you. I've not lied to him. Of course he doesn't understand. He's only three, after all." Percival smiled at the boy across the table, clasping his glass of milk in both hands. "I never lied to him about you. I always said you loved him. Always. I just couldn't explain to him any more than I can to myself why you weren't in his life. I didn't realize how much hostility my mother had nurtured in me and my sister toward men especially black men. Her own self-image had been so deflated, destroyed by years of being married to such a weakling as my father. I know it, now. She taught us to hate ourselves, first by teaching us contempt for our father, and through him, hatred for the race. Except, of course, the better class of Negro which, according to her, we were. What made that so, besides our complexion I don't know. It was with the welfare mothers that I came to realize the blatant error of my mother's point of view.

"I was simply too young and still very much under the spell of my mother's influence when we first lived together, I'm ashamed to say."

"Nobody took you away from your mother. I didn't, you came 'n found me to my everlasting regret."

"If I were too young for you, to love you, too naive, it's because my mother had not raised her daughters for womanhood. Instead, she tried to shelter us in a well spun web of lies and grandiose misconceptions of which my sister and I are the sad products. My mother had single handedly arrested our development; and I didn't know how to respond to a man. I'm terribly sorry for all of it and wish I could make amends," she said hungrily, a look of poverty on her face, a look of helplessness from which he had to harden his heart for fear of falling under her influence. "I've come to see how wrong my mother's been; how wrong I've been.

"God knows, I was frustrated. No man wanted to deal with my mother. So I drank to compensate for the void in my life, the absence of a man in my life. You were the only one my mother couldn't scare."

"You give me too much credit, she scared me alright. Stupidity always does. Then again I'm scared of you too, 'n no less scared for 'r son, Malek."

Percival's face reflected the despair he felt.

"I was a fool to let you go," she said, plaintively. "To have listened to my mother. What a fool I was.!"

"Too little too late."

"Do you forgive me?"

"For what?"

"You know."

"If I forgive it's cause things 'r different."

"You're still the only man for me, but you've spoiled it all," she said, petulantly. "I despise you. I do. And I hate her for interfering." She titled her head as if flipping a switch. "No I don't mean it." She reached for his hands, which he quickly withdrew. "I can't hate you but you do make me miserable."

A mocking silence followed, after which she added, "You and your god damn nobility. You were always too good for me, weren't you?'

"We were jus' kids."

She crushed the cigarette in the ash tray, grinding it out, and glowered at him. All light seemed to drain from her eyes and a nasty look came over her face. It was not going to be pleasant.

"You're the big up 'n coming Percival Jones," she said, falsely. "You've left me and Malek behind."

"I thought we were gonna keep it civil?"

"You've scorned me."

"I don't see how."

"I came to you on my knees. I've shown you my scars; spilled my heart out to you and this is how I'm repaid, you humiliate me." She paused as a wicked smile formed on her face. "She's white, isn't she?" She spat as if accusing him of murder. "Your wife! You married that white bitch, didn't you? You mangy black bastard!"

"I thought you came because Malek needed a father," he said, barely containing his rage, "not to cast wild accusations. As for that bitch, as you put it, she's dead. She killed herself. Are you satisfied?"

Joleen's face colored and she tried to look contrite. "I'm so confused. I've not had a drink in so long a time but I sure could use one now."

"Let me order you another cup of coffee." Percival looked at Malek and a terrible pain gripped his heart.

"You sure there's no chance for us?" She crooned.

"We're no good for each other," he said, exasperated.

"We were good enough to have a child," she insisted. Percival didn't respond. Joleen laughed. "I just knew this would be a bust." She stood up. "I'll be right back," she said, and headed for the bathroom.

"Well, young man," Percival said, "n how 'r you?"

"Okay," the child raised his infant's face. "Am I going wif you?"

"You're mother 'n I 'r talking 'bout your coming to visit me sometime. Would you lik that?"

"You my daddy?" the boy asked in baffled wonderment.

"Yes, I am."

"Oh," said the boy in awe, delighted to be in his father's presence.

Joleen returned quickly.

"You all right?" Percival asked, watching as she stared off absently.

"I'm upset," she said. "Can't you see that? I can't stay. I can't talk to you. I've got to go. Come, Malek, mama's not feeling well."

"I thought we were going to try to reach some arrangement about the boy," Percival pressed.

"I don't think you're sincere."

"You came looking for me 'n I'm trying hard to ave it work." Percival sighed. "Look, Joleen, I want'a know my son – r son, I want'a be able to provide for him."

She collapsed onto the seat, folded her arms on the table and buried her face. She began to cry. "I'm wretched and loveless and you don't want me. I knew you didn't."

'What now,' he thought. He reached into his pocket, removed a couple hundred dollars from his wallet and offered it to her. "Here take the money, I'll have my manager contact you to make arrangements for more 'n visitation rights. I see you're in no condition to discuss this further. What'a you say, ay?"

She raised her head from her arms and gave him a look of savage hatred. "You think you can buy me off with a measly few hundred dollars?" she railed, as the eyes of customers turned to them. "See if I don't squeeze you for all you're worth!"

Percival's face hardened. "No one's gonna squeeze anyone! So let's not go that route."

"I have no wish to see you anymore," she said, standing. "I don't need to humiliate myself like this again."

"I promise my manager will take care of everything." His heart blackened with rage. "You won't have to see me. I jus' want'a care for Malek."

Joleen clasped the boy's hand and dragged him off. Malek strained to catch a glimpse of his father which broke Percival's heart.

"See what you've done," she shouted to him, standing at the open door. "I'm going to get stinking drunk off every penny of this," She said, holding up the bills he'd pressed into her palm. "Thanks for nothing!"

Percival sat awhile longer in a stupor feeling wounded. He paid the check and walked home. When he got there, Lisette asked, "Is everything all right? What I told you this morning didn't distress you, I hope."

"No, far worse, I'm afraid. Joleen showed up at the gym t'day with Malek. Ta shake my confidence, no doubt. If she wanted to upset me, she succeeded."

"Is she very beautiful?" asked Lisette.

"Funny you should ask," he said, recalling Joleen asking the same of her. "Yes, she is, cloyingly so."

"How's that?"

"She's like a sweet that's come to sicken you."

"It was that bad between you?"

"It was never good."

***

No sooner had Percival given Derrick the go ahead than everything was taken care of. Child support and visitation rights were set up within a few days. Derick had big plans for Percival and had no wish to see them jeopardized. In fact, he had even wrung a concession out of Joleen in which she gave Percival a month in which to reacquaint himself with his son, while she took a paid vacation.

"It's amazing what you can accomplish when you grease the right palms," Derrick explained, a sly twinkle in his eyes.

Jonas took Malek under his wing. He became his big brother. He enjoyed the boy. He had felt strongly that his father and elder brother, Tony Jr., had failed him miserably and that given half the chance he could do better, and, in as much as Percival was his mentor, he would become Malek's big brother.

He took Malek with him everywhere and the boy grew to love him. And they loved Lisette who loved them in return. Malek, at first, was a little afraid of his father and found Lisette comforting, reassuring.

Percival took both Jonas and Malek with him to the gym. Jonas would watch Malek, keep him out from underfoot, while Percival worked out. Jonas would entertain the boy, demonstrate the mechanics of the sport, point out various fighters and discuss their styles and shortcomings. Even though the boy was young he seemed to absorb it all. And Jonas had nothing but praise for Percival which made Malek look up to his father as well. Jonas also told him that his father was going to be "a World Champion, as good as Sugar Ray, jus' you wait!"

"As good as Ali?" the boy asked, not knowing Sugar Ray Robinson.

"Better," said Jonas, emphatically. "Well, as good anyway."

Much in the same way that Jonas helped Malek to see his father, so too he helped Percival to see his son. Jonas enabled Percival to see Malek for who he was as opposed to who he wished him to be. Jonas understood Malek intuitively and, as much as Malek needed one, he was his voice, his go between. Although Malek could be quite vocal for a three-year-old. Percival was grateful for Jonas and his input. Jonas had become an integral part of the family and could be found at Percival's more often than his own home. He would eat with them, as often as not, which was fine with Jonas' mother, Riva, grateful for one less mouth to feed. Jonas would also spend the night, secure in the bosom of his adopted family.

Jonas loved the gym even though he was too young to work out. You had to be sixteen. And he still had four years to go. He liked the rancid smell of the place, the overlay of winter green on the ripe stench of pugs locked in mortal combat. He found it all invigorating like nothing else.

"Look!" he turned to Malek, excitedly, pointing to the ring as a fighter took a spill. "See that?" Jonas was convinced, he was born to be a pug.

Derrick waved to Jonas and Malek on entering the busy gym. Percival had just started for the showers following a grueling work out. Derrick called Percival and Punchy aside. They followed Derrick into the office, closing the door, which muffled the noise from the gym. Percival paced restlessly. Derrick sat on the desktop. Punchy leaned against a side wall, crossing his legs.

"Here's the deal," Derrick proposed. "I got a call from the Garden's promotion office. They're looking for a substitute for Velez on the O'Leary card coming up in ten days. Velez busted his hand in training. They want to use Percival as a replacement. They think the fans won't be too let down if Percival can account for himself like he did his last outing. I assured them he could. The fight's ours if we want it. It's an opportunity. If Percival's up to it, that is," he said, presenting the offer. "It could be a sweet deal!"

"It sounds tempting," Punchy said, coldly. "But you forget to say they don't figure Percival can beat him any more than Velez. They jus' want a good show before Percival tanks out."

"That's their mistake then, isn't it?"

"They want someone to warm O'Leary up before his upcoming championship bid – preferably a stiff, but they can't risk having it look too much like a fix; it has to be someone with potential, but lacking experience."

"That's how they figure it. I don't. The question is, should we take it?"

"Can we beat O'Leary is the question," Punchy said. "The guy's got 36 professional fights under his belt to Percival's 13. They've been grooming O'Leary awhile. He's no journeyman. He's a contender. Eight ranked but no less so. One of the best. He's white, Irish, 'n with a following. Percival can only win if he knocks him out or cripples him, 'n that's only if he can beat him at this stage. I'd say they're booking he can't."

"What do you mean, not beat him?" Percival spoke up.

"Can you?" Derrick asked.

"I'll be damned if I can't!"

"Let's not be too hasty," Punchy cautioned. "We've been following a timetable here. You've only thirteen fights so far 'n you don't want your first ten-rounder to be with someone that experienced."

"Wasn't it you who said we can't pick 'n choose anymore?" Percival argued. The pressure was on and sweat began to trickle from his armpits like crawling insects. He was giddy with fear and excitement. Could he win? And if he did, he would at long last be a contender.

"I also said not to believe your press, either," said Punchy.

"Okay," Percival said, exasperated, "I'm either the best or I'm not, so what do we do?"

"If it were anyone but you I'd say no. You don't have the experience, but on the other hand, you're right, you happen to be the best n I guess y'll ave to prove it sometime."

"So why not now?"

"Why not," Punchy relented, ambivalent.

"Do we take it?" Derrick prodded.

"We take it," Punchy and Percival sang in unison.

Derrick sucked his breath in hard. "Well, Punchy, you've enumerated the difficulties, now how do we go about surmounting them?"

"We've two weeks to iron em out."

"Less."

"I can take him, now," Percival boasted.

"We'll take the allotted time in which to prepare, anyway," said a more pragmatic Punchy.

"I'll call the Garden to confirm," Derrick said, dialing the phone with an index finger.

"This is gonna be one hell of a challenge."

"It was bound to come," Percival said, undismayed. "I'll measure up."

"You'll have to," said Punchy bitingly, anxious over what he thought of as a premature encounter. "You best go shower off before your sweat dries n you catch cold."

***

When Percival gave Lisette the news that evening of his upcoming fight, she in turn informed him that she would be going upstate to Amelia's with a group of kids from the Settlement House the following Friday and would be gone a week. "I won't be here for your bout," she said, guardedly. "Unless you'd rather I not go?" He loved her beyond question. She had become his best friend and confident. He hung on her every word. He called on her judgment, her discernment. Since their marriage the previous Thanksgiving weekend, they had kept in touch by phone and correspondence while she was away upstate at college. Not a day went by that they had not spoken, if only to say "Goodnight." And they would continue that dialogue, nestled in each other's arms, discussing routine matters before falling asleep. "As the song goes," "'I've grown accustom to your face, it almost makes my day begin.' Or

589

something like that," he said, and they laughed. "Malek goes back to his mother that Sunday, too."

"You two have had such a good chance to become acquainted. It's been lovely for me to see."

"Yeah, he's a chip off the old block. It's been heartwarming for me to ave him around. But your going away is something else. I'll miss you."

"It's just as hard for me. I don't want to go. They had no one else. The Settlement accepted it because of my relationship to Amelia. I was pretty much put on the spot and couldn't refuse. It'll only be a week, then I'll be back home."

'Then I'll be home.' The phrase had never held such poignancy before. It denoted a feeling of belonging—one to the other. He was home, as she was home. Bound one to the other.

"You started to say about your upcoming fight?"

"Nothing really."

"Just because I can't bear seeing you fight doesn't mean I'm not interested in every facet of your life. I'm sorry for not being able to be with you, but we'll talk."

"Of course. If I win there's going to be a celebration –"

"If? What's going on? Come clean," she demanded. "Since when did 'if ' enter your vocabulary?"

He told her of the second thoughts he was having with regard to the bout. That perhaps he had been hasty in accepting because he felt indebted to Derrick for his intervening on his behalf with Malek.

She tried to reassure him. "If Punchy didn't have confidence in you I'm sure he wouldn't have agreed to such a match."

"He did so reluctantly."

"I wish there were something I could do."

"So do I but you can't." He sighed drowsily, already missing her.

They talked until they grew tired then they rolled apart and fell asleep.

Percival went into training fiercely, as if his life were at stake: He extended his run by four miles, putting in nine miles a day. Not to overly exhaust him, Punchy wouldn't let him work out any more than usual in the gym. Instead, he had him work on things like cutting off the ring; stealing the ground out from under his opponent's feet and forcing him to fight. "Ya don't wanta give O'Leary a chance to use the ring," Punchy told him. "You want'a minimize his ability to fight defensively. You want'a draw him out. Ya don't wanta get caught up fighting his fight." It was contrary to Percival's style. He was a boxer-puncher, and chasing an opponent was grunt work, awkward, like tramping through swamps in combat boots. Punchy worked on his fight by way of teaching him the art of cutting off the ring, anticipating his opponent's move and greeting him with an unexpected barrage of blows, preferably body blows, hoping to slow him to a crawl. He had him work with numerous defensive fighters. Percival picked up on the tactic quickly like the natural he was and had it down to a science before the week was out. He was a veritable compendium of tricks and had almost as many in his arsenal as "the mongoose," the greatest trickster of all, Archie Moore, back when he was in the game.

Punchy and Percival also studied the Joe Louis/ Billy Conn fight, wherein Joe had famously said, "You can run, but you can't hide." Conn had run well enough throughout the 'bout that he almost stole Louis' title until Louis caught Conn in the last rounds to hold on to his championship.

Punchy was satisfied that he had done all that was possible given the time in which they had to prepare.

It was Friday, the morning of Lisette's departure. Her bags were packed and ready to go. She looked around, hoping she'd not forgotten anything. "I guess I have it all," she said. She could barely stand the idea of leaving. Percival, Jonas, and Malek stood about eyeing her, feeling helpless. Percival felt as if the apartment were being stripped bare by looters and it's spirit put to flight. But it was not the room that stood bare, but he himself. It was overwhelming, the sense of emptiness welling inside him from her impending departure.

She picked up Malek and squeezed him to her. "I'll miss you, little one," she said, and kissed him tenderly. "You take care of them, especially Percival," she instructed Jonas, kissing him, too. "I'm sorry I can't take you upstate with me this trip but I promise another time Percival and I will take you, with your mother's consent of course. You'll love it."

"I'll take good care of em, don't you fret," Jonas promised.

She returned Malek to Jonas and he swung onto Jonas' back like a little monkey. Then turning to Percival she said, "I guess I'm as ready as I'll ever be."

"Let's flag a cab." And taking up her luggage, they started out the door. "I'll only be a minute," Percival told Jonas. Lisette waved as she departed. "Bye, guys."

"Bye," they piped.

Percival flagged a cab on 3rd. Avenue. He set her suitcases in the trunk. They said their farewells and kissed. "I don't feel good about this," she said over her shoulder as she climbed into the back of the cab. She rested her arm on the open window frame, eye gleaming.

"I'll be waiting for you," he said, dryly.

591

"My sweet," she said, reaching toward him as the taxi drove off.

***

A reluctant Malek was returned to his mother that Sunday. Crying, he pleaded for Jonas to stay, as if he would never see Jonas again. They had bonded, Jonas had become his big brother, telling him bedtime stories in the dark as they fell asleep in bed together. They were pals. When Malak wouldn't let go of him, Jonas reassured him, "Don't worry, we're brothers, see? I'll see you every weekend when you visit, okay?"

"Can't you stay wif me?"

"I'd like that, but I promised Lisette I'd watch out for your dad."

Malek sighed, defeated, as his mother pried him loose. She faulted Percival with her eyes. She wrenched Malek away, eyeing Percival crossly as if he'd committed some grievous offense against her as she slammed the door in his face.

Percival and Jonas returned to Manhattan without a word. That night, for the first time in weeks, Jonas went home to eat and sleep. The next morning as usual, he waylaid Percival returning from his run and in a burst of speed Percival could not match no matter how hard he pumped his legs, Jonas outran him by a building's width.

Jonas was greeted by applause from the tenants as they stood about discussing pressing issues of the day. They derided Percival roundly as he came from behind.

"You beat him today. You beat him fair 'n square," Ashton congratulated Jonas, clapping him soundly on the back. "We knew you could do it!" They laughed all the more at an out of breath Percival who, gasping for air, could not speak.

Jonas paced back and forth preening, his plumage fully spread.

"You'll have to do better against O'Leary than you just did with Jonas if you're going to win Wednesday night's fight," chided the printer. "I've got tickets so don't disappoint me after all I've heard."

"Jonas is bound to be better than O'Leary," Percival responded, catching his breath. "After all, I train him – right Jonas?" He chortled, laying a hand affectionately on Jonas' shoulder. Since Lisette's departure Percival had put all his energy, all his concentrated nerve force into preparation for the fight against O'Leary, the 8th. ranked middleweight contender. He would enter the big time or be sent scrambling back to square one – for which he had no taste. "You got me t'day. You got me good," he said, a little shaky, hoping it wasn't

592

an omen. Jonas smiled proudly, blushing. "I'll see you in the basement after I shower off."

"OK, coach, you're on."

Percival climbed the stoop, mocking banter at his back. He entered his apartment, showered off solemnly, sat down to a solitary cup of coffee, then joined Jonas in the basement.

He had Jonas work on the heavy bag for several rounds before they moved on the floor. Percival wore 16oz gloves to Jonas' 6oz ones. Percival slipped and parried punches while Jonas attempted to strike him with sharp jabs, right crosses and hooks, with little success. Afterwards, Jonas exercised out and returned home to change and shower off.

Percival encountered Jonas again that morning while out hosing down the sidewalk in front of the building. Jonas and a friend came swaggering down the block carrying fishing poles over their shoulders, Jonas' build noticeably developed more from boxing.

"What 'r you two up to?" Percival inquired.

"We're going fishing in the river off the rocks under the Drive."

"Beyond the rails?"

"Yeah, on the rocks."

"You be careful, hear?"

"We will, coach."

"R you going with me to the gym?"

"Nothing can stop me. Wait for me, okay?"

"I'll wait."

Percival watched the boys as they ventured off carefree as Huck Finn rafting down the Mississippi, the sap of life ripe in them, sweet as the flow of honey in their veins. The words of the song, 'Moon River,' sprang to mind, which he then whistled as the boys disappeared from view.

It was a common sight on these garbage strewn streets, young boys off to fish. The river wasn't fit for swimming, or for eating fish from, so they treated it as a sport, throwing any catch back into the murky water. City youth had few other ways by which to occupy themselves without getting into grievous mischief on hot, lazy summer days and Percival paid them no more mind.

Percival put away the hose then went inside to his reading. He had been immersed in Plato's "Republic," of late. Engrossed in the dialogue and expecting Jonas to rouse him, he lost all track of time and when he finally emerged from the pages of the book, from Plato's "Cave," he found himself running late. It was unlike Jonas to forget a promise, more so since he loved going to the gym and studying the other fighters, but Percival couldn't wait.

He left for the gym, without Jonas. for a final workout before Wednesday's big fight.

His work out was light, nothing strenuous. Punchy told him, after he'd showered off, "Go home 'n relax. Jus' take it easy. Take a long walk tomorrow but don't jog. Get your mind off things. We'll see you at the Garden fight time Wednesday."

Percival returned to his apartment wanting to talk to Lisette, but as he put his key in the lock, Ashton's door opened so Percival reckoned he would have to put that thought on hold for the moment.

He instantly felt something was wrong. Ashton's face was pale, his features drawn and his eyes teary; his lips trembled.

"You OK, man?" Percival asked.

Ashton faltered, "I – I don't know how t-to put it." He leaned heavily against the door jamb, his hand on the knob. "I-it's J-Jonas, h-he he's."

"Gone – gone where?"

"H-he's d-dead. drowned. in the river, him a-and a friend."

Percival's head swam as from vertigo, and his body broke out in sweat. He wanted to lurch his guts his knees caved. Ashton stepped forward to catch him, to support the strapping fighter. Percival yanked away. He stared blankly at Ashton. He hated him just then, hated him bitterly, this bearer of bad news.

Ashton drew back. "Can I get you some brandy?"

"I got'a sit," Percival said, steadying himself, grief sinking in, shrouding his heart. "I got'a sit."

They sat in Ashton's kitchen, silent. Percival clutched his head in his hands, numb, in a stupor, too crushed to cry.

Ashton put two shot glasses of brandy on the table.

"Wh-what happened?"

"It seems Jonas' friend fell in the river off those slippery rocks while they were fishing and he couldn't swim. Worse, neither could Jonas, but he jumped in to save him anyway and they took one another down. They were carried off by an undertow. Some other kids who were also fishing saw it and they tried to stop a car on the Drive, but no one would stop until a police car rolled up. It was too late by then. It took a Police launch to finally recover the bodies."

"They must'a been so scared," Percival mourned.

"It had to be horrible."

"It's odd," Percival said, numbly, "jus' this morning, for the first time, he outran me. This morning he was quick, fast, all of life in his limbs 'n now he's gone. How can you understand a thing like that? How? I can't take another funeral, not for someone so young. If I knew how to pray, I'd say one for myself."

"I can appreciate the sentiment."

"How's his moms taking it?"

"She's devastated. Would you believe, her mother and sisters are upstairs with her even as we speak."

"What 'r you talking 'bout?"

"Riva's family's upstairs. All of them. They got word of Jonas' death and came over dressed in ritualistic mourning. They looked like a flock of vultures. I guess they're Orthodox."

"Ya got'a be joking, man."

"I'm not."

"That doesn't make any fucking sense. Did the ole man show?"

"Her father? He led the procession, looking like something out of the pages of the Old Testament. It's crazy. While everybody was alive they'd have nothing to do with them, turned their backs on them, left them to struggle on their own. Then one of them dies tragically and they flock to them like carrion."

Percival shook his head, mournfully. "I can't figure it."

"Family," said Ashton, with a sigh.

"I got'a go," said Percival, leaving his brandy untouched. Back in his apartment he called upstate, hoping to speak to Lisette. She wasn't home. Lisette's mother said she would tell her he called. The phone rang within the hour. When he answered it he heard Lisette's voice effervescent on the other end,

"Percival, my love, how are you?"

"Not good," he began, and went on to tell her the tragic news.

"Dear God," she wailed. "Are you all right? Should I come home?"

"I'm sorry I had to give you such bad news, but no, it won't help your coming home early. I'm jus' trying to figure how I'm to support Riva."

"You've not spoken to her yet?"

"I don't know what to say."

"You'll find the words. Nothing anyone says will prove adequate, so just be sincere."

"I'm devastated. How much more sincere can I be?"

"Let her know her loss is yours too."

"I'll try."

"You'll succeed, my sweet."

"I'll keep your words in mind."

"Call me later."

"I will."

Percival headed up to Riva's apartment on the third floor. His mind was dark. He felt like the ground was slipping out from under his feet, like the walls were shifting. He felt as if he was slipping into another world. His heart pounded painfully in his chest. He was welcomed into the apartment with other tenants and friends already present. The immediate family members, starkly dressed, were discernible from the others. Riva approached him cautiously. They shared a death, and a life, in common. They had no words for each other. He looked around. He felt as if his presence were an intrusion into some occult ritual. Riva's gray haired sainted mother, her rabbinical father, sisters and brothers, all upset him considerably. He wanted to shake them out of their somnolence, tell them it was too late, ask 'Where were you these years?' He wondered where her husband, Tonio, Jonas' father, was. He remained no longer than was necessary, then left. He had to get his rest. Despite his grief, he still had a fight to win on Wednesday.

Though his head struck the pillow like a stone he still had trouble falling asleep. He could not escape the many faces of Jonas playing over and over again in his head like those of children on a carousel. Nor could he think of what he was going to tell Malek when the time came – and come it would. He rolled, restively, from side to side, sleep eluding him. He didn't realize that he had been crying. He turned his face into the pillow his body racked with sobs, a stream of unrestrained tears washed his cheeks. He loved Jonas and Jonas had been devoted to him. He would miss him sorely. The phone rang suddenly, rousing him with a start. He got up to answer it, glad for the distraction.

"'ello?"

"Percival," said Lisette, "I couldn't sleep thinking of Jonas. Have you been crying?"

"Me? How could I not. It's Jonas."

"I can hear it in your voice," she peeped.

"I was trying to drop off."

"Me too. I'm so sad. I miss your arms."

"It would fill a void if you were here."

They talked on, trying to comfort one another over the distance, until they fell asleep with the phone to their ears. They each woke up, discovering the dead space on the line and wished the other "goodnight, my love," into the mouthpiece. Percival set the receiver back on its cradle and fell fitfully asleep.

After a difficult night, Percival took a long, solitary walk in the predawn light along the East River and paused to look over the fateful spot at which Jonas would have lost his life. The water sparkled in the rising sun of a rosy morning.

That afternoon Ashton met him and together they strolled round to the funeral parlor where Jonas was laid out. The chapel was stark, no flowers or candles according to the families religious customs. The family occupied the front row seats. Riva, more alluring for her loss, was central. The rest of the family fanned out around her protectively as with angels wings which enfolded her once again to the bosom of the clan.

The room was full. People stood around visiting or sat in silent contemplation. Each mourner eventually approached the small casket to view the remains for a final time. Percival dragged himself forward, acknowledged the family, then viewed the casket, the familiar body, Jonas. At sight of the slight corpse, he faltered. His heart ached and he was moved to tears.

Mr. Sapistano, appeared, staggering through the door, causing a small commotion as he did. Drunk and disheveled like a wronged man. "I got'a find out my boy's dead from fucking strangers on the goddamn street like I'm some fucking derelict," he carped, appealing to the mourners. His eyes took in Riva and her family as a cruel, bitter expression crossed his surly, olive face. He careened forwards drunkenly. "Ain't this a sight. I ain't seen the like since hell froze over. But here they are, turn up like bad pennies all in a row." He laughed, harshly.

Riva's family lowered their heads, embarrassed for her.

"Please, Tonio," she implored, "don't."

"Don't fucking please me. Please them instead. Remember when we was kids 'n you got knocked up 'n when we got married – when I did right by you – they disowned you, said you was dead to em," he whined, swaying on his feet. "It's their fault. They cursed us. Cursed our marriage 'n now they come round to gloat over the handiwork of that curse. Where were they all these years, Riva? Where were they?" he demanded of her.

"Where were you, Tonio? Where were you?" Riva cried in response. "Where were you, my darling husband, with your other wife?" She broke into tears, and her mother draped her arms around her like a mourning shawl.

"Where w-was I?" Tonio asked, stumbling backwards against the casket, almost toppling it, surprised by the question.

Percival sprang up and gripped him by the arm, steadying him. He gave Percival a cold, hard look of recognition:

"I know you," he cawed, liquor speaking, jealous that Percival had taken his place in Jonas' heart. "You're the janitor. The broom sweeper."

"Don't test me," Percival warned quietly. "Now let's go. You've had your say for the day."

"Get your hands off me you black devil," Tonio cursed. "I ain't going nowhere with you."

Percival glowered at him and tightened his grip considerably. "Let's go."

Tony Jr. started to rise, but Riva caught him by the arm. "It's better this way," she said, choked with tears.

Percival escorted Tonio onto the sidewalk. "Listen," he said through clenched teeth, "the reason your son Jonas wanted to learn how to box was cause he wanted to kick y're ass, 'n if you fucking ever give me an excuse again I'll gladly kick y're ass for him, dig?"

Late evening found Percival relaxing in his easy chair in front of the T.V., watching the late news. He had only recently finished speaking to Lisette and was now trying to inch his way to bed but had little taste for sleep. He had been debating without much success whether or not he would attend Jonas's funeral the next day – fight day. While he had no stomach for it, he knew he would go. Meanwhile he was thinking he might watch the Johnny Carson show on television when there came a knock at his door. He perked up and listened. The knock was repeated. He got up and cracked the door surprised to find Riva standing there clasping a silk robe close to her chest.

"Can I come in," she asked?

He stepped aside for her to enter.

She closed the door and leaned against it. She wore no makeup. Her face had been scrubbed for bed.

For the first time Percival saw how lovely she truly was, how fragile.

"I want to thank you so much for today," she began, averting her eyes. "You were Jonas' friend. You were a father to him. He thought of you as such. He loved you like he'd never loved Tonio. I owe you something for that and it can't be less than what I owe his father, Tonio. You did more for him than he did," she said, shyly. "I'm grateful beyond words and this is the only way I have of repaying you." She removed her hand from her robe and unleashed the sash, the robe parting, exposing her nakedness beneath.

She had taken a ritual bath and came to him scented and perfumed as for a nuptial bed.

Percival sucked in his breath at the sight. Taken aback at her boldness, he was abashed by her forwardness. She was certainly more lovely than he had ever allowed himself to imagine. Her flesh was as smooth as porcelain and white as alabaster down to the inverted, sable hairs which nestled sweetly between her thighs, perfuming the air. His nostrils twitched, and he felt himself sinking.

"Besides," she said, scornfully, "it'll serve Tonio right if the first man I give myself to outside our marriage bed is you." She snaked her arms around his neck.

How could he refuse her? He couldn't. Yet, contrary to all desire and lust, he did. "No," he said, unsettled in himself. "I admit I'm flattered." He backed off, unable to take his eyes off her. "But it's no more complementary to me than it is to you. Besides you don't really wanta do this. Y're actin' out. It's your grief speaking, your loss and your pain," he said, voice cracking. "Tonio might be deserving of something, but we're not, Lisette's not. If we do this we'll only be taking it out on ourselves."

"You like me, don't you?"

"Yes! More 'n more," he confessed, looking her over. "But we don't want each other like this. Not in this way," he said, removing her hands from his neck. "We don't wanta sully Jonas' memory like this."

She fell back, clutching her hands to her face and sobbed.

He raised her robe back over her shoulders and closed it round her, fastening the sash.

"I see now why Jonas was so attracted to you." She lay a hand on his chest for support. "Don't blame me too harshly will you?"

"It never happened."

"I'll go now," she said.

He watched as she moved down the hall like a ghost.

It was a wet, rain-soaked morning. The funeral service was brief and unencumbered. Jonas' father, Tony Sr., as expected, didn't show. "I'll catch you later. I'm going home to rest up for the fight," Percival told Ashton, as Ashton climbed into the car to be driven to the burial site.

"I'll see you at the fights," Ashton said.

The printer, riding in the same car as Ashton, shook Percival's hand. "If I don't see you before fight time, the best of luck to you."

Riva kissed him on both cheeks, squeezing his hands in hers, her face contorted and washed with tears. "Thank you for everything," she said, politely, and slipped into the back seat of the lead car.

Percival compressed his lips into a veiled smile, then started homeward in the rain.

***

Derrick was late. It was expected that he would be. He had called the Garden and had asked that they inform Punchy that he was running behind schedule. The main event was about to start, and he had not yet shown. Percival mounted the ring steps and climbed through the ropes in advance of O'Leary, as the restive crowd settled back in their seats following a brief intermission. Then, garbed in a hooded purple robe and gloved fists, O'Leary pranced down the aisle to the hoopla of the fans, "O'Leary! O'Leary!" He entered the ring to rousing applause. There was no doubt who the crowd favorite was. He bowed to the four corners of the arena, to the bellicose approval of his fans.

The bell tolled, drawing everyone's attention to the ring. The official stood in the flood of lights.

"Ladies 'n gentlemen," he barked into a mike and went on to introduce the combatants. Hearing his name Percival took a curt bow and raised a gloved fist in observance of the gladiatorial maxim: "We who are about to die salute you." The response of the crowd was tepid, a faint mixture of applause and boos. But when O'Leary's name was called the fans went wild and whistles echoed from the rafters. O'Leary acknowledged the applause by blowing kisses off his gloves to the fans.

The referee summoned the fighters to center ring, and as they huddled, he gave his final instructions. "I expect a clean fight," he began. Percival had not met O'Leary prior to weigh in, though he had seen him fight on T.V. Both men were of equal stature with similar arm reach. And both were in excellent condition. The tale of the tape was inconclusive. "Shake hands now 'n at the bell come out fighting," the referee concluded.

At the bell Punchy slipped Percival's robe off and Percival moved out of his corner to face O'Leary. O'Leary was a straight up fighter with a more European style, accustomed to using a lancing jab to get through to his opponents. He quickly learned that Percival's jab was equally good, if not better. And so he resorted to circling, changing up, and forcing Percival to pursue him, which, for the first round, Percival did, needing to warm up. It was a lackluster round in which neither fighters claimed an advantage.

The second round was similar to the first, although O'Leary took the round by eluding Percival more effectively and landing a fairly good hook, which Percival shook off as inconsequential.

"Okay," Punchy told him between rounds, "start cutting off the ring. Don't waste time!"

O'Leary took the third round handily. Percival was unable to get off, unable to reach into his bag of tricks and pull out a better fight. He was lethargic, uninspired and unable to rise to the occasion. He fared better in the fourth but was still not exhibiting enough of a fight to pull off an upset, especially against a crowd favorite.

"How's it going?" Derrick asked, coming up on Punchy from behind, having finally arrived.

Punchy replied without taking his eyes off the action. "His performance to now ain't worth talking bout."

"Have him take a look to his right at ringside when he gets back to his corner."

Punchy peeled his eyes off the ring for a moment and saw Lisette and Malek in two front row seats, and, in the same motion, his eyes returned on the action in the ring. "I'll be glad to." He smiled.

At the end of the round Punchy had Percival look at the front row ringside seats. His heart stopped when he saw Lisette there with Malek. She flashed him a smile, and Malek waved. And there, too, he thought he saw Jonas in an empty seat next to Malek. He looked again but the specter had vanished, dissolved into mist like vapor. He felt his innards churn. But when he saw Malek again he knew that he could not explain both Jonas' death and the loss of the fight as well. Nor had he any wish to have Lisette see him suffer an ignominious defeat. He sucked in his breath and refocused himself for the fray.

"How long have they been here?" he asked, anxiously asked.

"They jus' got here with Derrick."

He spat into the water bucket his eyes fixed on O'Leary. "I'm ready," he said determinedly, snorting like a bull. "I'm ready!"

Percival sprang from his stool at the bell like a cougar and met O'Leary at center ring with a barrage of blows. He snapped his punches off from the shoulder with spitfire accuracy, and his foot work was deft. He began to cut off the ring, outmaneuvering O'Leary. He slipped punches with precision, making O'Leary miss by a hairs breath, and then he would counter. He ratcheted up the pressure a notch, allowing O'Leary no room in which to escape. O'Leary realized that the dynamics of the fight had shifted, and that he was fighting an altogether different opponent.

So, too, had the crowd realized that Percival had nimbly upped the ante.

The next round Percival took an even more decisive lead. O'Leary fought back furiously, but, Percival, resolute, stalked him with the stealth of a big cat, caught him coming off the ropes with body blows followed by a crashing left hook that pitched O'Leary face forwards to the canvas. O'Leary struggled to his feet, shook the cobwebs from his head realizing to his dismay that he was in a fight he had not bargained for. He returned to his corner at the bell a much-confused fighter.

And the once partisan crowd found themselves more impressed by Percival's ringmanship.

O'Leary's corner advised him, "Move, box 'n stick."

He tried to follow their advice but Percival was unrelenting and not to be denied, ripping off punches to the body, followed to the head with unerring accuracy. With seconds remaining before the 7th. round bell, O'Leary found himself wobbling about the ring at the gong.

The next rounds, more or less, were replays of the 7th. Between the 7th. and 10th. rounds, O'Leary found himself climbing off the canvas two more times for a mandatory eight count. Try though he may, Percival could not put him away. By closing bell, when Percival's hand was raised in victory, the fans were on their feet shouting approval. Not only had Percival won the fight, but he had won the crowd as well.

"I know you didn't think I knew what I was doing when I made this match," Derrick said to Punchy.

"You didn't. You were playing a hunch."

"Your damn well right I was."

"Well it turned out. But we'll not be giving this guy a rematch any time soon."

"Agreed."

Lisette hugged Percival passionately as he left the ring basking in the glow of his new ranking. He was a contender. Malek was swept away on the waves of accolades raining on his father.

The fans blocked the aisle along which Percival was to pass. They wanted to touch him, congratulate him. "Great fight!" they shouted at him. "Great comeback! You the best! Congratulations."

Punchy and Derrick did their best to clear a way through the tumultuous crowd, as Lisette, with Malek in her arms, brought up the rear, all bursting with pride.

Once inside the locker room below, Percival sat on a massage table, exhausted, spent like a faded, threadbare dollar bill; his limbs sore and spirits ebbing. He was breathless, besides. Lisette stood in front of him, a vision for sore eyes. He took Malek's hand in his and looked into Lisette's eyes.

"W-what brought you? What made you change your mind? Not that I'm not grateful – I thought," he spoke in bursts, "you – you weren't gonna come to – to any more fights."

"That was an emotional reaction, senseless and selfish of me. It took Jonas' tragic accident to shake me, make me see. We're in this together, whatever it is."

He panted. "Anyone tell Malek yet?"

"I thought that best left to you, as his father."

"So it is," he agreed, lowering his wary head against her bosom. Tears of mixed emotions sprung to his eyes and mingled with the sweat cascading down his face, running in rivulets over his drained body.

"I don't know if I could ave done it had you not shown."

"You would have found a way." She cradled his damp, wooly head to her. She understood better than anyone the conflict of emotions he was going through.

Malek tugged insistently at the hem of his robe. "Where's Jonas, daddy?" he asked, looking for him. "Where's Jonas?"

***

Following the fight, O'Leary demanded a rematch. He told the press he had not prepared for Percival and that expecting someone like Velez, he was caught off guard, hence he was demanding a rematch. When asked about a rematch, Punchy was emphatic. "There will be no rematch for a while." He told the press, "It's clear, O'Leary had been preparing for Velez, for a major fight, otherwise Percival would 'ave knocked him out." Everybody had a good laugh. "Remember, Percival only had ten days to prepare for a man so much more experienced. No," he said, "there's no percentage in giving him a rematch at this time. We have a schedule to meet, 'n we'll fight him again down the line when 'r schedule permits."

O'Leary got his return match, as promised, down the line. It was Percival's 21st. outing and he won, disposing of O'Leary in short order. After dominating the fight for the first four rounds Percival knocked O'Leary out in the fifth.

This encounter came shortly after their European tour which took place in conjunction with winter school break, thereby permitting Lisette to travel with him. The first fight on the tour, which took place in Paris, Percival won on a decision. The second was in Bonn and the third in Rome, both fights won by knockouts, and, as he went on to build a Trans-Atlantic reputation, the tour culminated in a victory against the reigning European middleweight champion in London. He won that fight in ten rounds by a unanimous decision, wooing judges, fans, and sports writers, alike.

He and Lisette managed to steal away on an occasional day trip and took in some of the sights. He was becoming popular and was recognized almost everywhere they went. And so, for more romantic dalliances, they'd rendezvous in their hotel suite and order in. It was as close to a honeymoon as they had yet to have. Lisette complained to Punchy and Derrick with a whimsical, teasing smile, "I'm fully grown now, as is Percival. We don't need to be chaperoned anymore." They took her attempt at levity in stride, recognizing that Percival's schedule for the past year and a half had been excruciatingly tight, and that they had kept watch over him like mother hens.

Lisette graduated university that May and was promoted to program director for the Settlement House. Percival continued his studies and despite his demanding schedule he still managed to maintain a B average. His professors thought it laudable that he persisted as he did, given his rigorous outside schedule and the substantial purses he was now able to command as a contender. They were all fans for whom, at one time or another, he had procured ringside seats.

After his twenty-fifth win against the second ranked contender, Amos Kincaid, which he'd won in the 7th. round with a knockout, contracts for a championship bout were drawn up and signed at the Boxing Commissioner's Office with the press in attendance. He would fight the then reigning title holder, Arturo Cruz, a Colombian born transplant, raised in Miami's Little Havana. Because he was an outsider he had had to fight his way up through the streets of the barrio but in the end he had won the respect of its inhabitants with an unapologetic fist. In due course, the exiled Cuban community embraced him as one of their own, especially as his star began to rise.

At the time of the signing he was at the height of his fight and had dominated the division for the past three years. He was as vicious and cruel a product of human intelligence as the fight game ever produced. It was said he took sadistic pleasure in injuring his opponents. Certainly, the evidence in the wreck of fighters he'd hospitalized without a sympathetic word, gave weight to that conviction. It was also rumored that he was *connected* and the evidence for that was present at the signing in the person of Alfonse McGraw, who was to be one of his New York handlers.

The papers were, signed, and a media-op photo taken for press release the next day, with the two fighters posed as if about to duke it out. The caption under the photo in the Daily News read, "May the Best Man Win!"

Punchy thought it best they relocate their training sight to the country upstate. Percival was amenable. He consulted Lisette. She asked Amelia who was more than willing – excited even. Renaldo was brought in on it, and he was happy to turn an old, unused barn into a gym for Percival, his son-in-law, for his middleweight title bid. In fact, nothing could have pleased him more; nothing that is save for Lisette and Percival to present him with a grandson. Terms were agreed upon and money advanced for the project, and they could look forward to bringing up their squad within two weeks. Punchy then scouted out the best gyms in New York's five boroughs to put together a string of the best fighters available in the city. He was thorough in his search and circumspect in his selection of sparring partners brought on board.

Lisette obtained a three month leave of absence to be with Percival for his championship bid.

After the tickets were printed, Percival was given six complementary ring side seats, making it possible for him to fulfill a promise he'd made to himself two years earlier, the morning after he'd left Jamal asleep on a bench on Eastern parkway. Jamal had reminded Percival, who had been sunk in despair, that he was "arguably the best fighter alive, pound for pound." Percival had promised himself there and then that if he ever made it to a title fight he would make sure Jamal was ringside. Now all he had to do was locate him. He would start his search at Jamal's parent's home in Bed-Stuy.

Lisette braked the Volkswagen to a stop in front of a brownstone, and parallel parked in a tight spot between two other cars. Percival gazed out at the Atlantic Avenue between the buildings across the way on the far side of the road, listening to the rumble of a passing train as it careened on its wheels like a juggernaut, drowning all else out. They climbed from the car, passed through the front gate and pressed the bell for the ground floor apartment.

A well preserved, gray-brown skinned woman in her mid-forties in an Islamic hijab, answered the ring. "Yes?" she said, scanning their faces.

"Ello, I'm Percival Jones, 'n this is my wife, Lisette. I'm a friend of Jamal Ibraham 'n I believe this is his home?"

"Percival Jones," the woman echoed, her teeth flashed white in a charming smile of recognition. "You're the boxer. I'm Jamal's mother, but I'm sorry Jamal's not here."

"Oh?"

"He's not been home for quite some time. He's gone to India, in fact."

"India?" Percival said, surprised.

"Yes."

"How did that come about, may I ask."

"Would you care to come in for a minute? It would be more comfortable inside."

"Thank you, we'd like that."

Jamal's mother directed them to the living room. The room was pleasantly fragranced with incense, immaculately clean and well furnished with a sole photo of Elijah Muhammad. She invited the couple to sit.

"May I get you a cup of coffee or tea?"

"We wouldn't want to put you out," Lisette responded.

"It's no bother at all. It's not often you get'a future champion in your house," she said. "My husband will be sorry to have missed you."

"If you insist," Lisette said. "We would love to have tea."

Percival nodded his approval.

She went off and shortly returned with a pot of hot tea and cups and saucers on a tray. She set the pot down on the coffee table between them, and took a chair across from them, observing them wonderingly. "Jamal spoke quite highly of you," she said to Percival. "I want'a thank you for talking him into coming home that night. He spoke of it often – the night you two met on Eastern Parkway. It was a turning for him, an epiphany I guess you'd say. I don't think he would ever ave come home had he not met you there that night. N I wouldn't'a seen my son again 'n I don't know I'll see him again now."

"It was a fortunate encounter for me, too. I was at my rope's end. Jamal reminded me of who I was—am."

"Jamal did not fare well for a time," she said, softly. "He 'n his father didn't get on. His father wanted him to go for his master's degree or get a job— one! He refused to go back to school. He thought it a waste. He said school was bogged down in empty details, 'n churches, including Mosques, were sepulchers of 'dead gods,' something from Nietzsche. It horrified me, but it was blasphemy to his father. His father wouldn't listen. Jamal was difficult for his father cause he was more intelligent than the both'a us together. His father couldn't handle it. He was intimidated by Jamal's genius. He often used his intelligence as a barrier, 'n so his father couldn't get close. He, more or less, shut his father out. But I was non-threatening. I was not in competition with him. I'm his moms and he's my son. I nursed him at my breast. Genius or simpleton what's it matter to a mother?

"I'm also a nurse, an LPN, and I only read medical journals these days but as a devoted Muslim I read my Quran faithfully every day for inspiration. I'm not cleaver in the sense Jamal is. No one in this household could say that though, unlike the others, he and I 'r close and I gained many insights on account. We use to have such delightful discussions. He would open up to me. And I remember a great deal of what we spoke. It meant so much to him. He always appreciated it when I would cite something of which we'd talked," she said in fond remembrance. "Back in school, when Jamal was a boy, he was skipped from grade to grade ahead'a his elder sister and brothers 'n graduated high school early, at age fourteen, along with his oldest brother, Kareem, who was eighteen. He then went on to graduate Brooklyn college two years later with a fellowship to MIT, while Kareem struggled through junior college bitterly envious at how easy it all was for Jamal. There was a bit of contention there. He saw things others could not see easily. Which made his brothers and sisters leery of him, they were uneasy in his presence for fear he would upstage them. As a nurse in a hospital setting I'm always dealing with unseen possibilities, so I didn't feel half so threatened by what he saw.

"Don't get me wrong, I love my family, my children, and admire my husband tremendously. He's a man of deep conviction and faith. Jamal is different, that's all. And I harbor a special place for him in my heart. It's true, in the past his father had been happy to acknowledge Jamal's scholastic achievements, but when he defied him and turned his back on our Islamic faith, especially since my husband is a member of the FOI, the Fruit Of Islam—the defenders of the faith— he became utterly disgusted with him and was increasingly unhappy when he joined the Black Panther Party. He saw it as yet another slap in the face. And he denounced him at our mosque. I dared not defend him, as a woman it was not my place. I only wish his father could see what a fine and brilliant son he'd sired in Jamal, but to do so would be to take a wrecking ball to his world view and, all too sadly, he has nothing else to replace it with. My husband, Jamal's father, grew up hard on the streets of Hell's Kitchen and everything he has was hard won. Unlike Jamal he didn't have the advantage of a father's shoulders on which to stand. He does not see Jamal as standing on his shoulders either, viewing the world from a better position. Though his father doesn't see it Jamal does."

Listening with unflagging interest, Lisette sat on the edge of the couch, her teacup poised gingerly between the fingers of her hands.

"I'm the one who went to see him in jail when nobody else would; not his father, his brothers or sisters. N ya'll Panthers cut him loose cause you had no further use for him. He says it was on account of his insubordination but, uh-uh, under the circumstance, that's no excuse," she said, her eyes steadfast, condemning. Percival shifted his gaze, shamefaced. "He was jus' a kid, seventeen, 'n ya'll cut him off."

"We were making it up as we went along," Percival said. "Sometimes we got it right, but as often as not we got it wrong."

"That's cold comfort," she responded.

"Ours was a Faustian bargain from which few of us emerged unscathed," he said with regret. "I know I didn't." He smiled wanly. Lisette took his hand. "It was my good fortune to have found Lisette."

"As it was mine to be found," she added, smiling.

"Never mind. Jamal did not fault you nor shall I," Jamal's mother continued. "Still you Panthers broke his heart, broke his trust. Ya'll almost kill his spirit," she said, with a sorrowful shake of the head. Percival felt a pang of guilt. "When he saw you on the streets I think it helped pull him together.

"Oh, he tried to find work, but nothing come of it. He would work on 'n off, here 'n there, but nothing stuck. He was uneasy in his mind 'n restless in his spirit. He felt the culture was a wasteland, had nothing to offer 'n he had no wish to contribute to it. He took to listening to a Bob Dylan song he'd play 'n play again, 'There must be some kind'a way out'a here said the Joker to the Thief—'"

"'There's so much confusion I can't get no relief,'" Percival said, picking up the lyrics where she left off. "Yes, I know the song. It's called 'All Along the Watchtower.'"

To their credit, neither one tried singing it.

"He played it a lot," she said. "And reading heavily, too, both day 'n night. He searched into philosophy, religion, absorbing everything on which he set his mind. He avoided his father. He would take his books 'n go to his room when his father got home 'n read till early morning. I would get up sometimes late at night 'n find his light burning 'n if I was to look in I'd see him absorbed in some book or other. Sometimes I'd sit 'n he'd talk to me about whatever it was he was reading. His appetite for esoteric literature was insatiable. He read 'n reread Dostoyevsky 'n Hesse. He found 'Siddhartha,' he told me, 'Spell binding, 'n the way of the Buddha irresistible.' He was deeply influenced by 'The Brothers Karamazov.' For a good time there he only read Nietzsche; but, after much thought, he put him aside saying, 'after you break the code, his philosophy amounts to no more than that of a precocious adolescent.'

"'He's engaging at first,' he said, 'because it's surprising that an adult could possibly be, at one and the same time, so brilliantly astute and naive in the same breath. His father was dead and, as a consequence, he denied the existence of a heavenly One. His father was dead and so too was God. He required the one to have the other. And since he was denied the one, he would not have the other. His father, a minister, died early on in his life, and he was left in the care of his sisters and aunts. They had a telling effect on his intellectual growth. When his father died, God the father died, too. Maddened by an overwhelming feeling of abandonment, he cried out to a dumbfounded world, "God is dead!" And the deaf overheard him! His views are as sour against women as against God. No, mama, the best of western thought is summarized in the words of Plato's Socrates, 'I know that I know nothing.' It's quite Zen, you know?' he said, 'Knowing I didn't know.'

"Anyway, he went on to become involved with the "I-Ching'— the Chinese book of changes— the 'Tibetan Book of The Dead,' Tarot, and other things occult. The bible, your bible, the Christian bible. The New Testament. He had been raised on the Holy Koran 'n could quote it chapter 'n verse, but he found himself attracted to the mystical Christ. Then he started to meditate for hours on end. One day he told me that he had decided to go to India to pursue his deeper interest. He decided he wanted to study under a holy man, a sage, he said, a man of God, as if Elijah Muhammad was not." She sighed, "'n that was another source of contention between him 'n his father," she offered, by way of an explanation. "Anyway, he had been writing to people with a hermitage in the jungle in a place called Tivunmali, where a group of Sadhus gathered round the shrine of their Rishee, 'n he was invited to join em. 'Their spirits were one,' he told me. 'N within the month he had enough money for the trip, 'n off he went to India lookin' for a way 'out.' May Allah grant him the 'out' he seeks," she said resignedly. "He's kept in touch. He doesn't write often but I've received at least three letters over the past year." She paused in her story. "If you want I can share em with you?"

"I'd like that," said Percival. "I'd like that a lot."

She scurried off and quickly returned with three envelopes and passed them to Percival. He opened the first letter and read,

Dear Moms,

I've entered another world of time and space. If not for the poverty of its people I should think that I had found the Peaceable Kingdom. This is how it seems at first blush. I'm intoxicated, for lack of a better word. The people are more Black than we are. Beautifully so, I might add. And for the most part I go unnoticed, except when someone wants to know whether I'm African or American. Apart from that, my skin color goes unrecognized. My American accent is more recognizable than anything else about me, oddly enough.

Needless to say, the caste system here is no less vile than that of American racism. Worst still, much of it is carried over into the religious system, as racism is carried over into our political and economical system. Yet, the wise men here, as wise men everywhere, see beyond all temporal illusion and are capable of transcending our earthly existence.

I was greeted at the Ashram as if I were an emissary of God's. I learned quickly that all who enter this abode are welcomed in equal fashion, as if we'd arrived in a king's carriage where, in fact, we'd simply dismounted a bullock. My room is clean. Monastic. There are a small number of religious books. A pallet for my bed. And not much else. For the most, after the Rishee has given his Dashan, which is conducted in silence, we pray or meditate.

My duties are to work in a clinic among the poor. Although I clean the sick and aged for a period of my day, I am not long distracted from my prayers. I am, as I say, in a new world. A far different world. A place where love and peace abide. Where tears of joy grace my face every day and often more than once a day. I am relieved of our nation's sorrows, which are well known to you and need not be entered into here.

I pray for all of you, but remember you most fondly, my angelic mother.

Your son, Jamal."

Percival passed the first letter on to Lisette, then went on to the second shorter one.

Dear Moms,

I know I've written you and have received an answer in reply, but time here has virtually no meaning. Moreover, we are delving into timelessness, the emptying of Maya, the illusion of life – not as you might imagine the denial of existence. No, but to plunge like a dagger headlong into the very heart, the valley of existence. The timelessness of being where the wheels of thought

609

grind to a standstill, and you're left naked in the company of your Lord and Master – your selfhood. There are unsung masters here as yet, and the mountain itself is magnified with spiritual energy. I have had the good fortune to have been taken under the wings of such a one, a holy man, who knew the master in the flesh, a man of remarkable spiritual attainment in his own right, and in whose gaze my lowly soul often soars to the most dizzying, unimaginable heights of unfoldment. A glorious mountaintop view of the inner workings of the cosmos. That's as best I can describe it. This is the kingdom in which I've come to dwell. It is real for me now and shall become real for all as we learn to overcome the shackles of our engagement in, as our Indian brethren call it, Maya.

Your loving son, Jamal.

Percival went on to the last and more recent letter.

My dear moms,

My stay in India at the hermitage is rapidly drawing to a close. As a result of my daily routine of prayer, meditation and work, I realize my obligations are to humanity as a whole. I shall therefore leave here and travel the world as a mendicant, working among the poor of the world to reestablish myself with its people. It is a thing we in the Panthers attempted on a political front and failed for much the same reason. Here, it is as an individual savant, a monk, if you will, that I shall return to the world and claim my stake, guided by the light of God, which alone illuminates the chandelier of my conscience.

And while I strive among the poor, so too shall I beg among the rich that I do not loose communion with any of my kinsmen and to remind them, as Jesus said, 'The poor will be with us always,' making no mention of the rich, save, 'It would be as hard for a rich man to enter the Kingdom of God as it would be for a camel to pass through the eye of a needle.' As well I need must grasp the difficult lesson of humility.

I have gained much here. I can stay forever, but to do so would defeat the purpose of my having come. While long ago I seemed to have found God, I feared that I had lost contact with mankind. And now I'm endowed with the capacity to rediscover my root's in humanity's soil. Wish me well. And may the eternal be your guide in all things.

I pray that we might meet again in this incarnation for I fear it is not guaranteed. I leave here to journey through the Middle East, then I'll continue on to Africa. It shall be a slow journey, months if not years in completing.

Your loving son,
Jamal."

Lisette also read the final letter and restored it to its envelope. She looked into Jamal's mother's clay colored face. "You have a remarkable son," she stated simply.

"I don't pretend to understand him I know he's different from the rest of us, his family. I just pray that Allah protects him."

"You worship different Gods," Percival allowed.

"No," Lisette put in, "I think his is the nameless God, the unfathomable God to whom all names apply, as aunt Amelia would say."

Percival was visibly affected. "I want'a thank you for the letters," he said, then stood and for a second it was as if the earth had shifted again beneath his feet. "When you write Jamal again, please mention this visit."

"I will," said Jamal's mother, escorting them out. "N thanks for coming."

"Thank you for having us," Lisette replied.

"Thanks again," said Percival.

"What did you make of Jamal's letters?" Lisette asked, as they got back in the car.

"I don't know they affected me strangely. Other than that I can't say."

"You former Panthers are a breed apart," said Lisette, as she steered the car into traffic.

Lisette's remark was not entirely without merit. In the days to come, when Percival tried to contact Silva, he found that he, too, was out of the country, in England, enrolled at Oxford as a doctoral candidate and would not be in the states at the time of the fight. He wired Percival to wish him "luck." Meanwhile, Raschelay was attending Columbia University on scholarship, as well as having to care for her child, and, regrettably, could not commit to a date so far in advance. Leroy and Nora, both enrolled in the local community college, said they, "Wouldn't miss it for the world!"

Much to Percival's dismay, Rufus was still catatonic and confined to an Army mental hospital. True to her vow, Lily patiently waited as would a sailor's widow. Sadly enough, Priestus had succumbed to the ravages of heroin and had become a drug fiend, lost like Lancelot, broken and confused in his quest for the Holy Grail. Percival had also wanted to invite Tzi but he had become hopelessly lost in Chinatown, lost as all the others scattered without a trace.

Percival therefore awarded the remaining tickets to his dear friend, Nina Koestler, and Renaldo and Dominick Poincare. And finally, despite the fact that Big/Black was in prison on a twenty-five year to life sentence for arson in South Carolina, Percival gave him his last ticket which he autographed, and sent off with a brief note— "Whenever you get out, I'll redeem it somehow or other. Look forward to visiting you after fight, hopefully a champion.

Your friend & comrade, Percival.

Since Big/Black was basically illiterate and another inmate had been writing his letters for him, but, this time, his letter was in a childish scrawl and in his own hand,

My man,

You going to be the next champ. Sweet. I told everybody that. I said I know you but these cats don't believe squat. When I show them the ticket you sent me for the championship fight they just gawked. I can't use it, but I'll hold on to it anyway. Some guards ask me for it, say they'll take care of me. Bull crap, I'm a keep it, know?

"You surprised to see me writing, I bet? I met a guy here. My good friend, Carl Moore. A white dude. He's the only person I know smarter than you. Course you ain't kill your folks off either. He did, so that might explain it. He wiped them out. He know something you don't, sure. He-he. Anyway, he taught me to read and write and do math, too. He white, like I say. But he be my man. He be teaching me all kind of stuff. Stuff I was shoulda know. Hell, for the first time I'm getting a fucking education. Ain't that something? I had to burn down a school that taught nobody nothing and go to jail to get an education. Ain't that some shit? I mean, man, like I finally know what a dialectical materialist is, after calling myself one so long. Now I ain't so sure. Yeah, he's my ace. We tight. He's a good dude, even though he be a little bit crazy.

I also want to thank you for the lawyer. With some luck, I'll even get a new trial. Thanks for being such a pal. I won't wish you luck cause I know you don't need it. Till next time, champ.

Your friend & comrade,
Sundown."

***

Since early adolescence Percival had been training, both mentally and physically, for a professional championship bid and now, in his mid-twenties, he had attained his first objective. To realize the second, winning the title, he ran fifteen miles per day – a mile for every round to be fought. He ran the lonely, desolate pre-dawn rural roads of Saratoga County, as Lisette bicycled alongside. Only one of the other fighters, Leon Bell, an up and coming welterweight, the best boxer Percival had yet to encounter, would rise early enough to run with him. He was an intelligent fighter, brilliantly fast, dangerous with both fists, and no less exacting than was Percival. In a pinch, Percival was not reluctant to use his weight against the lighter man. It was his only advantage. Percival worked with Bell every day, if for only three rounds; and he was sure to put Percival through his paces. It was a brutal psychological game played, even with road work, pushing each other to the brink of exhaustion. The competition between them was much too fierce for them to be friends, but they respected one another tremendously, otherwise they could little bear the sight of each other.

After a breather from his run, Percival would join Renaldo on the wood pile and face a mountain of logs, a daunting workload. Renaldo had estimated that it would take upwards to eighteen cords of wood for them to properly heat the barn and loft for the next twelve weeks. Renal would cut the logs with a chain saw and Percival would then split them with an ax, mallet, and wedge. Sweat flew along with wood chips and every consecutive fall of the ax. They would work unceasingly for the next few hours, and Percival would be soaked through his clothes, every muscle in his body thrumming. He would shower off, take a light breakfast, and then rest up until it was time to go to the gym.

The autumn was brisk and the smell of snow rife on the air. The wooly bear caterpillar, indicators of a severe winter to come, were plentiful that fall. "It's going to be a cold winter," Amelia predicted, a fat wooly bear caterpillar curled in her palm. Thus, Percival and Renaldo were kept busy on the wood pile, mounting up cord after cord and stacking them to dry in a woodshed behind the barn.

Percival watched films of Arturo Cruz's fights with Punchy and Derrick, night after night, until he could little think of anything or anyone else. He would fall asleep and wake up with Cruz on his mind; beating Cruz, upending him and becoming champion in his stead. A month and a half into training – midway to fight time – Alfonse McGraw appeared among those of the many local viewers who'd paid three and a half dollars a head to see Percival work out. The old barn, converted into a gym, was warm from the fires burning in the wood stoves, keeping out the chill. An early pre-Thanksgiving snow had blanketed the surrounding fields and woodlands and dusted the rooftops with a crystalline sheen.

Punchy was unhappy to spot McGraw in the packed gallery. He pointed him out to Derrick, who was momentarily surprised.

"He wants something," Derrick warned, under his breath.

"No doubt," Punchy agreed, sneering. "I've a bad feeling 'bout this."

"You should have," said Derrick. "But let's not hedge our bets as yet."

The gym was a beehive of activity. Percival was impressive. His team of sparring partners showed him off to advantage. Some were preparing for a fight of their own on the same card. Leon was one of them. The viewers got a lot for their money. Since SPACC and the racetrack had closed for the season, the rural gym had taken up the slack and became the center of attraction in the county, where the gentry hobnobbed with the locals.

Predictably enough, after the session, Alfonse waited around for all the others to leave before approaching Punchy, Derrick and Percival, as they conversed outside the ring.

"Hello sports fans," he began cheekily, the world being his oyster and a source of amusement for him. "You look good in there," he said to Percival, sitting on the apron of the ring, his eyes cast to the floor. "It ain't surprising in itself, is it?" he reached for a lighter to light Derrick's dead cigar.

"No thanks," said Derrick, with a shake of the head.

"I guess you're wondering what I'm doing all the way up here out of the city, other than spying on your boy, of course."

"Care to get to the point?" Derrick said, impatiently.

Alfonse looked about the empty gym. All the guests had gone and the other fighters had retired to the loft to lie down, play pool, watch T.V. or just lounge about.

"What'a you want?" Punchy asked.

"I'm just a messenger," said Alfonse, with spread hands. "It's like this, the boys want a guarantee."

Percival was immediately incensed: "The boys 'n I 'ave never had any dealing 'n that's why you're on the other side of this conversation!"

"It's not so simple." Alfonse cleared his throat. "The boys think Arturo can beat you. But I dissuaded em of that notion. I told em I've known you from jump; from your early amateur days 'n that if I was placing odds I'd bet on you to win on a KO in the mid to late rounds, after frustrating Arturo the first number of rounds. We studied some films together 'n they came round to seeing my point."

"And?" said Punchy, pointedly.

"They have a big investment in Arturo. They owe him. He can't lose. He's their prize possession. These are new boys on the block. They're a Latino syndicate, macho as all hell. They play by rules that would make the old mob blush. Take what I say seriously. They're anti-communist and, quite frankly, they don't like your politics. In fact, they think they stink!"

"But Arturo can lose," Percival assured Alfonse, angrily. "My politics my ass."

"That's just the point of my visit," said Alfonse, "he won't," engaging Percival's unsmiling face. "He won't!"

"You're talking to the wrong person," Percival said, turning to go. "I got'a shower off." He was furious. "You can see yourself out."

614

"It's not that easy," Alfonse said, shifting his gaze to Derrick. "You owe us."

"Owe you? Owe you what?"

"Recall the small service I performed for you on Percival's behalf?"

"What service?" said Percival, angrily, looking from Alfonse to Derrick.

"Expediting your child visitation rights. You didn't think it came off so easily in your favor, cause your ex ole lady had a change of heart, did you? It was more the twisting of an arm 'n a promise of more to come if she didn't comply." From the vacant expression on Percival's face Alfonse knew that he did not know anything about it. "You care to explain it to him, Derrick?"

"Explain what?" said Punchy, with a doubtful look on his face.

"He wants me to tell you that I had some of his cohorts lean on Joleen in order to secure visitation rights for Percival with his son. She wasn't seeing reason. But that didn't involve you. Alfonse, here, owed me. And it was not to come up again."

Punchy walked over to a wood burning stove and nervously stoked the hot coals in the grate, then set in a few logs. The air was suddenly tense, as everyone waited in solemn silence. He returned, hands in pockets. "I never did like you, Alfonse," Punchy said, almost casually. "You destroy good fighters for no more than a few lousy dollars. You've mounted em up in a garbage heap over the years, you 'n your sort. I won't let you do that to Percival."

"There's not too much you have to say about it, ole man."

"We'll see about that, won't we?"

"It's not like you'll walk away empty handed. You'll make a bundle between you, betting against yourself plus your share of the purse."

"I'm gonna beat your boy," said Percival, sharply. "I'm gonna beat him bad. N now you don't give me reason to let it go long. I'm gonna take the son of a bitch apart 'n leave him for you to put back together like Humpty Dumpty, dig? N that's my final word," Percival said, turning abruptly for the showers.

"I'm sorry to say," said Alfonse, "but if you don't agree there won't be a fight."

"The contract's been signed," Percival spat, strolling off.

"Contracts can be broken easily enough," Alfonse shot back.

"I'm not impressed."

"By the time we're done with you, you won't be able to get a fight in Podunk. If what we got on you gets into the papers, you'll have a lot of explaining to do to the Boxing Commission – as well as to the police."

"What's he talking 'bout," Percival said, livid, taken up short. "There's nothing for the police to question me on," he said, his brows twitching in rage.

He felt his dreams shattering and he could hear them tinkling like so much broken glass.

"Maybe. But the damage would have been done. Wouldn't it? Think of the press, how savage they can be. Joleen doesn't like you, not a little bit. She said a lot about you. Your past, your brother's death. And, yeah, Priestus. Do you remember him from your Panther days? He hardly cares to remember, but you'd be surprised at what a person can recall if you withhold their junk from them long enough. All of a sudden they become a fount of information. All of which the news boys will eat up. Unless you got something else to say to me, I'll be on my way. You think it over and have Derrick get back to me in a week's time, no more."

Tension filled the air, a raw sense of malice. Percival balled his sweaty fists, his guts screaming. He gnawed at his under lip. He felt everything that he had ever struggled for in danger of collapsing, as if someone were trying to snatch back hard-won food out of his mouth. He felt cornered and without room in which to turn, his eyes as fiery as a cat ready to spring. He growled, "There's nothing for Derrick to get back to you on. It's no deal!"

"You think it over, anyway."

"You heard the man," said Derrick. "There's nothing to consider."

"Is that your last word?"

"My very last!"

"If that's the case you can tell me again in a week's time."

After Alfonse's departure Punchy spoke up, irate, "What the hell is this," he said, addressing Derrick, outraged – perfectly incensed, "how'd you get us entangled with that slime?"

"It's no good turning on Derrick," Percival interjected. "If it's anyone's fault it's mine. He only did what I wanted. I would ave done most anything to get to see Malek. There was no way round it for me. Without Derrick, I would'a been stuck. God knows, I'd wanted to strangle Joleen. N probably would'a too. Joleen could'a ruined me back then. No, let's not fault Derrick. It's because of him we've come this far, this fast. You got'a remember Derrick's been damn shrewd for the most part. Damn shrewd. The question is, what'a we do now?"

"I'm afraid," said Derrick, "the next hand is theirs. All we can do is wait to see how they play it."

"N you know damn well they will play it," said Punchy.

Percival informed Lisette later that evening of Alfonse McGraw's visit.

"So what are you going to do?" she asked.

"Do?" he said. "I'm gonna kick Cruz's ass."

Adhering to the old adage that, "No news is good news," they scrutinized the papers daily, expectantly, in trepidation. Within a week's time the Boxing commissioner's office summoned Derrick to appear with Percival before the Commissioner the following day at two o'clock. Percival objected, he was to take Lisette to the doctor's. Lisette was more compliant, "It's okay, if it's important. I'll go with my mother."

Percival conceded. The meeting was brief. The Commissioner was corpulent, in his mid-fifties with a bull dogface, jowls and double chins to match. He looked like an ill at ease, roughneck kid in a suit and tie. He occupied a sumptuous chair behind a sumptuous desk in a palatial office, his back to a picture window overlooking 34th. Street below and the entrance to Madison Square Garden.

Although he acknowledged Punchy and Derrick, who flanked Percival, he kept them standing while he scrutinized Percival. "I don't know what to say to you, young man," he said at length, his tone curt, manner brusque, "You had the promise of being among the best. 'Incomparable,' I believe the paperboys say. In a game full of heartbreaks, you disappoint me the most. The boxing game is froth with difficulties enough, but you present it with a whole new set of problems, which would be unpardonable under ordinary circumstances. As a champion, you're supposed to be a role model. The allegations made against you, if borne out, would do nothing to enhance the sport. I mean, as if having your brother set up isn't bad enough, you're a communist, too. A commie of all things, Jesus Christ," said the Commissioner in disgust. "Why couldn't you be a crook like everyone else?" He squirmed in disgust, in his sumptuous chair.

Percival was not to be cowed or intimidated. "None of those accusations can be substantiated. If you mean to say I was with the Black Panthers – well, yes, I was. As for the other, none of it can be proven."

"Don't give me your sarcasm. This has already been leaked to the press. They've held off long enough to give us time for this interview, but when your back strikes that door on the way out you're shark bait as far as I'm concerned. As I've said, these charges against you, if proven, would do nothing to enhance the sport. Therefore, until further evidence is forthcoming one way or other, I reserve my decision for at least another week. But in all honesty, I don't see how having you for a champion could be good for boxing. Good day!"

"Our lawyers will be in touch with you," Derrick declared, as they turned to go.

The reception room to the Commissioner's office was full of reporters, cameras and handheld microphones.

"Is it true you set your brother up to be killed?" came the first crass, indelicate question, as flash bulb after flashbulb exploded in Percival's face.

He grimaced. "I'm gonna do you a favor 'n not dignify that question with a reply."

"But you can't deny you're not a communist?" came another hostile voice out of the crush of reporters blocking the passage.

"I was a Black Panther, yes."

"They're Marxist, are they not?"

"Marx himself wasn't a communist. He was a dialectician no less than we were."

"You're just mincing words.

Percival gave the camera a fierce look as his thoughts cast back to the first time he'd ever knowingly shaken hands with a communist and feeling like a virgin about to lose her virtue. From then on he would tread the path of a heretic. As the old saw goes, "He who passes beyond these doors abandon all hope." And so he had.

"Is this an inquisition? I thought the McCarthy era had passed. Okay, you asked. First off, do you know what a communist is? Any of you?" When he received no reply, he said, with a smirk, "That's what I thought. I'll not hold your ignorance against you. I'll tell you since you don't seem to know. A Communist is nothing more than a Christian soul grown sober waiting for the meek to inherit the earth."

"Is the fight still on?" a lone, more friendly, voice asked, which Percival recognized as Ashton's.

"It's under advisement. Our lawyers will certainly press for it," Derrick said. "Hopefully you will, too."

"Are any criminal charges pending?"

"None! Not at all! Why would there be? No crime was committed. This is all a smoke screen, a setup, an attempt to stop a legitimate contender. The only one Arturo has faced since becoming champion. Percival's a real threat. And that, in a word, is what this is all about. Arturo's camp is afraid," said Derrick, bluntly. "And rightly so. And that's where these charges originate."

"You claim these accusations are unfounded?"

"You're investigative reporters, do the footwork for yourselves."

"One more question," shouted another.

"No more questions, please," Percival begged off.

"Can we get by?" Punchy implored.

"Let us through," Derrick added his voice to the fray, as they tried to elbow their way through the crush of reporters. Just then the Commissioner came out of his office and the reporters surged forwards with a barrage of questions for him, allowing Percival, Punchy and Derrick to make their escape.

618

Shortly after his return from the city, Lisette found Percival in the darken gym striking the speed bag listlessly, adrift in thought. The other fighters had since concluded training for the day and withdrawn to their quarters in the loft overhead. A discernible light from the loft filtered down the stairs and sifted through cracks in the ceiling. A murmur of voices drifted down as well.

Percival looked so lost in the shadows. Lisette had come to tell him their good news, that she was pregnant, that she was going to have a baby, and she could little contain herself she was so full with the joy of it. But when she saw Percival in the shadows, tapping lightly on the speed bag, by himself, she knew things had not gone well with the Commissioner, and that her good news would have to wait.

She approached him. "Is everything okay?"

He caught the speed bag in his hands. "Hi," he said, casting a melancholic gaze her way. "How'd things go at the doctor's?"

"I'm fine. But tell me your news. I want to know how things went. Is the fight still on?"

"I won't know for another week at least. Seems I won't make a good role model."

"And Cruz does?"

"Seems he's not a communist."

"And you are?"

"Sam's dead, killed by the cops but they want'a know if I'm a commie or not—can you imagine?" He shook his head like a weary hound.

"What did you say?'

"I told em differently in the only way I know."

She escorted him to a bench where they sat facing each other in the shadows. "The thing is," he said, "this country of ours sends you off in search a' your ethnicity, your racial identity, your place of national origin –paying lip service to diversity while honoring none of it. Invariably, it sends you in pursuit'a the God almighty dollar to the exclusion of all else – which, if the truth be told, is why I return'd to the ring, for lucre, not love of the game. And love it I do. The fight. But more than anything else I needed a payday. Something to get me over; get me outa the daily grind – the nine to five. Boxing was my ticket; my way out. Poverty circumscribes one's horizons, not that I'm afraid of it. It's the misuses to which the powers that be put it to control us. But it can also keep a good fighter lean 'n alert like a lone, hungry wolf."

"Is that what you are, Percival, a hungry wolf?"

"Hungrier than anyone might care to think. Hungrier than Cruz, surely. Hungry for his crown. Hungry to take my place at the top of the heap." He sighed. "I'm hungry, but it's not a hunger one has from lack, want, or insufficiency. It's a hunger only self-fulfillment can alleviate.

It's a hunger Cruz knows nothing of. Of all the fighters I know, Ali is the only one who knows what I mean. He's always been hungry in that sense. That's why he'll regain his championship. 'Truth crushed to the earth—' As for myself as of today, it's all in doubt."

She could feel his isolation, his despair. The abyss into which he was sinking. She could not fault him. He had labored, struggled, sacrificed, and bore up under the most grueling tasks imaginable to find it all, at the end of the day, slipping away. She shuddered, seeing him for who he truly was. Not, the legendary Arthurian hero, Parzival, as Racine had thought, "growing slowly wise." She saw him as Hector, the vulnerable Trojan prince and tragic war hero arrayed in armor and plumage ready to face Troy's most formidable foe, the great warrior and King, Achilles, demigod and Greek champion who had littered the battlefield of Argos for years with the broken remains of his victims. And Hector, failing to heed his sister, Cassandra's prophesy, would also find himself counted among the fallen, the victims of Achilles wrath.

Lisette knew Percival was a good fighter. A very good fighter. The best. Indeed, he had been dubbed by the press as "incomparable." He had objected saying, "Ali's incomparable. I'm to be likened to Sugar Ray Robinson." Nevertheless, she had recently overheard Punchy caution him, "Don't believe your press." And rightly so, for as she knew Cruz had two fists, too, and would, to the best of his ability, use them in defense of his title. In addition, Cruz was a fearful, brutal champion, and she could little imagine her husband, Percival, as a fearful, brutal man, any more than was Hector before him. Besides, Percival's career was in doubt. The fight might well be cancelled. She felt some relief in that though she would not admit it even to herself. Lacking the ability to protect him, provide him with a shield, she refrained from commenting for fear of divulging her concerns. She was afraid for him, for herself and for their unborn child.

"As I was about to say, it's a sad fact that in this greedy, selfish economy, freedom depends on the size of your paycheck, the balance in your bank account. The larger the balance, the freer you are. And I have no wish to spend my life in service to the money market. I have no wish to be bought or sold, or a desire to be anyone's boy!" He shook his head.

"I know," she said. "In that you're much like my father."

"God forbid," he continued, "you should take it in to your head to go in search of your humanity, a humanity easily lost in this country. It's why so many artists expatriate to Europe, Africa, or wherever else they go. Ginsberg is not alone in his complaint— 'the best minds of our generation, too, are being destroyed by madness.' Like the Jazz song goes, 'You took the part that once was my heart— '" He leaned forward as if sinking. "That's what I should do. I've been trying to recover myself for a long time now; to pass beyond the animus that informs so much of American life. I need to get out of here for a while. I need to go on a pilgrimage, somewhat akin to Malcolm 'n Jamal; not a religious quest but a spiritual journey to revivify myself. Hell, even Ashton had a spiritual awakening of a kind on his European sojourn." He smiled recalling the face of his dear friend. The one friendly face in the pack of jackals disguised as sportswriters in the Boxing Commissioner's outer office earlier that day. "I don't need an analyst's couch. What I need is to put back the fragmented pieces of my shattered humanity for which I've searched so long in all the wrong places. I need to find a place where I can lower my guard, lay down my sword 'n shield, 'n bare my soul as the Poet Walt Whitman suggests. That, above all, is what I yearn for, *'To invite my soul.'*" He sighed, "Instead, I feel like an old warrior broken on a wheel of sorrows more ponderous than the Christian cross. Your Jesus was, for all his humanity, the son of God, whereas I am the son of man born of mortal woman made of clay, blood 'n bones. I could cry. Only I won't! I didn't cry at Sam's funeral," he said, sadly, on reflection. "I've cried since but—." He succumbed to remorse and, in the words of his namesake Percival D'Gales, Knight of the round table, he lamented, *"Oh unhappy and wretched man that I am."* He sighed from exhaustion, weary of it all. "I thought finally, in the ring, against Cruz, to take my stand; make my play; put the past to rest! Now, I just pray however the chips fall, wherever they land, I still have your hand. The rest, for all I know, might not be possible."

Lisette raised her eyes to his and saw his face in a stream of light passing through a crack in an overhead floorboard, in which they solemnly gazed at each other. A murmur of voices reached their ears from the sleeping quarters above. She brought his hands to her lips, then pressed her face sideways to his breast. *"Wherever thou goest I will go,'"* she quoted Ruth from the Old Testament, deciding to keep the news of her pregnancy to herself for the moment.

While other news columnists busied themselves exposing Percival's dubious past, Ashton, in his column for the New York Post, picked up the gauntlet on Percival's behalf and lambasted the hypocrisy of the press and Boxing Commission for denying Percival the right to work because of his political convictions while, "the sweet science," as he put it, "has hosted more champions with underworld connections including Arturo Cruz." At this stage in his career, Ashton had become one of the most respected columnist of the day. His column, "Word on the Street," was syndicated nationally and had a wide readership. He was convincing because he was also apolitical. He was moreover, as Percival had observed, and his readership picked up on, "of a rare honest breed and told the truth as best he knew it."

The mood in camp was low, spirits damp, though Percival worked as hard as ever. In fact, he fought furiously. He had struck a hitherto untapped source of fury and it had started a fire in his bowels and everyone in his way was made to pay. Even Leon Bell could little withstand the onslaught of his newly found fury and found himself reeling defenselessly like everyone else under Percival's withering assault.

"Man," said Leon in the showers after a particularly grueling workout, "you're fighting like the devil's to pay."

"One way or the other, he'll ave to," Percival said, tersely.

Punchy said to Derrick, "This is what I've been waiting for. Percival's now ready to capture the championship."

"If they allow the fight to take place, you mean."

Within days of Ashton's article, other sportswriters also came out in favor of the match. When interviewed, Arturo had said, "If I don't fight him I look like I'm afraid. I've something for his communist ass. That's how deep I'm gonna bury my fucking fist in his face. They'll have to unlace my gloves from his asshole. I spit on him. The traitor. The killer of his own brother. I pity his mother." It was shaping into a grudge match, the kind of fight fans love. It promised to make for a thriller. The Boxing Commissioner could not go against popular demand and so the fight was given the green light. Ticket sales soared. The fans hoped to see Percival get his comeuppance.

Punchy put it to him so, "Fans don't think of fighters as having an IQ above their own. They like to feel you don't matter. They don't wanna know you as a person. They jus' want'a see you bleed or bloody someone else's nose. You come across as much too complicated. With Ali it's a religious issue, 'n since the country's founded on the concept of religious freedom, they can't fault him overly. But they see you as Cain 'n, not caring for the facts, fault you for a cultural taboo. It gives em a readymade villain. Someone they can boo! It's like in the movies. You're the cowboy in the black hat. The one who gets the boos. You'll have'a few fans only. Count on it. You're gonna have to turn the rest 'round like you did with O'Leary—with ya fist!"

A few days before camp broke, Percival caught sight of Julius among the thicket of fans in the gym conversing familiarly with Lisette, as he and Leon Bell fiercely sparred. Percival caught Leon in a clinch, and quickly sized Julius up from the ring. Rich, handsome and sporting a casual nonchalant ivy league style, Julius looked every bit the '*eternal, fancy free frat boy,*' pursuing his vantage.

After the day's workout and the gym cleared of spectators, all the other fighters, but for Percival who hung back, headed for the locker room to change and shower off. Cloaked in a full-length terry cloth robe and holding a towel with which to wipe his sweat-bejeweled face, Percival sensed something amiss, as Lisette approached him purposefully, smiling noncommittally.

"Was that Julius I jus' saw you with?" he asked, tautly.

"Why, are you jealous?" She asked.

"Should I be," he said, tonelessly.

"I don't mind your being a little jealous," she preened.

"You're not my possession but I adore you as such," he said, winningly.

"You possess my mind, my heart, my body and my soul. You command my love. I would have you right here right now on the gym floor were you not soaked in sweat," she said, cheekily.

They laughed with the affection of love birds cooing.

"Yes, it was Julius," she said. "And I was no less surprised than you. I've not seen him since Renaldo's funeral; and that's going back awhile. I was curious as to why he was here, too. He put me off by saying, 'we're old friends. And besides, I'm a boxing fan, remember?' He then looked me over and said, 'I still retain a soft spot for you.' I replied, 'I never heard that.' To which he responded, 'If you ever need a shoulder on which to cry you know where to look.' I said, 'Let's not do this!' I started to walk away but he held me back. Then he shrugged and said, "As you like but I'm also here on sort of an errand.' He told me his father's firm was hired by an Alfonse McGraw a fight manager interested in some properties in Saratoga County, and his father wanted him to oversee the transactions. But when he met Alfonse there were also two Latino guys who didn't say a word, just stood with their hands over their hearts, or maybe concealed guns. Alfonse told Julius to get me to give you a message— He knew Julius and I had once been romantically linked— And Alfonse figured the message would carry more weight coming from me. Julius said they must have considerable interest in this fight. The message was, 'Percival can't beat Cruz even if he can. That if you were smart you'd make book on it!' Julius said he had learned from his farther early on that it was in the interest of a man of influence to count on the friendship of gangland figures such as Alfonse. I feigned a naive response and said, 'I know you're aware that I'm not familiar with these things. Tell me, why does this sound to me like a threat?' He seemed amused and said, 'Certainly, not from me.' It struck me he was not being entirely honest, and I told him, "You come with a veiled threat for me to deliver to my husband in the guise of an old friend, from a man seeking his ruin. Am I right?' I suggested he leave before you climbed out of the ring, found out why he was here and take him apart. I also added, 'I won't try to restrain him either.' He watched you spar awhile longer, then said he'd seen enough. He said you looked good, like a champion. He said he was banking you'd fold and take a dive. That I'd see the real character of the man I chose over him. I was furious, as you might imagine. I asked him why he would care, since it wasn't his money he'd be throwing away, but his father's. Then I told him, as for character, I've just discovered a vile and unflattering side of you I'd never known.' At that he left. There was something chilling about the whole encounter." Lisette shivered.

"If I'm right, it was intended to be," Percival said, adrift in thought.

"What are you thinking?" she asked.

"Your ole playmate Julius is, as might be expected, a spoilsport, whereas Alfonse McGraw is a born snake. These boys play dirty – involving you this way! They're unscrupulous bastards 'n will resort to any trick to throw my game. They're trying to rattle me. They hope to scare you to scare me."

"I'm far from scared." She was angry at Julius for daring to deliver her a proxy threat in hopes of scaring her into cowering her husband. She set aside all previous ambivalence about the fight, now in favor of Percival winning out over Cruz, and winning big. "You can beat this guy – this Cruz. And you deserve to be champion. Don't lose heart on my account." She then took his sweat drenched face between the fingers of her outspread hands. "Remember, Punchy and Derrick are in your corner, but I'm in the ring with you. Win!"

"It's a game of nerves I've played before. I'm no less versed in it than they are. Let's forget them 'n not dwell on it. As you say, 'I've a fight to win.'"

"Then chase that frown from your brow and shower off. We have a supper engagement with my parents in Saratoga this evening," she said, bravely. "Hurry now."

"I don't know I'll make good company."

"Try," she urged.

He smiled.

They broke camp in mid-February, the week before the fight. The winter had proven bitter, as had the wooly bear caterpillars predicted. Snow blanketed the landscape as far as the eye could see. Amelia's house and barns were covered in snow, tree branches creaked under the weight of snow. Everything in all directions was bedazzled by reflected sunlight off the snow, striking the eyes with blinding force. A frosty wind tore all around them and gusts of snow flew up and howled in their faces as they huddled in their overcoats against the biting chill, saying farewell to the departing fighters, as one by one they piled into the waiting van until, at last, only Percival remained.

Amelia, who seldom visited the gym, stood knee deep in snow. A lone sparrow came to rest on a shoulder of her snow dusted overcoat. Although a pacifist, she had ruled in favor of her heart over her head to attend the fight since Felicia and Lisette would not be able to go. "I have a stomach virus," Lisette had explained, "and that's why I've been sick these mornings." And she would need her mother, Felicia, to attend to her.

"I believe in you," Amelia said, her voice swallowed by the wind. "I'll be there with Nina. Good luck. I'll see you at the fights."

"You're a great fighter; a man of substance," Renaldo said, clasping him fiercely by the hand. "And I'm proud to call you son. I'll be there rooting for you."

Felicia embraced him, warmly. "Good luck, my son," she said, snow blowing around them. "I love you."

Percival faced Lisette. "You've been especially radiant these weeks," he remarked. "Maybe it's because I'm even more in love with you than ever or is it something else?" He broke off with a laugh.

Lisette smiled, her hands in his, the wind tearing at them. She was both saddened and afraid for him, going off as he was in pursuit of an uncertain destiny. "I'll have something to tell you once you've won this championship, too."

"We can then go on that promised honeymoon," he said, as the driver started up the van and he climbed on board, leaving her with a heartfelt kiss. Renaldo and Felicia backed away from the vehicle, as did Lisette and Amelia, looking on with frost on their breath. The van pulled away and the fighters waved.

The last days of waiting were the longest, loneliest and most anxiety ridden. One moment he'd be elated, then the very next he'd be downcast, like a condemned man about to face the gallows. His mood would swing back and forth.

Saturday, after supper, while trying to relax, he was summoned to the telephone,

"You were told once you can't win this fight, so let's not have to tell you a third time," warned a smooth Latino voice on the far end. "Profit by it. Bet against yourself. "

"Who's this?" Percival demanded.

"You're a bad ass nigger. You figure it out."

Percival dismissed the call, only mentioning it to Punchy in passing. Punchy was noncommittal, not placing much store in it.

Sunday Percival dropped by Our Lady of Victory to see Dominick and attend mass. He had started going to church with Lisette in Saratoga and felt that this would be a way by which to keep a spiritual connection with her, something like pressing petals of flowers between the pages of a favorite book of poems, the memory of the fragrance perfuming the words. And he took in mass and afterwards had a spirited conversation with Dominick. He mentioned the previous night's call.

"I'd say they're trying to throw a scare into you."

"I got'a win this fight, no matter."

"You are who you are by no accident of fate and it's your destiny, surely."

Two days before fight time, Percival took solitary walks in Prospect Park. Then the day of the fight arrived. The two fighters, Percival and Arturo, were weighed in separately with observers from the others camp in attendance. The rest of the day, waiting for the opening bell, was unnervingly long. He was restive. It was no less so in the locker room that night. Derrick went above to see the preliminaries. The hour was drawing near and the fight uncomfortably close. More than a little was at stake; his whole sense of self was on the line. Punchy taped his hands. He shadowboxed, working up a sweat, then stretched out on a cot. Punchy covered him with blankets to keep his sweat flowing. His pulse was racing no less quickly than were his unruly thoughts, one into another. The phone on the wall beside his head suddenly rang, startling both him and Punchy. He sat up, seized it, and stiffened perceptibly on recognizing the suave, unctuous Latino voice from the other night.

"I told you I didn't want to tell you a third time –"

"H-how'd you get this number?" Percival asked irritably. "Who' 'r you?"

"You know who it is and you know we're not playing," the words rolled menacingly off the callers tongue. "You don't know your wife's pregnant do you? Well she is."

"Pregnant?" Percival stammered stupefied. "H-How would you know that?" he demanded.

"We know things the F.B.I don't." He snickered. "Maybe your child's gonna need a father more than the boxing world needs a new champion. Think on it, can you stomach the sight of your pretty wife raising your child with another man? A man such as Julius?" the voice was cruel and vulgar. "Well that's how it's gonna be If you win this fight, you won't live long enough to enjoy the victory celebration."

Unable to dismiss the menace in the caller's voice, Percival struggled to get hold of his emotions, as a cold chill took hold of him and his brother's face, Sam's ghostly face, came into view. Sweat broke on his brow and ran in rivulets down his flanks. "Ah, Sam, Sam," he thought, feeling the cold hard steel of Damocles sword dangling over his head by a frayed cord ready to drop. "I sense the mis-spilt blood of your restless soul. Sorry I can't help you now, I have other obligations to meet." The ghost dissolved into vapor. He had a championship to win or lose. Trying to mask his fears from Punchy he averted his pale, damp face. When the line went dead he clutched the phone to his ear a moment longer – concerned.

"Who was it?" Punchy asked, eyes riveted on Percival. "You're sweating like a geyser."

"N-no one," he said, sporting a poker face. "Just a fan wanting to wish me luck."

"Oh? It looks to me like y've seen a ghost."

Percival laughed. "A friendly one."

A man stuck his head in the doorway. "Fifteen minutes to championship."

Derrick rushed in moments after looking about anxiously. "Ready?" he asked, leveling his gaze on Percival.

Percival felt that he would lose himself if he were to throw the fight. And how could he hope to love Lisette if he were lost to himself? Indeed, he would love her less and fault her too. Julius be damned! And she, in turn would lose her respect for him, which he prized above all else. Her love for him. No, everything in him railed against throwing the fight. Besides, he could kill Cruz for this outrage; more so now that they would draw Lisette into it – to try and hamstring him. He would take Cruz apart, piecemeal, like a locksmith picking a lock. He would kill Cruz for it. He'd struggled too hard too long to do otherwise. "As ready as I'll ever be," he said, decidedly, choosing to ignore the threat as nothing more than a bluff, thinking to himself, "If you're not man enough to threaten me face to face, then you're probably not man enough to squeeze the trigger, either." No matter, he would risk it.

"I've been waiting on this all my life," Punchy said, his eyes watering. "Win, lose or draw, you've made me very proud. It's a dream come true."

"Well then," Percival said, with a defiant light in his eyes, "let's go out 'n win us a championship!"

The End